Madge Swindells

SHADOWS ON THE SNOW

Madge Swindells

SHADOWS ON THE SNOW

BOOK CLUB ASSOCIATES LONDON

This edition published 1987 by
Book Club Associates
by arrangement with Macdonald & Co Ltd

Printed and bound in Great Britain by
Mackays of Chatham Ltd, Kent

ACKNOWLEDGEMENTS TO:

Lawrie Mackintosh, Susan Fletcher, Susan Schwartz, Lana Odell; *Sports Illustrated Magazine of America*; Mr M.E. Millard and Colleen Millard; Roger Rosenblatt, essayist *Time Magazine*; Organizing Committee of the 14th Olympic Winter Games, Sarajevo; *The Guinness Book of Skiing* by Peter Lund; *Ski Sunday* by John Samuel; Peta Sokolsky; the British Ski Federation.

CHAPTER 1

Sarajevo, Yugoslavia. January 26, 1983

She was a young city-bred woman. She knew her way around the world's capitals, and understood the complexities of managing international sports superstars and turning the daring, the winning and the public acclaim into hard cash. She was American, twenty-six, good at her job and ambitious, and she had come to watch the World Cup ski events at Sarajevo to search for talent and, if possible, sign it up there and then. There and then! That was the way Megan Carroll operated.

It had been raining when Megan left London and she had been glad to go, but her enthusiasm had dimmed after waiting several hours in Belgrade airport's draughty halls for the connection to Sarajevo. Delayed by fog, the domestic flight had left five hours late, and the uncomfortable journey had been a fitting continuation of one depressing day. And now this dismal airport. All the pinching and scraping of a poverty-stricken nation was evident in the dim neon lights, the makeshift decor and total contempt for comfort.

Megan hurried to the restroom to freshen up. She was about to dab cold water on her face when a drab airport cleaner placed one hand on her sleeve. The woman, who had once been very rich, looked overawed.

'You are American, yes? In America one can find such beautiful clothes.' She stepped back and appraised Megan's long brown mink coat tied around her slender waist with a leather thong and her fox fur hat from which a few brown curls straggled. She noticed the grey eye shadow which lengthened the large, deep blue eyes set wide apart in a squarish face, and she saw how the freckles of her smooth pale skin were subtly disguised with matching foundation. Her sensitive lips seemed to live a life of their own, curling and flickering into a smile.

7

There was self-confidence, compassion and honesty in that beautiful face and the woman stared longingly as she thought about the background that could produce such an expression. Then she noticed that she was embarrassing the girl. 'Excuse me,' she murmured. 'I am very rude ... I forget ... but to see you ... to smell your perfume – to see your clothes – to know that these things still exist – that is wonderful for me. You are here for the skiing, yes? And there will be more like you ... many more! Things will get better ...'

Megan stepped back, feeling touched by the woman's poignant longing. She took off her embroidered Swiss scarf and handed it to the cleaner. 'Take this,' she said. 'No please ...' as the woman backed away. She pressed it into her hands and felt her eyes sting with tears at the woman's gratitude. 'A gift from the West. Really ... it's a very small thing.'

The woman was still murmuring her thanks as Megan left hurriedly. She felt saddened by the encounter and she had to make an effort to pull herself together. Megan had a surfeit of caring and she tried to protect herself from this. It was a weakness which prejudiced her business and left her the loser in every relationship. Now she shivered and glanced round. How bleak the faces; how drab the clothes. yet the smiles of the airport personnel were warm and genuine as they murmured: *dobrodosli, bienvenido, bienvenue*, welcome – welcome to Sarajevo!

To the young skiers, flooding through the doors to collect their gear, it was just another airport – no big deal. It was the snow that mattered and the mountains. Nothing else! They were not expecting too much. For the first time Sarajevo had been included in the World Cup ski circuit; it was virgin territory and they were all excited.

Organisers, coaches, skiers, medics from almost every nation were crowding the foyer. Megan pushed her way through to the luggage ramp as the voice on the loudspeaker announced yet another arrival.

The main hall was chaotic. Hundreds of youngsters in multi-hued ski gear were clambering for taxis, information, maps, buses and change. Their shouts echoed in German, Norwegian, English, French and a dozen more languages.

Their currency flooded the counters as they examined their near-worthless Yugoslav dinars with disbelief. 'Hey, Mark, take a look at this. You reckon I can buy the Taj Mahal?' Thick handfuls of paper currency were stuffed in woollen pockets and wallets. 'Hey, you guys. I'm gonna take a bagful home and paper my loo.' 'Now I know what it feels like to be a millionaire.' The smiles of the officials were becoming strained and unaccountably Megan felt guilty. The kids were noisy, over-exuberant, buoyed up with that strange, wild feeling of being part of a group and far from home, so they swaggered a bit, and showed off.

The police, to whom foreign visitors meant complications, disruption and inevitably more overtime, put on a show of bluff friendliness; the cafeteria girls overlooked the insults about stale rolls and muddy coffee and kept smiling; and taxi drivers pushed their shoddy vehicles along the curbside to conserve petrol as they moved to the front of the queue. The Slavs were not a smiling people, that much was clear, but when they said 'welcome', you could see in their eyes they meant it.

Megan felt vaguely irritated as she watched the antics of her countrymen. I'm becoming a snob, she told herself sternly. Who cares if these kids take over? After a year in London, British mores were invading her psyche.

Megan heard someone murmur close beside her in a voice that was so deep that the words came out like a growl. 'Many more Yanks like these and the Slavs will give up gate-crashing the West.'

Megan turned in surprise. The man behind her looked so exasperated that she could not help smiling. His cheeks were flushed and his lips were set in a taut line. She wondered why he should care so much.

'I guess they need us more than we need them,' she replied, surprising herself by her involuntary patriotism.

He was tall and athletic-looking, dressed casually in grey flannels, a dark blue shirt with a sweater and windcheater – yet there was nothing sloppy about him, quite the contrary, for he wore his clothes as he would a uniform. His face was quite distinctive with his deep blue eyes, his prominent features and high cheek bones. He had thick brown brows and a mop of dark curls cut short and brushed back vigorously, a straight nose that was blunt and short above a long, deeply grooved upper lip. A strictly British face, with his rosy cheeks and freckles, she decided. He flashed a short, searching scan at her and his mouth curled into an expression of wry concern.

'Not you, I assure you. Merely your dollars, ma'am,' he said pointedly. 'My apologies. I saw you at Heathrow and jumped to the wrong conclusion.'

He hurried on. For a moment she could not place his accent which was almost public school English, but not quite: his consonants were too harsh and his vowels rounder. He's a Scot, she decided with a flash of intuition. 'Quite a guy,' she muttered.

'Jeeesus! Have you seen the cafeteria?'

It was a young girl speaking. Megan had heard her agonised, pampered voice list every one of the airline's deficiencies during the tedious flight. What was she doing here? She was so obviously rich, spoiled and discontented. She might have been commonplace in St Moritz, but she seemed to have none of the *joie de vivre* shared by the serious skiers. Her clothes were bizarre: a cheap knitted ski hat and a thigh-length ermine jacket over her padded ski trousers.

'I'm goddamned fed up with it. I don't care about the frigging budget. Just don't give me any more of that economising shit. I'll stay where I damn well like,' Megan heard.

'You'll stay with the rest of us, Jenny. I can't have the team scattered.'

Megan recognised the Highland accent of the British team's coach. He was a man she liked and admired and he seemed to be on top of the situation. So the girl was skiing for Britain; yet she was clearly American. No end to the surprises today.

Jenny's retort was drowned by shouts and laughter nearby as the French team tried to fit their skis and gear into three ramshackle taxis.

Megan smiled with pleasure as her snow boots crunched the packed snow. Far away she saw the lights of Sarajevo twinkling softly in the early twilight, but except for the airport there was only emptiness for miles around and she saw now that Sarajevo was built in the centre of vast flat plain with mountains rising sheer on all sides, giving the impression of a gigantic amphitheatre.

Megan took her place in the queue and eventually squeezed

into the back of a beat-up yellow Lada and found to her surprise that she was expected to share. The man who had been standing behind her in the queue was told firmly to hurry up and get in.

He lifted his fur hat and squeezed beside her and Megan did a quick double-take. He was too good to be true: thick black hair and brows, soulful brown eyes, even features set off by his smooth tanned skin, flashing white teeth when he smiled, which seemed to be all the time. The shock of his flamboyant good looks was downright intimidating. His smile was strangely intimate, as if they had known each other for years, but she had never set eyes on him before, Megan was sure of that, his was not the sort of face you could forget.

'What luck,' he said with a strong French accent. 'I was hoping to meet you. Fate has played into my hands.'

Megan groaned inwardly. What a cliché-ridden goon, but she smiled absent-mindedly and gazed back at the empty plain.

'Where are you going?' he persisted, his eyes caressing her clothes, luggage and handbag.

'The Sarajevo Palace Hotel.'

'So am I.' He spoke rapidly in Serbo-Croatian to the driver.

Megan glanced sharply at him and her surprise showed in her eyes.

'Michel Juric,' he introduced himself. 'Freelance feature writer, currently domiciled in Paris, but originally from Yugoslavia.'

'I'm Megan Carroll.' She smiled charmingly. 'Sports agent.' The press was a valuable tool of her trade so she knuckled down to smile throughout a boring half-hour.

But he was not boring at all, she discovered as their taxi raced them to the hotel. He was a shrewd, devious man who knew a great deal about the sports world and the big stars. He even claimed to have heard of her.

'You must be International Sports Agency's young whizz kid who's been sent to shake up the British sports world,' he told her.

'No kidding,' she exclaimed. 'I can't lay claim to any such title. But you've heard of ISA? How come?' Megan looked up, feeling surprised and pleased, but her smile faded as she caught a glimpse of steel behind the glamorous facade. For a moment she was caught off guard and Michel, noticing this, almost softened. She was so young and so different from the woman he had imagined.

11

Nevertheless he was here for a purpose, Michel reminded himself – information – and like a true professional he homed in to find her weak spots and break her defences. Smiling quietly to himself he said: 'Your outfit's getting known. Challenging the big names. Besides, I've met John Oberholtzer a few times.'

'No kidding? You know my boss?' Megan felt a surge of warmth towards this stranger who was no longer quite so strange. Nice to have a friend here, she thought, but her relief was short-lived.

He grinned nastily. 'Perhaps you read a recent article of mine published in *The Athlete*.'

'Why, yes – surely not you?' Megan could not disguise her dismay. The article had slated all sports agents and ISA in particular. It had been vicious, biased and altogether unfair and it had claimed that the big agents were taking over sport to the detriment of everyone in the business.

'Oberholtzer threatened to sue, but nothing much came of it eventually. It never does.'

'Well,' she said doubtfully. 'At least you're straightforward. Goodness! This is uncomfortable,' she said as a sudden lurch sent her bouncing against him.

'Doesn't it worry you – this unpopularity in the sports world?' Juric asked, smiling as if he were paying her a compliment.

'Depends which side of the fence you're on,' she said, tight-lipped and offended. 'Our clients think we're pretty good. We make them a great deal of money. We take the rap for anything that goes wrong and they take all the credit.'

'And you split their earnings,' he continued in a manner so smooth it was hard to believe he was deliberately insulting her.

'We deserve our commission,' she snapped, speaking rapidly. How did she get into this mess? she was wondering. If she had not been so fed up and depressed after the flight she would have been on her guard. 'Our athletes earn a fortune when we're out there toting for them. They don't have the time, the experience or the expertise to go out and sell themselves.'

'And you do?'

'Sure I do.' She could feel her temper rising. 'Last week I went out and sold a deal for a well-known tennis star. Two point five million over three years. That takes some doing, Mr Juric. She could never do that for herself.'

They were moving towards the outskirts of town which rose

out of the snowy plain without warning. Suddenly they were amongst highrise buildings on either side of the road. They were ugly and utilitarian. Megan felt disappointed.

'Don't judge Sarajevo by the new town,' Juric said softly as if reading her thoughts. 'There are three completely different Sarajevos, the Austrian town is beautiful, quite different from this and then there is the Turkish town which is our showpiece.'

Our showpiece! That was curious, Megan thought. 'So you're from Sarajevo?' she asked.

'No. But I'm a Slav. The new city hurts me.' He turned away from the window with relief. 'You aim to hold back any of the scheduled competitors this time?' Juric asked in his deceptively gentle voice.

Megan forced a smile. 'I never do that,' she said. 'I know you're referring to the Cologne Invitation Meeting. You think I pulled a trick there when I cancelled two of our runners' appearances. You and the rest of the world.'

'And it didn't come off.' Amazingly, he was still smiling.

'I pulled my clients out on doctor's orders; not to pressurise an increased fee – which is what you wrote in your libellous article, Mr Juric.'

Megan took a deep breath. It was time to put Mr Nasty in his place. 'I don't mind being interviewed without an appointment,' she went on more quietly, 'but I object to the innuendoes. Any time you want to write an unbiased report I'd be happy to answer your questions. Just so long as I have your guarantee. This is neither the time nor the place for it and right now I'm tired of your inquisition.'

But Juric would not give in. He chuckled. 'Too many people are asking if agents are really in the best interests of sport or merely lining their pockets. What do you think?'

'If we didn't perform a service we wouldn't make profits,' Megan retorted. 'I'm running the London office and it's out of the red after just six months in business.' She paused; she knew she was talking too much, but now she was furious and uncaring. 'I aim to break a few records, too. It's very important to me. I gave up skiing for business, but I still want to win and so do my clients. That's why we pull together. It's tough if some of the losers don't like what the winners make.

'Are you a loser, Mr Juric?' she went on. 'Is that why you're so sour?' Her voice sounded hoarse and she was trembling a

13

little as she struggled to keep calm. How could she be so naive as to let this monster get under her skin. She should have known better, she chided herself.

She glanced out of the window and saw, with relief, that they were driving towards a curious structure which presumably was the hotel. It was square and painted bright mustard. Sickening! The morning was becoming unbearable.

'I've decided I'll write an article on you,' Juric said. 'ISA's new tiger woman.'

The taxi was coming to a halt so Megan bit back an angry retort, jumped out, thrust some notes into the startled driver's hand and stalked into reception.

She heard Juric's stupid chuckling. What an oaf! He sounded genuinely amused and that was disconcerting.

Megan could never hide her anger. How could I be such a fool, she wondered? She knew her cheeks were burning and that it showed and it was just her bad luck that the foyer was crowded with cameramen standing amongst piles of equipment.

She was conscious of a sudden silence and as she hurried to the reception desk she felt the men's sullen appraisal as something alarming. Megan had always been intimidated by the curious phenomenon of a group of males; to her they seemed predatory and threatening. Yet individually she liked men and preferred their company to women. A soft wolf whistle came from the crowd that was staring unabashed with twenty pairs of admiring eyes.

Trembling with indignation she signed the register and handed in her passport. Then she fumbled in her bag for change, but glancing over her shoulder she saw that it was not the hotel porter bringing her bags, but Michel Juric. He was smiling triumphantly. She should have know there would be no porter; after all, she was in a socialist state. Now she would have to thank him.

As she turned to do so, she was saved by the Scot she had encountered at the airport. He stepped forward and placed one hand on her shoulder. 'I wanted to give you a lift,' he said, 'but I could not find you.' With a practised nonchalance he stepped forward and thrust some bank notes into Juric's top pocket. 'You can leave Madam's bags here,' he said. 'Have them sent up, thank you.'

Turning to Megan he winked and said: 'I like to see a fellow who smiles as he works. Come along dear.'

'Do you know ...' Megan began breathlessly as she followed him towards the lifts, trying not to laugh. 'Do you know who he is?'

'Of course I do: Michel Juric, self-opinionated wimp.'

'And he knows you?' she persisted, allowing herself to be guided through the foyer.

'We've had a few encounters, but he's none too swift with the repartee, so he usually loses. I could see you were upset.' His chuckle was warm and friendly. 'Anyway, let's forget him. I wanted to invite you for a drink, or preferably lunch. I owe you an apology for my rudeness, and I like to pay my debts.'

'You don't owe me anything. I didn't think you were rude – just over-reacting. I'm sorry I can't make it. Perhaps later.' She smiled to soften the refusal. 'I'm here to work and I have to be at the Men's Downhill race this afternoon.'

'I'll probably see you there,' he said. 'I'll introduce myself, if I may. Ian Mackintosh, freelance script writer, here as advisor to the British television crew.'

As the doors closed, Megan gazed into the mirror, her fingertips pressed against her flushed cheeks. 'What a fright,' she murmured, tucking her hair into place. She knew that she would see Ian that afternoon and she was looking forward to it. Then she frowned at her reflection. She was here to work, she reminded herself sternly.

Nikola Petrovna sat quivering as the Soviet jet transported the youth ice team from Moscow to Sarajevo, Yugoslavia. She had travelled outside the Soviet Union many times in the past eighteen months, but this time was different. She was not going back.

It seemed to Nikola that the truth must be etched on her face and in her eyes for all to read, but no one gave her a second glance. If they had, they might have noticed a certain tension in her body, and a frown on her otherwise smooth wide forehead as she sat ramrod stiff, gazing straight ahead of her.

She was a slender girl of seventeen and exquisitely beautiful, although she did not know this, with wide-set elfin eyes of shimmering green, small and slightly pointed ears, a fine, straight nose, a wide mouth with large, but perfectly even white

15

teeth, a pale complexion, and ash-blond hair which she wore braided and coiled around her head. When she laughed, which was not often, she became immensely captivating, but for the rest her beauty was marred by the tragic look in her eyes when she was not consciously looking gay. Hardly anyone looked beyond her beauty, but if they had, they would see courage and sensitivity and pride, but her pride was excessive, so much so that her first consideration in every calamity, was to show a brave face to the world. Today, however, there was a trace of desperation in her expression. There would never be another chance like this. It was now, or never.

It was over a year since she had first left the Soviet Union to skate at a youth programme in Helsinki. She had not been the star, far from it, but she did have a short solo performance. Afterwards, when she was leaning over the railing watching the next turn, a young French cameraman had approached her and whispered: *'Bravo! Miss Petrovna, you are by far the best. You're overlooked here. you should come to the West – you'd be a sensation. Where I come from they don't waste talent – or beauty.'*

Just that. Nothing more. He had merged into the crowd. But later it had happened again and again: in Düsseldorf, in Dortmund, in Vienna, Budapest and lately in Moscow – whispered voices, unknown faces, but always the same message. It had been flattering, amusing, exciting, but that was all, and she had told no one. Madness to tell anyone.

It was in December that she had made up her mind to defect. She had been excluded from the special training squad of the country's top figure skaters, and two other girls, whom she knew were not as good as her, had been chosen. The shock and unfairness of it had made her ill, but later, when she recovered, she had begged an appointment with her head coach to demand a reason for her exclusion. As usual, he had been politely evasive and very careful about what he said. 'I'm not denying your talent, Nikola,' he repeated several times. 'The decision to exclude you from the team was made higher up.' He pointed to the ceiling and shrugged significantly. 'I don't argue with the authorities, Nikola.'

Shortly after this hurtful interview she had been informed by her father that it was time to give up international skating. Perhaps she could teach a little, he had suggested in a voice

16

that was unusually gentle for Papa. Or take more interest in running the household. After all, their housekeeper was well past retirement age. No explanations, no excuses, but she knew that it was Papa's fault that her skating was to be sacrificed. No, not just her skating, but her life. There was nothing else that meant anything to Nikola. It was then that she had decided that she would rather live in exile amongst the bourgeois Westerners, with their greed and their grasping ways than become a housekeeper. But how could she escape?

After that, she had begun to investigate ways and means of leaving Russia, and she had read, to her amazement, of people being turned back at the border. You had to be someone important to defect, she discovered, and she was not important. Far from it, her importance was sinking daily as she was excluded from every international team. It was deliberate and it was cruel. Lately, as if in cahoots with the skating officials, Papa began to seek her assistance with hours of typing and editing which prevented her from training properly. What was happening to her dreams? They were becoming more hopeless by the day.

Nikola was close to despair. She hoped that they would come again – these whispered voices – for loyalty had fled now. So when, at Leningrad, a seemingly casual onlooker had whispered: '*My dear, in the West ...*' She had turned, fiercely attentive, and murmured: '*Yes! Yes! But how? Help me!*'

After that there had been two words scribbled on a sheet of paper placed in her locker at the ice rink. '*At Sarajevo*' the message had read and that was all.

Sarajevo? But how? And why?

Sarajevo, she had discovered when she looked it up, was the provincial capital of Bosnia-Herzegovina and a centre of fierce resistance when Hitler invaded Yugoslavia in 1941. It was also where Gavrilo Princip, a nineteen-year-old student, assassinated Archduke Franz Ferdinand, heir to the Austro-Hungarian empire, and so precipitated World War I and indirectly freed their Yugoslav comrades from Austrian Imperialism. The Winter Olympics were to be held in Sarajevo in February, 1984. That much, at least, she had known, since she had only recently been excluded from the Olympic team.

She had begun to take the message seriously when the skaters in her club were told that a special Youth Team was to

17

be sent to Sarajevo at the end of January, in order to give a display of Soviet skating talent. From other sources she learned that the various teams of the World Cup Ski Circuit would be there at the same time to try out the newly constructed ski slopes and infrastructure which had been prepared for the Winter Games.

Hope began to grow, but not for long, for she was not chosen for the team. It was only weeks later, when Katya Oblonsky had mysteriously fallen and twisted her ankle during a rehearsal – Katya had tearfully claimed she was tripped – that Nikola had been hastily summoned to take her place. There was no one else available at short notice.

So here she was, and she had no idea what would happen next, only that she was prepared to grasp any slim chance to reach the West. She was born to skate – she longed to be the best in the world. she had always wanted this and she would fight for the chance to prove her worth.

Nikola was jolted back to the present by a sudden lurch. The jet was losing height and slanting slowly earthwards. The wild and desolate mountain peaks, part of the Dinaric chain of over fifty mountain ranges, were giving way to a sudden flat emptiness, with here and there an unpretentious boxlike house, squalid and lonely beside the road. As they began to circle the snowbound, featureless plain that surrounded Sarajevo, prior to touchdown, Nikola gripped the armrests and tried to quiet her fears. I will never go back, she vowed silently. Never! Never! I'd rather die. Her destiny lay in the West and somehow she would get there.

CHAPTER 2

The road wound higher into the heart of the Igman Mountains, with the forested slopes rising gently upwards on the left side of the narrow road, but on the right falling steeply away, so that Megan could see the immense snow-bound Sarajevo plain bathed in a purple haze with the domed Turkish roofs sparkling in the distance.

She was looking for the site of the Men's Downhill race. She had a client competing, a young British-born boy of Norwegian parentage, called Conrad Soerli, who was the best skier the British team had seen for many years. He was also the idol of Vanguard Sports, who were the largest multi-national ski manufacturers in the world as well as chief sponsor of Megan's clients. Megan, Vanguard and the British team were hoping Conrad would win a gold in the Winter Olympics next year and Vanguard had lavished a costly campaign around this golden-haired ski racer's exploits.

Megan had high hopes of signing some new talent, too. Winners were hard to come by, but Megan had a flair for finding them. Hence her job, her top salary and her profit-sharing bonus. She was a good saleswoman; she knew it and she was proud of it. Part of the reason, she often claimed, was that she always followed her hunches.

She found the turn off at last and drove along the narrow track which cut across the Malo Polje Valley to the base of the Igman Mountain and the ski lifts. A crowd had gathered, but the race had not yet started. Everyone was excited; there was a feeling of exhilaration, a sense of expectancy; it was all around them in the tingling air, the spruce and pines standing tall and straight and laden with snow, the snap and crackle of new snow underfoot, the sharp repetitive echoes of the loudspeaker announcing the names and numbers of competitors, the shouts from the crowds. Megan's eyes were smarting with cold, her feet glowed and tingled in her new Swiss moon boots and she

19

felt joyously alive. Far away a dog howled and the sound echoed eerily through the valley, while above her the sombre Igman Mountain rose to 3000 metres of snow-laden forests and icy mists under a washed-out sky.

Michel Juric was there, looking very Slavonic in his fur hat and sheepskin jacket, his dark eyes glowing with excitement. He smiled and waved and Megan smiled back feeling too happy for grudges, just glad to be part of it all. It was far colder than she had realised. She pushed her collar up and pulled her hat over her ears as she saw Michel hurrying towards her.

'Did you hear the wolf howling?' he asked.

'No kidding? I thought it was a dog.'

He glanced at his watch. 'They may cancel,' he went on worriedly. 'It's too dangerous. When the clouds bank up on the summit like that it means a bad gale's coming. The blacker the clouds, the harder it blows. Even the wolves don't like the look of it. Temperatures can drop by up to forty degrees within half an hour in these mountains; a deathtrap for the unwary.'

By the time the race began it was bitterly cold and gusts of wind were shredding the mist and blowing it away. Megan peered toward the summit, trying to catch a glimpse of competitors as one by one their indistinct shapes materialised out of the clouds.

'Look out for Number Fifteen,' Michel shouted to her above the clamour of the loudspeaker. 'Rob Scott, an American. I saw him race in Austria; I was impressed.'

'I know him well,' she yelled above the wind. 'You'll never believe this, but I trained him a few years back.' When was it, she tried to remember, eight years ago – or nine? He had been thirteen and pretty good even then and he had soon progressed out of her class at the ski school where she taught in college holidays. Now he was making a name for himself in the US Giant Slalom team. 'I've been following his career,' she said. 'He's pretty good. I suppose our Denver office will be signing him up one of these days.' She made a mental note to remind them to do so.

Shortly afterwards Number Fifteen hurtled down the piste hugging the gates and making good use of his size and weight in the fresh soft snow. The television crews and spectators were cheering by the time he entered the home run, half a second ahead of the best time to date.

'But you're right. He's better than I realised, in fact, he's tremendous,' Megan said excitedly.

She waited until the skier emerged from the huddle of congratulations and then went over. Rob was looking gloomy. 'Hi, Rob! Remember me?'

'Megan,' he yelled. 'Of all the places.' He cheered up and gave her a great bear hug. 'It's good to see you, Megan. What are you doing so far from home?'

'Home's in London nowadays,' she said. 'I'm running the London office of ISA?'

'An agent? You?' He pulled a face at her and pinched her cheek. 'Boy, you've grown well,' he said taking in her figure at a glance.

'And you're mighty uppity for a skinny little teenager,' she laughed. 'How d'you find the piste?' she went on.

'It's a real phoney,' he burst out. 'The whole damn course – man-made and full of blunders. You can't do your best speed because you're too damned scared.' He noticed Michel whipping out his notebook and grinned wryly.

'You'll see – there'll be some spills today,' Rob said. 'First problem is you have to make a left-hand turn before any speed has been built up; this ruins the start completely. After that there's a pretty good run down for the next several hundred metres leading to a really fine jump, with a nice smooth landing. Then trouble starts – it's just one mean obstacle after the next. When you get into the tree-line for a really fast schuss, you find they've shoved a Giant Slalom section into the course with a bulldozer. Riding through those darn flags is pretty tiresome. Downhill racing means getting from the top to the bottom of a mountain in the least possible time. It's always meant that.' He broke off and wiped the sweat off his forehead. Then he grinned. 'I'll probably get my ass kicked for saying this.' Then he peered back at the piste. 'Weather's worsening,' he muttered. 'They should cancel.'

He looked worried as he turned back to Michel. 'Those last jumps are designed to create a few more paraplegics. Disastrous! Landing bang into the flat. Then down near the finish there's a launching pad to send you into outer space. They'll have to get this place fixed up before the Olympics. You can quote me on that.'

'Nevertheless, you made good time,' Megan said. 'One of

these days my Denver office will be trying to sign you.' She was impressed how the skinny, thirteen-year-old youngster had grown into this huge, bluff, athletic all-American boy with his wide-set candid grey eyes and his mop of ginger-brown hair.

He grinned. 'Megan, there're a few guys in my team would like to talk to you, but I'm building my own place.' He lifted a ski and showed her the logo: a blue star with Scott brand written in white in the centre. 'Got a small outfit, Denver-way and I'm aiming to grow pretty fast. Right now I design custom-made skis for serious skiers. Maybe one of these days we'll talk business – but I'll be the sponsor.'

'Well, good luck,' she said. 'See you later.'

'That's one hell of a nice guy,' she told Michel when Rob had joined his team mates.

Conrad had drawn number forty and by the time his turn came, the wind had reached gale force and snow was falling heavily. Visibility was so bad that they did not realise Conrad had collided with a gate until stretcher bearers raced down the mountain bearing the unconscious skier to the First Aid hut. Shortly afterwards race officials announced Conrad's accident and the cancellation of the race over the loudspeaker.

But too late, Megan thought angrily as she raced towards the hut. The boy was conscious and groaning with pain from a badly fractured leg and Ian Mackintosh, whom she had not known was there, was bending over him, trying to reassure him. Ian was smiling and joking with Conrad as the attendant gave him a pain-killing injection. A few minutes later, the boy managed the glimmer of a smile. He seemed to know Ian well. Megan hung around awkwardly, wanting to help, but having nothing useful to do and then she sat on a bench in the corner listening to Ian questioning the stretcher bearers in fluent Serbo-Croatian, which surprised her.

'The helicopter's on the way,' he told Conrad. 'There's nothing to worry about. Hospitals are first class in Sarajevo. You'll be all right.'

Nothing to worry about! She listened incredulously. All the medical services in the world could not make it up to Conrad. She knew he had lost out – easy to see from the lie of his leg that he would never make big-time skiing again. He'd miss the Olympic Games and a medal was so desperately important to Conrad. Besides, he was counting on the winning bonus

22

Vanguard sports had promised to put him through university. She felt depressed both for Conrad and herself. There went her hopes for an Olympic gold, as well as Vanguard's million-dollar advertising campaign.

Then she wondered if she could squeeze Vanguard to pay him compensation. After all, he wasn't just a skier. Conrad was also retained by Vanguard as a winter sports promoter. This could be construed as full time employment, she thought. She would telex ISA's legal department as soon as she returned. Surely they'd come up with something. Meantime there was nothing she needed as much as a replacement for Conrad in Vanguard's advertising campaign.

Shortly afterwards the helicopter arrived and to her surprise Ian climbed in beside the boy. She watched as he took off in a swirl of snow and ice. She was still staring at the blurred shape disappearing into the blizzard when she felt Michel's hand on her elbow.

'Please don't worry. He'll be all right,' Michel said in a voice that was meant to sound comforting. She felt a surge of irritation at Michel, knowing he would get full mileage out of the tragedy. Well, he'd get nothing out of her.

'I'm not worried,' she snapped, although she was. She stood moodily stamping her feet and clapping her hands for warmth as she considered just how far she could push Vanguard for compensation. Did she have a case at all? she wondered.

Juric watched Megan cautiously; she looked pale and sad and she was obviously fighting back her tears. He was puzzled and intrigued by her. He would have liked to reach out and comfort her, but she was not the sort of girl to invite sympathy. Was she really as tough as she would like everyone to believe? he wondered. Megan had a reputation in the sports fraternity for being brilliant, but heartless, and for seeing sport only in terms of credits and debits, yet Michel felt instinctively that there was a warm, genuine woman under her glossy facade. She was worth a little effort, he decided. He would dig into her soul and write a superb in-depth personality piece. With luck it would be syndicated. 'I'll drive you to casualty,' he said quickly. 'Please don't argue. I know the way. You don't.'

'No thanks,' she muttered feeling too miserable to be polite. 'I'll stick around. I need a replacement in a hurry. I'll wait in the car in case they start again.'

She turned abruptly and Michel watched her jaunty step as she hurried through the new snow. 'Bitch!' he murmured under his breath. She deserved her reputation.

CHAPTER 3

Megan was reluctant to go down, although she was dressed and ready for a pre-dinner drink. Conrad's accident had thrown her, she could not shake off her grief, and when she had arrived at the hospital in the late afternoon, it was to find Conrad heavily sedated with his leg in plaster. Now she would have liked nothing more than an early night, but she was looking for talent, she reminded herself, and the only way to find it was to go out and get known.

She walked out of her room and leaned over the balustrade. The curious architecture of the hotel puzzled her, until she noticed its resemblance to a vast concrete and glass tent, with the rooms built in tiers around the perimeter of the building, leaving the interior as a huge empty dome. Suspended over one side of the main foyer was a circular mezzanine section containing the bar and over this hung a vast purple-and-mustard-striped silk canopy. It was flamboyantly oriental, reminiscent of the Slav's nomadic heritage, but the shouts echoing from under it were blatantly Anglo-Saxon. It seemed that most of the American and British teams were letting off steam.

There was a startled silence when she appeared in the bar. Perhaps it was her clothes which caused the astonishment. She wondered if she should have dressed more casually. The skiers were clad in their ski gear while she was wearing a stylish red jersey wool dress. There were a few wolf whistles which she pretended not to hear, but Ian was there and the sight of him brought the blood flushing to her face. How stupid of her to react this way she told herself as Ian introduced her to the people he knew, which it seemed was just about everyone.

'How d'you know my name?' she asked curiously. 'I keep feeling that we've met before. Have we?'

'I would be bound to remember you if we had,' he said. 'I

must admit I cheated.' He gestured over the balustrade towards the information desk. 'Have you met Čana yet? She's in charge of keeping tabs on all of us and she checks the passports. I simply asked her. I hope you don't mind.' He stared at her searchingly and a smile slowly appeared, first in his eyes and then spreading to his cheeks and lips. Suddenly, he looked carefree and boyish. She noticed that his lips were full and sensual, although cracked by the cold, and his eyes were an unusually dark shade of blue. How old was he? Megan wondered. Not more than thirty-two – or -three, yet he had the manner of an older man, or a man in authority, which was strange, since he was a freelance scriptwriter. Megan prided herself on her ability to read faces and he puzzled her. What was so different about him, she wondered? Perhaps his toughness. Yes, that was it! One hell of a tough guy lurked behind that smiling, boyish appearance. Suddenly he was too close and too real. She saw him off-guard like a wild creature brought sharply into focus with a telescopic lens. The hearty, modest manner was just a front, she decided. He was a clever, introverted man and he was intent on getting to know her. Suddenly she knew that she had seen Ian before. But where? She could not recall ever having been introduced to him, yet she had seen him, she would swear to that. Perhaps in passing at some sports event, she decided as she excused herself and moved towards Rob and his friends.

Soon she was being teased by some of the athletes. 'Sign me up, Megan,' one of them begged in mock supplication. 'I wanna be a millionaire.' Most of the athletes and their coaches had heard of her company, ISA, and knew she was doing a good job and she felt happy and accepted. There was a great deal of laughter and cries of '*Zivjeli*!' 'Bottoms up' in Serbo-Croatian, as the athletes downed their fruit juices and the rest drank *slivovitz*, a potent aperitif made from plums.

The American and British TV crews were heatedly discussing the Russian refusal to allow them to film their youth group, which had arrived that morning to perform at the Zetra Stadium. The Americans were determined to increase their offer to a point where the Soviets could not refuse; the British were wondering if it was worthwhile. There was only one star worth filming, they told her, and that was Nikola Petrovna, the Soviet free-skater. Best skater in the world, one of them

26

claimed, but he was shouted down. They could not agree on her status, but they wanted to film her anyway, just for the hell of it.

'Did you ever see the Russian ballerina, Galina Ulanova?' an older man slurred his words and without waiting for Megan to reply, went on: 'Probably before your time, but she has the same ethereal quality. You can't believe she's human.' Then he hiccupped loudly and apologised.

Michel arrived. He seemed to know a great many people and he was obviously a popular guy judging by the back-slapping. He homed in to target as soon as he saw Megan, although she was doing her best not to notice him, and behaved as if they'd known each other for years.

'For goodness sake stop drinking *slivovitz*,' he warned, as she picked up her glass. 'Don't be hoodwinked by its pleasant taste. It's almost pure alcohol. I recommend apple juice.'

'Thanks for the warning,' she said and smiled briefly as she pushed her glass away. 'I'm here to work.'

'All work and no play?'

'You've said it.'

'Well, I can combine business and pleasure – your business, my pleasure – by taking you to see Nikola Petrovna one of these evenings; preferably tonight. She's the best free-style skater you're ever likely to see.'

'Hey, wait a minute; that's a pretty strong claim.' Her eyes flashed challengingly. 'I represent the Swedish champion, Maria Stenmark, and I'm tipping her to win a gold medal next year at the Winter Olympics. They don't come much better than that.'

'But Nikola is better,' he insisted. 'I promise you – or else I'm no judge.'

She would go, Megan decided, but not with Michel. She made her excuses, explaining that she was tired, and stood up to leave. Glancing round she noticed Ian was looking towards her and as she hurried down the stairs to the information desk, she heard footsteps behind.

'I just wanted to reassure you about Conrad,' Ian said. 'I know you went there earlier this afternoon. He woke up round six and he's feeling quite comfortable. He'll be all right. The doctor is satisfied with the set, but of course he'll be in plaster for some while.'

27

Looking up at his serious, concerned face, Megan could not help thinking that Ian was a really great guy. He cared and he did something about it. 'I was so glad there was someone around he trusted. You being there meant a lot to him. D'you know him well?'

'We used to ski together,' Ian said.

'So you ski?'

'Nowadays I ski for fun.'

'And previously?'

'I was more serious about it when I was young.'

'Just how serious were you?'

'Americans are very persistent, aren't they?' He frowned at her. 'I skied for Britain in the Olympics twelve years ago. Of course, in those days we were just showing the flag.'

'So what's new?' she said.

He stared at her thoughtfully, eyes narrowed, with a strangely challenging look on his face.

Megan quickly changed the subject. 'He'll never make the big time next season,' she said. 'His career's ruined.'

'I think you're right,' he said gravely, 'as skiing goes, but there are other things in life besides sport. Don't take it so hard. It's a risk all skiers take.' He spoke impatiently, as if annoyed with her depression and suspicious of her compassion. Then he made a visible effort to charm her. 'You need cheering up. How about dinner? There are some very good restaurants around.'

She smiled and shook her head. 'Right now I'm going to ask Cana here,' she gestured towards the information desk, 'to buy me a ticket to see Nikola Petrovna skate. Everyone here seems pretty impressed.'

'You're wasting your valuable time, Miss Carroll,' Ian said, his dark eyes mocking her. 'You can't sign her up. Nikola Petrovna will never skate in the West. Although I have no doubt she'd like to. Her father's unpopular views are killing her career. It's unlikely she'll be allowed to leave the Soviet bloc again. Oh, hang on.' He fumbled in his pocket and produced several tickets. 'Have one of these free press tickets. Or would you like two?'

'One's fine. Thank you very much.'

'Don't thank me. Thank the Sarajevo Publicity Bureau,' he said gravely.

As she hurried to her room to fetch her coat she felt slighted. Ian's inference that she would only be interested in the Russian skater if she could make a profit out of her had hurt. Good grief, she muttered. How could he think such a thing? She wondered why she wanted Ian to think well of her. 'I should care!' she muttered. All the same, she could not help wondering if Ian would ask her out a third time. If he did she would probably say yes, she decided, but she knew that would be unwise. The prospect of spending an evening alone with Ian Mackintosh excited her. In some strange way that she did not understand, she found him very disturbing.

CHAPTER 4

She had been waiting in a queue outside Zetra Stadium for twenty minutes in sub-zero temperatures while officials opened only one door and treated spectators like inmates of a boys' correction centre. Megan kept reminding herself that this was the East, not the West and it was not her business to complain, but her indignation was getting the upper hand, and the snow was piling up on her hat and shoulders.

After a while, Ian Mackintosh, who was a few metres ahead in the queue, saw her standing hunched in her coat and hat and moved back to join her. She tried to draw him out, but failed, and eventually subsided into silence as they shuffled forward. Ian was scowling as they slowly moved towards the door.

'They've never heard that the consumer is king in this part of the world,' Megan muttered.

'What's that?' Ian asked, looking bored.

'Oh my! Where've you been all this century? It means the consumer comes first and foremost – what else?'

'I see.' Ian was grinning sceptically. 'A very American concept and totally foreign to the Slavs. Still, they're aiming to become a ski resort for the West. Why don't you show them how?'

He was setting her up. 'Why don't I just?' she muttered. She strode out of the queue to the main gate. 'Hey. Anyone here speak English?' she shouted to the ticket collector. 'We're freezing to death in this blizzard. Doesn't anyone care? Why don't you open another door? Stupid ... really stupid,' she fumed.

With amazing speed they were ushered out of the queue and into the bar, presented with complimentary programmes and two glasses of *slivovitz* on the house.

'What about the rest of the queue?' Megan said, feeling amazed that ordinary people could be treated so off-handedly.

30

'What about them?' She gestured towards the frozen, patient people.

'Please don't concern yourself,' the stadium manager murmured smoothly in passable English.

'He means mind your own business,' Ian told her when the manager was out of earshot.

'Under every comrade's skin lurks a lackey,' Megan retorted, still shivering, her cheeks flushed and her nose blue.

'Don't you believe it,' came a voice from the doorway. 'They just need your currency.'

Looking round Megan saw Michel Juric standing in the doorway, white teeth shining in a mirthless smile. 'I thought I'd find you two here.' Megan could see from his eyes how hurt he was. His expressive, gypsy eyes were burning with righteous indignation. Once again she felt stunned by his extraordinary good looks, but since this morning she had seen a dozen more men just like him. On the whole Yugoslav men were very good looking, she decided.

'We just met outside in the queue,' she said smiling apologetically. 'Ian gave me a press ticket.'

'No doubt it's the seat next to his.'

'Yes it is,' Ian put in quickly. 'Tough luck, Michel. See you around.' He turned away and after a second's hesitation, Michel left.

'Why are you so mean to Michel?' she asked.

'He's a pest. Besides, whatever you say to him is taken down and used in evidence against you – and publicly, what's more.'

'You're just jealous because he's so handsome,' she teased.

He looked at her quizzically. 'I admit he'd make a good gigolo. Forget him,' he said, holding up his glass. '*Zivjeli*! Here's to your beautiful Irish eyes, unimpaired by three generations of American smog.'

'You've got it all wrong,' Megan said incredulously. She wondered if she should take a stand. 'It's you guys who have the smog.'

He was looking pretty good himself, Megan noticed, in his Harris tweed jacket, Paisley cravat and grey flannels. She was noticing things that she should not notice, how black hairs curled around his wrist over the functional black watch he wore, and how his thick brows nearly met when he frowned, which was often. He was a big, gruff, fierce man and his face

31

was a continual change of contrasting expressions. She sensed that he could be ruthless when he needed to, or gentle when he was loving, and either way he would be deadly.

'What are you smiling about?' he asked.

'Well, just look at you,' she replied, saying the first thing that came into her head. 'It's like you're in disguise.' She saw him stiffen as if she had neared the truth in some clumsy, hit-and-miss manner. 'The dour and terrible Scot dressed as a pukka Englishman.' She wanted to hit back at his anti-American sentiments. But then she laughed to show that it was all a joke, anyway.

'If you had had a less parochial education you would know that Harris tweed, Paisley patterns and brogue shoes all originated in Scotland – like whisky – often imitated, never equalled.' He reached out impulsively and pinched her cheek. 'Now for your next display of ignorance.'

'No kidding? A few evenings with you and I'd be the best informed kid on the block.'

'You're welcome,' he said seriously.

Megan wondered what was going on behind that guarded, buttoned-up expression.

'What are you thinking,' she asked on impulse.

Ian was thinking that it would be a terrible mistake to take advantage of the invitation he could see shining in those candid, blue eyes which were smiling up at him so provocatively. He had never seen a lovelier woman. She had a perfectly delightful profile and her red cheeks were glowing brightly against the white of her skin. A real Irish beauty with her deep blue eyes and near dark brown hair. A waste! he thought. She was both efficient and resourceful and she was probably what the Americans called an over-achiever, and a go-getter. He found both expressions distasteful. His idea of female beauty was the soft and feminine clinging type. The Irishness was there, too, and so was her latent warm and passionate nature. He wondered if she knew about this side of herself, and if she had yet discovered who and what she really was. Efficient women repelled him usually, but this time he felt strangely drawn to Megan and he was excited by her nearness and her obvious interest in him. But why were his thoughts sliding into dangerous channels? Madness to think like this. Only a damn fool would fall into his own trap, and Ian had never been a fool. Anyway, he was not free. Besides, the women in Ian's world were soft and pliable, patient and happily domesticated. Preferable without many brains. A line of poetry from the bard came to mind: 'A gaudy dress and gentle air may slightly touch the heart; but it's innocence and modesty that polishes the dart.' Hardly a fitting description for the girl who was gazing up at him, confidently anticipating a compliment of some kind.

'I was thinking that it's going to be cold in the front row right next to the ice. Drink up,' he said, refilling her glass. It will help warm you.'

'Quite a place,' she said a few minutes later when they had found their seats and were shivering from the shock of cold air rising around their feet. Zetra Stadium was huge, with seating capacity for about eight thousand people and an intricate network of spotlighting from the scaffolding in the roof. This was the first performance, Ian told her. The stadium had only recently been completed for next year's Winter Games. Behind them the frozen Slavs were gradually filing into the hall.

'What's numb toes to a hardy Scot? I'm sure I'll get frostbite. The question is – will it be worth it?' She turned and smiled questioningly and there was both tenderness and friendliness in her smile.

Ian reached out and put one arm around her shoulders. She looked up so trustfully and placed her hand in his. Against his wishes Ian felt himself warming to her and a feeling akin to panic welled up inside him. What the hell was going wrong with him? Fortunately, at that moment, the music blared from the loudspeakers and a team of folk dancers zoomed around the ice in national costume.

'Good grief,' Megan whispered an hour later as the fifth team of national dancers assembled. 'Only the costumes change, I can't take much more of this.'

At last Nikola Petrovna shot out onto the ice. In a split second the cold and discomfort were forgotten. The amazing personality of this intense young Russian skater struck onlookers like an electric charge. She dazzled and shocked with her rapid changes of mood, one moment expressively tender and beautiful and then gay and abandoned in a modern interpretation of a Russian dance.

33

Megan watched in a daze of astonishment and admiration. Nikola was skating like a mischievous pixie, she was a ball of natural talent and energy.

Her beauty was as breathtaking as her skating: long flaxen hair braided around her head, shining green eyes and a full mouth that smiled often, showing perfectly even white teeth. She had a figure that could make *Playboy*. Even her tightly-laced bodice could not disguise her full, high breasts, and her frilled skirt revealed her lovely long legs.

Looking sidelong, Megan could not help noticing that Ian's attention was riveted on the skater. Let's face it, she thought, Nikola Petrovna has everything.

The music was a disaster until the end when they played traditional Cossack folk songs and Nikola tossed her head, laughed and spun into a Cossack dance, kicking her legs in the air like a demented can-can dancer with some movements Megan had never before seen on ice and never would again, she was sure of that.

The performance lasted ten minutes. It passed like a dream. Suddenly Nikola had finished and there was that small moment of quietness in the audience that only comes after a deeply moving performance.

There was no encore. Nikola Petrovna simply curtsied and disappeared.

'I'm in a daze,' Megan raved as they trudged along snowy pavements searching for a taxi. She hardly felt the cold, she was so excited. 'I'm ecstatic,' she raved. 'If only she were American, or British,' she added as an afterthought. 'My God, with her looks I can just imagine the film contracts rolling in, the sponsors on their knees pleading for Nikola. Oh, what a dream.'

They found a taxi and Megan huddled in the corner, trying to keep warm as she analysed Nikola Petrovna's performance. She was a splendid individualist and her free-style dance had included three triple jumps and a triple toe loop in combination with a double jump which she had performed faultlessly. But the music had been badly chosen and the mood of her dance had little to do with the emotion portrayed in the music. The performance had been over-choreographed in most places and the seven or eight highlights had not been strung together to make a composite whole, but rather presented in a rough and ready fashion. The entire effect had been rather frenetic and breathless.

Yet there was no denying her raw talent. With the right coaching she could reach the top. Her beauty was an added bonus, Megan thought. She tried to analyse the girl's appeal, but she could not. Neither talent, nor beauty alone could electrify the audience as she had done. Perhaps it was the combination of the two grafted together, plus a strange beam of ecstasy conveyed from this diminutive dancer to her audience. Megan felt haunted by her lovely smile and her glittering sea-green eyes.

'Oh, if I had her ... my goodness, with the right music, the right backing, the best coaches, can you imagine? She'd be a sensation. She'd make a fortune.'

'The ultimate accolade,' Ian said, grinning cynically.

Ian's hired car started as soon as he turned the key. This surprised him and for a while he concentrated on speeding smoothly along the icy straight road which was almost empty at this hour except for a few dilapidated Ladas. Poverty and hardship was reflected in every figure hurrying by. What docile people the Slavs had become. Their eyes were bleak, their bearing subservient. In World War II they had impressed the world with their bravery and their irrepressible passion for freedom. Yet the system, like an insidious, debilitating cancer, had taken hold, weakened their courage, dampened hope and ruined the economy. Freedom was one of the few things Ian felt really strongly about.

Megan said goodnight to Ian in the foyer, refusing his invitation to coffee and a nightcap. He did not seem very disappointed. It was chilly in her room, the central heating was hardly lukewarm and the stark beige decor was depressing. The lights were dim from yet another of the country's energy brown-outs. Megan decided that she did not want to be alone, after all, so she walked down to the bar and ordered a glass of hot milk, hoping that she would not bump into Ian.

Jenny was sitting there, huddled in her ermine jacket and jeans, her black hair dishevelled and a look of desperation on her face. Then Rob Scott walked past Megan, waved and sat opposite Jenny. They were talking in a low, confidential manner and suddenly Megan heard: 'I'm goddamned fed up with it.' Jenny's voice was shrill and tinged with hysteria. 'I don't care about the frigging race. I just don't wanta hear anymore about your good intentions. Piss off!'

Rob stood up, looking embarrassed and hurt and walked quietly back to Megan's table. He sighed. 'Hi, how you doing, Megan?'

'I'm fine. What's up with our prima donna?'

'Pre-race nerves. It's a bad course, but whisky isn't going to help her tomorrow.'

'That's her business.'

He sighed. 'Did you know she's a brilliant skier? But she's suicidal. Can't you help?'

'I suppose I could try,' Megan said reluctantly, 'but I can't see her listening to me either.'

At that moment Jenny stood up and sauntered to the lifts, ignoring Rob and Megan. She was so young, Megan noticed, watching her upturned haughty profile; hardly more than eighteen.

'Perhaps she's taken your advice,' Megan said smiling. Rob was looking thoroughly upset and Megan wondered why the best guys always seemed to fall for absolute bitches. 'I can see you care, but I don't think there's much more you can do.' She squeezed his hand. 'Hope it works out.'

Rob left and Megan felt utterly alone and curiously reluctant to face that dismal bedroom, but there was no point in sitting there all night. Eventually she went upstairs.

It was starting to snow. Looking out she noticed for the first time a three-storey-high portrait of Marshal Tito on the wall beyond the square. He seemed to be glaring at her.

She pulled the blind and switched on the light beside her bed.

Then she noticed a tray with a bottle of wine and propped against it an envelope addressed to Ms Megan Carroll. A welcome note from the manager, she supposed, but the handwritten airmail envelope was curiously out of place.

She opened it.

Inside was a single sheet of paper. The untidy script read: '*Nikola Petrovna wants to defect. Can you help her?*'

CHAPTER 5

Megan felt tired after a restless night spent worrying about Nikola Petrovna and her plea for help. She wanted to help her, but what could she do alone? she wondered. How could she even contact her? After some soul-searching she wondered if it would be safe to confide in Ian. He exuded an air of dependability and she admitted that she was very attracted to him, but could she really trust him? And would he want to be involved?

Eventually Megan had decided to ask Conrad. After all, Ian and he were old friends. He knew what sort of a man Ian was.

She arrived at nine am and found Conrad looking a little more cheerful than he had when she last saw him. Although it was not visiting hours, the nurse allowed her into the ward. The Slavs seemed to have two sets of rules, one for locals and one for their much-needed foreign guests.

Conrad told her he would be able to go home in two weeks' time, although in plaster. Later, he would set about looking for a job.

'I was surprised to find that you know Ian – Ian Mackintosh,' Megan began casually. 'He told me you used to ski together. Was that recently?' She hoped it did not sound too obvious that she was prying for information on Ian. Evidently it did for Conrad was having difficulty concealing a smile.

'He's a straight guy,' he told her. 'The sort of man you'd trust with your life, in fact, I have once or twice ...' he broke off and grinned ruefully. 'We belong to the same skiing club and the same mountaineering club. Ian's always been a man's man, Megan. I don't know what he'd be like with women – you, for instance. To tell the truth I've never seen him with an intelligent woman. He goes for the fluffy sort – no brains, big boobs. For the rest, all I know is hearsay.'

'Well, go on,' she prompted him.

'Ian comes from some old established family with a strict naval tradition. He was doing pretty well in the Navy, I believe, after a typical establishment education – Fettes College, Dartmouth Naval College then Greenwich Naval College where he studied languages – he was all set to make Admiral. Then – out of the blue – he opted to become a writer. I've heard his family were pretty cut up about it. The story goes he was invalided out after an accident in the Falkland Islands War. Maybe he'd just had enough.' He smiled sadly.

'I don't think he's all that successful nowadays.' He broke off and tried to shift his back on the bed. 'Megan give me hand to wriggle up a bit. I want to sit higher.'

She put one hand under his shoulder and pulled hard.

'That's better. As I was saying, Ian writes the odd script for the BBC. He's always talking about the novel he's working on, but it never seems to see the light of day. It must be tough because Ian's very competitive – always has been. But it's his choice. At any rate I know he used to be an underwater salvage expert, so he's always got something to turn to.'

'I think he'll make the grade as a writer,' Megan said staunchly. She had the impression Ian would succeed at anything if he set his mind to it.

'All I know is, if I had to choose a man to get me out of a tight spot – it would be Ian, that's for sure. But why are you asking? Come on, tell me Megan. Be sensible. Don't set your cap at Ian!'

'It's just that something's come up, I need help and I didn't know who to ask. I'm sorry to sound so mysterious.' She smiled apologetically.

'Well, if it helps I'll tell you about the summer of eighty-two when a team of us went to climbing in the Andes.'

Megan sat listening to Conrad, who obviously hero-worshipped Ian, telling her of how Ian, single-handed, had saved the lives of two members of the expedition by carrying them through a blizzard to safety after an avalanche. All her resolve not to be affected by Ian's charm crumbled. She would have liked to sit there all day, but she had to watch the Men's Giant Slalom at Bjelašnika.

When she left the hospital shortly afterwards she was fully convinced that she could trust Ian. What was not so apparent was whether or not she could trust herself.

It was dark by the time Megan returned to the hotel at six pm that afternoon. Cana came hurrying across the foyer to say that Megan had missed an urgent call from Monaco. They would keep calling, Cana told her.

It could only be Vanguard Sports, Megan decided as she hurried to her room, and shortly afterwards the call came through, but she only heard static and the voice of the operator speaking in Serbo-Croatian. After two more attempts, she picked up the telephone receiver and dialled the bar. 'Can I speak to Ian Mackintosh, please. No, he stays in the hotel, but right now he's waiting for me in the bar. Yes, you've got it. Ian Mackintosh.' She groaned. 'M ... A ... C ...'

Drumming her fingers on the bedside table, Megan gazed round moodily at the dull beige and dusty pink decor and at the snow falling heavily outside the window. She felt depressed and guilty and she had a vague foreboding that things were not necessarily going to turn out right this time. Conrad's accident had shaken her more than she cared to admit. She had telephoned Ian when she returned from the hospital that morning, telling him that she had a problem and needed his help and he had asked her to meet him for drinks and dinner. It had been a long and anxious day for Megan and she had found it difficult to keep her mind on the Men's Downhill, although she had managed to interest Gunter Erath, Austria's leading skier, in signing up with ISA to replace Conrad.

Then she heard Ian speaking. Unaccountably she felt comforted and a warm glow started in her stomach and spread to her fingertips.

'You're late,' he said.

'I'm stuck here. There's a call coming from Monaco, but they keep breaking the connection.'

He laughed briefly. 'Americans are so spoiled,' he said. 'You expect things to work all the time. All right, I'll bring the drinks up.'

'Scotch on ice, please,' she said. Then the telephone rang and Megan pulled the door ajar before she picked up the receiver. As she had feared, it was Vanguard Sports on the line. Megan recognised the voice of Nigel Wilder, sales director.

'Hello Megan, sorry to hear about the accident. Just

checking to see how young Conrad is.' He sounded friendly, which was unusual.

'How did you find out so fast?'

'It was on the radio.'

'It's a bad break,' she admitted. 'The doctors say no skiing for a year. Maybe longer. That'll put paid to his chances in the big time.'

'That's tough,' he said. Suddenly the friendliness had faded. 'I must remind you that the contract is null and void if he can't fulfil the specified number of races this year, so don't expect us to foot the bills for hospitalisation, or any further travel expenses.'

'Hey, there. Hey, wait a minute,' she yelled over his voice. 'Listen Nigel, you surely haven't forgotten that he's employed by you. He's on the payroll as the winter sports promoter – now he's met with an accident during the course of his duties. Sure you'll foot the bills – until he's back in Oslo. And then there's the small matter of his compensation and his bonus. It's almost the end of the season. You can't expect to get off free.'

There was a long silence. Then he said: 'I wouldn't try that if I were you. You can be very generous with other people's money, Megan. I'd like to remind you that this entire campaign was your idea – and it's cost us hundreds of thousands of dollars. I can't tell you how angry Miss Douglas is.'

'I've found a replacement,' Megan yelled triumphantly into the mouthpiece. 'A West German called Gunter Erath ... very ambitious ... he's holding out for more cash ... but don't worry ... I'll clinch it when I see him in Frankfurt next ...' She wondered if Nigel could still hear her. 'But I'm determined you'll pay compensation. Otherwise ...'

'That sort of attitude can cost you your job.' Nigel's voice began to fade into the static which was worsening. She heard him in snatches: 'Most annoying ... vital marketing time ... owe us an immediate replacement ... you're bound by your contract ...'

He was still talking when she replaced the receiver.

Megan crumpled on the chair and buried her face in her hands.

Ian, who had been walking quietly down the corridor with the drinks, paused in the doorway and watched her silently. Megan's slim shoulders were shaking and although her face was buried in her hands he knew she was crying softly. He felt puzzled and cheated. Was this the hard-boiled Megan Carroll he had heard so much about? The girl who was always on the make? In a moment of truth he realised that the Megan Carroll he had sought was a creation of bad press reports and his own imagination. He felt inadequate to cope – women's tears always threw him – he should comfort her, but he could not. Instead he knocked gently on the door.

Megan sat up with a start. Then she glanced round, nervously smoothing her hair.

'Here,' he handed her a glass. 'Cheers.'

'Cheers,' she muttered absent-mindedly. She grinned shyly. Why did she feel so at home with Ian? When he appeared, the room seemed to brighten. It was as if the sun came out. She tried to disguise her relief as she said: 'I loathe that guy.'

'Who is he?'

'Nigel Wilder, sales director of Vanguard Sports, our biggest sponsor. When I say biggest, I mean – they just about own us.'

'You're too tense,' he said. 'You should learn to handle these situations. Losing your temper doesn't help.'

'You're right of course, but I hate to see these kids get dropped when they're no longer useful.'

'That's business. Why should Vanguard pay for losers? Presumably you have insurance for hospital bills, that sort of thing?'

'Yes,' she said slowly, 'but nothing can protect them from ...' She broke off, unable to find the words to explain what she meant.

'From not winning?'

'Okay, so you're putting things into perspective, but it still hurts. You think I'm being a fool?'

Not a fool, Ian thought to himself, and not the tough bitch everyone mistakes her for either; just a mother hen with a clutch of chicks and Nigel was threatening one of them. He decided not to answer.

'I suppose I am,' Megan answered herself. 'Particularly since everyone knows Nigel's only a mouthpiece for Vanguard's chairman, Eleanor Douglas. I've never met her. Hardly anyone does nowadays. She stays in her ivory tower overlooking the harbour and she runs her empire through her henchmen. Nigel is the chief of them. Eleanor Douglas is the ultimate meanie.'

'Maybe, but she's also a very clever and a very able woman,' Ian said. 'Scottish!'

'My God, we're patriotic aren't we?'

'It takes more than meanness to build a company into the biggest sports distributor in the world,' he added, somewhat pompously, Megan thought.

'You wouldn't sound so impressed if you'd been on the receiving end of her contracts,' Megan snapped.

Ian put down his glass and leaned back with his hands clenched behind his head. There was a slight aroma of after-shave and freshly laundered shirts, and the delicious tang of his Harris tweed jacket. He caught sight of her strange expression and raised one eyebrow as he stared at her thoughtfully.

Megan felt her face flushing. It was hard to ignore Ian's physical attraction. He was so intensely male. She had the feeling that he was physically attracted to her, too, but that he was holding back.

'Another drink?' he asked.

She thought: I wouldn't want more than just sitting here like this. It's my idea of a perfect evening. But she said: 'I'm hungry and it's late, so let's eat in the hotel.'

'I've booked somewhere else,' Ian told her. Evidently the matter was not up for discussion. She shrugged and took her coat. 'Let's go,' she said.

Ian looked pleased as he followed her out of the room.

They went to the Café Constance, a private club to which Ian had temporary access through a friend, he explained.

The exterior resembled the entrance to any business building, and Megan felt disappointed, but inside, the night club was dark and intimate, with a decor reminiscent of Sarajevo's Austrian rule: thick Persian carpets, red velvet curtains between the alcoved tables and gilt mirrors on the walls. There were massive silver candlesticks and flowers in cut glass vases on every table.

'How's this for imperial decadence,' Megan murmured, admiring the polished rosewood furniture and gleaming silverware.

A group of Russians were eating in the dining room. They

ignored Megan and Ian, but she could feel the fierceness of their disapproval as they swept past. She knew they both looked so obviously Western, affluent and free. Megan felt a sudden surge of complacency – for the evening, for Ian, for her job and her home. 'Have you ever seen one of them smile?' she asked when they were seated in their alcove.

'It's not their style. They either laugh, or they don't laugh. To the Russians, smiling for nothing is a foolish pastime, but they laugh often.'

'Is Nikola Petrovna like them, I wonder? Somehow I don't believe she is.'

'I don't know,' he said. 'From what I've heard, she seems to be a bit of a misfit.' He broke off as the waiter approached their table. 'Do you like shellfish?'

She nodded.

'Well, why don't you let me order for you?' The *slivovitz* arrived and they listened to the floorshow, a Yugoslav-style Country and Western group singing soulful ballads in Serbo-Croatian.

Megan watched the Russians ordering their next course. 'They seem to be very condescending towards the Yugoslavs,' she whispered. 'Have you noticed? Rather contemptuous really. I don't know why that is. I like the people here. It's just a pity they're so poor.' She smiled winsomely at the waiter carrying their food and he smiled back. 'They've set their hearts on joining the West and the twentieth century via the Olympics. I hope they make it,' she said.

'You're a very perceptive woman,' Ian said. 'But over-sensitive. You care too much. In business that's disastrous.'

Something about the look on his face troubled Megan. What was it? He looked regretful, she decided. A mugger might look like that before he snatched your purse. She gazed at him mistrustfully.

'A woman like you would be better off running a family. That's all these clients of yours are – substitute children. Have you ever worked that out?' Ian said slowly, as he tasted the wine. Then he looked up and she was surprised to see that he was not even smiling.

'Good grief, but you're freaky. Where did they find you – on some palaeontologist's site, frozen stiff and well preserved?

Someone thawed you out and let you loose. Don't worry, your secret's safe with me. Just don't try to club me and drag me back to your lair.'

Looking at her at that moment, with her crazy, courageous ideals and her sensitive, beautiful eyes full of warmth and shyness and too much caring, Ian thought that was exactly what he would like to do. She was so vulnerable and so trusting underneath her facade of worldliness.

She leaned forward touched his cheek with one finger. 'You hit a raw spot and we almost had our first fight. Let's talk about something else,' Megan said. 'Tell me about that documentary filmscript you're writing. The one about Yugoslavia. What on earth could you say that's pertinent to the West?'

Ian looked up and gave her a strange, questioning smile.

Pertinent? People are pertinent, aren't they? To all of us – or they should be. It could be you or I. Instead there's my friend, Daniel. He's just left university with a PhD in mathematical physics, but he can't get a job because there are no posts to fit his qualifications. So all he has are promises. He's still too young to admit defeat and take the job the State has offered him as a mechanic in a computer factory, years behind the West.

Or there's his wife who has had to leave Daniel, whom she loves, and take their nine-month-old baby to her parents, because the country's accommodation is reserved for workers, and there are no unemployment benefits after three months without work.

Or I'll write about Cana, the information chief at our hotel. Her job is to report on the comings and goings of Western visitors. She's clumsy, ill-trained, obvious and inefficient, perhaps because she likes us all. In reality, she's a fine and warm woman. Yet in spite of fifteen years in the Communist party, and her ten-hours-a-day job, she's in tears because the plumbing has broken in the wall at the back of the bathroom in her State-owned flat and she can't afford to get it mended. So her family don't sleep at night; they're too busy mopping up.

He smiled after a long silence. 'I shall try to explain that the system doesn't work and the real victims are the people,' he said. 'That's pertinent!' He spoke with conviction and anger and suddenly his Scottish accent was more discernible. Megan

44

guessed that he had not yet sold the script and that he was writing it because he wanted to write it and because his whole being was at war with all that he encountered here in the Soviet bloc.

'Okay, I'll buy that. Now tell me about you. How come you know so much about conditions here? How come you speak the local lingo?'

After a long silence he said. 'I learned Serbo-Croatian for a year in college. I used to come here for the skiing and sometimes for hunting. It's one of my favourite countries. Now you tell me how you knew about the film.'

'Okay, so I questioned Conrad about you and he told me about the film,' she explained a little shamefaced. I couldn't make up my mind whether or not to ask you for help. You see, I've received this note and I want to go ahead, but I don't know how.'

She took the folded sheet of paper and passed it to him. He read it silently and gave it back. 'Save it,' he said urgently. 'We'll talk about it in the car. By the way, I should burn it, if I were you.'

The food was delicious, but Megan had no appetite – she was too tense and worried. Ian told her about the skiing in the mountains and bear hunting and she listened with only half her attention. It seemed an age before he said: 'It's getting late. Let's go.'

'Why me?' She burst out in the car. 'Why should Nikola Petrovna pick on me? And who knows I'm here, or who I am?'

'This is no time for false modesty, Megan. You're pretty well known in the sports world. But in answer to your question,' he went on, 'I have no doubt that she, or they – and presumably someone is helping her – have picked on you because you are the answer to Miss Petrovna's prayers.

'We can guess that money is what she needs the most,' Ian went on. 'She's here on a Russian passport, so she could walk into the airport and leave now – if she could evade her keepers and if she could pay for her ticket. But,' he laughed briefly and Megan had felt annoyed because of the implied hostility in that laugh. 'Her real problems start at Heathrow. How's she going to convince them she can earn her living? I doubt she can without help. What's she going to do for a work permit? As for skating she needs coaching, sponsoring, a meal ticket – in other words – you! Half of Yugoslavia would have defected by now if they could. The world's tightening up. No one wants East Europeans. If I were you, I'd leave it alone. You can't help everyone and it might be a costly exercise.'

D'you think I haven't thought of that? Megan said to herself.

Ian drew up in the hotel car park and turned to her questioningly. 'Well, can you help her? Do you have that much authority?'

'I run the London branch my way,' she replied bluntly. 'Of course, I lean heavily on the expertise of head office, but when there isn't time to consult them I go ahead. I also take the rap when I fail.'

'Well, don't get caught out promising something you don't really mean. What exactly can you offer her?'

Megan stirred restlessly. This was the big question mark and so far she had not been able to make up her mind. 'Well, I guess I could sign her up – like I always do,' she hedged. 'A minimum of a million dollars over a three-year period plus bonuses for winning. Of course if Nikola Petrovna were to win a gold at the Winter Olympics she'd treble that amount. In that case,' she paused, 'we'd be talking in terms of millions. It's all supposition, not guarantees. The sponsors do the guaranteeing. I go out and sell the deal, bring the two parties together. Our standard contracts merely promise to do our best to obtain sponsors and we state what we think we can get, and in return they let us handle their careers.'

'She won't get far on promises,' Ian mused. 'Doubt she'll make it past Heathrow's immigration. Perhaps it's better like that.'

'What d'you mean?' Megan queried.

'Just because some damned idiot left a note in your room, it doesn't mean you're responsible. Let's define why you want to help her? What's in it for you? Let's measure the profit versus the risk.'

'Funny, but I hadn't actually thought about it like that,' she said icily.

'Why not?' he said, ignoring her sarcasm. 'What if she breaks a leg. You – or ISA – would be responsible for her upkeep and future security.'

'Oh don't go on and on,' Megan grumbled. She did not need Ian to tell her the risks of her tough, competitive business. Glancing sidelong she noticed his angry expression: sullen face, hunched shoulders, smouldering blue eyes – was it possible Ian was building himself up into a childish tantrum?

She said: 'Listen Ian. All my business instincts are saying: Go for it! Pick the plum out of the whole caboodle and watch them drool – all the sports agents. Nikola is tremendous.'

Now he was smiling and that annoyed her, too. 'But Ian,' she went on more seriously. 'Although business is very important to me and I'm ambitious and hard working, there is another side to life – even for me – and helping people does not come under the heading of business.'

She broke off and sighed. Ian's expression was a kaleidoscope of changing emotions: first surprise, then annoyance, then the blinds came down. All of a sudden he had switched off her.

Oh Megan, don't get involved. He's proud, he hates to be crossed and to Ian disagreement means betrayal. Do things his way or find yourself at war – a cold war.

'If you don't want to help me, then good grief, surely you can say so without this tedious preamble,' she added bitterly.

'I never said I wouldn't help you,' he said coldly. 'Don't try anything silly until I come back to you.' She looked up in amazement and held back the angry retort that had sprung to mind only with an effort.

'I'll bear your advice in mind,' she said.

Ian was strangely preoccupied on the drive back. The truth was he was shaken to the depth of his being. He had to admit that his first impression of Megan Carroll had been quite erroneous. The women in his private life had always been docile and willing. He had never before met a woman who was so stubborn. Megan had her holy cows, one of which was helping others, and nothing was going to shake her from her task. He had to admit that physically she was most appealing, but mentally she was like a roadroller, grinding on inexorably, running on the euphoric fuel of goodness and mercy. God protect him from do-gooders!

Back in her room Megan read a sports magazine for half an hour to cool off. After a while, she bathed, put on her pyjamas and a jersey and laid her coat over the blankets. She fell into a restless sleep and she dreamed ...

She was trying to find Nikola Petrovna, searching the snowy slopes of the Igman Mountains. She wanted to tell her something important, but she could not find her and she could not remember what it was, only that it was a matter of life and death. Then the stretcher bearers raced down and she saw the diminutive skater lying unconscious under the blanket. Michel Juric came up behind her, his face twisted with fury; 'It's people like you ...' he said twice and then backed away, the helicopter swirled into the clouds, the stretcher bearers disappeared into the mist and she was left alone and lost amongst the wolves in the dismal twilight.

Megan switched on the bedroom light and climbed out of bed. It was only a dream, she said, but she had the strangest feeling that it was not a dream at all, but a warning. She went to the window, hoping to see someone walking past, but the streets were deserted. Would it never stop snowing? She stared across the square and the portrait of Marshal Tito stared back at her. At that moment she felt absolutely alone. It was a terrifying feeling and it had been creeping up on her all day. She knew why.

Megan believed in God, the Bible, Thanksgiving and human decency. At church on Sundays she prayed to a democratic God who had created man in His image, so that man could create old age pensions, medical benefits and the wonders of science.

But where was the God she understood? For surely He had created this harsh and alien land where women, old before their time, herded goats and sheep through frozen fields and harsh, uncharted mountains. Was He perhaps a sterner, tougher God than she had prayed to in the village church with the rhododendrons, and the flowering herbacious borders and the lovely old stained glass windows? For the first time in her life she felt bewildered and unaccountably responsible. Why? She did not know why. Only that she had never before refused a plea for help and that in return she would never be refused.

At that moment she decided she would do all that she could to help Nikola Petrovna, with or without Ian's assistance.

CHAPTER 6

Megan felt like an impostor sitting by the fire in the Hotel Yahorina, watching the camera crew and race officials coping with the freeze outside. She had spent a restless night worrying about Nikola Petrovna and how she could help her to defect. Could she approach her, she wondered, without inviting the suspicions of the formidable-looking coaches who were usually hanging around the Russian team? It seemed to be an impossible task and Megan felt entirely lacking in resolve. She stretched her hands towards the hearth and tried to draw courage as well as warmth from the crackling log fire. Megan was meeting Ian again that evening and she hoped that he had persuaded the television crew to help them.

Megan had arrived at the hotel two hours ago after an early visit to the hospital to see Conrad, but the race had been delayed repeatedly, because of the blizzard and Megan was finding it difficult to muster any enthusiasm. She reminded herself sternly that she was here for business; to find winners which she and ISA needed so badly, and not just to worry about a defecting Russian ice skater. When she managed to put Nikola out of her mind, she could not help remembering Conrad's white face, taut with disappointment. They had worked hard on his career and it had looked so promising. If only the race had been cancelled earlier, but what was the point in wasting time with stupid regrets, she reminded herself. She would just have to press for compensation. Gunter Erath had won his race and taken Conrad's place at Vanguard.

It was so quiet here; stuffy, too. The hotel, built of granite and timber, resembled a modern-day hunting lodge, with stuffed trophies around the stone walls and one complete wall of glass overlooking the piste. No sound penetrated the double-glazed windows and she had the impression that she was watching the storm on a gigantic cinemascopic screen and that

49

the muffled figures seen dimly through snow were quite unreal. The tick-tock of the antique grandfather clock which chimed each quarter hour and the crackle and hiss of the fire seemed unnaturally loud.

From time to time technicians and race organisers drifted in for a drink to pass the time and left again, and even they spoke in hushed whispers. Everyone felt anxious, wanting the race to start and fearing the effects of the tension on the youngsters waiting up there in the starting hut.

Megan glanced at her watch. It was approaching half past eleven and if the weather did not soon improve they would have to cancel. Outside she could see the dark, fir-clad mountains squatting menacingly over them through a blur of snow and mist.

Below, at the last gate, the faces of the waiting TV technicians and race organisers looked pinched and grey as they stamped their feet, their breath rising in miniature hoary clouds. They were all feeling uneasy and Megan knew why. The piste met FIS requirements of a vertical drop of 805 metres and a length of around 3300 metres, but for the rest it was a disaster, with far too many stones and not enough mesh fencing for safety. It would be a dangerous race.

At hour later, it seemed to Megan that the sky was lightening in the north-east and the snowfall was lessening.

Then a cameraman waved and people began to move around looking agitated. Megan thrust her feet into her moon boots, grabbed her coat and scarf and ran outside.

The cold was shocking. Her fur coat was quite inadequate and so were her boots. She began to shiver and her ears burned unbearably. Then she realised it was the metal in her frozen earrings and she fumbled to remove them with numb fingers.

The loudspeaker crackled and a voice, echoing and re-echoing like a volley of gunshots around the mountains, announced the start of the Women's Downhill race. First would be Jenny Johnson of the United Kingdom.

Poor kid! They always sent the 'rabbits' first – the more inexperienced racers – to test the piste and the gates, so that the better skiers could learn from their mistakes.

Megan felt scared for the girl – however unpleasant her behaviour. Downhill skiers reach incredible speeds of over 130 kilometres per hour and to be one-hundredth of a second faster can clinch a victory. To ski at this intensity in a race that lasts two minutes requires an extraordinary level of fine-tuning, nerve and a great deal of luck. As far as luck went, Jenny had lost out; she would be venturing onto a new and alien mountain. All her team's careful testing and planning during the past twenty-four hours had been wiped out by this new, heavy snowfall. Even now – as they waited with bated breath – a thick cloud was drifting down from the pines obscuring some of the upper gates.

Suddenly there was a great roar from the crowd as the first competitor rocketed out of the starting hut. Megan grabbed her binoculars.

Far up, almost hidden in the mist, a tiny figure shot on to the slope. How slight and small she looked against the immensity of the mountain. Yet she could sense the girl's will as she plummeted down, leaving a trail of spray and snow behind her.

The first few gates were hidden in mist and Megan lost sight of Jenny, but she knew that the top part of the course was a series of sharp, icy bends lasting for about thirty seconds, testing the maximum resilience the skier can muster. Then Jenny burst out of the mist and there were excited yells from the crowd as her speed flashed on the electronic board. Twice she seemed to be out of control, but each time she made the gate and came on down, ever faster.

Now she was reaching 130 kilometres an hour and Megan watched uneasily.

Too fast, she muttered. She'll kill herself. At each twist the sheer momentum would push three times the girl's body weight onto her legs and back, the vibrations were punishing, but worst of all was the wholehearted pursuit of speed which Jenny must hold – totally disregarding all concepts of safety and self-preservation.

The track was running too fast, to Megan's mind, Jenny was coming off bumps at such speed that she was being carried into hollow sections before landing, with the result that her body sustained a crushing, jolting impact as soon as her skis hit the ground. 'She'll never make it,' she murmured.

'She's some tough kid,' the cameraman said beside her.

Now Jenny was in the homerun and she dropped into a textbook, aerodynamic tuck, fists together in front of her face, helmet down, back parallel to the ground. 'Smooth. Real smooth,' Megan muttered. She was letting the skis do the work as she guided them with almost fingertip control.

As she came through the last gate there was an audible intake of the crowd's gasp of relief. Then a burst of cheers as Jenny pulled off her goggles and helmet.

The electronic score board was flashing Jenny's superb timing – 1-16-04 – outstanding in these terrible conditions.

Megan knew very little about this tough seventeen-year-old American, only that Jenny Johnson had set her heart on skiing at the Olympics, but she had broken her leg in practice at Val d'Isère, France, last year and that had put paid to her hopes in the US team. Undaunted she had gate-crashed the British team and demanded that they give her a chance and here she was hell-bent on getting the points she needed to make the Games, wearing a specially-built ski boot to support her weak leg.

Megan decided there was a good deal more to Jenny than she had thought from her arrogant behaviour. Right now she looked like a cheeky gypsy, with her dark skin, flashing white of her eyes and teeth and her black hair falling in ringlets over her shoulders.

All that gamin charm, Megan was thinking as she watched Jenny grinning and waving at the crowd, but can anyone guess what it cost her to push herself down that terrifying slope at such phenomenal speed, in unknown snow? At that moment Megan decided she would sign her up – somehow – and it had better be soon.

The opportunity to approach Jenny arose sooner than Megan expected. The hotel's switchboard operator had managed to connect Megan with ISA's head office in Denver just before dinner and her boss, John Oberholtzer, had given her the green light to sign up Jenny with their standard contract, right away. After dinner, when Megan went to the bar to meet Ian, she saw Jenny sitting alone in the corner, clutching a Scotch and soda.

'Congratulations,' Megan said, approaching her firmly. She would not be put off by rudeness this time.

'What for?'

'Your run – it was brilliant. I was scared to death.'

'No kidding. I came in third.'

'But you were first down and the weather improved dramatically right after your run.'

'So what?' Jenny turned her head away, and stared obstinately at the table. Her knuckles were white against the glass and her foot drummed irritably against the table leg.

'Whatever you think about your performance, you're really something, Jenny. Everyone was cheering you.'

'Don't give me that well done shit. I ski for myself.' She looked up hostile, and on the defensive.

Jenny was as prickly as a porcupine. There must be a reason, Megan thought, but she just smiled sweetly, took out a business card and handed it to her. 'I represent ISA in London ...' she began.

Jenny flipped the card back. 'Megan Carroll! Everyone here knows who you are. Most of these creeps are hoping to be signed up. You've got a reputation. I could find myself on the treadmill – overbooked and under-trained.'

'I understand what you're saying, but it's not true,' Megan said firmly. 'I never overbook clients. It's not my style, in fact, I've often had to cancel a very profitable appearance because my client was badly in need of a rest.'

'Yeah, I bet.'

Megan shrugged and sat down. 'I wouldn't lie to you,' she said softly. 'That would be the wrong way to start a business relationship.'

'What makes you so sure we're starting anything?'

Megan shrugged. 'Maybe I sense a touch of desperation. Something's bugging you – I wish I could help you. You don't have to be a client to be a friend.'

Megan broke off as the gypsy eyes gleamed maliciously. 'Cut the crap,' Jenny said in a voice that sounded contrived and childish. 'We're talking about money, not friendship. What's your offer? Let's hear it.'

For a moment Megan was taken aback. Her lips quivered slightly and turned down at the corners, but after a long, quizzical glance she relaxed. 'I can almost guarantee to put together a million dollar deal over a three-year period. Much more if you win a gold, plus the usual winning bonuses, naturally.'

'Why me?' Jenny stared challengingly at her. 'Or do you solicit everyone in turn?'

'You could find a better vocabulary,' Megan retorted, feeling disappointed and depressed. It was hard to believe that this

53

rude, aggressive teenager was the same incredible girl she had watched hurtling down the piste.

'Hell! I hate agents. I always have done,' Jenny grumbled and then scowled as Megan placed her glass carefully on the table and stood up.

'You could just say "no". You don't have to be rude,' Megan said softly. She turned away feeling soiled by the encounter, and wondering why. It was nothing new, she reminded herself. Silly to feel hurt by this childish girl who was unsuccessfully trying to appear hard-boiled and aggressive.

'Why should I say no, when it's yes?' she heard Jenny calling after her. Jenny put up her feet on the chair opposite, folded her arms behind her head and leaned back, grinning cheekily.

Would she ever stop posturing and showing off? Megan wondered and checked a grimace of irritation.

'I mean it,' Jenny went on. 'You can manage me. I might as well go the whole hog. I need the cash. My mother's curtailed my credit facilities. Zup! Just like that. Every penny. If you've got a standard contract let's do it now.'

'You sound as if you're eloping,' Megan said.

'Top marks!' She grinned, looking Machiavellian.

Ten minutes later the contract was signed and witnessed by a waiter and the boy at the next table. 'You'll probably get more than the figures I quoted,' Megan said smiling with pleasure. 'I was being conservative. There's all sorts of extras like suntan lotion, deodorants and so on, if you're prepared to take the trouble of letting photographers take the shots they need. It doesn't take much time, but I won't do anything you don't want. After all, it's you who'll sign the contracts, not me. I just go out and sell them.'

Feeling pleased with her success, Megan ordered a bottle of champagne. It was the right gesture under the circumstances, she thought. Who knows, it might even make Jenny look a little less sulky.

'Perhaps I ought to tell you that my name's not Jenny Johnson,' Jenny said solemnly as the waiter popped the cork. 'I guess my signature's pretty hard to decipher anyway. I think you'd best just put brackets around the Jenny Johnson bit. Give it here. I'll do it.' She pointed to the top line. 'After all, the contract wouldn't be legal if you used my pseudonym? Or would it be okay?' For the first time she looked unsure of

54

herself as she gazed earnestly at Megan.

'Why do you need a pseudonym for skiing?' Megan asked feeling puzzled.

'Because of Mother,' Jenny said, moodily playing with her glass. 'She's dead set against me skiing. She's afraid I'll fail. Mother's cut my credit facilities until I agree to give up competitive skiing – in writing. I can't do that, even if she does disinherit me – and she usually keeps her word. She's a real tough woman.'

Megan couldn't imagine Jenny being frightened of any woman, yet her lips were trembling and there was a shine of tears in her eyes. 'So then I hit on this idea of a pseudonym,' she said shakily. 'I was hoping for a good season. 'Maybe then ...' She broke tremulously and gazed at her hands.

'Well, let's celebrate,' Megan said doubtfully as the waiter poured the champagne.

The waiter said he never drank on duty. The boy from the next table was in training, he told them. He looked peeved and left abruptly. Megan picked up her glass. 'To the future,' she said. 'I'll try to work on your mother for you.'

'Sure,' Jenny retorted. 'You do that. I don't drink that stuff, but you go ahead.'

It tasted sour and Megan had never liked champagne much anyway. 'So what's your real name?' Megan queried.

'Jacqui Douglas,' the girl said flatly. She stood up too abruptly, pushing over her chair. 'And there's just one thing I should mention,' she said firmly as the waiter rushed to pick it up. 'Don't try to sign me up with Vanguard.'

'Why not Vanguard?' Megan stammered. *Douglas! She thought with mounting dismay. Surely, it couldn't be ...*

'Because Eleanor Douglas is my mother. She threatened to sue if I lost a race and damaged Vanguard's image. We only sponsor winners,' she said with a sneer in her voice. 'Surely you know that. Not that she'd sponsor me,' she went on, 'but since I'm the only heir, I guess it would be even more damaging.'

Megan sat feeling bemused. Poor child, she thought. With her background losing was taboo. The company's slogan flashed through her mind: *'Vanguard – Valour – Victory'* the three V's emblazoned on every piece of equipment or clothing Vanguard produced.

'Jenny ... no, I mean Jacqui. Listen to me, Jacqui. The

55

press will find out about your background just as soon as you start winning. Don't hide, because it won't work. I understand your concern, but just think, Jacqui … what if your mother's competitors found out first? What if you get a good win on someone else's skis? So from now on, you're Jacqui Douglas. Leave it to me to fix this with the British team and the press. I just need a while to think of a suitable story. Tell everyone your real name – tell them Jenny's a nickname if you like, but drop this deception now.

Jacqui shrugged. 'Either way I'm in trouble,' she said. She grinned wryly over her shoulder and sauntered jauntily through the tables to the lift.

It's just an act, Megan thought, watching her go. Just a touch of bravado. She's a real nice kid underneath the hangups and the hurt.

You could hardly call this trip a success so far, Megan told herself, contemplating her bottle full of sour champagne and a contract that was one hundred per cent overflowing with trouble.

CHAPTER 7

Shortly afterwards Michel came into the bar. He stopped short when he saw Megan and his friendly smile changed to a grin of cynical amusement. 'I could write a play around this scenario,' he said. 'Something trite and weepy. Act 1, Scene 1 ...' He moved around, fixing imaginary lights and camera. 'Check props: one table, one bottle of champagne, two glasses – one untouched, one dismal heroine crouched over the table in an attitude of despair. We'll call the play: "Jilted in Jidda". Cut! The heroine's laughing. That's not in the script. She has to shiver and shake. She's about to be sold to the Sultan of Omar. Poor guy! She'll introduce Women's Lib to the harem and the sultan will end up castrated. *Mama Mia*, American women!'

Watching Michel's efforts to make her laugh and the warmth in his brown eyes, Megan thought, he can't be that bad. Somehow, I've got everything wrong.

'I've decided,' Megan said, 'that it's a mistake ever to take you seriously. Have a glass of champagne.' She filled the untouched glass. 'It's the only way I can get my own back on you.'

'It's not that bad,' Michel said, tasting it. 'You've been spoilt by Yugoslav wine.' He grinned. 'I just came from the hospital,' he went on. 'Saw Conrad there. He mentioned you'd been around a few times. He told me you'd replaced him as Vanguard's Olympic hope with Gunter Erath from the West German team.'

'Yes,' she said guardedly.

'And he told me you're trying for compensation.'

'That's right.'

'You don't look that naive.'

'Listen, it's not as naive as you might think. He's been operating as house model, PRO, research guinea pig and officially he's the Winter Sports promoter. I think I'll swing it. Depends how badly they want Gunter.'

'So why all the gloom?'

'I made a booboo,' she sighed. In fact, she thought, I might just have blown the compensation as well as my reputation. Then she said aloud: 'But don't ask me about it, because I'm not going to tell you.'

'So there's a story for me, is there? When it comes to news I have the nose of a bloodhound.' He placed one hand lightly on her shoulder. 'You'll work it out,' he said. 'And so will I. I have the greatest faith in both of us. I'm definitely going to write that article, but not yet ...' He broke off and gazed over the balustrade into the foyer below. 'I'm waiting for the witch's brew to brew ...'

He broke off and stared intently at the foyer. 'Here come the Russian team – arrogant, badly-dressed, faces like unbaked dough. Except her ...' He turned and smiled rather shame-faced, Megan thought.

'I've never liked Russians,' he said frowning, 'but then I've never before seen a woman as beautiful or as talented as Nikola Petrovna.' He drained his glass abruptly. 'Look at them all – no shouts or laughter, no fun; dour faces and suspicious glances. What must it be like for a girl like Nikola to have to live amongst people like that. If I were a knight on a faithful steed, I'd carry her away to a place where she'd always be smiling.'

'But since you're a journalist?' Megan queried.

He looked away uneasily and Megan suddenly wondered: could it be Michel who wrote the note? Why not? The more she considered it, the more plausible the idea seemed. Michel was obviously taken with Nikola.

'Michel, you're such an oaf,' she said. 'Always roman-ticising.'

'What's wrong with that?'

'Nothing, as long as you keep it out of print.'

'*Touché,*' he said. 'I know you're still angry with me. One of these days I'll make it up to you.'

He stared at her so intently that Megan had the impression she was supposed to take him seriously. Then she caught sight of Ian and forgot about Michel and his article.

Ian scowled at Michel's retreating back, his blue eyes blazing with fury. He's more handsome when he's angry, Megan decided. She wanted to reach out and touch him, but at the same time she wanted to run away.

'Let's go,' he said brusquely.

He drove aggressively, skidding around corners, gliding over the ruts and bumps of the gravel track, through the forested mountain trail, towards Yahorina.

Finally Megan said: 'Do you always drive like this – as if you're fighting a war?'

He braked unexpectedly and parked on a wide ledge overlooking the precipice.

'Sorry,' he said. He turned and stared at her until Megan reached out and took his hand. 'What is it? What's the matter?'

In answer he merely tightened his grip on her hand.

It was almost dark and wisps of mist were gliding down through the trees, towards the car. On the far horizon there was a streak of green-blue in the dark sky. The lights of Sarajevo seemed far away.

'Spooky,' Megan said staring out of the window.

'When are you leaving?' Ian asked.

'I should have been on tomorrow morning's flight, but I cancelled. I've left it open, but I don't know what to do ...' She broke off and stared at him hopelessly. 'I want to help her, but how?'

'It's arranged,' Ian said, seemingly reluctantly. 'One of the camera crew who speaks Russian slipped her a note today. She's to come to your room some time in the night. You can sign her up – if you still want to – as you said yesterday.'

'I'm certainly not going back on my word,' she said primly, but she was thinking: *Oh my goodness – so soon. What if something goes wrong? What if we fail? What will happen to her?*

'This weekend is the only opportunity you'll have,' Ian said. 'The skiing finishes today. Most of the team will be sightseeing for a while and leaving on the weekend flights. The Russians are scheduled to leave on Monday morning. They were only here to show us the flag.

'I've spoken to the rest of our television team,' Ian went on, 'and quite honestly, I'm amazed that they're prepared to get involved. But they think it's some kind of a lark. They're willing to drive Nikola over the border to Italy in the equipment van on Saturday night. It's not difficult to get her out of Yugoslavia. They're not breaking any laws. After all, she has her passport. They'll take her to the British Embassy in Rome and from there she'll be flown to London.'

'Hey, wait a minute, how can you be sure the Embassy will do that?'

'Standard procedure. She has a passport and she'll have your contract and guarantees, plus some cash. For the rest the Foreign Office will sort it out.'

'Uh huh! But how do you know she has money?'

'Simple! We'll all chip in and give it to her. Now this is the plan.' It seemed simple enough as Ian explained it in three sentences. Then he watched anxiously. 'How does that strike you?'

'Just great,' she said with a gulp. A wolf howled nearby and Megan shivered. 'Wolves scare me,' she said.

Unexpectedly Ian put his arm around her. She felt the sudden stiffening in his body and sensed his heightened tension. He bent forward and pushed her chin up. She felt his cracked lips hard against hers, and the stubble of his cheek scraping against her skin. The smell and the feel and the touch of him was violently sensuous and passion surged so swiftly that for a few minutes she was unaware of anything other than the need to be close to Ian, to clutch him, hold him, press her mouth tightly against his and feel his strong, hard body pressed against hers. Afterwards, when reason flooded back into her mind, she felt shaken by the force of her passion. She had never before felt like this. It was like a pristine memory brought sharply back to the present. She thrust her fingers into his hair, and pressed his head down harder, probing his tongue with hers, loving the strength and fullness of his lips.

How long did they stay like that? She did not know, she was entranced with the feel, and smell of him. Her fingers were searching his head and his face – like a blind woman's – needing to touch and to hold. She had the strangest yearning to take off her clothes, right there, in the car, in the dark, on the roadside, without caring, and to feel his naked body against hers. She had never felt like this before and she was shocked by her own sensations. She gave a short, sharp cry and pulled back.

'Oh Ian, I don't want this to happen,' she whispered.

60

Ian struggled against her withdrawal. He held her fast and an instinct as old as man made him struggle to push her thighs apart, feel the soft, clinging flesh in hidden places, force her to surrender. He pushed her back upon the seat and used the weight of his body to pin her there, thrusting his mouth over hers as if to stifle her words. At that moment he could have raped her, would have raped her, but reason surfaced as his knee struck the gear knob, and anyway there was no room. Reality hit home hard.

'Oh God,' he said pushing himself up and smoothing her skirt down. 'Did I hurt you?'

'No. I guess I frightened myself.'

'Me, too. I'm sorry. I can't explain my behaviour.'

'You can't?' she giggled.

'Don't laugh. You were saved by this damned awkward car. I wish I hadn't done that,' he went on eventually. 'I'm sorry. It won't happen again.'

'You didn't do it alone,' she said. 'It's just that I didn't want this to happen.'

'Neither do I, quite honestly,' he said gruffly. Then he rubbed his hand over her hair. A strange gesture! Like patting a dog, she thought.

'So let's cool it,' she said.

'Look,' Ian whispered. 'Keep still, but look there.' He pointed into the trees and she saw against the luminous glow of the snow, between the shadows of the trees, a grey shape gliding, moving down towards the car, hesitating – passing by. Then more of them.

'Wolves!' she whispered.

The pack moved past silently and for a long while she sat staring at the trees, but they did not return.

'I've never seen them before, but I've heard them,' Megan said. 'It's fantastic, but it's scary, too. This place ... it's so uncontrolled. There are no signs saying: Wolves are dangerous – don't feed them. There are no litter bins, no litter, no coke tins under the bushes ...' she broke off.

'Nature has things pretty much her own way here,' Ian said. 'Let's blame it on nature.' She noticed that his voice was hoarse as he started the car.

It was past eleven when Ian dropped Megan at the hotel and said goodnight. They had eaten mainly in silence, both too tense for small talk and neither really enjoying themselves. Megan sensed that Ian was as unwilling as she was to embark upon a meaningful relationship. It was all wrong – wrong time, wrong place.

Some guy, she murmured, as she watched his hired Lada racing along the main highway and out of sight. Oh hell, she thought, I wish the next few days were over and done with.

She walked through the swing doors and hurried to information. Cana was there, looking tired and strained, but her face was perfectly lovely, Megan decided, noticing her amber eyes and straight honey-blond brows. She looked so womanly. How could she be a spy? Ian was full of nonsense, Megan thought. Perhaps because he was a writer and lived on his imagination.

'Cana, my passport hasn't been returned,' she complained.

'I put it in your room an hour ago.' Cana looked up, smiling graciously – like a perfect society hostess. 'Have you had a good evening?' She looked genuinely concerned as she cross-questioned Megan about where they had been and what they had eaten. Once again Megan was struck by the curious group psyche which the Slavs seemed to share, feeling pride or shame in each other's achievements.

Megan fled to the privacy of her room and ran the bath. 'Ian, oh – Ian,' she whispered as she lay back in the hot water. She had the strangest impression that she was falling in love. Of course, that was impossible. It was the loneliness and being away from home and her business. The force of her need was something new and entirely unwelcome. Megan had only loved once before, at college and it had been a sad and lonely affair, leaving her bruised and suffering and vowing never to fall in love again. She climbed out of the bath shivering and towelled herself dry. Then she stood examining her body in the mirror. Would Ian like her? she wondered. She had small tight breasts, a narrow waist and long legs and she knew she looked good in a bikini, but she would have liked her breasts to be a little larger.

She was athletic and it showed, and she knew that Ian went for soft and feminine types. Was this love, she wondered? This desperate need to be naked and close to him. She could not recognise herself. Certainly it had not been like this the last time.

She sat reading the sports pages from a pile of outdated

magazines for a long time, but no one came and at one am Megan went to bed.

Much later there was a gentle knock on the door. Megan stiffened and lay without breathing ... listening. It was her. She knew it was.

'Oh God,' she whispered to herself as she crept across the floor, smoothing her hair and her dressing-room.

A small figure in a drab coat flung over a gown, stood in the dark. It was Nikola Petrovna and she looked scared.

Megan hesitated in the doorway, stunned by the impact of Nikola's incredible face.

Then the girl whispered. 'Please ... please ... let me in. I am so frightened ...'

When the door was shut, Nikola turned and faced Megan. She was so slight and so young and she was very beautiful with her perfectly even features, her smooth, unblemished white skin and ash blond hair. Yet there was something that marred her appeal, something to do with the expression in her bright green eyes – a bruised look. Women would not trust her, Megan decided instantly, but men would covet her.

'I have been told that you will help me ... Yes?' There was only a shadow of fear on Nikola's face and the slightest twinge of doubt, but it was there and Megan was touched.

'Who told you that?'

Nikki stood staring sullen and dumb.

'Yes, I'm going to help you,' Megan said after a fractional hesitation. 'I'm relieved you speak English. That helps, too.' She watched Nikola walk across the room and gaze nervously at the bathroom door and then at the window.

'I learned English at school,' Nikola said frowning, as she sat on the end of the bed. 'Later I learned with records. It is not bad, my English? Not bad. What you think?'

'Very good,' Megan said politely. Nikola was watching her with a mixture of trust, anxiety and impatience and she felt burdened with the responsibility of this young skater's hopes and ambitions. Here was Cinderella and she the fairy godmother.

'I'm going to speak slowly, so that you will understand properly,' Megan said, sensing that Nikola was afraid to be there. 'I'm going to offer you certain guarantees – enough for you to live on and train, and other possibilities, depending upon the contracts that I sell and the sponsors' optimism. Do you understand what I'm saying?'

'Of course. I understand how you operate in the West. I am prepared ...' she broke off. 'I need coaching, time to practise ... many things.' She gave up, her English inadequate to cope with the situation.

'I understand,' Megan told her. 'You will have all these things – if you work very hard.' She hesitated, not wishing to foster false hopes or tell lies.

'And I will have the best coach and an allowance, not too little, not to much, and I will skate for Britain. It is all here.' She took out a sheet of paper with her demands written in pencil in large, childish handwriting. 'You will sign here, da?'

'Well, that's not exactly the way we do business at ISA,' Megan said, grabbing her briefcase.

But finally Megan signed the grubby piece of paper. It seemed to mean so much to Nikola, more than ISA's signed contract, which she also gave her, more than Megan's reassurances or her promises of help from the British TV crew.

'Do you think you can come to my room at half past seven tomorrow evening? It's important that you do this,' Megan explained. 'You will be taken out of Yugoslavia to Italy and from there to London.'

Nikola thought for a moment. 'We are having a farewell party – I will pretend that I am unwell ... you understand ... please don't lock your door.'

She clutched Megan hard, kissing her on both cheeks. Then she went out clutching her contract as if it was a passport to heaven.

CHAPTER 8

Rob Scott walked moodily through the foyer. Some members of the Austrian team who were leaning over the balustrade of the mezzanine bar aimed a champagne cork at him. It missed, but the froth splattered his head. 'Come on up,' they yelled. He shook his head and smiled. Rob was in no mood for a party; he was looking for Jenny. Eventually he found her in the newly opened *Pizza Den* in the hotel and, as usual, she was creating a scene.

'You call this a pizza?' she yelled at the chef, who had been summoned by the waitress.

Jenny's tantrum did not affect the chef one way or the other. He would never eat this mess of tough pastry, smothered with tomato sauce and re-heated in the microwave. If he could choose, he would not cook it, either. He was merely following instructions to produce pizzas and hot dogs for Western tourists. He was renowned for his *sarma*, a fragrant dish of succulent minced meat cooked in vine leaves, and his piquant apple desert, *tufahija*, had once been praised by the great Tito himself, so now he regretted his transfer to this so-called International hotel where he had to serve up hash and listen to spoiled young women from the West, but one must live, he told his wife night after night.

His impassive expression was provoking Jenny even further. 'A pizza has cheese,' she yelled, 'and anchovies ... olives! You've heard of olives? Have another try for Christ's sake.'

Rob's hand shot out and grabbed the plate as it skimmed across the table. 'What you need is some good local food – and lessons in manners,' he added as an afterthought.

Jenny sat bolt upright looking amused. 'Why you bossy pipsqueak ...' Unexpectedly she laughed.

The waitress slammed the bill on the table and removed the pizza.

'She's got a nerve …' Jenny began, but broke off as Rob took the bill and signed it.

'You didn't have to do that,' she objected. 'They shouldn't … shouldn't get away with it.' She was stuttering with temper.

'Let up, Jenny,' Rob said. 'It cost exactly forty-two American cents. You don't need the big guns out for forty-two cents.'

'It's the principle,' she insisted sulkily.

'You can't expect them to be experts on junk food. Come on, I'll show you round the Turkish quarter. Have you tasted *begova corba*, or *bamija*? I had it yesterday and believe me, it beats pizzas.'

Jenny looked up and coolly studied this hulk of a boy who looked kind of nice, but you could never go by looks. He'd turned into a regular pest just lately and no wonder. She should not have told Megan who she was. When the word got around that she was the Vanguard heiress, they'd all be grovelling. Too late now, she thought gloomily. 'No, and I'm not sure I want to,' she said.

Rob was feeling dejected. He couldn't think of anything else to say to this skinny, oddly beautiful girl. Right now her upper lip was looking petulant, ready to pout. Obviously, she was accustomed to having her own way. Her brown eyes were staring up and boldly challenging him.

'Let's get out of here,' he said. He was not surprised when she followed him.

Rob called a taxi and they sat in uneasy silence as they were driven towards the Turkish quarter.

'You like to put on that big macho image, don't you?' she said after a while.

He turned and studied her coolly. 'No,' he said. 'It's something quite different. I feel for you. Don't ask me why. You're so prickly I get punctured each time I talk to you.' He wanted to say: You're lonely and desperate, but he didn't want to humiliate her. 'I know you're carrying a load of trouble. I wish I could help. That's all there is to it.'

Her face was dauntingly expressive. Right now she had 'distrust him' written all over it. Rob looked away. He did not want to see any more ugly expressions. He had another image: it was of Jenny when she made her legendary flight down the hillside. He had caught sight of her face as she pulled off her helmet – not the smiling, defiant skier she had showed the crowd a split-second later, but that of a small, frightened, troubled girl.

That was when he made up his mind that she needed looking after, and in Rob's opinion he was the best man for the job. She seemed to have a real talent for rubbing people up the wrong way. He knew, he'd seen her in action enough times. He knew she was a rich kid, too, he could tell from her manner and her clothes, and that might be a problem, but, after all, he was not without prospects himself. Rob was an intensely obstinate man, he set about each task with thorough preparation and dedication. This was the first time he had come up against a situation which he could not control and where he could not be sure of acquitting himself well. He felt baffled and anxious and he wondered why he should care so much.

They were passing through narrow cobbled streets with the shuttered stalls and intricate alleyways of beautiful, centuries-old Moorish buildings on either side; Turkish music blaring from every restaurant and groups of people poorly clad against the cold, thronged the doorways.

Jenny felt a little uneasy having her arm held. She wondered why she had come in the first place. But of course she was hungry.

'Tell me about yourself,' he said. 'About your home. Why did you sign up with Megan Carroll? I would have thought that was the last thing you'd do?'

'A month ago I'd have thought the same,' she answered with a shaky laugh. 'Mother's leaning on me to stop me skiing; blocked my allowance so I'm broke. She swears she'll disinherit me if I take part in international competitions. You see, if I fail I'll damage Vanguard's image – as I explained to Megan.'

Vanguard! Was her family connected in some way with the Douglases? Surely not. The poor kid seemed very mixed up, but Rob could hear the bitterness under her bantering chit-chat. 'Vanguard only sponsor winners – everyone knows that – and if I lose, that'll knock the image. More so – since I am Vanguard ... if you see what I mean ... or rather ... I will be, if I give up competitive skiing. Mother can't afford to take a chance on me. That's why I'm using a pseudonym. My real name's Jacqui Douglas. Mother doesn't even know I'm here.'

Jacqui took a deep breath and looked up to see shocked dismay on Rob's face.

'Your mother is Eleanor Douglas of Vanguard?' he asked sorrowfully. He had known she was a rich kid, but not this rich. The thought was too daunting to handle.

'Didn't you know? Yes Mother owns Vanguard – she's the chairman. They don't come any tougher – or richer. Surely Megan told you my name's Douglas. Why else would you still want to be friends with me?'

'You believe that?' he asked incredulously. 'But Jenny ... should I call you Jacqui?' he went on more gently, 'if you spend your life thinking every guy's after your money, how the hell are you going to gather some real friends? You're a walking cliché – the poor little rich girl – I feel really sorry for you.'

She peered at him with her strange habit of half-closing her eyes and tilting her head sideways, reminding Rob of an inquisitive bird. '*You* feel sorry for *me*?' She laughed harshly. 'Well, that's just droll. I've got everything,' she added.

Yet Jacqui could see that Rob meant it and she felt strangely insulted and upset.

The taxi drew up in front of an old Moorish-style building with the name, *Daire's*, written above the gateway. 'This is it,' Rob said. He did not seem to notice her angry glances as he paid the taxi and led her through the tiny Turkish garden to the entrance.

Daire's was a fifteenth century granary which had been faithfully restored. They were given a table in a room next to the kitchen and because they were visitors, the manager proudly led them on a tour of the building through a maze of rooms, with walls four foot thick: and they saw the original bread oven built into one wall and still in use; and the coal barbecue in the centre of the kitchen with its huge copper canopy; they dutifully admired the heavily-barred windows, doors of thick, intricately-moulded iron; and handmade woven rugs and cushions; and at last they were ushered to their table with a great deal of ceremony. The waiter, in a green velvet waistcoat and black trousers, placed a jug of high-octane *slivovitz* on the table and advised them to start at the top of the menu and try everything in turn.

Jacqui seemed strangely oblivious to her surroundings and Rob felt disappointed. She tossed off two glasses of *slivovitz* and pecked at the *begova corbar* soup, while telling him of Mother's villa in Cap Ferrat. Then she chewed her way through *skamplignje*, a spicy dish of squid, and told him solemnly that Mother's turnover for 1982 was in excess of one hundred and sixty million dollars worldwide. After that she tackled the *sogan dolma*, a spicy Turkish dish of minced lamb and onions, and recited the highlights of Mother's six-storey head office in Monaco, while gulping the mellow *samotok* wine as if it were water.

'Okay, so that just about describes Mother,' Rob said, looking thoroughly disgruntled. 'What about Father? Doesn't he figure in Vanguard?'

'Father?' She looked at him suspiciously. 'That's a real sob story,' she said. 'Mother had an affair and the man left her high and dry. That's all the info I've ever been able to get out of Mother. Who needs him?' she said contemptuously. 'And who cares anyway? He must have been a real shit.'

Rob's spirits were sinking. He wondered if he had made a terrible mistake and the girl he had fallen in love with was just a dream. He had listened and grieved for the brave, trembling girl who had hurtled down that terrible piste at a speed few skiers would contemplate.

'I'm surprised you have time for skiing with the exciting life you lead,' he said. 'So why do you ski?' he wanted to know.

Jacqui held her glass in her hand and swished the wine around, watching the changing yellow patterns on the white tablecloth. 'It's always complicated to find reasons ...' She paused and it seemed to Rob that she was having difficulty pronouncing the words. 'So many levels ... deep levels ... surface levels ... know what I mean?'

Rob nodded, relieved to see that she was no longer posturing.

'On the surface I ski because there's no way Mother's money can help me when I'm up there. I could crash, or die, or win, but whatever I do, I do it alone. Mother's power and her money ... why, it's just nothing up there. And then again, I ski to be me. I have this terrible fear ...' she broke off and gazed at Rob as if in despair. 'I have this terrible fear that I could miss my whole life. Just being Mother's daughter is a full time job – but what about me?'

She broke off and sat fiddling with her glass. 'I don't want you to get the wrong impression about Mother,' she went on eventually. 'I don't hate her – nothing like that – I love her in a way – it's just that she's always there, overshadowing me. She

69

wants to give me everything. I can freak out sometimes. She even tries to find my dates. That's not funny when you think about it. Then there's other things ...' She pressed her lips together firmly, as if determined not to say another word.

'And the other levels?' Rob pressed her after a long silence.

'Well, I really want to excel – at something – something that's really mine, and skiing's the only thing I'm really good at. So I aim to get better, just for its own sake. Just for no other reason.'

'The pursuit of excellence.'

'That's it!' She looked up, suddenly excited. 'You've got a way with words. I could never nail it down.' She picked up her glass and Rob put one hand over hers.

'Go easy, Jacqui. You'll get sick.'

'So what? The race is over.' She shook his hand off and drained the glass.

'There's still more to it,' she went on absent-mindedly as if she was far away. 'There's the joy of speed, the joy of feeling your body and your mind working like a unit, and then somehow you find it's not only you, it's the snow, the air you breathe, the trees, the clouds, all working together with you ... part of you. You're not even thinking. It's like being in a daze. That's when you ski your best.' She grinned self-consciously. 'You ever feel like that?'

'Yes, but not that often. When it comes it's good.'

'Sure is,' she said. 'But not today. Today I had to keep my mind on that goddamned awful piste. Where are you going tomorrow?' Jacqui asked abruptly.

'Back to Denver.'

Jacqui looked disappointed. 'I thought I might stay over for the weekend. Look around a bit.'

'I can't,' Rob said regretfully. 'I have a plant outside Denver making skis. It's coming along nicely, but I can't stay away so long. You ever heard of Scott brand?'

'Sure. You were wearing them.'

He felt surprised she had noticed. 'Custom-made for serious skiers! When I've built up a good enough reputation, and enough cash for the machinery, I'll start bigger production lines.'

'I'll tell Mother to watch out,' she said.

She was laughing at him. 'You do that,' he said, 'but it may take ten years before she need start worrying.'

Rob felt he had seen the real Jacqui, but now she was taut, aggressive, angry. Instinctively he knew that there were many other problems besides Mother, heaped on Jacqui's shoulders.

The waiter brought *baklava*, with its piquant jam sauce, and Jacqui gazed at it blearily. 'Oh my God I feel sick. Can we get out of here?' she groaned.

'You need some fresh air,' Rob said. He called the waiter, paid quickly and helped her outside.

Suddenly she groaned, gave a curious half-sob, looked up at him beseechingly and then vomited into the roots of the ancient oak tree which shaded the patio.

Rob should have been irritated, but he felt sorry. For a few precious moments she had shared her hopes, let him peer into her soul and he had sensed her isolation. Now she seemed pathetic as she leaned over the Turkish garden, her black ringlets damp with perspiration in spite of the cold, her face as white as the snow.

'It's that terrible, greasy food,' she sobbed.

'You drank too much,' Rob insisted. 'This could start a war. I'd better get you home.'

By the time they reached the hotel Jacqui had passed out. He paid the taxi and carried her awkwardly across the foyer.

Cana, the information chief, hurried towards them.

'Food poisoning,' he explained, lying awkwardly and feeling bad about it. 'Can you find a doctor at this time of night?'

'I'll find one,' Cana promised.

Rob carried Jacqui to her room and laid her on the bed. The doctor arrived with the housekeeper shortly afterwards and Rob waited outside. When he returned she was freshly washed and lying in her pyjamas smiling blearily up at him. Then she closed her eyes and fell asleep again.

'Tension!' the doctor said. 'She can't stand the tension after the race, so she took three tranquilisers, and drank too much. She'll have a hangover in the morning, but nothing more serious than that.'

They left and Rob stared down at Jacqui, looking quaintly virginal and sweet, with her black hair tangled over the pillow.

Rob was about to leave when Jacqui called out in her sleep and struggled up, her forehead damp with sweat. She opened her eyes and they were filled with dread and for a moment she did not seem to know where she was.

71

'Don't worry; it's over,' he said soothingly. 'You've got a bad dose of the eebie-jeebies. I've had them dozens of times,'

He went on. 'Once I was buried in an avalanche in Switzerland. I got out pretty quick. I didn't think much of it at the time, but that night when I fell asleep, I dreamed I was buried alive – the nightmares went on for a week. I can tell you, I was scared to go to bed.'

She laughed uneasily and told him about the terrible piste, and her fears beforehand, and how she nearly killed herself in one godawful skid towards the spruce forest where the nets were blown down, and of her need to win and to be the best. At last she fell asleep, only to wake with a jolt shortly afterwards.

Finally Rob took her in his arms and held her while she slept peacefully until morning.

Looking down at her, Rob had the strangest feeling that she was his responsibility, his girl to cherish and protect. He knew that he loved her, and that she needed his love, in spite of the tough image she was acting out. Yet Vanguard and Mother's money were obstacles that seemed insurmountable. How could he expect a girl like Jacqui to share his home and his prospects – although until this evening they had both seemed pretty good? The more he thought about it, the more despair crept into his soul. But Rob had never yet given up on any task he set himself.

At dawn, when Rob left, Jacqui was smiling in her sleep and he wondered what she was dreaming about and if she would remember anything at all about him when she woke.

CHAPTER 9

The first World Cup event in Sarajevo had not been the outstanding success that race officials had envisaged: snow was scanty, there were not enough storm fences, and the whole area was buffeted by gale-force gusts of wind. In particular the Men's Downhill course was slated by racers for its bad artificial design, with too many jumps into flat, jarring landings, no fast schuss for the gliding experts, and too many contrived leaps making it difficult to build up maximum speed so that even Franz Klammer remarked after coming third that he would have gone faster had he felt safe.

But that in no way dampened the spirit of the competitors who were letting off steam and sharing the triumphs and disasters of all, regardless of nationality. It was Saturday evening, the trials were over and the hotel reverberated with the parties which were starting to burst out sporadically in various parts of the hotel.

At a quarter-to-eight, only fifteen minutes late, there was a light tap on Megan's door. It swung open and Nikola darted into the room. She closed the door behind her and Megan hurried her to the bathroom. Nikola looked frantic, but as the door closed, she threw her arms around Megan and kissed her on both cheeks. Then she clutched at her as if she were drowning.

Megan recoiled slightly from the pressure of her breasts, the tang of perspiration and the smell of her unwashed hair. The thought came: don't they have deodorants? And then: no wonder she wants to defect. Megan hoped that none of this showed on her face. Nikola's eyes were wide open and glistening with fear.

'It will be all right,' she said quietly. She tried to smile, but her mouth felt as if she had just left the dentist. Nikola was gazing at her as a small Catholic child might gaze at a statue of the Madonna.

Oh, but it was too much, Megan thought, as she hid Nikola behind the plastic shower curtain and closed the bathroom door. Her fears were for Nikola, not for herself. What if she were caught? What if she were arrested, or sent to prison? These were the anxieties that had been tormenting her since the previous evening.

She glanced at her watch, dialled the bar and reminded the waiter that six bottles of champagne and three trays of snacks were to be delivered to her room promptly at eight.

At seven-fifty pm, four members of the British television crew came in and wished Megan happy birthday with a good deal of noisy laughter. They left the door open and at eight Ian arrived with a friend. He maneouvred her into a corner and muttered: 'Don't worry. The boys assure me that everything's under control. I'll go with them to Rome, then I'll fly on to Switzerland. See you in London.'

Champagne corks were popping, drinks were flowing and the shouting and laughter tempted several other members of the British and American team to drop by for a drink.

Michel arrived and gatecrashed the party. Then he tried the bathroom door several times.

Trust him to make a nuisance of himself, Megan thought angrily. 'A friend is ill,' she explained. 'Drank too much. You'll have to use the loo next door.'

The party was already spreading to the adjacent room where one of the TV cameramen stayed.

Michel smiled superciliously, and once again Megan wondered how much he knew about Nikola's intentions. Was it he who had written the note?

Soon the birthday party became riotous. At eight-thirty, Cana called to ask them politely to shut their doors and make less noise, but Megan shouted above the clamour that it was her birthday and why didn't she come up, and anyway, they were going out to dinner shortly.

At nine pm, Megan tapped on the bathroom door and walked in carrying her coat and hat and boots which Nikola put on. This time Nikola did not attempt to hug Megan. Perhaps she had sensed from Megan's manner that it was not her way.

She's altogether too sensitive, Megan thought as she wished her good luck and shook her hand. Nikola looked pretty good in her mink with the collar turned up, her boots with half the toes

74

stuffed with cotton wool, her fox hat pulled well down and, of course, her sunglasses. Her hair was quite concealed, but her milky white cheeks showed. Would it matter, Megan wondered? She would be walking out in the centre of a noisy crowd. Who would bother to look? At the same time, the Russian team managers were always hanging around in the foyer with their vodka and their bleak disapproving stares.

Megan snatched her foundation and some cottonwool and rubbed the girl's cheeks. 'There! That's a bit better. See you in London,' she said. 'Good luck.' And then, because she was scared for her, she reached out and hugged her. 'You'll be okay,' she heard herself say in a funny, high-pitched voice.

'Come on Megan or we'll be late,' she heard Ian's voice. He sounded petulant and slightly drunk, but he was none of those things. Nikola was shaking badly as she stepped outside.

The light went out and the door slammed. Their footsteps and noisy shouts continued along the corridor and down to the foyer and soon Megan heard their voices echoing as they crossed the wide marble entrance to the main door.

Megan opened the window, but the sudden shock of cold was numbing. Peering through the snow, she heard the group arguing about who would go in whose car, and she saw Nikola step into Ian's car. Two more men sat in the back and the rest piled into the TV van. They'll be able to change around outside town, she thought. A few seconds later they drove away and only Tito was left glaring accusingly at her.

Megan slammed the window. She pressed her hands on the central heating, but it was lukewarm and when she switched on the lights they were dim. Another of the country's brown-outs. For a while she sat cross-legged on the bed, but she could not stop shivering.

Suddenly she longed to be home. She was booked on the early morning flight, she consoled herself, but if her coat were not returned, she wondered what she would wear.

She was hungry, but the plates were almost empty, just two olives and a biscuit left and she ate them. They tasted stale and she longed for a plate of soup. She wondered whether or not to have a glass of champagne and then decided not to, she didn't much like the stuff anyway. She could hardly send down for a sandwich, she reasoned, when she was supposed to be out to dinner. Suddenly there was a quiet knock. Megan tiptoed to the bathroom and locked the door.

She heard her bedroom door being unlocked and for a moment she froze with fear. But then she heard the unmistakable sounds of the glasses and trays being cleared away. It was only the waiter after all. The door slammed and Megan waited in the icy bathroom for five more minutes before she ventured out.

Her coat was flung over the bed with her hat and sunglasses and her boots were on the floor.

Nothing else! Megan was left to wonder at Nikola Petrovna's strange accomplices, who delivered notes, fetched trays and handled defections. She had the strangest feeling that she was not in control of the situation. A pawn moved in a sinister game by unknown hands.

CHAPTER 10

Megan awoke to the sound of running footsteps and angry voices echoing from the foyer – Russian voices! Then she heard a siren faint and far away – but it was coming closer. She remembered Nikola and the desperation in her green eyes and suddenly she was wide awake.

Grabbing her dressing-gown Megan hurried to the window. Just as she had guessed the radiator was lukewarm and blinds were frozen. Impatiently she pushed them aside and blew on the windowpane, rubbing angrily with her fist until she had a small hole to peer through, but there was only snow, and it was falling so heavily even Tito's portrait was obliterated.

It seemed smarter to skip breakfast and leave at once. She would drop in at the hospital, en route to the airport, she decided as she hurriedly packed. Within fifteen minutes she was waiting at reception to pay her bill. The foyer was piled high with ski gear and bags, and it looked as if most of the teams were leaving today in relays.

Megan arrived at the airport with only five minutes to spare, feeling sad for Conrad. He had been wistful and lonely, but he was being flown home in ten days time.

There were no chairs in the airport cafeteria. Megan leaned against the counter and swallowed the bitter black coffee with distaste, having refused a stale bun, which was all they could offer. She gazed dismally through the window across the flat, featureless plain to the distant Igman Mountains and tried desperately to hang on to the image of those wild, magnificent forests with the spoor of wolf and bear, and the joy and exhilaration which she had shared there, but the pervading atmosphere of gloom was rapidly penetrating her psyche. She shivered and decided to eat a stale bun after all.

It was only then that she noticed the man with the

newspaper. He had been standing beside her reading for sometime, his paper spread out over half the narrow table, but when she carried her plate and cup to a space near the kiosk, he followed her, dumping his still open paper beside her. Perhaps it was a coincidence, she thought desperately and glanced at her watch. It was time to leave, so why weren't they calling the passengers to the exit doors? At that same moment a voice crackled through the loudspeakers in Serbo-Croatian. Megan glanced at the departure board in dismay; her flight was delayed for half an hour.

'Oh hell,' she muttered nervously.

Well, he couldn't follow her to the loo, she decided. Megan had learned to avoid Yugoslav public loos, but this time she lingered there for fifteen minutes before emerging to find the man leaning outside, having abandoned his newspaper.

He smiled slightly and looked directly at her. It was a strangely knowing look that seemed to impart a certain intimacy to their situation. 'Go away,' she said, but he just stared. Megan fled to the coffee bar and stood helplessly stirring her second muddy coffee, which she did not want, and trying not to panic, but when the flight was delayed a second time, she found it difficult to contain her nervousness.

It was fifteen minutes later when Megan noticed two policemen in their airforce grey uniform with the gold braid hurrying up the wide flight of stairs behind a plain-clothes man who was obviously in charge. Her watcher moved behind her as if cutting off her retreat. But where did the spook think she could run to?

'Miss Carroll?'

The man who had spoken was shorter than she, but broad and stocky. First impression was that he was running to seed, for his hair was grey and thinning badly, there were several warts on his brown, sagging skin and his teeth, which were held together by intricate dentistry, showed a thin gold rim along each edge. His neck was scraggy, and his nose and mouth were over large, but his eyes shone with intelligence and brought a certain nobleness to the chaos of his face. 'Will you come this way, please, Miss Carroll.' He gave a funny half-bow.

'What the hell ... no way ... I have a plane to catch,' she stammered, caught off guard by his unexpected politeness.

'The plane is delayed by fog and snow. It happens two or

three times a week here.' He sighed dramatically and spread his hands palms upwards. 'So – you have plenty of time – to kill – that is what you say in the West? Yes? So – we kill time together.'

He turned and walked ahead of her. As Megan hesitated, his two henchmen moved closer and leaned threateningly over her. She might as well go, she thought. As she walked across the hall she was all too conscious of the angry stares of waiting passengers who seemed to blame her for their delayed flight and their discomfort and cold.

The room to which he lead Megan resembled a VIP lounge. The two policemen were dismissed and Megan sat at the table, as she was told, and folded her hands in her lap. Was this the right time to ask for the American Consul, she wondered? Or should she brazen out her lies?

'Let me introduce myself,' he said and his voice was deceptively quiet, yet she could sense the unpredictable explosive beneath the calm manner. 'I am Zoran Banski, head of Sarajevo's district security police, a grand title, yes? But not a very grand monetary compensation, as you can see.' He shrugged and indicated his shabby suit deprecatingly. 'We are a poor nation, my dear. It is not at all like America here. However, my elevated rank ensures certain privileges and good coffee in the state lounge is one of them. It will be here soon.'

'What do you want ...' Megan began aggressively.

'Information,' he interrupted her. 'I assure you, Miss Carroll, you will catch your flight when weather conditions permit. There is no need to be afraid.' He spoke in an oddly stilted fashion which puzzled Megan. Then she decided that he was pausing to search his memory for the correct English words. Once, years ago, he had spoken English fluently. She guessed he had lived in England, perhaps during World War II.

'It is important for everyone concerned that I am able to persuade the Russian authorities that Miss Petrovna left of her own volition,' he was saying in his stop-start manner. 'They – the Russians – insist that she was kidnapped. Now if you would like to give a voluntary statement – simply that Miss Petrovna approached you for a management contract and some sort of financial security in the West. You are her agent, are you not? That is all that I need.'

There was a long silence, but Megan did not reply. 'Did you sign her up, along with your many other triumphs in Sarajevo?'

79

Megan stared at her hands. Then she looked up and said: 'No.'

At that moment the coffee arrived and Banski fussed unduly as he poured it. Megan wondered if she should tell him the truth. She felt strangely drawn to this curious man. Surely by now Nikola Petrovna was out of the country. But what if she'd been caught at the border? Silence might be her best strategy, at least for Nikola, Megan decided.

She stared hard at Banski and her face looked grave and puzzled. 'I've had enough of this,' she said. 'What the hell is going on here?'

Banski gaze was long and melancholy as if deploring the veracity of the young in general and Megan in particular.

There was a sudden commotion outside the door: loud voices raised in anger. She recognised Michel's voice. One of the policemen opened the door and spoke quietly to Banski.

'It seems that you have a friend looking for you,' Banski told Megan. 'He says he's an important journalist and we'd better be careful. He also reminds us that the Western visitors we need so badly will not tolerate this type of totalitarian inquisition. He's a bully, this friend of yours.' He smiled faintly. 'I think we will let him in.'

Michel's handsome face was the best thing she'd seen that morning. 'You're not safe to be let out of sight,' he said. He strode into the room, throwing off the restraining arm of a policeman and stood behind her chair, his hands resting on her shoulders.

He spoke to Banski long and earnestly in Serbo-Croatian. Then he sat down and Banski poured him a cup of coffee. I wish they'd speak English, Megan thought, but decided it might be wise to keep quiet.

At last Banski turned to Megan. 'Your friend has convinced me that you know nothing of this affair.' Banski was looking worried and she felt a shaft of pity for him.

No doubt Michel wants exclusive rights to the story in return for getting me out of here, Megan was thinking ungratefully as Banski showed them out of the lounge.

'You need a keeper,' Michel said. 'I'm volunteering for the job – at least on a temporary basis.'

She looked up at him in surprise and caught his unguarded expression: he was looking kind and that was the last thing she had expected.

The loudspeaker was calling her flight. 'Well, thanks Michel,' she said awkwardly. 'See you around.'

'I'll be with you all the way to Belgrade,' he declared. 'What flight are you catching at Belgrade?'

'British Airways,' Megan glanced at her watch in dismay. It was nearly noon. 'It leaves at fifteen hundred hours. Think we'll make it?'

He grinned at her. 'Even Yugoslav Airlines couldn't be that late.'

She smiled gratefully. Underneath that urbane exterior was a rather nice guy, she thought. But devious. She was seriously beginning to suspect that it was he who had implicated her in the first place.

'Megan, I tried to warn you ...' he began. 'There are many people here in Yugoslavia who are pro-Russian, and you, my dear, have made them very angry, so I'll just hang around and keep an eye on you.'

'And pump me for information,' she tossed out aggressively.

He ignored that remark. 'Do you play chess?' He patted his pocket and half drew out a miniature set.

She nodded.

'That's good. It will help to pass the time.'

The light was flashing over Gate 7 and a crowd was collecting there. The doors were thrown open by a woman in a grey uniform who looked and acted like a prison wardress. The passengers passed through silently, turning out their pockets and throwing their dinars on to a tray. Several passengers were searched inside a curtained cubicle, but Megan was not. Then they were ushered to a waiting room with no seats where they stood for twenty minutes. No one spoke and a heavy gloom descended upon them all, unrelieved by the weather. Afterwards they were called into a second room and the same procedure was re-enacted.

At last they were told to file out to the runway and Megan was caught up in the pressing, anxious mob and slowly, but inexorably pushed through. Another wardress checked her ticket, taking an extraordinarily long time about it and a third stuck a ticket on her. It was large and handwritten. *G 29*, it said. She was pushed on. Michel would be several seats behind. Well, that was probably fortuitous, she thought. She wasn't that good at chess.

They were herded out into the blizzard like a flock of silly sheep and they stood like sheep in a huddle while the passengers in front filed slowly into the cabin from one entrance at the rear of the cockpit. Snow gathered on their shoulders and heads and Megan began to despair.

The uncomfortable flight ended at last and there was Michel waiting at the bottom of the gangway. They retrieved their luggage, played chess, ate sandwiches and drank black coffee. Michel seemed in no hurry to cross-question her.

Eventually she said: 'Thanks for rescuing me. I guess I sized you up all wrong.'

He looked at her long and hard and then laughed curtly. 'You're not much good at chess, are you?' he said as he removed her Bishop.

'I just can't concentrate.' She flushed and then she said: 'No I'm not much good, but today I'm worse than usual. Do you think she's all right,' she began hesitatingly.

He reached out and pressed his fingers into her arm. 'The Yugoslavs don't want to stop Nikola from defecting. There's no love of the Russians here amongst most of the people. Banski just wants to extricate himself from trouble. He doesn't need a kidnapping right under his nose. Nor does he want the West's intelligence services operating inside his territory.'

'What do you mean – intelligence? Nikola's just a girl who wanted to get out,' Megan objected. 'So we helped her.'

For a few moments his shrewd eyes scanned her face. Then he laughed curtly. 'Megan, believe me, you're just the plum that garnished this affair for public consumption.'

She looked up and smiled. 'I think you're wrong,' she said. 'But you got me out of Sarajevo, so thanks.'

Michel leaned back and stared at her rather oddly. 'Let's talk about something else,' he said. He glanced at his watch. Another half hour to wait. 'I'm going to tell you what it's like here in Yugoslavia.' Then he paused and examined the board. After a few minutes he moved his Queen. 'Checkmate,' he said. 'Yugoslavia is a very poor nation, poor in cash, poor in skills, poor in power. It's a very new nation, a collection of various ethnic groups welded into a unit by Tito, who, in his wisdom, decided that the country would pursue a middle-of-the-road policy – or non-alignment.' He broke off and grinned as she sullenly watched her King being toppled.

'I couldn't concentrate at all,' she said. 'I'll have a return match some time.'

'Any time.' He was placing the pieces back in his pocket set. Each one had its own niche and it required his attention.

'It was Tito who succeeded in ousting the pro-Russian elements from positions of power in this country. Zoran Banski's job is to carry on his work in Sarajevo – in other words to make sure that only patriotic, non-aligned Slavs get into positions of power. No wonder the poor guy has four ulcers. Did he tell you about his ulcers?'

'No,' she said sullenly. 'I didn't know you knew him.'

'I used to know him rather well,' Michel said. 'He's my favourite uncle.'

'The result of this treasured, non-alignment is poverty,' he went on without a change of inflection. 'We Slavs are having to turn ever so slightly towards the West. We need your dollars and your pounds sterling. That is why we fought so hard to get the Winter Olympics. We are hoping to become a minor playground for the West. After all, we're not proud.'

Megan wondered why Michel felt it necessary to excuse his country's poverty to her. Even after ten years in the West he still shares their curious group psyche, she thought.

'So now they have started something daringly new for Yugoslavia – private enterprise – in a very small way, of course. But they have to be careful: only one-man businesses, one neon sign, modest expectations. They cannot afford to taunt that great Russian bear who is always at their backs.' He sighed.

'So for that reason they would not like to give the impression that they looked the other way while Nikola's defection was planned. They have to be careful. That is why my uncle was trying to enlist your support.'

'My support?' She broke off for at that moment her flight was called.

Relief sunk into the pores of her skin when her British Airways plane taxied down the runway. The pampering shown to first-class passengers was like soothing salve to her damaged psyche. Pretty hostesses were handing out newspapers, their smiles and deference promised a comfortable flight and non-stop attention.

Megan was back in the world of private enterprise, where consumer sovereignty reigned, and she had suddenly become a member of the royal family – not just number *G 29*. A hostess was demonstrating the safety routine and thanking them all for flying British Airways. Megan felt her spirits soaring. She allowed herself to dwell on business and profits. She wondered how soon the sponsors would start knocking on her door for Nikola.

Tea was served. Far below she saw the mountains and forests of Yugoslavia looking wild and roadless and untamed. She ordered a Scotch with ice and clutched the glass as she stared thoughtfully down. She muttered: 'Thank God,' twice, but she was not completely sure why she said that. It had something to do with the pliable, malleable human spirit that could be shaped and formed by Man, for good or for evil, for peace or for war, for freedom or slavery, just as Man shaped and formed the fields and towns and forests. I could be there, she kept thinking, down there, dressed in cheap calico, hoeing the frozen fields, sleeping in some shepherd's hut on the mountain slope, and then ... and then ...?

Megan jiggled the ice in her near-empty glass and a hostess promptly asked if she would like another. Megan said 'yes' smiling happily. Looking out of the porthole, she noticed that the terrain had become more orderly. There were more roads and clearly defined outlines of fields and dams and neat towns. Lights twinkled merrily through the haze as twilight fell. She was back in the West.

CHAPTER 11

'Oh dear,' she murmured as she squeezed the oranges in her electric juice extractor, in her London flat. 'I hope I've done the right thing.'

It was seven days since Megan had returned from Sarajevo and she had become involved in so many problems she was unable to worry about any one of them exclusively, her mind kept darting from one to the next and consequently the past few nights had been torments. The waiting was the worst, but so far there had been an uneasy silence on all fronts.

Overwhelmingly, her anxiety for Nikola was uppermost in her mind. Where was she? Had she escaped, or had she been arrested and perhaps imprisoned? Worse still, perhaps the British had returned her to Russia to face the music. But no, she must be all right, Megan reassured herself. Things that bad couldn't happen – not to people that you knew.

Her own role in Nikki's defection was uppermost in her mind. She should have done better. She should have gone with her, or hired a car and driven her out herself. Oh, if only she knew where Nikki was.

Then she would try to comfort herself. Any day now Nikki would pitch up. With that thought, Megan would remember her guarantees! Was she out of her mind? A flat, and an income – admittedly a small income, but add to that coaching, transport, clothes ... she could go on forever.

Absurd to worry really; of course she would find a sponsor. And if Nikki broke a leg? Well, there was always Vanguard to fall back on, but thoughts of Vanguard brought her up against her next problem: Jacqui!

She should have cancelled the deal when she discovered Jacqui's real name. Why hadn't she? Simply because of the pathos underlying the girl's arrogant behaviour. She had felt sorry for her. Now she was trapped in a no-win situation. If she sponsored Jacqui with a rival company, Eleanor Douglas would undoubtedly withdraw her sponsorship from all ISA's clients. In which case ISA London might as well close down.

At the same time, Eleanor would not sponsor her daughter. 'Oh dear, oh dear,' she muttered. It was all very well wanting to help people, but there was no point if you could not guarantee success. Signing up Jacqui and alienating her mother might have put paid to any chances she had of gaining compensation for Conrad, who was now back home, broke and jobless.

She walked into her tiny lounge and stared listlessly around. Usually Megan loved her Chelsea apartment. She was a dedicated Anglophile and her flat was ultra-English; it was all her own work, furnished with Victorian antiques from Portobello Road, with etchings of old London and some rather comical but excellent paintings of swooning maidens and kneeling swains set against off-white linen wallpaper. The dining room was classic from the elaborate candelabra to the ornate sideboard and gilt mirrors and the entire flat was furnished with wall-to-wall moss green carpeting.

This morning, however, she was in no mood to admire her home, so she returned to her all-American kitchen to drink orange juice and black coffee.

I'm getting morbid, she thought. Things aren't this bad, but in fact they weren't too good either, and she should have known better. She'd had a good training. In fact, the best.

She had been twenty-one when John Oberholtzer, her boss, met up with her at the ski trials near Denver. She had just won the Women's Giant Slalom event. Afterwards, she had found herself sitting next to John in the hotel bar, and somehow she knew that this was contrived and that he wanted to talk to her. He's going to sign me up, she had thought happily.

'I like the way you ski,' he had said for his opening gambit. 'You can tell a great deal about a person by the way they ski. You for instance.'

'Go on,' she had said.

'Well, your skiing shows intense training, good knowledge of skis and snow, it shows commonsense, strong discipline and a healthy respect for staying alive.'

'Somehow, you don't seem to be describing a promising champion,' she had said feeling let down.

'You're quick on the uptake, too,' he had told her. 'If you

86

hud to choose between winning and staying alive, which would you choose?' John was extraordinarily tall and when she glanced up she saw that he was grinning with amusement. 'Need you ask,' she had replied.

Megan had wondered why John was an attractive man when, logically-speaking, he should have been ugly. His shock of grey hair stuck out at all angles, his features were too large, his mouth crooked, and there was a harsh glint in his large green eyes. But she liked him anyway.

She had laughed then. 'Say no more. I get the message.'

'It's strange,' he had said thoughtfully. 'You beat the kid I'm signing up, but that's because you didn't mind taking a few chances today, letting rip a bit. It's a good safe piste.'

'Sure is?' she had told him. 'And I know it well. Bet I know who you signed up.'

She had been right and after that they talked about sport for a long time and then the business of sport and finally he had asked her to join ISA when she finished at business school where she was studying economics and law.

She had passed with honours and joined John when she was twenty-two, first as his secretary, then as talent-spotter, and later as general assistant. After that she had set up her own winter sports division and that had been a great success – so now she ran the London office.

This was her big chance. John had appointed her in the face of tremendous criticism a year ago, and she knew why he had chosen her. She was the only one who knew how precarious his business was, and to what extent his rapid expansion had left him short of liquidity. He hadn't dared send one of his managers – he just didn't have the cash. Instead he had taken her out to lunch and asked her if she could run the London end without much capital behind her. He could manage six month's expenses and a few thousand to get her started, he had explained, looking as if he was handing her a million-dollar contract. In return she would get a modest salary, plus twenty-five per cent of net profits.

She had said 'yes' there and then. It was a gamble and she intended to pull it off.

That was eighteen months ago. In the first week of business she had signed-up a middle-distance British runner, whom she had 'discovered' at Crystal Palace, followed by two tennis stars, not big earners yet, but she had high hopes of them; then there had been a bad period when she had run out of cash and without telling anyone had lent the business all her savings. After that she'd found a superb young swimmer, called Petunia, and shortly afterwards she had signed-up her star profit-earner, a handsome body builder called Adolpho, who was on his way to becoming Mr Universe, she hoped. Adolpho's flashy looks had enabled her to sign up suntan lotion, men's cosmetics, bathing suits, toothpaste and a new brand of Italian Vermouth.

Until now, Megan had been the rocketing star in the ISA stable. Admittedly she leaned heavily on head office, with their legal and statistical departments and their many sports experts and, of course, John's expertise was always available to her.

Megan had no losers in her stable. Winning! That was what counted, and in Megan's case winning was measured in profits, not time, and her fame came by proxy through her various clients. But she was a warm and compassionate woman and revered her winners, not for the profits they made, but for their grace and beauty and courage. Nevertheless, the facts of life were simple and unalterable. In the sports world there was no place for losers.

CHAPTER 12

It seemed to Jacqui as she trudged around the edge of the
frozen Alpine lake that there were two entirely different
villages called Arosa – one for the rich, which she had known
and loved for years, and another for the poor. Across the
snow-covered lake the lights of Hotel America twinkled merrily
in neon blue and mauve against the darkening sky. Never had
it looked so inviting. Jacqui closed her eyes and remembered
the grill room, and Emile the head waiter, and the view from
her favourite bedroom, which looked up to the towering
Weisshorn Mountain.

Arosa was no longer quaint, but hostile and frightening
when your pockets were empty and your stomach rumbling, for
Jacqui was almost out of funds. Never before had Jacqui been
in a face-to-face confrontation with Mother and she felt
bewildered, resentful and determined not to give in. She was
prepared to throw all her inheritance away, for the chance of
competing in the Winter Games. Skiing was something that she
had to do. She did not waste time wondering about the reasons
for this.

So she had rented a small room, with breakfast included, in
the village backstreets and she was trying to survive on a
sandwich for lunch and a plate of soup for supper. The daily ski
lift tariff was costing much more than her food and making a
frightening dent in her meagre reserves. This afternoon, for the
first time, Jacqui had tried to bum a lift to the top of the
mountain with Karl, a coach who had trained her when she
was still at school. She had been mortified when Karl had
refused. Jeesus! When she thought of all those tips she had
lavished on him she could cry.

Now it was dark and the temperature had plummeted well
below zero. Jacqui would have to go soon, but her small
bedsitter was not the least bit inviting. She missed the ski

crowd. Oh damn! She could just imagine the fun they were having across the lake.

Jacqui had been in Arosa for two weeks of intensive training and now the lack of adequate food was beginning to sap her strength. If only Megan would call. Jacqui knew of at least six companies who would be thrilled to sponsor her, so what was taking Megan so long?

She shivered and unwrapped half of her lunchtime sandwich, but a hungry duck, who had been eyeing her timidly from a man-made break in the ice at the side of the lake, waddled towards her quacking noisily as hunger overcame its fear. Jacqui eyed the duck compassionately; it seemed as hungry as she was, so she fumbled to divide the sandwich with icy fingers and flung half towards the poor creature.

'You and I,' she said. 'You and I both,' but she was not completely sure what she meant, only that the Swiss should have been feeding their shivering ducks and swans marooned in the middle of the frozen lake.

Suddenly Arosa appeared to Jacqui oppressive and dangerous. The tarted-up shops full of merchandise; the quaint streets and scenic views; the hotels' twinkling lights and superb service; the tantalising odour of *leberspiesschen* and *raclette*, the beautiful Swiss handiwork, all this was merely camouflage to hide the hideous, currency-eating monster called Switzerland, without a heart or soul, but one gigantic appetite.

She stood up, wiggling her frozen toes in her boots and said aloud: 'I'm getting morbid – it must be hunger.'

Then she heard the footsteps of some idiot ploughing his way through the tall bank of snow which had been piled up by the industrious Swiss to clear a path around the lake. She turned and called out in German: 'Careful. There's a path lower down.'

A deep American voice called back in English: 'Well if you wait till I get there I'll go find it.'

'Who on earth?' she muttered. A tall dark man walked hurriedly down the gloomy path under the bare branches of the spruce trees and turned towards the lake. He called out again, but Jacqui could not hear what he said. Then he turned into the circular path which bordered the lake and said something else. It sounded like: 'I've come to take you to supper.'

I'm hallucinating, Jacqui decided. 'What did you say?' she

called out. He did not answer, but merely pushed one arm through hers and hurried her back along the road towards the village.

'I know I'm feeling lightheaded,' Jacqui said, trying to sound dignified and rather amused by it all, 'but is this for real? Is this the way you normally pick up girls?'

The stranger chuckled tolerantly. 'I'm not picking you up,' he said. 'Merely feeding you.'

'I could do with feeding.' She looked up, but could not get a clear impression of what the man looked like in the dark, only that his teeth gleamed when he smiled and he smiled often. I guess I'll just shut up and eat, she thought. She knew she should be feeling alarmed and wondering what he wanted in return for a good meal, but Jacqui had reached a curious state of detachment, and she no longer felt real at all.

It was a stiff climb to the nearest restaurant and Jacqui had difficulty keeping up with her companion. It seemed as if each leg weighed a hundred pounds and they had to be picked up and moved forward so many times that she was sure she would die with the effort. Once she swayed slightly and giggled. 'I guess I overdid the skiing today,' she said. Her companion gave a brief, contemptuous snort.

The restaurant was brightly lit, filled with the aroma of a hundred mouth-watering dishes and the heat came up and hit her like a wave of hot water. Jacqui stood at reception peeling off her jacket, gloves, scarf and hat and rubbing her hands until her fingers came back to life.

She glanced up aggressively. 'You're probably saving my life and I don't even know your name,' she said. In the light now, she realised that she had seen her benefactor before – and recently, but right now she could not remember where.

'Wolf,' he said. 'Wolf Muller.'

A pretty Swiss waitress showed them to a table. 'Just how rich are you?' she murmured swallowing hard as she eyed the menu.

'Excessively rich,' he answered. 'Especially this evening.' She ordered barley soup – *engadiner gerstensuppe*, followed by *leberspeisshen* – succulent skewered liver, with *sauerkraut* and *rosti*, hashed potato fried with onion and *spätzli*, the tiny dumplings she loved so much. Followed by *zuger kirschtorte*, and then she pushed the menu away and sat dreamily watching the moon rise over the towering mountain peaks and shining on the brilliant snow, but all she could think about was how soon they would bring the soup and the bread.

'You must have some wine,' Wolf Muller said. 'Or better still, brandy.' He beckoned the waitress and ordered. 'It's a fine old Swiss tradition,' he said. 'Even the St Bernard dogs carried it in a barrel to resuscitate frozen skiers.'

'You don't look a bit like a St Bernard,' she murmured as she sipped the ten-year old Cointreau a few minutes later. 'But you're right about it warming you,' she murmured dreamily. 'Already I feel better and sort of floating ...' She leaned back and closed her eyes and thought about the absolute good chance of being wined and dined by this crackpot philanthropist.

'You don't look like the sort of girl who is used to deprivation,' Wolf said quietly. 'I've noticed the coaches and the lift operators know you pretty well. Even the shop keepers wave at you.'

'Waving doesn't cost them anything,' she said bitterly. Suddenly it all poured out. It had been so hard to battle alone against Mother, who was a most formidable opponent, so she let it all flow. She began by telling this sympathetic stranger about her humiliation when she tried to bum free lifts, then about her anger with the Swiss, and then with Mother and finally about Vanguard, and the company's image, and of her need to ski and Mother's determination to stop her. 'I'm going to be the best,' she told him with the excessive optimism of youth. 'The best – or bust! It's far more important to me than my inheritance. No one has the right to stop me.'

Wolf nodded.

'Seems to me wrong to bring a girl up to be so dependent upon Mother's wishes. What about your father? Can't he help?'

Should she tell him? Why not? He was a total stranger and she would never see him again in her life – not once she left Arosa. 'I'm illegitimate,' she mumbled and watched his face register shock. Well, at least he can be thrown sometimes, she thought. 'I don't know who my father was. Mother had an affair with someone and then he got himself killed in Viet Nam before they had a chance to make it legal.'

'Did your Mother tell you this?' He looked as if he didn't believe her.

'Sure, who else? She doesn't like to talk about it, so I don't ask.'

'You need someone on your side. Your mother seems to be quite despotic. She's a multi-millionaire and you're a pauper.'

'Well, not exactly a pauper,' Jacqui said uneasily. 'I own ten per cent of Vanguard. It's tied up in a holding company. I suppose it's worth millions, but right now that doesn't help me to eat.'

'Someone else in your position might have sold her shares.'

'I'm not sure if I can,' Jacqui argued. 'Besides there's a question of loyalty to Mother.'

He sighed. 'All you need is professional advice. I could put you in touch with a good lawyer. There's a hundred ways to raise some cash on your shares, without actually selling them.'

Supper arrived at last. Wolf smiled absently at her and turned his attention to his food.

Not the talkative type, Jacqui thought later as she slowed her pace in her gargantuan feast. He was quite old, she noticed, maybe as old as Mother, but he was handsome in a way, with his high cheekbones, deep blue eyes and thick, light brown hair, streaked with white. His nose was high-bridged, an arrogant Roman nose and this, together with his clever eyes, gave him a cool, watchful look. There was something predatory about the way he studied her from time to time which made Jacqui slightly nervous.

Eventually Jacqui gave up, pushed her plate aside and slumped back in her seat. 'I give up,' she said. 'All this food and I'm too tired to eat. So tell me,' she said, 'what's your problem?'

The waitress hovered over them to remove Jacqui's plate and Jacqui had to restrain herself from grabbing at it.

Muller studied her curiously. 'None that I can think of,' he said. 'Yours was definitely hunger.'

Jacqui slumped down further, as if trying to hide under the table. 'God,' she said, 'you're spot on. So now, let's hear what it's all about. What do you want?'

He laughed and waved to the waitress to bring the bill.

'Look, d'you have a communications problem? It's real kind of you to feed me,' she said. 'But I won't be able to return the treat – at least not for a month or two. I'm flat broke, see? I'm hanging in there until I've spent my last cent, but I'm hoping to last another week or two yet.'

'You can't ski without food,' he said firmly. His voice was deep and there was the faintest trace of something foreign behind his attractive mid-western American accent. He looked self-assured, but reserved. A man's man, Jacqui decided.

'Would you mind telling me what this is all about? I mean, I'm grateful for the feast, but you came down there looking for me and I'm wondering why.' She was starting to feel uneasy.

He grinned suddenly. 'It's your skiing I'm interested in, not your body,' he said. 'You're too damn skinny, and too young for me, so relax, kid. I've been watching you all week and wondering how you do it on two sandwiches a day. I wouldn't advise you to keep it up. I think you stand a pretty good chance of making the Olympic Games, if you don't starve first, that is. So I thought I'd feed you and turn you loose.'

'How would you know?' she said rudely. 'You don't ski. You're not the sort to be concerned one way or the other if someone starves. I bet you're not a kind guy at all, so don't try to kid me. You look a bit of a weirdo. Like someone partly dead. I think you're pretty rich, too. I know the look. Tough as hell!'

He frowned at her then laughed. 'Ninety per cent right, but I do ski,' he said. 'I used to ski seriously myself once, but I had a bad accident and that put paid to my chances. Nowadays I ski for fun.'

'Ah, wait a bit,' she burst out, her eyes widening with curiosity. 'I knew I'd seen you before. Aren't you the guy that was up in the blizzard on the Bruggerhorn piste when that Austrian kid broke his leg? That's right. You skied down and called the helicopter.'

He nodded.

Suddenly she smiled. 'I thought at the time you had style. Pretty slick at the turns.'

'Like I said, I was serious about it once.'

'Was it a bad accident?' she asked with morbid curiosity.

'I broke my back. I was almost paralyzed for a year. It was a bad time for me, but it's over now and I prefer not to think about it.'

She glanced up and caught hold of his expression – closed her eyes to hang on to it. It was a dead give-away – lousy memories and a king-sized hang-up. That's how he got that strange dead look, she thought. Obviously, it was a woman who did it, Jacqui decided, and for some strange reason she felt curiously protective. Good heavens, he was practically middle-aged, and rich, in fact he was a part of that odious world Jacqui was trying so hard to resist.

'Well you won't get far without a sponsor, Miss ...?' He paused and raised one eyebrow. 'I don't even know your name,' he said.

She laughed, an infectious girlish giggle that caused a few heads to turn their way. 'Jacqui Douglas,' she told him, forgetting about her pseudonym. I don't care if he knows who I am, she thought defiantly. He's not the type who would care anyway. The idea was strangely seductive and Jacqui felt comforted by it.

'Here's to your skiing, Jacqui.' He reached out and filled her glass.

'No, I don't think I should,' she protested. She blinked several times. 'I don't know if it's the food, or the warmth, or the wine, but I am feeling rather peculiar – sort of dizzy and sleepy and nice, all at the same time, but I'm not sure if I'll make it to the door.'

'I'll take you home,' Wolf said, signalling for the bill.

'No,' she said too quickly. 'I'll take myself home, if I make it.'

'You'll make it,' Wolf said.

Suddenly she felt his hand pressing down over hers. She looked up startled by the gesture and by the strange, intent look in his eyes. Then she stared at his hand. He had long, strong brown fingers and there were thick blond hairs around his wrist. Strange, she thought. I feel nice like this. Crazy really, and no doubt caused by drinking too much wine. But then again, she reasoned, he had practically saved her from starving to death, so it was only natural that she should feel grateful to him. She pulled her hand away slowly, at a loss for words. What was she supposed to say? What did he expect her to do? She was inexperienced with men, and she hid her fears with an aggressive, bullying manner. Right now her cheeks were flushing and her eyes smarting.

'Your hands are warm,' he said. 'Good! I think you'll last the night. Then I want to talk business to you – about sponsorship. Close friends of mine own a ski manufacturing plant in Scotland. They're looking for youngsters to sponsor and they asked me to keep my eyes open. Besides, I admire guts and I

95

don't think your mother has the right to force you to do anything you don't want to do. You've got talent, Jacqui. How about it?'

Jacqui leaned back and gave a big, self-confident grin. Now she was on firmer ground, she understood what this whole charade was about. 'What d'you think they'd offer?' she asked.

'That would depend on how well you do in Scotland, but from what I've seen of your skiing, they'd meet your terms. I'll give them a ring,' he promised. 'Meet you for supper here tomorrow. Eight suit you?'

'Well, actually – yes, why not? Thanks for the meal.'

'My pleasure, Jacqui.' She staggered out, grabbed her coat and scarf, shrugged into them, with the help of the waitress, and stumbled into the moonlit snow. She had the strangest sense of happiness as she trudged home. For the second time in her life she had met someone she really liked. She wasn't sure why but she had a strong instinct about Wolf Muller.

The streets were packed with tourists and from the sound of it, most of them were American. Everyone seemed to know everyone else, and suddenly Arosa did not seem so bad. Jacqui began to hum under her breath. She no longer felt rejected and the prospect of supper tomorrow and being sponsored at last was most appealing.

Wolf was the sort of guy you could trust, she decided. A tough, reliable, clever man and for reasons which she did not understand, he seemed to be interested in her.

'Oh Mother!' she whispered as she snuggled into her bed after a hot bath. 'I've found someone who believes in me. You never did – but he does. Isn't that unbelievable!'

She remembered his hand pushed over hers and for a few moments she allowed herself the luxury of wondering what would have happened if she had not pulled her hand away. She was still thinking about the warm comforting feeling of it when she fell asleep.

CHAPTER 13

It was seven-thirty and still dark when Megan reached her office in Belgrave Square. She switched on the light and felt a certain reassurance flooding through her as she glanced around. The large, open-plan area was totally functional – tiled floors with underfloor heating, three work stations and her own separate office. It was modern, plain and efficient, and on the walls were photographs of their winning clients – there were not many pictures yet, but room enough for more.

Megan usually arrived early. This gave her the opportunity to read the sports news, check the clippings from the agency and file any confidential telexes. This morning there was a strong smell of polish and she noticed the floor was gleaming and the bins emptied. Megan had moaned at the caretaker the previous day and obviously this had worked.

At seven forty-five came the tip-tap of stiletto heels, a swish of nylon petticoat against nylon pantyhose and a gust of perfume. Maureen Jessika, Megan's personal assistant, had arrived fifteen minutes early.

She found the kitchen full of steam and the kettle almost dry. This was not unusual. Megan gave her whole-hearted concentration to the job on hand and this morning she was hunched over the clippings, making copious notes and gabbling into the dictaphone.

'... check that Adolpho has fulfilled his personal appearances for the Burton aftershave account. We don't want to pick up any flack with this one ... he is, after all, our biggest money-spinner,' she added needlessly.

'Come off it, love! Am I likely to forget that handsome hunk?' Maureen murmured.

Megan looked up, smiled absently and wiggled her fingers. 'Hi,' she said.

As Maureen walked across the office, she heard a playback of the dictaphone. Megan's voice came out like Mickey Mouse: 'Number Six. Please contact the marketing manager of Lynton's Tennis Wear and tell him that Gertie Louw's outfits haven't arrived yet. She always beefs about them, so they should start well beforehand ...'

'I must get new batteries,' Maureen noted as she hurried back to the kitchen to make coffee, as she did each morning.

When she returned she gazed at her boss anxiously. As Megan's self-appointed keeper and guardian, she noticed signs that others missed: she knew, for instance, that Megan had skipped lunch for the past week and was sleeping badly; she was irritable and bad-tempered, which was unusual and Maureen wanted to know why.

Maureen had a curious love-hate relationship with her boss. She loved her for a variety of reasons: one was that Megan had been the first person to appreciate her own unusual abilities and give her the opportunity to use them. Maureen had a genius for organisation – she gobbled up work like a locust. She was also a pragmatist – cynical, distrustful, watchful. She could usually steer them clear of most of their looming disasters.

Megan, on the other hand, worked in fits and starts. She was too trusting, downright naive, at times, Maureen considered, and she relied heavily upon her instinct, her selling ability and her wits – to extricate them from the intimidating mass of problems they faced each day.

The two made a formidable and unlikely team. At the same time, she knew she often resented Megan, too: because Megan took too much for granted, and demanded that everyone else live up to the impossibly high standards she set.

Maureen sipped her coffee, jangled her bracelets and at last Megan looked up, frowning. Then she flushed. 'I sort of knew you were there, but I was concentrating. Have you been sitting there long? I'm real sorry. Well, hi. Thanks for the coffee.' She picked up her cup. 'Heavens, I can't believe an hour's passed already,' she said.

'I'm early,' Maureen told her. 'I wanted to talk to you. It's lucky I did because you left the kettle on. It was about to boil dry.'

'No kidding? That's terrible.' She pushed a lock of hair back and smoothed it down. 'Sit down. Talk away. Umm. Nice

coffee. You make it better than I do. So what's bugging you?'
Megan could not prevent her eyes from straying to her
assistant's exaggerated Afro hairstyle.

'You mainly,' Maureen said. 'Look here, Megan, it's none of
my business, so I won't get uptight if you tell me to get lost. On
the other hand, maybe there's something I could do to help.
You're not eating, you're not sleeping. In fact, you look a
wreck. One look at you, love, and people will think we're going
bust. Alternatively, they might think you'd fallen in love.'

Megan's face registered surprise, then annoyance. Oh what
the hell! she thought and smiled briefly. Maureen meant well
and her insight was a necessary part of Megan's business. She
would hate to have to manage without her, but she wished
Maureen was just a little less outspoken.

Maureen had an endless succession of boyfriends who never
lasted longer than a few weeks. Megan did not know why, but
supposed that it was something to do with Maureen's brains
being at variance with her looks. She was extremely pretty, and
this, together with her huge and shiny eyes, her crazy
hairstyles, clothes and wayout fashions, enforced the
impression of a scatterbrained girl. Underneath she was cool,
clever, cynical, and endowed with a sharp cockney wit which
left her men mortified most of the time.

Megan decided not to tell her about Jacqui, or Nikki. There
was no point in being teased by Maureen, to add to her shame.
Of course, she'd have to tell her eventually. But later.

'All right, Maureen,' she said crisply. 'Let's get into gear.
Any problems crop up while I've been away?'

Maureen took out her notebook. 'Nothing we can't handle,'
she said. 'Okay, here goes. On the subject of Adolpho, d'you
realise he has a good chance of winning the Mr Universe title?'

'Yeah, I had some suspicions – that's how I managed to sell
Adonis hair shampoo, Fitrix underpants, Phoenix ...'

'Don't go on and on,' Maureen cut in on her. 'I just thought
you ought to pay some attention to his name.'

'I'd rather not.' Adolpho Bartoli, was a mouthful that was
driving copywriters berserk.

'The press are calling him "Adolf" for short. It could affect
his chances.'

'It's too late to change now.'

'I don't think it is,' Maureen said blithely. 'Will you let me contact the sponsors and see what can be done. For instance, if we turned his name back to front ...'

'I'll leave it you,' Megan said gratefully. 'But all his sponsors must agree or it's no-go.'

'Trust me,' Maureen said. It was her favourite expression.

'You'll have to hurry. I aim to sell his name to a chain of health studios. If he wins, that is.'

'They'll love Adolf,' Maureen said scathingly. 'And he'll win.'

'We've a real problem here. Pitched up while you were in Sarajevo. Here's the file, it's full of legal documents. Gertie won the Women's Singles in Melbourne.'

'So, what's new?'

'She was cold afterwards so she borrowed a friend's jersey. It had Vanguard printed right across the front and that's how she was photographed leaving the stadium.'

For a moment Megan felt sick with shock. 'Is she half-witted, or something?'

'That's not all,' Maureen went on. 'After she won, a photographer on a minor daily, snapped her kissing her female room-mate too passionately to be kosher.'

Megan rested her chin on her hands and sighed. 'Have the sponsors found out about this?' she asked. *Frankly feminine* was the slogan for the new range of Bantex sports underwear which sponsored Gertie.

'Yes, in both cases.'

'Okay, I'll sleep on these. Next?'

'Petunia's father telephoned to say she's attempting a channel crossing in May. The youngest female ever, he believes.'

'Poor kid. She needs a new father,' Megan said feelingly.

'He wants fifty thousand pounds from the sponsor, not including the display ads on the boat. He's stepped up her training to eight hours a day and he's hired an ex-navy coach to follow her when she's training.'

'That figures,' Megan said angrily.

'Two to go,' Maureen said whipping through her notebook.

At that moment the telephone rang. Maureen reached for the receiver. A minute later she turned to Megan.

'Magnum Ski Manufacturers on the line.' Maureen's crisp tone was an indication of her disapproval. It must be Adele

Loots, Megan thought, the company's sales manager. Maureen did not like her. Adele was a tough, sophisticated, go-getter and this morning there was a ring of triumph in her voice.

'We want to sponsor one of your clients,' Adele began without any preamble. 'We're prepared to go to the top. Two million over a three-year period, some modelling, additional public appearances, and so on. Nothing that would interfere with training.'

Two million! That was excessive. Megan tried to think who she had on her books who could be that valuable to them. Only Jacqui. She felt her stomach lurch.

Could she fly up to Scotland this week, Adele requested excitedly. They wanted to get the deal signed and so did Miss Douglas.

Jacqui! Megan's mind was racing as she replied: 'I'm pretty tied up this week – I've been out of the office. I just returned from Sarajevo. Maybe next week. The fact is,' she cut in on Adele's protests, 'there are a couple of offers in the pipeline for Miss Douglas. I'd have to be satisfied that yours was the best.'

'Who else could offer two million pounds?' Adele shrieked into the receiver.

'Possibly her mother,' Megan said coldly. 'No doubt you're aware who her mother is – hence the two million bucks.'

'Pounds,' Adele retorted crisply. 'And her mother doesn't want to sponsor her. Jacqui is sitting here right now.' Adele was crowing with elation.

Megan heard voices raised in the background. Suddenly Jacqui was on the line. 'I'm taking the money, Megan,' she said coldly. 'What's the matter with you? I'm flat broke. Besides, Magnum are footing my hotel bill.'

'Can't do, Jacqui,' Megan retorted crisply. 'You'll have to pay them back. They're too late. I've just accepted two thousand pounds option fee from another company ... well, they got in first, Jacqui, and I think they're going to offer more than Magnum ... yes ... it's for one month ... where're you staying? I'll get some cash up to you today ... let me speak to Adele.'

Eventually Megan said goodbye and replaced the receiver angrily. Eleanor Douglas's daughter, the Vanguard heiress, would be major promotional material for Magnum Sports who were running a very poor second place to Vanguard in the ski clothing field and in hardware they were around tenth. She'd heard rumours that the company had been taken over.

'Good grief!' Megan moaned to Maureen. 'What Jacqui needs is a keeper, not a manager. I'll have to use my own savings.' She looked up and caught sight of Maureen's incredulous stare. 'Okay, I've made a booboo. You might as well hear about it now as later ...

'There's only one way out of this mess,' Megan said after she had told Maureen the full story about Jacqui. 'I'll have to speak to Eleanor Douglas. Try for a personal appointment. I'll fly over at her convenience.'

'Gawd! She only sees the President and the King. Don't you think that's a bit of a tall order.'

'Try anyway.' Megan said.

After five calls Megan told Maureen to give up. Eleanor Douglas did not see representatives from any organisation, nor did she speak to them on the telephone. Megan was welcome to see Nigel Wilder, but a brief telephone conversation with Nigel convinced her that it would be a waste of time. 'It's more than my career is worth to mention Jacqui's skiing to the Chairman,' Nigel had said pompously. 'Miss Douglas has taken steps to disinherit Jacqui – since she persistently disobeys her mother's orders.'

By four pm Megan was tense with worry and Nikola Petrovna was uppermost in her mind. The girl had vanished without trace and Megan felt sure that Nikola had been turned back at Rome or Heathrow. She decided to ask Maureen to check on the whereabouts of the BBC television crew.

'Very cagey,' Maureen told her later that afternoon. 'They cannot reveal the whereabouts of the crew, likewise they cannot reveal when they will be returning.'

Megan nodded. 'Any message,' she couldn't help asking.

Two black eyes were studying her with amusement. 'Michel Juric telephoned four more times since I gave you the last message. I've made up one silly excuse after another.'

'He wants a story from me.' Megan looked down at her papers in dismissal.

Watching her, Maureen felt a surge of irritation. Why did Megan always play things so close to the cuff? She wondered

102

peevishly. Never mind, before long Megan would let it all out. All the same – if there was a real problem, she should know about it.

Maureen went home in a huff sharp at five, leaving Megan hunched over her desk, absorbed with the accounts.

Megan found it hard to concentrate. The truth was, she had stayed on at the office hoping that Ian would contact her, since he did not know her home address. Perhaps he was still abroad. She had found it very difficult to think of anyone else but him during the past few days.

At six pm a telex came through from head office: It read: *Re: Jacqui Douglas stop. Are you out of your mind stop. Inform Adele Loots of Magnum no deal stop. Positively no deal stop. Concerned that you did not know Jacqui is the daughter of Vanguard's Chairman stop. ISA's largest single sponsor stop. Avoid confrontation at all costs stop. Your job and my business at stake stop. John.*

Megan sighed. Adele had lost no time in trying to by-pass her by contacting head office, where it was still early morning. She sat down to find a solution, but nothing occurred to her and eventually she decided she might as well go home.

It was dark and cold and the telephone was ringing. Megan moved sluggishly from her comforting dream and warm duvet and fumbled for the light switch. She felt angry and deprived as she grabbed the receiver. 'Hello,' she said hoarsely.

'That you, Megan? You caught a cold or something?' She recognised the voice of her boss, John Oberholtzer and instinctively glanced at the side table to check that her notepad and pencil were there. Then she pulled the duvet around her neck and cleared her throat. 'It's two am, John,' she protested.

'That's too bad.' His voice sounded high-pitched – a sure sign of anger. 'What the hell d'you think you're doing, Megan? even if she's as good as you seem to think ... well ... it's going to be messy. I don't like it ... what if she flops?' There was a long silence pregnant with condemnation. 'Messy' was the ultimate disaster in John's world.

'John, what are you talking about?' Megan said, but as she spoke, the whole Sarajevo nightmare came flooding back into her consciousness and she felt uneasy.

'Well, you should know. It's not as if you organise defections every day of the week ... or d'you have a few more lined up?'

'John!' Her voice sounded agonised and she took a deep breath and tried to calm her rising panic.

'Of course ... if she's as good as you seem to think.' His voice was more conciliatory now. 'Get her the top coaching ... the top ... no expense to be spared ... we don't want to get a reputation for collecting lemons. Quite honestly I don't see how we'd ever get her off of our backs ... if she fails, that is.'

'But how do you know?' she hurled against his voice and the transatlantic static.

'... contacted by the highest authorities,' he was saying.

Megan wondered what she had missed.

'... the very highest authorities ... this is big, very big indeed ... naturally I said we'd back you in anything you promised, particularly since you seem to have signed all your promises. We're holding the baby, honey, so you better make sure she scores.

'John ... I ...'

He was still talking; that was his way. 'Meantime it'll cost us a packet, Megan. She may never win anything. They're temperamental people – the Russians, so you must go for the publicity ... Recoup *your* outlay ... stress the philanthropic bit. In fact ... screw it for all it's worth. And don't ask me for cash. Get out and sell her, Megan.'

He rang off before she could reply.

Megan switched off the light and huddled back into the duvet, still half asleep. Then the implications began to sink in.

Suddenly she laughed. 'Nikki's made it!' she said aloud. 'She's safe and free and somewhere in the West.' Whistling merrily she put on her dressing gown and went into the kitchen to make a mug of hot chocolate.

CHAPTER 14

On Monday, February 14, 1983, a small news item appeared on the front page of *The Times*, headed: *RUSSIAN ICE STAR REPORTED MISSING*. The article read; *Reliable sources report that Nikola Petrovna, leading Soviet figure and free-style skater disappeared in Sarajevo during a Youth Display at the Zetra Stadium on January 29. So far there has been no evidence of foul play and kidnapping has been ruled out.*

It is believed that Ms Petrovna may have sought political asylum in the West, although to date there has been no news of her whereabouts.

A spokesman for the British Foreign Office reported no knowledge of the defected ice star, and American sources claim ignorance of the incident.

It was an altogether unremarkable piece of prose and would not have gained much readership were it not for a head and shoulders picture of Nikola Petrovna underneath. It was a photograph which gripped the imagination. So much humour and sadness lurked in that provocative smile, and her eyes blazed with a promise of secrets shared and a hint of mischief. She looked exquisite.

For the next forty-eight hours the newspaper's switchboard received a record number of calls, mainly male, asking if there was any news of her.

Megan telephoned the Foreign Office, and Scotland Yard. The former said they had no information at all, the latter that it was not in their territory, while *The Times* news editor said the press release had been delivered by hand from unknown sources. He was lying, Megan felt sure. In desperation she telephoned John, but he was somewhere in South America.

On Friday morning there was a slightly longer report: *Rumours of Russian Ice Star in Rome. Our Italian correspondent reports that a passenger called N. Petrovna left Rome airport on the morning of February 2, en route to Heathrow, travelling on a Russian passport with a four-day visa for Britain.* The report went on to describe Nikola's Russian career and the photograph showed her on ice during a Moscow performance.

Her hair was never so lovely as that, Megan thought wonderingly, studying the photograph. A first class hairdresser had changed Nikki's stringy locks into a cascade of ringlets, transforming her, and she was smiling enigmatically into the camera.

By the end of February, several newspapers were querying Nikola's safety. Rumours arose that the Russians might have shipped her back to Russia, or that the British or Americans had returned her to the Soviets.

It was a miserable time for Megan. She was dragging her feet with the problem of Jacqui, because she did not know what to do. Ian had not called her, or even written, so she had wiped him out of her mind, but not out of her dreams. Nikola was a constant worry, although commonsense told her that either the British or the American authorities were keeping Nikola in hiding, for reasons which she did not understand, and that Nikola would soon be free.

Free to skate, to eat, shop, drive her own sports car and enjoy her own London flat. 'Oh my God,' Megan muttered daily. 'What have I done?' Nikola would cost a mint of money which ISA would have to provide. Surely, she would find a suitable sponsor without too much trouble, she consoled herself, but meantime, she was forced to do nothing and the waiting was killing her. She began to receive telephone calls from reporters. 'Why ask me?' was her standard reply. 'I don't know anything about Miss Petrovna.'

The following Monday, a front page article in *The Times* read: *MORE CLUES TO WHEREABOUTS OF RUSSIAN ICE STAR. Ms Megan Carroll, 26, general manager of the London branch of the International Sports Agency (ISA) is believed to have signed up Nikola Petrovna, the Russian free-style skater, during her recent visit to Sarajevo. Ms Carroll denies all knowledge of the ice-star, but reliable sources state that the contract, which ran to a seven-figure sum, indicated that Ms Petrovna would join the élite band of high-earning*

106

sports stars in ISA's stable. It is believed that Nikola Petrovna feared that she would not progress further with her career if she remained in the USSR.'

'Oh Gawd, now we're for it,' Maureen said.

Megan was too angry to speak. By ten am, all four lines had been persistently blocked by enquiries about Nikola. Then Maureen came into her office. It's that Yugoslav bloke, Michel what's-his-name, on the telephone, and he insists on speaking to you.'

Megan picked up the receiver reluctantly.

'Congratulations, Megan,' he began aggressively.

'What do you mean?' she began.

'A superb publicity campaign, but I would have thought you'd send me an exclusive.'

'Michel ...' she said and then broke off. Could it be Michel who had sent out the press releases? Was Michel involved with the CIA? He had the perfect front and he frequently visited Yugoslavia. 'Michel stop playing games with me,' she said briskly. 'I'm sure you know that I haven't seen a sign of Nikola since Sarajevo. As a matter of fact,' she went on, feeling guilty because she knew she ought to say nothing, 'I'm worried sick.' There was a long pause. Then Michel said: 'In case that feeble whine was genuine, Nikola is in London, in a safe house, as a guest of the British Foreign Office. No doubt they'll be contacting you shortly.' He rang off.

'That's it. It's him! And I've had enough,' Megan stormed. 'I'm the fall guy. Everyone knows what's going on except me ... me ... the idiot who's going to foot the bills. I'll get to the bottom of this if I have to punch someone.' She grabbed the telephone and sent her work basket flying across the floor.

Maureen sighed and picked up the fallen papers. 'You're unlikely to find the right person to punch, so calm down.'

'Is that so!' Megan snarled. 'Well, let me tell you this, it's always *The Times* with the real news first. They're being tipped off and I'm going to demand an explanation.'

She grabbed her raincoat and fastened the buttons with shaking fingers. 'Bastards,' she muttered several times.

She was on her way out when an elderly man walked into her office.

'Miss Carroll?' He strode forward and produced his identification. Would it be convenient for you to come to the

Foreign Office now? They said to tell you it's very important – very urgent.'

'How dare you,' Megan said icily. 'How dare you take me for granted. What's it all about – that's what I want to know? All this publicity, all these damned lies?' She shook her fist under his nose and glared up at him, felt her temper rising in angry waves.

'I'm just a driver, Miss,' he said.

Half an hour later, Megan was shown into an austere office where a young man sat writing in a notebook. He was plump and white, with rosy cheeks and shining blue eyes behind thick-lensed glasses and he was waiting for her.

'Ah, Miss Carroll. Please sit down. We have a few things to discuss. You know, you've caused us quite a bit of trouble,' he said. His toneless English voice was very dry, like the crackle of dead leaves underfoot, hardly more than a whisper, really. It seemed to Megan like a deliberate cover-up, as if he had tried to cultivate anonymity, even in his voice. 'So we thought we'd better have a little chat.'

'Oh, we did, did we?' She was seething, but he seemed quite unperturbed by her anger as he opened his file.

'Now let me see,' he said. 'Nikola Petrovna arrived at Heathrow three weeks ago requesting political asylum. We noted that she has a contract with ISA and certain promises appertaining to ISA's management of her future career.' He glanced up and stared solemnly at her for a few moments as if to squash any opposition. 'Presumably you intend to honour these promises?' For a moment a touch of anxiety showed in his eyes. Then he glanced back at the papers.

'Just stop! Stop a minute,' Megan interrupted him. 'There's a few questions I'd like to ask you. For starters, what the hell are you playing at?' Megan hardly recognised her high-pitched voice. She swallowed and made an effort to gain control.

'I demand an explanation for the newspaper reports and hints and deliberate publicity. As for mentioning my name without asking ...' she was almost incoherent by now, 'while all the time ...' she nearly choked with temper, 'she was here,' she rammed her fist on the desk.

'Calm yourself, Miss Carroll,' he said and for a moment she glimpsed the steel behind the effete public school image, 'I'd like to remind you that you organised Miss Petrovna's defection and we have merely been looking after her for you,' he said eventually. Then he looked down at the file.

'You took a chance, Miss Carroll, and you were lucky. It's not always this straightforward. We have to be careful that defectors are not, in reality, criminal elements fleeing Soviet police. In that case, we simply return them.'

'Nowadays, not many countries will allow East European nationals to defect,' he went on gloomily. 'Seamen who jump ship, or travellers who walk into foreign police stations and ask for political asylum, find it's not so easy. Even the socialist states send defectors back to Russia – although they know they'll be in for stiff disciplinary action there. However, when it comes to well-known performers or artists, we find the publicity their escape makes, reimburses us for the trouble we have with the Russians.' Megan opened her mouth to interrupt, but he lifted one hand to silence her.

'The Soviets invariably stir up trouble to pay us back for any defectors we welcome. Believe me, Miss Carroll, there are so many avenues open to them. So far we have received six requests for the extradition of Nikola Petrovna.'

Megan gasped. 'But she's here – she's safe ...?'

'Oh, yes, absolutely. We've also been accused of kidnapping her – hence the publicity,' he went on as if reciting a well-prepared brief. 'Firstly, it was vital that we let the Russians know she was here; secondly, that she came of her own volition. That immediately nullifies any attempts they may make to spirit her back and pretend she never left – if you see what I mean.

'Right now the world knows that Nikola Petrovna has defected and there was a small report in the latest issue of *Pravda*. So we feel confident that we can let her go – in your care, of course. Scotland Yard will provide a twenty-four hour surveillance team for the time being.'

'I don't believe it,' Megan said feeling dazed. 'I don't believe what you're telling me. It's not this simple and Nikola is not that good a skater, at least not yet, and even if she were ...' she broke off. What was the point in arguing? The man was smiling enigmatically through his thick lenses and pursing his thin lips.

Megan nodded. She felt deflated as her anger subsided.

'Now we come to the question of maintenance. You have promised to back Miss Petrovna and you must sign these papers to that effect. We can't expect the British taxpayer to foot the bill, but under the circumstances, and since it seems certain that Miss Petrovna will not become a drain on the Exchequer, she has been granted a work permit and temporary residence and she has applied for British nationality, with our help. Merely a formality, of course, but these things take time.' He watched her nervously as she scanned the pages.

'Look here,' Megan managed to interrupt the flow of words. 'I said I'd sponsor her, but I didn't envisage becoming her keeper. In fact ...' she broke off.

'But who else is there?' Then, unexpectedly, he tried out a shifty smile. Megan glared back coldly and he cleared his throat several times. 'Let's get the formalities over, shall we? If you would just sign there on the bottom line, on your company's behalf.'

Oh boy! Megan thought as she gave in. She'd better be good or my head is on the block.

'Well, I'm sure you'll have no difficulty in obtaining sponsorship,' he said and Megan wondered if she imagined a gleam of compassion in his eyes. 'After all, she was one of the Soviet Union's top skaters.'

'I'll do the best I can,' Megan murmured hostilely.

'Well, Miss Carroll, if you'll just follow me. Miss Petrovna is waiting for you in there.' He gestured to a door.

No point in ducking now, she thought as she entered the room. She'd been set up by experts.

CHAPTER 15

The most amazing coup of my business life, Megan though wearily as she lay in bed contemplating the day. Her initial excitement and joy at the safe arrival of this supremely talented skater, had been suddenly dampened by the discovery of just how taxing Nikki was proving to be. Nikki, the champion, was an asset which would make her the envy of the sports world, but Nikki the flesh-and-blood person might well drive her crazy, she considered gloomily.

Good grief! What a trial! Somehow the news of Nikki's appearance had leaked out and when they returned from the Foreign Office, ISA was besieged with reporters, while the telephone never stopped ringing.

Megan and Maureen had hastily organised a lunchtime press conference and there had been a mad scramble to find a caterer at such short notice.

The press conference had been exhausting with the reporters' sly, insidious questions: 'How did you talk Miss Petrovna into leaving?' 'What did you offer her?' 'How much do you expect to make on the deal?' 'What about her family?'

The implied criticism in the questions was aimed at Megan, not Nikki. Never Nikki! Megan thought sadly, for it was soon clear that this diminutive dancer had captivated the male reporters with her exquisite and unusual beauty, her slenderness, and her dazzling presence. When she smiled her green eyes shone with warmth and merriment, but there was something else as well – a certain pathos: *'please protect me – you will be well rewarded,'* her eyes said so clearly to every male present and they all wanted to be the lucky one, so they jostled and grinned and showed off. Nikki could do no wrong, they hung on every word of her monotonous reply: 'I'm sorry, my English ... it is not good ... perhaps Megan ...'

When Michel Juric stood up, Megan had flinched

involuntarily, for she had not known he was in London. *How did he always know when to be around?* She wondered.

There was a curious glint in his brown eyes – a touch of malice, Megan decided. 'Are you her keeper now, Megan?' he had called loudly. 'How are you going to cope?'

His questions had echoed Megan's fears exactly. 'I don't know,' she had answered truthfully. 'I'll just have to play it by ear. I'm just so thrilled to have Miss Petrovna – that is, Nikola – here.'

Eventually Michel homed in for the kill. He stood up and called a question in Russian. Nikki's winning smile faded as her face took on the furtive, sullen expression of a downtrodden peasant. Suddenly there was a trace of heaviness to her chin and eyes which Megan had not noticed before.

'I have put Russian behind me,' she had muttered, twisting her hands nervously. 'I no answer.' Suddenly there was that vague smell of mustiness which Megan found so disturbing. Nikki was sweating with fear. A stab of pity sent Megan rushing to the rescue.

'No Russian, please,' Megan had said firmly, glaring at Michel.

'What has she got to hide?' Michel had called out angrily. 'Why should she be afraid?'

After that there had been no stopping them – and hour later Megan was reeling from the cross-questioning, but she clung to the story the Foreign Office had advised: Nikki had approached her in Sarajevo because she wanted to be free to develop her art. She wanted British coaching and the right to enter international competitions. She had been held back in Russia, and she longed to be free and to have a chance to reach the top.

It was after two when Megan glanced at her watch and stood up.

'Gentlemen,' she had said calmly. 'This has been a tough time for Miss Petrovna. You can see she's tired and upset. The press conference is over. I'm going to take her to see something of this wonderful city she's chosen to live in.'

'And now what?' Maureen voiced her own fears when the last reporter had been turned out, and the switchboard girl had been asked to take messages.

Nikola was looking crumpled and bedraggled, so they had driven to Knightsbridge and spent a costly three hours fitting her out with a basic wardrobe of everything.

Oh Lord! Megan had groaned inwardly as she signed and signed. Nikki fell in love with everything she saw and it was difficult to say 'no'. Quite understandable and very human, Megan kept reminding herself. After all, Nikki had never, ever seen such lovely clothes. It must seem like a treasure trove to her.

Suddenly Nikki's English was much improved. She oohed and aahed over the pretty French underwear, and could not be dragged away. When Megan tried to say 'no' to anything, she became in turn tearful or insistent, and her manner varied from bullying demands to downright servility. It was clear to Megan, that Nikki had no idea what was expected of her, or of her worth. She seemed to be searching for an identity, it was almost as if she wanted to position them all according to their importance, and so find her own niche in the ladder. But she could not, and she was floundering in confusion. She was pointedly rude to the shop assistants and she pushed her way bodily through crowds, elbowing and shoving people aside without qualms.

Once she had made up her mind to have something, her will was absolute. She accepted the clothes, the cosmetics, the bags and suitcases, the skating boots and clothes, and all the rest of the paraphernalia she would need, in the manner of a queen accepting homage from her loyal subjects, with grace and patronising charm and a shrewdly calculating eye.

To make matters worse, wherever they went, people stopped to stare at Nikki. Not rudely, but nevertheless pointedly. They just wanted to hang around her. It was as if her beauty reached out, like the perfume of a flower, to captivate, so that passers-by were snared and stopped to gawp with open mouths and eyes brimful of admiration. It was an appeal which Megan had never known existed, and she felt as if she had caught sight of another kind of existence. What must it be like, to be Nikki? To have every man falling over themselves just to wave, or nod, or say hello? To have every woman filled with envy. Was it a blessing, or a curse?

Finally it was exhaustion, more than anything else, that brought Nikki's shopping spree to a halt.

The three women returned to Megan's flat where Nikki would stay for a while, but when shown to the spare bedroom Nikki's wail of astonished dismay had been genuine enough.

'This is not what they promised me,' she whispered. 'They promised me my own flat – and they said I'd be a star ...' She broke off and bit her lip.

'Who promised?' Megan said, but she could get nothing more from Nikki who sat on the bed and sulked.

'You don't understand how things work here, Nikki.' Megan had sat beside her and explain in glowing terms 'Lesson One' of basic economics in the West. To prove her point she had handed over Nikki's first month's allowance. The bank account would follow shortly, she said.

Her explanations were received in stony silence.

'Meantime, you will share my flat. There is plenty of room for us both.'

'I am prisoner here,' Nikki had said angrily.

'No, you are not. I promise you,' Megan had protested.

'Then I go now for a walk.'

'Why don't you just do that,' Megan had retorted, and turning to Maureen she snapped: 'Why don't you tag along just so she doesn't get lost.'

Avoiding Maureen's accusing stare, Megan had been only too happy to escape to the office, to catch up with the day's work. Her first lucky break was in persuading Eric Lamont, Britain's top figure skating coach, to take on Nikki.

She had returned to the flat at eight, feeling exhausted, but ready to take the three of them to supper, only to find a delicious smell wafting from the kitchen. The flat was full of flowers: daffodils, irises, snowdrops – all out of season. Nikki bought them, Maureen explained.

'My God, did she rob the bank?' she asked Maureen.

'Nikki's feeling contrite. She blew all her cash on those flowers for you, and now she's cooking supper. She has the stamina of an ox. Must be all that skating and training. As for me, I've had it for one day.'

Maureen had lost her usual jaunty air and her exuberance, Megan noticed. 'She's so lovely,' Maureen said, voicing Megan's own thoughts, 'that you feel like some sort of lesser being when you're next to her. I feel like an old auntie. I don't like that much.'

'Well, get used to the feeling.' Megan laughed to take the sting out of her words. From now on she's all yours during office hours,' Megan had warned her. 'Just double as nanny, interpreter, chauffeur, keeper, English teacher, tourist guide and, in the addition, find her a flat we can afford – something stylish. Start tomorrow at eight. It will be a new experience for you. It won't last forever,' she had added placatingly, but Mareen was too furious to answer.

Nikki's Russian *borsch* had been very good. She had drunk most of the bottle of red wine herself, and at eleven, when Megan had suggested going to bed, she had looked surprised and let down.

'But it is our first night together in London. My first night of freedom, so we go out – yes? Celebrate? Have fun?' Her voice sounded light-hearted, but her eyes were pleading. 'Are you still angry with me?'

'Later, some other night. And no, I'm not angry – I never was. Maybe at the weekend,' Megan had said firmly. 'I'm tired and you need your beauty sleep, too.'

There was that look again. It was amazing how Nikki's enchantment could suddenly switch off, and then you were given a chance to see how determined her face, how hostile her eyes. The original ice maiden. Nikki was wholeheartedly dedicated to having her own way.

Alone and in bed at last, Megan lay contemplating the future, it looked bleak, at least until she'd found Nikki a sponsor and her own apartment. She'll change in time, Megan thought, forcing herself to feel charitably towards her. She's merely the product of her environment, acting out her fears and her needs, fighting for her rights. Soon she'll find out that everything is within her grasp, and the way to get it is through her skating. She is, after all, a supremely talented artist all she needs right now is friendship and understanding, Megan told herself as she drifted into a restless sleep.

Nikola Petrovna switched off her bedroom light, opened the window and knelt on the bedroom stool, where she remained immobile and silent gazing over London's rooftops towards the Thames.

If Megan had crept into her room, she might have thought Nikki was in a trance, she was so still and so pale, with her head bent forward and her long, white fingers gripping the windowsill. But the stillness was deceptive, for Nikki's mind was in turmoil.

A thousand impressions and memories were crowding in on her in rapid succession: the flight from Sarajevo to Dubrovnik and the long journey by motorboat, submarine and helicopter to the pretty country cottage outside London, where she had been spoiled and cossetted for the past two weeks. And today ... today had been glorious.

Now she was free!

Free of her father and his colleagues, free of the staid Russian establishment, the irksome control of the skating authorities, of being told how and when and where she could skate, free of her boring, lonely life ... free of all restraints.

At last she was in the West.

She gazed around at the multi-coloured neon lights, and the headlights of so many cars weaving in and out of the traffic's mainstream in every direction and at the river and bridges. In the distance, she could see a pleasure-barge moving upstream. There was a party aboard: shouts, music, figures moving against the light. Here she was, right at the start of everything, poised for take-off. A surge of triumph raced through her like a flame as she thought about what she had done. She felt giddy with her success. It was truly fortunate that she was talented and beautiful and that people in the West held beauty in such high regard. Soon she would be invited to all the parties.

Right now, however, she was feeling cheated and let down. It was Megan's fault, of course. All her life, Nikki had been learning to thwart, circumvent, irritate and cheat those who in some way made up established authority. Megan and Maureen, she decided, would try to take over her life, but she would know how to evade them. Yet, she also liked Megan and wanted to please her. She was not quite sure why this was. Nikki had never trusted anyone in her life and more than anything else, she distrusted this new and unwanted emotion of caring. Yet there was something about Megan ... the way her eyes beamed warmth and obvious goodness. Nikki longed to reach out to her. Madness, she reminded herself. She forced herself to dismiss this weakness. After all, it was disgraceful that she was alone on her very first night of freedom. This was not what they had promised her.

She quivered slightly as she heard the sound of laughter drifting from the barge. It seemed to Nikki that fun was drifting in the wind. She would like to reach out and grab at it, as she had snatched at butterflies as a child. Were it not for Megan, she would go out and make friends, but she was still unsure of herself and of Megan. Perhaps it would be better not to, just for a while.

She sighed sadly. For most of her life she had felt as if she was encapsulated within a large, glass bubble, so that she floated apart, behind an unbreakable barrier, separated from human laughter or companionship and trapped in her own private hell. The bubble went back to her very earliest memory; so that tonight she felt exactly the same as she had years ago when Mama left.

She had crept along the corridor, in the family's gaunt Moscow apartment, to Papa's study, where she had crouched close to the door, listening to the voices in the meeting, unable to hear one word of what was said, but feeling strangely comforted to know that people were there. Her recollections shied away from the inevitable recriminations when she was found, blue with cold, in the early hours of every morning.

Nikki had always longed for her father's love, but eventually she had seen him for what he was: a harsh, ego-driven, ambitious man whose excessive energies were lavished on his career, with nothing left over for a small, lonely girl.

Later ... years later, she had discovered the warmth of a delighted audience and she had worked hard to gain and hold public acclaim. But it seemed there was no remedy for the emptiness between each public triumph. Sometimes it seemed to Nikki that her life was like a necklace of diamonds, each event sparkling brilliantly, but between the jewels only an aching void.

Nikki clutched the windowsill tighter as she tried to recall the day, and her small triumphs in detail: the press conference, the flashguns momentarily blinding her. Later her picture had been in the evening newspapers and they had bought them at the corner newsagent. Maureen had found a scrapbook and together they had pasted the press cuttings into it.

Nikki turned away from the window and switched on the light. She would like to wake Megan and they could go through the pictures together again, but Megan had been so tiresome,

117

complaining that she was tired and liked seven hours sleep a night.

How boring people were. How tedious to be with them, and how lonely to be without them. Somewhere, somehow, there must be others who were just like she was. She was a misfit — like Hans Christian Andersen's cygnet, hatched into a family of ducks. If only she could find her own kind of people, but she did know what to look for.

After a while she opened the scrapbook and examined the cuttings of herself. There were several shots, and she was laughing in all of them. That was good, she thought. She hated to be photographed looking serious, for then her sadness was revealed.

When Nikki reached the end, she drummed her fingers on the table for a few seconds, then she turned to the drawers where her new clothes had been crammed in and began to examine each new item, one by one. Eventually she lost interest and after putting them away, she returned to her vigil at the window.

The doorbell rang.

'Oh damn,' Megan muttered as she got out of bed and reached for her dressing gown. Glancing at her watch she saw it was one am. 'This can only be yet another disaster to add to this disastrous day.'

But it was Ian.

He was standing at the door holding a bottle of champagne and a small gift-wrapped box and he was smiling with his lips, but questioning with his eyes. She gazed at him in shocked relief. Her first impulse was to shut the door on him. You're being absurd, she told herself sternly. There was no point in losing your cool, even if he had stayed away for two weeks without even a telephone call or a postcard to explain his absence.

'Come in,' she said. Why should her stomach lurch just because Ian was here? Megan felt angry with herself and reacted by scowling ferociously. Yet something about the line of his cheekbone, the way his nose was shaped arrogantly, yet perfectly, even the deep groove in his lip, and the stubborn chin — all of him was so familiar. Now she understood well enough why she had been missing him. Absurd — really absurd, she told herself for the second time. But how could she ignore the power of his body, the sheer brawniness of him. Only his eyes looked gentle, the rest of him was compacted power, like a coiled spring. Then she noticed that he looked tired and cold; he had lost weight and there were deep shadows under his eyes. He'd been having a rough time, she decided and some of her annoyance fled.

She offered him a sandwich and coffee, but he merely shook his head and took off his raincoat, which he folded neatly over the back of a chair, moving with an economy of movement and with the grace and precision of a hunter. Yes, he was predatory, she decided, a dangerous man in spite of his carefree smile and ready humour.

'You're rather late,' she said pointedly, determined to ignore the warmth in his blue eyes.

'I've just returned from Switzerland, so I came straight here. I read the evening news on the plane and I thought you might need a drink.'

'Oh Ian, I need so many things, but a drink's not one of them,' she said, rigidly polite. 'But thanks anyway.'

'Where's Miss Petrovna?'

'Here – until I find a suitable, furnished flat. She's none too pleased about it and to tell the truth, neither am I.'

Suddenly he caught hold of her hand and lifting it, kissed the palm. My God, she thought, trying not to gasp. He's practised, cool, deadly and I certainly won't be deceived by his pseudo-gentle approach. 'It seems a long time,' he said as he handed her a gift-wrapped box.

It was a Swiss scarf with pretty floral embroidery. 'I didn't expect ... oh, but it's beautiful ... thank you, Ian,' she said politely, trying to conceal her joy.

At that moment the passage door was flung open.

'Ian,' Nikki said, in her low contralto voice. She paused dramatically in the doorway, arms upraised. 'We meet again – and in London at last.'

Watching her glide into the room with her arms outstretched, Megan wished that she had not chosen quite so pretty a peignoir. Ian's eyes were glinting in a manner which she had never seen before. Triumph? Pride? What was it for God's sake? What did Nikki have to do with him, anyway?

Ian was slipping another package out of his raincoat pocket.

Nikki swooped on it laughingly and made a big fuss about the pretty paper and the pretty string which she carefully untied and folded.

You'd think he'd given her the crown jewels, Megan thought as Nikki screamed with pleasure at the perfume he had given her and flung herself at him.

Why had Ian brought Nikki perfume — and why bring it here? Had he known she was staying here, or had he only come to find out where she was?

Next Nikki pounced on the champagne. They must drink it at once, she insisted. Together! Ian made a laughing performance out of popping the cork as Nikki held the glasses.

'Here's to champagne,' he said.

Nikkie giggled childishly. 'Here's to laughter,' she added in remarkably good English. She sat on the edge of Ian's chair and wrapped one arm around his shoulder. They looked so happy together, and so well matched, Megan noticed.

'And here's to little Nikki, safe in London,' Ian added.

'Here's to the three of us,' Nikki said, generously remembering Megan.

The three of us, Megan thought peevishly, as she lifted her glass, could become an unfortunate habit.

CHAPTER 16

It was late March and there was no sign of spring in Scotland. It had rained non-stop for four days, turning the snow to slush and freezing it, layer by layer. Even the Cairngorm plateau was a dome of frozen slush. Around and below lay trampled snow and ice with the occasional rock washed clear by the downpour. A really bad piste, Rob reckoned, viewing the slope pessimistically. Below he could see the lochs and vast forests of Scottish pines and the towers of some ancient castle in a clearing and beyond were patches of purple heather amongst the snow and the barren hills.

Rob took off his goggles and thrust them into his pocket. He did not need them, the sky was leaden, the glare minimal. He was frowning as he gazed around. What was he doing here? He cursed himself for being a fool and hanging on. It was a week since he had telephoned Megan for Jacqui's address and flown over from Denver to see her. He should never have left his plant at this time of the year, but his longing to be with Jacqui had overruled his commonsense. He was curious to find out why Jacqui was training here, but then she had told him of the promise of sponsorship and Megan's obstinacy in refusing the offer, and of her hopes that Megan would soon sort out the best bid. Meantime she was hanging on here because it was cheaper.

A pity, Rob thought. Jacqui was not happy here, he knew that. The trip had not been a success. Jacqui had been moody and unresponsive and they had not achieved that sense of togetherness they had shared briefly in Sarajevo. Rob could see that Jacqui was tense and preoccupied – and it was not about money. Since Megan had sent the mysterious option money Jacqui had been able to pay her own hotel bills and eat three meals a day. Still, Rob sensed her unease. Outwardly she was her usual overbearing self, but inwardly she seemed to be torn

121

in two. Jacqui had not confided in him, but Rob had heard her on the telephone two or three times talking to some guy called Wolf. He had questioned her, but she had been evasive, and that had hurt Rob more than anything else. Eventually she had admitted that she had an older friend, more like a coach, than a friend, whom she had met recently in Switzerland. Just someone who wanted to help her train, she had explained defiantly. A most unlikely story! Not that he thought Jacqui would lie, but she was far too inexperienced to understand why some guy would be hanging around her. But how the hell could he compete when he lived five thousand miles away in Denver?

He knew he should cut his losses and fly home, but he could not do that. Not yet. He loved this truculent gypsy girl with all his heart. So, this morning, he had trailed along because of some crazy feeling that she might need him, as he had done every day for the past week, but in spite of their camaraderie on the mountain, he had not succeeded in penetrating her defences.

Rob stood poised on the steep slope and gazed after her. She was far below, yelping with joy, he knew. Speed envigorated her. She was like a swallow, swooping and turning and falling just for the hell of it. Right now she was fast disappearing from view and doing at least fifty miles an hour.

He frowned as he saw her pushing too hard on her super-long skis. 'Jees!' He gasped. The next moment Jacqui was cartwheeling in the air, boots, arms, skis flailing as her body was bounced and buffeted in a series of collisions with the ground.

Like a rag doll, he thought as he raced to the limp body spreadeagled on the snow. He bent over her, his heart pounding.

Jacqui opened one eye: 'What took you so long?' she gasped. Then she sat up giggling. Suddenly Rob's fears melted. She was unharmed and she was just a kid after all. Absurd to get uptight about her older admirer. She was probably teasing him. He grinned, picked her up and shook her. 'Come on,' he said laughing happily at last. 'I'll race you to lunch.'

They spent a carefree day and returned to Jacqui's hotel at dusk, trudging side by side in happy silence, both content to be together and finding words unnecessary. But that evening Jacqui was unusually quiet, but with a tense sort of quietness.

122

There was a build-up of pressure there; a sense of too big a load on those slim, brave shoulders. She was like the mountains back home in the spring, Rob thought, piling up with snow and ice and more snow balanced on ice, so that the whole structure could come crashing down at the slightest provocation.

Rob had almost given up trying to find an opportunity to talk to her. He knew that he loved her and that she was the only girl he would ever really want. He did not know why this was? Perhaps it was her bravery, he rationalised in sleepless hours in the night, or some strange, inexplicable emotional bond too deep for his conscious mind to analyse. He was sure that she felt the same way, but she would not admit it. Ever since he arrived she had been sniping at him.

'How long are you aiming to stick around in Scotland?' he asked at dinner. The room offended him: with its monotonous buzz of discreet voices, over-heated air, cigarette smoke and the smell of stale beer. Ugh! 'How can you bear it?' he whispered.

Jacqui shrugged. Her world was divided into two classes: skiers and non-skiers, the former belonged to some heavenly commune, the latter were beneath contempt. 'You're right, it gives me the creeps,' she muttered. 'Trolls and ghouls.'

'Unless it stops raining, the season will be washed away. The snow's had it. Back home the season lasts until the end of April. Even longer in the glaciers.'

'Denver's my home town,' she said, sounding bored.

Rob was too surprised to answer. Then he thought: I should have known. Everything about her shrieked of home – her ready smile, her candid manner, her courage. She'd be happier back there, he decided. He had a sudden vision of Jacqui standing in the field behind his house. She was smiling. He saw her hair tumbling over her shoulders, her dress billowing round her slender legs.

With a sudden shock, Rob realised that he had never seen her legs. Were they fat, dumpy or scarred perhaps? It did not matter, he'd love her anyway, but the question kept tormenting him. 'Yeah,' he said. 'I forgot that Vanguard began in Denver. They've still got a manufacturing outfit there. You must have been pretty spoiled – even then.'

'You bet your life I was,' Jacqui lied, remembering lonely days and nights when Mother was out at work and there was no one to care for her. Mother had worked like a dog in those days, selling by day, doing the accounts at night and rushing back to the plant at odd moments to bully the packing staff. Jacqui had learned to cope with housework and cooking her own suppers, and helping with stocktaking in the store evenings and school holidays. Those were her happiest memories. When she was twelve they had moved to Monaco and she had been thrust into boarding school, and that was worst. She used to long for the stockroom in Denver. It was the only time she had ever been close to Mother.

She looked up suddenly and her face was hard and old before its time. 'Sure it was swell. That's why you're here, isn't it? Because of Vanguard. You've been licking my ass so hard you must have blisters on your tongue.'

Rob stood up in shocked dismay. Crudity disgusted him, but when Jacqui unleashed her virulent tongue it was not for the sake of crudity, but a form of self-defence; a porcupine erecting barbs of pain.

'Let's get out of here,' he said. He walked to the desk and paid the bill without waiting for Jacqui. When he walked into the comparatively clean air of the foyer he felt Jacqui's hand tugging his arm.

He turned round and smiled sadly at her. 'Jacqui,' he pleaded, 'don't do this to us.'

'Us!' She uttered the word contemptuously. 'Don't kid yourself. There's no such animal.'

Rob swore quietly under his breath. Then he leaned forward and muttered in her ear: 'You're a lousy judge of people, Jacqui.'

Jacqui stared at him, feeling bewildered by his obvious concern. He was not angry, as she had intended, but hurt. You could be fooled by a face like his, she thought suspiciously. She said: 'What could you possibly see in me, apart from Vanguard, that is?' Her brown eyes were tense and watchful. She looked so much like a homeless animal that Rob forgot how angry he was.

What could he see? Right now he saw hope lighting her eyes with a curious incandescence, and fear of rejection so strong it could consume her. A lost girl, he thought. How did it happen and why? He reached out and grabbed her hands and held them in his.

'Listen to me,' he said urgently. 'Come back with me, Jacqui.

124

Come and train with me for the rest of the season. I've got a sweet wooden house up in the hills amongst the woods. And a workshop that's more than just a workshop, it's a small factory and I've a name you can say proudly for twenty miles in any direction. Every man there knows my word is as good as a signed contract. That's important where I come from.

'There's a field behind the house and one day I aim to make a garden there, but right now it's wild and pretty and my horse grazes there and Johnny – that's my spaniel – keeps him company when I'm at work. The house is all wood: wooden floors and walls and ceilings, and there's the prettiest view you could wish for over the maples and the pines, way across the valley. You'd love it there, Jacqui. Why ... you might even want to stay a while longer. Say yes,' he whispered urgently.

'Yes to what?' She asked, taken aback by his silly torrent of words which, for reasons she did not understand, had brought her arms out in goose-pimples.

'Yes, you'll come and see my home. Stay a while,' he urged.

It was absurd. Of course she could not. Yet something about the longing in his large, grey eyes made her hang back from saying 'no' outright and hurtful. With his tousled tawny hair and his big broad brow he looked like a kindly bear. He's a good man, she thought, and then wondered why she should care.

'It sounds real great – your home I mean, but it's not so simple for me. I've made other plans.' She looked round and grimaced with disgust. 'There's no place to go without these creeps listening in. Let's go up to my room. I'm kinda tired anyway,' she said, 'and we can order coffee.'

She didn't know how to tell him how absurd he was to keep after her. All this love stuff belonged in romantic novels. All the same, Rob was a pretty nice guy, handsome, too, in a bluff sort of way. How strong he was, yet gentle. Ever since she'd first met him she'd wondered what it would be like to feel his arms around her and his body pressed against hers. She flushed at the thought and then felt angry with herself.

'You know something?' she said, when they had closed the door and she was sitting on the bed, looking shy and tremendously brave and he was sitting on the room's only chair. 'You'd like Monaco where we live. We have a pretty nice place there, too. It's right on the Mediterranean at Cap Ferrat. We've got a couple of oil sheiks on either side of us. Spoils the neighbourhood, Mother says, but nowadays they get in everywhere. Still we don't see much of them because there's acres between us on either side, but sometimes we meet on the beach. I could take you round the place. I've got a pretty nice Lotus – all white, with white upholstery and dark green trim. Mother had it made in company colours. Boy! When I park at the Casino there's always a crowd hanging round admiring my car. I don't like gambling much, do you? It's a bore ... I mean ... if you win or if you lose ... what's the difference? It's a drag. Maybe you'd like it ... just for a change.'

'Okay, I get the picture,' Rob said sullenly. 'My place must seem pretty silly compared to yours.'

He stood up and grabbed his windcheater. 'See you around,' he said.

'Now you're angry,' she complained. 'What'd you want to rush off for?' She pouted and crossed her legs. 'You're really kinda nice, but old-fashioned. You don't screw around, do you?' She tilted her head sideways again and peered up at him.

Suddenly she flushed and put up one hand to wipe the moisture off her forehead.

'I don't get much time,' he confessed, wondering who he was the most sad for, Jacqui or himself.

'Well, don't rush off,' she said pleadingly. 'I could do with a nightcap. What d'you say to a nightcap?'

Rob stood up and pulled her towards him, amazed at the strength of her, in spite of her delicate shape and size. 'Do you?' he asked.

'Sure. Why not?'

He cupped one hand around her chin and thrust his lips down on to hers, probing her mouth with his tongue. He felt her lips tighten and stiffen and their teeth clash together. Then her nose got in the way. It was a virginal kiss – blundering, searching. He felt her body shrinking away from his as his mounting desire overcame his self-control. She had been bluffing, he knew. He let out a long sigh and hugged her closer.

'Who d'you think you're kidding, Jacqui?' Rob stroked one cheek gently and blew the hair from her face.

'I thought it might be nice,' she said wistfully. 'I've elected you to be the first.'

'It's always nice, but I don't think that now would be the right time.'

Jacqui giggled again. She flung herself face down across the bed and leaped up and down. The bed made a noise like an animal in pain. Jacqui beamed up at him. 'This is a real dump,' she said as if she'd just made an important discovery. 'It's a good place to be screwed for the first time. Wouldn't you say so? Sort of sleezy and yucky and very smelly.'

I'm going to teach her what it's all about, Rob thought as he took off his clothes. To hell with Wolf, whoever that creep is. If there's only going to be one beautiful thing in her life, it's going to be this.

She was sitting on the bed, her arms tightly clasped around her virginal knees, staring at him with a troubled frown creasing her brow. Her colour had heightened, too, staining her cheeks which glowed rosy and dewy-soft, in the soft chiffon-pink light. The way she was staring made him feel slightly ill at ease. She looked troubled, there was a touch of appeal in her eyes and in her humility.

'Are you sure?' His voice was husky. Something was holding him back. What was it? Her purity? Innocence? It was all there shining in her eyes.

When she stammered: 'I've never seen a man naked before. Never, ever,' he knew it was the truth. For a moment he had a crazy impulse to flee out of the room with the groaning bed and the dusty carpet. He wanted a field, a stream, tall white lillies reeling in the moonlight, the air charged with perfume. That was what she deserved – only the best. But it was too late now, he reminded himself. After all, he was naked.

Instead he sat next to her; clasped her knees in his hands and slid her body along the quilted eiderdown until her legs were sprawled over his and then he hoisted her on to his lap.

'You look kinda funny, but sort of nice,' she said, smiling mistily through her embarrassment.

Rob gazed at her with something close to desperation in his eyes. The truth was, he'd had half a dozen girls, but none of them had been virgins and they had all been hot in the pants for him, so there had been no need to wonder what the next move was. It had all taken care of itself. Yet he knew without doubt that he was going to make love to Jacqui and soon. The knowledge of this brought his skin up in goose pimples and his thighs thickened and stiffened, and a sense of urgency kept the blood pounding in his head and a lump in his throat so big he could hardly swallow.

'Jacqui, I love you,' he whispered, as if to condone all that he was about to do. 'I always will.'

He pulled her jersey up over her head and heard her gasp as he caught her nose on the buttons.

'Oh my ... I sort of imagined something ... sort of more ... well, you know,' she whispered. 'I'll do it.'

She began to unfasten the buttons of her blouse, and Rob, whose main ambition now was to wrench the stupid offending garments off her in one fierce movement, felt her thighs moving on his legs, driving him half crazy with desire.

When she reached her bra her hands faltered. 'It's cold,' she complained.

'No, it's not cold.' Yet unbelievably she felt like an ice block, so he carried her to the bed and pushed her in between the cold sheets and scrambled in beside to warm her.

Poor little thing, she was shivering. How slight she was, so small, Rob was amazed that so much courage and skill could be compressed into this slight, girlish body.

He wrapped his arms around her, felt her thick hair tickling his face, pushed her hard against him until the shivering stopped.

But then, at last, when he bent to kiss her, she complained about the light. He switched it off reluctantly, groped for her in a blind way, felt her hands groping for him, feeling, touching, exploring. He knew then that she wanted him as much as he wanted her and a wave of hot love raced through him, leaving him feeling exalted, and envigorated.

His eyes became accustomed to the soft glow from the moonbeams penetrating the crack between the curtains.

He bent over to examine her. 'Oh Jacqui, my love,' he murmured. Her breasts were quite perfect, two swollen mounds of firm flesh with the wider circle of brown skin surrounding her nipples which were small and pointing out now. He ran one finger around one, felt the firmness, heard her gasp. Then he clasped his hand over her breasts and thrust his mouth on to hers.

She was lovely. Lovelier than he could possibly have imagined, he discovered when at last he could see all of her naked on the sheet. Her skin was smooth and soft to touch – like velvet. Her legs were long and lithe, her tiny waist amazed

128

him, and the swelling fullness of her thighs filled him with desire.

Yet he would wait. She must be the aggressor, just this one time, he knew, or else he might lose her forever. So he nuzzled her back, and her stomach and ran his hands over her skin, loving her delighted oohs and aahs and the little shivers of joy she gave.

He wanted to kiss every perfect part of her soft skin, feel each piece of her with his tongue, taste her, devour her, starting with the spaces between her toes, then her delicate proud ankles and her calves, while she lay shuddering, groaning, clutching the pillow and giggling girlishly.

But soon she could stand it no longer, an unquenchable need was driving her into a frenzy.

'You must ... I must ...' she whispered. 'Oh Rob ... I don't know what I want, but you must do something ...' She began to cry, until Rob lay on top of her and the sweet thrust of his love stilled her anguish.

Astonishing pleasure, each time it was unbelievable – each time always like the first time, but now there was an added dimension, no longer merely physical pleasure, but emotionally satisfying, too. She was his woman for life, he knew that, even now as he thrust softly, slowly, deeply inside her and heard her cries of agonised desire. She began to move, thrilling to the rhythm of his body, but blindly he held back, softly he nourished her with the maleness she was craving. He was drenched and drowning in this panting, untamed, nymph.

'Oh God, oh ... do it, do it, don't ... don't stop.'

He gave a long shuddering sigh and felt her body stiffen and contract. Then she was crying softly on his shoulder: 'So beautiful ... so beautiful ... Oh Rob ... I never knew anything so beautiful ...'

It was midnight and the sky had cleared slightly. A wintry moon shone through the bare branches of the silver birch making weird shadows on the whitewashed wall. Jacqui felt confused and angry with herself. It had been her first time and because it had been beautiful, she felt overwhelmed and rather sad. Mother doesn't know what she's missing, she thought and wondered if she should tell her about it. It wasn't for laughs or

129

for kicks or anything like that at all. Rob had been tender and wonderful and for the first time in her life she had trusted someone and been rewarded. 'Beautiful,' she murmured looking down at the sleeping giant in her bed.

He would make some girl very happy, she thought, and for a moment experienced a feeling of regret. He loved her now, she was sure of that, and that was why she had decided that he must be the first. Maybe he'll be my only lover, she thought with teenage melodrama. They had made love and now he could go home and forget about her. As for her, it meant nothing – just an interlude, admittedly a lovely interlude. She stirred and stretched luxuriously, remembering how it had been.

He had told her she was lovely and that in all his life it had never been like this before and he had cried out and shouted, and something in her had quivered to fruition in response to his ecstacy. Afterwards she had cried and she did not know why.

Rob stirred in his sleep and flung one arm possessively over her and then one leg.

It was heavy and she moved restlessly. That was how it was with men, she thought. They fell in love and then they hoisted an arm and a leg over you, and there you were, trussed up like a Thanksgiving turkey ready to be devoured. She shivered and gently eased herself out of bed. Jacqui was intent on avoiding the whole business of caring. Emotions were yucky things, and love was some sort of a high that people imagined when they could not stand being alone.

Skiing was the opposite. There was no time for emotions or thinking up there. Up there was real! The sting of cold on your cheeks, the split second timing, the race against yourself and against the elements – that counted, that was meaningful. All the rest was a load of crap.

130

CHAPTER 17

It was seven am on a dreary Monday morning and the weather seemed to match Megan's mood exactly. It was two weeks since Nikki had defected and Megan's normal efficiency was beginning to crumble under the strain of her house guest and Ian's constant attendance on her. This morning she had arrived early in order to catch up on the paperwork she had missed for the past few days. Her 'urgent' basket was overflowing and taking the top sheet she leaned back with a grimace of despair and read: *'HAS NIKOLA PETROVNA SOLD HER BIRTHRIGHT FOR A MESS OF POTAGE?'*

Megan frowned and examined the cutting more carefully. There was a note from Maureen pinned on to it: *'Michel's getting nasty, perhaps you should stop being so rude to him.'*

Sure enough, Michel Juric was the name at the bottom of the article and it had been published in an influential European sports journal in three languages:

We question the ethics of ISA entering the political arena and organising the defection of a young ice skater who, it seems, was only too willing to abandon the socialist bloc for the glitter of the West and, in this case, all that glitters is gold, for Nikki is to be seen driving around London's streets with a learner licence plate on the back of her brand new sports car, part of the list of expensive demands she made ISA prior to defecting.

The speed at which the British Foreign Office opened its arms to this young Russian ice star and bestowed British nationality upon her, brings the whole question of sport and ethics into focus.

Will the various competing countries be wooing each other's champions to defect? Will a red MG sports car, a London flat and a British passport be the norm for prospective gold medalists, or is this a stepping stone to greater glories? Possibly

Ms Petrovna will be sporting a Chevrolet and Manhattan flat together with an American passport if and when she wins the European championships.

It seems that we have reached an absurd position whereby nationality can be awarded, rather as sports bursaries are awarded, to promising young athletes. And if this is the case, to what extent will ...

'Oh hell!' Megan grumbled. She skimmed through the article until she caught sight of her own name: *'John Oberholtzer's new protégé, Megan Carroll, — a luscious hand-maiden who has wiggled her way up through ISA's ranks, and now runs the London office — is trying to plunge her company into show business by capturing the role of Tarzan in the new French production, for her body-building champion Adolf Bartoli, whom, we hear, is about to be renamed. Adolf is on the short list together with ...'*

'Wiggled her way up.' Oh, how unfair, she moaned, but it was not the first time she had been slated in this way, and lately she had learned to be philosophical about it. There was only one profession men would ever recognise for women and that was the oldest. All other successes — however remarkable — were pigeonholed into the same category. 'Just spite!' she said aloud several times. 'You wait, Michel Juric.' Amazing how quickly the news spread. She had only just approached the French film company.

At nine sharp Megan's bank manager called on her private line. 'I don't want to worry you, Miss Carroll, but you're running over the limit.'

'If you could just cover me for a few more days ...' she said breathlessly.

'Oh, good grief! What a time to choose,' she grumbled as she took out her cash flow sheets and studied them anxiously. Where was she going to find the cash to tide them over? Ah! Poor Petunia. There was scope for instant cash in that channel crossing — good for a couple of thousand in advance, whether or not she made it. After all, ITV were bound to show up.

Conscience-stricken she rang Petunia's father instead. 'Did you get my letter?' she queried. 'Good. I just wanted to record my protest in writing — my feeling on the whole matter of

132

Petunia's channel crossing is that she's not ready for it. It might even prejudice her training – let's face it – it's nothing more than a publicity stunt and quite frankly she doesn't need it.'

She listened incredulously for a few seconds. 'What's that? Not for the publicity – only for the cash? That figures! Well, if you're determined, I'll see what I can do,' she said and feeling guilty hastily rang off.

Megan heard the jingle-jangle of Maureen's approach. She hurried in, wearing a crimson and brown jazzy toga with dangling gold earrings and shiny turban.

'What's this, Jamaica Day?' Megan called out.

'Roots! I'm remembering my roots,' Maureen called out as she disappeared into the kitchen.

'Maureen,' Megan called. 'The bank manager wants five thousand. Now where can I lay my hands on that much by Thursday? By the way, I telephoned Petunia's father and asked him what his daughter thought about attempting the channel crossing. D'you know what he said ...?'

'She does as she's bloody told,' Maureen said as she entered the office.

'How d'you know that?' Megan looked up in surprise.

'That's what my Dad would have said, if I'd been able to swim. Here! Know what he once did? He entered me in a teenage dancing competition. The winner got a hundred quid. I came last so he boxed my ears.'

'You probably got off lightly,' Megan said, thinking of their child protégées.

'Maureen, did you get hold of the original picture of Gertie kissing her girlfriend?'

'I did.' Maureen sat down and took out her notebook.

'And did you send it round to the newspapers?'

'Sure.' Maureen was burrowing through the 'urgent' pile. She drew out two cuttings and pushed them across the desk.

'*Happy reunion for long-lost cousins,*' Megan read. '*When Gertrude Mullins won the Women's Singles in Melbourne recently, it was a cause for double celebration, for Gertrude's long lost cousin, whose parents emigrated from Britain ten years ago, was there to see her win ...*'

'Well done. Did you tell her to keep private life off the courts?'

'I did. Bantex have agreed to be magnaminous over the jersey *faux pas*. The PRO is sending a selection of their latest – in case she gets chilly again.'

'Megan,' Maureen began, looking troubled. 'This Michel Juric has asked me out to dinner tonight. I know what he wants – to pump me for news about Nikki. You know what they're saying, don't you? That you bought a lemon; that she's not so hot and you're too scared to let her make a public performance; that Eric Lamont is working day and night to lick her into shape.'

'What do you think, Maureen. You've seen her at coaching.'

'She's fantastic ... when she tries.' Maureen frowned and examined her pointed nails. 'Shall I tell him that?' she said without looking up. 'I'd like to go, but if you don't want me to ...'

'I'd rather you didn't, Maureen. He'll get the better of you. We'll go through those press releases Ian dreamed up, you can memorise a few and send an article.' Megan nodded: 'Two can play at his game. We'll use him as our mouthpiece, but Maureen, I don't want to intrude on your private life, but I think it's information he's after.'

'I'll tell him to get lost,' Maureen said with a sigh.

If you can, Megan thought silently, but she said: 'Business is coming along nicely, except the cash flow situation which is critical. If only I hadn't signed up Jacqui – we'd be laughing.'

'It's not the cashflow that's wrong – it's you,' Maureen said with her usual lack of tact. 'You've lost your sparkle – and your concentration. Your mind's not on your work.'

Megan scowled at Maureen who shrugged. 'I'm sorry, I'm sure,' she said in a sing-song voice. Then she grinned cheekily and hurried off.

Why am I scowling at her? She was only telling the truth. I'm getting through the workload, but only because I force myself to do so. My creativity has gone for a loop and work has become a burden instead of a joy. Why? What's gone wrong with me?

Part of the answer, Megan knew, had to do with her incredibly cluttered home life. Her flat was chaotic, not just in terms of fearful disorder, for Nikki left her things all over the place, but in every other possible way. Nikki adored music. She was either singing or playing classics loudly – or both. She was rigidly cultured in the arts, and became quite hurt if Megan complained about the volume. She never wanted to sleep, and most evenings Megan was bullied or cajoled into going to plays or concerts or visiting art exhibitions. After that, she usually wanted to play cards. She had made friends with curious people of a dozen nationalities who took to dropping into the flat at odd hours and staying far too long. She would telephone the office several times during the day to ask questions and advice, and she seemed to have absolutely no consideration for others. 'If I don't soon find her a flat, I'll collapse,' Megan muttered.

But is Nikki the whole story? The sole reason for my waning creativity? Not really. I can't keep my mind on my business because I spend too much time day-dreaming about Ian – like a frivolous teenager. It's not like me at all, and goodness knows I haven't had much encouragement from Ian. Yet he's always around. Why? He arrives here every day on any excuse, but usually with helpful ideas for Nikki's career or publicity and, let's face it, he's a real genius at this. Most nights he takes us out to supper, or pops into the flat for a snack. At the same time, Ian doesn't seem to mind if he sees me ... or Maureen ... or Nikki ... Is he looking for freelance work? Or trying to learn the business? Yet when I offered him a fee for writing Nikki's press releases he laughed and refused. If only he weren't so capable. If only I hadn't fallen in love.

She had to admit that right from the first day, the man she was so attracted to, was an enigma to her; and after a month of close association he remained a mystery. There were just too many contradictions. He was charming, clever, but, as yet, he had not achieved success in any field; he hated business, but spent most of his time helping her with ISA's business and in particular with Nikki's career; he detested the link between business and sport, yet he was masterly in manipulating sponsors for Nikki's benefit; he scorned plastic values, detested cities, but lived in one. All of which didn't add up. She longed to know how much was simulated, how much was real?

Megan vowed to push Ian out of her mind from that moment on, but five minutes later he walked into the office with cakes for everyone. Megan was taken by surprise. Her heart lurched and her stomach contracted with painful barbs of pleasure. He was glowing from the cold, and his eyes looked twice as blue this morning, while his dark hair was curling from the damp air. He noticed her glance and ran his hand over his head.

'Damn weather. I'll get a crew cut this afternoon.'

His full lips were cracked from the cold, and he looked lean and strong and vigorous. 'Oh my,' she said, hoping he had not noticed her pleasure at seeing him. She glanced at her watch in surprise. 'Good heavens, it's only ten-thirty.'

'Tea-time,' Ian said happily. 'Hasn't Maureen taught you about our tea breaks yet?'

'Oh, we don't stop for tea,' Megan retorted loudly. 'We gulp our coffee while we work.'

'Take a look at this work of art,' Ian said, plonking a thick manuscript on the desk and handing the cakes to Maureen. 'It took all night to finish.'

From the way he handled it, Megan could see how proud he was. 'Is this the fateful documentary on Yugoslavia?' she teased.

'No. Guess again! It's a film script written around Nikki's defection. It's a little romanticised, but Nikki won't mind – in fact I checked it with her. I've included a love affair – which is vital to the story. Now Megan, I want you to be my agent. Try to place it with a film company. After all, they'd have to offer Nikki the lead role, so it would benefit all of us. You do see that, don't you?'

Megan hardly knew how to tell him the absurdity of his idea. He was so enthusiastic. He'd be so disappointed and that was a pity. It was incredibly difficult to market a film – so many intangibles had to become reality – an interested and successful producer, a financial backer, production house, distributing network – and only when all of them had agreed, jointly and severally, could you say the script had got off the ground. After that were hundreds of other hurdles and a chance in a million of ever seeing it on the screen. Oh dear! But Ian should know all that. After all, he was in the business.

'I'm not a film agent. I don't have the know-how, Ian,' Megan explained.

'All the same, send it round to the British companies. I'd do it, but I need a covering letter on your letterhead.'

'That's no problem,' she said, knowing that she was taking the easy way out.

'Where's Nikki this morning?' he asked casually.

'Training. At least I hope she's training. I think there's a little romance brewing with her coach, Eric Lamont.' She searched Ian's face for signs of jealousy or annoyance, but he looked only mildly interested.

Megan broke off and frowned. There was nothing attractive about Eric; he was slightly effeminate-looking and definitely middle-aged; a pale, insipid, ginger-haired man, but a superb coach and she had a sneaking idea that Nikki was finding it easier to push her own ideas through from a pillow position. He had certainly given in on any number of points concerning classical stance and the feasibility of introducing Nikki's own new steps. She made a mental note to talk to Nikki about Eric. Not that she wanted to interfere, but Nikki was throwing herself away on him.

She sighed. 'Nikki's a bit of a problem right now. We're rather overcrowded in the flat.'

'Well the good news is ...' Ian began after an awkward silence, 'I have a cottage for Nikki. It belongs to my batty old aunt. She lives alone in a ruddy great mansion on the moors and never leaves her home. The place is empty and it could do with a tenant. The bad news is – I'm not sure for how long Nikki can have it. Maybe a year – I just don't know.'

'Why that's wonderful, Ian. Saved my life – no really. I'd like to pay rent, of course. How much will it be?'

'The point is, my aunt can't let it. It's tied up in a family trust, but of course, friends can live there. I should have thought about it before.'

'Well, who cares if it's not forever,' Megan said, her face alight with joy. 'Nikki will be delighted and as for me – it's a reprieve, let me tell you. Oh for peace! How soon can she move in.'

'Here are the keys,' Ian said, taking them out of his pocket. 'Please yourself.'

How about today? Megan thought eagerly. There and then she decided to take the day off work to move Nikki in.

CHAPTER 18

It was absolutely charming, a gem of a cottage leading off a tiny cobbled cul-de-sac, with white walls, pretty striped awnings and flowers in painted window boxes. Megan was delighted to discover that it was furnished even down to kitchen utensils. What a relief!

Nikki was ecstatic. She even stopped moaning about her guard, who took up residence at the lamp post opposite. Maureen and Megan helped her to pack and move in. Then they went back to work, but Megan returned at six that afternoon to make sure Nikki had everything she wanted.

There was the sound of music and shouting coming from the front room. Nikki had thrown an impromptu party and it was amazing how many people she had already gathered around her. Nevertheless, when she caught sight of Megan standing in the doorway Nikki ran across the room with a whoop of joy and flung her arms around her neck. 'Now you are here ... now I am complete ... I have everything ... Oh! My English! Oh Megan ... if I could only explain.' She broke off and peered intently into Megan's eyes and for a moment Megan was suffused with a feeling of warmth. Megan did not understand Nikki fully and they seldom agreed about anything, but there was no denying Nikki's friendship and this made her feel good. Nikki rushed back to her friends and for the first time, Megan saw Nikki intent on enjoying herself. She let her hair down, sang Russian songs, guzzled vodka, taught them all Russian dances and was particularly tough on poor Eric whom, she insisted, must learn Cossack dancing.

'Let's hope he has more energy for dancing than he has in bed,' Nikki said in a stage whisper and then collapsed into giggles.

Megan was shocked. She could not understand why Nikki was making fun of Eric.

138

'Nikki, please remember, he's the top coach in England,' Megan said, pulling her aside. 'If you offend him, he might refuse to coach you, even though you are paying him top rates.'

'I am *paying* him?' Nikki's voice echoed her incredulous expression. 'You mean, he is working for me?'

'In a manner of speaking, but not quite, because it's an honour to be coached by Eric. You have to be pretty good for him to take you on.'

'I assumed the State had organised my coaching.'

'Good grief! How many times must I explain how things work over here. The State controls the government and you control your own life and your own career. I engaged Eric on your behalf and I pay him out of your trust fund, which has been set up to hold your sponsorship money.'

This was not the right time to add that so far there was a large debit balance in the trust fund which ISA was covering and that she would have to find a sponsor soon.

'You should have told me,' Nikki said, her eyes narrowing into quite a cruel expression. 'I really can't stand that odious little man,' she said petulantly.

'No one asked you to go to bed with him,' Megan said tartly.

Suddenly Nikki's expression changed. She was contrite and smiling again. '*Nichevo*,' she said, and tugging at Megan's arm she led her off to the hastily erected bar for some fruit punch.

Nichevo, (it doesn't matter) was a word Megan heard several times a day. Nikki would create incredible scenes when she did not get her own way, and then, just as quickly, she would give up, murmuring *nichevo*. It was a word which even Megan was starting to use.

Megan excused herself as soon as she could and returned to the office at eight. She had been putting off asking John for bridging finance, but the position was critical and she had no prospect of any immediate funds coming in. She explained this in the telex she sent.

At eight-thirty pm John telephoned, his voice flat with anger: 'You balls up our biggest sponsor by gate-crashing their family vendetta and you're out on your ear, honey, and as for that Russian skater you saddled us with; get out and sell her a meal ticket before she eats us out of business.'

No point in complaining, she thought. I knew it would be tough when I took on the job. There was no alternative. She

139

would have to find Nikki a sponsor, even if it meant by-passing Vanguard. She would start in the morning.

It was her first evening without Nikki, and Megan had planned a mammoth clean-up. She was washing the kitchen floor when Ian dropped by. Oh good grief, she thought, glancing in the mirror at her perspiring face and dishevelled hair. She had been so sure that Ian would spend the evening at Nikki's cottage.

She offered him soup, but he insisted on helping her clean. Later, he said, he would take her for supper.

For an hour they worked together to restore the flat to its former tidiness. Ian polished and cleaned and talked to her of his plans for Nikki's career. It was amazing how quickly he had learned about the sports world, and exactly how far one could go with sponsors and where to draw the line. Then they discussed the play they had seen last week, and the books he had lent her, and once again Megan was struck with the similarity of their viewpoints. They might have been an old married couple, they had so much in common. What a curious complex man Ian was, Megan thought watching him sidelong as he polished the table intently. His manner was totally and arrogantly male, he always wanted to make the decisions and any form of resistance irked him, yet he had no qualms about knuckling down to housework. 'It's my naval training,' he laughed when she broached the subject. 'I like things to be shipshape, too.'

'I can't tell you the joy of getting Nikki out of here,' she confided when the flat had been restored to its former order. 'Not that I don't like her, but she's ... well, she's a messer ... the place is always untidy ... I hate untidiness.'

'I don't understand why you don't sign up Nikki and get some cash in,' Ian said later, when they were sitting in the little Italian restaurant on the corner of her block.

Perhaps it was the wine, or her delight in seeing Ian unexpectedly, that led Megan to tell Ian about John's telephone call. 'I was hoping to use Nikki to sell Jacqui preferably to Vanguard in a package deal, and thereby get myself out of an embarrassing, if not dangerous situation,' she admitted in a rare moment of candour. 'You see, I made this terrible mistake.' She explained about Jacqui.

140

'Of course, I'm not actually harming Nikki at all. Vanguard are the best sponsors she could hope for. They're the toughest, but the richest and they'll be able to splash out on big promotions.'

'I've got a couple of ideas that might help you,' Ian said. 'I can offer you the films taken at Sarajevo, Nikki skating at Zetra Stadium, and Jacqui hurtling down Mount Yahorina. Would they help?'

'Would they help?' Megan gasped. 'Why, Ian, that's all I need. You're a dear, you're a darling. You've solved my problem – now if I can only gatecrash her establishment, I'll have something to show Eleanor Douglas.'

'I've heard she's a very kind woman, under a hard exterior,' Ian said thoughtfully. 'She used to be out selling herself, that's how she built up Vanguard. If you go there and sit it out – eventually she'll see you.'

Megan reached forward and grabbed his hand, pressed it between hers. His hands were strong and muscular, which was strange for a writer. She gently ran her fingers over his wrist and noticed the thick black hairs curling around his efficient, multi-dialled watch. Lately Ian seemed to be solving all of her problems – except one, she thought as his hand was gently withdrawn.

She looked up at him, a long, quizzical look. There was this indefinable barrier between them. Something he had erected. He was holding back. So why was he here? Why had it all been so different in Sarajevo?

'Remember Sarajevo and the wolves?' she blurted out. Then she flushed.

'I'll never forget,' he said.

He's married, she thought suddenly. What else could possibly explain his inexplicable restraint in the face of her many and varied invitations? She might as well find out. 'There's something I want to ask you,' Megan began in an undertone as lightheartedly as she could manage, while the waiter cleared away the coffee cups and brought the bill.

'Are you married?'

She glanced round sharply to catch him off guard and succeeded, for Ian's eyes looked troubled. Not guilty at all, just sort of sad. Without answering he paid and walked her to the door. Outside there was a cold wind blowing and Ian took her arm as they hurried through the streets.

'Megan,' he began at last, as they walked through her front door.

'Don't Megan me,' she said icily. 'Are you ... or aren't you?' She clenched her fist and shook it involuntarily. There should be a special punishment for married men who fooled around. Not that Ian had done much fooling, she thought regretfully.

'What is it that you want?' he asked as if he were genuinely baffled.

'The truth. What else?'

'No, I am not married.'

'Well then,' she said.

'Well then?'

Megan sat down abruptly without grace, like a sack being dumped, knowing that she had blown her defences and made a fool of herself. 'Well then why are you always here?' she asked. She might as well go the whole way, now that she had begun.

'For so many reasons, Megan, one of which is to help you with Nikki's career. I promised you in Sarajevo. Do you remember?'

'I remember many things in Sarajevo.'

'Megan, come here.'

She remained stubbornly hunched in her chair until Ian sat beside her, tilted her face round and kissed her on the lips.

She thrust him away, but Ian pushed her down on the couch and wrapped his arms tightly around her.

'If you knew ...' he was whispering. 'If you knew how I've been longing to do this ... and so much more. Megan dear ... you're driving me crazy, with your silly ideals, your courage, your crazy business drive. My God! How you drive yourself and everyone else you meet. I've never known anyone like you. And you're so lovely, you've been causing me sleepless nights ever since I met you. What am I going to do with you, Megan Carroll?'

'You could try loving me,' she said and instantly regretted it for Ian pulled his arm away and sat up, staring down at her with a rueful look on his face.

'One of these days I aim to do that,' he said. 'But not now.'

He stood up. 'Right now I must be getting along.'

Her shoulders sagged as she watched him reach for his raincoat. 'Megan,' he said, looking sad, 'be patient. I have another commitment. No, not a woman, but far more

142

demanding. It's my work. Something I must do. I think you understand how I feel about you – but just give me a year.'

'A year?' she spluttered. But Ian had already left.

After this embarrassing evening, Megan hardly expected to see Ian again, but the following night he arrived at her door with a bottle of Scotch and a large folder.

'My film script. I need help,' he admitted ruefully. 'This lacks the woman's angle.'

'Well, I don't know how much help I'm going to be,' she said as he dumped his manuscript on the table.

Surprisingly, she seemed to be able to find a good many points he had missed. Midnight came and they were still at the start of it.

'I had no idea what a tough job it is to write a film script,' Megan admitted a month later after they had worked together for at least three nights a week.

'I don't know how I ever wrote anything without you,' Ian said softly as she kicked off her slippers and curled up on the settee to drink the cocoa Ian had made.

She gazed long and hungrily at Ian who was scribbling some last minute adjustments. He had promised to hand over the script to an interested producer in the morning. Megan felt sad about this. During the past month they had built a wonderful camaraderie and to some extent they had learned to size up each other's strengths and weaknesses as they drove each other to the limit to finish the work by Ian's deadline.

Nevertheless, it had not been all work and no play. Some evenings they had put the script aside and gone for walks in the park, and Ian had identified the various birds for her and told her about the wildlife in the forests and moors of his beloved Scotland. When he spoke about home you could hear the yearning in his voice and she often wondered why he was living in London at all. Surely he could write from further afield? But Ian had explained the importance of being on the spot to a freelance writer. They had taken Nikki out to dinner or a show on several occasions and the three of them were drawing closer, as they learned to understand each other.

'Well, it's over,' she said. Ian picked up the sadness in her voice and one eyebrow rose mockingly. 'Let's celebrate,' he

143

said. 'We'll have a glass of champagne to launch this venture.'

'Oh Ian, I'm sorry. I don't have any,' she said.

'Didn't you check the provisions I bought?' He sounded quite hurt. Amazing how quickly he had made himself at home at her place.

'Well, no,' she said.

'I restocked the groceries you were running out of. Let's hope you're good at business, because one day you're going to make someone a really terrible wife.'

She aimed her slipper at him and caught him on his shoulder. 'This month has been a bit unusual,' she admitted. 'Normally I just sleep here.'

'Excuses, excuses!'

He disappeared into the kitchen and returned ten minutes later with a well-stocked cheese board, biscuits and champagne bubbling over the glasses.

'Well, I can't return the compliment,' she said as she took her glass. 'You'll make someone a really superb wife.'

The barb was intended and Ian stared long and hostilely at her. 'What time are you delivering the script?' she asked hastily to change the subject.

As Ian answered her, it was easy to see that his mind was not on the subject. Shortly afterwards they emptied their glasses and he left.

Something was wrong, she thought dismally as she tipped the rest of the champagne down the sink. She loathed the stuff anyway, and had only drunk it to humour Ian.

She returned to her lounge disconsolately and sat gloomily surveying the empty room. Ian had a self-sufficiency that appalled her. Yet she had to admit that they had grown very close mentally. She knew he liked her, maybe his feelings were stronger than this, as hers were, yet he had made no move to seduce her. Every night he gave her a brotherly kiss on her cheek before he left. Occasionally he took her hand. He was friendly, uncomplaining, helpful, but still a stranger. It was almost as if he were playing a part and deliberately keeping his emotions free.

Something would have to be done about it, she thought gloomily, as she bathed. It can't be too soon for me.

144

CHAPTER 19

'It's just too ridiculously perfect,' Megan muttered as she waited nervously in Eleanor's private reception area on the sixth floor of Vanguard's head office. She had never seen anything like this room, with its high domed ceilings and bay windows overlooking Monaco and the Mediterranean. The decor was white – white walls, ceiling, carpet, furniture, even the telephones and typewriters were white so that the larger-than-life photographs of Vanguard's winning athletes seemed to be the only reality there.

Several girls were sitting at their desks or passing through. They wore white imitation suede track suits with the Vanguard emblem and their white jogging shoes made no sound on the deep pile of the carpet. Megan was woefully aware that this was not a place for gatecrashers and she doubted Eleanor Douglas would see her at all.

For the third time, a pretty blonde girl in the Vanguard gear hurried out of an adjoining office. 'Miss Douglas has not said whether or not she'll see you,' she cooed felicitously. 'She's still tied up, but she'll be back soon. Won't you have another cup of coffee?' She tossed her blonde curls over her shoulder and hurried away.

Any minute now, Megan thought irritably, an all-white angel with an all-white harp is going to perch on that table and serenade me with a company hymn.

But instead two hours later the white lift doors slid silently open and Eleanor Douglas burst into the room. 'Megan Carroll!' she exploded. 'Still waiting. My God, but you're persistent. All right, all right,' she said to her secretary, 'I'll see her now.'

'Come on then,' she said turning to Megan. 'Have they given you coffee, or tea? I prefer tea. Bring some more tea,' she yelled at no one in particular. 'Here, let me take something.' She grabbed Megan's video console as if it were weightless and rushed on ahead.

It was almost impossible to grasp the full impact of Eleanor Douglas, there were so many parts of her, all of them bombastic, unexpected and staggering – her voice, for instance, which was broad Scots on acquired American. It was a deep voice, made for laughing and shouting, and she did both of these things frequently and never stopped talking, or so it seemed to Megan.

From the back view she looked absurd in her tight black leather trouser suit stretched to breaking point over her generous backside, and when she turned, the buttons of her red satin blouse gaped over her voluminous bust. Yet her dangling gold earrings, her permed brown hair, her ridiculous outfit and her excessive jewellery – all of that was insignificant besides her shrewd brown eyes, her all-seeing and judging eyes which made the rest appear to be some ridiculous disguise. A whizz kid disguised as a middle-aged woman, Megan thought, feeling totally incapable of coping with the interview. Suddenly all her preparations and her sales pitch would have to be discarded. Eleanor would not be persuaded, or influenced. That, at least, was very clear.

When Megan had the chance to study the rest of Eleanor's face, she saw that her mouth was too large, and smeared with crimson lipstick, her nose too prominent, yet her features were in harmony with each other and the overall effect was that of a sexy, bedable woman. How does she do it? Megan wondered, trying to analyse Eleanor's appeal.

Eleanor led the way to her private suite of offices and Megan sank gratefully into a comfortable, white leather chair. 'How d'you like my office?' she babbled as she took off her jacket and hung it behind the door. 'My interior designers refuse to come in here. They say I've ruined their decor with my junk. Junk? I ask you,' she flung her hand around expressively.

The room was like Eleanor, cluttered, costly, and immensely appealing. Two bookcases were crammed higgledy-piggledy with ornaments and priceless works of art. Megan recognised Chadwick's *Iron Bird*, Boccioni's *Space Form* and there was a beautiful jade horse which looked oriental. Around the walls were some beautiful wildlife paintings: a water colour of an African Loerie by Ingrid Weiersbye; a Kudu in oils by Paul

Rose; *African Eagle* by Leigh Voigt. She tried not to stare, but could not conceal her surprise.

A white clad nymph brought a tray of tea and left. Eleanor rose briskly. 'Milk, lemon?' she barked. 'I never see anyone if I can help it,' she went on briskly. 'I haven't time. One can lose a day, or a month, or half your life talking nonsense, so it had better be good, Miss Carroll.' She smiled warmly and Megan began to feel optimistic, but her hopes faded when Eleanor reached forward, grabbed a cooking timer and set it for half an hour.

'When the bell sounds, that's it,' she said. 'It helps if we both know where we stand. This damned gadget rules my life,' she added as if to excuse her rudeness.

As the minutes ticked by too fast and too loud, Megan reached forward and switched on the video machine. 'I've got two competitors for you. I want you to sponsor both of them,' she said hurriedly. Her mouth seemed to have stiffened and it was difficult to pronounce the words; her hands felt clammy and her throat was dry; and she could hear John's words ringing in her ears: *You balls up our biggest sponsor by gatecrashing their family vendetta and you're out on your ear, honey – and as for that Russian gal you saddled us with, get her a meal ticket before she eats us out of business.*

Eleanor seemed to be having difficulty in sitting still, as she watched the video of Nikola re-enacting the Sarajevo show. She scratched her head, grabbed a ruler and rubbed her back, she wiped her arms surreptitiously, crossed and uncrossed her legs and fidgeted and jingled throughout Nikki's brief performance. Obviously she was bored.

'Nikola Petrovna is very talented,' Megan said angrily.

'I can see that,' Eleanor said between the twitches. 'Natural talent, insufficient coaching, no finesse, she may or may not make the grade. Am I right?'

'She'll make the grade,' Megan argued. 'She has to – that's why she left home and went into exile. You know as well as I do that there's always something extra – not talent, not skill, some extra factor that drives these youngsters to the top. Nikki defected because she's driven by something inside her – the obsession with perfection which drives these kids to the limits of their endurance – and beyond. It takes more than guts.'

'You're talking shit,' Eleanor said flatly. 'Fame and fortune

147

every time. They're egotistical and they're greedy – every last one of them. If they win, they're set up for life, but most times they lose. They know that when they take the risk.' She smiled grimly. 'You're an idealist, Miss Carroll. I was once, but that was a long time ago. Life wiped the stars out of my eyes. Now I see things for what they are, plain and straightforward. These kids are in business to make a fast buck and so am I. It helps when you understand what it's all about.'

Megan mumbled unhappily, not wanting to become embroiled in an argument which had little to do with the reason she was there.

'You're a bit of a softie,' Eleanor went on, smiling ruthlessly at Megan. 'You'd like them to get the same rewards – whether they win or whether they lose. Come now, admit it. You're costing us a fortune in lawyers fees over that young Conrad Soerli of yours. You'll lose in the end and you'll pay the piper – how is he, by the way? I bet he's not grumbling. The kids know the odds when they go into it.'

Nikki's performance was over. Megan took out the video feeling crushed and disappointed. Eleanor had hardly bothered to look. 'You're trying to pull sport down to a business level. You can't do that,' she protested. 'You're taking something beautiful – and trying to evaluate it in terms of dollars and cents, profit and loss. Have you ever considered, Miss Douglas, that you're privileged – yes, I mean it – you're really privileged to link your products with these kids and their heroic struggles.'

Eleanor's eyes were shining black and beady now, a bird about to peck the worm. Don't squirm, Megan, she warned herself. Eleanor would strike without mercy.

'Horseshit, Miss Carroll,' Eleanor said.

'I didn't come here to argue with you,' Megan said. 'Particularly with that clock ticking away.'

'Honey, it ticks whether you hear it or not.'

'Miss Douglas – listen to me!' Megan said determinedly. 'Nikola Petrovna is a brilliant young skater. She's only eighteen and there's a year before the Games. We're backing her all the way with ISA finance and the top coach in London, but we're looking for sponsors. I want to offer you her skates and clothes on a non-restrictive basis. I aim to sign her for toothpaste, face cream, hair spray, and so on. All the cash will go into a trust account, of course, to maintain her amateur status. Naturally, you would be the only sports sponsor.'

'How much are you asking?'

'A million dollars over a three-year period, made up of basic yearly annuities in advance, and bonuses for public appearances.'

Eleanor laughed. 'That's what I paid for your Finnish ice dancer and she's proven. This one's only hopeful.'

'Yes, but in terms of public exposure she's better. For starters, she's beautiful, and the fact that she defected will catch people's imagination. She'll be a household name long before she's the world champion. I can guarantee heavy non-sports exposure.'

Eleanor paused and waited while her secretary cleared the cups away. 'That just makes her famous – not Vanguard.'

'Not at all,' Megan argued desperately. 'You want to gatecrash the public's attention – well, I'm offering you someone who'll do just that. How you angle the association between Vanguard and Nikki depends on the skills of your advertising people.'

Eleanor chuckled. She sounded genuinely amused. 'You know something, Miss Carroll, you remind me so much of myself – in the beginning. I started off with selling and if there's one thing I admire it's a strong sales pitch. Why don't you show your other video to Nigel? Marketing is his baby and he doesn't like me interfering in his domain.'

Megan's heart sank as she gazed at this tough, hard-working woman, whose attention was already wavering.

'Miss Douglas, I've got ten minutes left. You promised,' Megan said desperately.

'Okay, okay. Sorry!' She raised both hands in mock defeat.

Megan changed the video tape, blessing Ian for extracting this one from the BBC. 'This skier is going to make a monkey out of everything you said about kids on the make,' Megan said quietly.

Eleanor shrugged, looking grim.

The screen flickered and flashed and then stabilised. Sarajevo, 1983, the commentator began against the howling gale. Megan reached across and switched off the sound.

She saw Eleanor stiffen slightly as the diminutive figure of her daughter came racing down out of the driving snow.

149

'That's boy's suicidal,' Eleanor gasped.

Megan watched her in amazement. Did she have no idea her daughter was skiing for Britain in Sarajevo? Impossible! Surely mother and daughter weren't that estranged. And surely she kept up with the sports news?

'Fantastic!' Eleanor gasped and then peered forward over the desk. The two minutes seemed to last forever, as the skier raced against time on that terrible piste in the blizzard.

Eleanor let out a deep sigh as the girl passed the last gate and slowed towards the camera. She disappeared into a huddle of wellwishers. Then, suddenly, she emerged with her helmet off, grinning cheekily towards the camera.

Eleanor's cup fell out of her hand and shattered on her desk, but she did not seem to notice.

'Can I have that tape?' she asked shakily after a long silence.

'Sure.' Megan took it out of the console and handed it to Eleanor. Suddenly the timer buzzed loudly and Eleanor whipped round and swept it off the desk in a single compulsive movement. 'She broke her leg last summer,' she began dully, 'so she didn't make the US team. I thought that was the end of that.'

'I'm amazed you didn't know,' Megan began.

'I do the finance and the sales. Sport and marketing is Nigel's baby.'

Megan sighed. She wished she could be anywhere, but here right now. This was not selling, this was moral blackmail. 'I signed her up in Sarajevo,' Megan began shakily. 'At the time I didn't know who she was because she was using a pseudonym. When I found out ... well, you can probably imagine how upset I was. I mean ... it's wiser to steer clear of family tangles – particularly if they involve your biggest sponsor. I tried to sort it out with Nigel, but he told me you were against Jacqui skiing. Well, I guess I was determined you should know how good she is.'

'I know she's good,' Eleanor said flatly.

'Jacqui skis because it's the only thing that means anything to her. She's run out of cash, she's desperate, but she's determined to hang in.'

'She skis because I don't want her to,' Eleanor said obstinately, 'and she's throwing away a fortune to do so.'

'Doesn't that tell you something,' Megan shouted. Oh God,

what was she doing. She heard her voice go on and a part of her wished she could stop while the other part wanted to knock some sense into this stubborn woman. 'Can't you see yourself – battling to succeed on your own. How would you have liked to have inherited Vanguard – on a plate. That doesn't sound like you – and she's like you – you're both winners and both obstinate.'

Megan leaned back feeling spent and depressed. She knew she had blown everything. When she looked at Eleanor, she saw a large tear rolling down her haggard cheek.

'I'm so sorry,' Megan said softly. She stood up and stared out of the window at the sea. 'I just thought you ought to have a chance to sponsor your daughter. If she wins a gold, it could mean a great deal of publicity. Someone else could score and that might increase the load she's carrying on her back. I'm not a psychiatrist, I don't want to blackmail you, I just want you to know the score. Then you can make a decision.'

'Why should you care?'

'Because I'm caught in the middle of this thing,' Megan blurted out. 'I didn't know what to do, so I bought an option on Jacqui with my own cash. Two thousand pounds for one month.'

She had intended to say a great many clever things, but the sight of this haggard woman with the tears rolling down her cheeks was too much.

'D'you know what it would mean to ISA if I cut all my sponsorship?'

'Disaster!' Megan said truthfully, 'and right now Magnum are getting rough because they've got her contract lined-up – two million dollars over a three-year period, bonuses for winning and breaking records. The usual thing, plus a first-class technical back-up.'

'Huh! They can't compete with our expertise.'

'So – Jacqui'll just have to try harder.'

'Don't try to blackmail me,' Eleanor said sharply.

Megan looked round abruptly and saw a face ravaged with grief and dark with smudged mascara. 'I guess I'd better leave ...'

'No,' Eleanor interrupted her. 'You were right to come here, Megan,' she said. 'I'm in your debt, but I won't be bulldozed into anything. If I sponsor Jacqui, I'll want a special contract

drawn up. I'd hate to think of my daughter on the receiving
end of one of my contracts.

'Right now I'm going to buy time from you,' she went on.
'I'll take over that option on Jacqui and since I wouldn't
consider sponsoring someone I've never seen perform, I'll do
the same with Miss Petrovna. What do you say to ten thousand
dollars for a two-month option on both of them.'

Megan sat down slowly, letting her breath out in a long sigh.
So they'd reached the bargaining table – well that was
something she understood.

'It'll cost you much more than that,' she said determinedly.
She looked up and to her surprise saw that Eleanor was smiling
at her.

'So? Don't waste time – name your price,' the older woman
said softly.

CHAPTER 20

After Megan left, Eleanor picked up the video, to lock it in her safe, but looking down she caught sight of her large, tanned hands with the knotted veins and drying skin and it seemed that her daughter's safety lay in her hands and she whispered: 'Oh God, Oh God. Such ugly hands.'

For most of her life she had been climbing up and away with savage concentration – but away from what? From poverty, she often thought, yet she was excessively rich. Not rich enough, she thought. Never rich enough to save her from anxiety and fearful premonitions. Consequently, she was always searching for something on which she could unleash her fears, some concrete thing, for she was a resourceful woman and she had always coped with reality. Yet lately it seemed that even real problems were becoming insurmountable and that the retribution she had evaded all these years was creeping up – oh so slowly and so silently – up and around – like icy flood waters at dead of night.

For a while she sat staring at her desk. Then she came to a sudden decision. She pressed a button on the intercom and a few seconds later she was speaking to Lawrence Bain, head of her legal division.

'I don't know if you've met my daughter,' she began. 'No? Well, I'm hardly surprised, she's seldom here. I've not been able to interest her in Vanguard although I'd dearly like to. She's always been crazy about speed skiing and now she's made the British team in the World Cup Series ... Yes, that's right. Well, I don't think congratulations are in order, I'm dead set against her racing, but I haven't been able to prevent it.'

For a few seconds Eleanor drummed her fingers on the desk. Everyone always had to have their say. Quite unnecessary really, since only she knew what she wanted.

'Well, we're going to sponsor her,' she broke in on him when

153

she lost patience. 'Why? Because Magnum made her a very good offer. Two million dollars over a three-year period. Think up a better deal, without any compulsion to win and try to tie her up with some sort of job in Vanguard. Something to catch her interest.' She drummed her fingers impatiently as she listened again.

'I disagree, what's so difficult about that? Offhand I can think of public relations officer for winter sports?'

She replaced the receiver cutting off further views and disagreements. For a while Eleanor stared out of the window at the sea, wondering why it had turned so deep a turquoise. She could see her yacht, *Sea Shanty*, moored in the yacht basin, tossing from side to side. Waiters in the quayside café were running to take down their gay, purple-and-rose striped umbrellas which were flapping wildly in the wind. Looking up she saw a bank of purple clouds racing across the sky. She turned away. It made no difference really – no difference at all. Not to her. In Vanguard's offices it was always warm, always bright, always the same. So why did she feel chilled and out of sorts this morning?

She collapsed into her chair and stared for a long time at the folder on her desk. It contained a complete daily record of share trading of Vanguard stock on the New York stock exchange. Lately too many shares were changing hands and prices were rising. There was no obvious reason for this and it worried Eleanor. Her stock had always been highly rated, near-blue chip. Her dividends always modest, but adequate for the investment value, and investors had been assured of a slow, but steady capital appreciation. Suddenly prices had taken off. Why? Who was bidding enough to persuade so many long-term investors to take their profits now? What was behind it?

Eleanor hesitated, her fingers poised over the intercom. She felt tired after a restless night and the interview with Megan had upset her. Perhaps she was over-reacting. Nevertheless, it was disquieting. She made a sudden decision and switched on the intercom.

'Nigel, are you very busy right now? If you've a minute to spare could you pop in? I want to discuss something with you. You can? Now? There's a dear.' Nigel was her oldest business associate. He had been with Vanguard even longer than she. Their friendship reached back to the days when she was a penniless rep and he a counter salesman.

Nigel had aged a bit lately, but still retained his stern and upright military appearance. He looked like a retired colonel nowadays, she decided, with his sparse, six foot frame, his clipped moustache, shrewd grey eyes and crisp New England accent. This morning he was looking particularly kindly and she wondered why.

Eleanor fiddled with her pen. 'I don't want to worry you unnecessarily, Nigel ...' She gasped, clapped one hand on her arm and pressed hard, frowning with the effort of not scratching.

'No better?' he asked sympathetically.

'Worse!' She relaxed and pulled up her silk sleeve to reveal two large red weals containing small white patches, like a blemish from stinging nettles. She shuddered. 'Nerves, or so the doctors say. I've tried three of them, but they all say the same thing. It's the very devil trying to sleep at night.' She shrugged, dismissing the problem.

'Nigel, this is strictly between you and me. Of course, I don't have to tell you that,' she added hurriedly. 'Someone's started a take-over bid for Vanguard. Unbelievable, isn't it?' She smiled, a tired, apologetic smile. 'Too much is being traded and prices are rocketing for no obvious reason. I've always worried about this,' she went on. 'Ever since we went public.'

There was no need to spell it out to Nigel. He knew as well as she did that she had retained only thirty per cent of Vanguard's shares, in her and Jacqui's name, and Nigel owned another eight, while other key directors shared three between them. The remainder was in the hands of the investing public and some large institutions.

'Look Eleanor,' he began reasonably. 'You really don't have a thing to worry about. Between you, me and the staff, we have forty-one per cent. It's well nigh impossible to persuade all the public shareholders to part with their shares.'

'Then why is someone bidding so hard for Vanguard shares? Why are share prices rocketing? They seem to be buying at any price and the investing public's getting the sniff of profits – like sharks when they smell blood.'

Nigel allowed himself one of his rare smiles. He had a strange way of smiling, Eleanor noticed. First he would fix you with a penetrating stare, then his smile would come and go as

155

quickly and you were left with the feeling you had witnessed something extraordinary, like the evanescent trail of a comet. He was making comforting noises and Eleanor could hardly be bothered to listen. 'More little men are going into the market nowadays and sport's the in-thing.'

'D'you really think I'm being silly?' she interrupted him.

'Let's say over-cautious,' he humoured her.

In spite of her uncanny foreboding of disaster, Eleanor felt cheered by his confident manner.

'Yes,' she said thoughtfully, 'but something's bothering me. Something's wrong and I can't quite ...' She broke off, flushed heavily for no apparent reason, and wiped her brow with a tissue.

Watching Nigel, Eleanor could read his thoughts: If this is the menopause do I have another ten years to suffer? 'I think I'm getting a touch of flu,' she said.

'We all have our problems,' he said. 'Mine's Megan Carroll. She's still hammering for compensation for that Conrad Soerli. You won't believe the trouble she's got herself into and she's hoping I'll bail her out.'

'Is that so.' She frowned. 'By the way, Nigel,' she said with a sudden change of mood. 'You must have known Jacqui was on the World Cup circuit for the British team. Why didn't you tell me?'

'Didn't want to worry you, my dear. To tell the truth I tried to talk her out of it.' He smiled apologetically. 'I didn't succeed.'

'You're a dear,' Eleanor said with a quick smile. She stood up and walked around the desk. Placing one hand on Nigel's shoulder she squeezed gently. 'Thank you for coming so promptly.' This was her favourite way of ending interviews. It always worked. She was an expert at getting rid of people, and half the time they weren't even aware of it. Nigel was, and he went out scowling.

CHAPTER 21

'Get me Doctor Chatwitz,' Eleanor told her secretary. A few minutes later his voice came on the line. 'You were lucky to catch me.' He sounded aggrieved, obviously he was not so lucky.

'It's my itch,' she said flatly. 'If you don't do something about it, I'll land up in the nut house. You should see me! Large weals on my arm. They look like nettle stings, only they itch. God, I wish it hurt instead.'

'I know what it looks like, Eleanor. I've seen it before.' There was a pause. Then he said abruptly. 'I've told you what to do about it.'

'I don't believe in shrinks.' She said flatly. 'They're cons. Quacks!'

'I know how you feel.' The inflexion in his voice reminded her that they were repeating an ancient conversation.

'What am I going to do?' she said, and the whine in her voice brought her sharply back to reality. 'Your ointments don't work and neither do the tranquilisers.'

'They're only of short-term benefit. We've been through this before.'

'Jesus, I pay you enough,' she snarled.

'Not enough to establish a research institute – which would be the only other way of finding a stronger cortisone ointment. The effects wear off, Eleanor. That's why I suggested therapy. I've suggested it before.' He sighed.

'You expect me to see a guy with a name like Gundelfinger?'

'What's wrong with Gundelfinger?'

'It sounds like Rumpelstiltskin. Part of this Mickey Mouse world you want me to join.'

'Eleanor, you're *in* the Mickey Mouse world. I'm trying to get you *out* of it,' he snapped. 'Okay, can I go now? I've got an ante-natal, an insurance medical and a lacerated foot in the waiting room.'

'Goodbye,' she said wearily and replaced the receiver.

'Oh Lord,' she groaned. Now it was her stomach. It was worse than Chinese torture. She walked into the private bathroom adjoining her office and locked the door. Then she pulled up her skirt and examined the weal on her stomach, a great purple blaze that would go again in an hour or two. Meantime, she sighed and taking the latest ointment she carefully rubbed it in, taking care not to scratch. One scratch and she'd be climbing the walls, she knew. She'd tried that before.

Eyes blinded with tears of frustration, she rummaged through her work basket for Gundelfinger's telephone number. He answered his own telephone. Surprise surprise!

'Doctor Gundelfinger, I was referred to you by Doctor Selwyn Chatwitz. I'm Eleanor Douglas.'

'Yes?' The voice sounded guarded and cautious.

'Did he mention me to you?'

'No. That wouldn't be very ethical of him, would it?'

'Well I don't know. The fact is, I don't really want to come, but I have this ... this eczema. I'm desperate, but I don't believe it's going to help a bit.'

'Yes, I see. Well, that's not uncommon. Look here, it's lunchtime. Come over and share a sandwich with me. I don't have a free appointment anyway. Now let me tell you exactly how to get here.'

Dr Gundelfinger's rooms were situated in a very exclusive building, not another doctor there, which was hardly surprising considering the high rents. Christian Dior and Cartier jewellers shared the ground floor shops. The plaque on the door read simply: Dr P Gundelfinger, consultant, and the door was unlocked, as he had promised.

She walked into an empty waiting room. A moment later the interleading door opened and Dr Gundelfinger beckoned her inside. He did not look as she had imagined him from his voice. He was a tall man, in his late forties, sandy-haired and running to fat with horn-rimmed glasses and friendly grey eyes gleaming through them. She could not place his accent. German perhaps – with a long stay in America? Not that it mattered.

158

'I hope you like egg and lettuce,' he said, handing her half a sandwich, and pouring her a glass of orange juice.

'I don't want to take your lunch.'

'As you can see,' he said patting his midriff. 'I don't deserve lunch. What's the problem?'

'I don't have a problem,' she said. 'At least, nothing mental. As a matter of fact, things couldn't be better. It's just this eczema.' She rolled up one sleeve. 'I'll tell you now, I don't believe this nonsense about physical symptoms have a mental source.'

'Emotional,' he corrected her.

'Whatever.'

'You've never cried?'

'Of course I've cried.'

'Well, that's caused by emotions, but your eyes get red and water pours out of them – that's physical.'

'And now,' she asked when she was sitting comfortably facing the window, with Dr Gundelfinger behind her. She felt a fool, but after all he had given up his lunchtime.

'Is there anything you'd like to talk about?'

'Heavens no. If there were I'd talk to my friends. I wouldn't have to pay ...' her voice tailed off.

'One hundred and fifty dollars an hour.'

'Don't you think that's exorbitant?'

'I do it for less when my patients are very poor. Are you very poor?'

'Quite the opposite.'

'Okay. Now tell me what your friends say when you tell them about your problems.'

'Well, in fact I don't discuss my problems with them.'

'That's what friends are for, isn't it?'

'Maybe they're more like acquaintances,' she said.

'Okay, tell me about your home.'

'Well, it's sometime since I was back,' she began.

'Miss Douglas, your home in Cap Ferrat is world famous,' he argued.

'Yes, of course,' she said tonelessly. 'Is that what you want me to tell you about?'

'No. I want you to tell me about real home.'

She laughed. 'It consisted of a three-roomed croft in the Scottish Highlands.'

'Go on,' he urged her.

'I left home when I was eighteen,' she said, 'so you're asking me to think a long way back.'

'Take your time.'

Where should she begin? What confused cacophony of disjointed fragments and impressions could she dredge up from her forgotten past? It was years since she had thought about her parents. They were both dead. She'd gone back once and the ruins of their home, so poor and exposed on the windy moor had made her cry. Could anyone have survived there? she had wondered. But they had; and in a way they had been happy. She closed her eyes and remembered Invergordon, the school and the docks which were always full, for it was World War II and that tiny village had suddenly been transformed into a vital naval base.

'Eleanor Douglas, wake up, lass.'

The teacher's fingers pressed into her shoulder and shook her gently. Eleanor sat up, face burning with embarrassment. To her shame, she felt her eyes prickling. The next minute tickling teardrops were running down each cheek. If she rubbed them away the class would notice and if she ignored them they would splash on her desk.

She heard laughter behind her. Not real Scottish laughter, that came from the belly in gusty guffaws, but Sassenach's laughter, like tinkling bells, not laughter at all really.

Compassion glittered behind teacher's spectacles. Don't be kind, Eleanor's eyes pleaded silently in return. Kindness weakened her, made her cry. Eleanor was so well equipped to cope with anger or fear. In the playground she could take on the worst bullies and win. But kindness! Eleanor had no defence for it.

So two great balls of tears rolled down her cheek and splashed a mess of ink on her neat handwriting and Eleanor sat up straighter and stared hard at the blackboard.

She was first out when the school bell rang and first to grab her bicycle and pedal through narrow Invergordon streets, to buy Dad's newspaper, and then race towards the mountains.

Most of her class were going to the cinema that afternoon and Eleanor had been invited, but she had refused, having little interest in the latest Veronica Lake movie. But it worried her, as she stood on the pedals, zig-zagging to offset the steepness of the track. She wanted to be like the other girls and the fact that she was different made her feel uneasy and increased her longing. She had never discovered where the difference lay.

It was becoming too steep to ride. Eleanor climbed off her bicycle and pushed it up the hill. She glanced at her watch and quickened her pace. She must finish her homework and her chores before high tea and be back to her job in Invergordon by six-thirty. If she were to fall behind, father might stop her from working, and that would be a bit like dying for Eleanor.

It was late June and hot, but the higher she climbed the colder the air as she followed the winding track high up the slopes of the mountain, amongst the bracken and the heather. Now and then she stopped for a few minutes to swat at the tormenting bog flies. Far below she could see the Cromarty Firth cluttered with warships at anchor and the village of Invergordon spread around the busy seaport.

Up here it was another world – the crofter's world – and just as wild and free as it had been for centuries. Here the road was rougher, and quite deserted; hardly anyone came this way, for the road lead to nowhere, petering out high in the mountains beyond the last crofter's cottage. But sometimes the red stags came creeping down from the mists and forests and in the season you could often see the salmon leaping up the rivers, wild and frenzied with the lust for life.

The Douglas family lived in a gaunt stone cottage with a corrugated iron roof. There was no garden fence or anything silly like that, but a clump of flowers clustered round the front door. The narrow beaten path led off the road, over the moor and right into their livingroom and as usual, in summer, the door stood open.

From inside came the delicious smell of scones which her mother had just taken out of the oven. Eleanor's brown eyes lingered for a moment, taking in the blue flowered wallpaper, the polished wood of the floor and ceiling, the embroidered flowers on the tablecloth. And there was her mother, wiping her forehead on her apron and pushing her faded blond hair into place with nervous fingers. She smiled briefly, wiped her floured hands on a cloth and pushed a dish of scones towards Eleanor.

161

Eleanor took one and crammed it into her mouth. 'Too much salt,' she complained as she took another and piled a heaped spoon of homemade red currant jam onto it.

'Dad likes them salty.' It was an old argument – for the scones, porridge and haggis were all too salty, made to suit her father's taste. In spite of his bad legs and the poverty-stricken life she led, her mother still put him first and Eleanor ate what Dad liked or went without.

'Got any tea, Mum?'

'You can make a fresh pot if you like.'

Eleanor went out of the back door and threw the tea leaves on the apple-mint which grew in great tatty armfuls by the kitchen door.

The water was always boiling on the old wood stove and Eleanor made tea and poured a cup for her mother, stirring in the globules of fat from their own creamy milk.

Eleanor's room was grand, now that she had it to herself, for her brother was in the Navy. A double-bunk, a wooden table with Mum's second-best cloth over it and a cupboard for her books.

Now she was fourteen, Eleanor had two hours of homework a day. She sat down and finished half of it and then she set about her chores: collecting eggs, feeding chicken, stacking the wood by the stove, feeding the rabbits and laying the table.

Her father arrived at dusk with a salmon in a bag under his arm. He'd been poaching, she knew. She and her father seldom spoke, strangers since the war, for he had been away four years, but there was a certain fondness which shone from his eyes, despite his lack of words. He sat outside, scraping the scales, silent, content, his lips muttering silently. Then he washed the fish in a bucket of water and brought it inside.

'Finished your homework?' he asked as he settled down behind his newspaper, in the old armchair by the window, which was his special property.

'I have indeed,' she snapped, feeling guilty for lying. 'And the chicken and the pigs and the rabbits. So now I'll be doing the wood.'

He looked up sharply, pale blue eyes framing a rebuke, but Eleanor ignored him.

'It's late, Eleanor lass,' her mother warned her when she returned with an armful of twigs. Eleanor flew round the table, setting the knives and forks and making fresh tea again. They had herrings and a cucumber with home-made bread for tea.

Her father stood at the end of the table, eyes closed solemnly. 'For what we are about to receive may the Lord make us truly thankful. Amen,' he said sonorously and sat down at the head of the table.

'Truly thankful!' The words were like blows in Eleanor's head. What did it mean – this truly thankful that her father was always prodding her with? Did it mean content? Satisfied? Making do and never striving to grow. For she was not satisfied. Oh no! There was so much more she wanted and, on impulse, she told Dad about her dreams and ambitions as she munched her herring and washed away the salty taste with strong, sweet tea.

Her father's face became stern and set. He got up and fetched the Bible and started reading '... *turn ye not aside for then should ye go after vain things, which cannot profit or deliver; for they are vain ...*' then he whipped over the pages, fast and furious with his gnarled, arthritic hands and read; *'There is that maketh himself rich, yet hath nothing; there is that maketh himself poor, yet hath great riches.'*

Eleanor burst into tears, rushed into her room and slammed the door. Nothing would stop her, nothing, she vowed and certainly not Dad and his silly readings.

She knew she was going to have that house by the sea; not any sea, mind you, but a warm, deep blue sea – definitely not a pale Scottish sea – and her own yacht lying at mooring. Her house would be all glass and pillars and marble floors and every room with a lovely view.

'You'll see, I'll have it all when I grow up,' she said defiantly to her mother when she returned to the kitchen later.

'When you grow up ...' her mother began incredulously in her soft Highland accent. 'But Eleanor you're fourteen, as good as grown up. Nowadays they keep you over-long in school. Oh my, I was working when I was your age. In three year's time you'll be working, too – though God knows how you'll find a job round these parts when the war's over.

'Still, dreams are good,' her mother added. 'You hang on to your dreams, lass. It's dreams that keeps folks like us going – dreams and prayers.'

To Eleanor it seemed as if they were trying to drag the

163

blackout curtains over her brilliant future. 'Not dreams,' she snarled. 'That's how it'll be.'

Eleanor watched her parents surreptitiously. It was contrary to her nature to be deceitful, yet she had a secret and that was her skating. Of course, they knew that she worked at the skating rink four nights a week, but they did not know she also skated. Free tuition was one of the perks. That was her dream – her way out of the poverty-stricken life she led – her skating. And that was why she worked all hours and finished her homework by candlelight at midnight when Dad was sleeping.

Soon she was racing down the steep track to work. Her bicycle was like a mysterious part of her own body; an extension of her personality, the best part of her. On it she could reach incredible speeds, bolting down the hill like the wind, up and down on the saddle over the rough track, winding, curving, and never for a moment losing that queer watchfulness, which was always a part of Eleanor whatever she was doing – a part which hung back and kept watch over the rest of her.

Then, at the next bend, she saw a deer, a great red antlered beast grazing quietly beside the track. It took fright and bounded down the hillside, with Eleanor racing alongside. Away they went, the two of them, with the wind rushing against their faces – all-conscious of the magnificent thrust of speed. Eleanor was rattled and jolted, her bones jerked almost out of their sockets, her hands were numb as they gripped the handlebars. But away they went, wild and free.

The great red deer turned, almost as if in mid-air and bounded up and away into the heather and bracken, and disappeared into the trees, while Megan went on down and down towards the village. But it seemed to her as if her soul went with the great antlered beast and only her body crept through the mean streets of Invergordon.

Oh, but she would be a deer … she would … she would … if only she could.

There was a long silence which jolted Eleanor back to the present. She felt confused and tearful, but she did not know why. How much had she told him, how much had been in her mind?

'Funny how you remember things,' she said weakly. 'I used to be so ambitious, but even in my most extravagant dreams, I never imagined I'd get this rich.'

She looked round cautiously and saw that Dr Gundelfinger was sitting with his elbows on the refrigerator, his head resting in his hands. 'I've got everything I ever wanted.'

'Everything?'

'Yes, everything I could possibly want,' she said emphatically.

'Yet there does seem to be something lacking. Wouldn't you say so?'

'No I wouldn't.' She was rubbing her hands nervously, pulling her fingers and making them snap.

'Would you mind not doing that? It makes my flesh crawl and if there's nothing wrong, then there's no need for it.'

'Well, there's a bit of tension with the business. Nothing I won't solve.'

'I'm sure of that,' he said.

'I do have a wee problem with my daughter,' she admitted. She noticed she was speaking with a pronounced Scottish accent and she concentrated on losing it now. 'She ... that is Jacqui ... left home. We had a bust up because I didn't want her to ski; I mean downhill racing, but she went ahead anyway.'

'Do you think your relationship is irreconcilable?'

'No, but I've not decided whether or not to give in.'

'Daughters have a habit of taking after their parents,' he said. 'What was her father like?'

'She doesn't have a father.' Even to herself her voice sounded flat and suspect.

'A virgin birth! That's just swell. You're my first!'

'You're a snide bastard,' she said, sitting up abruptly and glaring at him over her shoulder.

'And you, Miss Douglas, are a woman with a heap of problems. No home — just a big, expensive house — no friends, no family, an estranged daughter, and a heap of money, but no one to share it with. Once you used to share tatties and you got one hell of a lot of joy out of that. Now you get very little joy out of anything.'

165

She jerked her head around, feeling astonished that anyone would dare to speak to her like that. 'Do you always insult your patients?' she asked icily.

'It's odd that you should think that,' Gundelfinger said, 'but never mind. I think that somewhere, between the innocent young girl with the big dreams and the tycoon with the famous house and yacht, something went wrong. I think you picked up a massive trauma, something you're hiding from yourself, some emotion you can't face.

'You'll have to face it, Eleanor and it won't be pleasant. The alternative is nervous problems. It's up to you. If you want to see me again, please telephone and make an appointment. By the way, I don't charge for lunch dates.'

Eleanor staggered towards the door feeling weepy, stunned and altogether thrown off balance.

She pressed the ground floor button and emerged at the back of the shopping centre in the exclusive arcade. She could have been any smart woman in search of a Dior dress or a Cartier necklace, if you discounted her dazed expression and shaking hands.

CHAPTER 22

It was bright and sunny in Kensington Gardens. Nikki, clad in a pale blue track suit and matching shoes, her hair firmly braided around her head, Russian-style, was jogging over the grass. She looked angry. Volts of impatience and frustration were surging out of her. It was spring and she was missing it all. She ought to be in the countryside, she ought to be looking at rolling plains of spring flowers, with glorious space everywhere you looked. It was space that Nikki missed, more than any other thing. Even the clouds hung low over this claustrophobic island, so that there was hardly room to breathe. Horrible ... truly horrible.

Today Nikki was being herself, without her snazzy costumes, her new fashionable dresses and lacy blouses, and consequently without that aura of sophistication. She looked so young, but so determined. Hers was a face to register simple emotions: love, anger, grief, with childlike intensity, but you could sense her strength as her sinewy legs pounded the earth. She was obstinate, you could see that in the way she ran; never faltering, keeping the same rhythm over hills and flat ground. Sometimes she was more breathless than at other times, but that was all. This morning she was angry because she was so lonely. She had avenged herself on the English by outpacing her bodyguard some way back. Hopefully he would get into trouble.

After the early morning drizzle, the leaves and blades of grass, and the spring flowers were sparkling in the May sunshine. It was very pretty in an English way, if you liked English prettiness, that was. Nikki did not, but she was grateful for the park, all the same. It gave her a chance to escape from the rows of grey houses and dreary streets, all so ugly and disappointingly uniform.

Absurd to see the flowers stuck in straight rows like soldiers

167

standing to attention. The prim flowerbeds offended Nikki's passion for nature. She had never been able to relate to people, and in all her young life, her pent-up passion had been lavished on flowers and trees and the countryside. In Russia now, there would be miles of primroses, scattered in profusion over fields and banks and under trees – everywhere you looked, she remembered. If she could see them – just for a moment. Oh how she longed for Russia again.

She was an exile, she thought melodramatically. Torn up by the roots, but unwilling to be transplanted into English soil. She did not know why this was. God knows, she was not homesick, she hated the Russian establishment. No, it was simply a yearning for the Russian countryside, and space, but only because it was spring.

Nikki brought herself to an abrupt stop. Madness to think this way. She looked over her shoulder cautiously. Her guard was far behind, but she could hear his voice calling faint and far away, and then a dog barked. In the oak tree overhead a blackbird was singing, and beyond the peaceful country sounds was the persistent hum of the city's traffic.

There was no escaping this city – she was trapped in a world of sponsors and agents. She had been sold piecemeal to so many of them it was hard to understand it all.

Nikki shuddered slightly and buried her face in her hands. She thought about Megan, who had made her re-enact the Richmond show four times last week for prospective sponsors. Megan was constantly nagging her to try harder, train longer, wash her hair more often, be polite and sweet when scruffy children nagged for her autograph smile at the press. It was too much; most times she longed to be downright mean.

She stood moodily kicking at a turf of grass, thinking about Megan and sponsors. Of course, Megan had been right – she loved her red sports car and her cottage and her new clothes and consequently she was as trapped here as she had ever been. The good life – it was here, waiting for her. Her skating would bring her everything, but she had to conform. Wasn't that what Megan had been telling her for weeks? But it was so humiliating to have to pander to decadent, imperialist money-makers; a slave to the system.

'Oh, oh, oh,' she wailed. Suddenly her eyes were pricking and there was a suffocating lump in her throat. Wiping her eyes

168

with the back of her hand she glared round, hoping no one had noticed her outburst, but someone had. A man stepped from behind a tree, holding a camera which was pointed her way. The flash dazzled her several times.

'Bastard!' she screamed. 'You were hiding – spying on me – following me – how dare you! Oh I hate you – hate you all!' Her good intentions forgotten, she turned back and swung a vicious punch at the camera. She gasped at the pain in her knuckles and this made her even angrier. Then she lunged forward and hit him across the nose with the side of her clenched fist.

The man was amazed at the fury in her eyes and her ugly expression. 'Hey, hey there,' he said, fending her off. 'Is it that bad?' And then: 'Where's your guard?'

Nikki realised belatedly that the man was speaking Russian.

'Who are you?' she began, nervously, backing away.

'No, wait,' he called.

Nikki turned and fled into the trees.

'I'm not Russian,' the man called in English. 'Trust me.'

Nikki fled faster as she heard his footsteps gaining on her.

'I'm Michel Juric ... from Yugoslavia,' he panted. 'Megan knows me ... you've met me twice ... at the press conference ... surely you remember ... and later, at Megan's office ... come back, Nikki ... I'm writing an article about you ... oh! shit!'

Nikki was losing him now. When she looked round she saw him bent double, holding his side and looking exhausted. He could not be a Russian agent, he'd be fitter, she thought, smiling to herself. Juric! Surely she knew that name? She had heard Megan mention him to Maureen.

Laughing over her shoulder as she went, Nikki did not see the branch lying across the path. She fell heavily, grazing her knee and let out a stream of abuse in Russian.

Michel caught up with her and pulled her to her feet. He took out a handkerchief and tied it round her knee.

'Be careful, or you'll spoil your pretty legs,' he said, humouring her.

'They're not my legs,' she retorted furiously. 'They belong to Arla Hosiery. Megan sold them.' She stamped her foot and Michel was reminded of *Alice in Wonderland*. I guess she is, too, he thought smiling to himself. 'And my clothes belong to Vanguard,' she rushed on hysterically, 'and my skating belongs to Megan, and my teeth belong to Blanchette toothpaste, and my hair to Alpine shampoo. My God, there's nothing of me left. I wish I were dead,' she cried out with Russian melodrama. 'Do you believe me? If I were dead they would leave me in peace.'

'Come,' Michel said, linking his arm with hers. 'I have to warn you about something very important. Only yesterday I discovered that Megan had sold your hair to a wig maker, your heart to medical research and your black soul to Reborn Christians. It's to be exhibited as a warning to others. And ...'

'Don't tease. Don't play with me. And never speak to me in Russian again. I must forget that language.' She suddenly burst out laughing. 'Oh, I like you,' she said, wiping her tears on her sleeve.

Looking up she examined him dispassionately. He was a very sexy man, she decided. Quite tall, with black hair, a squarish face, hooded eyes that were so dark as to be almost black and flashing white teeth when he smiled. A handsome gypsy, she decided. Instinctively she trusted him, and she hugged him tightly against her.

'Things not working out quite as you expected, Nikki?' he asked sympathetically. He smiled gently.

'You look as if you understand. I think you really do,' she said hopefully. 'It's so ... different,' she burst out. 'Not terrible, just different and the difference hurts. I don't know how to say. My English ...'

'You don't have to say anything,' Michel said gently. 'I understand. It was difficult for me, too.'

'It was? And now you are happy here?'

'Yes,' he said after a long pause. 'Not here, but in France.'

'I have my own car, my own cottage, beautiful clothes – all the things I was promised ...' She broke off, frowning.

'Who promised you these things, Nikki?' Michel asked casually.

For a moment Nikki looked startled. She looked away evasively, but then her eyes glowed with amusement. She laughed her thrilling, low-pitched laugh. 'You are always a reporter first – and a friend second, *da*? I,' she said, touching her chest, 'I promised myself all these things.'

Watching her, Michel felt strangely drawn to her. She was glamorous, sexy, but only a kid, he decided, but a fascinating, talented, beautiful kid.

The guard arrived and Michel waved cheerily. 'Have to get into training, won't you?' he called out.

The two walked arm-in-arm while the guard hung back. Worry and guilt showed on his perspiring face.

'So what can I do to help you?' Michel said when she had told him exhaustively of all her complaints.

'Just be my friend.' Her green eyes were sparkling now and she looked happy and confident.

'I'm flattered to be the friend of the beautiful, famous Nikki Petrovna.'

'Now you're teasing again,' she said, but he could see that this was what she wanted to hear.

She turned away. 'I must go,' she said. 'I will be late for coaching and Megan will be oh so very angry with me. I will see you again?' she asked pleadingly.

'Of course,' he said.

'And you will not publish those terrible pictures of me?'

'Not if you don't want me to.'

'I trust you,' she said, with childlike simplicity. Then she kissed him slowly on his mouth and rushed off with a wave.

'And I really mean that,' Michel whispered at her retreating back. He stood staring after her feeling profoundly disturbed.

CHAPTER 23

It was bitterly cold weather for May. The cobblestones were wet and slippery and the north wind gusted under her umbrella, throwing her off balance and making it difficult to make headway in the dark. Megan did not know which house was Ian's, but looking around at the luxuriously-converted, fashionable mews cottages, she was amazed that he could afford to live in this street. She had parked her car at the end of the cul-de-sac, in order to find the right number, but as she searched her spirits sank and it no longer seemed such a bright idea to drop in unannounced.

She had not come empty handed. Good news had been waiting on her desk when she returned to the office earlier that evening. It was a letter from the film company, stating that they were ready to go ahead with the script Ian had written around Nikki's defection. It was strange that this whole matter should be resolved so quickly, the script must have been pretty terrific, she thought. It had been accepted within a fortnight of posting and she had hardly finished witnessing the ninety-page contract Nikki had to sign when they were ready to start production. Megan had experienced the frustrations of dealing with the film world on many occasions and she knew that it was never this simple. Well, she thought, just one of the many glimpses Ian had shown her of the smooth road paved with friends in high places. Nevertheless, it was pretty thrilling for the three of them and she knew Ian would be pleased.

She flashed her torch again and read number thirty-six; she must be near at last. She should have driven up, but the road was so narrow there was scarcely room between the parked Jaguars. She was beginning to feel faint-hearted. What if he had lied and was married after all? That might explain a great deal. Better to find out now, Megan Carroll, she told herself sternly. So why shouldn't she arrive unexpectedly? Ian dropped in on her almost nightly. At the same time, she knew that under Ian's charming exterior lurked an over-secretive male whose home was his burrow, which she was intent on invading.

Now she was getting cold feet in more ways than one, and when at last she found number forty-one and saw the lights shining inside, she shuddered involuntarily.

She rang the bell and endured Ian's astonishment and half-hearted welcome as she stepped inside and took off her raincoat.

'Surprise, surprise,' she said. 'I managed to get back early and I popped round to give you the good news.' So far so good! She handed him the letter.

'Nice place you have,' she said insincerely taking in the room in a quick glance. In fact, it was very austere: brown wall-to-wall carpeting, black leather furniture, a solid wooden desk. There was no clutter or untidiness. Where were the books, pictures, ashtrays, bric-a-brac? There was nothing at all here. A word processor and a computer took up most of the desk and an efficient filing cabinet stood next to it. Megan tried not to show her disappointment.

Ian took her wet coat and hung it on a stand. 'Well, come in,' he said. 'Drink?'

'When you've read the letter,' Megan replied smiling sweetly. 'Can I help myself? What would you like?'

'The usual.' He waved his hand towards the liquor cabinet which contained the more obvious requirements. It looked as if he bought his glasses in a supermarket. Nothing personal here, either.

Megan poured two drinks and handed one to Ian.

He folded the letter, replaced it in the envelope and handed it to her. 'Well done,' he said.

Watching him, Megan felt slightly ridiculous. Ian always seemed to be one step ahead of her. He knew why she was there and he disapproved. She could read the signs in his mocking eyes, his raised eyebrows, his lips curling into a smile that was almost a sneer. She could almost see his aggression rising – like hackles on a dog's back. She had challenged him, gatecrashed his home, and now she could take the consequences.

So be it, she thought, smiling coolly. There was a limit to the time they could spin out a platonic relationship. She said: 'Oh no, not me – all the credit goes to you. Let's drink to Nikki's film.'

'Have you eaten?' he asked.

'No.' There was that damned sarcastic smile again. He was trying to hide his annoyance. What the hell was the matter with him? Other men had to be fought off.

'I'll take you out.'

'Oh I couldn't ... Ian really, the thought of battling with that rain again ... What's in the fridge?' she said making a sudden, clumsy movement towards the kitchen. 'I'll make some sandwiches, – shall I?' she added, faltering for a moment.

'If you like.'

'Aren't you going to show me round?'

'Help yourself.'

The cottage was carpeted throughout in the same dreary dark brown carpeting, the furniture was uniformly light oak. It was modern, functional furniture and the furnishings appeared to have been put together hastily by an interior decorator who specialised in offices. Even in the bedroom there were no pictures on the walls, no books lying around, no untidiness, but a Paisley silk dressing gown was hung on the back of the bathroom door and minimal toiletry requirements were placed on the bathroom shelf. On the double bed was a large plaid rug, it was sort of rusty looking with faded green and blue. That was the only item in the house which looked personal and slightly out of place.

'It's all so impersonal,' she complained. 'What a strange man you are. You're real, aren't you?' She punched him on the arm playfully, to show that she was half-teasing. 'Or are you the clone of the real Ian who's lurking somewhere else in time and space? Do you live here?' she asked as she returned to the lounge. 'I mean do you really *live* here, or do you just exist?'

'Mainly I work,' he said stiffly,

'And that rug on your bed?'

'It's the Mackintosh hunting tartan. Not a popular tartan, but I like it.'

'You have your own tartan?'

'Not mine – the clan's.'

Now I know the meaning of the world 'clannish', she decided, watching Ian's lips fold into a tight line. She noticed that there were no discarded papers on the floor, even his bin was empty. Then she saw the shredder. That figures, she said to herself. 'Don't you ever buy a book?' she asked. 'Don't you

174

have any snaps of yourself at school? There's just nothing here of you.'

'Ah,' he said. 'I take most things home.'

'Home?' she echoed stupidly.

'I have a wee croft – in the Highlands.'

'Funny, I can't imagine you shipping everything back to your parents.'

'My father's dead. My mother lives in France.'

'France?'

'Dammit Megan, stop echoing everything I say. There's nothing extraordinary about living in France, particularly if you're French. Mother's French – or she was French. Technically she's British, but she hates Scotland.'

'So you look after her cottage in the Highlands?'

'Actually, it's mine. Most of my things are there. Now how about supper? Let's see what we can find.' He turned away, but too late to hide his expression and his eyes which were glacial with fury.

'So did you have a good day today – what, for instance, were you writing today?' she persisted. 'I mean, just where are all those pages of deathly prose?' She knew she was overstepping his sensitive limits of endurance, but she was too disappointed to care. She had the oddest sensation that she had fallen in love with a carbon copy and that the original was somewhere else. She wanted to tell him that, but was afraid of hurting his feelings. 'My, this is pretty efficient,' she said as she walked into the kitchen. 'I thought I had the ultimate in gadgets.'

'I took the place over like this,' Ian explained grudgingly. 'I don't know what half the things are. The good news is ?' he went on, rummaging in the refrigerator, 'I've some venison left over – and home-made pork pie and bread and butter pudding. Ah! I'd been wondering how to get rid of that. Can't stand the stuff myself.'

'Why d'you make it then?'

'Oh I can't cook much – trout, venison, game, that's about it.' He laughed briefly. 'Someone made this for me.'

'A friend?'

He turned slowly and glared at her. 'Would you like to help carry something?'

The venison was superb and so was the red wine. Even the bread and butter pudding was wholesome and Megan began to

175

feel warmer and a little more cheerful as they ate supper and Ian entertained her with naval stories from his past.

'The meat's gorgeous,' she said. 'Did you cook the venison?'

'No. I shot it.'

'Oh.' For some reason she felt sad about that.

'Do you hunt?'

'What is this? Twenty questions?'

'Tell me, why do you hate questions so much?'

'Because they're unnecessary. I'm me. You're you. We're here together and we enjoy each other's company – well, most of the time. That's enough, isn't it?'

Foiled again. Return to start and throw a double to move, she thought dismally. No it's not enough Ian, she wanted to say. You know that I care for you and I think you care about me and I want to know more about you. I want to be close to you, I don't know why this is so necessary for me, but it is.

Dinner was over, but Megan had never felt less satisfied, she took another chocolate and another spoonful of bread and butter pudding, another coffee, another chocolate. She took a deep breath and gazed long and hungrily at Ian who was watching her with a mixture of cool appraisal and mocking amusement. It was not food she craved, but Ian. More and more of him. He had no right to be so destructively handsome. The candlelight was shining on his hair, reflecting purple glints in the dark brown. His rolled-up sleeve showed the strength of his tanned arm with strong black hairs curling over the skin. His neck was sinewy and strong and invitingly touchable, his shirt hung half open. He was flaunting the goods and playing hard to get. Right now she'd like him on a plate, here and now, served up ready for eating.

Megan allowed her sense of humour to bubble up through her frustrations and she laughed.

He smiled back. 'Can I share the joke?'

'I was thinking you'd look good trussed on a plate garnished with a sprig of mint behind your ear,' she said aggressively, wondering why he had not made the first move. He'd had plenty of opportunities since they met a hundred years ago in Sarajevo.

What was she saying? She sounded like a female predator,

176

but now was not the time for weighing each innuedo, she was
obsessed with the nearness of him; the smell of his hair; his
after-shave and the faintest musky tang which was Ian's own
smell and which could send her brains zooming to her navel
whenever she was near enough to touch him. She could not
stop herself, she moved forward, an impulsive, clumsy gesture,
intending to run her finger over the back of his wrist, that
strong and infinitely beautiful wrist, but instead she sent his
glass flying across the table. The deep red stain could have been
her own blood.

'Oh,' she said. 'Oh, Ian, I'll buy ...' This was no time for
talking. As Ian rose, looking murderous, she flung her arms
around him, pushing him back onto the chair. 'Oh Ian, kiss
me,' she moaned.

She tilted her head, trembling with anticipation, her eyes
tightly shut, her mouth soft and yearning.

There was no kiss. Tentatively Megan opened her eyes. Ian's
buttoned-up expression was firmly in place. His eyes had a
strange expression, what was it? Regret?

He glanced at his watch, but Megan grasped his head in both
hands and kissed him on the mouth gently. She opened her eyes
and studied the expression again. Surely there was more lust
this time? Tightening her grip, she kissed him again, moving
her tongue over his lips and thrusting into his mouth. Then she
pressed her body tightly against him, feeling the luxury of his
hard back, strong as iron, and his shoulders which felt like a
rock, and the strength of his neck. Slowly she moved her fingers
up into his hair, and all the time she was insidiously moving her
body, closer, moulding herself around the concaves and the
convexes. We fit perfectly, she thought rapturously.

She unbuttoned her blouse, feeling herself flushing furiously,
but knowing that this was no time to be chicken-hearted. She
felt glad of the expensive, dark blue French underwear she had
bought especially for this occasion. She took his hand and
pressed it over her breast, felt him tense and suddenly his arms
were pressing her tightly against him. 'Is there any reason why
we shouldn't go to bed?' she asked decisively.

'Megan, when I feel like a romantic evening, you'll know. I
promise you.' He stood up, lifting her with him and dropped
her none too gently onto an armchair.

Megan flushed deep red. She was horrified to see how

detached he looked. She buried her face in her hands, but when she looked up she saw that he was laughing at her. Laughing! Oh God! The evening had turned into a nightmare.

'How is it possible that I want you so – and you don't want me?' she said, her eyes stinging with tears. 'How could I have been so mistaken? I've never been so humiliated.'

'Humiliated!' he roared.

'Sit up, Megan, and stop making a bigger fool of yourself,' Ian said sternly.

'Get lost, Ian. There's a limit to any girl's patience.' Megan tried to cover her confusion with aggression, but she was feeling mortified. 'You know how I feel about you. I feel ... I feel ...'

'Presumptuous? Bossy? Immodest? Spurned?'

'Now you've had your fun, I'm going home.' She stood up and groped through misty vistas for her handbag and coat.

'Well, I'm delighted to discover that a fair portion of femininity still lurks under that fearful feminist shell. Surely you can see that your reaction to being spurned is hardly up-to-date? I've been spurned hundreds of times. I can't win them all. It doesn't bother me the least bit, but you, who no doubt feel that women have every right to be as aggressive as the male, are reduced to a shuddering jellyfish by your first refusal. Am I your first refusal?'

She looked up feeling appalled that he could laugh in the face of her humiliation.

'You know something?' she said. 'I'm glad to see you can be cruel, because I was thinking you must be some kind of animated robot. No feelings – or emotions. Just a clone, walking around pretending to be Ian. But where's the real Ian? What did you do with him?'

He looked suddenly serious. 'The real Ian is in the Highlands which is the only place he can be happy – and free,' he added as an afterthought. 'And I'm not being cruel, I'm teaching you a valuable lesson. Don't play the game if you don't like the rules. Remember that, Megan. If you have the right to act like a male, then I sure as hell have the right to act like a female. It was all too sudden,' he said in a croaky falsetto.

'Oh Ian,' she said, laughing and crying at the same time. 'You're freaky. I'm going home. I couldn't face you anymore for one night. Or maybe ever.'

'Oh, no,' he said softly. 'I'm going to show you how it's done.'

'Get lost, Ian,' she said, looking round for her coat. 'I'm not in the mood.'

'Well, that's just tough, because your striptease turned me on beyond control.'

'Oh God,' she whispered. She had the feeling she was standing on the edge of a cliff and that she could fall, far out of control – drift and fall.

'I'm leaving,' she said fiercely. 'Don't try to stop me.'

'Why?' Because you're not in the driving seat? Things must go your way, Megan,' he whispered gently, 'or not at all? Is that it?' He leaned forward and smothered her outcry with his mouth while his hands pulled and wrenched at her clothes.

'Give over. You'll tear my dress,' she gasped.

'I'll buy another.'

She was angry and fighting furiously, but Ian was stronger. He held her hands over her head with one hand and pulled her dress with the other. Then she realised she was naked to the waist.

'Oh, oh,' she yelled angrily as she tried to pull up her dress.

Ian stood up, locked the door and put the key in his pocket. 'We have all night,' he said with infuriating good humour. 'Lesson two: don't give up too easily.'

'I'm going home. Don't you understand plain English?'

'I understand you all too well, Megan. But I wonder how well you understand yourself.' He hoisted her over his shoulder and carried her kicking up the stairs to the bedroom, where he dumped her roughly on the bed. 'Did you really envisage a gentle seduction with me playing the part of a coy young virgin and you the seductress? Och, Megan, you're a very confused young woman. No doubt that comes from being the boss eight hours a day.' He closed the door, switched on the bedside light and began to take off his clothes.

Half of Megan wanted to run away, but the other half thought: *I won after all, only he thinks he has.*

Then she saw the scar on his back: a deep ragged gash, and there were many more, she discovered. A small round, shrivelled hole that was probably a bullet wound on his thigh, and several scars on his belly.

'You don't feel safe unless you live in a controlled

179

atmosphere, Megan,' he was saying. 'And guess who has to control it?' His hands were removing her clothes, hard, implacable hands with a will of their own. 'You want a housetrained wimp for a lover, someone you can bully and seduce when you feel like it. The trouble is, you'll feel less and less like it and finally, one day, you'll gobble up the wimp, trussed on a plate with mint behind his ears, and find another victim.'

Now his fingers and his lips were moving slowly over her body, seeking, finding, exploring, approving. She groaned softly. The thrust and pull of his passion was filling her body with sensations she had never before experienced.

He was gentle and strong and he loved her passionately and she said: 'Oh Ian ...' and, 'It's so wonderful ...' and, 'It was never, never like this ...' and, 'Oh God I love you so.'

And he shouted and clung to her and afterwards he pulled her beside him and she lay with her head on his shoulder, one leg tossed over his hips, with his arms wrapped around her.

'I tried so hard not to love you,' Ian told her, wrapping her closer in his arms. 'But it didn't work and now I don't know what I'm going to do with you. Oh Megan,' he whispered. 'I'm not free to love you. If you would only wait for me. Just a year, that's all I'm asking. Is a year so much really?

'No, I can't tell you why,' he said, running one finger over her lips to silence her outburst. 'But you were right. You're a wonderfully sensitive, clever girl, and you were spot on, as always. You've fallen in love with a clone. Wait for me, Megan. Is that too much to ask?'

She opened her eyes, smiling happily. 'As clones go – you're tremendous,' she said.

180

CHAPTER 24

Jacqui paused as she entered the impressive Vanguard foyer and glanced around. Photographs of the company's latest winners, blown up to larger-than-life proportions, hung on all sides of the towering white marble walls. There was a new one, she noticed, Gunter Erath, West Germany's Downhill champion had replaced Conrad. It was an excellent photograph, shot as Gunter took off from a mogul on the Bjelašnica piste. He was crouched forward, and from his stance you could sense his tension and his will to win.

For a second she hung around indecisively. Then she heard the doorman approaching. 'I'm Jacqui Douglas,' she said in answer to his query.

The doorman eyed her dirty jeans, sloppy sweater and tangled hair and decided that she just might be who she said she was; that's how the rich kids ran around in Monaco nowadays. Best not to take a chance, though. He rang through to Ms Douglas's secretary, and shortly afterwards his expression of distaste changed to respect as he ran to call the lift.

As the doors slid open on the top floor Jacqui experienced an unpleasant sinking in her stomach. The all-white decor, the trim clerks in their white tracksuits, the opulence, all conspired to make her feel out of place and downright scruffy.

Why am I here? To plead with Mother? Because I love her in spite of our fight? Because, deep inside I long to be loved by her? Or is because I'm scared of Wolf and his smooth-talking — scared I might just give in one day and exchange my shares for a quick profit and to hell with mother ... and loyalty ... and all that jazz?

There and then Jacqui wanted to turn and run. Her fight with Mother had reached a pinnacle of destructiveness. Mother had shown a formidable single-mindedness which frightened

181

and repelled Jacqui. Not once had Mother weakened or shown any compassion for her daughter's plight.

She's lost, all the same. I will never give up skiing. Never! No matter what she says – or what she threatens. Wolf has shown me how. But is this what I really want?

Jacqui tried to look nonchalant. As she strolled across the thick pile carpet, she was suddenly conscious of her dirty jeans and the way the office girls were eyeing her. She hoped her shoes would not leave dirty smudges.

When she was asked to wait in the reception area she was not surprised. Whatever Mother was doing would take precedence over an unscheduled call from her renegade daughter.

Half an hour passed. Jacqui's nerves were taut and her mouth dry.

Why don't I get the hell out of here and swop my holding for Wolf's?

Once again Jacqui recalled their last conversation which had been uppermost in her mind ever since. She had explained to Wolf that her Vanguard shares were held by an Off-Shore Trust company called Young Endeavour.

'Jacqui, listen to me.' Wolf had been unsmiling, but overtly affectionate. 'You're a very wealthy young woman, but living like a pauper. You personally control twenty million dollars of Vanguard stock which is currently almost twenty-five percent above its true value. It's absurd – stop dithering. I'll arrange everything. We'll do a simple swop between your company and mine, called New Enterprizes, which is the holding company of a brand new oil producing company I've just launched; so instead of owning Vanguard stock, your company will own oil wells. In a year's time – if you still feel the same way about Vanguard – I'll resell your Vanguard shares to you at a far lower price. You'll retain a good profit – perhaps as much as four million dollars. You'll also make a packet on the oil shares because you're coming in on the ground floor of a profitable venture.'

Mother would never know, he had promised and Wolf was even prepared to give a legal guarantee that he would sell Vanguard back to her in twelve months' time.

Why was he doing this for her? That was the question Jacqui had put to Wolf repeatedly and to herself during restless nights that followed.

182

'Because I don't want to see a talented kid squashed flat, before she's even made the grade,' he had replied carelessly. Jacqui knew it was for far stronger reasons. He was in love with her. She sensed that and she was unwilling to take advantage of his love. At the same time she was also filled with doubts about her debt of loyalty to Mother and to Vanguard.

So here she was. Her morbid self-analysis broke off as Mother came rushing into the reception.

'Well, well, well,' she said, feet astride, hands on hips. 'Cut off the purse strings and Jacqui returns to the fold, albeit unwillingly.'

Jacqui stood up, tossed her hair back and pouted. 'Is that the best greeting you can manage?' she said sulkily.

'What should I say? Welcome home stranger! How kind of you to call! Funny, but I can't believe you've come willingly.'

'You could try Happy Birthday,' Jacqui retorted and saw her mother flinch.

'God! How time flies! Is it really?' Her mother glanced guiltily towards the calender to check that it really was April 13. 'So you're nineteen today. That's a great age, Jacqui. Congratulations,' she said flatly. 'Come in my office. We'll have some coffee and later I'll take you to lunch.'

Mother was blustering now, Jacqui noticed. For some strange reason that did not make Jacqui feel any better. If anything, she felt worse.

It was the same ... always the same ... Jacqui thought moodily. The moment they sat in Mother's office the endless telephone calls began and between calls there was scarcely time to say hello.

At last her mother stood up. She raked Jacqui with a searching glance and said: 'Good grief! What do you look like? A tramp. It's time we did a little shopping for you.'

The chauffeur was called and Jacqui was rushed unwillingly to *Cartier's* for a jewelled wrist watch, to *Gian Franco*, and *Valentino's*, two exclusive dress shops Mother patronised, for a dozen fashionable model dresses, and on to *Le Sporting* in *Plas due Casino* where Mother tried unsuccessfully to wrest the old jeans and sweater from Jacqui, in return for several jazzy sweat suits.

It was only when they were seated in the exclusive, *Salganik* restaurant that Jacqui realised Mother was deliberately

183

showing her the rich world she was supposed to be living in. Surely, otherwise they would have lunched in *Le Mistral*, which was Mother's favourite place where she kept a table permanently reserved.

Eventually Jacqui plucked up courage to voice her fears.

'Mother, I came to ask you to give up this ... this war ... Yes, you know it's true – you've declared war on me and my skiing.'

'You're darn right I have.'

Jacqui toyed with her knife and fork unable to eat the *salade nicoise* which Eleaner had insisted on ordering for her. At last she made a decision. 'Mother, I came to tell you that you're losing. Stop now before it's too late,' she said softly.

'Too late?' Eleanor queried. 'You mean too late for you to make the Olympics?'

'Too late for us,' Jacqui retorted. 'I'm not giving up skiing Mother. I'm going to be right up there with the rest of them doing my darndest to win. You can't disinherit me, I've done some checking. The Trust Fund you created is irrevocable. Just empty threats – that's all you've been using.'

'That's all I ever wanted to use,' Eleanor said, looking quite unperturbed. 'The Trust Fund was set up because I wanted it set up like that. How else? Everything you've got, I gave you. Doesn't that mean anything to you?'

'Yes, it does.' she answered miserably.

How can I explain to Mother, of all people, that I'd love her even if she'd never given me a penny? That all I want is her approval and her love. If she loved me, she'd want me to be myself. She loves herself much more and that's why I must become a miniature replica of her. All she gave me, does not give Mother the right to live my life for me. It's my life and I have some basic rights, don't I – for Christ's sake?

'Don't think I'm not grateful,' Jacqui stammered, 'but you know something, I can't allow you to dictate to me how I'll spend my life. And why are you so so scared I'll fail and disgrace Vanguard? Can't you just trust me a little bit? I don't suppose you know I've been using another name to ski under. Well, I intend to carry on skiing. Sorry, Mother,' Jacqui went on, ignoring Eleanor's protestations. 'I think it's best if we split. That is ... for a few years, at least. Maybe forever ... I don't see my future in Vanguard. I don't see myself as a big business tycoon – or anything like that.'

'All this ...' She waved her hand, indicating the restaurant in particular, and Monaco, in general. 'All this is not my world. However, if you could just give me time. Just give me until the Olympics. Right now I can't think further than that.'

'No deal,' Eleanor said quickly. 'Don't be a fool. You're under age and I'll prevent you from Downhill Racing somehow, if I have to apply to the courts. It's dangerous and downright ridiculous for the Vanguard heiress, and I want you in Vanguard, right beside me where you belong. You owe it to me, Jacqui. All my work all these years ... it was for you. Don't you think it's time I had a rest? You've had a good upbringing – in fact, the best. Now earn it, for goodness sake. You can't be a drone all your life.'

'That's hitting below the belt,' Jacqui complained. 'Why do you always bulldoze your opponents flat into the ground? You're about as subtle as a buffalo. Unconditional surrender, no terms, no saving face, just do things your way, or else.'

Was that what happened to Father? Did he, too, run away to Viet Nam because he found you too formidable to live with? Jacqui sighed. However much she longed to know more about her father, she seldom found the right time to ask Mother. If she ever ventured a question, Mother shut up shop and usually remembered some urgent appointment. As far as Mother was concerned, the subject was taboo.

'So,' Eleanor was saying, 'spend the next two years in Vanguard. Then you can leave if you're really so sure it's not for you.'

'But Mother, this life, all these rich people, the power, ... it's not me at all.'

'Jacqui,' Eleanor said firmly. 'That's exactly why I cut your credit facilities. So that you could find out just how the poor live. You seem to be having difficulties continuing with your training. Let's face it, skiing is costly. Perhaps wealth has it's advantages after all. Just don't try to sign up with another company, because there's a few conditions under which you hold that Trust Fund. Go ahead and try. Why don't you?'

Jacqui glanced surreptitiously at her mother and was amazed to see a tear running down her mother's cheek.

'Here!' Eleanor opened her bag and thumped an envelope on the table. 'I didn't forget your birthday, I just forgot the date this morning. Your present is in the garage at home. Here are the keys for it. Although I doubt you remember where home is. If you decide to sell it, don't take less than two hundred thousand francs, or you'll be a bigger fool than I take you for.'

'You're right, it doesn't seem like home,' Jacqui said, standing up coldly. 'I don't understand you, Mother. I never will. You see the world in terms of debits and credits, everything has a value, even your own daughter's affections can be bought – or so you think. All I ever wanted from you was love and moral support,' she found she could hardly speak from the lump in her throat. 'Well, to hell with you and your world.'

Blinded by tears, Jacqui rushed out, leaving the car keys, the dresses and all the paraphernalia Mother had heaped on her. For the first time, now, she was seriously considering selling her shares.

CHAPTER 25

Eleanor lingered over lunch. She was sitting by the window in the *Venezia*, a restaurant she patronised a great deal lately. She told herself that it was convenient, but the truth was it overlooked the harbour, so she could see her yacht, *Sea Shanty*, rocking at its moorings not a hundred metres from her table and if she looked up she could see Vanguard House, framed by the *Corniche*, and she had a delightful sense of well-being and could enjoy her lunch of oysters, *salade nicoise* and Perrier water with orange juice.

It was Friday and her appointment with Dr Gundelfinger was at two, but she was not sure she would go. The unbelievably dreary man kept harping on the past, which could have no possible bearing on her present condition. Eleanor did not believe in anything which she could not touch, calculate or sell. Yet the results of her last meeting with him had been traumatic. She had felt depressed for days afterwards and she did not know why. Absurd to bring up the past – it was over and done with. Besides, she had enough trouble with the present.

She pecked at her salad and thought about Jacqui. Their last fight had been traumatic and for once Eleanor deeply regretted the rift with her daughter. She was keenly aware that Jacqui was all she had in life, and that she was in real danger of losing her daughter. Why was she so good at running a business and so hopeless at managing a relationship, she wondered? If only she had been able to convince Jacqui that her anathema towards Downhill Racing was caused by her fears for her daughter's safety and not anxiety for Vanguard's image. Yet, for some reason, she had not even tried to expiate herself in Jacqui's eyes. *It's my damn pride. I'm too arrogant to excuse myself or try to explain. Besides, how could I explain the terrible trauma of what ski racing means to me.* Jacqui was just

187

as bad – for the first time it occured to Eleanor that she and Jacqui were very much alike.

Should she give in? She would never forgive herself if her daughter were injured. At the same time ... For the first time in her life Eleanor could not make a decision on a matter which must be settled. Megan Carroll had telephoned three times in the past week, until Eleanor had instructed her secretary not to put her calls through. So what should she do? Oh dear, when it came to emotional problems she was quite inept.

With a sudden shaft of pain, she found she was raking her arm with her long red fingernails. Eleanor gazed down in despair and wondered whether or not to see the shrink. Might as well, she thought, frowning at the rash. She ordered coffee and sat sipping it. After a while, she paid her bill and walked the few streets to Gundelfinger's office.

She walked in without knocking and found him gazing out of the window looking moody and sad.

'I'm sorry I'm late,' she said.

'So am I. You pay for the time you waste.'

'I can afford it.'

'Okay, okay, let's get started.' Hc glared at her until she sat on the couch and lay back. 'I want you to tell me about your childhood.'

There was a long silence. Then she said: 'I don't know where to start.'

'Well,' he paused. 'last week you were telling me about the war.'

'It ended,' she said flatly, 'and the sailors went home, the ice rink closed and there was no market for our eggs.' She sighed.

'I remember VJ day quite clearly. It was my birthday you see,' she began hesitatingly. 'I was sixteen. I was given a new pair of school shoes and a Bible of my own. Mum had saved and scrimped to buy a lipstick. I was surprised.' She broke off and for a few minutes was lost in memories.

The gift had been delivered in secret and she had known very well that Dad must not know about it. What strange longings and rebellion had led her mother to scrimp and save for the glossy pink stick? Was it a warning? Or compensation for all that she did not have ... or would not have?

'Go on,' she heard his voice behind her.

'I kept staring at that lipstick and thinking about my mother

188

and the life she led. It was the first time I realised how lonely she was.' She broke off and bit her lip. She had a sudden vivid recall of the faded woman who lived her last fifteen years alone in Invergordon, unwilling to move or to share a life of luxury, accepting only a small pension and a stone cottage by the sea.

'There was a cold, east wind blowing, poppies were blooming and so was the heather and there was a drone of bees and the persistent buzz of bog flies. I climbed to a rocky peak overlooking the town and watched the distant firth packed with ships. All the hooters were blowing. All of a sudden there was silence and the ship's crew right down the firth began a hymn – then the next ship – and so on, so that the song passed right up the firth, from ship to ship, but the sound was intermittent and far away. Church bells were ringing and the sound of a brass band came in snatches.

'I felt so depressed. I remember thinking that all my life, whenever anything terrible happened, there was always a brass band playing: when my father joined up; when he returned with a shattered knee; when my brother's ship left harbour at the Clyde; and then, later, I was nearly deafened by the brass band at the memorial service for the sailors who would never return.

'So I wondered what the brass bands had in store for me this time. I ran home feeling afraid. Mum was cooking kippers on the stove and Dad was reading the newspaper. Watching them I felt my heart lurch and my knees stiffen. What if they died? What if Mum fell ill? I trembled at the prospect. What if we were were all trapped, here in Invergordon with the heather and the bog flies? I felt responsible, particularly that day. I think I saw them as children, both of them. They were so ... so defenceless ... and Dad had his wonky knee.'

She broke off and for a while there was silence.

'So you loved your home and your parents,' Gundelfinger said eventually.

'That's not unusual, is it?' she said, managing a laugh.

'In this room, it's unusual. Tell me then, why did you leave home?'

'It's a long story.'

'That's what I'm here for – listening to long stories. Carry on.'

She turned and glared at him and her face looked tormented.

Then she sank back on to the couch and twisted her hands nervously.

'When I left school,' she went on angrily. 'I got a job coaching beginners at the ice rink, but when the sailors went home, the rink closed down. That was a blow. I'd been pinning my hopes on skating. I was quite good, or so I thought. The only job offered in Invergordon was helping out at the village store for fifteen shillings a week. Hardly what I'd been dreaming about, but I took it anyway.'

'And then?' He waited, but Eleanor sat very still staring at the wall.

'So you left home to seek your fortune? Romantic, isn't it?'

'No,' she said in a tired voice. 'Finally they turned me out.'

'Uh huh,' he grunted.

'I became the local fallen woman.' She laughed. It was a harsh, grating sound devoid of mirth. 'No woman can fall quite so low as a Presbyterian fallen woman,' she said.

Abruptly she reached forward and snatched her bag. 'It's three o'clock.'

'Never mind – we can go on.'

'Maybe you can, but I can't.'

She stood up, her face ravaged with grief. 'I can't talk about it. Not yet. Maybe never.' She walked out, slamming the door hard behind her.

Dr Gundelfinger opened the door to his waiting room and said hello to Eleanor. It was a week since Eleanor's last visit and once again she was late. Gundelfinger knew the trauma behind her tardiness, but that did not lessen the irritation. He noticed that she looked as if she did not sleep at night, but she had obviously taken a great deal of trouble with her appearance. 'Come in,' he said.

He could not help admiring the way she swept in. She was the type of woman who would stand out in a crowd as someone rich and elegant, Gundelfinger decided, no matter what she was wearing. Yet there was a certain pathos about her – a sadness. He knew that he was going to discover the reasons for it one of these days and then he would sleep as badly as she. In all the years he had been practicing, he had never managed to acquire absolute detachment, which was his only self-defence. He said:

'I'd like you to carry on where you left off last time, Eleanor.'

'Where was that?' she asked coldly.

'You were getting to the part where you became the local fallen woman, or so you said. I believe you used that expression; to tell the truth I've only read it in Victorian literature ...'

Eleanor laughed without bitterness. 'You're jumping the gun,' she said. 'Besides, you're far too young to understand.'

'If you say so,' he said mildly.

'But if you had lived with Dad and his terrible faith ...' she broke off and fumbled in her bag. Gundelfinger put the ashtray on the table beside her. He was allergic to cigarette smoke, but some of his patients needed the comfort.

'In those days it wasn't the poverty that irked me, as much as the code Dad imposed,' Eleanor was saying. 'If I hurt myself it was wrong to cry, ill-bred to lose my temper, pain had to be endured stoically, pride was vain. The Bible was the only book in the house and I was brought up listening to Dad's readings.'

She glanced over her shoulder and smiled at him. 'Do you want to hear all this?'

'I do,' he said, smiling back through the smoke.

'You see, Dad was a lay preacher and he used to leave early on Sundays and hobble over the moor on his bad leg. Before the war he used to win prizes for tossing the caber at the Highland Games, afterwards he deserved a medal each morning, just for walking ...' She settled herself more comfortably, leaned back and closed her eyes. 'Dad's leg became more bandy, buckling out sideways, his face all twisted-up with the pain of it, but he never complained. Watching him I used to get a lump in my throat so big I could hardly swallow. But he didn't feel sorry for himself. The concept of desiring anything was quite foreign to Dad.

'I could never understand him. For me, God was all around – in the sheep and the deer and the trees and specially in the beauty. But I had this conflict – my own pagan God and my Christian God. So half of me was filled with joy and the other half felt guilty because I was so happy. And uneasy. Yes, half of me was afraid that my happiness would anger God.'

She sighed and pushed her fingers through her hair. 'Of course that was long ago.'

She moved restlessly and clutched her hands together. 'I used

191

to cycle five miles down to the village to work and every morning was ... well ... just great! How else can I describe it? I wish I could paint you a picture: the deer moving like wraiths into the mist, the mist itself hiding away in hollows as the sun rose, sparkling prisms of sunlight on dew, the crisp crunch of hoar frost under my boots ... and I used to know that my God loved beauty, because the world was so beautiful, and I used to wonder why it was good to feel guilty and wrong to feel joy ...'

'Then one morning ... one particular morning ... well ... it was misty – so misty that it seemed I was quite alone, safely hidden from Dad's peeping-Tom deity who would strike me down if I were happy. So I hopped and danced and sang loud and clear. *Ye banks and braes of bonnie Doon.*

She began to sing softly and Gundelfinger was taken with the clarity of her voice, a pure fresh girl's voice and quite lovely.

'So I finished the song, holding the last note for a long time and it sounded quite grand to me because of the echoes from the mountain. But again I felt guilty because I was being vain – the unforgivable sin.

'Suddenly clapping came from the bowels of the earth, right at my feet. I screeched, and staggered back. "Who's there?" I cried, but hardly more than a croak came out of my throat. You see, I was so sure it was the Devil coming up to claim me for my terrible ambitions and my vanity.

'There was a chorus of boyish giggles, coming from a ditch at the side of the road, hidden behind tall grass and bracken. A face appeared. "Oh mercy me," I cried But I could see it was not a face to be frightened of – it was a face for laughing and such deep blue eyes with crows' feet at the corners, even though he was so young. His hair was light brown and cut in a shapeless crew cut, he had rosy cheeks, white teeth, but he was so thin the poor lad, my heart went out to him. When he climbed out of the ditch I saw how tall he was and that his German army coat was threadbare and far too small for him.

'I felt scared at first. All that propaganda in the war had made the Germans seem like monsters, but he looked shy and very civilised and after all, the war was over, so I plucked up courage and walked to the edge of the road. Peering in I saw another two boys looking up at me. They looked younger and smaller and they were shivering in spite of their big coats. I asked them what they were doing there.

' "German prisoners, Ma'am." The blue-eyed soldier touched an imaginary cap. "We have been told to dig a ditch along this road." He laughed and pointed upwards. "All the way up the mountain." Then he shrugged. "We'll be here for some time, I think. Ja?"

'So this was the Hitler Youth, I'd heard about; boys taken from school in the last days of the war and pressed into the army to defend Germany. "You will indeed," I said, trying to sound severe. "Since you Germans knocked half of Britain down, it's only fair you should build it up again. Well, good morning. You'll have plenty of time to reflect on the sins of war as you make your way up the mountain."

' "Yes, ma'am," the prisoner said. He stared at me long and seriously and then he smiled. The smile started in his eyes and spread over his cheeks to his mouth – a lovely smile which sent a shiver of feeling through my stomach. I don't know what that was, but it was a very personal smile which seemed to make too many unwarranted assumptions.

'So I walked on, but after a while I felt bad about the way I had spoken. So I turned back.

' "You look hungry."

' "Yes ma'am,"

' "And those poor wee boys," I said, peering past him into the gloomy ditch. "They're little more than children. Twelve are they?"

' "Fourteen ma'am."

' "And were they in the army, too?"

' "Yes, ma'am."

' "Och, the poor wee lads," I said. "Well, I'll be away off to work."

'Three pairs of eyes started up defiantly, the friendship gone. It's my pity I thought at the time. They can't stand pity. I could understand that.

'When I walked home that night, I shone my torch into the empty ditch. "What a job!" I muttered. The ground was frozen rock hard. For some reason I lingered there, although I did not know why.

'It was good to get home. The kitchen was steamy and filled with the aroma of boiling mutton stew. I kicked off my wellies and warmed my feet in front of the stove. Then Mum fished around with the ladle for a meaty bone and some carrots and dumplings. I balanced the plate on my knees and sat as close as I could to the stove and thought about the prisoner with the lovely smile and wondered how he was coping with sub-zero temperatures and no wood stove and no mutton stew.

'I rolled up a dumpling in my handkerchief and stuffed it in my pocket. Then I said: 'It's terrible to be hungry when it's cold.'

' "We haven't done too badly," Mum said. "It's the people in the towns I'm feeling sorry for. Well, I suppose rationing will be over one of these days."

'Dad spoke up from the table: "Did you remember to say grace, lass?"

'I bent my head and mumbled the ritual before the next mouthful. Then he said: "It'll be years before rationing's over. You mark my words."

' "Know what I saw today?" I persisted. "German prisoners-of-war. But really only children," I was lying a bit because I knew that one was just about my age. "They're digging a ditch all the way up here for services. Of course it will take a good while. They look frozen and so skinny. I thought perhaps we could spare them a wee bit of bread and dripping. I could drop if off mornings, like."

' "We canna be wasting good rations on them that forced the troubles on us in the first place," Mum said quietly, but not quietly enough, for Dad heard.

' "Och woman, have you no charity in you. We can spare a bite of bread or maybe an egg from time to time. We're not asking you to feed the men entirely, just a little extra now and then."

' "So it was arranged, as I had expected, and every morning I gave them a packet of sandwiches and occasionally a wee bit extra. Our brief conversations, were the highlight of my day. I discovered he was six months younger than I, and that he came from Austria, and he had been recruited into an Alpine regiment just before the end of the war. His family spoke English well because in peacetime they kept an inn which relied upon the tourist trade, so they made sure their son studied English at school.

'Every morning I heard the thud-thud of pick-axes on frozen ground from far off. When I approached the prisoners were always higher up the hill and I would see their steaming breath rising from the ditch. They were becoming thinner daily, in spite of the sandwiches, but never once did I let my pity show.

'One day he took hold of my hand, pulled me to one side and asked me to meet him after dark. He could get out of the camp, he said. Oh his voice, soft, soft yet strangely compelling; a dangerous voice. It would haunt my dreams, I knew.

'I answered sharply. "That would be like starting a fire in the bracken in August. Only a fool would do that. It can run away with you, you see and in no time – no time at all. And here's you an enemy prisoner and I ... well, why should I explain. You can see it yourself, as plain as the nose in front of your face. I know you can."

He smiled painfully. "Right now I would long for a fire," he said in his beastly, beautiful voice.

'I felt I hated him as I raced down the hillside ...'

'I'm afraid it's time to stop.' Gundelfinger had often wondered about the wisdom of his forty-five minute appointments. Eleanor had been talking non-stop for an hour and he could hear his patient pacing the carpet in the adjoining room. It was a pity to interrupt her.

She was staring at him hostilely. 'Good God, what time is it?' She glanced at her watch, 'I feel as if I've been here forever.'

'We'll carry on next time. Perhaps you could come earlier,' he suggested, glancing at his diary.

'Friday will do,'' she said flatly. 'Let's not go overboard.' Gundelfinger looked up sharply. Her voice had been pitched too high and now he noticed the tears glistening on her cheeks.

'I don't know why I waste time here,' she said bitterly. 'I have really pressing problems to solve. Take my daughter, for instance. I've tried so hard to impress upon Jacqui the importance of wealth. I've spent this week showing her the best in Monaco – well, reminding her would be a better word – after all, she was brought up here. She has no idea of the value of all that she's going to be handed on a plate. All the years of back-breaking toil ...' She broke off. *Not just work, but luck, too. Being in the right place at the right time. It could never happen again now. Never ever. Those days were past.*

'She wants to ski. I want her in the business.'

Gundelfinger looked up from his diary. A silky smile on his face. It was a look she had learned to distrust.

'Two headstrong woman and you both want your own way.

I'm sure you'll win, Eleanor – all the muscle is on your side, but what will it do to Jacqui – losing? Is she the type who can survive losing? I rather gathered she took after you. Perhaps I'm wrong.'

Eleanor's eyes opened wide and her cheeks paled. Then she pulled herself together with a grimace of anger.

'Is all this ... this talk ... is it going to help me?' she asked.

'The benefits of psycho-analysis are always long-term, but yes, it will help you find the root of your nervous condition. Trust me, Eleanor.'

'I have so many problems ...' she began. She gazed at her arms in despair. 'I've only shown you my arms, but of course it's ... it's everywhere.'

'It's possible that your present problems could exaggerate your condition,' he began cautiously, 'but all trauma is rooted in the past. Something you've blocked out of your mind perhaps, we'll see. It's possible that you are deliberately punishing yourself.'

Eleanor stared at him long and hard. Then she laughed briefly. 'I knew I should never have come here,' she said hatefully. 'Now I've heard everything.'

She left without saying goodbye.

196

CHAPTER 26

When at last Eleanor Douglas telephoned, Megan was discussing next year's sponsorship programme with one of her promising tennis stars. Megan apologised and rushed outside to take the call in private.

'Hello, Megan. I decided to call you personally, rather than let these proposals go through the normal channels.' Eleanor's voice sounded apologetic under her bombastic American Scottish accent.

Megan groaned inwardly. Come on, come on, she was pleading silently. Don't do this to me Eleanor. Yes or no.

'I've decided to sponsor both of your clients, so from now on we can work through Nigel ...'

Megan felt a surge of elation; her skin was tingling, her hands damp, she felt a strange desire to shout aloud. Instead she took a long deep breath.

'Remember what we agreed,' Eleanor was saying. 'If I accept your terms for Miss Petrovna, which I do – with two minor changes; you'll accept mine for Jacqui. I expect you're wondering why I've given in. Well, I'll be frank with you; I have no choice, unless I want to lose my daughter. I'm sending her contract over by special courier. You'll have no difficulty if you play it right. Try to persuade Jacqui to accept my terms, before you tell her it's Vanguard. That way you might be able to swing it.' There was a touch of wistfulness in her voice now. 'You'll need all your selling ability, Megan. So don't forget – the two contracts are tied in with each other. It's like that song: *you can't have one without the other*. That's my decision, so please abide by it.'

Megan was still remembering Eleanor's sad voice as she flew to Scotland two days later. Eleanor had sounded unsure of herself, desperately wanting Jacqui to sign the contract, but doubting that she would, understandably so, since it was so blatantly manipulative. Why did Eleanor always use the big stick to force through her wishes? Megan wondered. And was that why her daughter rebelled against all types of authority?

There was no point in worrying about these two hard-headed women, Megan reminded herself, she had a business to salvage. Somehow she had to persuade Jacqui to sign.

Jacqui was training at Aviemore. From Inverness airport, Megan continued her journey in a hired car. After four days of heavy snowfall, the road was slippery and dangerous. Megan had no eyes for the sylvan beauty of the snowy highlands, or the distant mountains rising like phantoms against the leaden sky. She was planning her selling strategy.

Eleanor's contracts had arrived by special courier that morning. Nikki's had been exactly as Megan had planned except for two alterations which she had accepted on Nikki's behalf. First, concerning the twelve, non-skating public appearances, Eleanor was insisting that the Vanguard emblem be clearly visible in at least half of them. How was she supposed to do that? Megan wondered crossly. Tattoo the brand on Nikki's forehead? Secondly, Eleanor was insisting that some additional publicity should be created by ISA concerning the choice of skates for some of Nikki's new and difficult skating movements.

Jacqui's contract was just too good to be true – over-generous, with large bonus payments if Jacqui came in the first fifteen, instead of winning a medal. Furthermore it tied Jacqui to four periods of promotional work in Vanguard's Monaco offices, several advertising sessions where Jacqui would be photographed in skiing gear, and the compulsory attendance at the company's board meetings. How on earth was Megan going to sell this to Jacqui? she wondered dismally. Megan knew that Eleanor's generosity and manipulation would rankle in Jacqui's mind. If she was going to sell it to the girl, she would have to package it in an acceptable manner. But how? She had not yet worked out a solution to her problem, but she was still two hours away from speaking to Jacqui and she had boundless faith in her own imagination.

Jacqui was skiing and Megan had to wait until dark at four o'clock before she returned.

'I don't know why you went to all this trouble when you know I've agreed to accept Magnum's offer,' Jacqui told her when at last they met in the bar.

Jacqui was lounging against the counter with a dreamy look on her face and she kept shaking her drink, and listening to the sound of ice tinkling against glass, like a child with a rattle. She was wearing a bright red Angora sweater and white ski pants and she looked exhilarated and very young. Her hair was a little longer than Megan remembered and her natural black ringlets were falling haphazardly over her shoulders.

'But Jacqui, this is a much better deal,' Megan began, feeling her way. 'The cash offer is doubled, there's far less in the way of promotional ties, which means most of your time is free for training.'

'So where's the snag,' she said with her curious smile, which was more of a sneer, and which Megan loathed. 'There's bound to be a snag, isn't there.'

'Not necessarily,' Megan countered.

At that moment Jacqui's face lit up with a smile of genuine welcome as she beckoned towards a tall man who was watching them from the doorway. Megan watched curiously as the man walked purposely, but unhurriedly towards them. His light brown hair was streaked with grey, and he had extremely cold blue eyes with faint white wrinkles at the corners which grooved frequently when he smiled. He was smiling now as he looked down at Jacqui, but when he turned to greet Megan, something about his expression annoyed her. It was as if they were protagonists in a boxing ring and Megan wondered what this was all about and who he was. He was clearly older than Jacqui, perhaps twice her age, but he still had the body and movements of an athlete. He was sun tanned, lean and big-boned and his shoulders were very straight and held back stiffly, which was not an affectation, she decided, but the result of vigorous, sports training. He had big hands and prominent features and his most arresting feature was his nose – a classic Roman nose which belonged on a statue and lent his face a sense of nobility.

He walked over to the bar and pulled up a stool next to Jacqui.

'Megan, this is Wolf Muller,' Jacqui said. 'Wolf, meet Megan Carroll, my agent. She's trying to talk me out of signing Magnum's contract.'

'I have a better offer, Jacqui,' Megan said firmly. 'And I'd like some time with you alone,' she emphasised, 'so that I can tell you the terms.' She smiled to soften her brusqueness. 'If you'll excuse us,' she said.

'That's not necessary. Wolf's my business advisor.' Jacqui twisted her head sideways and shot a shy glance at him. 'You might as well add that to the long list,' she said to him with an intimate glance. Then she giggled.

It's times like this when you remember how very young she is, Megan thought, trying to curb her irritation.

'Wolf's been coaching me,' Jacqui told Megan. 'We've been racing today. He's pretty rough. It was something else.'

'So what's the offer?' Wolf asked. He smiled pleasantly enough to Megan, but she noted his antagonism was stronger now.

'Double what Magnum offered, fewer personal appearances, far better training back-up. In fact, Jacqui, they're prepared to throw the full weight of their research department behind you.'

'So where's the catch?' Jacqui asked. 'It sounds too good to be true.'

'There's no catch. You're going to be the company's figurehead. They're demonstrating their faith in you, with a million dollar advertising campaign.'

Jacqui laughed shakily. She looked as if she did not believe Megan. 'That's if I win,' she said. 'Come on, Megan, you're giving me the good side. Let's hear the bad side.'

Megan took a deep breath. 'The bad side is – if you don't win a medal, any medal, and you get dropped from the British team during this three-year period you make up your time as their public relations officer for winter sports working in the company. That means grooming other champions and operating from head office, except when you're off skiing.'

'Why would they want a loser to do that?' Jacqui asked. Her eyes had narrowed and Megan could see her temper was rising from her flushed cheeks and smouldering eyes.

'They've seen the film of you skating at Sarajevo. They don't consider you to be a loser.'

'Let's see the contract,' Jacqui whispered.

'I'll give you the contract later, but I'd like you to say 'yes' in principle first. There's the usual clauses: wear company garments, use company skis, a maximum of twelve modelling sessions a year on the ski slopes and some other company attendances, limited to four times a year.'

Jacqui's face crumpled. 'Oh shit,' she said quietly. 'Shit, shit, shit. I told you not to go to Vanguard. Mother'll knuckle in and take control – like she always does.' Suddenly her pent-up anger surfaced and she crashed one fist on the table. 'Shit!' A few heads turned their way. The barman scowled at her, but Jacqui did not notice.

'I'd stick with Magnum, if I were you,' Wolf put in casually. 'They've offered you a good standard contract. You can't expect more. This deal's going to keep you right where you've been struggling to escape from – under Mother's thumb. Now's your opportunity. You're nineteen years old and quite capable of running your own life. Take the deal I offered you and get out now. You'll be a world champion and a millionaire.'

Wolf signalled to the barman, who ignored him. 'Jacqui, you've been struggling for years to leave your mother behind,' he said. 'Go for it now. This is your chance. If you sign up with Vanguard, you're back where you started, but this time it's for life.'

'Are you a lawyer, Mr Muller?' Megan asked casually, glancing coldly at him.

'No.' He grinned lazily.

'An accountant perhaps?'

'No. Oh no!'

'He owns oil wells,' Jacqui said quickly. 'Can you imagine that? Dozens of oil wells. Beats Mother!' She grinned derisively. 'We're thinking of doing a deal,' she added defensively. 'My parcel of Vanguard shares for stock in Wolf's new oil production company. I stand to make a million on the swop.'

Megan stirred restlessly. 'So tell me, Mr Muller, on what basis have you decided to become Jacqui's business advisor? As Jacqui's agent, I must advise her to contact our legal department if she's contemplating any type of business deal.'

Wolf hesitated before answering, subjecting Megan to a keen, searching appraisal, from her feet to her hair. It was disconcerting and Megan guessed that he did it to all women with whom he had business dealings, in order to throw them.

Megan sipped her drink and waited for an answer.

'Let's say that a lifetime in business has given me a certain amount of experience,' he told her coldly. 'The business world is full of sharks out to make a quick buck, particularly agents. I'll tell you straight, Miss Carroll. I don't like agents. When Jacqui told me she'd signed up with you, I felt real sorry for the kid. Now I can see your strategy. Not bad really, I have to hand it to you. Patch up a family quarrel and net a cool three hundred thousand dollars. What was it – a day's work? Two day's work?' He gazed at her evenly and Megan glared back.

'This is a private conversation between Jacqui and I,' Megan said. She turned to Jacqui. 'I think I deserve your attention Jacqui, having come all this way. You can say yes or no, but for goodness sake let's talk about it.'

'Wolf's right,' Jacqui said sullenly. 'Magnum's offer is better for me. I don't know how you managed to get round Mother, to get this offer out of her, but it's no dice. I want to succeed on my own.'

Megan stood up. There was no point in trying to talk Jacqui round with Muller there. 'I've done what I think best for you under the circumstances,' she said coldly. 'I want to talk to you privately about it. I'm going to wait in the lounge.'

Wolf grimaced. 'Don't worry. I'll leave you two together. Now watch out, Jacqui. Don't sign your life away,' he said as a parting shot.

'I can see how quickly Mother twisted you around her finger,' Jacqui said meanly as soon as Wolf was out of earshot.

'Jacqui, I've just about had enough of you and your rudeness,' Megan said, feeling self-righteous and justifiably hurt. 'You're spoiled silly and you're behaving absolutely recklessly. What do you know about this Wolf Muller? I find him highly suspicious, to say the least.'

'Why? Because someone's on my side, for once in my life.' Jacqui was scowling as she fumbled through the contract. 'At least he's not trying to buy me body and soul.'

'Don't tell me your mother wants to control you. I'm fed up with that overplayed story. She's given in on anything you ever wanted except just one thing: competitive ski racing. You know why she didn't want to give in on that – because she's afraid you'll be injured? For some reason or other you hate your mother.

'No, let me go on,' she said, holding up one hand as Jacqui's mouth opened and shut. 'You must work out how much you

202

hate her. Enough to throw away a fortune? Enough to win a gold on Magnum skis – a public slap in the face for your mother? Do you hate her that much, Jacqui?'

Jacqui did not answer. She had screwed her eyes shut and she was frowning heavily, pushing her fingertips together.

'You've got it all wrong,' she said eventually. 'I don't hate her at all. I just don't want to keep living in her glory. I want to be me. This is not a business deal.' She flung the documents across the table. 'This is mother-love taken to extreme lengths – which is the way Mother takes everything.'

'That's perfectly true,' Megan said, 'but you must now examine your alternatives. They're not exactly what they seem. You can't be just any girl from any town, because you're the Vanguard heiress. You have to learn to take the bad with the good. You've heard that before, I'm sure.

'You know what your mother told me to tell you,' Megan went on relentlessly, when Jacqui did not answer. 'She said: "Tell Jacqui that if she wins a gold on Magnum skis she'll lose Vanguard twenty per cent of the British market, and five per cent of the American. She'll understand that sort of reasoning." That's what your mother said. But Jacqui, I'm going tell you this for free: when your mother saw the video of you skiing at Sarajevo, she burst into tears. She said: "Oh God, if I can't stop her then I must help her."'

'There,' she dropped the contract into Jacqui's lap. 'Read it. Sign it. Or tear it up. There's another clause you might note. It says that because this is a family arrangement, and because you will not need any further sponsoring, I hereby resign as your agent as and when you sign this contract. I don't want any fees.

'Don't bother to tell that to your precious Wolf Muller,' Megan went on, 'because I don't like him any more than he likes me.'

Jacqui was staring up at her and looking bewildered.

'Hey! Hang on, Megan. Where's that clause?'

'Amongst the addendums at the back.'

'Where's the pen? Hey! Wait a minute! We're always sitting in bars,' she said. 'Let's get out of here.'

Finally they signed the three copies of the contract at the hotel reception desk and the receptionist witnessed them.

'Listen, Megan,' Jacqui said, 'how come you want out?'

'It's a matter of ethics,' Megan said. 'This isn't really a business deal, Jacqui. You said that? Remember?'

'Sure,' Jacqui said, 'but I want you to be my agent. I've got a feeling I'm going to need you, too.'

She picked up the addendum and tore it into pieces. Then she pushed the contracts towards Megan. 'Tell Mother ...' she began. Then she broke off.

'On second thoughts, there isn't much left to tell Mother,' she said with a wry grin.

CHAPTER 27

It had all been so simple, Megan thought with a surge of triumph that made her fingers tingle and her cheeks flush. She had just solved two pressing problems in one evening. She wished she had someone with whom she could share her good news as she watched Jacqui saunter jauntily across the foyer. No doubt she was going to find Wolf. Megan hoped there was nothing serious brewing between these two. Wolf was far too old for Jacqui and she did not like him, nor trust him. She wondered if she should warn Jacqui about him, but then discarded that idea. Jacqui would be insulted if she tried to intrude into her private life.

Megan was left alone in the foyer wondering whether or not to book into the hotel for the night. Could she make her flight back to London? Hardly! She frowned as she glanced at her watch. Much as she hated the idea of staying under the same roof as Wolf Muller, she did not seem to have an alternative. She picked up her bag and briefcase and walked slowly towards reception, but there was a large busload of tourists checking in, so Megan glanced at the ski pictures around the wall while she waited.

It was then that she recognised Ian. The snapshot was indistinct, but it was definitely Ian. He was standing on a platform, shaking hands as he handed a cup to a young girl in ski gear. Megan gasped and stooped forward to peer closer. In the background was a great deal of snow and the corner of an ancient building beside a forest.

No wonder she had always felt she had met Ian before – Megan thought as she straightened up. She remembered clearly now: she had been looking for talent and she had flown up to see the Scottish Games where she had signed up a young marathon runner. Ian had been handing out the cups and certificates. She had never really connected her casual, cheery freelance lover with the dignified, kilted Scot whom she had seen only fleetingly, otherwise she would have remembered. Megan had an excellent memory for names and faces. She frowned as she read the caption to the photograph. So this was Ian's 'wee croft' in the Highlands, she thought bitterly as she hurried to the porter to ask the way to Inverewe House.

It was starting to snow again when she set out from the hotel, but her destination was only twenty miles away. She hoped she'd arrive within the hour, but the road was winding and the surface slippery, there were no road signs and after an hour she guessed she had taken the wrong fork and when she tried to return to the main road she could not find the way. There was no sign of the forest which was clearly marked on her map.

She knew she was lost. It was cold and dark; the car headlights caught a few errant snowflakes whirling in the wind. The road became narrower, the snowdrifts deeper. Then she skidded on an icy corner and the car ploughed into a bank of snow. It would take some shifting, she reckoned.

Megan climbed out of the car and looked around for help, but the road was quite deserted. The temperature was minus ten degrees in the wind, she guessed, and she was well aware of the danger of freezing to death out here on the unprotected moors. She jumped up and down for a while, but the prospect of staying there all night was unappealing, so eventually she set off in the direction of the nearest village, or so she hoped. She wished now that she had stayed the night at Aviemore, but at the time her temper had gained the upper hand. Even now she could hardly believe Ian's deception. How could he have lied to her? They had grown so very close to each other in the past six weeks since she had gatecrashed his London home – or so she had thought, and she had been so happy. They had seemed to have so much in common. They laughed at the same sort of jokes, viewed the world and the people they met from identical viewpoints. Megan had never met anyone with whom she was so perfectly in tune. And now this – this treachery! Surely the caption to the photograph was a mistake, or perhaps a joke. Some joke, she thought grimly as she trudged on.

The moon rose: a shining silver ball that reflected eerily on the snow, making the shadows twice as dark. Megan kept walking clapping her hands and humming to herself. Long ago she had lost all feeling in her feet, but now the numbing cold was creeping into her head and she was beginning to feel drowsy, and that was a bad sign, she knew.

The road must lead somewhere, she promised herself as she hummed to keep up her spirits. An hour or more later, she saw lights in the distance. At first she thought it was a village, then a hospital, or perhaps a hotel, but as she hurried closer, she saw that it was a large and gloomy-looking mansion built of granite, with turrets, and ramparts and whirly bits. Or maybe a small castle.

It took a long time to walk the length of the driveway, but at last she reached the huge, carved door. Inside she could hear snatches of voices talking and laughing, faint and far away, and then the sound of a bagpipe tuning up. She summoned the last of her strength and rang the bell. Looking up she saw granite gargoyles grinning at her and there was a crest with an evil-looking cat prancing on its back legs. 'Oh my!' she whispered. 'Walt Disney Productions should know about this place. I could earn a cut just by sending pictures over,' she thought with amusement. I guess it's a real, genuine stately home,' she drawled Brooklyn-style, through chattering teeth to keep her spirits up.

The door swung open with enough squeaking and whining to satisfy the spookyist film set, and a red-faced woman in a starched grey pinstripe dress and permed white hair said: 'Oh you poor lamb. Come in, come in, and warm yourself before you freeze to death.'

'My car broke down,' Megan explained, 'and I lost my way.' *Why was she lying? She had found her way right to Inverewe House, hadn't she? But it all seemed so unreal and her head was ringing in a most peculiar fashion.*

'Och, save your strength, lassie, until you're a wee bit warmer. It happens all the time here. There's no proper road signs. His Lordship has given the police a bit of a mouthful lately and we're thinking it's over time they did something about it.

'Well, we'd best not stand about here. This draughty old hall's not much better than outdoors.' Her broad Highland accent was difficult to understand, but Megan followed her gratefully into the library and crouched beside a roaring wood fire.

'I'll go speak to his Lordship and he'll be helping you in no time. It's his birthday. That's why we have a piper from the village. Young Rob Faulkner it is and I'm thinking he's a mite off-key, or maybe it's my ears that are going a bit.'

Oh dear! A birthday party! She felt depressed and unwanted and not far from the surface was the knowledge of her narrow escape. She might have died of exposure.

She glanced around wonderingly. She had never seen anything quite like this room; it was a great draughty barn of a place – a huge room for a library, with heavy timbered ceiling and floors and oak panelling everywhere. The glassed-in bookcases covered two walls from floor to ceiling. Above the door hung a portrait of an ancient Scottish chief who seemed to be glaring down at her. She tried to read the inscription, but it was too dark.

You could tell the family's history from this room, Megan decided. There were several paintings of ships, going back for hundreds of years. The carpets were old and there was a smell of mildew in spite of the roaring fire. There was a naval sword hanging on the wall, several framed photographs of ships, a moth-eaten tiger skin lay before the fire, an overt relic of the Colonial era, and there were hundreds of books – books on guns, warfare, tactics, naval history, geography, and travel guides. There were dictionaries, books in several languages including Russian, and a bookcase full of textbooks on hunting, fishing, estate management and forestry, besides the novels and leather-bound Scottish classics. A strange collection.

She heard the housekeeper returning from the bowels of the old house. Evidently there were no carpets and her footsteps echoed eerily on the stone floor. 'His Lordship wants you to join his dinner party, miss,' she said cheerily when she opened the door. 'They've a very nice salmon his Lordship caught, and venison he shot not a week back.' As she led Megan along one corridor after the next, she chattered on about how well they lived when his Lordship returned to the estate, which was not often, Megan gathered. He knows how to live off the land, she thought.

Oh boy, she shivered as she passed the portraits of his Lordship's ancestors: a fierce, proud, raggle-taggle mob, in their kilts and clutching their swords.

'No women?' she asked.

'Their Ladyships are hung in the long gallery,' the housekeeper said.

I bet they are, too, Megan thought, noting the cold eyes and fierce mouths of the old Scottish chiefs glaring angrily down at her.

A door was flung open and the housekeeper ushered Megan into a vast baronial diningroom lit by the dim light from one hanging chandelier over the table. Like the library, the room was all wood, from the oak panelling to the timbered ceiling and floors and on one side a huge fire blazed. There was a long, highly polished, dining room table, and a small party was gathered at one end of it.

'Here she is — our waif from the storm,' the housekeeper announced cheerily. 'Lucky she was wearing this lovely fur coat, or she might have frozen stiff. She wouldn't be the first. I'll warm up a hot toddy in a jiffy and she can eat while you drink your coffee.

'Now you tell her,' she said bossily to the laird at the end of the table, while she fussed around serving the food. 'Tell her how dangerous it is to go wandering around the moors at night.'

His Lordship was unable to say anything. He had leapt to his feet when Megan entered the room and he was still rooted with shock. He was dressed in a kilt and a green waistcoat with some fluffy stuff around his silly neck and the sight of his eyes registering horror and his cheeks burning very red in patches, was almost worth the rejection and the pain of catching him out.

She heard Ian saying: 'Let me introduce ...'

She felt the oddest sensation: she was so cold and she seemed to be sinking into the floor and the room was slowly turning around her.

She awoke feeling cold and uncomfortable and she did not know where she was. She only vaguely remembered being revived with brandy and Ian carrying her up the stairs to his vast, musty bedroom. The housekeeper had brought her soup and bread and explained that Ian had insisted she take the only aired bed in the house. He would be sleeping in the library the housekeeper added. Yet Megan seemed to be pinned down under some heavy object, a familiar feeling, since Ian always slept this way. Exploring with her hand she satisfied herself that it was indeed his leg that was flung over her. What a cheek, she decided. She was not quite sure why that was, since they had been sleeping together for the past six weeks. Somehow it seemed all wrong now, but she was cold, while Ian felt warm and comfortable and after a while she shifted gently towards him. Ian murmured something in his sleep and turned away, so she snuggled up behind his back.

Reality came flooding back. What a nerve, she thought, and why had he lied about his background? She would have it out with him in the morning, but now she was so tired. She snuggled up and soon fell asleep again.

It seemed only a second later that the telephone was ringing beside her. Sleepily she reached out and groped for the light switch, but she could not find it. The room was pitch dark. Then she heard a movement beside her and Ian's voice saying: 'Mackintosh here.'

'I just had dinner with Sir Geoffrey Houghton,' Megan heard the caller's clear, incisive voice saying. 'He's given the go-ahead for your project.'

'About bloody time!' Ian sounded angry, but he seemed unconcerned at being woken in the middle of the night.

'You're always so damned impatient, Ian. He wants you to get started on it right away. He also asked me to tell you that your girlfriend, Petrovna, is causing him an inordinate amount of trouble.'

'Tough,' Ian murmured.

'Well, I'm sure you're making the most of it. Houghton said he's never known you to miss a trick.'

'If Houghton were forty years younger he'd think it was well worth it, too,' Ian said in a noncommital voice.

'You naval men deserve your reputation.'

Ian swore quietly and replaced the receiver.

Megan turned away in the dark. She heard Ian replace the receiver on its cradle and knew she was shaking with rage. That clear, cold voice kept ringing in her ears: *Your girlfriend, Petrovna!* It hurt both ways. Over the past six weeks Megan had grown fond of Nikki, seeing her aggression and temper for what it was – the defences of a lonely, frightened woman. Underneath her sophisticated and often prickly manner lay an emotionally immature child, a victim of her orphan-like upbringing and because her emotional development had been stunted, she had thrown all her energy and her determination into the development of her art. She needed love neurotically, but she could not give love. All that she had to give went into her skating. Megan had grown to love her, because she understood her. It hurt to think that she and Ian had been deceiving her. What a bastard Ian was.

'I think you're a bastard,' she said loudly.

'Hush. Mrs Gilmour will hear you,' Ian replied sleepily.

'I don't care if she hears me. Let her think what she likes. She might as well know the sort of man she's working for. What are you, some sort of a psycho playing the part of a poor, freelance writer in London and living it up as the local laird in Scotland? You're despicable.'

'What difference does it make. The fact is I'm a bit ashamed of it,' Ian said mildly. 'Without the cash to go with it, a title is particularly nonsensical.'

'So why did you lie about your home?'

'Megan, I did not lie to you,' he said coldly. 'You're confusing modesty with lying. Hardly surprising, given your background.'

'How dare you ...' Megan began.

'You should have waited for an invitation before you came snooping after me,' Ian went on, interrupting her. 'Please don't think for a moment I believe your silly story of losing your way in the snow.'

'Snooping!' she snarled. 'Oh, this is too much.' She buried her face in the pillow. She had been about to tell him of the snap she had seen on the wall in the hotel reception, but it was too late now. 'I *was* lost,' she said quietly. 'I don't care what you think, but I want you to know that I couldn't help overhearing your telephone call. The caller, whoever he was, has a most penetrating voice.'

Megan felt the involuntary stiffening of Ian's body. So he does have something to hide, she thought dismally.

'So?' he said quietly.

'So he must know you pretty well to call in the middle of the night and I heard that comment about Nikki being your girlfriend and you making the most of it ... and deserving your reputation – yes ... that's right ... I heard that, too.'

'You can think what you damn well like,' Ian said and

211

turned his back on her.

After that he pretended he was asleep, but Megan knew from his breathing that he was awake. She lay tense and miserable, not wanting to say anymore and wishing she was back home, not wanting Ian to know how unhappy she felt. Eventually she turned her back on him and she, too, pretended to sleep. After a while she heard Ian climb softly out of bed, fumble for his dressing gown and tiptoe out of the room.

Let him go, the liar, the cheat. He had pretended that he loved her, yet his mysterious friends, whom she had never met, thought that Nikki was his girlfriend. No doubt Nikki had met all of them. Hadn't he told her, too, that he was a struggling freelance writer, with a croft in the Highlands? Instead he was deeply entrenched in the British establishment. He patently wasn't wealthy, she thought, remembering the threadbare rugs in the library and the housekeeper's obvious joy at the venison and the salmon Ian had procured for the table.

Still, there was no excuse for his behaviour. Oh how miserable she felt. And how strange to think that they had been loving each other for only six weeks. Surely it was forever. The realisation that Ian had been lying to her for all this time was a hurt as physical as it was mental; like a cold, hard lump in her entrails. Had all that love and loyalty she had lavished on Ian been misplaced?

Breakfast was a lonely affair which she ate in the morning room, a small room close to the kitchen decorated with gay chintz curtains and hand-painted plates on the Welsh dresser. It was warm and cosy, but outside the clouds hung low and dark and matched her mood exactly. Mrs Gilmour, kept popping in and out with more hot coffee and toasted scones, but Megan was feeling feverish and upset.

'Master Ian says I'm to show you round the house. He says you'll want to see it all,' she went on in cheerful ignorance of Megan's depression. She told Megan that Ian had gone to tow her car to the village and have it fixed. He was expected back for lunch and afterwards he'd drive her to the airport himself.

Megan felt miserably in the way and could not stop apologising. She had no desire to be shown round Ian's country seat, but the housekeeper was so obviously delighted to have someone

212

to talk to, she couldn't refuse. At least it would pass the morning. She laughed bitterly when she remembered how much she had wanted to find out about Ian's background. The man she had fallen in love with did not exist.

'For generations,' the housekeeper was saying as she led her through the main hall, 'the Mackintosh men have gone to Fettes College, followed by Dartmouth Naval College. The late Lord Mackintosh, did the same, but he died five years ago. Ian, however, broke the tradition to study languages and then he was sent to Greenwich Naval College to become a language specialist.

'When he became the youngest Lieutenant Commander in the Navy, we thought we had a budding admiral in the family, but suddenly he quit the Navy, just like that. He wanted to be a writer, he told us.'

Well at least he tells the truth sometimes, Megan thought.

'So he spends his time writing TV documentaries, quite successful, I'm told.' She sniffed to show her disapproval, and Megan could hear the disappointment in her voice.

'Have you worked here for a long time?' she asked.

'All my life,' Mrs Gilmour told her. 'I don't consider it my job, it's my family. I brought Ian up when his mother returned to France. He was only a wee bairn then. Of course, she used to come back from time to time, and sometimes the family went to France for holidays. She was a poor thing, Lady Anne, she couldn't stand the weather, she said, but she was just as obstinate as her husband and she would not give in. Ian changed after Lady Anne left. He used to be such a happy child. I can still see him running through the house, always laughing, he was. Afterwards he became a bit wild, right ferocious he can be when the mood takes him. He's too introverted, wraps himself up in his precious animals. Woe betide anyone who meddles with the wildlife around these parts.

'Of course, I shouldn't be telling you this,' she confided as they wound their way through long, musty corridors, 'but last year Ian caught a poacher stealing Osprey eggs from a nest by the loch. You probably know how hard the wildlife folks are working to woo the Osprey back to Scotland and Ian's in with that lot, of course. Well, he tarred and feathered this poor bloke. A Londoner, I believe. He dumped him at the local pub in the village with a note stuck on his back stating: "I steal

213

Osprey eggs." Then the villagers roughed him up a bit, too. Nothing serious. Quite a to-do, it was. Ian was charged, and brought up in court, but let off with a caution.' She sighed. 'I never did have much influence with Ian, although I loved him as if he were my own. He'd do anything for his mother, though. She's still living in Roqueville. Ian is planning on spending Easter there.'

At the end of the hall they saw the shield with the cat again. 'That's the Mackintosh crest,' Mrs Gilmour told her proudly: ' "*Touch not the cat, bot a glove*." '

'What does that mean?' Megan asked.

'It means what it says: Don't touch the cat without a glove on. Don't meddle with a Mackintosh unless you're well protected.'

I should have read that first, Megan thought miserably.

She was led to the library, where the family's hero sat in solitary splendour. It really was a magnificent painting and now she realised how much the ancient chief resembled Ian with his penetrating blue eyes, dark brown hair and striking features. She went closer and read the inscription: "*Calum Mackintosh, 1696-1745. Hero of Culloden, who died for his King.*" They went on to the long gallery where the Mackintosh women sat smiling in wintry splendour with their shawls and fancy lace. Megan could take no more. She pleaded a headache and returned for a cup of tea in the breakfast room. But Mrs Gilmour was determined she would see everything and after a brief rest, off they went again. And by the time Ian arrived, three hours later, Megan was just completing the tour of his stately house, each room lovingly shown off by the ever-bubbly Mrs Gilmour.

'It's not a crime to hide a title, or this musty old house,' Ian protested, when they were sitting alone in the diningroom and the housekeeper had placed the food on the sideboard and left. 'Up here I can't get away from it, but in London I can just be myself.'

'Be yourself,' Megan repeated furiously in a stage whisper. 'What is yourself? Nothing, I tell you. Just an empty, impersonal shell. Up here at least you are yourself, your tradition and all the paraphernalia of your life — it's all here.

'This is you, so what are you hiding it for? You lied about yourself and your life and you lied about Nikki and you.'

'Have it your own way,' he said infuriatingly. 'Serves you right for spying on me. I hope you've had a satisfactory morning. I instructed the housekeeper to show you absolutely everything. Did she show you the cellars? Good. I expect you'd like to examine the pedigrees of our Highland and Galloway cattle, and the sheep, of course. They're in the filing cabinet. You must see it all, before you leave.'

'What the hell are you saying?'

'Come off it, Megan. You came spying on me and I don't want you to waste your valuable time.'

One look at Ian's face told her she would never convince him of the truth. 'Let's chuck it,' she said. 'Who cares? If you've finished eating you can take me to the airport.'

It was a long and miserable drive to Inverness. 'Please don't wait,' she told him icily when she stepped out of the car.

Later she discovered he was waiting behind her, while she argued with airport officials about her reasons for missing her flight the previous evening without cancelling.

'So what were you doing in Aviemore,' he wanted to know. He looked better tempered, but Megan was still furious.

'I don't want to discuss it,' she said icily. 'Do you want to discuss the telephone call?'

'No,' he said furiously.

'Well, then,' she said. 'It's goodbye!' She turned away and when she passed through the 'passengers only' exit, she did not bother to look back.

CHAPTER 28

Megan was feeling nervous both for herself and for Nikki as she hurried to her seat at Earls Court. Tonight was Nikki's London launch and after the publicity she had received she'd better be good – oh, boy, she'd better be good, Megan muttered. Nikki was a household name in Britain and America, yet no one had seen her skate. Megan had delayed her debut for three months of hard training, while press and public alike clamoured to see Nikki perform. The publicity had been tremendous, but now she had to deliver the goods. What a build-up! But tonight Nikki was on her own – the coming performance would make or break her. Impossible to ignore the tension – it was like static electricity before a storm and it was everywhere, particularly in the wings where the skaters were dressing for the show.

The seats were filling rapidly and well before time. The audience was excited – you could tell by the sharp staccato of conversation and the high-pitched laughter. It was a well-heeled audience; tonight's performance was in aid of the Save The Children Fund; seats were prohibitively priced and at least three members of the Royal Family would be attending.

ISA had a block of ringside seats near the wings and so far there was only one person there: Eric Lamont, and he was looking unhappy. His gold-rimmed glasses and his cuff links glittered in the light, but he looked haggard.

Poor Lamont, Megan thought as she hurried towards him. Since he had been so ignominiously kicked out of Nikki's bed, he seemed to have shrivelled into himself. Nikki had cruelly described him as a lovesick 'puffing billy'. Eric could not cope with her excesses – her joy seemed to disturb him as much as her anger. Lately, Nikki's tantrums were becoming as famous as her defection; she charmed or abused as the mood took her and during rehearsals she ranged from superb to indifferent.

'Hi Eric,' Megan said, sitting next to him. 'D'you think she'll pull it off?'

'What an insane question,' he shrieked. Then he shuddered slightly and gave her a strange half-smile. 'Sorry,' he muttered. 'I'm satisfied with the choreography, *if* Nikki sticks to it; *if* we could only discipline her ...' He broke off and Megan was reminded that his reputation was on the line, just as hers was.

Megan's heart lurched when she saw Ian approaching. She had tried to snub him since her night at Aviemore five weeks ago, but Ian appeared to be unusually thick-skinned. He still came to the office almost daily, he watched Nikki's coaching sessions, thought up new ideas for press releases which he conned Maureen into typing and posting almost daily. In fact, he carried on just as before, and Megan had grudgingly decided that he had turned his attention to Nikki. Who cares? Megan told herself once again.

Nevertheless, Ian looked superb in his evening suit, and Megan noticed he had lost weight and there were shadows under his eyes. Oh, why did he have to come? Megan had always had a tight grip on her intellect, but lately her body and her emotions seemed to have a mind of their own, acting insanely whenever Ian was nearby. What's the matter with me, she wondered miserably? Why can't I forget that monster?

Abruptly, she sat on the other side of Lamont and began scribbling in her notebook.

'We had a mint of trouble forcing Nikki to skate to Russian music,' Lamont was saying to Ian. 'Of course, the audience expect something Russian for at least part of the programme. Nikki gave in when we hit on the idea of miming her flight to freedom. It's rather a novel idea of mine,' he simpered in his high-pitched nasal tone.

Oh, how smug Ian was looking. Of course, he had a right to look pleased, didn't he? This show was his brainchild – the royal turn-out, the audience, the publicity, everything!

'First there's the opening gambit, very grand, very Russian – Prokofiev, naturally; then the Cossack dance bit: plenty of triple toe loop combinations, two double axles and a variety of spins. You saw something similar in Sarajevo, but this time the choreography and music are much better; followed by the flight to freedom. I won't spoil it for you by telling you what the music is ...'

Oh, God, can't he shut up, Megan moaned to herself. She noticed that the press seats were filled to capacity, several prospective sponsors were present and she could see Vanguard's Nigel Wilder sitting in the front row. It was a shame Eleanor had not come instead. She noticed Ian was looking restless.

'The best bits come later.' There was no stopping Lamont now. His eyes were gleaming, his lips were moist and pursed. 'You'll see a triple Lutz, followed by a triple flip – where all her work is done on her right foot – very difficult. Then in quick order there's a dance section, giving a display of intricate straight-line footwork that explodes into a Hamill camel, melting fluidly into a sit spin.'

'I'm afraid it's absolutely meaningless to me,' Ian interrupted him. 'Either I get goose pimples or I don't. If I do, she's made – if I don't, she's a flop. Works every time,' he said in a tone designed to silence Eric.

'That's all very well ...' Lamont began.

Megan stood up and excused herself. She hurried over to Nigel and shook hands. 'So glad you could make it,' she murmured smoothly. 'I know you'll have a lovely time. Nikki's costume has the Vanguard emblem right across the front and no doubt you've noticed the rink is decorated in Vanguard colours. You'll be very pleased, Nigel, I promise you.'

She nodded to her boss, John Oberholtzer as he took his seat in the front row. He had arrived in London that afternoon specially for this performance. She wondered how Nikki was making out in the wings.

For Nikki the past few days had passed with agonizing slowness as her debut loomed nearer and now she was close to despair. It seemed that the bubble was about to burst, the illusion which she had so carefully nurtured, was going to melt away. Who was she, after all? A failed Russian skater who had never once been chosen for world championships. She peered forward and gazed searchingly into the mirror as if to convince herself that she really existed. She saw a stranger there; a girl with an exquisitely made-up face, in a green velvet skating dress with a deep-V neckline, outlined in dark green satin ribbon, and a white embroidered bodice underneath. Was it really her? She put up one hand and touched her hair which was golden now,

218

and piled up in a cascade of curls. Then she let her arm fall in a gesture of despair.

What if she failed to please these strange Westerners? Would they send her back to Russia to face her father's wrath? And did they know what would happen to her if they sent her back?

But of course she would prove to them now that she was the best. Yet there was this nagging suspicion, something shameful, which she had pushed to the back of her mind, out of reach, which suggested other reasons for them wanting her. But of course, that was impossible. She was insane even to consider such a possibility. Even more important was to prove it to herself – to squash her suspicions for once and for all. For weeks she had been practising day after day, for as long as she had the strength and sometimes longer. At night she would fling herself on her bed fully dressed and surface to reality in the early hours of the morning. She had to be the best – or else she would die of shame.

Maureen burst in to her dressing room, shattering her soul-searching. 'Ready?' she asked in the manner of a nurse about to wheel her into the operating theatre.

'Don't creep up on me,' Nikki shouted. 'Why can't you leave me alone?'

'Pull yourself together,' Maureen snapped. 'Just pretend it's a rehearsal.'

'A rehearsal! You're crazy,' she shrieked. 'Oh, but I don't mean to shout at you Maureen. Forgive me, really. No, no, you must say that you forgive me for being so rude. I want so badly that we be friends.' She reached out her hand imploringly.

Maureen grabbed it and squeezed it to keep the peace.

'I'm so scared, Maureen.'

'Scared! Why? Nothing to be scared about, is there? You've been through this old routine a million times. You'll be all right. You've got butterflies. That's all.'

'It's the orchestra,' she said, wondering why she had confided her fears to Maureen. 'Their beat is not quite ... you understand. I have a very good ear. An excellent ear. And I can hear ...' She shook her head impatiently. She would rather die than admit that she was worried about her own ability. That would be quite shameful, and of all the things that Nikki dreaded in the dead of night, being shamed was the very worst that could happen.

'Here! Come on.' Maureen massaged her fingers into the back of Nikki's neck. 'You're going to be a sensation. I promise you.'

'But of course.' She looked up haughtily. Why was Maureen being kind to her? There must be a reason for that, and it could only mean trouble. She drew away from her and began patting on more face powder. How could Maureen ever understand her trauma. She had to be the best. That was her destiny. Nothing else was good enough. She could not live with mediocrity.

'The Princess is here.' The call sent a ripple of tension through the wings; the band began the *Children's Overture* by Quilter.

Megan saw John hurry down the aisle and reach his seat just as the first wave of infant skaters burst upon the rink, enacting children in literature and nursery rhymes, to the delight of the audience.

Megan's irritation was forgotten as she turned to Eric. 'Fantastic Eric. Really well done.' The guy was a genius at his work in spite of his cranky manner. Now, the Pied Piper of Hamlin was in the centre of a long line of kids: Little Bo-Peep, Tom the Chimney Sweep, Peter Pan and a host of other characters, whirling them faster and faster around the rink. Suddenly they raced off-stage behind him and the audience erupted into a torrent of applause.

'Pretty good skaters, Eric,' she said. 'Maybe I should sign up some of them.'

The last act before interval was Megan's Swedish skater, Maria Stenmark. She was so good Megan wondered if she had made a mistake in putting her on. Nikki had to be better. Otherwise ...

She remembered Nikki's performance in Sarajevo. Since then she had watched her being coached daily, and Nikki had been precise and polished, but there had been no sign of that elusive magic which had captivated the Slavic audience. Was it all a mirage, created by her own emotional state of mind? Megan sat twisting her fingers nervously. If Nikki failed to excel, Megan would be the laughing stock of the sports world. She'd probably be out of work, too.

Interval came and Megan excused herself and hurried backstage. 'She's too nervous for my liking,' Maureen whispered to her, pointing towards Nikki's dressing room.

Megan hurried over to find Nikki vomiting into a basin. 'Go away, go away,' she screamed at Megan. Wiping the perspiration from her forehead, Megan hurried back to the stalls and sat aching with pity for her temperamental Russian skater.

At last it was time. The moment Nikki burst out with her electrifying smile, looking sensational in her Vanguard costume and skates, Megan felt Eric freeze beside her. 'This is not the routine we planned,' he whispered to Megan.

'But it's fantastic,' Megan reassured him.

'I forbade it, utterly forbade it,' he groaned.

'Why?' Megan whispered, her eyes following Nikki's slender form.

'Because she can't manage it, that's why. There's a movement she dreamed up herself. She calls it the Cossack Whirl. Trouble is, it can whirl her straight onto her backside. It's a variation on the Triple Inside Axel Paulsen, but more difficult.'

Suddenly it didn't matter what it was called. Megan forgot her fears and could only press forward and gasp and cheer – at one with Nikki and the spectators as she alternatively teased, thrilled and frightened them. She had her audience on the edge of their seats, breathless with admiration. Then she burst into the Cossack dance with a devilish grin, gathered speed, using the full perimeter of the rink and zoomed into the centre to perform her dynamic Cossack Whirl, a movement that sent a thrill of fear through the audience and left them gasping with admiration. As she landed, one leg slipped awkwardly and for a moment there was a gasp of dread, but her momentum helped her to recover as she whirled into a one-foot spin.

She was well into her flight to freedom now, to Stravinsky's *Petrouchka*. She seemed to be airborne over great swathes of ice and yet came wheeling out of these manoeuvres serenely, arms out as if she had changed tempo in the air; and all of it at a dazzling speed that whirled her from one end of the rink to the other while the music swirled and crashed around her. The illusion had taken over: the audience were with her to a man in her imaginary flight across snow and ice. Ian was leaning over the rail, his knuckles white as he gripped the edge. The press were spellbound, their faces moving from side to side, following the diminutive, graceful figure.

221

There was a breathless silence in the audience during the entire ten minute performance and when Nikki reached safety and danced a graceful mime of thanks rising to a pinnacle of joy the effect was stunning. Suddenly she moved into her final spin and the music exploded to a crescendo as she spun like a top and finally dropped into a curtsey.

There was a moment of stunned silence. Then the audience rose to applaud her – the press, the public, the royal guests – in a spontaneous roar of welcome and praise.

After nine curtain calls the band struck up the national anthem and Nikki stood clasping armfuls of flowers with tears running down her cheeks.

'She did it, she made it, she's superb,' Megan gloated to John Oberholtzer as they hurried backstage. 'My God, when I see her skate like that, when I watch her, I forget all that irritation. Suddenly I feel privileged.'

Lamont was boasting to everyone. 'She's a born performer. She never came anywhere near this perfection in the practice runs. I don't mind telling you, I was close to throwing her up. It's been one tantrum after the next. But when I watch a performance like that I have to admit that if it only happened once in my life, all my coaching would be worthwhile. I won't stay for the party,' he said. 'I've had about all I can take for one day.' He looked close to tears as he hurried away.

The show was over and Nikki was an established star, but the party was just beginning. Nikki was to be presented to members of the Royal Family together with three other skaters. Some of the children would present bouquets, and the press conference would take place in an adjoining room shortly afterwards. The presentations were over and Megan hurried Nikki to the press room. As they walked in, they were caught up in an explosion of flashlights.

In no time, John Oberholtzer was beside them, expertly taking over. That was John for you, Megan thought treacherously. He'd kept out of the way until Nikki came up trumps and now he was there to catch the accolades.

'As soon as I heard of this amazing phenomena – this superbly gifted ice skater, I sent my assistant, Megan Carroll, to woo her to the West,' he was saying in his lazy mid-western drawl.

What a liar! Megan slipped aside as soon as she could and sat at the side of the room. John loved the limelight and he was welcome to it. She felt like a wrung out rag.

John was looking pretty good for his age, she thought. He was fifty-four and his hair was dead white and cut short in a crew cut, but his six foot four body was broad and athletic. John was a big success with women, although he was ugly in the conventional sense of the word with his clumsy, too-large features and his lined, sun-tanned skin. His eyes were too shrewd, his mouth too hard, but his brilliant smile and sense of humour made up for the shortcomings. He was bad news for women, for he never hung around for long, and he had remained a bachelor. With his hyperactive, restless mind, she doubted he would ever marry. Right now he seemed very taken with Nikki, Megan noticed.

Megan looked for Ian, but there was no sign of him. He was probably in the next room with his fancy titled friends.

It was Nikki's turn to face a barrage of questions. They asked if Mr Right had appeared yet, and Nikki said she was looking hard and would anyone like to volunteer; they asked if she missed her home and she said her home was in Chelsea and she loved it; would she defect if she had the chance to choose again? Yes, but sooner.

Watching Nikki, Megan suddenly realised that she was an extremely clever woman. She had never thought of her in that way before and it surprised her.

Nikki's act had been televised and it was followed by a personal, live interview. It was all such an outstanding success that Megan sat bemused and happy, nursing a glass of champagne behind the cameras. 'Perfect,' she murmured, enjoying her sense of well being. 'A triumph.'

She was only half listening when she heard the commentator say: 'Miss Petrovna, I noticed a very difficult new movement performed during your Cossack dance. Would you tell us a little about it?'

Nikki babbled on happily.

'I noticed your foot seemed to skid when you landed. You recovered quickly, but for a moment you were in danger of falling. Is this the first time you have performed this movement in public?'

'Yes,' she replied with an angelic smile. 'It needs very good skates. Unfortunately my skates are far from perfect.' She shrugged charmingly. 'Next time, perhaps.'

223

Megan leapt to her feet and signalled wildly over the cameraman's head.

The commentator, who was a friend of Ian's and who liked Megan, deftly changed the topic. He had no wish to cause problems. How was she coping with the British weather? he asked. Better than all that snow? But Nikki's mood had changed. She was petulant, aggrieved and ready to air her grievances. After one more try the commentator wrapped up the programme. 'Well done to Nikki Petrovna,' he said, 'and on behalf of all our viewers, welcome to the West, Nikki, and good luck in the European championships. And with that goodnight from ...'

Megan grabbed Nikki's arm and pulled her to the dressing room.

'You fool,' she snarled. 'You ungrateful, self-opinionated idiot. You slipped because the movement is too difficult and you changed the routine. D'you know how much trouble your statement will cause Vanguard – and me?'

'But Megan,' Nikki began, faltering between arrogance and her fondness for Megan. 'It is the truth. The skates are clumsy.'

Then Megan heard Ian's voice behind her. 'Cool it, Megan. I'm sure Nikki didn't understand the importance of her silly excuse. She did brilliantly this evening. Don't spoil her triumph.'

'Ian,' Nikki whirled round and grabbed him tearfully. 'I am the best in the world, aren't I? Tell me again ... you've told me so often.'

When? Megan wanted to scream. When has he told you?

Nikki turned to Megan imploringly. 'They said it was a triumph,' she said tearfully. She felt a wave of self pity gush through her. She had tried so hard to please everyone, but Megan was angry and she so much wanted Megan to love her.

'D'you know what your 'silly excuses' will cost Vanguard? Millions of sales! I'm telling you one thing that's sure – you don't have a sponsor as from this evening. What's more, they'll probably sue.'

Then John arrived looking breathless and upset. 'Is it true?' he demanded and as Megan told him, Nikki burst into tears.

'Hell, Megan. I blame you,' John said, wrapping one arm around Nikki who was sobbing appealingly on his shirt front. 'She didn't understand the score. It was your duty to look after her.'

'You all make me sick,' Megan said bitterly. 'Nikki, you

224

haven't a hope of hanging onto that fancy Vanguard sports car,' she went on spitefully, enjoying Nikki's horrified expression as she clung to Ian's arm.

She felt Maureen's arm tugging her strongly, but she could not stop. 'Jesus! Is this the way you repay your friends?'

'Megan, stop it! You're obsessed with money and sponsors,' Ian said bitingly.

Megan glanced up at him in surprise.

'Have you nothing to say about her performance? Doesn't that mean anything to you? Is all achievement measured in dollars, in that mercenary world you inhabit?'

'Don't you preach to me,' Megan snapped.

'I don't understand,' Nikki said pathetically. 'I skated well, da? I am the best, da? How can Vanguard take that away from me?'

The men made comforting noises and led Nikki towards the party.

As Megan neared the door, Ian stood blocking her way, his eyes blazing with fury. She felt his hand grasp her elbow so hard that his fingers bit into her flesh. 'Megan,' he said low and urgently. 'The position is not irreconcilable, but if she flees to Russia it will be. Now get some control, for God's sake.' He closed the door in her face and she heard the key turn in the lock.

For a moment Megan tugged the door. Then she turned to Maureen looking bewildered. 'He's locked us in. Of all the ...' She broke off and crumpled into a chair.

'Never underestimate the power of beauty on the male ego,' Maureen said placidly. 'Beats brains anytime.'

Megan was too miserable to answer. A thousand images were flashing through her mind: the telex that would arrive from Vanguard tomorrow, the cheque due at the end of the month which they would never see, Nikki's expression, pleading and disappointed when she had berated her, but worst of all the sight of Ian and the fury in his eyes as he slammed the door in her face. Intuitively, Megan understood that Ian's first priority was to protect Nikki and nothing was going to stand in his way. It was so obvious. He was totally obsessed by her. What a fool I am, she thought. And then, to her embarrassment, she burst into tears.

225

CHAPTER 29

It was a night for recriminations. Megan tossed and turned and relived the evening a hundred times. At two am she gave up trying to sleep, put on her dressing gown and stumbled into her kitchen, hoping that a cup of coffee with honey would offset the effects of an overdose of champagne and guilt. The champagne had been a little premature, considering the chaotic finale of the evening, and her own undisguised fury had been overplayed and ill-mannered.

Megan felt wretched and ashamed. It should have been enough to point out the error of Nikki's waywardness and the financial effects of her silly lies on both her pocket and lifestyle. Until this evening Megan had not realised that her tension had been activated by a surfeit of old-fashioned jealousy. Instead she had blamed it on their cash flow, their sponsors – anything rather than face the truth. And the truth was she resented Nikki and her marvellous beauty, her vulnerability, her talent – or whichever of these assets kept Ian hanging around like an urchin at a cake shop, uninvited, but always there.

She should have faced up to the truth long ago. After her disastrous visit to Aviemore last month, Ian had made no effort to make amends, or to explain his behaviour. He had not even stayed away, but simply carried on as usual. Most of Nikki's publicity was due to Ian, and his friends, that network of old boys who seemed to control half the British institutions.

'Damn! Damn! Damn!' she said aloud. What a fool she had been to believe that Ian was pushing Nikki to help ISA! What short-sighted complacency had led her to believe that his interest in Nikki was merely professional?

At two-thirty Megan decided to dress and try to work, but when she stared at her accounts, she could only see Nikki's tragic eyes and stricken face.

Megan hated to be cruel, yet she had been, she decided as she put on her tracksuit and fur-lined boots. The memory of Nikki's hurt expression was tormenting her. Nikki had been wrong to blame her skates, but she was new to Western ways and had not understood the consequences of her mistake. She had skated superbly and deserved a little more kindness and less censure. Overwhelmingly, Megan had to admit that she had allowed personal emotions to cloud her judgement. She had been wrong to blame Nikki for Ian's infidelity. She must apologise for her rudeness and she would.

Five minutes later Megan was in her car and driving towards Nikki's home. It was two am, but she knew how much Nikki hated to sleep. She would see if her lights were still on and if they were she would go right in and apologise.

There was a dim light shining behind the rose curtains of Nikki's bedroom and Ian's car was parked at the curbside. For a moment Megan lost control and nearly slammed into it, then she recovered, accelerated and drove aimlessly away.

She parked at the Embankment and walked along the side of the Thames. Her breath was coming in short, sharp gasps, she was cold, but sweating and her stomach was aching.

I fell in love with a man who doesn't even exist, she told herself after a while to try to ease her pain. She had simply created the man she wanted – a dear, loving, unsuccessful scriptwriter whom she would cheerfully have supported for the rest of her life, while he tried and tried again. Her tough and elusive Ian with his deep blue eyes and his stern face which could melt to tenderness and love. There was no such man, she told herself. How stupid can you get, Megan Carroll?

But who was he really? She had to admit that this man whom she had made love to and who had claimed to love her, was a complete mystery. Was he just a Scottish laird in mufti, trying to live down his title? Or was he serious about his writing? Did he yearn to find a niche for himself in the city – perhaps a career in public relations? Well, what business was it of hers, she thought bitterly, because right now Ian was in bed with Nikki. The thought brought a fresh flood of scalding tears to her eyes. God damn you, Ian Mackintosh, she whispered.

Not knowing or caring where she was going, but obsessed with her loss, Megan walked through the night. At dawn she took a taxi back to her car and drove home.

CHAPTER 30

Nikki, too, was walking the pavements, as the first glimmer of grey lit the eastern horizon. She hated to be alone, and after the glamour and excitement of the party following her debut, she could not bear to let joy slip through her fingers. Ian had brought her home, but she had slipped out the back way, avoiding her guard. Parties should last forever, she thought sadly.

How strange it was in the West, in some ways better than she had expected, but in other ways not. It was satisfying to have her own stylish red sports car and soon she would have a licence – amazing to have her own pretty cottage and soon it would be filled with people all the time. She felt dazzled by the amount of expensive possessions she owned, and she had done all this herself, with her skating. Recently her self-confidence had surged to the point of vanity. She knew this, but at the same time she had something to be proud of, she told herself frequently. She could laugh when she thought of those terrible days in Moscow when she had to fight to get on the ice.

At the same time, she had to admit that her new and exalted position had not brought her much happiness – or friends. She was lonely, and angry because she was lonely.

She walked for hours, past curtained windows, a few with lights shining, past closed pubs and restaurants, while her grief was flowing through her like the ebb tide. She felt it trickling into her bloodstream, permeating each part of her until she was engulfed by the flood surging through her body and her limbs. She gave herself up utterly, devotedly, preferring sorrow to guilt which in turn had replaced the euphoria of the excitement and champagne. It was not her fault, she thought crossly. Her skates were faulty. Yes they were. Was she to be punished for telling the truth?

Nikki felt sad about Megan. In some strange and inexplicable manner, Nikki had felt a bond with her and even with ISA's office team. It was the closest she had come to a family feeling. Now Megan had repudiated her, just because she had blamed her skates for slipping. The truth was, Megan hated her.

Why? Why? She longed to be accepted, to have a friend, but there was no way to penetrate the barriers Megan and Maureen had created. The sternly-guarded privacy and individualism of the people here frightened Nikki. Russian comradeship and the habitual intrusion into each other's privacy was entirely missing. In a way, it was a relief, but it also made for loneliness.

Nikki had hardly ever been physically alone, but as far back as she could remember, she had felt lonely. She was convinced that no one knew about the lost girl who cowered behind her extroverted behaviour.

Nikki could remember exactly when her loneliness began.

She had been five years old and hiding behind the coatstand near the front door of their Moscow apartment, waiting for Papa to come home. She had been very cold there, but if Nana found her she would be carried off to the nursery. Papa loved her, she knew, but Nana tried to keep her away from him. Then, at last, she had heard his footsteps. She waited until he was in the hall, then rushed to smother him with her hugs. Papa had pushed her away and called the housekeeper. He had not spoken to her at all, not even hello, but he had shouted at the housekeeper. He had an important meeting and the child must be kept in her quarters, he had said. When he wanted her, he would send for her.

The housekeeper was not all that bad, after all. She had carried the sobbing Nikki to the warm kitchen and given her some cake. Afterwards, Nikki had curled up on the settee pretending to be asleep and listened to Nana grumbling to her friend: 'It's a crying shame the way he hates that child. Since her mother left he hasn't said two words to her. His blessed party meetings – that's all he thinks about. If this poor lamb disappeared tomorrow he'd be relieved, and that's a fact.'

Slate roofs and window boxes full of spring flowers. It was April and dawn was breaking earlier than usual. The river was gently lapping at the embankment. In time she would make friends, she promised herself. She thought about the evening and her triumph on the ice, and relived the applause and the praise many times, until she had sucked every shred of satisfaction from her memories.

On impulse she walked into a telephone kiosk and telephoned the number Michel had given her. Her change was almost exhausted by the time she was put through. He sounded sleepy and irritable.

'Hey Michel,' she called out. 'Nikki here. I'm walking round London looking for a party. Do you know where I can find one? ... You do? ... Of course two's enough for a party – those are the best parties. I'll wait here for you,' she said, giving him the name of the street on the sign opposite.

She hated to replace the receiver, but she did. Glancing at her watch she carefully counted the minutes that she would have to wait. Twenty minutes at the most. Michel was not that bad. A bit of a tease, but she sensed his underlying kindness. No, not bad at all, she decided, although at that moment anyone would be better than no one. At least with Michel she could be sure that she would not be lonely for the next few hours.

CHAPTER 31

Spring in Arosa. Although the season had been officially closed since just after Easter, the snow was still thick on the ground and light flakes were drifting in the wind. The streets were empty, the shops shuttered and one by one the villagers were leaving for their six week holiday before welcoming the summer season.

The small inn felt and smelt like all Swiss inns during the off-season, Wolf thought gloomily as he waited in the tiny foyer which was just large enough for two armchairs and his luggage. Most of the staff were on holiday. The dreary rumble of the vacuum cleaner echoed in empty corridors and the room smelt musty.

Wolf rang the bell for the third time and endured the sour face of the manageress who plodded out to see what he wanted. The season had closed, she told him impatiently, and so had the hotel.

'But you have a few skiers staying here,' Wolf insisted.

She sniffed and pressed her lips together. Her expression defined her views of skiers who hung on when ski lifts, shops and restaurants had closed, and who made their way up the mountain on foot each morning, risking avalanches and the villagers' displeasure.

She was an obstinate old woman and would not book Wolf into the hotel. Eventually Wolf left in a temper. He telephoned his London travel agency from the public telephone in the post office, who, in turn, contacted Wolf's airline to put pressure on the hotel management. When Wolf returned two hours later, his luggage had been moved to a bedroom and the manageress, looking furious, informed him that he could stay until noon the next day. This was her holiday, he must understand. She worked hard for two seasons a year; she must have her rest.

'Tough!' he thought angrily, feeling amazed that the change

231

of season could turn the amiable, smiling hostess he remembered, into a bad tempered old frump.

Jacqui was on the piste, he was told, and would probably return at dusk. Wolf decided to spend the next few hours searching for off-season accommodation and research the possibility of using the hospital's helicopter pad. He returned to the hotel in the late afternoon and passed an hour drinking beer on the balcony overlooking the road. He was still there when he heard youthful voices yelling to each other. Why do the young always shout? he wondered, as the skiers gathered in the doorway of the ski room, kicking the snow from their boots. Jacqui was at her quarrelsome best.

'I'm staying here until the piste's melted,' she shouted. 'If you don't like climbing, why don't you piss off home?' She was bareheaded and hunched with the cold. Then she looked up and her eyes widened with shock. Exhaustion and joy showed on her face as she smiled at him, ran up the stairs and flung herself into a chair. 'Wow!' she said. 'Whatever? Nevermind, I'm starved. Feeeed me! You can tell me all about it while I eat.' Then she laughed. She had a low, musical laugh and Wolf was jolted by it.

'On second thoughts I'm cold, let's move inside,' she said. 'Can I have a drink? Something warm; I'm frozen right through.'

The restaurant had been painstakingly decorated to look exactly what it was – an alpine restaurant, from the dark wooden beams in the ceiling and alcoves to the painted plates and cuckoo clock. There were dried summer flowers in the vase on the table and a tantalising aroma of barley soup drifted from the kitchen.

Wolf ordered drinks for both of them, Scotch on ice for him and mulled wine for Jacqui, and soup for both of them, followed by *fondue bourguignon* and fruit tart with cream.

Jacqui was drinking steadily. 'Now,' she said. 'now that you've satisfied my thirst and my food is being prepared, you can satisfy my curiosity.'

Wolf leaned back and told her of the joys of summer skiing on a glacier, and how vital it was that she train throughout the summer months. That was why he was there, he explained, although he had been afraid he would miss her. Business had kept him in America until the previous day, but he had arranged to spend most of summer skiing with Jacqui. He had found a small chalet for hire, and persuaded the hospital to share their helicopter pad in the off-season.

'A helicopter drop – wow, that's tremendous,' she said shyly.

He tried not to notice how lovely she was, and the way her eyes shone with happiness when she looked at him, or the disturbing pleasure he felt at seeing her again. He was here because she was part of his plan. She fitted into the scheme he had dreamed up years ago in Denver, and which he had carefully activated year after year. He said: 'How long are you planning to stay here?'

'I don't know,' she grimaced. 'Come up with me tomorrow. Please! It's a real slog. It takes six hours to get up there and half an hour to come down. The snow's fantastic. I don't know why they close the lifts this early.'

'Even the Swiss need to rest occasionally,' Wolf said smiling. Jacqui reached out and grabbed his hand in an impulsive gesture. Then she grinned as if to apologise. 'The others are packing up tonight,' she explained. 'I wanted to stay on. Say you'll come with me tomorrow. Then we'll call it a day. I don't think I can take much more of the climbing. My legs are killing me.'

Wolf nodded. 'I can't return until mid-June. What will you do meantime?'

She made a mock grimace. 'Megan insists I placate some of her sponsors. There's four different photographic sessions scheduled for May and June and I'm supposed to open a new sports centre some time in May. I try to forget these things.' Jacqui took a long gulp of her wine. 'Well it's been grand here,' she said regretfully.

Jacqui's voice rambled on describing the many thrills and spills of the past month.

Wolf hated the feeling of warmth that was flooding through his whole being. He smiled, pushing love away, and forced himself to concentrate on his plans, but he could not squash all of his regrets. She was so tender, so brimful of youthful emotions, so trusting.

'Have you been keeping up with the finance news?' he asked her casually. 'Vanguard stock is still rising. It can't go on forever. You should take your profits now and sell out. Why don't you give me your power of attorney?' he argued persuasively. 'I'll sell your shares as they peak, hold back enough cash to buy them back for you when they fall to more realistic levels. With your profits I'll sell you a parcel of my new oil producing company. Jacqui, listen to me,' he said earnestly. 'You'll be right in at the ground floor. What have you got to lose? You land up with the same amount of Vanguard stock and an oil well or two.'

'You're a dear,' Jacqui said, suddenly hugging Wolf. 'I don't deserve to have you looking after my interests. I don't know why I held back for so long about those shares. Some misguided feeling of loyalty, I suppose. I guess I'm just a coward at heart.'

'Not you. Never you,' he said. 'As for loyalty. What harm can it do anyone? You'll land up much richer.'

'Well, I don't know about that, but I'll sign the documents whenever you like.'

'How about now,' Wolf said. 'I was hoping you'd come to your senses while they're still at their peak, so I brought the documents with me.'

It took only a few seconds and the grumbling Swiss housekeeper was lured from the kitchen with a hefty tip to witness the deal.

'Now about my plans for us,' Wolf smiled falsely and painfully at Jacqui. 'There's plenty of snow up there on the glacier throughout the year, and the best way to get there is by helicopter. So I've hired a helicopter, a pilot and a chalet from mid-June through to August. How about it?'

'Sure,' Jacqui said in a small quiet voice, thinking: 'I hope to God Mother never finds out.'

CHAPTER 32

Mother was standing at the window of her office staring out to sea. She was feeling depressed and uneasy and she wondered why. There was no time for emotional weakness right now. Eleanor was at war. The sports industry was dominated by a handful of powerful, multi-national companies who fought for every per cent of market share with all the clout they could muster – fierce and merciless as ancient gladiators – and the world was their arena.

The real winners were not the skiers and the swimmers and the athletes who gave their all in heroic pursuits of excellence and who basked in the glory of public adulation. No, they were the legitimate prey for those whose ambitions depended upon manipulating public attention – to sell their creeds, or their products. She should know, she was leading the pack. To Eleanor, a gold medal at the Olympic Games meant one thing only, another few percentage points notched up in world markets with the subsequent millions of dollars of additional sales.

It hadn't always been like that. Heavens, no. She was as responsible as anyone else for the change. When she first joined the sports industry it had been wide open: a happy retiring home for ex-sportsmen.

She remembered her first year in America so vividly. Within a month of her arrival, she had landed a job with a large sports wholesaler, selling winter sports gear to retailers. In those days she had never asked for a signed contract. The sports dealers' word was their bond and you could count on them to pay their bills within thirty days and buy you lunch into the bargain.

Then big businessmen had climbed in and most of the small men had been forced out in the next few decades of thrusting growth into international markets. Now the big expansion era was over. Most markets were at saturation point, and growth was restricted to the population increase. Vanguard was facing a period of consolidation, which made it all the more remarkable that someone was after her business. Meagre profits were on the cards for the next few years and with the increased competition she would have to fight even harder to retain her worldwide market share. Briefly, she thought of Nikola Petrovna and gritted her teeth in temper. Then, on impulse, Eleanor grabbed the telephone and dialled her broker in New York.

'Yes, it could be a straightforward takeover bid,' he agreed hesitatingly in response to her question. 'On the other hand it could be corporate raiders. Let's face it, Eleanor, your shares were slightly undervalued and dividends have been on the low side.' He paused to give Eleanor time to disagree vehemently. Then he went on: 'So far I've not been able to find out who the buyers are. They're hiding behind several nominees, but I'll get there eventually. I'm sorry Eleanor, I told you all I knew yesterday. I don't think you should be over-anxious. Between your family and members of your staff you control forty-one per cent of Vanguard stock, I seem to remember.'

'That's correct,' Eleanor said.

'I would think you had nothing to worry about.'

'Yes,' she said without conviction and replaced the receiver.

For a while Eleanor sat quietly doodling on a pad, investigating a dozen ideas in her mind. Then she sat up and called her secretary. Five minutes later she was speaking to the managing director of her New York advertising agency. '... a massive advertising campaign ...' she was dictating forcefully. 'Build it around the new blood at Vanguard ... the younger management, as well as the young champions we sponsor – and particularly my daughter. Yes, that's what I said, my daughter, Jacqui. She's being groomed for the Winter Olympics. This has got to be the biggest campaign you've ever done for us and I want it in a hurry,' She went on to explain the ideas she had. When she flung down the receiver she felt drained; her blouse was wet with perspiration, but she felt more confident.

It was time for the shrink, and since she was too tired for anything else, there was no point in cancelling her appointment.

As usual, Gundelfinger was sitting in the corner on his high-backed chair looking grave and pale and not very healthy.

'You're getting a paunch,' Eleanor said rudely. 'Comes from sitting here all day. You should try to take some exercise from time to time.'

'I'll note your advice,' he said dryly.

'Don't you ever get any fun,' she said. 'I'm beginning to worry about you.' She took off her gloves and bag and threw them on the table beside the couch.

'I want you to tell me about your home again,' Gundelfinger said without any preamble.

'We've been through all that.' Eleanor squirmed with irritation. 'Must I keep repeating myself every damned time.'

'I think it's relevant, Eleanor. There's something that seems to upset you whenever you tell me about your home.'

'Poverty, that's what upsets me ...'

'No,' he interrupted her. 'I don't think poverty ever upset you. You're a fighter, Eleanor, you can cope with tangible problems. It's the intangibles you can't handle.'

She sat hunched and sulky glaring at her fingernails until Gundelfinger said: 'Cycle home from school and tell me all about it.'

'What's there to tell? It was a long way; sometimes I was tired, but it was always lovely because you could look right down over the firth and you could see Invergordon in the distance,' Her voice was warming to her story. She came alive when she remembered her home and she sounded younger and fired with enthusiasm. 'Further up the mountain there was a bend and after that you could only see the moors,' she explained, 'and sometimes the deer would go bounding away over the fences up into the mountain mist. Most times I could see the croft from far off and I used to cycle faster until the track became too steep and then I would walk the rest of the way, pushing my bike. I used to wonder what Mum had on the stove for tea. I was always that hungry.'

She broke off and once again Gundelfinger noticed the almost imperceptible stiffening of her fingers as they crushed a ball of tissues. It was always the same.

Then she said: 'Of course it was warm in the croft ...'

'Hold it, Eleanor. I want you to go back to the bend in the hill, where you can see the croft for the first time. Start walking

237

towards it and tell me what you see?'

'Why, nothing of course, nothing more than what I've always told you. The heather, the stream, stepping stones over it.' Once again she shivered slightly.

'And?'

'What do you mean *and*?' she asked aggressively. She sat up abruptly, swung her legs over the couch and glared at him.

'If it's too painful, Eleanor, we can skip it.'

'Painful? Daft would describe it better.'

'Well, humour me, then. You can do that, can't you?'

'At one hundred and fifty dollars an hour?'

'Okay, we'll take this session for nothing.'

'I'm sorry, I didn't mean that.' She sighed and lay back. Then she closed her eyes. 'I see the croft and heather and the stream and I'm making my way across the stream and Lucy is running around in circles splashing me and barking and making a nuisance of herself.'

'Lucy?'

'My dog.'

'You never mentioned your dog before.'

'I guess I forgot.'

'Did you love her?'

'Most kids love their dogs.'

'And what happened to her?'

'She disappeared.'

'That must have been hurtful?'

'Not as hurtful as having her at home.' Her hand was fumbling towards the tissue box. Gundelfinger leaned forward and kicked it towards her.

'I can't see the point of talking about a dog,' she said in a high-pitched, croaky voice.

'Because you always avoid remembering. There must be a reason for that. Why is that, Eleanor?'

'It was a sad story.'

'Tell me about it,' he said gently.

'Must I?' she said in a small muffled voice.

'I think you should try.'

'Well, you must remember times were hard. The war was over, but we were still on rationing and one day Lucy stole a chicken. She killed it and ate a bit of it. Dad found her and gave her the thrashing of her life and he took the remains of the chicken and he tied it around her neck.'

'I see.'

'No, you don't see at all. You couldn't possibly imagine the smell – later that is when the chicken went rotten. It was the habit, you see,' she went on tonelessly. 'To teach the dog not to steal, but this was the first time Lucy had done that. I expect the temptation was too much for her. We were all short of meat in those days.

'The chicken went green and its feathers fell out and the smell became so bad that we couldn't let Lucy in the house. But still Dad wouldn't let me take the chicken off. She had to learn, or else be shot. Lucy came out in sores – a sort of eczema, I suppose – and she was all itchy and stinking and she took to crawling around on her belly. Couldn't look any of us in the face. And one day she ran away. I never saw her again. Maybe she was run over, maybe she died. I searched for her for days. I don't know ...' Her voice trailed off disconsolately.

'Is that what happens to people who steal, Eleanor? A bad dose of itchy eczema?'

She looked up startled and angry. 'I don't like whatever it is you're implying,' she said, but the rigidity of her shoulders revealed her inner tension.

'So what did you steal, Eleanor?'

There was a muffled sob. 'Amongst other things I stole Vanguard,' she said.

'Do you think there could be a link between this childhood nightmare and your present condition? Are guilt and eczema synonymous in your mind?'

There was no answer. Then Eleanor sat crouched forward with her hands over her face.

'Eleanor,' Gundelfinger said, gripping her tightly by one shoulder. 'Whatever you did, I'm sure you had a good reason for it. I have the greatest admiration for you. I'm going out for lunch. You've got an hour here. No one will disturb you. Put the catch down when you leave.'

Eleanor held her breath until she heard the door shut and the lift open and close again. Then she flung herself onto the couch and sobbed as if it had happened only yesterday.

CHAPTER 33

Seven-thirty am on a cold Monday morning. It was the second of May, but so far there had been no sign of warmer weather and rain was pounding the windowpanes, but in typically British fashion, the central heating had been turned off for the summer months and consequently it was freezing in the office. It was mornings like these that made Megan long for home. She shivered and turned her attention to her work basket as she tried to come to terms with a bewildering variety of problems.

First and foremost was the lawyer's letter that had been delivered yesterday. 'The Vanguard-Petrovna contract was hereby cancelled because one of the clauses (specifically clause 15) which stated: *"The athlete shall not publicly ridicule or criticise any articles of sports equipment or clothing, manufactured or distributed by Vanguard"* had been broken.' In addition, Vanguard were suing for three million dollars, for damages sustained firstly, by the derogatory statement made live on British television, and secondly, for losses sustained from the break-off of the current advertising campaign centred around Ms Nikola Petrovna. There was much more, all of it bad. Megan flung the document on her desk.

Since yesterday she had tried repeatedly for an appointment with Eleanor Douglas, but Eleanor refused to see her.

There was nothing else she could do right now. It took a great effort of will to pull over her file and start on the rest of the day's problems.

Vanguard had won as far as compensation for Conrad was concerned. Her lawyer had advised her to drop the case; Vanguard would not pay and there was nothing she could do about it. There and then she decided to try for an American athletic scholarship for him. She settled down to dictate several letters to American universities and she was still busy when she heard the tip-tap of Maureen's shoes and the scent of heady perfume which always preceded her.

'Hi,' she called. 'You're early.'

'I thought I'd find you here,' Maureen retorted 'and I didn't want the kettle to boil dry – but it did. I think it's still working.'

She hurried away and returned shortly afterwards with a tray of coffee and the morning's mail. 'Hark at this,' she said as she opened the first letter. 'Petunia's father wants the Channel crossing to be brought forward to June.'

'Forget it,' Megan said, snatching the letter. 'I spent a week selling the advertising. I'm not going to waste more time changing the dates. Besides, August is warmer. Everything's been organised and booked, right down to a light aircraft with a streamer reading: "Kola-pep for those who dare." '

'Ugh! A pantomime!'

'Well, I could have done better,' Megan said thoughtfully, 'but my heart wasn't in it. Let's get a press release out. Maybe a few more sponsors will jump in boots and all.'

Maureen picked up her notebook.

'On August five, Petunia Prestwick will attempt a Channel crossing from Calais to Dover,' Megan began. 'Aged fifteen years and four months, Petunia will be the youngest girl to attempt this ... this ... Maureen, do you think she's the youngest?'

'Leave it to me,' Maureen said. 'I'll check it out, draft a press release and show it to you in the morning.'

'Good,' Megan said.

'Megan,' Maureen began hesitatingly. 'Do you think we're doing the right thing with Petunia?'

Megan looked up guiltily. 'Right from what point of view – from the bank's point of view – really – need you ask?' She drummed her fingers angrily.

'Sorry I spoke, I'm sure, but Megan, a year ago you would have refused to handle something like this.' Her full, blood red lips turned down in a pout and black eyes flashed angrily.

Megan ignored Maureen, but she was seething with temper. How dare she be so rude? No wonder she could never keep a man. She was far too outspoken and never pulled her punches. 'Have you tried to get me an appointment with Eleanor Douglas?' she snapped.

'Twice a day. She refuses to see you.'

'I'll have to eat humble pie outside her office again.'

' 'Fraid so. Michel Juric telephoned you three times yesterday. He's in London and he wants you to have lunch with him. He's drafted his article on the London branch of ISA and he wants to check it with you.'

'Tell him to put it in the post,' Megan said angrily.

'I'll try. I don't know why you can't meet him.'

'Because he's an opportunist. Anything interesting in the mail?'

'Bills, several requests to be sponsored. I've put them in the applications file for you to study later. There's a letter from Gunter – he's been selected for the West German Olympic training team and travel documents for Nikki, for two weeks only, enabling her to travel to Sweden for some of the film shots.'

Maureen sighed. Megan was in a filthy mood this morning, which was usually the case lately. She feared for the business, for Megan's stream of creative ideas which kept them going, seemed to have dried up. She flipped over the pages of her notebook. 'We had three calls from Adolpho yesterday. He needs another puff from your famous bellows. He's feeling blue – he's hurt his back and he can't face opening the gym in Manchester.'

'Listen, I'm in no mood to reassure anyone, least of all that nut. Can't you take him off my back?'

'I could try,' Maureen said doubtfully. 'What exactly do you do?'

'I show him the press clippings again, tell him he's wonderful and send him on his way.'

'Is he still on line for the Tarzan part?'

'Only if he wins the Mr Universe title,' Megan explained. 'They're bound to choose the best.'

'Well, I'll give it a go.' She sounded doubtful, which was not like Maureen.

'Next!' Megan cried crisply.

It was almost lunchtime when Ian walked in. 'How about lunch?' he said. 'It's a perfect day for something hot and spicy.'

Megan leaned back and glared at him angrily. 'No thanks,' she said. 'I'm busy and quite honestly you're not welcome here, so I wish you'd stop calling.'

242

'I must see you. It's important – and private. Come on, let's go.'

You monster, Megan thought, but she said: 'All right, sit down – I'm available for a few minutes, and it's private enough here.'

'I was talking to the head of the British Ski Federation a while back,' Ian began, 'and he let slip that the British team will need one hundred and fifty-two thousand pounds to cover their expenses at next year's Winter Olympics. Any chance you can do something to help?'

What's so special about that? she thought, but she said: 'I can try to raise the cash, subject to my company's usual twenty-five per cent commission.' She frowned at him feeling puzzled. 'You've proved yourself an expert at this game, so why don't you do it?' There had been times when Megan had wondered if Ian were hanging around just to learn the business.

'Good heavens. I'm not going to get involved with this sort of thing. Handle it in the usual way.'

Strange guy, she thought. Hadn't he spent weeks doing exactly 'this sort of thing' for Nikki.

'Let's put out a few feelers,' she said. No one could say she let emotions interfere with her business drive, she thought piously. A few minutes later she was speaking to Adele Loots at Magnum. 'There you are,' she said putting the receiver back a few minutes later. 'I'm ninety per cent sure they'll do it.' She did not add that in a roundabout way, they would also be sponsoring Jacqui at the Winter Games – if Jacqui made the Games that was, nor that such a prompt and direct approach had seldom reaped positive results. However, Magnum had been taken over recently by an unknown buyer, and she'd heard they had money to burn for advertising.

'Pretty easy way to make several thousand pounds,' he said sourly.

Megan scowled at him.

'I came to see you about Nikki,' Ian went on. 'Did you know that Nikki and Michel Juric are having an affair? He's bought her a ring. Five small diamonds set around an emerald. For some reason Nikki is being particularly secretive about her relationship with Michel. Did you know about it?'

For a moment Megan felt as if she had been kicked in the stomach. She had difficulty breathing. She wanted to shout:

but what about you … and she? Had Ian been dumped, as Eric had been dumped? 'Can't you run your own romances without coming to me for help?' she snarled. 'You see, Ian, I know everything. I saw your car parked outside Nikki's home in the middle of the night.'

'Checking up,' he said mockingly.

'Actually it was right after her debut. I wanted to tell her I was sorry, but your car was there so I … I drove home,' she said remembering that long and bitter night's walk.

For a moment she thought he was going to walk out: eyes blazing with fury, lips compressed. He ran his hand through his hair in a quick, hesitant manner, turned and opened the door. Then he changed his mind, closed it softly and turned back.

'Megan,' he placed his hands on her desk and leaned forward until he was staring intently into her eyes. 'My car was outside Nikki's door because she went missing. Afterwards she was discovered in Juric's hotel. That's when it started – this affair of theirs.'

She stared up at him in shock. What was he saying? She watched in a daze as Ian sat down and leaned across the desk. 'My address was in the cottage, I mean, my aunt made me the official caretaker, so it was there if the lights went wrong – or anything. So they called me and I came round to help,' he was saying softly.

'Perhaps marrying Michel would be the best thing that could happen to Nikki,' she gabbled, trying to conceal the joy that was surging through her like some physical force, numbing her senses and her limbs. 'She's such a strange girl – difficult to love. I sort of feel responsible and I don't think I'm doing a very good job. But you were so … involved. I assumed a romantic attachment. Wrongly, it seems.' She stared hard at Ian who was watching her with a curious expression on his face.

Then he shrugged. He was still angry with her. Evidently, in Ian's world, people had to trust him. What makes him so special, she thought bitterly.

'Let's just worry about Juric,' Ian said. 'If he plans to marry Nikki she could claim French citizenship, and then I don't know if she'd ever get the British nationality she's been wanting for so long. She would be unable to skate for Britain – I doubt she'd make the Olympic Games. What's more, she'd lose her chance for a gold medal. You might explain that to her, so that she knows the score. On the other hand if he jilts her, it might be even worse. Nikki's a very unhappy young woman lately, and I'm not sure if she could cope with being jilted.'

'She's usually the one who does the jilting,' Megan said. 'Nikki seems to me to be a very tough girl, who's quite capable of looking after herself.'

'You're wrong, but never mind. Just look at it this way,' he said coldly. 'If Nikki goes to France, you've lost your biggest potential profit-earner.'

Ian walked out, leaving her open-mouthed with astonishment. 'Why should Ian care? Was he acting out the role of the jealous, jilted lover? Somehow she did not think so. And did he really think that she would put profits in the way of Nikki's happiness?

Megan leaned back and pushed her work aside. She was feeling emotionally bruised and violated. She felt too confused to think clearly. Instead she leaned back in her chair, folded her hands behind her head and allowed herself the luxury of feeling happy for the first time in weeks.

When Maureen came in later with a cup of coffee she found Megan looking cheerful and quite her old self again, curled up in her favourite armchair, doodling in a notebook. She looked up – a faraway look in her eyes. 'Hi,' she said. 'Oh, thanks for the coffee. I've had this simply *marvellous* idea about Nikki. What d'you think of this?'

CHAPTER 34

Eleanor was sitting in her office scowling unhappily when her secretary knocked and entered.

'Miss Douglas, this parcel came by special delivery,' her secretary said. 'I was asked to put it on your desk personally.'

'You were?' Eleanor glanced at the parcel distastefully. 'Has it occurred to you that it might be a bomb?'

'It's not a bomb,' her secretary said tartly. 'I'll open it myself on my desk and bring it through.'

She returned a few minutes later carrying a mini-video machine, rather similar to the one Eleanor used in her selling days. Reaching forward she switched on the dial, but Eleanor leaned over and snapped it off. 'I'm busy,' she said, looking affronted. 'It's some damned advertising gimmick. Take it through to Nigel.'

'But Miss Douglas ...'

Eleanor frowned and pretended to read the folder on her desk. In fact, she was furious. She should never have hired an American secretary, with her new world democratic views and her irritating habit of taking control. Her previous French secretary would never have dared to interrupt her.

'Please excuse me,' she said, looking up coldly. She returned to her folder. The past four months' share trading in Vanguard stock was alarming reading. No point in trying to hide the obvious – someone was waging war against her. A war she might lose.

She frowned as she skimmed through the papers. Over twenty per cent of publicly held stock had changed hands in the past four months, but her stockbroker had been unable to discover the identity of the major buyer, because a Panamanian offshore company was acting as nominee.

It was not just the trading that was worrying her. Lately there had been a spate of bad press on three continents – the latest was in the morning paper. She skimmed through it:

'*Vanguard Sports, whose image has traditionally been associated with winners, is losing out in the management stakes. For three consecutive years growth and profits have been declining and it looks as if shareholders could be facing a no-win situation in the future with decreased dividends and minimum capital growth ...*'

There was much more but Eleanor could not be bothered to read it since it was obviously biased. How could she possibly maintain the growth rates Vanguard had enjoyed when they had first entered the British and European markets? She had a forty per cent market share in skis, which was phenomenal, and she'd be lucky to hang on to it. To maintain growth she was branching into after-sport fashion sports clothing, but the days of big market growth were over. Manufacturers were hanging on grimly to what they had.

But would the shareholders know that? She thought not. It was a well-known strategy: break the public's faith in the corporation's management, buy the shares up, grab control.

The name of the game right now, was shareholder confidence, but Megan and this wretched Russian skater had played into the enemy's hands with her damaging televised statement.

Eleanor leaned back and thought about the twenty-five years grind which had pushed Vanguard to the forefront of the world's winter sports goods manufacturers. Rapid expansion had cost money, more cash than she had available. That was why she had offered the parcels of Vanguard stock to the public, on three occasions. God, how she had worked: she had walked the pavements for eight hours a day, lugging that damned video machine and the video tapes which featured the big names she sponsored to sell her products.

With a sudden feeling of shame, she remembered how well she had been received by the sports traders when she trudged in with just such a gimmick as this. They always brought her a comfortable chair, a cup of tea and biscuits and listened politely, even if they weren't really interested. No doubt there was some eager sales person waiting downstairs for her secretary to call them.

On impulse she leaned forward and switched on the machine: The music was vaguely familiar, although Eleanor did not know what it was, she had no time to listen to music. It was definitely Russian and as the scene began to materialise from a blur of changing colours, she saw an ice rink and out on to it shot Nikola Petrovna, dressed in her Vanguard outfit, which was a damn cheek, considering they'd dropped her.

She zoomed to the centre of the rink at speed and leaping into the air, performed a movement that Eleanor had never before seen. It was dangerous and damned difficult and remembering her skating days, Eleanor felt a surge of envy for this sprite-like Russian skater as she sat spellbound for the next five minutes watching Nikki skate and perform her difficult piece twice more before the finale.

The scene faded and the commentator, who sounded remarkably like Megan Carroll, took over: 'You have just witnessed Nikola Petrovna performing her unique Cossack Whirl – the first public viewing of the most difficult skating step ever attempted. It was made possible by the creation of a unique skating blade, a perfect cutting edge, designed by Vanguard Sports for Nikola Petrovna to perform her intricate skating routine. Naturally, the boot is called Petrovna.'

'Oh God!' Eleanor switched off the set, but on second thoughts ran it back to the beginning and watched Nikki skate again and again. She was a winner – that girl. A natural public draw – and for her beauty and personality, as much as for her skating. She knew it would be madness to allow any other sports manufacturer to sign her up.

There was a timid knock on the door. Her secretary pushed her head around the door. 'Excuse me, Miss Douglas, I heard you switch on that video. Don't you think you ought to see poor Megan Carroll? She's been sitting downstairs for hours.'

'Oh, show her in if you must,' Eleanor said angrily. 'Thank the Lord you never took up advertising,' she said as Megan walked in.

Megan flushed. Then she laughed. 'Well ... of course ... your agency will work on the idea.'

'What idea? If I had to rely on you, I'd go bust. Forget that crazy idea. What I have to say won't take long, Megan. I've decided to reinstate Miss Petrovna's contract. I've come to the conclusion that she was misinformed about the contract, that she is unused to dealing with business people, and quite honestly she said the first thing that came into her head to excuse her slip. If anything, you're to blame for not anticipating it.

'Let's face it, Megan, I've never seen such exquisite skating, or such beauty. She looks kind of pure and a little lost. I'm sure she meant no harm. The poor child must be hopelessly confused in the West. Let's just forget about it. Now if you'll excuse me ... oh, and take that video with you.'

'Thank you,' Megan said. 'That's it then.' For a moment she hesitated. *When you've made a sale, shut your mouth and make yourself scarce. Don't overkill.* She could hear Oberholtzer's words ringing in her ears as she stood up and walked out. Of course, Eleanor didn't really have an alternative, Megan told herself as she hailed a taxi for Nice Airport.

CHAPTER 35

At that moment this 'Poor child' looked neither pure nor confused. She lay immodestly spreadeagled, naked on the bed, and beside her lay Michel, propped on one elbow, moodily watching her. She was examining her arms with a slight frown. There were freckles appearing on her white skin after their day in the country and clearly she was displeased with this. She kept rubbing her index finger over the marks as if this would erase them.

She glanced up and smiled at Michel, and her green eyes lit up from some inner glow, while her mouth curled into two dimples, revealing her large, glistening teeth. Watching her, Michel thought that her smile, like her love making, was for herself.

'It was good, da?'

'Yes,' he lied.

Nothing could be further from the truth, he thought unkindly. Their love-making had been exhausting, gymnastic and for him, at least, quite unsatisfying for there had been no emotional rapport. Nor would there ever be, he thought watching Nikki moodily.

Since their meeting at the park a month ago, he had fallen in love with her beauty, her pathos and her incredible skating. He had made love to her for the first time after her Earl's Court debut, and even then he had been puzzled by her overwhelming enthusiasm for sex, her lack of curiosity about him and her inability to relate to him. This had not changed during their hectic affair. He knew her now about as well as when he first set eyes on her. If he lived with her for the next ten years he doubted he would know her better. Emotionally-speaking she was a child and he wondered why. What scar had damamged her so badly that she could not relate to others and had to take refuge in herself and in skating?

There was nothing lacking in her physical desires, he noted as he watched her stroking his belly. She bent over swiftly and ran her tongue around his belly button. He squirmed and in spite of his tiredness he began to feel a stiffening in his loins and legs.

'Let's give it a break, shall we?' He made a half-hearted attempt to sit up, but she pushed him back with one hand and clasped her lips around his penis.

'Oh God, here we go again,' he groaned as he leaned back, unwilling to miss another lunge into this incredibly nubile nymph.

When his penis stood up erect and purplish-swollen she sat back on her heels and smiled triumphantly.

'Help yourself, Nikki,' he said, grinning painfully. 'I haven't the energy. You want it? You take it!'

She sat astride him, her slender waist gyrating, hips swinging forwards and backwards and breasts bouncing to her rhythmic thrusts. Her eyes were turned upwards half-closed and cat-like, her lips hung slack and open and every few minutes her pink tongue darted over them. Two red dots were appearing on either cheek, but slower than usual.

'Hurry Nikki or you'll be left behind,' he said.

'No wait, wait ... please, wait for me,' Nikki gasped.

Michel closed his eyes, blotting out that erotic vision and wondered what the hell he was going to do about Nikki. He had fallen in love, but he was thirty-two, almost double her age. Would it be fair to marry her? Or would it be fair not to? These were the questions that were tormenting him lately. He sensed a tragedy around her, and he wanted to prise it out of her, but he had not succeeded. Michel's talent as a journalist was equal to the most efficient cat burglar. He knew how to gain entry to all types of premises, it didn't take him long to work out if there were valuable secrets locked in the safes hidden deep in every mind, and he had a talent bordering on genius in discovering the precise combination of sympathy and emotional rapport which would unlock these safes and reveal their secrets. Nikki's security system was beyond him, however. The slightest intrusion set off a warning siren which put Nikki into full retreat. He had Nikki's character pretty well taped: apart from her talent, she was not all that different to the average Russian and therefore dominated by three big 'S's: saving-face, suspicion and secretiveness. The former was the overriding drive in Nikki's case and he assumed that shame was responsible for her formidable safety mechanism.

That was all he was ever going to find out. In the meantime he had fallen in love with her. Or was it love? Sometimes he wondered if it were just an overdose of compassion. Nikki needed looking after and he felt himself to be the best person to do this. Who else would ever understand her, as he did.

She was blatantly extroverted about those things that were not of any great importance to her. He knew, for instance, exactly how that poor sod Eric Lamont made love, or failed to make love and numerous other intimate details that Nikki should never relate, but if something was dear to her, then it was held close, away from all others, as if too precious for public exposure. So she had flatly refused to tell Megan, or anyone else, about their relationship. This bothered Michel. He could not see the reason for her secrecy – but felt consoled that he knew at least she cared a lot about him – *or about them*, which was not the same thing at all, he reasoned.

Michel's calculations faded as desire took over. He could feel Nikki's body stiffening as her movements became less contrived and more jerky. He opened his eyes and saw a look of fierce concentration on her face; her fingernails were piercing his thighs and she was groaning softly. Suddenly she gave a soft: 'ooooh', and sat gazing at the ceiling as if entranced by a holy vision. Then she crumpled in a heap on his belly.

Sometimes Michel envied Nikki. Whatever she was doing, she did it in excess. Joy sent her into ecstasy, grief numbed her from all other thoughts and actions. When she made love there was no other thought in her mind, she was all animal passion and afterwards all love and she would coo and fondle him for the next hour at least.

Should he – shouldn't he? he wondered as she wiggled up, eyes closed to snuggle into his shoulder. Yeah, why not? He'd had a dry season lately. He caught her under her shoulders and hoisted her up the bed on to her back and climbed in. Jesus, she was silky smooth and still quivering and pulsating when he came.

Physically she was superb, but she left him feeling sadly rejected. It was not him she loved, it was her need to feel loved that drove her to such erotic lengths. Or perhaps he was getting paranoid about their affair, possibly because of the age difference.

Michel surfaced, abandoning his self-flagellation at last, and saw Nikki watching him. There was a curious smile lurking around her lips and eyes. 'That's the best part,' she said. 'When you come.'

'Why?' he asked feeling surprised, and groping for his cold coffee.

'It's hard for me to explain in English.'

'Try Russian.'

'No, never.' Her lips folded with that superhuman obstinacy he knew so well. Once Nikki had decided to think, speak and live in English that was the way it would be. Pointless to argue with her.

'It is because all your mind and all your body are just for me,' she was explaining. 'For that little moment. Then I don't feel lonely. Then I know you love me. You understand, da?'

Suddenly he did understand – and the realisation was sad. Only physical coupling could fend off her solitude. He sat up, but there was no stopping Nikki now.

'All my life I have felt like an exile, sort of ...'

'Alienated?'

'Yes, thank you – like that. I never feel that I belong to anyone or anything. Do you know, sometimes I have the most curious sensation. I feel as if I have been dropped from outer space, perhaps some flying saucer visited earth and popped me into the nearest available womb. So I have human form, but I don't feel quite like I should, yet I don't know why. Do you believe in flying saucers?'

'No.'

'Oh, but you are crazy,' Nikki gasped. 'It is proved ... too many sightings ... our governments have been trying to keep it quiet.'

'Believe what you want,' Michel said briefly and sleepily. 'I won't argue with you.'

Briefly compassion touched him. She had no religion, that was too bourgeois for Nikki; no patriotism because she had been torn up by the roots; no family; nothing to cling to, and she was taking retrogressive steps into superstition and silly beliefs.

'I believe in love,' he said firmly. 'Nikki, I want you to do something for me.'

'I will, anything,' she murmured, snuggling into her favourite position.

'Everytime you feel like an exile I want you to remember that I love you very deeply, and at that very moment I will be thinking about you and wondering how you are, and what you are doing. Always, and I'll be loving you very much. Will you do that?'

'If you want,' she said without much interest.

Pulling Nikki closer into his shoulder, he hugged her tightly and fell asleep.

CHAPTER 36

The alarm rang and Jacqui opened her eyes reluctantly. The room was dark and for a moment Jacqui could not remember where she was. Then she gave a grimace of irritation as it all came flooding back. She was in Mother's serviced flat in Mayfair and she must stay there for weeks while she modelled for various sponsors.

Why? Dammit, why? Surely Mother's money was enough, but Megan had sold her hair to Glamour, her skin to Lux soap, and ten hours of modelling to a famous name in aperitifs. She had argued bitterly, but Megan had taunted Jacqui with her desire to be independent. 'You know perfectly well that the money is kept in trust for you. When you relinquish your amateur status, the trust fund will be released. You'll be well off in your own right. Surely that's important to you?'

Independent? Big joke! That was something she would never be, Jacqui thought ruefully. So this morning Jacqui had to finish an assignment at Greenwich studio, where she would sit under spotlights in an imitation Swiss inn, coyly sipping an aperitif, while a freaky model gave her the big come on, although he was really trying to date the photographer.

There was much worse to come. This afternoon she had to attend the opening of a winter sports shop in Kensington and give a talk about skiing. She sat on the edge of the bed and pressed her hands over her face. 'Oh God,' she groaned. 'How horrible!' She knew she was being absurd, but that did not help, either. She would be exposed and vulnerable and she would try to say something meaningful and they would laugh at her. 'It's easy,' Megan had bullied her. 'Tell them why sport is meaningful to you. And for goodness sake be natural. Don't read the speech, learn it by heart. If necessary carry a few key words on a slip of paper to prompt you.'

'Damn,' she murmured. A sudden lurch of her stomach sent

her rushing to the bathroom. I'll never make it, she thought.

How did the darn thing go again, she agonised as she sat in the bath? 'Ladies and gentlemen. Shit! Whoever heard of saying anything so silly,' she mumbled. 'Fellow skiers ...' And then what? She had learned it thoroughly last night. Megan's fault! She had this crazy notion that everyone was as poised and self-confident as her.

Doom was moving inexorably closer. She was going to make a fool of herself and botch-up the opening, which would be tough, because the new and swish sports centre was stocking mainly Vanguard skis and gear.

The shop was filling rapidly with happy young skiers and Jacqui hung around miserably, hiding behind ski racks.

This can't be happening, she thought, as she was led to the temporary stage, introduced and given the microphone. She heard clapping and looked down at a sea of eager faces. Then she opened her mouth, but no sound came.

'Fellow skiers,' she began at last to a titter of laughs.

She seemed to have cotton wool where her brains should be, because her mind had blanked out. 'That so many of you have attended the opening of this new winter sports shop, raises a question I have been thinking about for the past few days – why is skiing so important to us?' she stammered. Now it was all coming back to her.

'For my mother, at Vanguard, the importance is to do with making skis that go faster and bindings that are safer – the technology of sport and its profitability,' she paused and looked around, but that was a mistake, for having caught the eye of a man in the front row, it was difficult to look away again. 'For my agent, the importance of sport is winning. Not winning for its own sake, but for the profits which can be made out of winners by big business which promotes them.'

'Hear, hear!' she heard.

A bit rough, but Megan, you deserve it.

'I'm not good at expressing myself, but when I'm up there, alone on a difficult piste, I'm not in competition with the others, I'm battling against myself, pushing against the limits of my own human ability: "the pursuit of excellence" – that's a phrase I borrowed from a friend. It symbolises the desire in all of us to rise above a humdrum existence – hence the tremendous public adulation of winners.

256

'In turn, this adulation attracts those who would influence public opinion – the marketeers, and the politicians; so the athletes become their natural prey.

'For most of us skiers there's not much to be made out of sport, but a lot of expense goes into it. It's time-consuming, sometimes dangerous, it means making sacrifices, and above all, it's expensive. Just lately it's been brought home to me, just how expensive skiing is and how vital it is that good skiers should be able to get the right financial backing. You can't ski without cash and it would be a pity if it remained a sport only for rich kids. That's why I feel we have to bring our regulations on amateurism up-to-date. As they stand now, it's a sham.

'Today, we serious sportsmen and women, all know how politicized, professionalized and commercialized sport has become, but it's all right as long as we remember that it's only superficial. The compulsion to excel is what's real and important – it's one of the very special heritages of mankind. It's our job to cherish this gift we've been given – and to make sure that all the rest is seen in the right perspective – the wrapping paper round the gift.'

There was a long silence. Jacqui clasped her wet hands together and glanced round nervously.

'Well, that about ties it up,' she said, to a few polite claps. 'Any questions?'

An hour later, the opening ended with a short speech from the manager, and wine with snacks.

It was then that Jacqui came face to face with Rob and for a moment she was so overjoyed to see him she almost lost control. Her stomach lurched, her eyes were pricking. 'Oh! Wow!' She was bursting into tears. She struggled to pull herself together. 'Hey, this is great,' she said shakily. 'What a surprise. What are you doing here?'

'I've sneaked a three week holiday,' Rob told her happily. 'And I checked with Megan when I landed this morning. She told me where to find you.'

'Were you here all the time? I mean? Did you hear?'

'You were tremendous,' he said, wrapping one arm around her. His grey eyes shone with pride and looking up at him, she thought he looked so dear and reliable, with his tawny hair, prominent bone structure, and his kind expression. He seemed to have grown, or had she forgotten how tall and how broad he was. He was muscular, yet he had that look of gentleness about him, which turned her on.

'Let's get out of here,' he said. 'Are you free now?'

'Was it all right?' she asked nervously and urgently when she had said her goodbyes and they were waiting for a taxi.

'I told you – you were real – a real person. The girl I saw hurtling down Mount Yahorina. I've been missing her ever since.'

'I'm never going to do that again,' she said vehemently. 'The wear and tear on my nerves was terrible. It's not worth it.'

'Forget it. I'll take you to supper,' he said.

Jacqui grinned happily. 'I haven't eaten all day, but suddenly I'm starving.'

They ate scallops and prawns at a Soho restaurant, wandered round London's streets, window shopping and watching the crowds, bought grapes from a barrow and ate them together, held hands and laughed, and thought how wonderful it was that ordinary, daily things could be so different when they were shared.

At midnight they returned to Mother's Mayfair flat and Jacqui became haggard and frowned a great deal and complained of feeling tired. She had enjoyed the day carelessly, with no thought of what might follow and now, remembering Aviemore, she loitered at dreary shop windows and became snappish and rude, trying to create a fight.

'I'll leave you then,' Rob said, feeling disappointed. 'I believe you're tired. You don't have to snap and snarl. I understand and I'll go.'

'Don't be so hostile. What are you mad at me or something?' she whined. She looked up sidelong, head tilted, eyes burning, and stood legs straddled, hands on hips, reminding Rob of a chipmunk defending its nest.

Rob caught hold of her, pulled her roughly close to him and tilted her face towards him. 'Goodnight,' he said. Then he kissed her briefly.

'Well, I guess I don't really want to be alone all that much,' she said softly. 'How about coffee? I mean, just coffee.'

'Now you're talking.'

'I guess you think I'm a bit of a prude,' she said when she

had exhausted all the small talk she could think of, finished coffee and washed the mugs. 'It's just that it's such a binding thing, this sex bit. I mean, the last time I felt I sort of belonged to you. Mushy really, but it took me a while to get over it.'

'I quite understand,' Rob said, trying to look older than his years and worldly wise.

'I mean to say, sleeping around is okay on its own. I mean really, who cares? But I can see it sort of chains you up. That is, unless you're a lot tougher than I am.'

'How about snuggling? Is that allowed?'

She giggled. 'You make me feel so silly. I mean, really childish.'

Rob pulled her to her feet and picked her up. She was so light, surely lighter than last time, he thought wonderingly as he carried her through the door to the adjoining room and placed her gently on the bed. 'Just lie next to me, only for a short while. I want to hold you close, for the rest I'll rely on my memory.'

Jacqui snuggled into bed and reached over to switch off the light. Rob smelt delightfully familiar, just like last time, and the softness of his lips and his cheek reminded her of so many feelings and desires she had tried to put out of her mind. She flushed in the darkness and pulled away, but then, after all, it was so pleasant, so she nuzzled back again.

'You and me,' she whispered. 'It's sort of special. Like there's something wonderful about it. What is it?'

'Love,' he murmured hoarsely, pulling her to him. 'I love you, Jacqui.'

They lay close for a long time, content with the nearness of each other and the wonder of touching hands and rubbing noses and lips softly melting into each other. But then she wanted more, and more. She undid the buttons of his shirt and nuzzled her face against his broad, hard chest.

'Why can't I do that?' he whispered.

'I suppose you could,' she murmured. She closed her eyes tightly as she felt Rob fumbling with her clothes for what seemed forever. Then she caught her breath and nearly choked with the sensation of his naked skin against her breasts. 'Oh,' she breathed. 'Oh Rob, it's so dreamy. It would be nice all over. Wouldn't it be nice all over?'

Abandoning shyness, she scrambled out of the rest of her

clothes and tugged and pulled at his trousers. 'Terrible things you men wear,' she said giggling. 'I mean, really, on a balmy May evening – you have all this.'

'Watch out, be careful,' he said flinching.

Jacqui's eyes were becoming accustomed to the dim glow that came from London's lights shining through the curtains. She saw the sweet softness of his penis, moist and wet and gently throbbing against her hand. She bent down and brushed her lips briefly against his skin.

Then Rob moved her gently from his shoulder and bent over her to kiss her breasts and her belly and the beautiful soft skin between her thighs. She made little whimpers of joy as she lay, eyes closed, mouth curled into a gentle smile.

'Oh dear, oh dear,' she moaned gently. 'You must do it. You must. I can't stand this feeling of wanting you so.'

Yet Rob held back. Far greater than sexual need, was his desire to make her his. To marry her and take her home where he could guard her and protect her. Surely she could feel they were indivisibly entwined – as married as ever they would be? What else was necessary? He stared down feeling fiercely possessive, longing to show the world that she was his girl.

As if sensing his mood, Jacqui frowned and opened her eyes. 'Just love me,' she said. 'No ties, no mushy feelings. Let's just enjoy this – this night.'

She pulled him down, wound her legs around his buttocks and her arms around his neck.

No ties? What was the matter with her? She was so elusive and immature. Tenderness fled. Rob thrust long and hard and pushed his mouth over hers. She groaned slightly and moved her head aside. At least at this moment she was wholly his. He longed to prolong this act forever.

Even after Rob climaxed he hung on tightly, unwilling to loosen his grip on her, or to roll back on to the bed.

So they lay close together, nose to nose, smiling secretly at each other. Then Rob thought. It's all right. I was imagining things. She's mine. She always has been. He chuckled softly to himself.

'Why do you laugh?' she asked, snuggling hard against him and brushing her lips over his chest.

'I was trying to picture you coping with housework. I wonder how you'll manage. I think I'll have to try to get a housekeeper.'

She stirred uneasily, and he felt the tension in her body and it alarmed him.

'You must marry me,' he said urgently. 'Why else are we here? Why would we do this if we didn't love each other?'

'I love you,' she whispered, 'but I have other commitments. I'm not ready for marriage, Rob. First I'm going to train and try to make the British team for the Winter Games. I wouldn't let anything stand in my way,' she whispered.

'I'll wait,' Rob said. 'But come back with me now, for the off-season. Have a look round. I know you'll love it back home.'

'I'm going to train on a glacier with someone – actually it's Wolf Muller,' she mumbled, feeling embarrassed. 'You haven't met him, but I mentioned him before. And I'm leaving next week. It's something I have to do,' she said determinedly. 'He's hired a helicopter and we're going to fly up in the early morning and ski down. It'll be something tremendous. Don't you think so?'

'Why?' he said, moving away from her. He rolled over on to his back and clasped his hands behind his head. 'Why would you want to do that? I thought you said you loved me. Didn't I hear you say that. Not once, but many times.'

'I love you and I love Wolf, too,' she said miserably.

'Have you ...?' His voice came out like a growl.

'No,' she said. 'It's a different sort of love. What you and I share ... well, I'll never feel that way about someone else.'

'Give him up,' Rob pleaded. 'I'll make it up to you. We'll have a holiday in South America. Don't go with Wolf.'

'I must,' she said softly. She turned her back on him and pretended to be asleep. How could she explain that in some strange way Wolf was a part of her life. And even if she married Rob one day, Wolf would still be a part of her life. It was impossible to explain a crazy thing like that.

Rob fell asleep eventually, but Jacqui lay listening to his deep breathing worrying about her dilemma. She knew she loved both Rob and Wolf passionately. That wasn't right. Yet she could not bear to part with either one of them. They were both so dear to her, but in different ways. Suddenly she hated this new feeling of caring which made her so vulnerable, and so powerless.

Eventually she, too, fell asleep.

Rob woke in the early morning, lifted himself on his elbow

and gazed long and hungrily at Jacqui. She looked so young, with her mouth slightly open, her hair tangled over the pillow and the dark smudges under her eyes.

He felt he was beginning to understand her. All her life she had been spoiled in possessions, but deprived of love. She had always had her own way, but lately she was discovering that she did not have the things she really wanted – her own self-respect instead of her mother's wealth, and her parent's love. A father! Rob knew about the penchant fatherless girls have for older men. He would just have to wait and hope. Yet the thought of Jacqui spending three months with Wolf was anathema to him. His pride would not allow him to wait around and see what was left for him at the end of the day. Besides, he was scared for Jacqui. There was something wrong about Wolf's interest and feigned affection. Instinctively Rob knew this.

He got up quietly, took his clothes and tip-toed into the bathroom. When he returned Jacqui was still asleep. There was a writing pad on the dressing table with a pen and he pulled it towards him and wrote: *'If you ever need me – if the real Jacqui ever needs me, this is where you can find me. I love you. Rob.*

He wrote down his address and telephone number. Then he left, closing the door quietly behind him.

CHAPTER 37

Adolpho's studio was in a plush block overlooking Hampstead Heath. Maureen arrived sharp at three and stood gawping in the open doorway. She had never seen anything like it: one entire wall was a montage of girlie posters pasted over each other in a riot of buttocks and boobs; ultra modern easy chairs of white suede stretched over black tubular steel frames into weird shapes were strewn around the marble floor, a jacuzzi in the corner was reflected a dozen times in the mirrored wall behind. It was warm and steamy, ideal for the jungle of plants which were flourishing under their ultra-voilet spotlamps in the ceiling. Maureen was already perspiring as she flung her coat over a chair.

'Come in, little one. Come in and join me,' Adolpho bellowed from one faraway corner. His voice was deep-throated and masculine, but his phoney Italian accent jarred on her ears.

'Damn,' she said. Except for his sun-goggles, Adolpho was naked, stretched on a couch under three revolving suntan lamps.

'You're supposed to be packed and ready to go,' she called out, tremulously. She could not take her eyes off that magnificent hulk spread out on the slab.

'Come and join me, baby,' he called out. 'Strip off and treat yourself to a tan.'

'I am tanned,' she retorted, 'by forty centuries of African sunshine. So you know what you can do with your silly little lamps.'

Adolpho looked round in amazement as she strode belligerently into the room. 'You can get your ass off there, Adolpho. You've got a train to catch and I'm here to make sure you catch it. Tell you one thing, you've got a real talent for dodging your commitments.'

Adolpho sat up cautiously, grabbed a towel as he slid off the couch and wrapped it round his waist. 'Are you Maureen?' he asked in amazement. 'I always thought-a you were English.'

'I am English, you cockney creep,' she said bitterly.

'I'm not a racialist,' he said. 'Want to come over here and find out?'

Maureen's eyes roved over the famous torso longingly. Every square inch of him screamed sex appeal: from his bushy black hair and thick long eyebrows, his brown eyes with the blatant message 'love me' beaming out of them, his square jaw and white teeth, his strong sinewy neck to his rock-like shoulders and his broad torso covered in black hairs, not forgetting those well-shaped strong legs. Looking down she felt she could even fall in love with his feet. Pity about the towel.

'Don't give me that Eyetie crap,' she said crisply. 'I know you're London born. Your Dad was Italian, your Mum's a Londoner. I even know where you were brought up.'

He shrugged. 'That makes me Italian, too. Doesn't it?'

'Have it your own way,' she said shrugging. 'But hurry.'

'I think you are very brave,' Adolpho said, letting his eyes rove lasciviously over her body. 'Coming into my den all alone.'

'Nothing brave about it,' Maureen retorted. 'I've come to put you on the train. You must get to Manchester, Adolpho, or they'll have your nuts in the cracker. You can't monkey about with Universal Bodybuilding Inc. Tough crew! They get their money's worth and you've spent your share of it, I bet a shilling.'

'Money, money money, you sound-a just like your boss.'

'I expect I do. She taught me the business. Phew, it's hot in here. Clammy really. It's all right for you, stripped half naked, but I'm slowly cooking. Come on, let's get your overnight bag packed. You're going to be on that train to Manchester if I have to carry you there.'

'That's-a very funny. You think you're in charge, huh? Well, I'm not-a going. I'm ill! They can manage without me.' He backed away to a couch covered in towels and sat heavily on it. Then he leaned forward with his elbows on his knees, cupping his chin in his hands and stared at his feet with an expression of deep melancholy.

Maureen sat on the couch beside him and put one hand on his shoulder. 'What's up, Adolpho? You don't have to worry, you'll be a wow. All you have to do is flex those famous muscles – they only want to look at you.'

He sighed. 'Like hell. They're gonna look for trouble. Every kid who's ever thrown a punch is going to try to pick a fight. Just to boast they laid me out.'

'Well, you've got to go anyway. I'll pack. Be back in a jiffy.'

'Want me to get you a bodyguard?' She called from the small adjoining room where Adolpho slept. 'You could say he was your assistant.'

'Last time I tried that I got labelled as a poof, so Megan made me get rid of him.'

Maureen stopped short, mouth open with astonishment. She walked slowly back towards Adolpho, with his dressing gown over one shoulder, like a sleep walker with her face set in lines of lustful curiosity. 'Well aren't you?'

'You're revolting,' he said. 'Go back to Megan.'

She said: 'It's just that you've never been seen with a girl.'

'Girl's don't-a like me.'

'Ever given them half a chance,' she said sidling closer. 'Ever had a girlfriend, Adolpho?'

He turned and glared at her in a feigned indignation. It was phony, Maureen decided, like the rest of him. All the same, he couldn't conceal the longing in his cocker spaniel eyes.

'Ever had a boyfriend?' she persisted.

Adolpho winced visibly and closed his eyes.

'I'm sorry. Don't mind me. None of my business. You're just like you were made – nothing you can do about that. Takes all sorts. That's what my Mum always used to say.'

Oh Lord. Now look at him. Megan should have come, she thought. Next minute he'd be telling ISA to get lost and she'd never hear the end of it. Yet, watching him she recognised the mute appeal in his eyes. His obvious pliability was a challenge that Maureen could not resist. He was like raw clay, malleable, workable, and she the potter.

'Here, I'm real sorry,' she said sitting down close beside him. 'Really I am.' She stroked her fingers over the back of his hand and since he did not seem to be objecting, moved them slowly up his arm and over his shoulder.

'You keep doing that,' he said 'and I'll fuck your arse off.'

His sudden touch of bravado, with its boasting, macho arrogance fired her temper briefly.

'So where's this great seduction scene to take place,' she said glancing round as she unbuttoned her blouse. Then she caught sight of his expression and compassion surfaced. 'Oh Adolpho, who'd you think you're kidding? Everyone knows you're a ruddy great poof.'

'But that's not true,' he said in a voice that was hardly more than a whisper. 'You've no right to say that? You don't know, you see. It's just that ...'

'You don't fancy girls?'

'Look. Why don't you piss off,' he said, his Italian accent suddenly forgotten. 'Get lost and take your horrible insinuations with you. Go on now. Get!'

'You asked for it,' she said mildly. 'But I'll just help you on that train because it's more than my job's worth to let you miss it.'

She minced into the bedroom and flung open the wardrobe door and stepped back in amazement as she stared into the lifeless eyes of a full-sized plastic doll.

'Female,' she noted. 'Oh my! Wonders will never cease.'

'Here, Adolpho, how'd you like the real thing?' She sat down hard beside him and pressed his hand against her breast. 'Beats plastic, doesn't it?' She ran her fingers over his belly and down over his thigh. 'What a lovely chest,' she said. 'About the best I've ever seen. Perfect!' She brushed her finger down his chest and groped over his crotch, felt his flaccid member through the towelling and moved away over his belly.

'It's no good,' he said and stared at her, his face registering horror, despair and embarrassment.

'So what,' she said firmly. 'I could do without that for a bloke like you. Think you're the only one who's lonely. Not a bit of it. Men ... well most men that is, don't like girls as tough as me. I don't mince words, and I sure as hell can't put up with these arrogant wimps who think they know it all – when most times they know very little.'

'I would never be like that,' he said painfully. 'You think I like men. I hate men.'

He stood up and walked to the mirror, posturing this way and that way, as he flexed his many muscles and watched his skin rippling.

'Here! D'you spend all day admiring yourself then?' she asked. 'How about me? I've got a pretty good figure. How about looking at that?'

'I look in the mirror and I can't believe all this – this hulk,

Adolpho Bartoli – is real. I did all this with plain hard work, if you want to know the truth. Underneath is plain Johnny Bart, a skinny little rat the gang beat up daily,' he said. 'Weight training, exercises I got it all out of a book and afterwards I went to a gym. All because I was so skinny. I wanted to frighten them off you see. I can't stand fighting, but the English seem to love it.'

He looked agonised. 'I don't know why I'm telling you this.'

She reflected for a moment. 'Perhaps because I'm the first person who asked,' she replied thoughtfully. 'Johnny Bart! That's a much better name for you. I can just see that name up in lights. Johnny Bart's gymnasium. I can see the newspaper articles when you win that title: "The story of a skinny kid's climb to success." You are going to win Johnny. I promise you.

'Know what,' she went on. 'I want you to get up there on the platform in Manchester and tell them what you just told me.'

'Are you crazy? Just forget all I said. It was something personal. Not for public consumption. I trusted you.'

'Come here, Johnny, come here.' She pressed her breasts, naked under the thin silk blouse, against his chest, wound her arms around his waist and slithered like a snake as one black leg curled around his calf. Then she kissed him violently on the mouth, tasted mouthwash, and toothpaste as her tongue probed his mouth.

'That's all I want,' she said stepping back and scanning his eyes. 'Just a snuggle from time to time. Wasn't so bad, was it? Forget the rest. Who needs sex?'

He didn't look disgusted. Quite the contrary. He looked like an orphan kid who'd been taken out for a treat. 'You mean that?' His eyes were like windows – he'd never be able to lie – all the longing and the shame of the crippled ego, the uncertainty and the need – it was all there, locked inside that massive macho hunk.

Someone should take him in hand, she thought, and it might as well be me.

'Want me to come along – to Manchester I mean? I'll get the day off if you like. Hold your hand. Tell you what to say. You can pretend I'm your secretary. I'll keep my notebook handy.'

'If I told you to get lost again, would it make any difference?' he asked coolly and she noticed the Italian accent was back in place.

'Yes, it would,' she said gently. 'I've got to feel wanted. Otherwise it's no go.'

'Come if you like,' he said.

Well, that was a start, Maureen thought. 'Johnny Bart,' she whispered gently to herself, 'I'm going to turn you into a man.'

CHAPTER 38

'Eleanor, I want you to tell me about *yourself*.' Gundelfinger
studied the unhappy woman stretched on the couch. She was
still attractive and if she weren't so plump she could pass for
thirty-five, most of the time. The miracles of modern surgery,
he thought cynically. He had to admit that he felt attracted to
her, more because of her personality than her looks. However,
after their breakthrough during her visit in May, he had not
been able to penetrate her defences. Instead she had told him
about her current business problems and the opposition's
probable share percentage, versus her own. He had let her talk,
because he could see that quite apart from any psychological
trauma, she was also a very worried woman, with very real and
pressing problems. 'Lately, you've told me a great deal about
your business, but very little about yourself ...' he began.

'That is myself,' Eleanor said irritably. 'It's what I think
about and feel about and do – all day.'

'Exactly. All I hear about is business – business worries,
business strategy, business hopes – but what about Eleanor's
hopes? There is a real you, isn't there? Sometimes I wonder if
you can be yourself, apart from Vanguard.'

'I am Vanguard.'

Gundelfinger shrugged. 'You seem to have all your eggs in
one basket. No wonder you're so uptight over this takeover bid
you keep mentioning. What will you do if you lose – if they take
Vanguard and merge it with another company? You'd survive,
wouldn't you? So tell me about the real you.'

Eleanor shrugged irritably and fell silent. Gundelfinger's
words had hit home. 'I don't understand,' she said and noticing
the whine in her voice, she struggled to regain control. 'What
about you – don't you live for your work? Or d'you go home to
a wife and kids and forget about your patients?'

'No, I never forget about my patients,' Gundelfinger replied
warily.

'So what's different?'

'You tell me what's different? You're a clever woman, Eleanor. If there's one thing I appreciate it's working with an intelligent patient.'

Eleanor lay staring at the ceiling, frowning slightly. Then, as if by instinct, her hand moved up and smoothed her brow. Frowning was taboo. 'Emotions brought me a lot of hurt,' she said. 'Twice! So I gave up the silly business of caring. I prefer business.'

'Tell me about this hurt,' he persisted.

She sighed. 'I'm tired,' she grumbled.

'I'm sorry you're tired,' Gundelfinger said after a long silence. 'But I think you should continue.'

'What do you want me to talk about?' she asked hostilely.

'Tell me about the Eleanor you used to be – before hurting and caring became synonymous. He must have meant a great deal to you – this young German. What did you say his name was?'

'I didn't say,' she answered sullenly. 'I didn't really want to know. I didn't want to feel what I was feeling. I tried to remind myself that he was the enemy – a German – so I called him Jerry and that stuck – really it did – it used to make him angry and it was my form of defence against ... against him.'

'Yet you loved him very deeply. Think back. When did you first discover you were in love? How did you feel?'

'So long ago ... yet I'll never forget,' she began haltingly. 'It was unusually cold I remember, even for Scotland. Day after day the wind roared down from the arctic, hurling snow and ice over the village until it seemed we would be buried alive. Temperatures were thirty degrees below freezing, so Dad gathered the sheep and penned them in the field near the house and we fed them lucerne.

'One night we were snowed in; I woke to see a strange white glow coming from the window. When I tugged the frozen curtains aside, I saw that the snow had fallen so deeply, it was halfway up the window. There was no sign of the barn or the pigsties, or our sheep in the field. Nothing! Everything was buried by snow.

'I yelped with shock, pulled on my clothes and rushed into the kitchen. Dad was finishing his porridge. "Well lass," he said. "There's a fair bit of work ahead. Looks like you'll have to help me out. There'll be no getting to work for you today. Road's blocked. It's likely to stay blocked a few days yet."

'I would have started right then, but Mum insisted we ate a good breakfast first. "The sheep have been buried all night, another ten minutes won't make much difference one way or the other," she said, "but a good breakfast will." She had eggs and bacon ready – a rare treat.

'It was exciting, but awful, too. We couldn't get the door open without the snow falling in, so I squeezed out of the kitchen window and started to dig around the front door with the coal shovel to let Dad out. Then I heard the snow plough chugging up the hill in the distance. We knew the prisoners had been trying to clear the road; they'd been moving up towards us for days. Somehow I knew he – Jerry – would help us, but when he came and I saw him striding up the hill – well, that was something tremendous. When he reached the track above the croft he waved and ran down.

'At that moment, his rough army greatcoat, his flapping trousers, his close-cropped hair, all this was meaningless compared with the grace of him and his speed and strength. He was really alive, as some men are never alive; and he was all male, showing off and glad of the chance to do so. He'd been too long in that muddy ditch. He wanted to stand tall.

'He worked like a demon to clear the snow and I stood around helping half-heartedly, but really I was admiring his ruddy skin moist with sweat, the stubble of his beard gleaming, his breath steaming, nostrils extended, and the expression of exaltation in his deep blue eyes. It was then I realised how much he had suffered, working like a mole in the ditch and eating all our charity sandwiches.

'Later, Mum and I made a big pot of steaming stew, for by then the other two prisoners had arrived on the snow plough. They took off their coats and hats, bowed stiffly, murmured their thanks and hung around looking very Germanic. Dad said grace and Mum handed out bread and big plates of boiling stew, with thick mutton-fat bubbling on the surface and chunks of meat, turnips, potatoes and dumplings.

'I could see from Jerry's face that he was bewildered and unhappy. Later he told me that he had never seen such poverty. He was sad for me, he said afterwards, but at the time I thought he was struck dumb with gratitude because of the meat and the warmth from the stove.

'Then Mum and I started washing the dishes and he came up behind me and picked up a tea cloth from the hook.

' "Be off with you," Mum said. "We'll be done in no time at all."

' "But I can borrow a hand," he said.

' "Lend," I hissed at him. I was furious. I so much wanted Jerry to make a good impression. He was always confused by English idioms – and he could never resist experimenting with them.' Eleanor's hand groped instinctively for the tissues. Her voice quavered on a higher pitch. 'Funny,' she said. 'He never got them right.

'We fell in love,' she said. 'It didn't seem wrong to us. Our love seemed very special, and pure. It seemed sacred, like going to church – something holy. Can you understand that?'

'I've always believed that love is holy,' Gundelfinger murmured.

Eleanor seemed not to have heard him. 'It was cold at night, so we used to meet in an abandoned barn. It was easy for Jerry to get out of camp.' She broke off, remembering one night ...

'The full moon, white as death, glistened on the snowy moors so that the barn was lit with an eerie glow and we both felt a little strange. Ours was a clandestine relationship that needed the wrap of night, whispered secrets in the shadows. Now, for the first time we were able to look into each other's eyes and read each other's longings and witness all our guilt and pent-up desires. It was all wrong, we both knew this, but we could not stop ourselves from loving.

'It was twenty degrees below zero that night. I had a quilted coat, but it seemed more like paper for all the warmth it gave me and my feet were frozen inside my wellies ...'

She broke off. How could mere words express her overwhelming love and her sense of belonging. Jerry was real, in him was her life, her future, her womanliness, and at that time it seemed that all the rest was falling off her like a discarded skin. Loving him had made her feel purified and new – another person altogether, but she was unwilling to put the memories into words. All the same, she would never forget.

That night they had talked for a while of their plans, and giggled to find how similar their dreams were, but Eleanor was shivering fit to break and after a while he opened his grey,

272

great-coat and folded her inside it, warming her with his fierce, burning excitement.

She put her hand on his chest. How strong he was, yet he was little more than a boy, and his arms sinewy hard. She had never felt a man's body in all her life and curiosity overcame her.

'I would like ... why I would like to be a tiny hair, growing in the pit of your armpit, and I would stay there all my life and never stray away from you.' She stroked his arm dreamily, warmed with her own sensual desires, the cold and snow forgotten.

His silence was something alarming. Like a warning bell that shattered her calm. 'What is it then? What's the matter with you?' she asked petulantly.

His voice was hoarse with emotion when he eventually answered. 'I'm to be sent away. We're being repatriated. We were told yesterday. I don't know how or when I'll ever get back here.' He shivered and pulled her closer to him.

Eleanor cried out in alarm. Then she said: 'But what shall I do?'

'Wait for me, of course.' His words were brave, but she could hear the uncertainty in his voice.

'Forever,' she vowed, likewise agitated and afraid. The thought of life without him was empty beyond endurance.

'Promise you won't forget me,' she pleaded.

'Yes,' he said, and then he said: 'No. I mean, I won't forget you. No, why would I?' He cried out. 'I'll work and save and be back for you within a year. Or maybe two,' he added after a long, doubtful silence.

So they sat and promised and made plans and Eleanor said she would learn German and earn more money and save all of it, and he promised to write, but all the time they were living in a state of split consciousness, their words so formal and stilted, but their hands exploring, touching, intimate and knowing, and their bodies nudging closer, shifting and moving and finding a way to touch each other almost everywhere.

Then he said: 'Let's take those sacks and make a bed on the floor.'

And she said: 'Oh God.'

So finally, she sat in a daze unable to move, or to speak, while he hastily gathered the sacks, pushing and kicking in his

273

frantic haste. He picked her up and laid her on them and covered her with his greatcoat and then he nuzzled beside her. They were so solemn, noses to noses, her arms around his neck and his around hers, lying on their sides. There was a great urge inside her to feel his naked skin against hers and she fumbled with his shirt and her clothes and pushed and pulled trying to keep the coat over them, until her bare breasts were against his chest.

'Oh God,' she whispered. 'I never felt anything ... I never knew.'

'Little Eleanor, my Eleanor, I love you,' he moaned. His voice was hoarse and then he whispered in German and Eleanor could not understand what he was saying, but she knew it was the most beautiful thing she had heard in her life.

Urgently she tore down her pants and felt his penis throbbing and burning hot against her navel. It was so lovely, the sensuous, burning warmth of him, the soft, soft skin and his breath which was coming in quick gasps, warming her cheek.

'No, don't ... don't ...' he murmured, but an urge as old as Eve made her fling one leg over his hips and wriggle and move until at last he was firmly thrust inside her and they lay like that for a long time, entranced with their holy communion, unable to move for fear of breaking the spell, gazing into each other's eyes.

How long? She did not know. But later, much later, he moved and exploded and they were both quite shattered at their loss of innocence. Then she kissed him, and her woman's grief welled up inside her for what she had lost, and what more she would lose when he was taken away.

'Oh dear,' she said to Gundelfinger. 'Oh dear.'

At last she said: 'For weeks we met at night until eventually we were discovered. He was marched off between two policemen in handcuffs. He looked anguished as they led him away, but I knew he was only scared for me. He was confined to the camp, and I learned that he was repatriated shortly afterwards.

'I appeared in court and received a suspended sentence. They shouldn't have bothered,' she said bitterly. 'I had already been sentenced by the local community – a life sentence!' She shuddered. 'So from then on I was considered contemptible. Dad's face was full of pain. He never looked at me again. Mum

274

looked haggard, I knew she was suffering for me, but we never spoke about it. I even lost my job at the store ...'

'I find all this hard to believe,' Gundelfinger said after a while. 'All this punishment, just for loving. It seems incredible to me.'

'You're too young to remember the hate that lingered after the war and the narrow ways of a small community – the spite and the gossip.'

'I was desperate to get away, but home was the only place where Jerry could find me. So I waited a year – and heard nothing. Then I left – worked my passage as a stewardess and began a new life in America.'

'But you missed your young German and you missed your parents?' Gundelfinger questioned her.

'No, I blocked them off. I can do that anytime I want to.'

'I don't quite follow you ...'

'Well ...' she lay rigid, unmoving, deep in thought. 'Let's say it's like building a wall, the Great Wall of China and I wall up my enemies in the cement – only the cement is deep inside myself.' Her voice faltered a trifle. 'It worked fine until I started seeing you ... but remembering makes cracks in the concrete and ... all these corpses smell horrible.' She peered over her shoulder. 'I suppose you think I'm crazy?'

'On the contrary, I think you're very perceptive. You're also extraordinarily resilient. But I must warn you that the purpose of psychotherapy is to help you to break down the walls, haul out the phantoms and give them a proper burial. It's a painful process, as you are finding out. Many people don't have the courage to go through with it.'

'Okay, okay! I know about motivation.'

'I bet you do.' The doctor watched her shrewdly. He could see by her face she was back in Vanguard. He spoke quickly: 'So that was the last time you saw your young lover?'

She looked round and smiled bitterly. 'Why, no! The last time I saw him was years later. He was drunk and he was sitting on the floor crying and his last words to me were: 'You took something precious from me and destroyed it. One day I'm going to do the same to you, Eleanor.'

Abruptly Eleanor broke off. 'Losers always threaten,' she said with a shaky laugh. Then she shivered. 'Time's up,' she said glancing at her watch.

'Not quite,' Gundelfinger replied. 'Are you in a hurry?'

'I've had enough for one day, thanks,' she said over-casually. Then she grabbed her bag and fled.

CHAPTER 39

High in the Swiss Alps there was fresh snow after last night's blizzard, but temperatures were rising and the north-east wind was reaching gale force. To Jacqui, who was waiting on the crest of the next slope, it seemed that the leaden sky was resting on the mountain tops, and she had a curious sensation of being shut-in, like a trapeze artist at the top of a gigantic tent. She shuddered involuntarily and looked back for Wolf.

She had a bad feeling about the piste, although she did not know why. If only she knew more about the mountain and the formation of this winter's snow. Presumably the glacier slopes had been skied on through last summer and therefore, underneath the thick and unseasonable snowfall on which she was standing, was a steep and treacherous platform of slippery pack-ice, stretching down to the mist shrouding the valleys.

'Scary!' she said aloud, but there did not appear to be an alternative route. Typical of Wolf – danger excited him, just as it did her. She loved the sensation of adrenalin racing through her veins. A safe piste was boring.

Resting on her stick, she thought about the past month with Wolf. Fantastic! There was no other way to describe their savage concentration on enjoying themselves. They had trained day after day – trying out scary routes through rocks and trees, ignoring the locals' advice, and doing their own thing. He was reckless; enjoying danger for its own sake; squeezing the most out of every moment. Each day they had chosen a more difficult target, and in the evenings they had been exhilarated and Wolf had been full of fun, never tired. Wolf was pretty good, she had to admit, in spite of his age. Not just at skiing either, she couldn't think of a darn thing that he wasn't good at. She admired his go-getting ways, his verve and his vitality. With the helicopter on call, the evenings had been as exciting as the days. Wolf had the art and the power of using money –

something that Mother had never achieved in spite of her millions.

She felt a surge of pride as she thought about Wolf. That morning, when the private helicopter had dropped them at the top of the mountain, she had decided that she loved him, but she did not know why. It was because of his deepset, serious eyes that scanned the peaks for the best run, and his toughness and strength of character, and his funny way of walking – and it also had something to do with the power he had, and which he loved to use, and his courage. He made her feel safe. She knew that he did not love her, for he had not tried to make love to her. They were comrades – that more or less described it, Jacqui decided.

She knew Wolf had been married once, he seldom talked about it, but she could sense the hurt and that made her feel protective and compassionate towards him.

One night he had told her that his life had changed direction because of a skiing accident. His business, his marriage and his health had gone for a loop, and for two years he had sat around drinking and feeling sorry for himself. That was all he would tell her. She knew that he had built himself up from a cripple to a fit and powerful athlete. She admired him more than any person she had ever met. He was every bit as dogmatic as Mother, too. He's one hell of a guy, she thought as she searched the slopes for him.

Then she saw Wolf racing towards her and for a moment she felt a twist of fear in her stomach. Surely he must have seen how dangerous the piste was. She waved and he skidded to a halt and pushed up his goggles. His whole face shone with exhilaration, his streaky, sun-bleached brown hair was powdered with snow, his blue eyes were gleaming with excitement, and he was laughing. It was a face which Jacqui had learned to love and trust.

'Scared?' he asked out of the blue – challenging her.

'Sure I'm scared. We're poised on a killer slide. Did you know that? D'you know how much snow there is resting on a slippery platform underneath us? Round about sixty centimetres all the way down. I checked with the chief of the mountains. They had two nights of thaw before the freeze; then a heavy snowfall.'

'Why did you come then?' He looked disappointed in her.

She shrugged. 'You can't tell till you get here, can you?' Then she laughed uneasily. 'This wind doesn't help. It could blow any time,' she said moodily. She leaned on one stick and stared far down into the hidden valley. 'What'll we do if it goes?'

'You're chickening out on me,' he said.

Smiling up at him, Jacqui felt reassured. There was always that sense of quiet reassurance about Wolf. She just had that feeling about him. If he said it was okay, then what the hell?

But her doubts persisted. 'All the same, we need an escape route. I've been standing here trying to figure one out. We should cross that way.' She pointed to the side with her stick. 'We must go only one at a time and Wolf, listen to me, we should keep along the eastern edge of the piste, or even go right off it if necessary. Agreed?'

He gazed at her long and hard; his expression a curious mixture of impatience and affection. Then he winked and she felt fine.

'I'll go first, Wolf. I'm lighter – and I'm faster ...' She broke off as she realised how frightened she was for Wolf. Of course it was dangerous, and more so for the leader. But if the snow could take her weight, then it would probably take his. 'Please God,' she prayed.

She felt puzzled by her concern. Caring makes you cowardly, she thought inconsequentially. 'Gently, softly, Wolf,' she called over her shoulder.

She grimaced and shot off traversing rapidly to the east side of the piste. She negotiated the turn expertly as she approached a granite rock jutting through the snow and then tucked her head in for a fast schuss down.

Wolf watched Jacqui uneasily. Their fate was indivisibly entwined. She was his nemesis, and through her he would strike the first blow which would inevitably result in Eleanor's and Nigel's destruction. In a way he loved her, but only as a painter loves his brush, or a carpenter his chisel. But perhaps it was also because she was the image of the young Eleanor whom he had loved so and who had tried to destroy him. The moment he felt the first stray shafts of caring he realised that the intensity of his feeling for Eleanor had never diminished – not an iota in all these years – but there were two sides to passion, love and hate and Eleanor had chosen which side she wanted. Eleanor – Jacqui; Jacqui – Eleanor, they were indistinguishable. He stared across the snow at the woman he had hated every conscious moment of every day for nineteen years.

Jacqui was intent, concentrating on every movement she made and every mogul and twist of the snow. False snow, she knew – a brittle icing resting on melting snow. One error ... just one error. It didn't bear thinking about, so she kept to the eastern edge of the piste, hugging the rocks and clefts, close to an escape route, she hoped.

'So far, so good,' she murmured when she paused on the crest of the next cornice overlooking a steep fall between rocky crags on either side. The wind was strengthening and gusting up to forty miles an hour. It was picking up loose snow and depositing it on the lee side of the ridge.

'Real wild,' she said. Anxiously glancing round she saw Wolf catching up with her.

Whoom! There was a sudden crack from under her feet. As the snow slipped forward, the air trapped beneath it exploded around Jacqui, blasting snow into her lungs. Then she was zooming headlong down.

The world had spun into a different time zone. Every second lasted an eternity. The suffocating pressure was relentless as she fought to keep on her feet. She fell headlong to the ground, felt her head hit the snow with a snap which stunned her momentarily, but then she was spinning, cartwheeling, falling as the ground beneath her raced down the mountain. Her arms felt insecure in their sockets, as though stretched beyond capacity. She was helpless, blinded by snow, propelled at this insane speed to the bottom of the slope where tons of snow and ice and gravel would pile on top of her. She could see nothing but blinding white; there was no air – only powdered snow; she fought to breath, but some gigantic hand was squeezing her lungs and she was in agony.

Wolf heard the crack, felt the sudden blast of air which knocked him backwards, saw the snow ahead of him begin to move and then gather momentum as it raced down and away, reaching a speed of a hundred miles an hour within seconds, as Jacqui was carried out of sight.

Wolf scrambled to his feet watching – wondering at his mounting horror. He saw Jacqui's small body catapulted into the air. Then she was cartwheeling into a cloud of snowdust. The noise was deafening. Then silence – and a white mist that blotted out everything.

CHAPTER 40

'Oh Christ! Christ! Jacqui. JACQUI ...' Blind panic took over
and for a few crazy seconds Wolf was shouting and racing
down the slope in a vain bid to catch up with the avalanche.

Then reason surfaced. Madness to go down now. He might
set off another killer slide and destroy any chance Jacqui may
have of being saved. For the same reason he could not call the
helicopter. The noise could upset the delicate balance of
toppling snow and ice. Instead, he glided to the eastern edge of
the mountain slope where there were patches of bare rock
amongst the snow.

Wolf waited.

He felt an ache in his throat and his guts as he gazed at the
cloud of snow particles which rose high into the air, obscuring
the mountain. It seemed to hang there forever. What the hell
had gone wrong with him? This was his plan, brilliantly
conceived and executed. But now, inexplicably, some other
feeling had surfaced and he saw Jacqui as herself, not a replica
of her mother, or a tool to be used for his vendetta. She was a
living, caring, lovely girl – a girl he loved.

'Oh, God, Jacqui,' he sobbed. 'What have I done?' What
madness had led him to stifle his emotions and go ahead with
his mad plan? Yet he knew that he had never really expected
this to happen. Not consciously. He had willed it to happen,
visualised it in his mind, known that by taking these insane
risks he was flaunting danger and inviting disaster for both of
them. In a way he had been wreaking revenge in his
imagination, not really expecting the reality of the dream to
catch up with him.

What insane quest for danger had led him to bring Jacqui
here? He acknowledged now that all his life he had been bent
on a course of self-destruction, gambling every cent he owned,
time after time; gambling his life, his reputation, his health and

282

strength – never caring for a goddamn thing. Yet he had always emerged unscathed and lately he had considered this to be his right. Now he had someone to care about, but the knowledge had come too late. Or was it too late?

The snow dust settled, but there no sign of movement or even any clothing to show where she might have been. Wolf had difficulty in trying to control his panting breath and the thumping of his heart. 'Keep calm,' he said aloud several times. Panicking would not help Jacqui. If indeed, she was still within reach of help. 'Please God,' he muttered. 'Let her be alive.'

He stood up and stared long and anxiously down the mountain slope. Jacqui had been at the tail end of the slide, therefore she had a chance, but the terrible statistics were throbbing through his mind: three tons of ice can destroy a house, ten tons a spruce, a hundred tons can destroy a concrete building. The airblast alone can exert half a ton of pressure per square metre. The avalanche had been a soft slab type, disintegrating into powder as it ran and it had reached up to two hundred miles an hour, before it piled up, he reckoned. Looking up along the fracture line, he saw it was a good hundred metres wide and knocking his stick into a side of the piste, he noted that there was another layer of hoar sixty centimetres below the first slide.

Time to move. Below, he could see nothing but the billowing snow clouds slowly subsiding so that the vista looked like a coloured photograph from a damaged film with the bottom half white, and the top in shades of blue and purple.

Two hundred metres down the path of the avalanche, he found one stick and further down the end of another protruded, but he could not see her skis. Now an icy wind was gathering strength and Wolf began to lose hope. Keeping to the edge of the piste, he rummaged through the debris.

To Jacqui, the slide had seemed to last for hours. She remembered to get rid of her sticks and somehow she released her skis. Then all at once the snow came whirling, swirling, crashing over her head.

Suddenly there was complete silence. No rumblings, roarings. Nothing but complete blackness. Everything was so still, so dark, only the pounding of her heart seemed as loud as thunder. She had fallen on her hands and knees, protecting her face and allowing her air space. She lost all self-control and screamed, but soon realised her error.

The pain in her lungs was excruciating. She tried to breath deeply several times and clear her lungs, but each breath brought a fit of coughing and choking, there was hardly any air left.

Don't scream, she told herself urgently. There was no air for screaming. She must get more air – make an air space. She tried to push her arms and raise her body, increase the gap, but it was futile. She seemed to be cemented into the snow and could not move a muscle.

Then, as quickly as panic had surfaced, peace took its place. She inhaled the small breaths of air, thought of Rob and Wolf and Mother, and calmly accepted her fate. She began to hallucinate, floating on a cloud, rising and falling, like a large, quilted duvet, rocking up and down in the sky. Eventually, there was nothing at all.

Using his skis as probes, Wolf was working desperately down the avalanche debris. At last he contacted something solid with his stick. Sweating and shouting, almost out of his mind with panic, Wolf began to shovel the snow away with his hands. They were bleeding and raw, but Wolf did not notice.

He found a foot and moved down to her body, frantically clearing around her head. She lay, face downwards, her face on her hands, unconscious and blue.

Shouting at her, demanding that she answer him, Wolf wrapped Jacqui in his ski jacket, blew his breath into her mouth, rubbed her skin and pummelled her. Slowly she began to regain consciousness.

It was then that panic set in: screams of horror, relief, and the pain of thawing limbs. Unimaginable pain, as she fought to get up.

Then, murmuring Wolf's name, she lapsed into unconsciousness again as the helicopter zoomed down the mountainside.

'Concussion, shock, exposure and exhaustion.' The doctor

pronounced the verdict gravely to Wolf after Jacqui had failed to regain consciousness by the following morning.

It had been a long night in the hospital ward, with ample time to think about his motives and his mistakes – and the past.

He had thought back to the last time he saw Eleanor nineteen years ago ...

He might never have known Jacqui existed, if he had not returned to the ski club to say goodbye. He had lost everything: his health, his wife, his business, but he still had his friends, and he was strangely sentimental in those days. They had told him that Eleanor was pregnant, and although he found the idea ludicrous, he drove back to the factory, intent on discovering the truth. He had always wanted children, but Eleanor hated the idea and in ten years of marriage she had never once slipped up.

Going in had been painful. Seeing Eleanor had been worse. 'I came because I heard you were pregnant,' he had told her bluntly.

She had looked strangely joyful, which was the last thing he had expected.

'I'm touched you should care.' She had patted her stomach in a strangely conspiratorial gesture.

'Damn it, Eleanor. Why now? I always wanted a child. You know that.' He had tried to keep the condemnation out of his voice – for his child's sake. 'When I heard ... when I discovered ... I didn't know what to do ... it's not just us. Now there's three of us to consider. I decided to cancel my flight.

'Eleanor,' he began again, trying to break the barrier of contempt she had erected between them. 'There's so little love left between us, but there's the child. If you can forgive me for ...' For God's sake, he thought angrily. What had he ever done. 'For recovering, I can forgive you for ... for ...' what could he say? For stealing his business, his hopes, his future and his happiness. 'For your over-zealous business attitude,' he had eventually stammered placatingly. 'For the sake of my child I'm prepared to put the bitterness behind us.'

She had laughed, and it had sounded like a laugh of genuine amusement. 'But it's not your child, Wolf,' she had told him looking soft and gentle and sweetly virginal in spite of the bulge, just as Jacqui was looking now. 'It's Nigel's! Surely you must have guessed about us.'

Wolf's fingers gripped the bed rail as he remembered the scene that followed. He had ran into the plant, grabbed Nigel and punched him hard in the face. Nigel had slithered to the floor, whimpered like a puppy, looked up puzzled and contrite and passed out. Wolf had reached forward to grab him. He had intended ... hoped ... to bring him round and beat him to a pulp, but his back injury had sent him staggering to the floor, gasping in pain and by the time he regained his feet, Nigel had crawled out. He heard his car hastily revved and skidding out of the parking bay.

'I'll get you back, Eleanor,' he had vowed, when he was drunk and crying. It had taken him almost twenty years to accumulate the cash and the power to do that. Now he intended to keep his promise, but he had needed the help of Eleanor's daughter and her shares. Strange that Eleanor had never married Nigel and never told Jacqui who her father really was. Presumably Eleanor did not consider Nigel good enough for her.

Jacqui was stirring at last, mumbling under her breath and moving her head. He thanked God for that. How was it possible that he loved his enemy? Assuredly Jacqui was his enemy: the sole issue of Eleanor and Nigel – a product of their joyless lunge in love. He pondered for a while on the vicissitudes of hereditary genes. Jacqui was a replica of the youthful Eleanor, with her mannerisms and her voice – a daily agonising reminder of the woman he hated. Yet, mentally and morally the two women had nothing at all in common. Oh no! Jacqui was moulded from finer material. Here was no stern and grasping heart, no treachery, no viciousness. In the seven months since he had engineered their meeting, he had learned to know her and all her prickly ways. Tough outside, a stern, unbending virago to strangers, but warm and compassionate to those she knew and trusted. There was no doubt at all about her loyalty. A truly noble spirit, he thought, with her quest for excellence and her love of sport.

He acknowledged that until now, in his mind, mother and daughter had been hardly distinguishable and he had wanted to use her to punish both Eleanor and Nigel, her father. He thought back to those first agonising months when he had searched for a physical or mental resemblance to that wimp, Nigel, but clearly Eleanor's strong genes had saturated those of her mate.

Now, Jacqui lay here unconscious, as if in answer to his destructive thoughts. She must get better. He began to picture them skiing again, and exploring the quaint Swiss villages, skating on the lakes and buying her beautiful Swiss embroidered blouses and scarves – as they had done for the past three months between her arduous training sessions.

She would get better, he decided, and he would marry her. Perhaps, after all, that would be a fitting revenge, for he would turn her away from her mother in time and Eleanor would be left alone – without family and without Vanguard. Something tickled his cheek and putting his hand up he was amazed to find that he was crying.

'Oh God.' Wolf buried his head in his hands and prayed. It was the first time he had prayed in nineteen years. He continued to pray until Jacqui regained consciousness three hours later.

CHAPTER 41

Megan was waiting at the Richmond ice rink, leaning over the railings, watching Nikki train. She had been there for an hour, but the time had passed quickly. Even without the lights, music or costumes, the magic was there, as it always was.

Technically-speaking, Nikki's skating had improved remarkably in the past few weeks. She performed with a new intensity: it was as if all her frustrations, pent-up anger and longings were suppressed and channelled into her art. It was not difficult to see how unhappy Nikki was, but Megan did not know why. Was she really in love with Michel? Somehow Megan did not think so. For Nikki, men were stepping stones; she had a neurotic desire to be loved, but little ability to return that love. But if it wasn't Michel, then what could the problem be? Megan sighed, wishing that she could draw closer to Nikki. She knew something was upsetting her, but she had no means of finding out what it was. Nikki was so proud, and confiding her troubles was far beneath her dignity. Besides, the warmth that Nikki had at first showered on Megan had dwindled in the face of Megan's unresponsiveness. Too late now for Megan to explain that she had been so hurt because of Ian, and so mistaken. Megan sensed that Nikki would withdraw over a hurt and find it difficult to forgive or forget. Lately she was more withdrawn than ever before and Megan felt vaguely worried. Nikki had everything on her side. She had won the Southern England championships with ease, outstripping every other competitor and she had been nominated for the British championships in November. Admittedly, they had not yet managed to obtain her British citizenship, and without a passport, Nikki was not able to attend the European championships, or any of the European shows to which she had been invited. Unless she succeeded in getting temporary permits for each occasion, as Megan had done for Nikki's filmshots in Sweden.

The filming was going exceptionally well, too. Megan had seen some of the shots taken on a Scandinavian outdoor rink, which looked like a lake and they were superb.

Yet Nikki herself was never satisfied. She moaned about the look-alike English actress who was performing the role of Nikki in the non-skating shots. She would have liked to have played that role herself, and she never ceased complaining. Lately Nikki had become extremely temperamental. She criticised her skates, quarrelled with sponsors, tried to skip public appearances, spent too much time at parties and kept herself going on pep pills. She grumbled that the sponsors' demands laid severe restraints on her freedom and she could never stop moaning about Western ways, but she ploughed through her cash at an alarming pace and Megan had difficulty persuading the skating authorities to allow her to make further inroads into her trust fund without impairing her amateur status.

She drove recklessly around London and collected handfuls of speeding and parking tickets and had tantrums when Megan tried to caution her. She was like a moth fluttering against a candle. Megan sensed that Nikki needed help, but she could not break through to her. Nikki was a difficult child, but to watch her skate left you breathless with admiration. Perhaps talent such as hers deserved other standards, should one make special allowances, Megan wondered time and again?

Right now Nikki was having an argument with Eric, her coach, stamping her skates on the ice and shouting abuse. The row was about the choreography Eric had chosen for the British trials. Nikki wanted something more dramatic, but Eric was winning, Megan could see. Suddenly Nikki shrieked with temper, threw up her arms and raced off the rink.

'That's it,' she shouted. 'I refuse, I positively refuse to train with that odious little man. He is disgusting, *da*? A real wet blanket, as you say. With free-style skating one should be innovative, imaginative, do something new and startlingly different. You understand, Megan?'

Green eyes flashing like an angry cat. Any minute now she's going to wag her tail, Megan thought unsympathetically.

'So sorry, but you have been there a long time, *da*?'

If you knew I was here why didn't you take the trouble to come and talk to me? 'I want to talk to you,' she said. 'It's important.'

'I'll meet you in the canteen in ten minutes,' Nikki answered with a quick smile. 'I'll have cheesecake and coffee – with real cream,' she added.

Megan waited ten minutes and then another ten, as she had expected. Half an hour later Nikki arrived looking smug.

'Your coffee's cold,' Megan greeted her sourly, her good intentious wavering.

'I like cold coffee,' she retorted with a brilliant smile. She was wearing a pretty red and blue dress which looked vaguely Austrian with the deep, square neckline. Above it the rounded crests of her breasts looked smooth and full and her eyes were glittering with that strangely mocking expression, as if she would burst with secret mirth any minute. 'So? I am all ears, as you say.' She reached up and pushed an errant strand of blonde hair into the thick braids around her head.

'There's something I feel I should remind you, Nikki. You're free. Just remember all those silly statements you've been making about wanting to skate in freedom. Well, this is it. You've got it. All these tantrums and these fights with Eric and with me and with your sponsors – well, what's it all about Nikki? Why don't you go right back there and sack Eric? He's the best coach in Britain and you know it. But if you don't like him, get yourself the second best – or anyone! Be my guest, Nikki, but don't keep kicking against imaginary controls.

'That's your game, isn't it? You fight against authority imposed upon you, but there's no longer any authority. It's you. You're making it up because you haven't the guts to live without it, and because you're so used to fighting, you can't stop. You moan about me – well, good grief, you can sack me. The contract says three months' notice, but I'll take three days. You moan about your sponsors, but you can't stop spending their money. You can get out of all your contracts quite easily. You can even give up skating. Why don't you do that? So make up your mind what you want and stop making everyone's life miserable. Grow up, Nikki. You're becoming one big bore.'

Ignoring Nikki's shocked eyes and open mouth, she went on: 'I must tell you the truth, Nikki. I'm battling to get your passport, but I just can't break through the red tape. I'll keep trying,' Megan tried to smile, tried to soften the blow, but she felt as guilty as if she were the one responsible for the whole sorry mess. For weeks she had been calling one department after the next. She had a sneaking suspicion it was a deliberate put-off. 'I'm sorry you'll have to miss the French invitation show, Nikki.' She had finished her coffee, paid the bill and she wanted to leave, but there was something else she had to say as well, and she was not looking forward to it.

Nikki was gobbling her cheesecake and scowling between mouthfuls. 'Perhaps I can do without a British passport,' Nikki said recovering her poise and smiling maliciously. 'Perhaps I prefer a French one. I've been thinking about marrying Michel.'

'Fine,' Megan said with inward relief. This was precisely the direction in which she had hoped the conversation would go. 'I just want to make sure you know what you're doing. If you were to marry Michel before you had actually gained your British nationality, you might never get it. They might not push it through.'

Nikki laughed outright. 'Why would I care?' she asked.

'Because you would no longer be able to skate for Britain. Because the French might not select you for the Winter Olympics, but the British surely will, and because Eric Lamont does not intend to go to France,' Megan replied carefully.

'This is blackmail,' Nikki burst out. Glittering eyes and flushed cheeks. Megan knew all the signs of Nikki's tantrums, but this time she looked scared as well.

'No, it's not,' Megan said standing up. 'It's just the plain facts of life. I only wanted to warn you, so that you know the score before you make a choice. Remember, you're free and it's your choice. Now d'you want me to engage another coach, or would you rather do it yourself?'

'I'll stick with Eric,' Nikki whispered.

To Megan's amazement, the tears began to roll down Nikki's cheeks. 'I am totally manipulated here,' she blurted out, wringing her hands like a child. 'Where I may skate, what I may wear, how much I may spend, and now – even – loving. Why is this? Did Vanguard say this? Did the government say this? Why could I not keep my British nationality when I marry – like other British girls?'

'It's simply because you don't have it yet.' Megan retorted. 'But I'm trying Nikki,' she said more gently. 'I'm really trying. Hold fire for a while.'

Later, as she drove home, remembering Nikki's temper and

291

her eventual tears and her confession that she was not intending to marry yet, anyway, Megan felt guilty and wretched. If only she didn't react so badly to Nikki's rudeness. Surely she could be more understanding? Perhaps there was some truth in Nikki's lament after all. Perhaps she was being manipulated from all sides.

'I'm just as guilty as everyone else,' Megan muttered to herself in a burst of painful remorse. She had deliberately explained the odds to Nikki in order to prevent her from marrying, and herself from losing a valuable client. All the same, she rationalised, Nikki should know the facts of life before taking any detrimental steps. She didn't defect just to find a husband, did she? It was lucky Ian had reminded her of these dangers. Or was it lucky, she wondered suddenly, or superb strategy?

Reluctantly, she was beginning to suspect that she herself was as manipulated as Nikki. A nagging doubt was lurking in the back of her mind. Could Ian be involved? Was he a smooth, tactician masterminding every move with his helpful suggestions? Oh no! Her suspicions were so abhorrent to her. Once again she pushed them away vigorously, but she could never entirely eliminate them.

CHAPTER 42

The following morning, when Nikki emerged from her cottage for her morning jog round the park, she noticed that the guard was not waiting at her door. It was the second day running, and so far she had told no one about this. She felt uneasy and ashamed and she tried to push the nagging feelings of inferiority out of her mind.

After all, it was six months since she defected, she thought as she set off alone across the park. I'm free, she told herself uneasily. Free!

There was no joy in the knowledge; instead guilt was penetrating each particle of her being. Why feel guilty, she told herself repeatedly. She felt stunned by the realisation that while she was physically free, emotionally she was tied by a massive burden of guilt and that she would probably never throw it off. It was last night's news that had ruined her night's sleep. Her father had been sent to a sanitorium where he was resting. Resting! That could cover a wide variety of alternatives which she did not wish to investigate. She had never been fond of her father, she reminded herself repeatedly. He had never been a true father. That hard, despotic man who shared the same house had been devoid of feeling for his own family and totally obsessed with loftier considerations. Six months ago, she had no compunction at turning her back on her home and country. So why was she so upset by this news?

She progressed through her morning routine with a feeling of dread, performed particularly badly at her coaching session and endured Eric's reprimands without a whimper.

Afterwards, on impulse, she drove to Megan's office, but stopped on the way to buy some flowers. How lovely they were, she bought a bunch and then another. Eventually she had an armful of daisies, lupins and roses. Why not buy a cake, she thought as she put the flowers in the boot. The idea was tempting and she succumbed at the cakeshop around the corner from

293

Megan's office. Megan was the only one who could cheer her.

'Hey there, this is terrific,' Megan said, when she had recovered from the shock of seeing Nikki laden with cake and flowers. 'You should do this more often. You've come at a very good time. I have some good news for you. But first, is this a passing visit, or is there something specific?' Megan asked, noticing that Nikki looked tired and upset. She busied herself fetching plates while Maureen made the coffee. Megan had always felt guilty about Nikki, knowing that in spite of her cultured upbringing, Nikki was a simple girl, who saw life in terms of black and white. Things were either right or wrong, people were her friends or her enemies – there were no half measures and she had been elected to be Nikki's close friend – a position she felt she did not always fulfil, mainly because she had very mixed feelings about Nikki. She simply did not understand her. Nikki could be ruthlessly cruel one moment, and incredibly kind the next, but she was always an enigma.

She watched Nikki sit down, gulp her cake and launch into a tirade against Eric and his latest dance routine, but the implied insults and the skilful tactics for inveigling Megan's support, were below standard. It was easy to see that her mind was on something else.

After a while Nikki said: 'Megan. Why did you help me to defect? Was it because you were told to do so?'

Quivering lips, eyes brimful of tears, her chin thrust out aggressively, but a slump of defeat in her shoulders. She was childishly obvious in all of her moods. Megan read the signs well and decided to lie. 'I helped you because I knew you would be the world champion one day and I wanted to sponsor you.'

'And that is the truth, *da*?' Her eyes were brightening. This was obviously what she wanted to hear. 'It was simply a business arrangement. One of those deals you do so well, my dear Megan. But now we are friends, yes?'

'Well, of course. What else? Nikki, is there something wrong? You seem strangely preoccupied. Although it's lovely to see you, to be honest, it's a little unusual. What's the problem?'

'Nothing's wrong; everything's right,' Nikki said with a dazzling smile which did not quite make it. 'My guards have been removed. Just like that.' She snapped her fingers, but her hands were damp and there was no sound, so she smiled rather pathetically. 'This is my very first day of real freedom. It's been wonderful,' she lied.

Megan watched her shrewdly. 'And lonesome – or maybe just a little frightening?' she queried.

'Frightening. No! Maybe a little strange, *da*?' Nikki admitted.

'So now you're on your own. Congratulations! But we might as well find out why your guards have suddenly abandoned you.' She buzzed the intercom for Maureen. 'To tell the truth, Maureen, I don't know who to ask.'

'I expect Ian will know who's in charge,' Maureen said tartly. 'He seems to know everything.'

A few minutes later Ian was on the line. 'Nikki's here,' Megan explained. 'Her guard didn't pitch up.'

'I'll find out why and ring you back,' he said after some hesitation.

Ten minutes later he was on the line again. 'They should have let you know,' he said. 'They don't consider there's any danger to Nikki – it's almost six months since she defected and so far the Russians haven't tried to contact her. There's no reason why they should now.'

'Now?' Megan queried, but there was no reply from Ian. 'So that's it then? Back to normal.'

'I'm sorry if Nikki was alarmed, but tell her there's no need to be. She can settle down to lead a normal life. She's gained all she wanted, hasn't she? Tell her good luck from me.'

'You can tell her yourself. You are organising her next charity show, aren't you?'

'Actually Megan, I'm busy on a new script. Afraid I'll have to bow out for a while. I'm sure you'll manage brilliantly without me.'

'But Ian ...' she broke, not wanting Nikki to hear her protestations. This was absurd. Then it occurred to her that in six months she had never once managed to organise a public appearance for Nikki without Ian automatically taking charge. She'd been fighting him off most of the time. And now for some reason he was bowing out.

'Of course I'll help you if you need me.' He sounded reluctant. 'Listen Megan,' he hurried on, 'how about dinner later this week? If you have any problems we'll discuss them then.'

'I'm working late and then Nikki has a rehearsal. Will Thursday do?'

'Fine,' he said. 'Pick you up at the usual time.' He rang off.

How casual he sounded. Uninterested would describe it better. Megan had hoped that their relationship could return to normal now that her fears and jealousy had proved groundless. She felt disappointed, but none of this showed on her face as she turned to Nikki with a smile. 'The police consider you to be absolutely safe,' she told her. 'There's been no attempts to woo you back to Russia. You're considered part of the British scene,' she said, embroidering a little. 'In other words, you're no longer at risk – isn't that wonderful?'

'Or no longer useful.' Nikki closed her mouth firmly, as if ashamed of her outburst.

'Why, what do you mean, Nikki?'

'I mean nothing,' she snapped. 'I don't know why I said that. I was being silly.'

Megan could see the tears rolling down her cheeks. 'Nikki, what is it?' she asked. 'Something's upset you. Please tell me. You know you can count on me.'

Nikki gazed stubbornly out of the window, her hand over her mouth. Useless to question her.

'Listen Nikki, is there something I ought to know?'

No answer.

'If you don't feel safe we can employ a guard. D'you know how much money you have in your trust account? Almost half-a-million dollars. Doesn't that make you feel tremendous?'

'It's not enough,' Nikki said. She stood up abruptly, toppling her chair. 'Not nearly enough – not for what they've got out of me.'

Her eyes looked wild and tragic. Despair seemed to radiate from her and for the first time Megan wondered if she were slightly paranoid.

'Come on, Nikki, don't talk like that,' Megan said hurriedly. Could she be threatening a breakdown, she wondered? She knew she had been pushing Nikki too hard. Too many public appearances and long hours of coaching, and then the film on top of everything. 'You've got the world at your feet. You're young, beautiful, famous and rich. You're starring in a film and you're going to skate at the Olympic Games. That's official, as from this morning. Isn't that absolutely fantastic?'

'Wonderful! Yes, truly wonderful,' Nikki said. Then she burst into tears.

CHAPTER 43

It was seven-thirty, on a warm, August evening. The weather had been far too lovely to work, so Maureen had asked Megan for the afternoon off to walk over Hampstead Heath with Adolpho, or Johnny Bart as he was now known. I deserve it, she reminded herself guiltily. She had worked all hours for months and her holiday was weeks away. By then summer might have fled.

Johnny had needed the break, as much as she. Megan had been overbooking him, that was for sure. One appearance after the next, besides the hours he put in training and coaching at Universal's gym in Cheapside, now known as the *Johnny Bart Gym*. He was starting to look tired and that would never do – not with the championships coming up so soon.

She continued to file her nails, no longer red and pointed, since Johnny had objected to her talons, as he put it, but rounded and pearly pink. She was humming softly under her breath. She always did that when she was thinking. She was wondering how Johnny could get out of the whole Universal deal Megan had talked him into. If he made Mr Universe the bank would back him with his own gym, she was sure of that. Silly to waste his looks and his energy making other people rich.

Maureen looked up sharply and found herself gazing into Johnny's eyes. He was sitting across the room, in his shorts and shirt, and he was looking tremendous, if you ignored the shadows under his eyes. He was bronzed and muscled, with thick black hair on his chest. A real macho image, but he was saved from looking brutish by his sensitive face, and fine features. He was a hell of a looker, she thought for the umpteenth time, as she watched a thick black eyebrow rise in a question mark and his mouth curl into a lazy grin. Just one film, she thought. Just one miserable role as Tarzan and the women would go nutty for him. He didn't have to act, he just had to look as he looked now, not sensuous at all, but friendly and compassionate. He made you feel cared-for and sort of safe – which was a bit crazy when you thought about it sensibly.

'What were you thinking?' Johnny asked. 'You looked ferocious; your nail file was sawing away as if you were sawing someone's head off.'

'Then it must've been Megan's,' she said. 'because I was wondering how you could get out of this Universal deal.'

'I live on the Universal deal ...'

'No, not really. There's all sorts of bits and pieces coming in nowadays and it mounts up quick as anything. I want you to have your own gym. You will, you know, one of these days.'

'Then I would like it in Monaco,' he said, grinning like a naughty boy. 'I'd have all those fabulous French girls clamouring to get at me.'

Maureen felt hurt. 'Wouldn't do you much good though, would it? Nor them neither. Not the way things are,' she retorted pertly. Then she looked up and saw his hurt expression. 'Go on with you, I was only joking,' she said.

'How could you be joking, when you were telling the truth,' he said softly.

'True.' She smiled bravely, but she knew she'd rather bite her tongue off than hurt Johnny. She rose from the stool in a lithe, catlike movement and walked towards him, frowning thoughtfully. 'I was jealous when you talked about the French birds,' she said. 'Fact of the matter is, I'm in the same boat as you. Perhaps that's why I feel at home here.'

He gazed at her sceptically. 'That wasn't the impression you gave me when I first met you,' he said.

'Well, it's not the sort of thing you like to spread around, so I put on a bit of an act. You know, sort of sexy.'

'You look much sexier when you wear the clothes I buy you,' he said.

'I believe you,' she said smiling happily. Johnny had objected to her razzle-dazzle jewellery and brilliant colours and he had taken her out and bought smart tailored suits and dresses with expensive accessories and nowadays, with her hair scraped back and her face made up by experts, she had to convince herself it really was her when she looked in the mirror.

'Johnny, would you do me a favour?' she asked. 'The water

pipe's burst in my flat and the place is damp as anything. Drip, drip, drip, all bloody night. I hardly get a wink of sleep. The plumber's coming one of these days, but meantime I wondered if you could put me up.'

'Why-a not?' He shrugged. 'Help yourself. I'll even give you my bed. I'll sleep on the couch,' he added.

There was that pseudo-Italian accent back again. She'd scared him, she knew. 'Oh, there's no need to do that,' she said. 'I know I'm safe with you, Johnny. So I won't have to worry, will I?'

'No,' he said, looking glum.

It was midnight. Johnny was spreadeagled on the bed, the duvet kicked on to the floor and he was breathing heavily. They had left the curtains open and moonlight was flooding the room with its soft, sensuous glow. Maureen sat up softly and gazed longingly at this beautiful hunk she loved so much. If this is all there is, it'll do me, she thought. But that wouldn't stop her from trying for more.

They had dined well at home on grilled lobster, salad, a bottle of claret, followed by cheese and biscuits and they had sat for hours nibbling more cheese, drinking more wine and talking until they had decided to go to bed, which they had done laughingly, to break the tension. She'd felt really virginal putting on her newly-purchased lace nightie and scrambling into her side of the bed with a discreet: 'Night Johnny.' She had never felt so close to anyone in her life. Johnny felt the same way, too. She could tell that.

She pulled off her nightie, moved over the bed, lay her head upon his shoulder and snuggled up tightly. She felt his body stiffen and his breathing stop and then continue lightly. He was awake. 'I had a terrible nightmare,' she murmured. 'Hold me tight, I'm scared to death.' What's one more lie? she thought, after the whoppers I've told today.

His arms folded around her and he gently kissed her forehead. 'Go to sleep,' he said.

'Oh Johnny, I feel so safe when I'm with you,' she said.

He grunted and fell asleep.

Maureen ran her hands gently over his body, caressing and feeling, she pressed her lips on his belly and his thighs and tickled his skin with her tongue. He was languid and unwilling to wake, enjoying the dream, she knew, pretending he was unconscious of her movements and her intentions; falling into a state of drowsy euphoria, trusting her. Silly boy!

She reached down smoothing her hands over his belly and thighs and eventually touched and took hold of his flaccid member, rubbing it between her fingers and the palm of her other hand. Surely she felt a faint stirring and stiffening. There was a feeble twinge, a certain change in texture. The patient was not completely dead. There was hope.

She bent over in a swift, urgent gesture and pressed her lips around the tip and gently nuzzled – a kiss of life.

She knew he was awake. As wide awake as he would ever be, but still as a mouse. She knew he was hoping and that was exactly what she was trying to avoid. 'Maureen,' he whispered. Her patient suddenly froze, swooned and fell back limply unconscious.

'It's no good, Maureen,' he said. 'It's happened before. I'm sort of ... well ... shy.'

'You been to the doctor?'

'Sure I have.' He turned away from her and curled up facing the wall.

'What did he say,' she whispered as if they were indeed at the bedside of his gravely sick friend.

'He said there's nothing wrong. It's psychological.'

'Like me,' Maureen lied, still talking in hushed whispers. 'That's why I had that nightmare – just now I mean. Just the sight of you-know-what gives me the eebie-jeebies. I'd run a mile before I'd let them – well – you know. I can't even say the word. I just thought that touching yours might help me to overcome this phobia. You being safe – I mean you're not going to rape me, are you?'

'No,' he said miserably. 'That's not very likely.'

'So maybe I'll be able to lose my fear with you,' she said, 'if you'll let me. Will you let me?' She was running her finger round and round the tantalising problem.

There was no answer. Was that a tacit agreement that they should continue the lie? Or that her ridiculous sham was beneath his dignity. Or that he despised her for needing more than he could give?

She slipped off the bed and crouched on the floor, lay her

300

head upon his belly, heard the rumbling and the far off beat of his heart. At this moment she felt she loved him more than she loved herself. If dying would make him whole, then she would die happily. She knew without doubt that if some other bird could make it with Johnny she'd hand him over gladly. Just so that he could be happy. How lovely he looked with his head silhouetted against the white pillow. She bent forward, a quick, impulsive gesture, and pressed her soft, warm lips around him and sank her head upon him and lay there happy in the knowledge that all that was precious and tender – the very essence of Johnny – was tenderly trapped within her mouth.

'Oh Johnny, I'm not really a cheat,' she whispered a long while later. 'There's something you ought to know. I love you Johnny.' She waited but there was no answer, only the deep stentorous breathing which showed he had fallen asleep. 'I love you like I never loved anyone in all my life,' she went on. 'You could be my brother, or my son, or my father, or something. You must be something, not just another man, because I feel we're one and the same. Know what I mean?'

Why was this necessary, she wondered? Why would she never really feel loved unless their love was allied to physical coupling? Or was she kidding herself? Was it plain old-fashioned lechery? Just because of the way he looked. All she knew for sure was that she would never rest until Johnny was a whole man.

CHAPTER 44

It was a grey London morning following a night of intense heat. By midday it would rain. There was hardly any light in the corridor of London's Home Office, where it was stuffy and uncomfortable.

The room was empty except for Megan who looked out of place in her smart, white, Christian Dior dress, with a white snakeskin bag, navy boater hat and matching navy sandals. From a distance she looked elegant, poised and confident. A closer glance, however, showed the shadows under her eyes and a sense of anger in the quick flashes she darted at the door.

It was monstrous, absolutely monstrous. She smothered a cry of exasperation and tried to control her rising temper. They're enjoying this, she thought. Civil servants! My God! Big Brothers! with a capital B. It takes a special breed to keep people waiting like this, hour after hour. Good heavens, you silly old pig, no one's been in your office for the past hour, so what on earth are you doing in there? Having a snooze? Or playing power politics?

Trying to recover her poise, she fumbled for her notebook and began to write her day's programme. A quick glance at her watch showed that half the morning was already wasted. Good grief!

This was her tenth visit to various departments of the civil service, and so far she had made no progress, but merely endured the unnecessary waste of time, the polite indifference of various department chiefs, and the denial of any knowledge or responsibility.

She looked up frowning slightly as the door opened and the Under Secretary of the Home Office appeared.

'Miss Carroll? Delighted to meet you my dear young lady. I apologise for keeping you waiting, but I had a number of urgent telephone calls to attend to.' His manner and his voice were equally condescending and Megan's false calm rapidly evaporated. He was the sort of man she disliked on sight: plump and with gold-rimmed spectacles, shrewd grey eyes and the calm, unruffled manner of a man who has assured his pension and paid off his mortgage.

A real shrewdy, Megan decided, as she gripped his moist, soft hand.

'Well, Miss Carroll, I won't pretend not to know why you're here,' he said when she had sat down. He frowned and then thought better of it and forced a glimmer of a smile which made him blink several times. 'You've been stirring up my department with your impatience. We can't pretend to run the Home Office quite as you run your business, my dear. We have to keep to more orthodox methods. To tell the truth, I don't usually see people about citizenship applications, but in view of your persistence ...'

Megan ignored the jibe and cleared her throat. 'Mr Owen, I'll come to the point immediately. My client, Nikola Petrovna, is anxious to attend various skating competitions overseas. This is absolutely vital for her career. The European championships are being held in Hungary this year. She must attend. And then there's the small matter of my boss, John Oberholtzer, who would like her to give a number of exhibitions in America. Quite a reasonable request,' she rushed on, overriding his interruption, 'I'm sure you'll agree, but without a passport, for which she needs her citizenship papers, she is unable to leave Britain.'

She could see his expression hardening and she tried to soften her voice and disguise her hostility. 'Miss Petrovna was promised a passport when she defected in February. That's almost six months ago. Don't tell me it takes six months to produce a passport.'

'It's an unusual case,' he began primly. 'I don't believe that her file has reached my department yet ...'

'I've been shuttled from one department to the next for three months,' Megan blurted out. 'Someone is deliberately withholding my client's rights. You underestimate me – all of you – I'm telling you this now – I'll take the matter to the press. I'll raise such a storm of publicity. I feel totally responsible for Nikki's plight. It's a case of blatant manipulation, loss of human rights and dignity. She's no better off here than she was in Russia.'

'Shouting won't help, Miss Carroll. Let me explain how these

303

matters work. First, her file has to be cleared by the Foreign Office. There could be international implications in delicate matters such as these, he folded his hands and gazed at her solemnly for a few seconds, 'then the Minister will decide whether or not to grant British nationality. It's entirely at his discretion, you know. From the Ministry, her file is passed through to the Home Office and I assure you that we would not delay issuing citizenship – that is, once we have the authority to do so. After that, her passport is merely a formality. Passports are not withheld from British citizens. This is not a police state, Miss Carroll and I object to your tone and your innuendoes.'

He stood up. 'This is a matter for the Foreign Office,' he said firmly. 'I suggest you take it up with them.'

'I have six names here, all people I've been to see in the Foreign Office and each time I've sat waiting for hours – only to be told another story to explain the delay: the Home Office is overworked, a backlog at the Ministry, and so on. But I've seen the Minister's secretary and I know for a fact that Nikki's file has not yet reached his desk. Where is it? Who has it?'

He raised his hand to try to stem the flow, but Megan was too angry to care about good manners. She told the man exactly what she thought about his department and all other civil service departments in the British Isles.

'Miss Carroll, kindly control yourself,' the Under Secretary snapped.

Megan stood up. 'You're right,' she said contritely. 'That was silly of me. But it's like being tossed headlong into a Kafka novel.'

He smiled icily. 'Yes, I see, Miss Carroll, but if I might caution a little patience. Rest assured the matter will be processed expeditiously, the very moment Miss Petrovna's file reaches my department.'

'Could you tell me something,' she asked with all the appeal she could muster, catching him off guard. 'Where is this file? Who, or what, is holding it up? You know, don't you?'

He hesitated. For a moment she thought he was going to help her. Then his eyes assumed a bleak expression. 'Good day to you, Miss Carroll,' he said as he stood up and opened the door.

Megan had intended to go on to Nikki and tell her about the interview, but then she dodged that unpleasant duty. Nikki would be bound to throw a tantrum again. Why spoil her evening with bad news? Who knows what tomorrow might bring, she consoled herself. After all, they couldn't keep her prisoner forever.

She had a date for a quick drink with Ian, before returning home to catch up with her correspondence. He was waiting at their favourite pub and she ordered a Scotch on ice and poured out her troubles to Ian, who promised to try to help her. When she left an hour later, she felt much more confident about Nikki's plight. Ian had so many friends in high places, she felt sure that he would help her, but as far as their relationship was concerned, Ian was playing it cool. He seemed to be quite satisfied with a platonic friendship. Presumably she was not going to be forgiven for distrusting him. It's best this way, Megan told herself as she drove back.

She was home by eight, but after three hours of dictation, she felt very tired. She bathed and read for a while and eventually switched off the light, but found she could not sleep. She kept remembering the hostile grey eyes of the Under Secretary and the way he flushed each time he lied. Why? she wondered. Why did he have to lie? What was so goddamn special about Nikki's passport?

CHAPTER 45

Megan was dreaming. She heard the echo of a stag bellowing from high up in the misty mountains. The sound sent a spasm of excitement through the beagles milling around the courtyard and the stallions, too, pricked up their ears and their hooves beat urgently on the cobblestones at Aviemore.

Ian was riding a huge black stallion. He was wearing a kilt, with a pelt flung over his shoulders, but when Megan looked closer she saw that he was also the ancient tribal chief portrayed in the painting that hung in the great hall. His eyes were shining with excitement as he brandished his long spear and his mood was transmitted to the stallion who snorted and reared and pawed the stones with his hooves. Behind him a raggle-taggle mob of kilted men surged forwards and backwards on their ghostly mounts.

'Hurry,' Ian called to her impatiently.

'Will you kill it then?' she asked nervously.

Ian looked angry. 'That's the point of the exercise,' he said. 'This isn't a war game. Either you're with us, or you can't come here at all.'

Her mare was skittish and bit the other horses until she sidled next to Ian's great stallion, urging the rest out of the way.

Then they were off, side by side, galloping out of the gate, down across the moors, past streams and woods of silver birch, towards the mountains that rose dark and forbidding above them. She smelled the steaming sweat of her frantic mount, felt its nervous tension surging through her thighs to her whole body. They raced forward as one being, half-human, half-beast, fired with a blood lust racing through their joined veins.

Up and up they galloped, wild and frenzied, until they neared the summit of the Igman Mountains. Megan thought: how far we have come and how high on these magnificent horses.

There was a sudden sighting of the stag, the beagles bayed louder, a bugle blew and Ian shouted: 'Look! There!'

A dim shape moved wraithlike through the mist, racing higher, above the treeline. Ian was blowing his bugle. 'There! Can't you see it?' He looked fierce and cruel as he trembled with impatience.

Megan could only see Nikki, clad in a diaphanous white muslin dress that showed her white limbs and her thin trembling body. She was racing on skates over the rocks and snow and as they gained on her, they could hear the whimpers of fright and the rasping of her breath.

'No, no, no,' Megan screamed, but Ian was ahead and he charged down on the frantic girl with his spear held stiffly in front of him, piercing her arm. Nikki fell in a tangle of snarling dogs and Megan could only see blood.

'You're killing her. You're killing her,' Megan screamed accusingly. Trying to kick her horse ahead of his.

'Of course. That's the whole point of it,' Ian told her. 'Don't be squeamish, Megan. That's the whole point of her defection.'

There was a loud keening, like a hare in a trap, and something moved beneath the dogs. Megan thought: I must get down, and help her. I must. She struggled to dismount, but she was unable to move. She tried harder, groaning with the effort. I must, I must, but her limbs were leaden and would not obey her. She was sobbing with the effort, flailing her arms. Then Nikki stopped moving ...

Megan awoke drenched in sweat.

The room was stuffy and dark. When she fumbled for the light switch it was not there, nor was her bedside table. She lay still, trying not to panic. Was she still asleep? The dream had been so real, she had the impression that she would have rescued Nikki, if it had lasted a moment longer.

Slowly she fumbled around and then her hands encountered the brass rails at the bottom of the bed. She had been sprawled sideways, that was all. When she switched the light on she saw that her blankets and pillows were flung across the floor.

'Some nightmare!' she said, but there was no relief in being awake. She put on her dressing gown and went into the kitchen, but the bright lights and familiar paraphernalia could not dispel her fears. It was all there – an ominous foreboding of future crimes and the guilt of those already committed.

Why was she so depressed, she wondered? It was only a dream. Perhaps a cup of coffee would help. When she filled the kettle she saw that her hands were shaking badly. Lately she had not slept well, and she knew why. There were too many unanswered questions about Nikki's defection, lurking under the surface, but she had steadfastly refused to face her suspicions. Why? Was it because she knew that if she acknowledged that Nikki's defection was planned for reasons other than her skating, then she would have to accept that she, too, was as manipulated as Nikki. She was, in fact, merely a pawn, moved in a sinister game, by unknown hands and God knows what the outcome might be. The unwanted thought forced itself into her conscious mind. Was Ian the arch manipulator?

No! Her whole being shrieked in outrage. No, no, no.

Then who was Ian? He was not a bluff Scottish landowner, nor a failing, hopeful writer, although she wished with all her heart that he was one or the other. Either would do. Deep inside, she knew there was another Ian, a deeply committed and motivated man, a fiercer Ian, bred from ancient feuds and bloody battles, a man who would stop at nothing to achieve his ends. Whatever they were!

Nikki, too, had her secrets. Why had she cried when the guards were removed? What was it that she had said? It had sounded so odd at the time, but Megan could no longer remember.

She knew that Nikki needed her. Lately the girl had looked haggard and miserable, but Megan had avoided involvement with any problems Nikki might have, beside her career.

Why? The answer was simple. Because she feared the truth.

The kettle's whistling brought her back to reality. She felt so alone, she was tempted to telephone her mother, but that would be giving in. Then she thought: Why not? Back home it was still afternoon.

The sound of her parents' familiar voices made her feel worse instead of better. They were fine, she was fine, and she wished with all her heart to be back home right now. She tried to disguise the longing in her voice.

After she replaced the receiver, her small flat seemed more isolated than before.

It occurred to her that Nikki had no one to telephone when

she was depressed. Home, whatever that had meant to Nikki, was forever closed to her. For a bleak and terrible moment, Megan had a glimpse of Nikki's world. 'I must have been blind as well as spiteful,' She murmured, stung with regret.

Then she remembered her dream. She stood up briskly and dialled Nikki's number. The telephone rang for a long time, but there was no reply. Feeling numb with apprehension, Megan pulled on a tracksuit and raced for her car.

There were no lights on upstairs, no cars parked outside the door, it looked normal, but no one answered when she rang the bell. Feeling frantic with anxiety, Megan fumbled for the spare key, which she kept in her handbag, opened the door and rushed upstairs.

Nikki was sprawled on the bed amongst the blood stains. So much blood! Pale cheeks tinged with blue, her mouth hanging slack and loose, eyes closed and her hair damp and dishevelled.

'Oh my God,' Megan gasped. 'Oh my God!'

Overwhelmingly guilt was the uppermost emotion in her mind as she grabbed Nikki's pulse and held tightly, praying for signs of life.

I've pushed her too hard, neglected her as a woman or a friend, spurned her because of my stupid suspicions and then failed to heal the breach – and she needed me. Yet I treated her as a business asset. I have failed as a moral person and this is the result of my neglect.

There was no pulse. For heaven's sake, what was she to do? She could not think. 'I must pull myself together,' she mumbled. The blood was still oozing out of Nikki's wrists. Somewhere she remembered reading that the human body contains eight pints of blood. Surely there was more than this soaking the bed. 'Must stop it ... stop it ... somehow ...'

She raced to the cupboard, grabbed some filmy white material and began frantically ripping at it, binding the wounds, stopping the blood. Then the telephone ... Ian! He would get the ambulance faster than she could.

Megan prayed he was in. The telephone rang only twice but it seemed to last an hour before ...

'Oh thank God ... Nikki ... cut her wrists ... ambulance. D'you hear. Ambulance!' she cried out. 'Yes, I'm here at her cottage, but we may be too late.'

She replaced the receiver and stood bending over Nikki

309

frantically wishing there were something else she could do. Keep her warm. She'd read that, too. It couldn't do any harm. She took the bloodsoaked blankets and wrapped them round the pale form. Then she lay down beside her and tried to warm her. Still no pulse!

Was she dead? Had she really tried to kill herself? Perhaps the Russians ...? No, she dismissed that thought. What would Ian say? He would blame her, and quite rightly, too. She blamed herself. Oh God, why is there no pulse? Surely she's not dead.

'Dear God, don't let her die,' she pleaded, remorse and love swelling her grief. 'Just let her live.'

Then she heard the ambulance approaching at top speed. Even in her frantic state she realised that this was record timing.

Nikki recovered consciousness three hours later in a private ward of an army clinic outside London with two guards outside the door.

Megan was surprised when the ambulance had taken them there, but she had no cause for complaint; Nikki was surrounded by doctors and specialists.

Ian arrived before Nikki recovered. He stood staring at the unconscious girl in silence, then slowly turned on his heels to face Megan. 'Wrong method. Completely wrong,' he said. 'They hardly ever die this way; the veins seal over, you see. She'd have done better to jump out of the window.' Megan glared at him.

'Make sure no one finds out about this accident,' he continued. 'Particularly the press. It would ruin Nikki's chances of being chosen for the games.'

Would it? she thought silently. Or are there other reasons. Or am I going crazy. But why are you so angry, Ian? Why was Nikki pushed into the limelight and why have you switched off her now, and why have the guards been removed? Too many questions. If only she could ask him outright: Ian, tell me the truth for God's sake, do you work for British Intelligence? And is this all your work? But what was the point of asking? Ian would deny everything – even if it were true.

Ian was still glaring out of the window. Looking at him she

wanted to reach out and touch him, he was so achingly familiar with his brown hair streaked by the sun, and the Harris tweed jacket she loved so. She knew exactly the expression on his face right now – his buttoned-up look. But when he turned, she found she had been quite wrong – there was pleading in his eyes.

'Megan, apart from all this, there's also a question of you ... and I. I want you to come to Aviemore for the August holidays,' he said. 'We can talk there. There's so much I want to say to you.'

Megan's eyes widened in disbelief. 'I can't leave Nikki,' she said. 'Who would look after her?'

'She'll be better by then.'

Men can be so cruel, Megan thought. She shook her head.

'All right, bring her,' he said reluctantly. Then his face brightened. 'Of course, bring her. It will do her good to get away from London. She'll love the countryside and so will you. You've never been there in summer. Say yes,' he urged her. 'It would be so good for Nikki.'

'Yes,' Megan said, pushing away her doubts and fears, only too happy to believe in him. 'Just as soon as Nikki is well enough.'

CHAPTER 46

It was a scene for decorating chocolate boxes, Eleanor thought, and wondered for the umpteenth time if she had erred in her choice of venue. The altitude was making her feel dizzy. They were high up on a Swiss glacier, currently used as a training ground for at least three European countries. Crystal white mountain peaks soared against the deep blue sky, while gaily-clad skiers made vivacious splashes of colour against the snowy backdrop.

A group of advertising men and technicians were gathered in front of the halfway station restaurant. Eleanor's two secretaries were there, as well as sixteen top New York advertising executives, several porters and six Parisian models, one of whom was male, plus an expensive French freelance photographer, who had been flown in only this morning when the agency's photographer broke his leg. The ski crowd, sprawled on benches or sitting at the tables in the snow, were trying not to show their amusement as the ad team sweated in their arctic gear and slithered in brand new moon boots.

'Let's get the hell out of this Eskimo clothing,' Herb, the art director, groaned as he stripped down to the waist. 'The goddamn French have everything arse-about-face. Snow in the tropics! Who'd believe it? Doesn't make sense,' he growled to no one in particular.

They were filming a five minute TV commercial about Vanguard's *après-ski* wear, and it was intended that women, having viewed the commercial, would feel that it was not necessary to be a skier in order to wear these fabulously flattering ski fashions.

The morning had not been a success: the advertising team swore at each other, at the models, at the skiers who kept getting in the way and at the hundreds of takes that had been wasted.

Cretins, every last one of them, the French photographer,

312

called Pierre, had decided. As for that poor young Jacqui they had roped in from the British team as stunt girl and model, for some reason no one seemed to like her and Pierre couldn't imagine why she put up with them.

He glanced at his watch. It was time for her to begin her next descent, the fifteenth that morning. Five minutes later he was still wondering what was keeping her.

Much higher, on the very lip of the piste, Jacqui was crouched on her skis, elbows on her knees, holding her head in her hands. Here it was even more beautiful, and so peaceful with a curious absence of any sound. Jacqui was reluctant to start. 'If Mother beefs at me this time, I'll walk out,' she muttered. 'To hell with the frigging contract. She can frigging well sue.' She was not a model, never would be, and she was determined that Mother would find that out today, and that thereafter she would be spared from sessions such as this. The British team were training here and she was missing the day and she was fed up. Well, she might as well try again.

She straightened, dug her poles into the snow and shot forward for a fast schuss down, moving naturally into the skiers' classic 'skating step' with one ski pushed ahead of the other for extra speed as she came out of the turns.

Herb was standing in a huddle with the account director and the copywriter. They had already agreed that they would never please Eleanor, but eventually she would get tired of forking out four hundred dollars an hour and give up. Then Herb would be able to take a short vacation before flying home.

He glanced over his shoulder towards the video and screen where Eleanor was scanning each take. She was scowling ferociously.

'What the hell is delaying Jacqui?' he yelled. Then he saw her racing down, leaning well forward, arms together in front of her knees. He sighed. It might be a classic skiing position, but it was hell for showing the garments. Nearing the cameras, Jacqui straightened, squared her shoulders, as they'd told her to, and turned in a welter of snow spray. So far, so good. Jacqui took off her helmet, shook her hair and gave her own uniquely hostile sneer towards the camera.

'Shit!' he murmured. 'Shit, shit, shit.' There should be a special hell for clients who roped in relatives to appear in their advertising campaigns.

'Goddamn it, no!' he yelled. 'Cut!' He didn't need to look at Eleanor to know that they had notched up yet another failure. 'For Christ's sake, let's have a lunch break. If only she'd break her damn leg,' he murmured to his assistant. 'Then we could bring in a professional. Too bad if she teeters on the slopes, just as long as she can smile.'

Pierre caught up with Jacqui as she moved away from the chattering throng. 'Have lunch with me?' he called out in French. 'Let's find a table away from these idiots.'

She shrugged. 'Why not?' Mother would be annoyed, but Mother was angry anyway. Lately she always was.

'Why don't you throw in the towel?' Pierre asked halfway through lunch when they had both exhausted their small talk. 'Serve that formidable battle-axe right.' He was concentrating on his barley soup, wiping the plate carefully with his French bread, so he did not see Jacqui's astonishment, which left her open mouthed and gawping and afterwards the amusement in her eyes and the flickering smile around her mouth.

'You want to know something, *chèrie*? You're never going to make a model. You're too honest. You can't pretend. You're pissed off and it shows. But skiing – that's another matter. You're talented.' He looked up and smiled charmingly. 'Why not stick to skiing, Jacqui? You can make a fortune in France coaching kids in the season. Enough to last through winter. Hundreds of youngsters do it, and they can't all ski as well as you.'

'I'll think about it,' Jacqui said cautiously, smiling politely to acknowledge his compliment. She liked this diminutive, highly-strung cameraman with his rapid French, his graceful hands and his wrinkled brown face. She did not feel like embarrassing him. God knows, she needed a friend. Funny that Pierre did not know who she was, she thought, but then she remembered he had only arrived that morning and language problems had probably prevented him from gossiping with the American advertising team.

'Don't you know who I am?' she asked curiously.

'Should I? Sorry if I've offended you?' He grimaced and grinned again.

She giggled. 'I was only teasing,' she said.

He lifted his hands palms uppermost in a gesture of

314

resignation. 'You want to be a model, eh? All the girls do. Is that why you took this job, *chérie?*'

'I needed the cash to train – Vanguard sponsored me and modelling was part of the deal.'

'That figures.' His eyes surveyed her face, her hair and her figure, but for some reason Jacqui was not insulted. She sensed that it was not a sensual survey, but one of technical appraisal. 'You're part of their new campaign. Looks instead of expertise. It's part of their survival strategy.'

'Survival?' she queried.

'Sure. Vanguard is fighting a back-to-the-wall campaign against a takeover bid. The press has been full of it, but I don't suppose you read the financial pages, do you?'

'No,' she said, feeling shocked.

'This entire campaign was dreamed up by the great Eleanor Douglas herself – or so we were briefed. The agency aren't keen on it at all, but at four hundred dollars an hour they aren't beefing. The idea is to widen Vanguard's market by selling ski gear to housewives. It's trendy to be sporty! See what I mean? So the little woman will trot down to the supermarket in her smart new Vanguard ski jacket and kid herself she's having a good time. That's where you come in. You ski well, but you also look beautiful, so that creep,' he nodded at the male model, 'picks you up in your snazzy ski jacket.' He watched her quizzically, but there was no reaction.

Jacqui excused herself, insisted on paying for her own lunch and went to find Mother.

'Mother,' she called. She saw Eleanor sitting in the sun, her head thrown back and her eyes closed. Mother was dozing and Jacqui studied the familiar features dispassionately. Mother was ageing fast, she had puffy eyes, crows feet at the corners, and her neck was beginning to show signs of chicken skin. She should not sit in the sun so much, Jacqui thought. How absurd she looked in her skin tight, lurex ski pants. That was Mother – always outrageously dressed.

'Mother,' she said louder.

Eleanor opened her eyes and then closed them fast with a wince. She sat up and held her hand across her forehead. 'Can you see my sunglasses. They must have fallen off.'

Jacqui bent to retrieve them. No wonder they fell off, they were heavy with marquisette.

'They don't seem to make much difference,' Eleanor moaned. 'Oh my head. It's this glare.'

Jacqui fumbled in her pocket and took out her spare goggles. 'Put these on,' she ordered.

Eleanor did as she was told. 'What do I look like?'

'Absurd. Just as absurd as you did without them,' Jacqui said rudely. 'I just heard from the ski crowd that Vanguard are losing out in a takeover bid. That true?' she asked, tight-lipped and scared.

'Why Jacqui – don't be pessimistic. I've a few tricks up my sleeve. What's it to you? You've always hated Vanguard and either way you're rich. So, you have nothing to worry about, do you? You do? Surprise, surprise,' she went on without waiting for Jacqui to comment. 'I'm gratified, but don't worry, love, between us and Nigel and the staff we control forty-one per cent of the shares. It's most unlikely anyone could wrest the majority, particularly since a certain trust company controls another ten per cent and they happen to be old friends of mine.

'Why, Jacqui ... darling ... whatever is the matter? You look so pale. Don't be an idiot. Trust your old mother. We're in the winning seat.'

She grinned in surprise and sympathy as Jacqui collapsed on the bench beside her. 'However, it hasn't done shareholder confidence any good at all,' she went on. 'So this worldwide campaign is supposed to show them what Vanguard and the Douglas family, are made of.'

Jacqui looked away. She did not want Mother to see the tears in her eyes. She felt wretched with guilt. *But Mother; you don't control forty-one per cent, because I've exchanged my shares for oil wells. But I never dreamed ... never thought.*

Now, for the first time, she saw her mother as a vulnerable, middle-aged matron. What had Pierre called her? A formidable battle-axe. For some reason that had hurt Jacqui. It was okay if *she* criticised Mother, but no one else had the right to.

For a moment she was tempted to blurt out the truth. But possibly Wolf had not sold her shares yet. Perhaps she could still retrieve the situation without panicing. Meantime, what should she say to Mother?

God help me, but I feel more angry than guilty. What sort of a person am I? Some sort of a freak? But Mother, you had no

*right to fail; not to tell me what was going on; to behave like a
God and then grow old.*

A sudden flash of insight hit her like a slap in the face as she
realised that she had always taken their wealth and power for
granted. Of course, she had intended to join the company at some
far off future date, when she had found herself, or when she felt
like it. It was all Mother's fault, she thought moodily. How dare
she promise so much and then act like ...? Like ...? *Like she was
human*, a voice inside her whispered.

'Well, it's not working out too well, is it? Eleanor was saying
scathingly. 'Why don't we pack up now? When you're with me
you just can't help sneering.'

'I've read the score at least a hundred times,' Jacqui said, and
suddenly it was desperately important for her to get it right. 'But
that doesn't help me understand. Really Mother, I want to get
this thing off my back. Tell me where I'm going wrong.'

Eleanor sat up and peered suspiciously at her daughter. 'I've
just agreed to throw in the towel and let a model take over the
close-ups with you doing the skiing,' Eleanor explained. 'It seems
the sensible thing, but I thought ... I mean, just think what a
scoop it would be if you could pull it off.'

'Just explain,' Jacqui persisted. 'We'll give it one more go.'

'D'you know why I finally decided to sponsor you?'

'No,' Jacqui said flatly. 'I've often wondered.'

'It was that look on your face when you'd just hurtled down
the hill at Sarajevo. Pure ecstasy! Don't look surprised. Megan
played the whole run to me. I fought you on it for a while, but it
was then I realised that skiing isn't just a sport to you – it's a
source of joy. Your father was like that, but skiing destroyed
him.'

Jacqui turned around with a look of astonishment on her face.
'Tell me about him,' she pleaded.

'Oh I will, I will. One day ... but right now, at four hundred
dollars an hour ...'

Jacqui leaped to her feet.

To hell with Wolf, Jacqui thought as she clutched the tow bar to
the top of the highest piste. She was going to get her shares back.
She could not stick a knife in her own mother. She would have
liked to have explained to Mother exactly why she loved skiing,

317

about the intensity of each moment, speed and danger did that to her – in the Sarajevo video her expression had been one of rapt elation because she had won the race against herself.

'Well, if that was all Mother wanted ...'

'What the hell is she going up there for?' Pierre muttered to his assistant as he watched Jacqui moving slowly to the mountain peak. Maybe she was showing off to him, he thought, and grinned wryly.

Twenty minutes later, he swore when he saw her rocketing down. For a few seconds he thought she'd run out of control, until he saw the way she turned at the first mogul, and raced on down in a series of jump turns, using one pole for speed. 'Who the hell is she?' he yelled to his assistant. And then: 'Thank God I caught that shot.'

Jacqui was in a fast schuss now, reaching up to eighty miles an hour as she remembered Sarajevo. She heard the voice echoing from the loudspeaker, saw the throng of skiers as she zoomed through the last gate and slowed to a halt. Suddenly she wrenched off her helmet and grinned at the cheering crowd. It had seemed so real, she had almost expected Rob Scott to materialise out of the throng. Instead the creep was sauntering towards her, so she grinned at him instead.

'That's it, Jacqui,' Herb was yelling excitedly. 'That was terrific. Keep walking, not too fast, don't trip, for Christ's sake don't trip. You're going fine ... another smile like the last one, turn slightly this way, so we can see the jacket better. Shoulders back, Jacqui, sit down, slowly, slowly ... what's your hurry? Wave to the waiter. Fine ... fine ... fine. Now look up and smile one last time.'

'That just about wraps it up,' Herb said as the creep put his hand on Jacqui's shoulder. 'Cut everyone. That's it, coffee time.'

Jacqui did not wait around. She could not face Mother again today. She grabbed her skis and fled.

CHAPTER 47

'So you came at last, Eleanor.' Gundelfinger turned away, trying to hide his annoyance as he flicked over the pages of his diary.

'You haven't been for a month. I charge for sessions if patients can't be bothered to cancel. You know that, don't you?'

'I can afford to do what I damn well like,' Eleanor snarled ungraciously.

'Sure, if that makes you feel better. You might like to analyse the reason why you feel good when you mess people around. Do you do this to everyone?'

Eleanor pressed her lips tightly together and sat on the couch. 'I'm here, aren't I?' she said belligerently.

Gundelfinger caught hold of her arm and ran his finger along her skin. 'This looks healthier,' he said. 'I think the eczema is going to clear up.'

'It comes and goes.' She pulled her arm away.

'Eleanor, Eleanor! You're never really honest. You couldn't face coming here. Isn't that true?'

'I've been busy,' she mumbled.

'All right,' he said briskly. 'Let's not waste time. Carry on where you left off last time.'

Eleanor sighed and gazed out of the window with an expression of hopelessness on her face.

'You have to face it Eleanor.'

'The guilt?'

'Face your trauma. Your guilt may be imaginary.'

Unwilling to examine her memory, with its grief and treachery, she made herself think of pleasanter times, when she and Jerry had met again in America. It had taken him five years to finish his education, leave Austria and find her. He took only one month to court and marry her. She never called

319

him Jerry again. The name was outmoded and the war half-forgotten. Besides, Jerry did not want to remember his time as a prisoner. She never really liked the name Wolf, but she got used to it in time. Mrs Wolf Muller! She had always objected to having to change her name, but in those days there was no alternative. How happy they were. She loved him with all her heart and wanted nothing more than to slave for him and be with him.

Wolf was unemployed at the time; living on capital supplied by his mother, but she was pulling in good commissions selling winter sports goods for one of Denver's leading wholesalers. To her surprise, Wolf made no effort to find a job. He spent most of his spare time skiing and with the remainder of his capital, he speculated on the stock exchange. All Eleanor's Scottish ethics were affronted. She waited for the inevitable to catch up with him, but it never seemed to.

She remembered an evening during winter when he came back from skiing and rushed into the bathroom where she was drying herself after a bath. He was wildly excited and called out: 'I've made five thousand dollars today.'

'Nonsense. Don't tell me lies,' she had called out. 'You've been skiing all day.'

He had clasped her in his arms, picked her up, and carried her to the bedroom. 'Spentex shares have doubled their price and we have doubled our capital, so tonight we celebrate,' he had told her excitedly. 'So we make love and we drink champagne.'

'We don't have any champagne,' she had argued laughingly as he waltzed her around the bedroom.

'I brought some with me. Any more feeble excuses?'

There had been nothing wrong with their love making. Even now, twenty years later, she felt herself reacting to the memory of Wolf and his virile body. Then she remembered Gundelfinger and switched off.

'Wolf studied commerce in Vienna,' she began in a monotone. 'And then his parents gave him part of his inheritance. It wasn't much, but it was enough for him to come looking for me. We married and at first we were happy,' she said.

She tried to hang on to the happiness, but the memories were not potent enough to keep the nightmare at bay and it was relentlessly sidling up to her. She felt as if she would suffocate.

'You'll run out of tissues,' she warned in a feeble attempt at humour.

'No sweat. I buy them in bulk.' Like Wolf, Gundelfinger was always using American slang, but it never sounded quite right. 'Are you German by birth?' she asked out of the blue.

'Does it matter?'

'I'm curious, that's all.'

'You're digressing, that's all.'

Eleanor sighed. 'Okay,' she said, resigned and pitious. 'I stole the business from Wolf Muller and he fully deserved it.'

'Then good luck to you,' he said flatly. 'Keep going.'

'He was a vain, self-indulgent man and he turned out to be a total bastard.'

'Strange! The way you described him before, he sounded rather nice.'

'Well, I can describe him any way I damned well like, can't I?'

'Sure, be my guest.'

She peered over her shoulder and was surprised to see that Gundelfinger was yawning. Let him suffer, she thought.

'Wolf played the stockmarket and spent most of his time skiing. He was dead set on making the US Olympic team. That was all he thought about. That and making money. He wanted to get rich quick, but he didn't want to do any work. He used to laugh at me. He called me his little beaver, because I worked hard for my money – out selling all hours, all weather – yet he made as much as I did, sometimes more, and that used to annoy the hell out of me.

'One day, a ski workshop came on the market and Wolf bought it on the spot. I was so happy. I thought he would settle down and build up the workshop, but Wolf just kept on skiing. The previous owner was retained as manager and I helped plan the marketing evenings and weekends. I had no intention of quitting my job. So between us, and with the extra cash Wolf had borrowed from the bank, the workshop doubled its turnover.

'I used lie awake nights worrying about the cash we owed the bank, but after a year we managed to repay most of it. I was just beginning to feel secure when Wolf sold the workshop – just like that. He didn't even ask what I thought – or wanted. I nearly left him then.' Her voice tailed off and for a while she sat silently, gazing at her hands.

She had intended to leave. She could remember that

afternoon so clearly. She had felt belittled and rejected. How dare he shove her around; exploit her time and her skills only to dispose of their business without so much as asking. As if her opinion counted for nothing. She had told him so at great length. Eventually, Wolf had slunk off to the ski club, and she had packed and was bringing the car round to load the boot, when she had remembered the meat had been ordered, but not delivered and there was no bread, so she had left her suitcases in the passage and driven to the shopping centre to stock up. It had seemed unthinkable to leave Wolf with nothing to eat. When she got back, Wolf was carefully putting away her underwear and all her things were piled on the bed. He had hidden the suitcases.

'If you leave me,' he had said very solemnly, 'who will supervise our new pickling plant? We'll go bust.'

Our pickling plant. That was the magic word which had kept her from leaving. 'Goddammit, what pickling plant?' she had yelled, pretending to be furious, but in fact, she had been glad of a reason to stay.

Gundelfinger cleared his throat and Eleanor realised she had been thinking silently for a while.

'I was still working,' Eleanor said aloud. 'We lived on my earnings, Wolf's money was considered to be capital. We weren't allowed to spend a penny of it. Consequently, we were always hard up.

'We bought a pickling plant, but it lost money from the word go. Wolf borrowed the cash to buy up the manufacturing rights to a local chutney and I helped him market it nationwide. That was what saved us. I remember coming back from work tired out and putting in another five to six hours a night – for three years. A nightmare! Our expenses were five thousand dollars a month, our profit potential minimal, our loss potential enormous, but the chutney was doing well, and I reckoned we'd come right in time. A few years hard work and we'd have made it, but Wolf put the plant up for sale and we lost over half of our capital.

'Why did he do these things? I never could understand him, but his answer was always the same: "because our time is even more valuable than our capital; it is unextendable."

'For six months Wolf skiied and I found another job – with Vanguard Sports, a small wholesale outfit with a workshop attached for repairs and some custom-built skis. Wolf seemed to be wrapped up in his own gloom. It was hard to get through to him, but I loved him more then than at any other time. He felt guilty, so he went out of his way to make me feel good. He was really a giant of a man in many ways. He was so handsome. He had the sort of features that improve with age. His face became more hawkish, his eyes sterner, his nose more prominent – like an ancient Roman nobleman. In spite of his depression, his sense of humour made him fun to live with. He kept himself fit and watched his diet as if he still had a chance of skiing for America, but of course he was too old. He was almost thirty-three – and he still had not struck it rich, in spite of all his efforts, it was taking longer than he had expected.

'It was really through me that he learned about the opportunities in the sports industry. He started looking around and discovered a small retail business whose proprietor was due to retire. This time he wanted me to give up my job and take over the sales, but I wouldn't – and we fought like hell. He used to tell me I was a fool, a born worker, doomed to spend my life toiling to make other people rich. He was very persuasive. I used to lock myself into the bathroom, put my hands over my ears. It seemed to me that to scorn hard work was to invite starvation.

'And then one day he said it was my duty – well duty was something I understood. He said that I was being disloyal, a bad wife and I was upset, but still I couldn't pluck up the courage to leave my job. My earnings were what we lived on.

'Then one day my boss called us all in and told us he was facing bankruptcy, and he was expecting to be closed down very soon. We should all start looking for jobs, he told us. I came home feeling fed up and I said to Wolf: "Why don't you go right out and buy up the debts of Vanguard Sports. The creditors would probably settle for anything they can get. You can have my savings," I told him, "but I want my fair share of the company – tied up and legal."

'My Presbyterian upbringing cried out against this settling debts on a percentage basis and borrowing cash from the bank to finance the deal. I didn't sleep nights for a long time after this. In a way, it was like setting sail in a ricketty cockleshell boat and struggling through waves of debt with no sign of land in sight. I would never have let go of my secure job, but in some strange way, I felt I was employing myself and I would take damn good care that I was never thrown out of work again.'

She stood up, glancing at her watch. 'That's all Vanguard meant to me at first – steady employment.' She laughed grimly. 'That's the trouble with life; you can't hang on to a good thing and make it last; everything changes even companies have to grow or fail.'

CHAPTER 48

Megan was dawdling towards the Mackintosh homestead, feeling heavy with drowsiness, enjoying the country evening. She heard a sudden, shrill cry of a plover from the woods around the loch and the low of cattle in the distance. Warm, moist air caressed her face, there was a tang of damp earth and grass, and the murmur of innumerable insects' wings trembling in the summer air.

She was glad she had come. This morning she had fetched Nikki from the hospital and driven her to Heathrow for their flight to Inverness, wondering if she was doing the right thing. She was worried about Nikki, she looked so depressed and in spite of a heart-to-heart talk with her Megan had not yet been able to find out why she had attempted to take her life.

Nikki had always been secretive, she reasoned, particularly in emotional matters. Why, since their talk at the ice rink, Nikki had never again mentioned Michel, yet he had telephoned the office repeatedly, begging for news of Nikki. Maureen fobbed him off each time. Megan had no intention of letting Michel find out about Nikki's accident, as she euphemistically called it. Megan had reported all this to Nikki every time she visited her, but Nikki had not shown much interest.

However, with Ian, Nikki had immediately improved her mood. She enjoyed Ian's sense of humour and by tea time, she almost seemed her old self again. Consequently Megan had begged off accompanying the two of them to the village pub, insisting that she did not feel like going.

She turned at the gate and watched Ian and Nikki toiling up the distant hill until they disappeared from sight. They were taking a shortcut to the village and Megan had accompanied them for part of the way. She knew Ian was puzzled and annoyed because she was not going, but that was just too bad. She just wanted Nikki to be happy. She would explain later.

She paused for a moment to stare at the stone mansion, gaunt and massive, with no pretentions towards glamour or aesthetic appeal. It would still be there in a few hundred years time, with its twisted corridors and forgotten rooms. It could have been built snug in the valley beside the loch, she thought, smiling gently, but that was not the Mackintosh way.

She began to sing as she hurried home: '*So we'll walk up the avenue, since we haven't got a car ...*'

She was still singing when she reached the house ten minutes later. She walked into the hall and pulled the great oak door shut behind her. There was a smell of damp stone and the cold seemed to rise from the floor as if from an underground refrigeration plant. Megan shivered and opened the door wide.

'What this place needs,' she said aloud, 'is some fresh air and sunlight.' And so much more she thought quietly to herself. Warmth, children, noise, fun – and love. She ran her hands over the oak panelling: 'Perhaps a touch of wood preservative, too.'

'Och, I fancy myself as the Highland lady,' she said aloud, and clowned a Highland Fling as she hummed the music.

'I'm thinking it's a grand Scottish dancer you'll be after a few lessons.' It was the housekeeper's voice and Megan uttered a startled exclamation.

'Good grief! I didn't see you there in the shadows. I was just kidding,' Megan said, feeling her colour rising. 'You must think I'm crazy ...' Megan smiled at her.

'Och, no. Never crazy. The old place needs someone like you. It's right glad I'd be to see Master Ian married,' she went on curiously. 'Maybe put a bit of life into the house.'

'I'll pass on your advice,' Megan teased her.

'You can do that,' she said primly. 'I've told him so myself dozens of times. It's like a morgue here when he's in London.' She turned and hurried towards the drawing room. 'I made you some tea and scones. I'm sure you'll manage a bite of something.'

Megan sat in the vast, empty drawing room, facing the old silver tray laid for tea. The gooseberry jam was homemade, and the clotted cream was made of milk from the estate's prize Highland herd. Cook had been warming it on her antique coal stove all day. The kitchen contained a gas stove and a refrigerator, but Cook preferred the old ways.

Earlier that afternoon, the housekeeper had shown her round the old part of the house, which had been kept shut for years. 'There's not much point in opening the house for one lonely bachelor,' the housekeeper had rambled on, darting shrewd glances at Megan. 'But one of these days there'll be a family here again and the old place will buck itself up a bit.' She had rambled on, throwing out hints and questions.

Megan stood up decisively. She was looking forward to the next few hours. Ian and the housekeeper were perfectly amenable to her poking around in the cellars and so far she had found any number of fascinating objects: an old loom, which they had dusted and carried up to the great hall, some beautifully wrought swords and hundreds of old books. She was appalled by Ian's lack of interest in this wealth of antiquity which he kept packed away out of sight. But even Ian was pleased with the book she had found, written by one of his warrior ancestors, giving an eye-witness account of the Battle of Culloden.

The cellars were a rabbit-warren of rooms, corridors and pokey passages hardly tall enough to stand straight, and innumerable bricked-up cul-de-sacs. They had once been escape routes to various parts of the moors and woods, but they had been blocked by Ian's great-grandfather. They were stowed full of junk, with a rare treasure here and there, like a beautiful Spanish shawl she had just unearthed in a trunk full of Victorian clothes.

She was on her way to the cellars when Mrs Gilmour called her to the telephone. It could only be Maureen. It better be serious, she thought peevishly, to disturb my one and only holiday. 'Hi, what's the problem?' she said, trying unsuccessfully to disguise her annoyance.

'Sorry, Megan,' Maureen said apologetically. 'Petunia's Dad just called to cancel her cross-Channel attempt.'

'No! Good heavens, I don't believe it.' She thumped her fist on the desk in exasperation. 'Weeks of work on the advertising. What is he – crazy or something?'

'Petunia's three months pregnant.'

'Impossible,' Megan snapped. 'Her father never lets her out of his sight. Unless it was incest?'

'It was her coach. She took the only chance she had to get away from Dad, see? They were making it on the boat her Dad hired for her coach to follow Petunia up and down the coast.'

'I think the sponsors have a good case for suing here,' Megan said, feeling furious. 'I know there was a pregnancy clause. All that work ... my God ... what will the sponsors say?'

'What can they say? I expect they're all fathers, too.'

'All right, all right. There goes our swimming hopes for the Olympics. You'll have to ring everyone and tell them about the cancellation.'

'Will do,' Maureen said.

Megan dismissed Petunia from her mind as she replaced the receiver. 'Who cares?' she muttered. '*Nichevo!*' she added with a grin. London, and the business world, seemed far away.

'These things should be out on show,' Megan muttered later as she tackled another pile of books with a paper towel. Most of them were ruined with mildew, but some could be saved. Megan was allergic to dust and she felt her nose tickling, but she was too absorbed to care.

It was nine pm. Ian and Nikki had not yet returned and Megan was still rummaging through trunks when she heard the cellar door being quietly opened. She heard footsteps creeping down the stone stairs.

Megan shrank into the shadows as she heard the intruder calling: 'Nikola, Nikola Petrovna,' in a stage whisper.

Then he skidded, tumbled down the stairs and landed on his back in the dust. It was Michel Juric. He sat up swearing quietly in French.

'Michel,' Megan said.

Michel jumped and turned round fearfully. 'Oh, God, Megan.' He stood up painfully, clutching his back. He was wet through and covered in mud. 'I know Nikki's here and I'm warning you,' he blinked several times, and groped around the floor for his revolver. 'If you don't release her I'll have the entire British press behind me.'

'No kidding?' Megan said. She noticed with surprise that Michel looked pale and distraught. 'She's gone for a walk with Ian. They're in the village.'

'Do you expect me to believe that?' he said mournfully.

'I don't care if you do or not. Did you think she was down here – in the cellars? How quaint you are – all of you Europeans – really droll.' She chuckled to herself. Then she

328

stood up and brushed her jeans with her dusty hands. 'Well, come on then. We'd better clean you up. Lucky the dogs didn't get you, they would have torn you to pieces. My goodness, you're a mess,' she said as she pulled him into the light. 'You'd better take a shower. Mrs Gilmour will clean your clothes. You have some explaining to do, Michel, but I'll fix you a drink first. What on earth am I going to tell her – that you were organising a paper chase? Or bird watching?'

'Tell her the truth,' Michel said sourly. 'I'm in love with Nikki and I intend to find out why the two of you have kept her in hiding for weeks.'

'In love with her?' Megan queried sharply. 'We'll see about that when you next go to press.'

'I can't work out your connection with Ian and his outfit.' Michel said quietly, after he had downed his first drink.

Megan raised an eyebrow.

'Haven't you worked it out yet, Megan?' He grinned nastily. 'Ian is a spy. I don't know what he does exactly, but last year he was awarded the MBE "*For services rendered to the Crown.*" I read the citation, but no one seems to know what those services were. I don't know if you're one of *them*, or just an innocent victim who came in useful.'

Megan turned away abruptly, and walked to the sideboard to pour another drink which she did not want, unwilling to meet Michel's eyes.

It's true after all, she thought sadly, but she said: 'That's absolute nonsense.'

'Megan, the matter is not up for debate. His MBE is on record in the Queen's Honours list.'

Not for writing film scripts, that's for sure. It all fitted together – the family's long tradition to the crown, Ian's naval career, the Russian books in the library, the scriptwriter front, and even more damning, the guard calling him in when Nikki went missing. I should feel shocked, but isn't this what I've always suspected? It's just that I didn't want to acknowledge the truth.

She turned and smiled sadly. 'Another Scotch,' she said, taking Michel's glass. 'Of course, you know you're talking absolute rubbish Michel,' she said with a crooked smile, but all the time she was smiling and pouring the drink she was remembering half-forgotten words and disjointed impressions from the past.

The note on the tray: 'Nikola Pektrovna wants to defect.' *So who had sent it? Ian? Or one of his colleagues. Either way it made little difference, for Ian had used her to make Nikki's defection look like a business venture. He had ruthlessly created a relationship between them in order to be around where Nikki was and to mastermind her career. She felt bruised and violated.*

'I've been taken,' she said flatly and immediately wished she had not spoken.

'Not you,' Michel said harshly. 'Nikki! You're one of the takers.'

'You have no right to say that,' Megan retorted angrily. 'I've done everything I can for her.'

'Only when her ambitions happen to coincide with yours,' Michel retorted callously, 'but when she wanted to marry me, you made her choose – her career or her romance. I don't think that it was necessary for her to make that choice.'

'It's not that simple,' Megan flung at him, feeling her cheeks flush. 'She might have lost her British nationality. Besides, what's your hurry?'

'Nikki sees you as her friend,' Michel said, 'but you've been pushing your own interests.'

'Oh Michel, how could you. It's not true. I really do care about Nikki. After all, I found her ...' She broke off and clamped her lips together. But really, how mean of him. Was Michel so much in love with Nikki? Could she have been wrong about him?

A nagging guilt began to twitch in the back of her mind. She knew that Michel had been partly right; in some ways she had not had Nikki's welfare at heart, but ISA's. 'Okay, so I persuaded her to choose her career,' Megan acknowledged. 'But if I were her mother I couldn't have done a better job of it. She's only just eighteen and right now Nikki should be concentrating on her skating.'

'Fair enough, Megan,' Michel said calming down. 'But did you know you were also playing the game for Ian. And how did you both feel when Nikki tried to kill herself? It hardly fits with the public image you've created of the fun-loving playgirl.'

Megan flushed. 'How did you find out?' she asked, feeling shocked.

'Quite easily. I chatted up a nurse in the hospital,' he said, 'but it took me over a week to find out where she was. There's another thing you don't know,' Michel went on. 'While you've been conducting one-man sit-in demos at the Home Office, Nikki's file has been in Ian's hands. Her application, Russian passport, the whole caboodle. You've been pacing the wrong corridors.'

'But that's absurd. Insane!' She stared at him helplessly. 'Michel, tell me something. Why are you snooping on us all the time?'

'I told you – because I love Nikki.'

'Do you – do you really? I wonder if that's the full story,' Megan said bitterly. 'These days it seems to me that men use love too easily to push their own ambitions home. Perhaps you're also after a big story.'

She intended to say much more, but at that moment she heard the clip-clop of a cart horse and cartwheels groaning on cobbles. She heard Nikki singing, her voice was high-pitched and slightly off-key and she was obviously enjoying herself. Then a drunken chorus took over.

Megan ran to the window. 'So much for your prisoner theory, Michel,' she called out. 'She looks happy enough to me, but tipsy. So are the rest of them – a cartload of drunks,' she said wonderingly as she watched the men falling about and clambering over the wheels.

'Half the pub's coming in, by the look of things,' Megan groaned. 'D'you think they're here for supper?' She turned and glanced sidelong at Michel. How expressive his dark, Slavic face was, she thought. There was no sign of curiosity or journalistic zeal there, just old-fashioned jealousy blazed in his eyes. Ian was lifting Nikki down. He had his arm round her and he looked carefree and happy. Megan wondered suddenly if Nikki knew of Ian's role in her defection.

CHAPTER 49

For Megan, supper passed in a daze. She listened to the jokes and shouts of laughter, gulped her wine and tried to be a part of it, but all the time, she felt as if a wall of glass separated her from reality. The more she drank, the worse she felt and soon her eyes were staring, glazed and bewildered, at this perfidious world, where things were not what they seemed, and people were not what they pretended to be.

For there was her dear, her very own, dear Ian, the struggling scriptwriter, acting the part of Lord Mackintosh, MBE, British intelligence agent – whatever – with such aplomb, so sure of himself as he wielded the ancient silver carving knife with expertise and filled the silver goblets to overflowing, while he gabbled to his village friends, and joked with Nikki in Russian, under the fierce, but approving eye of his wild chieftain forefather. Insane! Only it was true and she could weep for the dreams she had dreamed.

Ian had not appeared to be the least thrown to find Michel in his home. All the antipathy he had harboured for the reporter, seemed to have fled together with his professional interest in Nikki.

Michel was holding hands with Nikki under the table. He looked carelessly happy and genuinely in love. Nikki had suddenly regained her good spirits, her eyes were glowing with laughter as she teased Michel for running after her. The village men were getting drunker and singing maudlin songs with Ian, who seemed to be even more besotted than them. Megan had never felt so miserable, or so excluded. She went to bed early, leaving them to their noisy party. Huddling into the blankets, she tried to sleep.

At midnight she heard voices shouting in the hall, the echo of the front door slamming, the clip-clop of the horse and cart, then footsteps on the stairs and afterwards silence.

Half an hour later there was soft, but persistent knocking on her bedroom door. She pushed a pillow over her head and clenched her fists, but the knocking persisted. How long was it? Five minutes? Ten? Surely the staff would hear?

Eventually Megan opened the door. Ian, who had been leaning against it, sprawled forward onto his face. He was naked except for his underpants. He raced across the floor on his hands and knees, jumped into bed and pulled the blankets around his neck. 'I nearly froze to death,' he complained. 'Come to the bed at once, wench, and warm me up.'

'How dare you speak to me like that.' She glared at him. 'Get out of here.'

For a moment Ian looked shocked. Then he grinned sheepishly. *'By the mass, I have drunk too much sack at supper.'*

'You're drunk.'

'I just said that,' he said, 'but you shouldn't. *Why, how now, dame! whence grows this insolence?'*

'Out of my bed, damn you.'

'The fact is, it's my bed. You'll be cold out there,' he said lifting one corner of the blanket. 'It's always damp here. Better come in.'

'Oh, Ian, go away please. Get out! Out!' Her voice rose in a shriek of fury.

'Out, damned spot! Out, I say! One, two; Why, then 'tis time to do't: hell is murky!'

'For goodness sake, stop quoting Shakespeare at me.'

'All right ...' He sat up, looking serious, one hand on his chest. 'Perhaps you prefer Robbie Burns: *Take away those rosy lips, rich with balmy treasure; turn away thine eyes of love, Lest I die with pleasure. What is life when wanting Love ...?"* '

'Oh, good grief!' she fumed as he carried on. She must talk to him, but he was too drunk. Useless to reason with him. She sank on the chair beside the bed feeling utterly miserable. 'Love,' she said bitterly, to herself. 'You call it love; I call it expediency.'

'Would you be unhappy here?' Ian was mumbling. 'I've always thought I'd never marry. I'd never want to see a woman as unhappy as my mother was, but lately I've changed my mind, perhaps because I need you here and because you're a capable woman. You'd make the most of what's available. How

333

about it, Megan?' *'As fair art thou, my bonnie lass, So deep in luve am I; And I will luve thee still, my dear, Till a' the seas gang dry.'*

'Oh, oh, oh, Ian, stop it.' Megan buried her face in her hands. 'Please don't propose when you're intoxicated. I find you disgusting.' She gazed at him repugnantly. 'Besides, you wouldn't propose if you were sober.'

'I am a little drunk, admittedly, but sobering rapidly. I liked it better when I was drunk,' he complained.

'Oh God! Now listen to me, Ian,' she snapped, sensing her advantage. 'Answer my questions or I'll just pack and leave right now.' She caught hold of his arm and peered tearfully into his eyes. 'Were you involved with Nikki's defection?'

'Of course I was. You made sure of that. You roped me in.'

'Even when you're drunk, you're still a liar,' she cried out hurt and out of patience. 'I know you wrote the note about Nikki wanting to defect. Michel's told me everything. Don't try to deny it.'

'I also tried to get you out of it,' he said sullenly, 'when I discovered that you weren't suitable for my purpose.'

'Your purpose. My God, you sound as if you were buying a horse. What d'you mean – not suitable?'

'Vulnerable,' he said, having difficulty pronouncing the word. 'Far too vulnerable! You care and that's a big mistake for this type of work. It can snarl up the whole job. I was wrong about you. I admit that, but I don't often make mistakes.'

'I know everything,' she said crisply. 'Michel told me you're working for British Intelligence.'

'Not true,' he said and hiccupped. 'Damn you, Megan. I'm on holiday and I was happily drunk. Leave it alone.'

She crouched forward and buried her face in her hands. 'Oh Ian,' she sobbed. 'You're a total stranger to me. I thought I loved you, but I don't even know you.'

'All right, all right, Megan,' he said. 'You've made your point. Now listen to me for once and for all and don't ever ask again. I'm bound by the Official Secrets Act and I operate on a 'need to know' basis. You don't need to know a damn thing. That is my final word on the subject.'

'You see ... you lied again ... you're still lying. Now you've admitted that you work for British Intelligence. A minute ago you denied it.'

'Wrong again, Megan,' he said more soberly. 'I'm in naval intelligence. I never left the Navy,' he said. 'Commander Mackintosh, at your service. I was lent to the Foreign Office for this tricky operation.'

'Operation? Nikki? That's crazy! What's so goddam tricky about an ice skater?' Megan gasped, more astonished than angry for a few moments.

'It's the publicity that's so special, not the ice skater. She's not special at all.' He sat up and pressed his hands on each side of his forehead. 'Oh,' he said. 'My head! It hurts. Megan, listen to me. Drunk as I am, or was, there's no point in questioning me. It's no secret that I'm in naval intelligence, so there's no harm in your knowing. Drop it now.'

'Not special?' Megan was staring at him in disbelief. 'So you and your pals conned Nikki into defecting, to get her in the limelight for some reason that you won't divulge – and all her life, her hopes, her art, were moulded and irretrievably changed for some official operation – as you called it … but she's not *special*. Because she's just a *tool*!' Her voice rose ominously. 'Nikki was wilfully manipulated and so was I. You led me to believe that you loved me and all the time I was being used – we were both being used.' Megan was nearly choking with rage.

'All right, I'm sorry, Megan.' I deliberately picked on you when I saw you at Aviemore. Remember what you said at Sarajevo? You said you'd seen me before and you were right. I was handing out the prizes, and when I saw you trying to sign up the winners, I realised that you were the answer. I had to get Nikki out and make it look as if she'd done it all herself.'

'How convenient that we met,' she said sullenly, torn between her longing for Ian, her pride, and her loyalty to Nikki.

'We met and I soon realised I'd made a mistake with you. Then I fell in love with you. The ultimate disaster.'

She turned away from him, unable to come to terms with his expert manipulation, unable to forgive.

'Listen to me, Megan. Nikki had no chance of making the big time in Russia. She wanted to be the world champion and she has a good chance of realising her dreams. She has everything she dreamed of having, plus the best coach in Britain. Now that it's over, Nikki will receive her British citizenship and passport.'

'What's over, for goodness sake,' she shouted.

'I can't tell you, Megan.'

'Is there some reason you know of that could have made her so depressed recently?' she persisted.

'I can't answer that either, Megan,' Ian said softly. 'Don't ask. I'm leaving the Navy in two years' time to run the estate. Hold on to that, Megan. Just ease off until then.'

'But if Nikki's come out of it with a credit balance,' Megan persisted, 'it's only by chance. It could have swung the other way. If she, or I, or both of us, had lost out, would that have altered your actions in any way?'

'I don't want to answer that question,' Ian said, 'because it's fiction. God damn it, Megan. I am what I am. I'm proud of my service in the Navy. You should be, too. Pull yourself together and quit moaning.'

'Is that what it's called?' she shouted him down. 'Now hear me out, Ian Mackintosh. Nikki's a loving, caring, talented person – and she's special. You hear me! And I think I should warn you that Nikki is not alone. Not anymore! She has me. If you dare to use her any longer, you'll find the consequences are not very pleasant.'

'I'm off the job,' he said. 'Calm down. She's of no further interest to the department.'

'Oh! You bastard!' She gasped as she remembered something else. 'You let me waste my time going from one department to the next trying to get a passport, and all the time Nikki's file was on your desk – why – you Machiavellian monster.' She was so angry now she had trouble controlling herself.

'Are you going to nag me all night or are you coming to bed?' he said in a voice that sounded hurt and offended.

She gasped. 'What exactly do you think I am?'

'A bossy, self-opinionated, female freak of the type mass produced by American plastic culture.'

'Freak! Plastic!' she shrieked. She hurled herself on him, pummelled with her fists with all her strength, trying desperately to hurt him.

Ian reached up and grabbed her wrist, pulling her off balance so that she tumbled face forward over the bed.

'How dare you ... how dare you ...' she shouted as he twisted her over. 'You're squashing me.'

He flung one leg over her knees and pinned her hands down

on the pillow. 'Let's dispense with extraneous details,' he said hoarsely pulling her nightdress off.

'I don't believe this is happening,' she gasped.

'Believe it,' he said. 'It'll be more fun.'

'You can't have me if I don't want you, Ian.' She punched him hard with all her force. She heard his teeth click and his head jerk back.

'You really meant that, didn't you?' he said, rubbing his jaw. 'Miss Goody-goody, but you want me just as much as I want you. It's written all over you, from here ... to here.' He brushed his hand over her body and Megan felt her stomach lurch.

She knew she was losing, even as she was fighting back, her body was playing traitor to her mind. He thrust her legs apart and knelt there. She wanted to thrust her knee into his groin, but she could not. It was too precious. The very essence of him was there. Fainthearted, she pushed him back, but what was the point in fighting? Her thighs ached to feel him clutched between them, her body was alive with desire, her physical need was rippling through her stomach and her groin, incapacitating her, like too much alcohol in her bloodstream. She wanted to clutch him and pull him down on her, feel his skin hard and quivering against hers.

Every movement of his body sent spasms of feeling darting through her, like swords of delight. She cried out, little feeble cries of joy that she was not even aware of. She was no longer a caring, thinking woman, but a cavern of feeling, where molten pleasure lapped and ebbed against the essence of her being.

She was clamouring for more of him, urging him to come, so that she could come, too. She urged him on, swaying, biting, whispering in his ear: 'I love you ... love ... love ...'

When he climaxed his cry drowned her own. Afterwards she lay for a long time inert on his shoulder, panting a little, and then feeling too heavy to move.

At last Megan stirred and said. 'I love you, but I despise what you are doing. I cannot condone your actions and it hurts.'

'Megan,' he replied, and she noticed that all trace of love and sensuousness had vanished from his voice. 'I never, ever doubt what I'm doing – not for a moment. I'm never ashamed of it. You must come to terms with that. I was born and bred for the Navy; it's a family tradition: my father and his father and grandfather. I was transferred to intelligence because I have a flair for languages. The Admiralty lent me to the Foreign Office for this manoeuvre, and the London house you hate so much is theirs. It's what they call a 'safe house'.'

She sighed, the woman's eternal sigh and longing for tenderness, to prolong the act, to make a bridge between passion and caring, sex and love. More than ever before she needed his reassurance, and his tenderness.

'To tell the truth,' he was saying in a matter of fact voice, 'I've been taken off the job now. Something more pressing's come up. Of course, I'll try to help whenever you need help, but I'll be doing it for you, Megan, not Nikki. So you must make up your mind what you want to do about us,' he went on relentlessly. 'I'm not going to beg you.'

Of course not. Not now. But you will be in a night or two. Right now, you're replete and filled with all the arrogance of the conquering male.

She sat up and stared at him coldly. 'And my final word on the subject is leave the service or lose me. I don't like what you're doing.' She turned her back on him, curled up into a ball and pulled the blanket over her head, feeling let down and sad.

'The estate's gone to pieces,' she heard unwillingly, although she was trying to ignore him. 'Lack of cash and an absentee landlord,' Ian went on gloomily. 'My grandfather planted three-quarters of the estate with timber – a long-term plan which is about to pay-off. There's money in timber, but there's also a great deal of planning and hard work ahead. I'm due to leave the Navy in a year or two. I've told you that often enough, but Megan, don't ever try to subject me to moral blackmail. My life is mapped out pretty much as I planned long ago. You must make your own decisions.' He stopped talking abruptly and soon fell asleep, or was he pretending, she wondered.

As she lay quietly and sleeplessly beside Ian, she realised with dismay that her love for Ian was something that existed despite her intentions or her wishes and that no matter what Ian did she would still feel the same way. She could leave him, she could go away and never see him again, but she would still love him and she would never be able to forget him. She felt completely bewildered by the force of her passion as she reached out like a blind woman, craving the touch of his strong body lying beside her.

'Wait for me, Megan,' she heard him whisper and suddenly

he turned and folded his arms around her. 'You mean more to me than anything else, but give me time to finish what I have to do. Just trust me.'

'Yes,' she murmured. 'Yes, oh yes.'

It's all right, she comforted herself. Everything's all right, after all. Nikki has recovered, she's no longer being used, I can forget the past and plan the future with a clear conscience.

Still she could not sleep. Her doubts kept racing insanely around in her mind like a wild creature caged. What if Nikki had died? What if there were other more sinister motives involved in her defection? What if she did not receive British citizenship? What if she were harmed, or extradited? Then could she truly forgive Ian?

She shifted closer against him, wrapped one arm around his waist and rested her cheek against his shoulder until eventually she fell asleep.

Michel had been waiting since midnight. He glanced again at his watch and shrugged with annoyance. Nikki loved to tease, she could not help it. Just because she knew every second would pass with agonising slowness, because he was anxious about her and longing for her, just because of that, she would tease, make him wait – spin out the agony.

He got up slowly from the old couch by the hearth and stretched painfully, feeling stiff all over from the day's unaccustomed activity. Then he bent with a gasp, grasped the tongs and put some more coal on the fire. Although it was mid-August, the house was damp at night and the housekeeper had lit the fire to dry his clothes which she had gone to some pains to clean.

'Lucky devil,' he murmured, thinking of Ian as he watched the flames flare and the coal spit. The smoke curled grey-yellow up the old chimney of the hearth. If I had this home I wouldn't be spying for anyone. I'd be right here looking after the place, he thought, remembering his flight through the Mackintosh forests earlier that afternoon – beautiful forests, filled with wildlife; rabbits, guinea fowl, partridges, fish eagles swooping into rushing rivers, salmon. One day he'd have his own place, too, but never like this.

He glanced at his watch again. One-thirty. Had they locked

Nikki in? He was about to go and investigate when the door slowly opened. She paused in the doorway for dramatic effect and he could see that she had gone to considerable trouble: she was clad in a diaphanous white satin gown. Her hair was plaited and wound around her head, she wore eye makeup which emphasised the green glint of her eyes against her white skin. Nikki stretched her arms out dramatically and raced across the floor to throw herself in his arms. That was Nikki, always posturing, she could never stop acting ... wouldn't know how, he reasoned gloomily as he kissed her. If she were in such a damn hurry she could have come an hour ago.

'Oh darling, darling Michel, you've come for me at last,' she gasped twining herself around him with her long, white limbs, nuzzling his neck, his ears, his mouth. In spite of his irritation with her, Michel felt desire rising, blotting out all other thoughts.

To hell with questions, he thought. Questions can wait until later.

Michel gently undid the buttons of her nightgown, and kissed the smooth white shoulders he loved so, then watched the smooth satin shimmer and shine in the firelight before he let it fall slowly to the floor. Nikki was quite perfect; she had exactly the type of feminine beauty he adored – wraithlike, her skin was white as alabaster and it gleamed smoothly inviting and unblemished. Her breasts were smooth white mounds, firm and taut, with small pink nipples that hardly marred the beauty of her form. She was a vision of perfection whichever way she stood or moved, graceful by nature, without an ounce of superfluous flesh, her muscles disciplined by years of vigorous daily training.

It was her beauty which snared him, but with her beauty came her tortuous character. To Michel, Nikki was like a perfectly formed bud on some mystical tree. He had been peeling off the petals, one by one, the deceit, the make-believe, the drama, all the stories she invented, the tantrums she deliberately created and the tears she falsely shed, but he never reached the essence of her – the true Nikki. Probably he never would. He had to be content with her marvellous exterior, and endure the mystery – grab the odd moment when her defences were down and she let a little piece of her real self show – or was it her real self? He never knew for sure.

340

Right now she was acting the martyr, because she was amused that he had thought she was being kept prisoner. So she had happily agreed with him, and was loving this new role.

'I thought you would never find me,' she whispered as she writhed against him.

Michel caught hold of her long blonde plait and gently untwined it, letting her silken hair fall over her shoulders.

'*They* are going to cut off my hair,' she said, teasing him again, he knew. 'The sponsors think I look old-fashioned. Megan insists. I shall give it all to you, since you love it so. You can make a cushion out of it.'

'Liar,' he said. He knew that she valued her hair almost as much as she valued her figure.

Whenever he saw Nikki naked he felt overcome with awe. She was so perfect, a statue of alabaster. She looked so pure, so virginal, he could never really believe how much she craved physical love. She did not seem to be in such a hurry tonight. That was strange. A feeling of panic welled up as he considered the possibility of Nikki taking a lover. Perhaps Ian? No, he dismissed that thought. Ian would not invite Megan along if he were interested in Nikki. But if not Ian, then who? Michel forced himself to quell his jealousy and think rationally.

'Did you miss me,' she was whispering as she darted little kisses on his body, here and there, as she deftly removed the striped flannel pyjamas Mrs Gilmour had lent him.

'Flannel pyjamas,' she giggled. 'Don't you think that is very right for Ian? And do you think Megan is sleeping in a flannel nightgown, too, with a lace collar, and a cap. What it is it called that funny cap you see in their films?'

'A mob cap,' Michel whispered, stroking her back gently.

Nikki gasped. 'Yes, I can just see her. They are right for each other. Don't you feel that?'

'I think you are just right for me,' he said and picked her up. She was so light, he could hardly imagine where she contained her strength in such a frail body. He ran one hand down her back, caught her buttocks and heard her squeal with delight as she caught hold of his neck and wrapped her legs around his waist.

'Not yet, no, wait,' he said, but he could not control himself. Her touch and scent and whispered words, and the movement of her body was driving him insane. He would never be able to

341

wait for her. 'Nikki,' he gasped.

He could feel his legs stiffening, every muscle in his body becoming taut like steel. Nikki was rocking to and fro against him and he wondered again, with the small part of his mind that could still wonder, how she could contain all of him. And then his ego fled down and away into a morass of pristine sensations. He was an amoebae; a mindless, floating lump of sensation, crushed and smoothed and stroked by the sea, this huge and throbbing, pulsating sea that contained him utterly. The grip was monstrous, total world, infinite pleasure and infinite pain throbbed in the waters that surrounded him and he was caught and helpless in the ebb and flow of the tide – contracting, loosening, flowing back to bring unbearable pleasure. He had to transform himself into a stream of liquid lust, to be one with the sea. For a few seconds that lasted a decade he was nothing more than a shooting stream of pleasure.

'You didn't wait,' he heard Nikki complaining as if from a great distance. Reluctantly he surfaced.

'I couldn't. I'm sorry. Just give me a few minutes.'

Nikki bent down and kissed him. An agonising pain shot through him as he grabbed her head and pulled her back.

'You can do it again, can't you?' A plaintive voice with a faint tinge of panic in it?

'Yes, but first I want to talk.'

'That's not fair.'

'Maybe not. I'm just going to be unfair.'

'All right talk.'

Now she sounded really angry, but he had the beating of her tonight.

'Nikki, tell me the truth. They told me in the hospital what happened to you. Why did you do it?'

'I did nothing. I was ill. Why it was just a breakdown, caused by overwork. They all told me that.'

'Nikki, that's not true. I know that you tried to kill yourself. Why? Whatever drove you to do that? All our plans, your promises, you said you'd call me if you felt depressed – or lonely,' he tried. 'You know I'll always look after you.'

She gave me a long angry look. Then her eyes glinted and her mouth turned up at the corners. She was laughing at him. 'Do you think that's all I want in life. Three meals a day and a roof over my head?'

'And love? You forgot the love.'

'Men! How blind you all are. You irritate me. Eating and sleeping and loving and a roof over my head. I never even think about these things. Well, maybe I think about making love,' she said, smoothing her naked stomach with her fingertips.

'Why do you persist in torturing me with questions,' she complained. 'You are as bad as all the rest.'

When he questioned her further, she burst into tears. 'Lies, horrible lies, they told you,' she sobbed. 'I was overworked. Perhaps I was a little depressed, but nothing much.'

'And this?' He held up her wrists to show the faint marks which London's top plastic surgeon had not been able to conceal entirely, although they were fast fading.

Nikki's face changed, as it did when she was confronted with some truth which she did not wish to acknowledge. She pouted. Her mouth became sullen, her face lost its ethereal loveliness and became heavy-looking, her eyes stared dumb and resentfully at him, like a savage confronted with the unknown. She would not acknowledge the truth – even to herself. She had blanked her mind to it.

'Come, love me,' she cried out angrily. 'If you can't love me, I shall go back to my room.'

Her fear was a real and tangible presence lying in bed between them. He could smell it on her skin, on her breath, in her damp hair. It was suffocating her. A tide of compassion and understanding swept through Michel. Poor angel, she could not face the truth. What event had driven her into the depths of despair? He would find out, he vowed, but not from Nikki.

CHAPTER 50

Maureen had dreaded this night for months and now it was almost upon her. She sat shivering with fright in Johnny's flat, hunched forward in a chair, her eyes fixed on the television screen as if mesmerised. She could see Johnny towards the end of a row of near-naked men. He was grinning, but to her mind he looked pale and tense. 'Come on Johnny, love,' she murmured, clenching her hands until the nails bit into her palms. 'Don't let them get you down.'

Wembley Stadium was packed to overflowing with flags and banners, pretty girls in sequined bikinis and the bandsmen dressed in shimmering red tuxedos. All the glitter and entertainment of this year's Mr Universe competition was about to break.

Everyone seemed to be having a wonderful time, while Johnny was dying back there. Did they care who won? Not a damn! What did they know about the tension, the scientific training, the years of brutish effort which were needed to produce the beef parading here tonight?

The competitors were filing across the stage, muscles flexed, teeth bared in fixed smiles. Maureen watched them avidly, hoping for flaws, but there were none. Here was the world's best – each as hungry as Johnny for the title.

If only he would win. If he won he'd be set to go pro and the publicity would help him to find the backing to open his own, *Johnny Bart Gym* in Monaco. They'd be set up and she'd be right behind him. She was making herself indispensible to Johnny: massaging his muscles, kneading away the stiffness and pain, she'd learned how to produce no-carb meals during training and to carb him up before a show, she was becoming a dedicated dietician – she was even into training. Eventually, she would run the women's slimming classes, under Johnny's supervision, of course. All that, and so much more. But to realise their dreams, *he had to win*.

Maureen shivered and gazed apprehensively at the screen. Unlucky to count their hopes right before the show. She crossed her fingers as she listened to the Master of Ceremonies go through his opening gambit of wisecracks, before introducing a team of singers and dancers. It seemed hours before the competitors returned to the stage.

There couldn't be many with Johnny's track record: first in the junior NABBA; Junior Mr SE Britain; second in Mr Europe; and first in the Midlands' Open Oscar? Still, she thought, there was plenty of beef on the stage and no shortage of good looks either.

It was Johnny's turn. He wasn't himself at all, she noticed, watching him nervously as he went through his routine. Hardly surprising either, after the way Megan worked him. He'd been forced into too many public appearances for the sponsors Megan had booked. She'd put a stop to that one of these days. Then an ugly thought occurred to her: if he didn't win, he'd be lucky to hang on to any sponsors; lucky to land a coaching job in a third-rate gym.

Oh God, what if he lost? It would be her fault, she knew that. 'Oh Johnny, I'm so sorry,' she whispered. What she'd done was unforgivable – no wonder he looked so pale and drawn. Why last night, for Christ's sake? Of all the nights in the past and the future – why did it have to be last night? A nightmare – and every second was engraved upon her mind forever. If she closed her eyes she could relive each moment without even trying ...

She was hurrying home from work, carrying his day's rations, three pounds of cod, a chicken, vitamins and milk, all of which she'd managed to buy in her lunch break. What a race it had been. Flinging open the flat door, she saw Johnny thumping away at the leg press and, to her dismay, Gloria, the tart from upstairs, starkers in the jacuzzi, watching him.

'Bugger off, Gloria,' she snapped as she raced to the kitchen.

'Here! Who d'you think you're talking to? I'm invited,' Gloria called out plaintively. 'Wasn't I Johnny?' she added in her husky drawl.

Maureen poked her head back into the room. 'Get!' she snapped.

Johnny stopped his leg work and propped himself on one elbow. 'Steady there, Maureen. Go easy, for Christ's sake. Why shouldn't Gloria use the jacuzzi occasionally?'

'Because she's starkers, that's why.'

'So what-a?'

She felt her temper rising as Johnny resorted to his silly accent.

'Worried?' Gloria had called, showing her claws. 'There's plenty there for both us, by the look of things. Don't be selfish?'

'Now look here ...' Maureen began, spitting venom as Gloria climbed out and stood casually towelling her body.

'Why?' she murmured now as she gazed at the screen. 'Why did I do it?'

The competitors were approaching the cameras, one at a time, and going through their routine. Pretty good, she thought watching Johnny with approval. There'd be plenty more hanging around besides Gloria, which thought flung her back into her horrid memories.

One thing had led to another and before she knew what was happening the two of them were going at it like a couple of cats. She pushed and clawed Gloria out of the door and turned to face Johnny's censure.

'I don't like you to act like a fish wife,' he said moodily, looking away shiftily, as if it was he who was to blame.

'Are you calling me a fish wife?' She yelled, hyped up and spoiling for a fight.

'Yes,' he said after a moment's hesitation. 'And I'm telling you now – I don't like it.'

'Well stuff you, too, Johnny Bart. I wasn't exactly thrilled to come home and find you lolling around with a naked tart.'

'She's not a tart, she just likes to be *au naturelle*,' he said. 'What could be more reasonable in a jacuzzi?'

Why did he take Gloria's part? More than anything else it was that which fired her fury. 'If I catch her au-bloody-anything in this flat again, I'll give her what for, I promise you.' Unable to control her rage, she hammered her fist on the table. Johnny's glass vase, his only heirloom from his Mum, toppled and smashed on the floor.

Johnny's face looked bleak and sad. He turned away without saying anything, and began to dress slowly. Where was he going in that silk shirt? she wondered with increasing dismay.

'Here! Where're you going?' Her voice was hoarse with fear and temper.

'None of your business,' he replied. Something about his tone hurt her badly.

'Oh, is that so? You think I've slogged my guts out these past two months: buying the food, making your meals, massaging your bloody aches and pains, just for you to walk out now, the night before the show. Get back on the leg machine.' She tried, but failed, to keep the desperation out of her voice.

'Listen Maureen,' he said, his voice deceptively calm, his face expressionless. 'If you know what's good for you – get lost.' Now he was searching for a tic.

'You bastard!' she screamed. She raced across the floor and slapped his face with all her force.

'Just mind out of my way,' he said making a visible effort to remain calm.

'Oh no, no I won't,' she yelled shrilly. 'You can't tell me it's over. Just like that. No ways!'

'No, it's not over,' he said with his infuriating dead-pan expression, 'because it never started. I prefer my women with a touch of class. You never managed to turn me on.'

'Why, you creep!' She lunged forward punching his face and reached up to slash his cheeks with her nails. 'I'll make sure you lose. Damn you, I will.'

Faster than she could see, he gripped her elbows and flung her back. Caught off balance, Maureen fell headlong into the jacuzzi.

'You bastard, look at my clothes,' she spluttered, climbing out half dazed.

'My clothes,' he yelled as she staggered back to the fight. 'I bought them.' He spun her round and zipped down her dress which fell in a bedraggled mess on the floor. 'I tried to turn you into a lady. A waste of time and money.' He was panting with temper now. 'There's a wardrobe full of your old trash in there. Put something on and get out.'

Maureen gazed up in astonishment. In all the time she'd known Johnny, he'd never lost his temper. She did not think he knew how.

'Now look what you've done. I hate losing my temper,' he roared. He was trembling. He pushed her aside and gazed at himself in the mirror. For a few moments he breathed deeply, flexing his muscles.

Maureen sensed that he was trying to hang on to his self

347

control, but the sight of his deliberate rejection, made her feel frightened and sick.

'Look at him! For Christ's sake. Fucking obsessed,' she muttered. Some dark, perverse part of her took control. 'Take this, you narcissistic sod,' she yelled and punched him on his shoulder. She caught hold of his silk shirt and ripped it half off him. 'Have another look before I scratch your skin off,' she cried out, pushing him hard. Then she lunged forward, reaching for his flesh.

'The show. I've got to look good,' he shouted, fending her off.

'Fuck the show and fuck you, too, you freaky eunuch,' she snarled. She caught hold of his underpants, and fell to the floor, taking them with her.

'You bitch! You want me to lose,' he growled.

Johnny was naked and fast running out of control. He hurled himself onto her and for a moment they were rolling and writhing on the floor.

Passion surged. She never knew how or when, but suddenly Johnny was on her, lunging into her. 'Bitch! Bitch!' he shouted. 'You deserve this.'

She did not know whether to laugh or cry, to scream abuse or murmur endearments. She was afraid he would recover his temper and with it, his impotence.

'Don't stop, Johnny, don't stop,' she thought. She wrapped her long black thighs around him and abandoned herself to the sheer joy of satisfying six months of pent-up longing. She cried out with joy when Johnny exploded in a paroxysm of rage and lust.

Johnny lay for a long time with his face turned away from her as she gently stroked his neck. Eventually, he propped himself on his elbows and gazed down at her with the strangest expression, part guilt, part pride, lingering anger and tenderness.

'I love you, Johnny,' she whispered. 'More than anything in the world. I'd do anything for you – except leave you. And I love what you just did.'

Johnny stood up, looking upset. 'Do women really like that?' He frowned. 'When I was a small kid,' he said in a low voice. 'I mean – really a whipper-snapper, I used to watch my old man beat up my Mum. And then he used to set about her like that. I used to peep, you see. Then one day she ran out crying and got run over by a bus. I was very young, too young for school. For years afterwards, I used to cry thinking about it. Dad used to clout me round the ear.'

He moved away from her and sat naked on the couch and Maureen went up to him and sat astride his knees facing him, and linked her arms around his neck.

'Forget all that, love. It's over. You've been crying inside a long time, but now you've got me, and I love you. Do you love me?' she asked contritely.

'Yes, I love you,' he said sadly.

He stood up, still carrying her, and stepped into the jacuzzi. He sat there with her on his lap as if it was the most natural thing in the world for him to do. 'Water's getting cold,' he said gloomily. 'I'll have to get a thermostat one of these days,' he sighed. 'If we stay here, that is. You don't have to worry about Gloria, or anyone, come to that,' he went on in the same tone of voice. 'You're all I want. Just don't make me lose my temper. That's all I ask.'

Later, when they had eaten and tidied the room, they went to bed and made love again, only this time it was tender and sweet and she cried a lot and eventually fell asleep on Johnny's shoulder.

She opened her eyes slowly and found she was gazing at a row of eight men – the finalists! For a moment she panicked. Then she saw Johnny standing at the end of the row. He was smiling at the camera and she knew he was smiling just for her with that special look that turned her on.

She'd been day-dreaming through half the show, she realised with a jolt of dismay. There was a girl in a feathered hat and not much else, calling the names of the finalists. 'Number three is ...' Maureen didn't listen to the name, it was enough to see the miniature Stars and Stripes she was waving slowly in front of her boobs.

'Oh God, I can't stand it. What must it be like for Johnny up there under the lights, trying to smile, whether he made it or not?

'Number two is ...'

'Pick it up. Please, please, pick up the Union Jack,' she

pleaded as she rocked backwards and forwards in front of the screen, but the girl was waving the French flag.

There was a fanfare of trumpets. 'Oh Gawd! They know how to prolong the agony ...'

'What's this then?' she muttered. The dancers were running in fluttering a ruddy great Union Jack, big as a van. Surely not ...? 'No, don't get excited,' she shouted. 'There must be other Brits besides Johnny.'

'Johnny Bart ...' The name exploded in her ears and Maureen let out a piercing cry. She didn't see anymore of the show. She was curled up on the carpet, sobbing out the tension of the past few days.

CHAPTER 51

Nigel Wilder parked his car outside *Le Mistral* and walked slowly across the pavement. Typical of Eleanor to choose Monaco's most expensive restaurant for 'a quick bite of lunch', as she had put it, and a business talk. The unassuming blue canopy and modest exterior gave no indication of its price and reputation. Nigel resented Eleanor's candid enjoyment of her money. Nigel had never acquired that art – but of course he was not as rich as Eleanor.

Eleanor had never been mean with money, but Nigel had always craved more than he had. Successful men were motivated by power, money, or fame, he knew, but with him it had always been a mixture of all three. There was nothing wrong with his motivation, but he had failed to achieve his objectives. Eleanor ruled the company tyrannically, a modern-day Genghis Khan in her management philosophy.

Nigel knew why Eleanor had summoned him – and outside the office, he noted – it was the increased campaign against Vanguard, portent of change. He felt a swift twinge of fear in his stomach as he walked into the room.

He hesitated in the foyer, but when his eyes adjusted to the gloom he saw Eleanor sitting alone in a discreet alcove, decorated in midnight blue and white.

Eleanor was nibbling a roll and salad, as he had known she would be. She was a compulsive eater when she was worried – and the current press war showed, he thought unkindly, particularly around her hips.

She looked up and smiled, but today there was a shadow of sadness in her normally warm smile. 'Ah Nigel,' she said and sighed, 'you're late, so I started – hope you don't mind. I was starving.' She passed him the menu.

He wondered if she realised how he loathed this place. The management were well aware of Eleanor's status as chairman of the company, after all she practically lived here, and invariably they gave her the wine list, poured first for her to taste and presented her with the bill to sign.

To Nigel, who hated to be belittled, it seemed like an exquisitely refined form of mental torture, but Eleanor had never noticed. She was not sensitive to other people's feelings. When she had something to discuss she approached it with the finesse of a sledgehammer, so he was hardly surprised when she said:

'They're gaining on us, Nigel, and I don't know what the hell we're going to do.'

'Let's order, shall we?' he said and raised one eyebrow mockingly. 'The situation won't change in the next half hour, so we might as well be civilised about lunch.'

'You haven't changed, have you?' she said affectionately. 'Still the same lovable prig I met back in Denver all those years ago. D'you remember the first time you asked me out to lunch in a Wimpy Bar. I was a new sales rep and you were practically buried alive in that ghastly basement, euphemistically termed 'research and development'. You wanted to tell me about your new combination skis. I remember how angry you were because the firm wouldn't back you.' She chuckled with amusement. 'You kept apologising because you had taken me to a hamburger bar and you were mad because they wouldn't cool your wine.'

'Is this a walk down memory lane today, Eleanor? Is that what it's all about?'

She pursed her lips and toyed with her fork for a few minutes. Then hunger got the better of her and she opened the menu. 'I'm having fresh *foie gras*, with a freezing cold Sauternes, followed by *potage Germiny*, followed by fillet of beef Richelieu, with a bottle of Beaujolais please, Nigel, topped off with *poires Bourdaloue*.'

'What's that?' he couldn't resist asking.

'You wouldn't like it,' she said. 'Too rich for your delicate stomach. It's a succulent tart with frangipani cream, topped with poached pears, brushed with an apricot glaze and sprinkled with chopped pistachio nuts and crumbled macaroons.' She turned her attention to the melba toast, which she plied with chips of butter and gobbled until the first course arrived.

Watching her out of the corner of his eye, Nigel felt peeved by the satisfaction Eleanor derived from food. She enjoyed every mouthful, and he found that nauseating. Nigel found very little satisfaction in chewing his way through anything. Even wine was drunk for the alcoholic content. Amongst his friends, Nigel enjoyed a reputation as a wine connoisseur, but it was all book learning and quotes from others. The truth was, he could just about tell the difference between dry and sweet wine, and that was all.

It was only after Eleanor had finished her meal and was drinking her coffee that she returned to the reason for the meeting.

'Mmn, good coffee,' she said. 'I wanted to talk to you outside the office, as an old friend,' she began diffidently. 'You see, Nigel,' she said, trying to soften her tone, 'it's becoming increasingly obvious to me that we may lose. I'm speaking confidentially, of course. Naturally, I'm doing my best, throwing everything we've got into the fight, but we're losing. No point in kidding ourselves.'

She placed one hand over his and pressed it briefly. 'So I just want you to know, that I'm sorry ...'

'Come on, Eleanor,' he said more roughly than he had intended. 'I don't know what's got into you lately; all this talk of losing. Between us – together with the NFF Trust Fund – we have fifty-one per cent. Even without NFF it's impossible for us to be taken over. How many times must I tell you this? The marginal shares available to make an opposing majority won't come on the market. It's totally inconceivable.'

'Nigel, NFF telephoned me yesterday,' she said sadly. 'The buyers, whoever they are, offered them a twenty per cent premium over current market values. Can you imagine that? It's the key holding you see.'

'Are they selling?'

'Probably. They're having a board meeting – later this month. We both know they'd be foolish not to sell.' She toyed with her cup and then beckoned the waiter for more. 'Right now I reckon that if NFF sell out our stock, the buyers could have control of up to thirty-five per cent. You and I, together with the other three directors, total forty-one per cent between us. We're running about even and it's up to NFF and the public to decide who's going to win.

353

'Our shareholders are facing a barrage of publicity on both sides. I've spent a hundred thousand dollars on the latest publicity campaign. Unfortunately, the enemy were ready to go before I knew there was a war. The advertising guys take a while to get geared up.

'Look at this.' Eleanor opened her briefcase and brought out a folder. 'Here's their latest effort which appeared in yesterday's financial press.'

The heading read: *'Vanguard's management losing ground. Vanguard must be more innovative if they want to retain the lead in winter sports. Falling growth rate, profits and investor confidence shows what happens when fat cats sit on their butts. It is ironic that a company which has gone to such lengths to associate its name with 'winners' should have a board of directors who are not winning. Against massive, hostile press coverage, Vanguard have thrown their reputation into a campaign modelled around a selection of young champions, including the chairman's daughter, Jacqui Douglas. Jacqui, a promising skier, broke her leg in Val d'Isère last year and lost her place in the US team. However, she joined the British team and came in 17th in the 1982/83 season in overall World Cup Circuit events. Hardly a safe bet. Is this sound business management, or the work of a doting mother?*

'They make it sound as if it's just Jacqui,' Eleanor grumbled. 'In fact, we have the pick of this year's ski crop, all under Vanguard sponsorship. Of course, they didn't mention that.'

'You stuck your neck out with Jacqui,' Nigel said sharply.

'With good reason,' Eleanor retorted. Her face settled into an expression of immovable obstinacy. Nigel knew that look. It was time to change the subject.

'What d'you think they're after, Nigel? This whole business gives me the creeps. We can't offer the juicy pickings raiders usually go for – and the sports industry has seen its best days. The lean years are approaching – time for consolidation. I don't get the reasoning behind the buying. To see Vanguard taken over and ruined would be like dying to me.' She broke off, remembering Gundelfinger and his silly warnings. Maybe she was going to find out how much of her would be left without her business.

Looking at her toying with her teaspoon, her face ravaged with worry, Nigel felt amazed at her arrogance. 'Eleanor, had it ever occurred to you that there may – there just may, be other entrepreneurs who could conceivably run Vanguard without you? You'd still own your shares – you'd still be a very wealthy woman.' That was a blunder, he knew. Eleanor's face was now crumpled with fear.

'*Better is a little with righteousness than great revenues without right.* My father used to quote the Bible nightly. Did you know that, Nigel? I still remember most of it by heart. It was the only book we had in the house. *Pride goeth before destruction, and an haughty spirit before a fall.* I should have remembered some of those sayings, these past twenty years.' She waved for the waiter, signed the bill with a flourish, tipped generously as usual and stood up. 'Just so long as you know I'm sorry,' she said.

Watching Eleanor, Nigel could not help thinking that she was as good as vanquished. He could cry when he thought of all these years when he'd put his faith in her strength. Look at her – a woman of straw. Crumpled, careworn, and itching with eczema. The investing public should see her now, he thought spitefully.

'Eleanor, sit down. I spoke out of turn,' Nigel said and reaching out he placed one hand over hers. 'Believe me, it's impossible. It isn't going to happen. NFF have always been loyal. If you like I'll fly over and see the board. I don't believe they'll sell to the enemy. It's not like you to be so negative. What you need is a holiday. Why don't you take off for a couple of weeks? By the time you come back this scare will have blown over.'

'I'll think about it,' she said unconvincingly as they left.

It was three pm before Eleanor's secretary managed to raise her London lawyer on the telephone. He was in charge of her private family affairs, including an offshore trust company, and her non-Vanguard investments.

'I want you to raise twelve and a half million dollars plus. I don't care how – sell my share portfolio, raise loans on the property, you can count on my house in Cap Ferrat and the yacht ... Yes, everything. It may only be a temporary exercise, but we're bound to lose on the deal ... Yes, that's right, up to thirty per cent ... no, I haven't taken leave of my senses, my assets are worth that much and I want the liquidity in a hurry. Got it? you've got forty-eight hours!'

Shortly after seven pm Eleanor telephoned the NFF chairman from her home.

'This is strictly confidential, Michael,' she said. 'I know how your loyalty has always been with Vanguard. You were our very first backer, but business is business and I don't see how you can refuse this offer you've had on Vanguard shares.'

She sat back patiently, while Michael rambled on about being caught in the middle of a two-day pull between investors and old friends.

'Well, I've worked out a way you can satisfy your conscience on both accounts,' she said. 'I'm offering you a twenty-five per cent premium on half your holdings. I can't afford more. Yes, I do realise that you might prejudice the deal for the whole parcel, but Michael, the other party can't afford not to take them, if I have half. You can even demand the extra five I'm offering you. This way you can take your profits without feeling bad about it.'

Twenty minutes later, Eleanor replaced the receiver knowing she had at least half the NFF shares. Forty-six per cent on her side. Forty-three, at the most, for the enemy. Nigel was right, it was inconceivable that all the public's shares would become available. She was safe. So why did she feel so damned uneasy? Eleanor poured herself a drink, went out on to the patio and stood staring at the sea, but her thoughts were far away. Time and again her female intuition had saved her and right now warning bells were ringing loud and clear.

CHAPTER 52

It was almost November, and Megan had cut short a holiday in the States in order to see Nikki compete at the British championships held at Solihull Ice Rink, the previous evening. Nikki had won with a brilliant exhibition of free-style and figure skating and several judges had congratulated Eric for his inspired tuition. That night they had all celebrated and Nikki had let down her defences and seemed her old self again. It was only two months before the European championships would be held in Budapest, but as yet Nikki had not received British citizenship. Megan was getting anxious. She had quarrelled with Ian about it, but Ian insisted that decisions were being made far above his head and that he was unable to help her.

This morning Megan had decided to take a few hours off in order to watch Nikki skating on the film set. Having repaired their friendship she did not want to put it at risk again. She had heard so many conflicting reports about the film making, Nikki's were not good, and she was curious to see for herself. Ian, she knew, was thrilled that they were following his script to the letter. Nikki, however, was continually moaning about the look-alike actress, Phyliss Symms, who was playing the speaking roles of herself. Nikki disapproved of her, mainly because she was so jealous.

Megan arrived at eight am but shooting had started and Nikki was speeding around the ice rink at Wembley Ice Stadium which had been hastily improvised to resemble a Russian lake. She was quite an actress, Megan thought watching her look of terror as she glanced over her shoulder, but she could not agree with Nikki, that she should have had the speaking role as well.

Watching Nikki, Megan felt quite stunned by her amazing performance. Nikki's skating had reached a fine peak of excellence. Lately she had been driving herself to ridiculous lengths, and training all hours. She had dropped her friends, given up baiting Eric, she did not even spend much of her allowance. She was obsessed with her skating. For Nikki it was one intensely gruelling day after the next. If she weren't so strong she would have collapsed, Megan knew, yet on the ice she looked ethereal and delicate, and certainly not vigorous enough to perform the graceful leaps and turns which required so much stamina and self-discipline.

Nikki's day began at six, winter and summer, with an hour's jogging, and after that it was one tough coaching session after the next, with gymnastics and dancing lessons fitted in here and there. She had been hard-pressed to find time for the filming.

It showed, Megan thought. Nikki was thinner, her face even paler and her eyes had a haunted look in them. She still had her radiant smile, but one saw it less often.

Megan's thoughts were brought smartly back to the present as she gripped the railing and watched Nikki perform a really hair-raising stag jump terminating with a sit spin.

The applause from the film crew was spontaneous as Nikki spun to the edge of the rink and leaned over the railing trying to catch her breath.

'That was stunning, Nikki,' the director called to her. 'Take a break everyone. Be back in ten minutes for the next sequence.'

Why was Nikki driving herself so? Megan wondered. She decided to speak to her. At this rate she'd crack up long before the Winter Games.

Megan, who was standing in the shadows of the props, was about to follow Nikki to the canteen when she heard Ian's voice talking to the director:

'Try to get the girl's skating shots finished before February, you may not get another chance,' he said.

Hardly listening, Megan walked up to Ian and pushed her arm through his.

'And why not?' she asked laughingly. 'Are you expecting her to elope?'

Ian looked shocked and guilty. 'Well, yes, why not? She'll be able to do what she likes. Good news,' he had said smiling over-brightly as he took her arm. 'Come on, I'll buy you coffee.'

In the canteen, Ian went to great lengths to explain that Nikki's British nationality had at last been granted. It was all over, bar the paperwork.

Megan felt pleased, both for Nikki and for herself. No more hanging around in dusty corridors. Nikki would be overjoyed. She decided to keep the good news until the passport actually arrived.

Back in the office, Maureen and Megan worked for the remainder of the morning to organize 1984's programmes for the champions ISA handled. These would be sent to their sponsors. They had over fifty-two clients nowadays and each one of them seemed to present unique problems which Megan had not encountered in America.

They worked quickly and sympathetically together, as they had done so often, planning the cash flow and answering the backlog of telephone calls. Maureen was on the same wavelength, Megan often thought, and it was seldom necessary to spell out her instructions.

'Maybe I'm over-confident, or simply stupid, but it seems to me that this is going to be one hell of a year,' Megan boasted to Maureen. 'Everything we've touched has turned to gold.'

'No, not everything,' Maureen warned her. 'A few problems cropped up while you were away. When we've finished here, I'll fetch the files.'

'Which would you like first,' Maureen asked later, after coffee break. 'The good news or the bad news?'

Looking up in surprise at Maureen's tone of voice, she was once again struck by her assistant's new image. The flash clothes had been replaced with smartly tailored suits, neat court shoes, pearl earrings and her hair was straightened and waved into a shape that resembled a bun. This was not an overnight transformation, Megan knew, but a deliberate change, executed step by step. Today Maureen was wearing a tailored navy suit, a white lace blouse and white accessories with a long pearl necklace.

'Maureen,' she began hesitatingly. 'You've changed. I've been meaning to ask – why?'

'The answer to your question is at the bottom of the list labelled: "bad news". So which d'you want first?'

'The other list,' Megan said sulkily.

'The good list is rather short, but here goes. First and foremost ...' She paused dramatically and mimed a trumpet player. 'Tum-tara! Johnny has landed the Tarzan role. The studios are getting their act together. The contract comes later.'

'Hey! No kidding? That's just great,' Megan said delightedly. 'Move over Johnny Weismuller, here comes Johnny Bart. But Maureen, how did you find out? I haven't heard a thing.'

'Johnny told me last night, after they called him.' She sat down with a self-satisfied smirk.

Megan watched Maureen fondly, pleased with the sight of her pleasure and her coy expression. She'd always thought Johnny was gay, but it looked as if she'd been wrong. She said: 'I'll dictate a letter to the film company later. We must make sure they give him a good deal. Anything else on the good list?'

Maureen looked annoyed, and Megan felt vaguely troubled. What else was she supposed to say about it? she wondered.

'The bank manager telephoned because he wants to advise you on company investments. Our excess liquidity could be put to work, he said. He has a plan for you.'

Megan smiled happily. 'We're making it Maureen,' she said and wondered why Maureen looked away guiltily. 'It's been quite a year, hasn't it?'

Maureen nodded self-consciously and watching her Megan was struck with the realisation that Maureen was leaving her. Obviously this had something to do with Johnny. Maureen looked coy and guilty, all at the same time. Megan felt a wave of panic run through her. How would she manage without her? She'd have to play down the loss, for Maureen's sake, and she would try to look surprised. 'Next?' she asked, forcing a bright smile.

'There's a letter here from the University of Michigan, offering an athletic scholarship to Conrad.'

'Wow! What a morning! I'll telephone him later today.'

'Next, Gerry Johnson wants you to be his agent.'

'*The* Gerry Johnson, the golfer?'

'The same.'

'Hey, Maureen, we're getting famous. Now they're chasing after us. We deserve it – but can you believe it?'

Maureen smiled, a strange, enigmatic smile. 'Darn it, Megan. Don't look so damned happy,' she said. 'The bad news is coming up next.'

'You've said it,' Megan said, watching through the plate glass window as Jacqui walked hesitantly into reception.

Maureen hurried off and shortly afterwards Jacqui stood at the door smiling softly and looking slightly hesitant.

Heavens, Megan thought, how she's changed.

Megan had not seen Jacqui since Aviemore and she was surprised to see how womanly she had become although she could not decide exactly where the difference lay. Perhaps it was the smart skirt and coat she was wearing, or the make-up, but mainly, she decided, it was Jacqui's poise, a certain self-confidence which she had recently acquired.

'I'm giving up skiing right after the Games,' Jacqui told her, 'so you might as well start cancelling those extra sponsors. I thought I ought to let you know well beforehand.'

'And Vanguard?' Megan asked. 'What do I do about Vanguard?'

'Don't worry about Vanguard,' Jacqui said slowly. 'I'm joining the staff.'

Megan felt shocked and showed it.

'Mother's collected a few problems,' Jacqui went on nervously. 'Don't tell me you haven't read about them. I guess I was the only idiot who didn't know. I've decided to learn the business. It's something Mother always wanted.' She paused and frowned at Megan. 'As a matter of fact, I haven't told Mother yet. We're hardly on speaking terms, just sort of giving each other space. I'll break the news to her after the Olympics.'

'Well ... Oh my!' Megan felt taken aback and could not think what to say. 'I'm glad,' she added eventually.

'Cut out the crap,' Jacqui said derisively. 'You're not pleased, I'm not pleased, it's just something that has to be done.'

'Did Eleanor pressurise you?' Megan asked cautiously.

'No.' There was a long silence. Megan sensed that Jacqui wanted to talk, so she ordered coffee.

Jacqui began pacing the office.

'Don't you want to sit down?' Megan asked pointedly.

'Not particularly,' she said off-handedly. 'All my life Mother's coped with everything. I mean she's a regular whizz kid, or so the newspapers say. The truth is, I know the other side of her. She can't cope with anything emotional ... retreats into herself. Consequently, I never got much attention in the things that count with kids, but when it came to money – well, I had everything, naturally.

'You know what, Megan?' she said gently. 'I used to envy the kids who had parents they could talk to.' She frowned, and glanced over her shoulder. 'Do you mind me talking like this?'

Megan did not think Jacqui wanted a reply, so she sat silently sipping her coffee.

'Whenever I needed help, she ran. Boy, she ran. I once asked her who my father was. You know what she said? She said: "Jacqui, I've started a family trust – for you. Ten per cent of Vanguard shares are in it as well as this property, the yacht – everything. When I die, you'll get everything. You'll be a very wealthy woman. Doesn't that make you feel secure?" Then she left for a business trip and I didn't see her for ten days. So I never asked again. I learned to be self-contained quite early in life.'

'Don't you want your coffee?' Megan asked.

'Oh sure.' She sat down abruptly and picked up her cup. 'Megan,' she went on in a low, urgent voice. 'I've watched Mother cope with problems that would capsize any other company. Nothing can beat Mother, if it's filed under the heading of "business".'

She looked up, pale-faced and angry. 'Until now! Which could mean that Mother suspects who's behind the takeover bid, and she won't face up to it. My guess is – it's someone in the company. At least four key directors have shares and between them they hold eleven per cent. Mother couldn't face that sort of betrayal.

'She likes you,' Jacqui went on. 'I want you to go and talk some sense into her. She must insist that those shares be held in trust until this takeover scare is past. And why doesn't she call in a firm of industrial intelligence agents? She ought ... oh, what the hell. She won't!'

'Have you told her what you think?'

'Sure.'

'And then?'

'We had another fight. Yesterday, as a matter of fact. We can't talk to each other, we've never been able to.'

'I'll see what I can do,' Megan said doubtfully. 'But it's not really my business.'

'If Vanguard sinks, you might go with us,' Jacqui said with her usual lack of finesse. 'Don't we sponsor three-quarters of your champions?'

362

'We?' So Jacqui was hooked, Megan thought with a smile.

She lay back thinking about the curious ambiguity of hereditary genes. Who would have believed Jacqui would emerge from the chrysalis of youth as another Eleanor and zoom straight back to Vanguard when the going became rough?

Perhaps Ian could help, Megan thought, remembering how he had always spoken so well of Eleanor. 'I have a friend who specialises in intelligence work,' Megan said slowly. 'If you like, I'll speak to him.'

Jacqui was twisting her hands nervously. 'Yes, do that Megan. There's something else, but you must swear you won't tell ... not yet ... not until I sort something out. I have ten per cent of Vanguard shares, but I exchanged them for a rather profitable percentage of a new oil producing company Wolf's floating right now. The idea was that I could sell now to Wolf, while the shares are sky high, and he'd buy back for me when they sink to normal levels. In the meantime I'll make a packet on the oil wells, too. So I stand to make quite a sizeable fortune.'

'You believe this?' Megan said ominously. 'D'you believe that this Wolf Muller is handing you a fortune on the plate?'

'Yes,' Jacqui said defiantly. 'He's doing it to help me.'

'How much are your Vanguard shares worth, Jacqui?'

'Around twenty million dollars,' Jacqui whispered.

'What makes you think you haven't been conned?' Megan said harshly. 'You knew your Mother would never have approved.'

'That's the whole point,' Jacqui said, her voice was hardly more than a croak now. She licked her lips nervously. 'In a year's time Wolf was going to buy them back for me. Mother would never know the difference.'

'She will if she's taken over, with those crucial ten per cent of stock making the majority for someone.'

'That's it exactly. I'm going to ask Wolf to give them back to me.'

'You think he will? No kidding? Looks to me like a case for a fraud investigation,' Megan said grimly feeling sorry for Jacqui who was starting to shake.

'In spite of what it sounds and looks like, I'd trust Wolf with my life,' Jacqui said.

'He probably doesn't want your life, just your fortune.'

Megan picked up the telephone. 'I know a lawyer who specialises in this type of thing.'

'No, Megan, wait. After all, you promised. Wolf would never defraud me.'

'Okay, prove it, Jacqui. Go to Wolf, tell him that you've told me and what I wanted to do and ask for your shares back. Tell him I wanted to start a fraud investigation. If he gives them to you ... well, then you're right. Otherwise ...'

Megan stood up abruptly and turned to the window. She was so angry and sickened by Jacqui's stupidity she could not look at the girl. Good grief! Twenty million dollars and Jacqui still wanted to make a profit. She'd heard that the victim's greed was the strong arm of all confidence tricksters. 'You owe it to your Mother to warn her. After all, she gave them to you. She'll be counting on that ten per cent in her fight to hold her company.'

'Yes,' Jacqui said. 'If I haven't got them back in a month's time, then ...' her voice trailed off, 'speak to your friend, please Megan. The one with intelligence experience.'

After Jacqui had left, Megan could not shake off her depression. She picked up the telephone and managed to raise Ian at the Admiralty. 'Ian please help, it's your sort of work and I know how much you admire Eleanor Douglas ... Yes, please, if you would meet me for dinner tonight, I'll explain the whole thing. It's messy ... to say the least.'

Maureen sent out for sandwiches and they made coffee, but it did not help Megan to feel any better.

'The problem file looks pretty thick,' she said anxiously, as Maureen produced a bulky folder right after lunch.

'Ten days is a long time in this business,' Maureen said smugly as she opened the pages.

'The smear campaign against Gorgeous Gertie was financed by Vanguard, and executed by a little creep running a two-roomed outfit in Soho. He specialises in this sort of thing on a freelance basis and he gets a good many commissions from Nigel Wilder.'

'How on earth ...?'

'Johnny chatted up one of the girls working there,' she giggled unexpectedly. 'Johnny's getting braver these days, but he had a lot of trouble getting rid of her afterwards.'

'You were playing a dangerous game, Maureen,' Megan said smiling with amusement. 'It could have backfired on you.'

'No, never,' Maureen said, her face radiant with the security of her happiness.

'I don't want to tangle with Vanguard again,' Megan said thoughtfully. 'Maybe I'll have a word with them. Wonder if Eleanor knows?' she murmured thoughtfully. 'Somehow she didn't strike me … Or perhaps I'll hand the matter to John.'

'I wouldn't bother if I were you.'

'Sssh,' Megan said. 'Let me think.'

Irreverently, Maureen continued. 'Gertie's sold the rights to her autobiography. It's to be entitled: *A frank confession*. Her exact words were: "She's sick and tired of hiding behind a web of lies mainly spun by Megan." She told me she can't wait for the publication date. She thinks the press will get off her back after this.'

'And Bantex? Does she want them off her back, too. Has she come into some inheritance, or doesn't she want to eat?'

'Who knows?' Maureen said with an enigmatic smile.

'Make a note to get our lawyer on the line for me later. Perhaps we – or Bantex – can prevent publication until their contract has expired. Bantex will back us.'

'But that would be very traumatic for Gertie,' Maureen argued. 'This book means a lot to her.'

'She can't have it both ways. She was only too eager to sign up as the *Frankly Feminine* champion. Next!'

'Lastly, here's my notice.' She flipped an envelope across the desk.

Megan opened the envelope sadly. 'Three months. I suppose I should be grateful for that,' she said quietly. She was feeling deeply hurt by Maureen's attitude, but she didn't want this to show.

Maureen nodded. 'I'm going to run Johnny Bart's career.'

'No kidding? You're going into competition with me? Hell, Maureen, I have Johnny on contract.'

'On a three month's notice basis,' Maureen retorted. 'And here's Johnny's notice.' She produced a letter from her bag and handed it over as if she was handling dynamite.

Calm down! If she's leaving there's nothing I can do about it and losing my temper will only spoil the memories. All the

365

same, I wish she'd wipe that self-satisfied smirk off her face.

'D'you think you're qualified to set up as a sports agent?' Megan asked, keeping her tone impersonal and light.

'No,' Maureen admitted. 'But I think I know what's best for Johnny.'

'How come?'

'We're getting married in a week's time.'

For a moment Megan beamed at her assistant. Then she leaped up and rushed around the desk. 'That's absolutely wonderful,' she said, hugging her and meaning it. 'Congratulations!' She took a step backwards and gazed at Maureen searchingly. 'Now I know what the difference is – love,' she said triumphantly. 'Hey there, Maureen, you don't put that sort of news on the bad list. I'm absolutely delighted for you. We must have a party to celebrate. What about tonight at my place? Are you both free?'

To Megan's embarrassment, Maureen began to cry. 'I misjudged you,' she said, dabbing her eyes with a tissue. 'Oh Megan, I'm going to miss this whole scene, but I've got to put Johnny first. You don't need love, not like I do. I long to have my own home, kids, a husband to hug at night. I don't want to be big-stuff myself. I just want to build up my man. I know that sort of thing's old-fashioned to you. You've no patience with women who just want to be women. You've always made that quite clear, so I thought you'd be furious. Quite frankly I was scared to tell you.'

'Is that what you think of me?' Megan said feeling genuinely bewildered. 'You're probably closer to me than my closest friend, and if you think that ...' she broke off and stood staring out of the window. It was cold, the trees were bare, and people hurried along, huddled in overcoats, eyes as bleak as the sky. She shivered, but she was not seeing the street, she was plagued with introspection and an unwelcome feeling that there might be some truth in what Maureen had said.

CHAPTER 53

For some weeks Eleanor had not mentioned Wolf. She restricted herself to telling Gundelfinger of her marketing strategy which had successfully thrust Vanguard into the lead among multi-national sports distributors. It seemed to Gundelfinger that she was determined to turn her back on the vulnerable Eleanor Muller she had once been. As the weeks went by she succeeded, but the eczema returned.

Her first step into the big time, she explained, had been to sell off Vanguard's manufacturing outfits to firms who would manufacture solely for her company's distribution. With her capital freed, she had been able to lay the foundation for what was destined to become the biggest sports distributing network in America. She lavished every spare penny on advertising the Vanguard brand, which became synonymous with winning. Her first stroke of marketing genius was to branch into sports clothing, and to employ a top fashion designer. The garments were made by various cut-make-and-trim firms, and in this changeable fashion market, stock was kept to a minimum.

At the end of her first decade, she turned to the Far East and particularly Korea for her manufacturing outlets and undercut all competition. When she had a thirty per cent share of the US market in her pocket she went public. Vanguard was quoted on the US bourse and shares were snapped up by eager investors including several growth funds. Eleanor's fame was spreading. She used the capital to set up exporting bases in Britain and Europe and shortly afterwards she shifted the head office to Monaco and bought back the original manufacturing base in Denver, plus four of the Korean outfits. She was now chairman of a diverse multi-national sports manufacturing and distributing company – a force to be reckoned with worldwide.

'How come you don't say much lately,' Eleanor complained

halfway through her next session. 'You don't make many comments and you don't help me like you used to.'

'I'm not a qualified business analyst,' Gundelfinger said quietly. 'I can only listen and wonder. I think you're some kind of genius at marketing and at finance.'

'You know I'm not a genius.'

'What are you then?'

She thought for a long time. 'I'm clever and I'm motivated,' she said at last. 'And I have a flair for marketing.'

'You sure do. I take my hat off to you.'

Eleanor looked round suspiciously. Then she said: 'I've been talking too much about business, haven't I?'

'You've been doing that most of your adult years,' Gundelfinger said gently. 'You've built up this wonderful, larger-than-life image of the great Eleanor Douglas, chairman of the board, so that no one would suspect that along with your other victims, you've walled up that young, caring, hurt Eleanor Muller somewhere in the depth of your whizz kid personality. But I think the real Eleanor would like to be let out.'

A slow flush spread up from her neck and blazed on her cheeks. 'Who's to know which one is the real one?' she said, swallowing hard.

'Let's find out, shall we, Eleanor?' the doctor said gravely. 'Or are you too scared to try?'

Eleanor hestiated. 'You don't understand how hurtful it is … I mean, all these memories …'

'Oh I do. Believe me, I do. I may not understand the complexities of business, but I know how hard it is for you to come to grips with your trauma. That takes real courage.'

'I've never been short of courage,' she retorted angrily.

'Let's go then. The last I heard of the real Eleanor Douglas was when she and Wolf were setting sail in a leaky cockleshell boat. You were really scared, Eleanor, weren't you?'

'With good reason,' she began determinedly. 'But I had one thing on my side: fifty per cent of the stock, so I reckoned Wolf would never be able to sell the company without my permission.'

Gundelfinger listened to the intelligent woman with the fashionable Balmain dress and the emerald jewellery thinking: you could have had any man you wanted Eleanor, how come you landed up alone?

'Together with Vanguard, came a colourless young man,

called Nigel Wilder,' she was explaining earnestly. 'He was an odd sort of guy, very pretentious. He insisted on calling himself Research Chief. He even had a sign put on his door, but in reality he was the storeman. Nevertheless, he spent most of his time down in the basement – which they called research and development, messing around with a new, faster ski he claimed he had developed. His idea was to make a metal sandwich of aluminium and plywood and fill the centre with honeycombed plastic. Most times he was either scavenging aluminium from the scrap pile of a local aircraft plant, or testing his skis. They broke, time and again, but Nigel kept on trying.' She chuckled suddenly, enjoying herself.

'When Wolf and I bought the company, Nigel was on notice to quit, but strangely enough, Wolf saw possibilities in his ideas and he borrowed ten thousand dollars from the bank and set Nigel up in a workshop.

'More debts! I was furious. Each morning when I surfaced, reality would hit me in the stomach like a kick from a mule. I used to add up the total of what we owed the bank and our creditors, and all the while the sweat would pour off me until the bed was wet through.'

It still happened almost nightly in her dreams. She would wake sweating with fright and only by listing her assets could she calm herself back to sleep.

'Eventually, Nigel produced a ski that Wolf liked, but we couldn't raise the cash to develop it, so the skis were shelved for a while. Six months later, Wolf's father died and he inherited twenty thousand dollars which he used to take out world patents on Nigel's skis and start manufacturing. Wolf had faith, but no one else did. No one knew if the skis would be successful and to tell the truth at first they weren't. Eventually, of course, they formed the basis of our success in the ski market.'

She broke off, twisting her hands nervously. The story, with its reminder of old, continuing guilts and regrets, disturbing her. Eventually she shook herself, like a dog shaking off water, and continued.

'We had nothing left to pay Nigel for his design so we gave him eight per cent of Vanguard equity instead.

'All the while as those two were counting on making the big time. I was patiently plodding on, building up sales and gradually we pulled ourselves out of debt.'

369

Sunday mornings at the club. Wolf skiing back for breakfast. Orange juice, bacon and eggs by the window overlooking the snow-clad slopes, sparkling in morning sunlight. They bathed in the admiration of their friends and the inevitability of their brilliant future. Oh Wolf! Oh God, Wolf, she screamed silently.

'And then?'

'The strangest things change one's life,' she said softly. 'In my case it was an accident. Wolf broke his back and that changed the whole course and direction of our lives.'

She crumpled into the chair and buried her face in her hands. 'When they carried him back on a stretcher I was so sure that he would die. I remember praying: 'God just let him live – if you let him live I'll do anything – anything.'

Suddenly Eleanor sat up and nervously fiddled with her hair. 'I can't take much more of this,' she said grabbing her hat and gloves.

Gundelfinger noticed that her forehead was damp with sweat and her eyes were swollen although there were no tears. 'Eleanor don't run away,' he said gently. 'Let's see it through. Otherwise it will bother you. I don't have a lunch appointment today. Stay and share my sandwich.'

Eleanor turned reluctantly. She said: 'I suppose I might as well get it over with.'

Gundelfinger fussed about making two cups of tea and dividing the sandwich in half, while Eleanor mumbled on as if not wishing to hear what she was saying.

'Wolf spent a year in hospital.' Eleanor's eyes were almost closed and her hands were clenched tightly on her lap. 'I felt utter despair. The nights were the worst. At the time I thought that nothing could ever be worse than that year. But of course I was wrong. Something inside me, some part of me, was pushed away out of sight. I had to be strong. I had to run the plant – for Wolf's sake.

'At first I was afraid of running Vanguard without him, but everything I touched seemed to go right. The sports retailers were pretty nice guys, mainly ex-sportsmen in those days, and most of them had heard about Wolf's accident. We had problems keeping up with the sales that came pouring in by telephone. From that day on the business took off.

'Once we were out of the red, I felt more confident – a different person. I commissioned a top advertising agency to build

370

Vanguard's image – and from then on I made sure all my sponsored athletes were winners. I even started skating again and wore Vanguard's after-ski wear exclusively. Nigel looked pretty silly in a track suit but I wouldn't let him wear anything else. I knew then that nothing could ever stop me. I was zooming right to the top. I remember how surprised I was when it dawned on me that I was much better at running the business than Wolf.' She looked up and smiled sadly.

'Eighteen months later, Wolf came back. They brought him home in a wheelchair and I cried when I saw him coming, but I tried to behave as if everything was wonderful. Of course he wanted to take over – just where he left off, but I just couldn't let go. How could I go back to debts, taking chances that might not come off, worrying myself sick? Besides, I knew he wasn't strong enough. I would not give in and we fought.

'Wolf seemed like a different person. He hated to be incapacitated, and missed his skiing. He was an impossible patient: demanding, irritable, bitter, throwing things around when he didn't get his own way, and he was always pulling himself out of the wheelchair on his wretched sticks and toppling over.

'I'd never wanted children, there wasn't time, but now I seemed to dredge up a surfeit of mother love which I lavished on Wolf. I held his arm when he tried to walk, picked up his sticks, bathed him, helped him to the toilet, there was nothing that I wouldn't do for him. Wolf was completely dependent upon me and I was happy once again. I liked him like that. I felt safe. Sometimes that used to make me feel bad.

'Wolf had nothing to do, and that irked him, so he plunged into the stock market with cash he borrowed from the bank on Vanguard's security.

'As his legs improved so did his sexual appetite.' She turned abruptly, looking flushed and girlish. 'Do you mind me talking like this?' she said.

'It's part of life, isn't it?'

'He wanted more and more sex but it was almost impossible to accomplish. I was so scared he'd hurt himself so I mothered him and Wolf played a passive role and this infuriated him.

Roll over I want to lie on top of you.

You'll hurt yourself: lie still or I won't do it.

Wolf, it's nice like this, you don't have to move and you always come. Please Wolf, close your eyes ... just enjoy.

Then it was over and there was no more fight in him.

'It wasn't just sex, this passive role seemed to shadow him in everything he touched and especially business. A number of deals went wrong at this time and Wolf became angry and frustrated.

'One day I was pushing him down the path in front of the factory when he said: "Turn left. I want to talk to Nigel". I was in a hurry and I said, "Later, Wolf. Right now we're going to the store."

'He turned and I caught sight of the expression in his eyes. For a moment I felt scared. He took his stick and thrust it through the spokes of the wheels. I fell over the chair and Wolf grabbed the armrest and pushed himself to his feet. He would not let me help him. I remember feeling a sense of regret as he hobbled away.

'He called over his shoulder: "Throw that damned wheelchair away, I won't be needing it again." After that he walked everywhere and improved dramatically.

'Then,' she broke off remembering, and her cheeks flushed deep red. 'It was a hot, Sunday afternoon in summer and I had been swimming. I walked into the house in a bikini ... Wolf wanted to make love as we had done before the accident and I refused. I was afraid he might injure his back you see.'

Be honest, Eleanor. Was it only that? Wolf had looked so full of vigour, his penis raw and swollen – ramrod hard, wilful, mindless but always demanding, and in Wolf's eyes there was the same wilfulness, the male imperative, to command, to bully, to seek compliance. Only his will counted, not mine. Yet I could see the entreaty behind the command. I understood then that the male ego is a fragile thing, easy to build, easy to destroy, and he needed me to thrust him into command so that he could take his rightful place as my despotic ruler, by reason of his genes and my own tacit consent. So I must lie spread-eagled in voluntary capitulation – submissive in love, submissive in marriage. A spark of revolt stirred in my breast.

'Go on,' Gundelfinger said mildly and Eleanor turned and gazed fearfully at him. 'I was afraid for his back,' she lied. 'I could not allow him to take a chance.'

I pushed him gently down, bent to kiss his mouth and eased myself gently on and around him, holding his hips still with my strong hands, swinging my hips forward and sideways, and then

I bent and cupped my hands around his cheeks, pressed my lips onto his and always my hips were gently swaying. 'Still, still,' I murmured and waited for the inevitable explosion.

She stared at the psychiatrist and he knew she was holding back.

'Wolf said: "I don't need a mother Eleanor, I need a wife," and I burst into tears. After all, I was only trying to get him better.' She looked round and saw Gundelfinger watching her with a strangely mocking expression on his face.

'After this, Wolf spent much of his time away. I should have read the signs, but I was busy − accounts at night, breakfast meetings with advertising executives, sales meetings weekends − there wasn't much time left for home.

'One day I received a telephone call from a woman called Isobel, a member of the ski club. She sounded sweet and mysterious and she said she wanted to talk to me about something very important. I thought she was looking for a job and was embarrassed to apply in the normal manner, so I invited her to tea. She told me that she loved Wolf; they were having an affair, she said. Wolf wanted to marry her, but couldn't bring himself to ask for a divorce.

'I remember I went berserk. I hit her − over and over again − I didn't know what I was doing, but suddenly I realised she was on the floor and I was standing over her, my fists stinging. I didn't care what happened to her, but I was mortified to have shown her how hurt I was. Somehow I reached the bathroom and locked myself in. I was very nauseous, but between my heaves I heard her slam the front door and then the sound of her car starting up and driving away. I must have cried for hours, but then I noticed it was dark and I was afraid that Wolf would come home and find me looking like ... well, you can imagine what I looked like. I didn't want him to get any satisfaction from my grief.

'I left a note, saying I had to stay overnight at a neighbouring city to clinch a sale and then I booked into a motel a few miles out of town and locked myself in a cabin. I nearly went mad there. I couldn't bear the pain, the thought of Wolf in bed with another woman − loving her − wanting to be rid of me. I thought then that widows are so much luckier than abandoned women − they have their friends' sympathy, they have their pride, and their love to hold on to. I had nothing. Everything I had lived for, worked for, day and night, year after year ... it was all destroyed. It took me days to get myself under control, but eventually my grief compressed itself into a cold hard ball in the pit of my stomach. I began to think about my revenge.

'Naturally, I did not tell Wolf about Isobel's visit. I carried on as usual, but I knew that I was just a walking shell; all that was meaningful had died.

'Wolf wanted to know where I had been, but he didn't seem too interested. Two weeks later he came home looking pleased and told me he'd found a buyer for Vanguard. 'Oil was the future,' he said. He looked self-confident and fired with enthusiasm. The old Wolf. For a while I wanted to kill him, but then I thought that was too good for him. I would be more subtle.'

She looked around fearfully as if waiting for a verdict. Her face was very white except for her flushed cheeks and for a moment Gundelfinger considered calling a halt until another day. But maybe there would not be another day.

'I pretended to play along while I enlisted Nigel's support. That wasn't difficult. He could not bear to see his skis owned by another party. Between us we had fifty-four per cent. We called a board meeting and sacked Wolf. I enjoyed every minute of it: his shocked white face, his bewilderment and then his fury. We made him a poor offer for his shares. After that, all hell broke loose, but short of shooting us there wasn't much Wolf could do. He took every penny he had made in stocks and shares to fight us in court – and he lost. Most of the cash he received for his shares went in legal fees. The last time I saw Wolf he was both drunk and broke and vowing he'd catch up with me. Later, I heard that Isobel left him and he returned to Austria.

'So that's the story,' Eleanor said astringently, standing up. 'Now you know everything, so wave your damned magic wand and charm away this itch.' She glared at him.

Alone in the room, with the suffering woman, Gundelfinger wished he had that magic wand. What was it she had said so aggressively? "Now you know everything!" Not everything. Not yet. She had looked sly and evasive and he wondered what else she was concealing.

'But Eleanor, not once have you mentioned your child, Jacqui – that's her name, isn't it? Surely Wolf made some effort to see his daughter?'

'Wolf wasn't the father,' she said sharply.

'Then who was?'

'It doesn't matter who her father was. It was a one-night stand, right after Isobel and that dreadful tea party. I didn't know what I was doing,' she added defensively.

'Is that what you told Wolf?'

'I told him that Nigel and I were having an affair.'

'And were you?'

'With Nigel? Don't be absurd.'

'But I don't understand why you didn't tell Wolf that you knew about Isobel.'

Eleanor smiled artfully and something about her expression bothered the doctor. 'I wanted him to feel as betrayed as I did. I didn't want him to make excuses for me. I was afraid I might weaken, one day. I never wanted to be hurt again, I never wanted to feel anything for anyone, ever again. I wanted Wolf to hate and despise me as much as I hated and despised him. After Jacqui was born I moved head office to Monaco. No one knows I was ever married – except Nigel, of course – Jacqui has always known she is illegitimate.'

Eleanor peered at Gundelfinger as though waiting for his reaction to her story. Gundelfinger kept quiet. 'Aren't you going to say something?' Eleanor demanded.

'Surely you realise that there was no other way you could have reacted,' Gundelfinger said helpfully.

Eleanor put one hand on his shoulder. 'You're young,' she said, smiling bitterly. 'You have still to find out that conscience is an occupational hazard of the old. I'm not sure if I'll come back again. I'll see how the itch behaves.' Suddenly she was gone and Gundelfinger sat bemused, feeling inadequate to cope with Eleanor's trauma. Self-absolution was what she craved; he didn't have the power to give it to her. He was a psychiatrist, not a priest. Sometimes he thought the old ways were best, the mumbo-jumbo of the witchdoctor, the priest's incantations, fasting and believing. Sins had to be punished and forgiven or the sinner shrivelled and died.

Eleanor had been brought up in a rigid code of values, a harsh evaluation of right and wrong. Her ambition to be rich was, in a way, a desire to abandon her Scottish upbringing and origins, but she never would escape; she would carry her Scottish mores inside her for the rest of her life. He could not give her the absolution she craved. Only she could do that.

CHAPTER 54

The 1983-84 World Cup Ski Circuit started at Kranjska Gora at the end of November, where there was no snow at all in the Julien Alps, but a brigade of hard-working Yugoslavs produced a narrow strip of man-made snow to ski on. It was a friendly little race with only a small crowd of local fans.

Jacqui was not surprised when Wolf arrived in time to watch her ski. She did not distinguish herself in any way, and she could see Wolf was disappointed after her race, but the truth was she was feeling on edge and uncomfortable.

Her problem was Rob.

She had met Rob on the very first day when she was watching the Men's Giant Slalom and she had felt cheered by the sight of this big, burly boy from Denver. Rob had come fourth, and when she had shyly congratulated him on his excellent timing, he had looked long and hard at her and the chagrin on his face had hurt her badly. She still loved him and longed to comfort him, but what was the point? Rob wanted her to give up Wolf and she could not do that.

He had stomped his feet moodily in the snow, and then, without looking at her, said: 'He's here – that middle-aged billionaire you're hanging on to, isn't he?'

'I expect he'll fly over from time to time.'

Rob shrugged contemptuously and Jacqui turned away to hide her tears.

For Christ's sake, why am I crying? Because he makes me so frigging angry? Because it's so unfair that he should judge me? Or because he looks so sad?

Rob had nodded coldly and turned away, and before Jacqui could stop herself she had blurted out: 'Rob, it's not like you think. Not like that at all,' but Rob had smiled grimly and joined his friends.

Well, to hell with him.

The prospect of a six-month season to endure with both Wolf and Rob at the same time and place was too awful to contemplate, but Rob was in the American World Cup Team, and he would ski his way around Europe with her.

So after that, Jacqui skied badly and felt ashamed of herself. After the race, Wolf took Jacqui to a restaurant for the local's favourite rose hip tea and pastries. Rob watched them walk off arm-in-arm and had difficulty in constraining himself. He had such a longing to beat up Wolf, but that would be uncivilised. 'One of these days, I'll get you, Muller,' he promised watching Wolf help Jacqui into the car he had hired.

Jacqui seemed ill at ease as she pulled a face at the tea and pushed her pastry aside. 'I'll be glad when we get to Switzerland,' she muttered.

Wolf could see something was bothering her, but it was only when they were about to leave that she plucked up courage to say: 'Wolf, about those Vanguard shares I swopped for your oil. Well, I'd like them back.'

To Wolf, her words were like a slap in the face. He flinched and took a few seconds to answer her. 'But Jacqui, honey, we did a deal and you have a parcel of New Enterprises stock which has been very well subscribed by the public. The shares are expected to take off pretty soon. That means you can make a tidy profit if you hang on a few months – or maybe weeks – who knows? Don't be a silly ass.'

Jacqui felt the first twinge of unease as she remembered Megan's warning. 'Wolf, I don't want the profits, I want my shares back,' she said. Then she looked at him long and hard. Let's not go overboard, she was thinking. I'm talking to a man I trust; he's not the crook Megan takes him for. I'd bet my life on that.

She smiled and relaxed visibly. 'Wolf, Mother's in trouble. Don't tell me you haven't read the financial news. Someone's buying up Vanguard shares and I want to make sure mine don't fall into the wrong hands. Have you sold them?'

'No,' Wolf said, wondering why he didn't make it all much easier for himself and lie to her.

'Then give them back.'

'You mean sell them back?'

'Sure. How much d'you want?' She gave him a mean stare. 'My oil shares returned, naturally.'

'Oh naturally. Well, you can arrange it all. You did last time.'

'Jacqui, I hate to see you lose out on this deal. Just think! You're in on the ground floor – just be patient and you'll reap the profits – and then you get your shares back, too. What harm can that do you – or your mother?'

'It can't do me any harm. I know you'd never do me any harm, but I feel disloyal to Mother.'

'What if I give you a written guarantee that your parcel of Vanguard shares will remain in my possession – that I won't sell them. Will that make you feel any better?'

'I might feel a bit better if I could figure out your angle,' she said, shocking him. 'After all, you were going to make a profit by selling them high and buying back later. Or that's what you said,' she mumbled.

'Finally, I didn't have time,' Wolf retorted, feeling irritated with Jacqui. 'My business is oil, honey. And you'll do all right with your share of it. That was my primary consideration.'

'Of course it was, Wolf,' Jacqui said smiling and feeling better again. 'So it won't make any difference to you if we cancel the deal. I'll sure feel a lot better.'

Later that evening, Wolf organised a party for Jacqui's friends and team mates in the inn where Jacqui was staying and where he, too, had booked in. As they ate and swopped stories of the day's experiences, Jacqui seemed to be content to drop the matter of the shares. Perhaps a lawyer's letter, proving that he was holding the shares in trust for her, would suffice, he wondered uneasily.

Outside the window, Rob Scott waited in the freezing cold. He did not know exactly why he was hanging around and he had cursed himself for being a fool more than once that evening. He had not been invited to the supper party and if he had, he would have refused, but he felt that he had to know what was going on between Jacqui and Muller. Was Jacqui telling the truth when she assured him that there was nothing physical between them? It seemed so unlikely after all this time. Besides, what else would Muller be hanging around for? Yet instinctively Rob knew that Jacqui was not a liar.

At ten pm the party broke up and the skiers hurried off to

their various boarding houses to sleep. They all had a strenuous programme ahead of them.

Rob knew which room was Jacqui's because he had hung around the previous evening, trying to pluck up courage to call on her. Muller, for some reason that baffled Rob, had taken a room at the end of the corridor on the floor above Jacqui's room. There was none of this nonsense about adjoining rooms, that much at least was clear.

Rob shrugged his shoulders and forced himself to walk home. What was he, some sort of freaky Peeping Tom? Yet, somehow, he could not find the willpower to go to bed, and after a cup of coffee in the dining room of his hotel, he walked back and stood like some lovesick fool in the falling snow under Jacqui's window.

These old places weren't built with burglars in mind, he thought. He guessed it was a pretty safe village where everyone knew everyone else, for there was a wood shed next to Jacqui's balcony and any fool could pull himself up there. Of course the window was closed, and curtained, but not shuttered.

The more he thought about it, the more determined Rob became to find out for once and for all whether or not Jacqui was sleeping with Wolf. After all, the guy had been away for weeks, tonight would be the night. If he was, then that was that, forever. He would never speak to Jacqui again.

As an experienced mountaineer, it didn't take Rob long to mount the roof of the shed and haul himself on to the balcony, but he did not realise that the gutter had melted during the night and the snow was covered with a layer of ice. He slipped badly and fell against the window with a loud clatter.

'Shit!' He lay sprawled on the ice cursing, and pulled himself on to his feet as the double windows were flung open.

'Rob? Or should I say Romeo?' Jacqui burst into girlish giggles loud enough to wake the entire inn.

'You'd better climb in,' she said. 'Hurry up. It's freezing.'

Flushed and embarrassed Rob climbed through the window, leaving a pile of snow and slush on the carpet beneath.

'Oh damn it, Jacqui,' he said. 'I really don't know what to say.' His eyes examined the room with care. It smelled of perfume and talcum powder. There had been no hasty retreat, the bed was hardly ruffled, just folded back blankets on one side where Jacqui had been and her clothes neatly folded over

379

the chair. There was definitely no one under the bed, either.

'Rob!' she burst out indignantly when she realised why he was there. 'You were spying on me. You thought ...? Oh, you freaky bastard. And I thought ...'

'What did you think?'

'Well, naturally I thought you'd come to ... Why don't you go fry your head?' she added ungraciously. 'How come you can't believe me when I tell you the truth?' Her gypsy eyes were flashing, her lips pouting, but to Rob she had never looked so lovely.

'How come he's still hanging around then?' Rob said moodily, unwilling to show her how pleased he was.

'Listen, how come you can't mind your own business?'

'Oh Jacqui.' Rob sat on the end of the bed, elbows on his knees, and buried his face in his hands. *Give him up. Tell him to go to hell ... get lost ..., Rob wanted to tell her.* Instead he looked up, smiling sadly. 'I'm sorry, Jacqui. I just had to know.'

'Since you're here, how about a night cap?' she said quickly, not wanting him to go and wanting very much to snuggle up in bed beside him. She noticed that he was blue with cold and his teeth were chattering. 'I could order some hot chocolate,' she suggested.

'Wouldn't that look a bit funny?'

'I don't see why. You've got to get out of here, anyway, or were you planning to go out the same way you came in?'

'I don't want hot chocolate,' Rob said gloomily.

'Rob, there's never been anyone, but you,' she said a little defensively, 'but I don't know why the hell I'm telling you that, because I'm my own mistress and I'll do what I damn well like.' Then she added in a small voice: 'it's just that, since I'm in love with you, there's not much point in fooling around.'

'Oh Jacqui,' he said. He stood up and walked across the room towards the door.

'No wait,' she called out. 'Someone might see you. Besides, you look kinda blue to me. How about a nice warm bath?' she added innocently.

'I'd be warmer in bed with you,' he pointed out truthfully.

'Hell! How crude can you get,' she frowned at him. 'If I let you stay, will you quit moaning at me. Just let me be. I want to be loved, not lassoed. Know what I mean?'

'You're calling the tune,' Rob said. He undressed hurriedly, before she changed her mind.

When he dived under the blankets, Jacqui squealed and jumped and thumped him because he was icy cold. Then he put his hand under her brushed nylon nightgown and felt her small, firm breasts, and soft curve of her belly, and his skin became hot all over. Soon he was damp with sweat and panting a little.

He pulled off her gown with awkward, hasty movements and covered her with his own body, keeping his weight on his elbows, not wanting to crush her, but needing to feel her skin close to his and the delicious moulding of her body trembling against him.

Her lips were moist and soft and her tongue tasted of toothpaste. She stretched her arms around him and hugged him tightly. 'I've been longing to love you again. D'you know that? All the time you were scowling and frowning and showing your temper, I just wanted to be loved.'

Why had they waited so long, Rob thought regretfully as they made love tenderly. When Jacqui was lying so trustingly in his arms, he knew that all he wanted out of life, was to look after her. He would never love anyone the way he loved her. He wanted to show her that, in every movement he made and so he loved her tenderly, and patiently, kissing and fondling her and waiting for her to come to a climax. Then they slept awhile and started all over again, but even when they lay in each other's arms, Rob's happiness was marred by Muller. He lay between them like a physical presence.

'You going to tell him about us?' He could not help asking before he left.

'When I'm good and ready, when the time's right for it. Right now it's our secret. I want to keep it like that, Rob.'

Tremulous lips, pleading eyes, why was Muller so important to her? Rob swore quietly to himself, but forced a smile.

'Be reasonable. You've got to think this thing through. You can't expect me to hide around forever. When Muller finds out, what d'you think he's going to say? See you around, Jacqui,' he said.

Oh men! They make everything sordid and ... well, different to the way it really is. How can Rob understand about Wolf? And Wolf ... well, he probably wouldn't understand about Rob either.

CHAPTER 55

Ian drew up outside the ornate wrought iron gates and pressed the button of the voice box. It was not yet dark, and through the twilight gloom he could see a long drive with shrubs on either side and beyond wide lawns, prim as a bowling green. The house was hidden beyond a bend in the driveway.

'Yes,' a metallic voice called from the box.

'Ian Mackintosh. I've an appointment with Eleanor Douglas.'

'You're late,' the box grunted. Then the gate swung open noiselessly and Ian drove through, conscious of watchful eyes from the lookout window of the caretaker's gatehouse.

Ian had often read about Eleanor's fabulous villa at Cap Ferrat and he was curious to see it, but now he felt disappointed as he neared the house. It was ultra modern: a study of symmetrical lines in shaded glass and concrete, reminiscent of dozens of modern office blocks in the city.

An elderly maid opened the carved ebony door and led him down a white marble passage with mirror walls and paused at a glass door. Indicating that he should enter, she said: 'Please sit down and wait.' She had a raw Italian accent and from her rudeness he gathered that she was an old family retainer.

Ian examined his surroundings with astonishment. He was in an enormous room with small, shuttered windows set in a vast expanse of wall. Presumably by day, most of the light came from circular glass inlays in the roof, but now he could see the stars faintly appearing in the dusky evening sky.

Luxuriant tropical plants with brilliant flowers grew into the room from circular holes, a giant rubber plant drooped over a fish pond, fever trees dripped on polished green and white mosaic tiles and lemon verbena filled the room with its pungent aroma. Between the shrubs were sculptured figures: a bronze by Henri Georges Adam, André Block's *Double Interrogation*; a torso by Hans Arp, and what looked like a huge marble eyeball which he did not recognise. The walls were crammed with works of art against moss-coloured parchment: two Gauguin's in brilliant tropical colours, a Picasso, three Mexican scenes by Orozco, a Matisse in purple, lilac and blue which Ian had thought to be in a museum. On one branch of the rubber tree a crimson and green parrot screeched incessantly.

He could hear the sea splashing beyond the room and he gathered that the house was built close to the beach. He knew that Eleanor had her own private beach and a rock pool built into the sea.

When the door opened a few minutes later, he gazed in astonishment as he stood up. The woman who stood there was beautiful, admittedly she obviously had not slept for nights, and she was not young, but still she was lovely. Her dress was a simple sheath of dark blue silk and she wore diamond studded earrings and no other jewellery. Gazing at Eleanor, Ian was quite unable to find a resemblance between this excitingly vibrant and sensual woman and the middle-aged frump Megan had described. Her face had been beautifully made-up and her eyelashes fluttered disarmingly. She had taken the trouble to look attractive and Ian felt touched and flattered, but no amount of make-up could hide the anxiety in her eyes and the tremor in her voice when she spoke.

'Miss Douglas, Let's get down to business,' Ian said, when he had accepted a Scotch on ice and he was leaning back on an ultra modern tubular steel chair which at first he had not trusted, but which turned out to be remarkably comfortable.

'It's an odd business,' she said quickly after that. 'To be honest, I was very reluctant to see you. Megan persuaded me, because my daughter enlisted her help.'

Ian had decided not to tell Eleanor about Jacqui's shares at this stage. If her boyfriend was still holding them, as he claimed, then possibly it might be a false alarm which would cause Eleanor a great deal of grief. First he must try to get them back.

'Nigel and I ...' Eleanor was saying hoarsely. 'Well, Nigel thinks that I'm worrying about nothing ... it's the waiting,' she went on in an agonised tone. 'Suddenly everything has come to a halt. No more press reports, no offers to shareholders. At least then I could fight back, but now – I don't even know if I'm still at war. Have they given up? Or have they won? Perhaps they're biding their time – any day now they might walk in and turn me out. It's just conceivably possible that they have the majority ...'

'Of course I should have explained everything ...' She broke off and shuddered.

'Relax! Start at the beginning,' Ian cut in on her. 'There's no hurry and I'd like to get it straight. But Miss Douglas ...'

'Eleanor, please.'

'Eleanor then, could you please shut that bloody bird up.'

'Oh ...' She smiled disarmingly. 'I'm so used to Tweedle-Dee that I don't notice him anymore. I bought him for the noise he makes. It takes away that terrible silence – you know what I mean – when there's only one person in a big house like this.'

The parrot was coaxed into his cage and covered with a black cloth and Eleanor sat down and began talking.

It was one am when Eleanor went to make coffee and Ian leaned back and studied his notes.

As Eleanor had said, she should be safe, but after a long and costly fight costing millions of dollars, why would the raiders suddenly give up – just like that? It didn't make sense.

Eleanor returned with a pot of filter coffee on a tray. 'The maid's gone to bed,' she explained.

'As I see it,' Ian began, 'you run a very tidy shop, Eleanor. All your clothing and your equipment is put out for manufacture under your brand, except for your Denver plant. Your big strength is your worldwide distributing network and your goodwill. The truth is your company is a really worldwide marketing network, selling a variety of products under the Vanguard brand. It's all in the image – and that's why this destructive campaign has hit you so badly. Sales are down, confidence is rock bottom and time is running out. You must be seen to be in the driving seat and to be winning as soon as possible. Are we agreed?'

She nodded and pressed one hand over her mouth.

'Eleanor, I want you to give me the keys of your offices, safe, and files. I want your wholehearted confidence and a *carte blanche* to act as I feel best. I'll work from a van parked outside your block and I'll need an alibi. Tell your staff I'm a filing consultant. Can you do that?'

Eleanor nodded, looking desperately disappointed. 'You won't find anything in my offices,' she said sadly. 'That's

384

clutching at straws, but if you insist ...' she broke off. 'I'm expecting the axe to fall at any moment.'

Two am Ian and his two assistants worked smoothly and quietly at a task for which they had been perfectly trained: examining, photographing, implanting microphones. They finished at dawn and by seven pm were back in their hotel for breakfast.

Their panel van, freshly painted to read: Ronex Micro-Filing Systems, which had been brought over from Dover on the ferry boat, was parked at the curbside, where it would remain for two days.

At the end of the third day, it suddenly disappeared and only Eleanor noticed its coming or its going.

CHAPTER 56

Wolf Muller had a problem for which he could find no solution, it was partly a problem of caring. Jacqui was more precious to him than his own life, and when he watched her sometimes he would catch his breath with the wonder of it all. Was it possible to contain so much love? Would it come bursting out of him in a great tide, as if from some overladen dam, and drown them both. Too much, he told himself. He could not handle this extraordinary excess of feeling. It was a dangerous obsession, he knew. He wanted to own her, possess her, take her to his home and feel secure in the knowledge that he had her by his side for life. He could not bear the prospect of a future without her; every minute of every day he wanted only to be with her.

That was not possible, he realised, and besides, Jacqui would soon feel claustrophobic, so Wolf played his cards carefully, treasuring every moment and etching the images of her in his mind: Jacqui's face blazing with exhilaration after a good race; her sadness when she skied badly and she knew she had let the team down; her youthful joy each morning. It was as if each morning was her first – her first sight of snow, her first mountain, her first race. There was something childlike and pure about her passionate love of every day.

Perhaps this was because the joy at being alive was a newly-acquired experience in Jacqui's life. It was something that Wolf had taught her and he felt deeply gratified with the way he had enhanced her life. He had brought her happiness and a sense of deep-seated security. He knew this, but he was not quite sure why, except that it had something to do with loving her. She felt secure in his love and she trusted him. With this had come the blossoming of her self-confidence. Lately, she had dropped much of her viciousness, he only saw it occasionally when she was scared or really angry. Her obsessive involvement, part-hate, part-love, with Mother's strong overshadowing personality seemed to have faded, too; perhaps because she had someone else in her life.

In November, Wolf returned after a business trip to find Jacqui strangely withdrawn and tense. There was none of her usual frankness with him. She seemed guarded and suspicious, and Wolf, who knew nothing of Jacqui's anxiety over her secret affair with Rob, was sure that her reticence was caused because he had not yet returned her Vanguard script to her.

So now Wolf lived each day in torment. He was deeply enmeshed in the trap he himself had set. He had planned to use Jacqui in his war of attrition against Eleanor, to make her fall in love with him and to obtain her shares, but winning the war might lose him his love, for it was he who had fallen neatly into his own trap. *Did he love Jacqui more than he hated Eleanor?* That was the question he had to resolve.

What if Jacqui were to discover his intentions and his schemes. Surely that would destroy all they had – the love, the trust, the comradeship? Of course, she must, eventually. What then?

This anxiety never left Wolf, and consequently he had prepared his ground – not once, but many times – by telling her about the woman he had once loved, the woman who had stolen his business and abandoned him when he was crippled and destitute. One day, he knew, Jacqui would see Eleanor for what she really was – a greedy, cruel woman.

That night at supper, which they ate together in the small inn where Jacqui was staying and where Wolf had booked in as well, he promised to bring her shares on his next trip.

'You're a dear,' Jacqui said, suddenly hugging Wolf. 'I never mistrusted you for a moment. But Wolf consider my position. If, God forbid, you were to die, whoever handles your estate might sell the shares without compunction.'

The silly goose. She seemed to know little about finance. She had a lot to learn if she ever joined Vanguard.

'You're such a good person,' Jacqui gushed, 'How could any woman have let you out of her life. It's beyond me. She must have been crazy – whoever she was.'

'Not crazy, simply greedy,' Wolf said sullenly. His face changed when he thought about the past, Jacqui noticed. An ugly, bitter expression sharpened his features and made him look years older.

'Want to talk about it?' she suggested shyly. He always wanted to let off steam about the way he was taken and Jacqui felt that it was good for him to talk about it. After a while Jacqui reached out and touched his hand. 'You weren't listening to me,' she complained. 'What were you thinking about?'

'Ancient feuds and promises broken,' he said. 'Once upon a time I was rich, successful, happily married and crazy about skiing. I had just invented a new ski which was set to make me a millionaire. Then I broke my back trying out a prototype in a ski jump I had constructed in the mountains. I had to spend a year in hospital. My wife took advantage of my weakness to steal my fortune, my business and my invention. That's it in a nutshell. I spent whatever was left, fighting her in court and lost. Then I went on the booze for a year, but eventually I pulled myself together and started again. Here I am, fighting fit.'

'You sure are,' she said, feeling desperately sorry for him and wishing she could make amends in some way.

'Wolf,' she said hesitatingly, reaching out and holding his hand with both of hers. 'I know you love me. I haven't been able to give you ... what you want,' she said flushing. 'I'm nineteen and you're a lot older. I think I'm a bit overwhelmed by you and to be honest I look up to you so much. I can't think of you as an equal partner. I can't,' she was getting into deep water and did not know how to extricate herself. Beads of perspiration stood out on her forehead and her cheeks were stained deep red. 'Maybe in time. Who knows? Maybe I'll be able to sort myself out. I'm very confused.

'Anyway ...' she laughed shakily after an awkward silence. 'Right now it's late and I'm tired and we have to get up early in the morning, so good night, Wolf.' She stood up, kissed him chastely on the cheek and hurried away.

Watching her, Wolf thought that she was ripe for plucking and if not him, then someone else would step in, but someone else would take her away from him. The thought was chilling.

Since Jacqui's near-disastrous accident he had fallen so deeply in love he had been terrified of losing her. He knew he had no claims on her at all. His many attempts at seduction had failed and although at first he had been furious, eventually he had grudgingly admired her for her self-control. They had a warm, loving relationship. After a good race, Jacqui would throw herself into his arms and he would whirl her round and hug her. She sometimes kissed him on the cheek impulsively, she took his arm when they were exploring the village and the countryside, she kissed him goodnight solicitously. He had to admit that she was a marvellous companion.

So where did that get him? Nowhere, he admitted. She could walk out of his life any time she wished, and he would have no claims on her.

He had kept the oil shares in Jacqui's name, but you could not buy Jacqui's affection. He would have to return her Vanguard shares to her, but lately another idea had been forming in his mind. There was yet another source which would give him the Vanguard majority he craved.

It was at Haus, in filthy weather, that Wolf met Jacqui again. The Obersalzburg was deep in the grip of the *Föhn* and the venue was a thin track through the brown fields of mountain farms. Haus proved to be a hard course, with its top gliding section, tough jumps in the middle part and big turns further down followed by a very fast zielschuss. It was also the longest piste the women had seen that season.

Jacqui scored brilliantly, however, by coming in eighth and first in the British team. She was chaired afterwards by her team mates and they rounded off the race with a celebration.

As the Christmas break neared, Jacqui became withdrawn and moody. She wanted to fly home and spend Christmas with Mother. The more Wolf begged her to stay with him, the more she insisted on going. Wolf resented her leaving, but eventually he flew back to Denver and Jacqui motored with friends to Monaco.

CHAPTER 57

There was music coming from the long gallery, a local Scottish dance band with piano-accordion and violins was tuning up and getting into the spirit of Hogmanay. They were brawny, tow-headed lads, in kilts that showed their thick knees and hairy legs, and they were settling in for the night's work with a barrel of homemade punch and a pile of cheese scones supplied by Mrs Gilmour to tide them over until a late supper. Boom, boom, boom, the fast, catchy beat reverberated through the house and everyone was smiling and giving a little hop and skip to the music when no one was looking. As Megan tripped down the passage with another armful of holly to decorate the hall, she heard their guffaws and jibes and she gathered that their celebrations had begun days before.

Well, just so long as they could play in tune who cares, she thought. Megan had spent most of that day, tramping across the snow in her moon boots to pick the holly in the woods. Amazing what a touch of colour can do, she thought, rubbing her muddy hands against her dirty corduroy pants. The housekeeper had found an odd job man to paint wood preservative over the panelling and the beams until they shone golden brown in the firelight.

Megan was not quite sure just how enthusiastic she was supposed to be about brightening up Ian's home, but today she had dispensed with caution and thrown herself into the joy of transforming the main rooms with some antique furniture, old copper urns and warming pans on long handles, discarded paintings, plaids and candelabra unearthed from the cellars. It had helped to pass the time, with Ian away.

The week had not been as lonely as Megan had expected. She had arrived on Christmas Eve, expecting Ian to meet her at Inverness airport. Instead Mr Foggerty had been waiting with the Landrover. Ian had received a sudden call from the

Admiralty, he explained, and left within the hour that afternoon. So Megan had eaten her Christmas goose alone at the end of the long table in the oak-panelled diningroom.

Later Ian had called from Aberdeen. He'd try to get back before Hogmanay. He was sorry. She and Nikki must ask Foggerty to drive them around.

Megan did not tell him that Nikki had opted out at the last minute because Michel arrived at her cottage bearing gifts and a Christmas tree.

Nevertheless, Megan had enjoyed her week, for it gave her a chance to indulge herself with some serious skiing on the Cairngorms, where the snow was remarkably deep and crisp for this time of the year. In a way she had been pleased Nikki had not come. Each day she had taken the Coire Na Ciste ski lift and skied until lunchtime. By then she was ravenous and she ate hot casserole with fresh rolls and salty butter, followed by thick, sweet coffee. There was still time to put in a couple more hours skiing before dusk fell. At four, she packed her skis into the Landrover and drove carefully home on icy roads.

It was so good to see the lights burning after the long drive in the dark, and better still to place her boots and skis in the gun room, drink a glass of steaming mulled wine, which Mrs Gilmour always had ready for her, and soak in the funny old tub with its ball and claw feet, filled with foaming scented water.

She heard Mrs Gilmour hurrying past, humming to the music. 'My,' she said, 'the old place looks a treat, but you haven't much time left for yourself, Miss Megan.'

Megan took the hint and raced up the stairs in time to the bewitching beat of the Gay Gordons. Ian would be home soon. The thought sent the blood racing to her cheeks. What a strange feeling she had, sort of light-hearted, with a sense of bursting exhaltation. Happiness! She thought delightedly. She had forgotten what it felt like. When had she last been this happy? Surely never! She wanted to sing and dance and she wished she knew the steps to the dances they would be playing tonight.

There was plenty of time, she saw, glancing at her watch. Megan washed her hair by ducking her head into lukewarm water in the bath and rinsing it under the cold tap. Boiling or freezing water, she had two choices, but she did not care. Then she rolled her hair in a towel and ran the bath. She was badly out of condition, she thought ruefully, examining her figure critically as the water lapped around her. To much sitting around at desks, too little sport and fresh air. No wonder she had been so stiff after skiing. She must change her lifestyle.

Warm foamy bubbles seeped into her aching limbs and grimy fingernails. 'Ah, at last,' she murmured. How wonderful to be far away from ISA, without a care in the world. She leaned back and closed her eyes.

Megan awoke as she slid lower into the water which was cold. She was late. She leaped out of the bath and began to dress for the party. She was wearing a frilled dress of crimson silk which had cost most of one month's salary, but which she knew Ian would love. She dried her hair with the dryer and combed it over her shoulders. Just right, she thought anxiously, adding a gold necklace. She was finishing her make-up when Mrs Gilmour hammered on the door.

'The first guests are arriving, Miss Megan, you'll have to manage on your own until his Lordship arrives.'

Oh my, she thought. I don't even know anyone.

The evening began with a great deal of formality. Mrs Gilmour, in a black silk dress with a pearl necklace, opened the door and introduced the guests to Megan and handed their coats to one of her many friends, who had come to help out. Mr Foggerty was keeping an eye on the barman and helping to fill the glasses. Megan did her best to behave as if she felt at ease and frequently played the hostess at Hogmanay parties in the Highlands.

There was such a variation of kilts, she had never known there were so many: she recognised the Barclays in their distinct yellow and black; Austin Buchanan, the garage proprietor, in his bright red, yellow and black; the Lamonts, who owned the haberdashery store, in their dark green and black; and so many others which she did not recognise. Mrs Gilmour had given her a list of names she must remember and one of them was Dr MacPherson. All two hundred pounds of him, clad in his crisp tartan of blue, red and black with yellow stripes, was advancing towards her with a glass of punch.

'I've been watching you, Carroll,' he said, 'and I've noticed you're not drinking. You'll never make a good Scot that way. It's Hogmanay, remember?'

A good Scot! Heavens! Was that what they were all expecting? Had Mrs Gilmour spread the word?

Shortly afterwards the band began the first Eightsome Reel, and Megan was thrust into the dance with the burly doctor who insisted on teaching her the steps and who was remarkably light on his feet for so heavy a man.

After a few more dances and a few barrels of punch, the party became less formal, and several people smiled, which was a nice change, and everyone insisted that she join in the dancing.

Between dances, Mrs Gilmour called her aside. 'I've been asking myself what we're going to do about supper, if his Lordship doesn't get back,' she said worriedly.

'He'll make it,' Megan said. 'He'll get here somehow. Let's wait until the very last minute.'

It was past ten, and Megan was flushed and breathless from whirling around on the arm of a brawny forestry official, when she turned and saw Ian watching her from the doorway. For a moment she was too astonished to speak. Ian in uniform was yet another shock to be absorbed. The truth was, he looked marvellous. She had forgotten how handsome he was, and seeing him now like this was like a dash of cold water in her face. It dawned on her that Ian must be one of the most eligible bachelors around. His vitality was beaming out of him like a visible force, you could see it in his blue eyes blazing with love, and his skin glowing from the cold, his mobile lips, that were always so expressive and his sensuous profile. A wave of hot love raced through her and she thought: tonight we'll make love and it will be the best ever. She wanted to fling herself into his arms, but restrained the impulse.

Ian tucked her arm under his and hurried around the room greeting his friends. Then he caught hold of her hand. 'I must change,' he whispered. 'Come with me.'

They rushed up the stairs into his bedroom and he slammed the door. A moment later she was in his arms as they hugged each other.

'We must hurry,' she said, when she managed to disentangle herself.

'Can you run my bath while I get out my things, love. I'm frozen.'

'I suppose you can't tell me what you were doing there?' she called from the bathroom above the noise of the tap.

393

'It was a false alarm,' he said. 'A case of suspected sabotage, but in fact it was an accident. Metal fatigue! I had to go down in the diving suit and quite honestly, I think I've got the flu coming.'

'No kidding? I'm glad I didn't know, I would have been worried to death.'

'No need to be,' he said lightly. 'Where's Nikki?'

'She's in London. Michel arrived unexpectedly, but I think Nikki was pleased to see him. She's been feeling down in the mouth. I don't think she's going to make the European championships,' Megan said crisply. 'No passport as yet. Now don't string me along, Ian.' She turned and saw a flush, like a red stain, spread over his cheeks and down to his neck.

'You're right,' he said as he stepped into the bath. 'She's not going to make it. She'll get her passport just before the Winter Games. The powers that be have decided that Nikki would not be safe in Budapest, and since it isn't necessary for her career, they want to keep her in Britain until then.'

'Why should Sarajevo be safer than Budapest?' she asked coldly, leaning against the bathroom door.

'Megan, this isn't my doing, but if it were up to me, I'd do the same thing,' he said brusquely. For a moment Megan thought he had mistaken her for one of his own staff. She glared at him. 'It's a completely different political climate there,' he said, hurriedly scrubbing his back. 'Mind your dress. It might get splashed. It's beautiful, by the way, and so are you. The Russians have very little muscle in Yugoslavia,' Ian went on without changing his tone of voice. 'And besides there'll be several guards, including myself. Officially I shall be writing a documentary on bobsleigh racing.'

'So you're back on the job again?'

'Until after the Games. Then it's finished and done with.'

'One day you're going to tell me what this was all about.'

'That depends on whether or not you marry me. You are going to marry me, aren't you?' He sounded very sure of himself.

Megan sat bemused, as he stepped out of the bath and raced back to the bedroom. He put on his shirt and kilt and sporran and fixed his bow tie in front of the rickety old mirror on a stand, while humming quietly. She had to admit that the evening jacket with the kilt looked very fetching. His legs were pretty good, she thought. All the same, she was both angry and pleased, liking him and disliking him, wanting him, but wanting to tell him to go to hell, too. It was all very confusing.

'Come on, yes or no?' he said impatiently, scowling at himself in the mirror.

'It's not like you to badger me?' she said defensively. 'You said you wouldn't pressurise me.'

'That was in August. That's very nearly last year. I'd like to make the announcement tonight; otherwise you'll have to wait another year before I'll ask again. Don't you want to bring a little joy into Mrs Gilmour's life?' he asked, looking perfectly serious.

'Ian, I love you, but I'm scared. I'm not sure if I could cope with your family fortress.' She smiled to take the sting out of her words. 'I fell in love with a poor, but gifted scriptwriter and I still love him – and I would marry him tomorrow.' She hesitated. 'I'm not sure if I know the real Ian Mackintosh and whether or not I could bear to live – well – here.'

'Then it's settled,' he said after a long silence. 'I'll renounce the title and we'll live in London. I'll write scripts forever.'

'It's all a game to you, isn't it?' she said, trying to keep the irritation out of her voice.

'No, it's not. So we'll be married, shall we?'

'I don't think I could give up my career,' Megan said primly. 'It means a lot to me.'

'If I'm to be a poor scriptwriter,' Ian said. 'We'll definitely need your salary.'

Megan could not think of a reply, although she knew that the conversation was all wrong and that Ian was sad, although he would never admit that.

'Ian,' she asked hesitantly, as he tried to pull her out of the bedroom. 'Are you giving in completely ... on everything ... just like that?'

'For the time being,' he said. 'Until you come to your senses. Besides, you'll find it hard to keep working with children to look after, but meantime it's all right with me. I still have another two years in the Navy, remember? Let's go.'

How would she ever forget this night? she wondered. The band getting louder and rowdier, the shouts and cries of the dancers ringing in her ears, the flash of kilts and heavy beat of footsteps thumping on the old wooden floors. Then dinner was served and three long tables were filled to overflowing with their guests.

'This place needs you,' Ian murmured. 'I'm amazed at the transformation.'

They ate salmon and venison and trifle and at the end of dinner Ian rose to announce their engagement. Megan was kissed and hugged and thumped on the back. Then Rob Faulkner arrived and strode round the table with his bagpipes. Their guests followed him back to the main hall to toast the New Year.

Megan was feeling tense and ill at ease as she lay stiff and unyielding in the double bed, listening to the fire crackling in the hearth and watching the firelight flickering on the walls and the beamed ceiling.

Ian's friends had lingered until it was almost dawn wishing them luck again and again, toasting the happy couple, teasing Ian, but she had felt so unreal, almost as if she was not there at all – merely witnessing the scene. Megan was feeling scared, almost alienated, and she wanted nothing more than to be alone. It had all been rather shocking, or perhaps overwhelming was a better word, she thought and she needed time to sort herself out.

She would have liked to have slept alone, but could not pluck up the courage to voice the thought. It seemed so unreasonable and anyway, there was no other bed aired. But it was so cold here. Megan lay as close as she could behind Ian, her knees tucked under his. As if sensing her withdrawal, Ian had turned his back and was feigning sleep.

Megan lay still and examined her anxieties about the future. The thought of giving up her career seemed a bit like dying. One thing was clear – one of them had to make the sacrifice. Could I live here? she wondered. Could I bear the loneliness, or living far from home, or having my children brought up in this alien land? She felt that this was the renunciation. Here and now! She was being forced to decide upon her future – the misty moors of Aviemore with her wild chieftain lover, or her career in London with their marriage squeezed into evenings and weekends, when she was not working overtime. Right now, Ian believed that he could live in London. He wanted her badly enough to promise anything, but when children came he would long to take them home, to be brought up as true Scots. Besides, what would be the point of him struggling to sell his scripts when the estate needed attention and the timber was waiting to balance the family's budget. Nevertheless, she loved Ian and he loved her. Megan hung on to that thought and tried to sleep.

An hour later she was still awake. It was something to do with the crisp feel of Ian's newly ironed pyjamas, the familiar smell of his hair and the faint healthy odour of his skin, with the tang of her favourite after-shave. How could Ian just go to sleep? she wondered.

She ran her hands over his shoulder, but there was no response. This was their special night, surely she deserved at least a goodnight kiss.

She leaned over him and ran her lips gently over his. Ian had lovely lips, she thought. She took his face in her hands and turned it towards her. Like a sleeping giant, and he was so beautiful when he was asleep. His features were softer, gentler, there was a look of sensuousness about him. She brushed her lips over his again.

What perverse impulse drove her to wake him? After all, she knew how tired he was, but she couldn't resist running her lips down his neck, opening his pyjamas to smooth her hands and her lips over the hairs on his chest and down further to his belly and his thighs. He was stirring, groaning slightly in his sleep, but his penis seemed wide awake. She watched it wonderingly.

Megan was burning all over. She fumbled at her pyjamas, tearing at the buttons, throwing the top on the floor as if it offended her. 'Undress! Undress!' she murmured. 'Oh Ian, hold, me, love me. I never wanted you so before.'

Her eyes were stinging, her lips felt feverish and dry, her breath was coming in short gasps, and her skin felt parched. The need to have Ian naked beside her had become unbearable. She reached forward and grasped his pyjamas firmly and wrenched them open. It was no easy task, but Ian just smiled sleepily. Then his hand caught hold of her arm roughly and pulled her down, pushing her under him. Her body reacted with spasms of pleasure from her bowels to her navel. She felt her breasts stir and firm and her nipples harden. 'Oh love me,' she whispered urgently. 'Love me.'

Ian too had kicked off his clothes and she felt his naked flesh caressing hers as he pushed into her. She could feel him gasp, and hesitate and the feeling of him in her belly was wholly enchanting and satisfying in itself. Then he began to move, and as his passion surfaced Megan felt strange new feelings of exquisite pleasure reaching an intensity that she had never before experienced. As if her body had woken like a bud to sunlight, a million nerve ends thrilled to this extraordinary sense of rapture. She was melting, molten inside, merging and flowing into his will, her feelings dependent upon his thrust and pull, she lay entranced, unable to move, incapacitated with the force of her passion. She could no longer grip and sway and urge him onwards, but hardly conscious of the low moans she was making, she lay helpless and softly clinging, obsessed with the movement that was filling her entire body and mind with ecstasy. She clung to Ian, immersed in her shared joy until it became unbearable. Pleasure of frightening intensity was piercing her body. She moaned and felt him climax; felt the sweet essence of him streaming into her womb, heard his cry, so that she too cried out with awe and followed him into a climax of blissful intensity. Then it was over and Megan felt as if she had cast off the traumas of a lifetime. She lay content, replete, filled with quiet joy, in Ian's arms.

'I always knew you'd be like this one day. It was only a matter of time and patience,' Ian whispered as she lay inert on his shoulder. 'That very first night at Zetra stadium, I saw the latent passion in your eyes, and your lips. Oh God, Megan, I want more and more of you. Darling,' he said, his voice hoarse with spent passion. 'I love you when you're like this, don't change, don't ever change, I couldn't bear it.'

'You're wonderful,' she said. 'This is all that counts. Nothing else. Just you and I, together here, loving each other. This is what it's all about. You know something, darling. I only just discovered that.'

CHAPTER 58

Wolf Muller stamped his feet in the deep snow, and moodily waited for Jacqui to come racing down the ... the what? Where the hell was he? He had lost track of these damned events and to tell the truth he was becoming a little less enthusiastic about skiing, although he was loathe to admit this, even to himself. Age – he wondered ruefully? No, of course not, merely the onset of commonsense. Sport was all right in its place, but the season's incredible whirl of travelling from one resort to another and fitting his business between was taking its toll. It had been one happening after the next and Wolf felt exhausted.

Jacqui had zoomed through the 1983-84 World Cup circuit with performances of outstanding mediocrity and had only been in the first fifteen, four times, although once she came fourth, so she had had her victories, although in Wolf's mind they had been overlooked by the press.

In the New Year, they had met in France. Jacqui had seemed anxious and depressed after a bad fight with Mother, but she would not tell Wolf about it. She soon recovered, he noticed.

The snows still had not come to the central Alps and the Pfronten venues were grazing lands, so the first events of the year were held at Puy St. Vincent. Jacqui had excelled by coming sixth. This was followed by Silberkrugrennen, one of the true classics of the women's tour, then Maribor, then Verbier, in thick fog and snow.

Wolf sighed. Jacqui was exhausted and it would be a miracle if she did well today. He had to admire her guts, she would never give up. He pulled his timetable out of his pocket. Of course, they were at Megève, the last pre-Olympic stop. For Jacqui the season was nearly over. And for him?

He must speak to her tonight, he decided.

He watched Jacqui come zooming down from the top part of the course. He thought she was landing a little off line over the ruts, but her timing was excellent. The press were beginning to notice her. He could see she was keeping her weight on the downhill ski and her shoulders low, but as she reached midway, she seemed to be losing ground and the press lost interest again.

For Jacqui the race was a nightmare. She had caught flu, and she was beginning to feel the effects of her high temperature. Her head felt as if it was rolling about her shoulders and her eyes were streaming. She desperately tried to concentrate upon that crucial final jump. The botch that she made of it cost her the race, for she hadn't realised how good her timing was up to that point.

Jacqui looked feverish when she pulled off her helmet and flung it on the snow. Her cheeks flushed, her eyes bloodshot. She greeted Wolf casually because Rob was in the throng. And then, when she realised she was fifth in spite of having flu, she burst into tears.

After a rest and a cup of tea and aspirins, Jacqui was back to her bullying self, Wolf noticed. She wanted to celebrate her good timing with her Olympic team mates, but Wolf used his muscle to persuade her to dine alone with him. He was leaving for Denver the following morning, he told her, and he had to talk to her. She gave in without much fight and they ate *fondue Bourguignon* and *Zuger Kirschtorte*, and touched rims to toast Jacqui's chances at the Winter Olympic Games.

Jacqui looked so beautiful, her young girl's eyes shining, her full lips trembling as she slyly teased Wolf about the parties she had attended in his absence.

Wolf, however, was withdrawn and serious. He was not sure how to get started, but Jacqui did not notice. When he opened his briefcase and solemnly handed back her script for all her Vanguard stock she looked gratified, but not surprised. 'I'm sorry I made such a fuss, truly I am, but if Mother were to lose because of me I think I would want to kill myself.'

The words slipped out: 'Marry me,' he growled and then flushed. Surely he could have done better than that?

Jacqui jumped and stared at him in alarm. A slow flush spread over her face and beads of moisture gathered on her brow.

'Marry?' she murmured, looking genuinely perplexed.

Watching her, Wolf felt himself go cold all over. His proposal had been received like a bolt from the blue. Obviously she had never considered marrying him, at the same time she would not make love to him either. So what the hell were they doing together? He struggled to retain his composure.

'I can't think of things like that, Wolf,' Jacqui said softly, feeling his pain. 'I'm too young to get married. Besides, I have too much to do.'

She poured out her story of Mother's business problems, and Wolf sensed that she was deliberately steering the conversation away from this embarrassing subject and that made him feel even angrier. She bored him with news of the takeover bid and how Mother was fighting back and vying for investors' confidence with an international advertising campaign, and how she herself was to be the bridge between management and the team of young champions Vanguard sponsored.

'We have to win back that winning image,' she said with her eyes shining. 'After the Games, I'm going to join Vanguard,' she added, as if that was the final solution to all their problems. The silly goose.

'But Mother will lose Vanguard,' he said roughly. 'At least,' he added when he saw her shock, 'that's what they're predicting in the market place.'

Jacqui began to tremble, and her eyes began to water. She could not come to terms with that idea. Instead she embroidered upon the advertising campaign and told him about her modelling sessions.

'You must understand that I have to win at Sarajevo,' she said with the earnestness of a child. 'Or die in the attempt. I'm going to ski harder and faster than I've ever done in my life. I'm not going to count the cost, I'm just going to go ... zip! ...' she held up her hand and brought it crashing down fast. 'Like that! No holds barred. You see, all my life I've been taking things out of Vanguard,' she went on slowly. 'At Sarajevo I'm going to start giving back.'

'Don't be a fool,' he said, feeling alarmed. Jacqui was not given to idle boasting. She meant what she said. Wolf felt a thrill of unease run through him. 'You don't need Vanguard. You don't need Mother. Marry me, Jacqui. Before the Olympics. You'll have all the money you could ever want.'

'Money?' she queried. Wolf sensed that money had never

been of much interest to Jacqui, except for the one time when Mother had cut off her credit facilities. Otherwise she had never been short of anything in her life.

'What a strange thing for you to say,' she went on, making him feel gauche and absurd. 'It's not money I want. I thought you knew that. I have to prove myself. Sometimes it's as if I'm only Mother's shadow. You've done so much for me, Wolf. You've helped me realise that I'm more than that. I'll never forget.'

Her words carried a strange ring of goodbye in them and for the first time Wolf felt his age as a massive handicap. In all his life he had never loved anyone as much as he loved Jacqui. His dreams were tormented by her, and even during an important business discussion he would find his thoughts sliding off to recapture memories of their last meeting. He could not bear to lose her. He knew that. He would not be able to stand it. He felt as young as he had ever been and as vigorous, or almost so. The difference was negligible, he reasoned. Admittedly when he saw that young pup, Rob, hanging around, he realised what a gap there was in their ages. Surely Jacqui would prefer experience, devotion, power and comradeship to an untrained, untried, unsuccessful boy?

'I love you, Jacqui. I didn't want to rush into anything, but after all these months we've spent together I think we've proved what a good team we make.' He reached out and grabbed her hand. She tugged for a moment and then let her hand lie in his.

'Oh Wolf, I don't know what to do,' she began miserably. 'Help me, Wolf. I love you so much. It's as if we belong to each other. I feel so close to you. As if we've known each other all our lives. I don't feel that way about Rob, yet I love him, too. Maybe not quite as I love you ... but in a different way.'

And then it all came pouring out. Her brief, but beautiful love affair, the three stolen nights on the circuit, when Wolf was in America, and the way she missed Rob when she was with Wolf and missed Wolf, when she was with Rob. She tried to tell him about the complexities of this new experience of caring.

She felt too ill, and too confused to notice how hurt Wolf was, but she promised to make a decision at Sarajevo. Rob or him! 'Yes, I promise,' she repeated. After the Games, no — sooner — after her race she would give him an answer. She would ... she would ...

Meanwhile, she was going to switch off emotions and live for skiing and let her problems sort themselves out.

She was so tired and run down after her race, and the tension of all the previous races on the Circuit. She drank too much wine and fell asleep over the table.

Wolf carried her to her room. He covered her with a duvet and left her lying on the bed.

The knife-thrust of her revelation had momentarily paralysed his senses. He was too shocked to react, but he could not banish a terrible sense of loss.

He packed, paid the bill and left. By this time he was feeling coldly furious, doubly betrayed, by both the mother and the daughter. As an afterthought he scribbled a note at reception. '*See you at Sarajevo.*' For what? For love? For revenge? He had so many alternatives.

CHAPTER 59

6 am, Monday, January 30, 1984

London was a God-awful place at the best of times, but in winter it was the bitter bloody end, Maureen thought as she peered moodily out of her office window at the dark clouds resting on the chimney tops and the drizzle beating against windowpanes. No sign of dawn yet, but the day wasn't likely to be much better than the night. She should have left long ago, the south of France was more her style, but she'd had Megan to think about. Well, now there was Johnny. God knows how Megan would run this ruddy business on her own next year. Megan had no idea of the hundreds of problems she had sorted out for her behind the scenes. Couldn't be helped. Johnny came first with her. He always would.

She wondered how Johnny was getting on in Monaco now, with his rusty French. He was looking for premises for their own gym. They had the backers – all the finance they needed – and she was going to run the place while Johnny did the body building. His pseudo-Italian accent wouldn't help him much-a there, she thought with a smile. Just as well he'd dropped it. He didn't seem to need it much lately.

She shivered and hugged her arms around her pale pink Angora sweater. Then she glanced through the glass enclosure into Megan's office and saw them arguing heatedly. They'd been doing that all morning, since they arrived at seven o'clock – Megan, Ian and his assistant carrying the telephone paraphernalia, plus two actors. She thought they'd probably like some coffee and she hurried off to the tiny kitchen to make it.

Bit of all right, that actor, she thought. She liked the way his hair rose up from a sharp widow's peak, with just a touch of grey at the temples. Distinguished-looking, he was. Not that she was supposed to think of things like that now she was betrothed. She looked down at the discreet emerald ring she wore and touched it lovingly with her index finger. She'd have preferred something a bit more showy, but Johnny wasn't like that. He had good taste, Johnny did.

She loaded the cups of instant coffee on to the tray and hurried back, trying to swing her hips provocatively, but this was a bit more difficult lately on the lower heels Johnny preferred.

'Whoops!' she sang out as she slopped the coffee on the tray. ''Ere you lot. Let's have a cuppa, warm the cockles before we start.'

She flashed a brilliant smile at them all, but they were too preoccupied to respond. Understandable really, she thought, as she darted a shrewd glance at the strange assortment of characters. Her hero was wiping his forehead with a handkerchief in spite of the cold. He'd been picked out of a long line of 'resting' actors who'd come in for an interview the day before. Poor blighter! He was getting standard freelance rates, plus a generous, unofficial bonus if he did his job well enough to hoodwink the other party. From the way he was sweating, it looked like he could do with the cash.

Then there was that dumb, American blonde Ian had roped in from a neighbouring pub where she worked as barmaid in the evening. Maureen had nicknamed her, La Boobs, because it described her well enough and because Maureen was learning French. She was frowning with worry, but the posh actor hadn't noticed. He couldn't take his eyes off her cleavage. Pity the way men fell for that type of thing. Oh well, she sighed, at least it proved he wasn't gay.

Ian was quiet and watchful, like a panther waiting to spring, she thought eyeing him warily. A real tough nut! Megan was welcome to him, she wouldn't have him as a gift. He'd been there since early morning with his assistant, rigging up some telephone equipment, which was strictly illegal, she knew. There was a loudspeaker so they could all hear what was going on, earphones and mouthpieces for the two actors, and Ian's chum was standing by with a tape recorder with static sounds in case they needed a quick break to think up new replies.

Megan's eyes were unnaturally bright, and two red spots were burning on her cheeks. Maureen had noticed that when

405

Ian was around, she always looked vulnerable. Her poised career-woman front seemed to crumble. She was far too good for Ian, Maureen thought. A real beauty – like Snow White, only right now her eyes were glittering with anxiety.

Ian glanced at his watch. 'All right, time to move. Away with the cups please, Maureen. Everyone ready? One more go with the tapes. Quiet please.'

There was a hum of the turntable and then a man's voice started speaking. It was a deep, authoritative voice with a pronounced mid-west accent.

'Wilder? Good news, Nigel. We've made it, at last. What d'you say to that? Not bad, eh? Now we can get moving.'

There was a startled exclamation and then Wilder spoke: 'Eleanor's very suspicious about the lull in buying activity – and the press releases. She suspects it's the end.' He was squeaking with suppressed anxiety.

'That doesn't matter a damn,' came the voice. 'There's nothing she can do about it. You'll be the chairman right after the Games. Just hang in there and keep your mouth shut.'

'I'm looking forward ...' Wilder's voice was cut off again.

'Even more important, you'll be able to run Vanguard like we'd both like to see it run. There's a few details to attend to. I'll be in touch.'

An impersonal click terminated the call.

'All right,' Ian said. 'Let's go over it once again.'

The actor groaned. When he began speaking, he was frowning with concentration: 'Wilder. You know who this is ... we've hit a snag ...,' he began.

Identical, Maureen thought watching him. Bet he could take off anyone, she thought to herself. Wilder won't know the difference.

'All right, this time it's the real thing,' Ian began as he picked up his earphones. We don't have any names. We don't know who the voice belongs to, so just follow the script. Answer slowly, complain about an echo on the line to give me time to jot down the answers, in case he comes up with something unexpected. If we get stuck, Morris here will come in with the static interference to buy time.'

The actor took out his handkerchief and mopped his head again.

'Okay, Maureen,' Megan said.

Maureen picked up the receiver of Megan's private line and dialled Vanguard's number in Monaco. After three attempts she was put through.

The barmaid clutched the receiver, a taut smile on her face. 'New York on the line,' she said briskly in her Brooklyn accent. 'I have a personal call for Mr Nigel Wilder.'

'Speaking,' Nigel said sleepily.

'Wilder!' the actor boomed. 'You know who this is. Since I called you last Tuesday evening, we've hit a snag. You haven't been doing your homework, Wilder. Now we've got to move fast, boy. We may have to move the coup forward by a couple of weeks.'

'Fine with me,' Nigel said smoothly. He sounded wide awake suddenly.

'Seems there's a ten per cent parcel of shares tied up with NFF Unit Trust. Did you know about that?'

'Yes,' Nigel said cautiously. 'We spoke about it. Remember? I thought you'd taken care of them.'

'So did I, but Eleanor's been on to them. Did you know that?'

'No,' Nigel said uneasily.

'I've just discovered they're prepared to give their proxy to the party with the largest shareholding. Without your shares, we're running neck and neck, of course. Eleanor's been a busy girl – and behind your back, Wilder. I presume you knew nothing of this?'

Nigel spluttered his denial.

'That's what I thought. Fact is, she might be getting suspicious. I'll have to purchase your shares outright immediately, to prove ownership. Then I can buy up NFF's holding.'

'But that's not the deal.' Nigel's voice was suddenly guarded and angry. 'What will my position be if I don't hold the stock?'

The actor gestured to Morris for static, while Ian scribbled on the notepad.

'No difference, my boy,' he went on. 'Can you hear me? It's a bad line this morning. It's your baby when this lot's over. I wouldn't be such a fool as to put the business into any other hands. As soon as the deal's completed, I'll sell them back to you.'

'What about the premium I was promised?' Nigel said angrily.

There was a long pause for more static. Ian was scribbling on a notebook and handing over the sheets.

'Now don't get greedy, Wilder. The fifty per cent premium was

407

your retiring bonus at the end of the day. Right now it's a temporary manoeuvre. You'll buy them back later.'

'Well, I don't know ...' Nigel began.

'Wilder, you sell me those shares or the deal's off,' he bellowed. 'You know as well as I do, investors always favour the incumbent.'

'Right.' Nigel said crisply.

'My London nominee will be over to fetch them tonight – with a bank draft. Be at your apartment at nine this evening. Can you have the script ready?'

'No problem. It's here in the safe. I'm sorry I didn't find out about this deal of Eleanor's.'

'As it happens – no problem,' the actor boomed, 'but it could have knocked our plans into a cocked hat.'

An impersonal click terminated the conversation.

Maureen flung down her notebook. 'Well, you've got to hand it to him,' she said. 'He pulled it off.'

It was ten pm. Megan was waiting with Eleanor and a magnum of champagne on ice. In spite of winter, the moist heat in the tropical lounge made Megan feel uncomfortable in her woollen two-piece. Eleanor, on the other hand, was looking cool and poised in a navy and white silk dress.

Half an hour ago, Ian had left Cap Ferrat with a cheque for sixteen million dollars, bank guaranteed by the London Branch of The Continental Illinois. It had taken him a day to raise the cash and when she asked him how, he'd replied: 'By pledging Eleanor's Vanguard shares and all I own.'

The two women were tense, and tried for a while to keep the small talk going, but eventually they had both subsided into a worried silence.

Ian arrived at ten-thirty and handed the Vanguard script to Eleanor. 'Like a baby with honey,' he said. 'Nigel swallowed everything without a question.'

Eleanor was overjoyed. She insisted that Ian open the champagne, and they drank to Vanguard's future.

'Eleanor, I have to admit to some failure,' Ian began, placing one hand lightly on Eleanor's shoulder. 'I haven't been able to find out who the buyers are, nor their shareholding. You haven't necessarily won yet, but you do have the advantage. Of course, I have a recorded voice, but I'm sure it's the voice of a nominee. I've heard him on two or three telephone calls and he always appears to be acting on instructions,' Ian confessed reluctantly.

Watching him, Megan realised with surprise that Ian found Eleanor attractive and furthermore, was flirting with her. She wondered what had happened on their previous meeting. Suddenly she realised that being married to Ian would not necessarily be a smooth passage. Women would always find him attractive and it seemed he returned the compliment.

'There wasn't enough time,' he was saying. 'Whoever he is, he thinks he's won; in other words he thinks he holds the controlling interest in Vanguard shares, including Nigel's proxy – which, of course, is no longer valid.' He put his arm around her. 'He'll be crawling out of the woodwork soon. Don't let on to Nigel that you know anything, Eleanor, or you'll never find out who the bastard is – or what exactly their holding is. Neither of you have controlling interest. It's up to you to bluff it out.'

'I owe you, Ian,' she said softly. She reached up impulsively and kissed his cheek. 'I can't pretend Vanguard's problems are over. The press war has damaged sales and growth. I need some really terrific publicity to regain our position.' She turned to Megan. 'We need some wins,' she said with a false smile.

Ian smiled at her reassuringly. 'Nothing you can't handle, Eleanor,' he said. 'You'll pull it off – I promise you.'

She smiled a funny, crooked smile. 'It was far too close for me to feel complacent,' she said. 'I can't help thinking of what might have been.'

CHAPTER 60

Countdown to Sarajevo! In Sarajevo, every man, woman and child had in some way helped with preparations for the coming Winter Games, cutting roads into remote passes previously traversed only by Tito's Nazi-fighting partisans, and preparing four beautiful mountains as lovingly as brides, for the Winter Games, but their task was not yet completed and everyone was panicing. On Mount Bjelašnica, five hundred soldiers were stolidly enduring cold and gale force winds to pack the first snowfall on the pistes; on Mount Trebević troops had been rushed in to complete the unfinished bobsleigh run; TV cables were still being installed while last-minute touches were being made to viewing huts, stands and ski lifts. Most of the nation's buses and taxis were moving towards Sarajevo in awesome convoys; doctors, translators, nurses, technicians and officials were collecting their brightly-coloured overalls and reporting for duty.

In Mother's luxurious Cap Ferrat mansion, Jacqui Douglas was gathering her ski gear in a mood of sombre determination. Mother and she had fought bitterly and Jacqui knew that it was her own fault. Three nights before she had demanded to know about her father, blamed her Mother for being thoughtless and selfish, and Mother had actually cried. That, more than anything else, had filled Jacqui with remorse. She saw herself as spoiled and selfish. A taker! But all this would change at Sarajevo, she vowed. At Sarajevo she would give the only thing she had to give – her skiing. She would gamble her life, her body and her skills to race faster than ever before. She would do this for Mother, for Wolf, for Rob and for Vanguard and in this way she would expiate the hurt she had inflicted on everyone. She was not expecting, or hoping, to emerge unscathed. She saw Sarajevo as an atonement – a purification by trial. This was what Jacqui was feeling as she packed and left. Without realising it she was nurturing a death-wish.

Ten days to Sarajevo. FIS (*Fédération Internationale de Ski*) officials, who had been sent to report on the facilities and pistes at Sarajevo, had reported to the pre-Olympic press that unpleasant jumps had been planed, and undulations in the ground had been removed. In addition, they had been lent six course vehicles, a hundred and twenty skiers, two hundred soldiers and almost the entire adult population of the town, divided into five detachments, to assist them with last minute corrections to the pistes and surrounds. Groups of young people from all over Yugoslavia were dragging turfs on to the courses, tons of stones were being dug out and removed and fifteen hundred metres of safety nets were being installed. All in all, they reported, the infrastructure was excellent and the newly-completed Olympic village was a model of its kind. Everything that could be done, had been done, they reported.

For Wolf, revenge had become a bitter taste in his mouth. At Sarajevo, he planned to destroy Eleanor utterly, and Nigel with her. But what about Jacqui? He loved Jacqui. That was why he had returned her shares to her, unwilling to risk losing her, even in the face of ruining his plans. Wolf felt obsessed with a sense of foreboding, and not only for himself. Jacqui was so young, and so fearless. He could not forget their last evening together when Jacqui had told him of her need and determination to win – in order to help save her mother's company. Wolf had not been able to talk her out of her absurd idea. What if she was injured? Or worse? It would be his fault, he reminded himself daily.

Nine days of Sarajevo. Fear of snowlessness has always haunted the Winter Olympics. By January, half a metre had fallen, enough for the troops to start packing the pistes, but not enough for the Winter Games. Climatic research studies that had been hastily prepared for the Sarajevo Games, showed that to date these regions had never been without snow in February. Nevertheless, throughout January, the townsfolk scanned the sky anxiously, and when the year's first good snowstorms came at last, crowds of youths had run out into the street to celebrate. So everyone kept smiling throughout a four-day blizzard which buffeted Sarajevo with intermittent, eighty mile-an-hour winds and played havoc with last-minute construction to the Games infrastructure. Olympic officials hastily brought in snow-removal equipment from Austria and Switzerland.

Meanwhile, Michel Juric was wining and dining a spinster from the British Home Office. He had been seeing her for weeks, but at long last she had brought him the papers he needed for his story. He could hardly wait to drop her home and examine the papers. As he had suspected, Nikki's real name was not Nikola Petrovna. In fact, she was Nikola Petrovna Kuznetsovna. Petrovna was her mother's maiden name. Suddenly a great many things became clear to Michel, but not enough. Hastily he booked a flight to New York, but with the instinct of a good journalist, he knew that the last chapter would still be written in Sarajevo.

Eight days to Sarajevo. Initial euphoria had passed and the Yugoslavs were in the grip of an unbearable tension. They were fiercely independent folk: six highly individualistic republics; two autonomous provinces; three mutually antagonistic religions, and five quarrelsome language groups (Serbo-Croatian, Slovenian, Macedonian, Albanian and Hungarian). Traditionally, they had refused to bend to each other, or to Russia, or the West. They went their own way in proud, poverty-stricken non-alignment, answerable to no one. But now they were united with a common goal. Hosting the Olympics had become a matter of fanatical concern to everyone. Why? Because they wanted to show the world what they could do, because they were a little lonely in their self-imposed isolation, because they were a warm and loving people and they longed to make friends. They would host the Games with all the passion and persuasion that won them the Olympics in the first place.

This was a time of lonely introspection for Nikki, despite her long hours of coaching. There was something which goaded her on – hour after hour, day after day – to do more, to try harder, to keep skating when her body was screaming for rest. Something which was too humiliating to acknowledge, yet was always there – like perpetual pain. A nagging fear which questioned the motives of all those whispered promises; the validity of their subtle flattery; the morality of the choice she made, which led her to defect to the West. Subversive voices! Self-doubts at dead of night!

At Sarajevo she would show the world – the West and the East and not the least her father – that she did not defect for fast cars and fancy flats and a million in the bank, but because she was the world's best and she deserved a chance to prove it. Only by winning would she be vindicated in her own eyes. And nothing else was acceptable to her. At Sarajevo all would be forgiven.

Seven days to Sarajevo. One hundred and eighty enthusiastic young Yugoslavs had joined the ABC team and were helping ABC technicians put the finishing touches to their complex installation. They were geared up to beam a total of sixty-three hours in thirteen days. In 1980 ABC paid ninety-one and a half million dollars for the right to televise the Sarajevo Games. Their nerve centre was the seventy million dollar concrete broadcast centre, on Sarajevo's main street. There were two control rooms, one with a wall of seventy flickering TV monitors, which would relay pictures from rinks and slopes around the city and mountains. The centre had been designed and constructed in Los Angeles, and shipped by boat in thirty mammoth trailers to Yugoslavia.

At her Monaco headquarters, Eleanor was waiting impatiently to discover the identity of her enemy. Someone, somewhere, thought he had won, might still have won. Surely he would be coming to claim his empire soon and she would have the pleasure of telling him – and Nigel – how she had outwitted

413

them both. But why was he taking so long? Eleanor's only diversion was watching Nigel's antics. Nigel was tense and arrogantly throwing his weight around. She could see how onerous the waiting was for her old friend. He could not wait to oust her. So she watched and laughed inwardly.

But Eleanor had little enough time to worry about past traumas. She had more than enough in the present. Vanguard was preparing for the Winter Games with all the drive and determination of the competitors themselves. They had staked huge amounts of cash on what they hoped would be a profitable investment – Sarajevo! Their technical back-up had to be the best. On the eve of the Games, almost everyone in the company had butterflies – and not for nothing. One million dollars spent on sponsoring a sporting event, or a sports champion, had the same impact on the public's attention as ten million dollars worth of other advertising. An embarrassing failure or disaster could cast a shadow over the sponsor's brand name.

Disaster, was the word uppermost in Eleanor's mind. She feared for Jacqui, and bitterly regretted their angry parting. Jacqui was right, she had belatedly decided. Jacqui had a right to know about her father. On the spur of the moment Eleanor decided to go to Sarajevo. She would try for a reconciliation and she would be there to see her daughter race. But what about Nigel? She was reluctant to leave him at Vanguard. Eventually she decided that Nigel would go with her. She called him in and insisted.

Six days to Sarajevo. At the Sarajevo tourism department, bookings were mounting daily. The new Holiday Inn Hotel, erected in the centre of the new town, only fifteen minutes from the airport, had three hundred bedrooms and sixteen luxury suites. Similar first-class accommodation had been completed elsewhere in the town as well as around every ski venue. Add to this miles of densely packed rows of three-storey apartment blocks painted in pretty pastel shades – which was the new Olympic village – and Sarajevans could be excused for feeling complacent. But then, advance bookings indicated they would be short on accommodation for several thousand visitors. In an unprecedented move, local townsfolk were asked to accommodate a further sixteen thousand visitors in their homes. There were no complaints – everyone was so proud that Sarajevo had been chosen. They longed to be known as the friendly city.

To Rob Scott, who was packing his gear, prior to joining the American team, Sarajevo represented another chance – to win Jacqui. He knew now that he would always love her and that his life would be quite spoiled if he could not share it with the woman he loved. He was praying that she had recovered from her foolish infatuation with a man old enough to be her father. His business was prospering, he had renovated his cottage in the woods, and if she would just say 'yes' he knew he could make her happy. He was counting the days and the hours to his departure.

Five days to Sarajevo. In 1978, when the International Olympic Committee awarded the Games to Sarajevo, they had a third-rate resort with a few lifts, no ice rink and no bobsleigh course. Now the proud and fiery Yugoslavs had succeeded against considerable odds in transforming their Balkan backwater into a first-class venue for the Winter Games. Banko Mikulic, president of Yugoslavia's Olympic Organising Committee, and a former president of Bosnia-Herzogovina, was jubilant. So were the townsfolk, officials, hoteliers, skiers, and politicians. *They did it! What's more, they did it for only $120 million.*

The mood was one of well-justified gaiety and self-congratulation. Barrels of *slivovitz* were being unloaded as Sarajevo awaited the world.

Sarajevo would make or break her, Megan knew. Her reputation for picking winners could change overnight. Unless she produced a good crop of winners at the Games, John would replace her. In this business no one could afford to hang on to losers. John had said as much to her in a long and hectoring telephone call just before she left.

Megan's Maria Stenmark, the Swedish figure skater, was good, too, but not quite good enough to win a medal, in Megan's opinion. Gunter stood a chance in the Giant Slalom,

415

but he was a temperamental boy and his performances ranged from very good to mediocre. Jacqui, on the other hand, was a persistent tryer – but was she good enough? And so on. Night after night, Megan had been lying awake evaluating the chances of her many other clients, but she could not achieve a great degree of confidence. As the time drew nearer, concern for Nikki became uppermost in her mind. She had decided that they would share a room at the Sarajevo Palace Hotel. This would enable her to guard Nikki and protect her from the scorn of her ex-compatriots. She feared for Nikki, and it was not just for business, either. She had grown fond of her and she doubted Nikki had the strength to face losing. She had to win. Lately, Nikki's skating had reached a fine peak of excellence and discipline, but she could be thrown off-balance so easily. So Megan prayed that the tension would not affect her performance.

Four days to Sarajevo. As the hours ticked away towards February the seventh, and the first tourists filtered into the town, the officials' pride gave way to edgy watchfulness. There were many more guards, thousands of blank video screens were waiting to be switched on, metal detectors appeared in every doorway. Zoran Banski had given the world an assurance that life and property would be safeguarded from the whole gamut of Olympic disasters, ranging from petty fraud to terrorism. As the deadline drew closer, all four ulcers started playing havoc with his stomach.

416

CHAPTER 61

11 am, Tuesday, February 7, 1984

Sarajevo looked like a scene from a fairy story, Zoran Banski, head of security for Sarajevo, thought sourly as he was driven slowly along Obala Vojvode Stepe Street, past the Princip Bridge beside the gently flowing Miljacka River.

Overnight the fairy godmother had waved her wand and Sarajevo was transformed into a blushing bride, decked in all her finery: flags of every nation lined the roads, windows were choked with Olympic souvenirs, there were flowers, posters, streamers – all the paraphernalia of pre-Olympic euphoria.

The city was coyly waiting to welcome the West, her long-awaited Prince Charming. Her dowry was the mountains, the snow, the new and glorious ice rinks and stadiums, the bobsleigh and *luge* runs, the ski lifts, the hotels, the barrels of *slivovitz* – all completed on schedule. The people were bubbling with love and friendship, hands stretched across the sea, from now on life would be ineffably richer, for the West was about to meet the bride, fall in love, and keep coming back, again and again; a joyful liaison between this lonely Balkan backwater and the twentieth century.

Temperatures were well below zero, but no one cared. The citizens of Sarajevo were out in the streets with flags and smiles and whispered words of welcome. 'You are beautiful, I love you,' was the message the bride was sending the West, in broadcasts, magazines, leaflets, videos, posters, pamphlets, and even printed on menus.

Zoran Banski was as full of foreboding as any other father of the bride. He harboured no such illusions; the bride would be ravished, abandoned and forgotten. Her dowry would fall apart, her joy would be dissipated. But no one wanted to listen to Zoran Banski, who was known for his pessimism.

Zoran was sitting in the back of a brand new Mitsubishi Combi, supplied free for the Games. He felt miserable. He missed his beat-up Lada with the broken upholstery into which he fitted so comfortably.

On the other side of the broad highway, most of the nation's taxicabs were proceeding bumper to bumper along the snowy street, horns blaring, as they transported tourists from Gordona airport to the many hotels in town and at the skiing sites. The pavements were clustered with noisy, happy visitors. Like swarms of multi-coloured butterflies, they circled aimlessly around, shopping, talking, or just looking.

The police, in their discreet, grey-blue uniforms were trying to seem invisible, but Zoran knew they were just as excited as the cheerful crowds, and determined to a man that no terrorism or hooliganism would mar their beautiful Games. No easy task: a city of five hundred thousand was playing host to forty-seven nations.

Bus loads of multi-hued skiers threaded their way to Mounts Yahorina, Igman, Trebević and Bjelašnica, where compulsory practice runs had been taking place for several days before the big races began. They waved as they passed and everyone on the streets turned and waved back.

Banski leaned forward and chuckled slightly at the long line of highrise office blocks, one of which was a glistening edifice of bright blue. Originally an ambitious plan of the seventies, the building had risen ten stories and then been abandoned, waiting for cash, which had never come, to finish it. But last month a gang of builders had filled in the gaping, crumbling holes with bright blue perspex and now it looked quite splendid, as long as no one went close enough to peer inside.

He sighed: they were so poor and saddled with a national debt of twenty billion dollars. Eighteen kilometres further along the road, lay the airport and adjacent to it the new Olympic Village. His driver parked in the official space and Banski pushed unnoticed through the arriving passengers, a small man in a shabby overcoat, perhaps the only man in Sarajevo who was not smiling.

And for good reason, he reflected angrily. He had received the news that morning – depressing news which had wrought havoc with his stomach. He was sagging slightly as he pushed his way through the crowded airport to a door marked 'private'.

418

The room was sparsely furnished, a few plastic chairs, two plastic tables. Someone had put an Olympic poster on the wall and he stared at it thoughtfully for a few seconds wondering who it was who cared enough to do that. The three policemen who had been drinking coffee, were now standing to attention.

'Why are you here?' He frowned and glanced at his watch. 'Why aren't you out there? Is there any coffee left?' He sat down cautiously, and unbuttoned his overcoat.

'I'll fetch you some, Sir,' the young sergeant said.

'No,' he waved his hand in a gesture of dismissal. 'Don't bother.'

'Nikola Petrovna is expected on the next flight, Sir, in approximately twenty minutes.'

He grunted and stared out of the window. His face took on a far-away expression which told them that further communication would be uncalled for, if not positively dangerous. After what seemed a long while to his subordinates, he stood up and left. Pausing at the door, he said, 'Millions!' He waved his arm around expressively. 'One hundred and twenty million, to be precise. That's what it's cost to get the West here. They have to feel safe. Remember that. It's important.'

'Everything's under control, Sir,' the sergeant said nervously.

The Sarajevo Palace Hotel bus was parked outside the airport. Cana was in the driving seat. Banski placed one hand gently on her shoulder. 'This time ...' he said. 'This time ...'

He turned away and listened to the loudspeaker announcing yet another flight. Then he took out a handkerchief with a flourish and noisily blew his nose.

Sarajevo had agreed to provide the playground for the world's Winter Games, not for their war games. They could find somewhere else to conduct their dirty business. Not in his territory. Oh no, not right under the nose of Zoran Banski. They underestimated him.

It was two pm. Rob and his squad were returning on the bus from another day's practice on the slalom piste on the slopes of Mount Bjelašnica. It was snowing again and winds were reaching gale force. Rob peered through the bus window; there was nothing to see but snow. Yesterday the view had been breathtaking: miles of snowy peaks and valleys spread out to the distant purple horizon. The mountain slopes were thick with spruce, their bare branches, uncluttered by snow, were dark brown patches against the white, and thick brambles on either side made a delicate web of snow and icicles; like lace, he had thought wonderingly. Today there was nothing to see and Rob was filled with impatience as the bus plunged down thirty-five kilometers of winding narrow road, newly constructed for the Games.

When they arrived in the Olympic Village at three, Rob was torn two ways: he was ravenously hungry, but longing to see Jacqui.

'Decisions, decisions,' he muttered to himself, grinning ruefully as he hurried along the pavement, past pink, blue and turquoise buildings. Each apartment block contained ground floor restaurants specialising in the traditional food of each competing country. As he neared the British section, he caught sight of one of the girls hurrying into the doorway. Presumably, they had just returned from practice, as he had. Perhaps he could satisfy both needs in one move, he thought, feeling more cheerful.

He joined the queue and as he neared the self-service counter, he saw Jacqui sitting at a table with her team mates. The sight of her lovely profile, her perfectly white small teeth glistening as she smiled, and her dark brown curly hair tumbling wildly over her shoulders, made him tremble. The cutlery and crockery rattled on his tray.

He put it down carefully and fumbled for change. He was always amazed at the ridiculously low prices. He paid five hundred dinars, which he calculated quickly, was around two dollars for soup, bread, cottage pie, peas, tinned fruit, custard, and a glass of apple juice.

Rob was in a quandary: should he sit near Jacqui, or move away? Their last encounter during the World Cup Circuit was a painful memory because he knew exactly how many times Wolf Muller had flown over to see her and although he understood her longing for a father-figure in her lonely life, that did not ease his suffering. In spite of her arrogant manner, he knew that she loved him, why else would she have made love to him while she was travelling with Muller, but she was so unsure of herself. No one else had made love to her, Rob knew that. She was still his girl. This was the only reason Rob was hanging around. He had set his hopes on winning her back at the Games. He would far rather win Jacqui than a gold medal. Not exactly the right attitude for a US squad member, he knew, but Rob was in love.

So how should he approach her? Finally, Rob compromised and chose a seat directly behind the British girls and unashamedly eavesdropped on their conversation. Jacqui had not noticed him yet, because she was arguing heatedly with a tall, angular woman whom Rob instinctively disliked, with her sophisticated city clothes. She was a faded blonde, of that indeterminate age between thirty and fifty, and she was heavily made up with a foundation too dark for her complexion. Her nails were red and pointed, her costume jewellery too flashy, and there was an impression of tension and uncleanliness about her.

'Look here, Adele,' Jacqui was saying, and for once she had not lost her temper. 'We all want to win, that's why we're here. It's not fair to suggest we're not trying. We'll do our best.'

He watched Adele, whoever she was, pick up the slip for lunch and fumble in her bag.

'I'm glad to hear that,' Adele retorted snidely. 'You girls have to be reminded of the facts of life from time to time. Magnum have paid two hundred thousand pounds to sponsor the British team and that kind of money deserves some public interest. So give the viewers what they want, some home wins – if you can't win, spice it up a bit, thrills and spills!' A bony hand reached up to pat her hair into place. 'We don't want viewers to switch off, do we?' Her tone was light and playful. 'We all know how badly the British team need sponsorship. Hardly surprising really, watching tortoises had never been a traditional pastime.' She was smiling, but her eyes flicked coldly back and forth. 'Okay, girls. Try harder,' she said, like a mother coaxing a child to do better at school.

'Just a minute, Adele.'

She spun round in surprise as a hand caught hold of her elbow. Looking up, she stared into the grey eyes of a powerful young man who was gazing at her with an expression of disgust. Unbelievably he was shaking her.

'Thrills and spills? Is that an order? From you? And who the hell are you?'

Adele tried to wrench her arm away, but failed.

Jacqui's eyes were wide with amusement. 'Hey there, Rob, give over,' she called out.

'No way,' he answered. 'Did I hear you right, Adele? Is this an official message from the British team's sponsor? Thrills and spills – or no more sponsorship. The press might find that interesting.' He gave her a harder shake, and for a split second Adele looked frightened. 'If you were a man,' he said in his deceptively quiet voice, 'I'd punch your teeth out.'

'Are you trying to be funny! Is this supposed to be a joke?' She looked up, scowling and shook off his arm. 'I'm their sponsor. So far this season British skiing has been one long bore. So we don't get the coverage we deserve for the cash we spend. It's simple economics. The girls must put up a bit of a show.

'Now, if you'd just get out of my way.' She pushed past and he listened to the sharp tap-tap of her high heels on the tiles as she hurried out of the restaurant.

'Hello Rob,' Jacqui's eyes were shining with happiness. 'Don't mind Adele. She's just trying to keep her job,' Jacqui said. 'Her new keepers want their money's worth. So would Mother. It's a tough business.' She pulled him down on the seat next to her. 'You should know, you're in it.'

'I wouldn't like to see any of you taking her seriously,' Rob began, and broke off to murmur goodbye to the other girls who were leaving. They looked rather subdued, he thought.

'Don't listen to that bitch,' Rob said moodily to Jacqui.

'Of course, I must,' she told him seriously. 'This race means the earth to me. Vanguard need a win. It's pretty rough being in the Cinderella team,' she laughed self-consciously. 'Of course, Mother wanted to go overboard and supply my own private technicians. It wouldn't look right, of course, but we could do with some backup. Every evening we skulk around the European teams trying to learn from their research.'

'Please don't talk about skiing.' Rob caught her hand. 'When this is over,' he said seriously. 'I want you to stay on a couple of days. Maybe we can see a bit of each other. Carry on where we left off. I've been missing you so much.'

She turned away evasively, and the look in her eyes made Rob flinch. 'He's coming here, isn't he?'

Jacqui nodded. 'Well, of course,' she said bravely.

'I'd hoped so much ... That's it then,' he said decisively. His face had blanched and his eyes looked stricken.

Jacqui could not bear to see him looking so hurt. 'Please ...' she began.

'Don't expect me to hang around playing the fool while you ... Oh, to hell with you, Jacqui. Make up your mind now – him or me. Right now!'

Jacqui looked up mistily and Rob wishing he could retract his words, felt shamed by her sadness.

She said only: 'Must you do this to me – just before the race? I refuse to be railroaded into anything. Do what you like. I won't stop you.'

Eyes glistening with tears, she walked quickly away. Rob glared at her feeling a heel.

As the port wing of the UTA jet bowed gently to the east, Eleanor caught a glimpse of the domes and minarets of the old Turkish quarter, and beside it an overcrowded medley of streets and buildings of the graceful Austrian town. Then they were cruising silently over the new proletarian centre, with wide streets, square buildings of glass and concrete and highrise apartment blocks. Only in the east, Eleanor thought, could you have a built-up city in the midst of so much desolation without the peripheral suburbs, parks, industrial centres and network of roads. It was if it had been dumped there.

It was bitterly cold in the airport. Eleanor was shivering convulsively by the time she had retrieved her luggage. Turning up the collar of her ermine jacket, she moved forward with the noisy, laughing throng of visitors and allowed herself to be thrust out of the airport building, to the end of a long queue.

She watched the convoy of taxis and buses moving slowly towards her. Incoming travellers – competitors, managers, visitors – were being packed and despatched with the speed and deftness of a packaging plant. A few minutes later she was hurriedly pushed into a taxi with three others who were also booked into the Holiday Inn Hotel.

Across the road from the airport was the new Olympic Village, their taxi driver told them with pride. She saw hundreds of pastel-painted apartment blocks and crowded pavements. Flags of every nation lined the route and everywhere you looked, files of people in different-coloured overalls were hurrying this way and that way, like ants in a strange, new technicolour world. 'Look for bright blue if you need a translator, dark blue and white for medical services, brown for Olympic officials ...' the taxi driver was reciting. His voice droned on and on. Half of Yugoslavia must be here to help the Games, Eleanor surmised.

'How could I have forgotten about the cold?' she murmured half an hour later when she had booked into her suite and was burrowing into her suitcase for warmer clothing. 'I should have remembered. After all, I'm Scottish, but I'd forgotten about real cold.' She would have to buy thermal underwear or she would freeze to death, but first she must see Jacqui.

By the time her taxi drew up outside the British block it was snowing heavily. Eleanor tipped the usual Monaco tip and to her surprise he smilingly refused to take more than a hundred dinars. 'You are all our friends,' he called out. 'We want you to come back.'

She was told by the British trainer that Jacqui was in the restaurant. She did not see her daughter at first, but then she noticed a crouched figure, bent over a table in the corner. It was Jacqui, head in hands, and unbelievably she was crying.

'Why, Jacqui, darling, whatever is the matter with you.' Eleanor was both touched and alarmed, she had never seen her daughter look anything less than abrasive. Jacqui fought sadness with anger, shrugged off her disappointments, and countered her fears with aggression. It was a characteristic she had been born with, not something she had learned. Eleanor had always admired this quality in her daughter. For a moment Eleanor wondered if she had been excluded from the team and a wave of happy relief rushed through her. There was nothing quite as meaningful to Jacqui as skiing.

'Jacqui,' Eleanor began gently, reaching forward and taking her hand. 'If you've been dropped from the team, there'll always be another year.'

Her daughter, sat up looking shamefaced. 'I had no idea you were coming,' she mumbled.

'Just as well I did. Now tell me why you're crying.'

Jacqui shook her head violently, screwed her eyes tightly shut and gripped Eleanor's hand harder.

424

'Mother,' she began in an agonised tone. Then she clamped her mouth shut as a party of tourists entered the restaurant.

'Shall we go for a walk?' Eleanor suggested. 'Or would you like to come back to my hotel for dinner?'

Jacqui shook her head. 'Too much work,' she gasped. 'Let's walk.'

The snow was heavier, the streets more crowded, the restaurants filling up, and the mood was one of exhilaration and youthful exuberance. The two women walked arm-in-arm.

'I came because I wanted to talk to you,' Eleanor began haltingly. She saw the withdrawal in her daughter's eyes, the involuntary flinching, the start of anger and she felt desperately hurt, so she ploughed on quickly before she lost her courage and her urge.

'I've never really talked to you about the things that matter. I've taken it for granted that you know how much I care about you. Maybe I haven't given you much affection, but that was because I try not to feel things – I mean emotions can be very hurtful,' Eleanor began, trying to rush through the speech she had rehearsed on the plane.

'I think it's time we both laid our cards on the table.' When Jacqui did not answer, she said: 'I'm sorry about our last fight, Jacqui. More sorry than you'd believe. I should have answered your questions. I know you want to know about your father. It was wrong of me. Forgive me.'

Jacqui clamped her mouth shut and looked away. The sight of her formidable mother looking so haggard and close to tears was too much for her. She could not bear to watch, could not trust herself to speak. She suddenly realised that she loved her mother desperately. She always had done and there was nothing she wanted more than to be close to her, but still she hung back.

'Jacqui, when I walked into the restaurant, you were crying. I've never seen you cry before. Tell me what's wrong?'

Jacqui shook her head. Trusting Mother could have the most awful consequences, as she'd found out to her cost in her childhood.

'Jacqui, darling, you're so young, why won't you let me help you? If we could only communicate.'

Well, if that's what she wants. In a moment of rare candour Jacqui tried to explain: 'Confiding in you, Mother, means total capitulation. In no time at all you take control, you bring out your big guns, use a cannon to kill a fly, which is your style, flatten everyone who opposes you – or me – into the ground and hand me victory on a bloody plate.'

Eleanor looked aghast. 'Yes, I do that,' she admitted with a shakey laugh. Then she paused, glared into the shop window and surreptitiously took out a tissue to dab her eyes.

After a long wait she said: 'I'll try to improve. But you're so young ... so inexperienced. I fear for you.'

'Oh Mother. I really don't know what to do. I'm in love, but with two men. I love them both desperately, but differently. After all, they are so different. Now they ... that is ... one of them wants me to choose. I can't do that. I can't bear the thought of life without either of them.'

My little daughter has grown up rather rapidly, Eleanor thought with a sense of shock.

'Well, tell me more about them,' Mother began. 'No, rather tell me about their parents. Let's start from the beginning.'

Jacqui mumbled and withdrew as she sensed that Mother was moving in on her act again, taking charge as she always did. Nothing would change; it never did.

'Take my advice, don't allow yourself to be bullied by either one of these men,' Eleanor was saying. 'He's probably bluffing you anyway. You choose when you're good and ready. They'll wait, I'm sure, or otherwise they're not worth having. But I'd sure love to meet them.'

There was a delicious smell of coffee coming from the Swiss block, and rows of strawberry cream puffs in the windows. 'Hey, feast your eyes on that,' Jacqui said pulling her mother toward the door.

Jacqui was obviously feeling better already. Oh to be young, Eleanor thought. 'Let's guzzle,' she said.

They ordered coffee and two puffs and sat in a quiet corner and Eleanor said: 'Trust me. I promise I won't interfere.'

Jacqui paused with a mouthful of cake and after a momentary hesitation, nodded her head. 'I'll do better than that. I'll bring them round to meet you. Then you can judge for yourself. You're going to love them, Mother. Both of them.'

Eleanor closed her eyes, determined not to be a coward. She had come here for a specific reason and she was not going to be sidetracked. She had been rehearsing her speech all the way from Monaco.

'Jacqui, you must know that I've been seeing a psycho therapist for a year,' she began. 'Mainly because of my allergies, but somewhere along the line I realised that I had buried my personality in the business and there wasn't much of me left. Once, long ago, I was hurt badly. I've come to terms with that,' she hurried on, not wanting to sound a martyr. 'Eventually, it wasn't the hurt that was the big problem, it was what I had become: an automaton, burying my feelings, my guilt, my anger, everything.

'I could never talk to you about ... well, about any of it, because I couldn't face the past myself. But now I think I can. I've been through it pretty thoroughly lately, I can just about manage to tell you without ... well ... you know.' She laughed shakily, fumbled for a tissue and dabbed her cheeks.

'You don't have to tell me, Mother,' Jacqui said quickly. 'I was wrong to ask. Your past has nothing to do with me. You've always done your best for me and I'm grateful.

'Oh Mother,' she said gently, as her mother gave a long sniff.

'I've always looked up to you and admired you. You know that. Let's forget about it.'

'No, it's no good soft-soaping me, Jacqui,' Eleanor said determinedly. 'I missed my chance at home and after you left I felt terrible. So I came here, hoping that it wasn't not too late.'

'Why Mother?' Jacqui looked up incredulously. 'Too late for what?'

'For us. I've been so afraid I might lose you. You're the only person I care about. You know that, don't you?'

She reached forward and clasped her daughter's hands and to her surprise, Jacqui did not pull away. Instead she hung on.

'I've always known that one day I'd have to sit down and tell you what I'm going to tell you now. You see, darling, I loved your father very much. He was just as keen a skier as you are, and if it weren't for the war I expect he would have been in the Olympics, too, but he broke his back in a skiing accident and from then on our lives were ruined.'

Skiing accident? A weird coincidence! Jacqui began to feel uneasy.

'I should have told you years ago why I'm so scared of you racing competitively. You see, Wolf broke his back and that ruined our marriage.'

Wolf! Jacqui mouthed the words and wanted to choke. She

put down her cup slowly with shaking hands, thrust them into her pocket and closed her eyes.

Mother did not seem to have noticed her daughter's reaction. She was leaning back, eyes half closed, searching for the right words, trying to tell the exact truth as she poured out her story.

'You see,' Eleanor said eventually. 'I was afraid I would lose you, too. You were all I had left of him. Can you believe that your old mother was once so much in love?'

'I believe you,' Jacqui said tonelessly.

'Let's have some more coffee,' Eleanor said over-brightly. She gazed at the tablecloth, waiting for Jacqui to say something and when at last she ventured a glance towards her daughter, she saw that she looked so white. Was she ill? Her fingers were clutching the table's edge as if she were hanging on for her life.

Eleanor peered worriedly at her daughter. 'Perhaps I should not have told you,' she whispered. 'Jacqui?' She reached forward and touched her daughter's hand. It felt so cold. 'I've learned that the truth is preferable to lies. Lies have a way of destroying you.'

'It's all right, Mother,' Jacqui said gently. 'You're right. I had to find out sooner or later.'

'There! I've said it all,' Eleanor said triumphantly. 'From now on maybe we can get along a little better.'

'Have you seen Wolf since then, Mother?'

'No ... I changed your name back to Douglas legally, by the way. I guessed he'd never find out he had a daughter.'

But he knew YOU had a daughter, Mother, and he came looking for me, to get my shares, to hit back at you.

The bile rose in Jacqui's throat; she thought she would throw up, but the moment passed. She pushed back her chair and Eleanor jumped up smiling gently.

Jacqui forced a smile. 'Mother, I've got to get back to the others. You don't have to worry about anything,' she said. 'Now I understand a whole lot of things.'

'Well, I wish that were true, but as long as we can pull together I'll feel better about everything.'

'Sure we will. Just as soon as the Games are over I'll be hanging in there with you – if you need me.'

How pale her daughter looked. Eleanor felt weakened by the

428

tide of caring surging through her. Jacqui was so young; too young to face what she was going to face. Why had she chosen downhill racing? She was nagged by memories and fearful premonitions. *'Oh God,' she thought, 'I wish these ten days were over.'*

Father! The concept was quite shocking. Wolf is my father and he's a cheat. He's been being lying to me and trying to cheat me. Yet, behind the angry thoughts and the desire to hit back was a warm glow deep inside her. Her own warm secret tucked away. A strange sense of belonging. She was not prepared to take it out yet, to examine it, not even talk about it. Not to Mother and not to Rob and especially not to Wolf. But Wolf kept telephoning and he had come round to the British block twice, but the team had agreed to tell him to get lost.

By nightfall, Wolf was feeling desperate. Jacqui had not turned up for their evening drink and he was sure that she was avoiding him. He had driven to the Olympic Village and repeatedly tried to see her, but her team mates would not let him in. Eventually she had agreed to speak to him on the telephone.

Even before he spoke she had demanded in a stranger's voice: 'Wolf, the woman you were once married to, the bitch who had an affair, stole your business and left you crippled and broke – was that Mother?'

'This is not the sort of conversation you hold on the telephone,' he had parried.

'Was it?' she had demanded imperiously.

'Yes,' flatly.

'You creepy bastard! You knew all along who I was, and you fed me all those stories. You only wanted my shares – to ruin Mother and steal Vanguard from us, but you pretended you were trying to help me. I know Mother pretty well and that's not the way she operates. You keep away from Mother, Wolf, and keep away from me, too.'

Wolf would not accept defeat. It was all true, and so was the love he had for Jacqui. Why all this sudden, misplaced loyalty for Mother? Where did it come from? He was not prepared to give her up. She could not throw away the bond they had built during the past year. He loved her and he would marry her.

'Jacqui, listen to me. Never mind how I started off; I ended up loving you. I gave you back your shares, didn't I? Doesn't that prove something? You still own your oil shares. That must tell you something.'

'Have them back.' An impersonal click terminated his call.

CHAPTER 62

Wednesday, February 8, 1984

The dainty, crystalline snowflake, designed by a leading Yugoslav artist, Miroslav Roko Antonic and chosen as the symbol of the 14th Winter Olympics, was entirely right, Megan thought as she stood in the blizzard beside Ian, chilled by intermittent eighty mile-an-hour winds in the Kosevo stadium, watching the opening ceremony.

In spite of the cold, she had been thrilled by the spectacle provided by the eager young Yugoslavs. Four thousand five hundred performers, dressed in brilliantly coloured, avant-garde snowsuits, had performed a gymnastic ballet with split-second timing, and a brilliant troop of flag dancers, had executed a startling visual display with flags. Watching them, Megan felt a thousand light years away from reality; it was as if she had been plucked from the world and dropped into some other existence in time and space; where people smiled all the time; where colours were more brilliant; where music played thrillingly from morning to night and the world was magically happy. Even Vucko, the wolf, the Winter Games's mascot, had changed from a bloodthirsty animal into a cute and cuddly creature frolicking happily with the gymnasts, cadets, folk dancers, ballet troupes and high school girls looking like gaudy visitors from another planet.

It was time for the march past. By now Megan was at one with the crowd, just another hyped-up, smiling enthusiast, cheering the teams, waving her Stars and Stripes, wide-eyed at the jazzy Olympic uniforms: the Canadians like red-hooded Santas; the Italians with striped scarves tossed over their shoulders; the Swiss in their smart red and white suits; the Swedish in all-blue with bright yellow hats; the Americans in their cowboy hats; four mustachioed Lebanese, handsome and smiling; cloaked Moroccans; and the lonely one-man squad from Puerto Rico.

But Megan had eyes only for Jacqui and Nikki, two slender marchers in the British team. Nikki held her shoulders back, chin out defiantly, head held high. Yesterday, she had been snubbed by members of the Russian team in the foyer, and later Megan had heard her crying softly in bed, so Megan had asked Jacqui to look after her today, and now the two of them were marching side by side.

There was no mistake where the Yugoslavs' feelings lay; when the US squad doffed their cowboy hats, the Slavs joined their voices to the scattered Americans in the crowd, and cheered them past.

When the fire department band from Lake Placid, the 1980 Olympic host, oom-pah-pahed their way through catchy American songs, Megan found herself singing joyfully with the rest of the stadium.

Eleanor was studying the competitors, trying to pick out which ones were Vanguard-sponsored and thinking what a pity it was she had missed out on the clothing side. She had desperately wanted to provide the ski suits and uniforms for the various competing teams, but had lost out to *Fila* and *Descente*. A pity, she thought. No doubt the takeover bid had diminished her usual efficiency, but next time she'd win, she promised herself.

Most of Vanguard's competitors were known to her by photographs only, but she had managed to find Gunter who was in the West German Giant Slalom team, and Maria Stenmark, the Swedish ice skater. Nikki of course, was marching side by side with Jacqui in the British team. How pale they both looked, she had thought, studying them carefully through her binoculars.

Then Nigel, who was beside her, reached in his pocket and jolted her arm. Suddenly she was tossed back twenty years in time as the binoculars jerked up and she found herself staring at the familiar features of Wolf Muller. It seemed as if he was staring straight back at her. But this was absurd. A hallucination. That's what comes from seeing a shrink, she thought with a grimace. Next thing she'd be hearing voices. *But why shouldn't he be there. Half the world was.* Anyway, by now he would look quite different. He'd look older, wouldn't he? Yet the man she had seen – or thought she had seen – looked just like the youthful Wolf of her memories.

For a moment Eleanor was overcome with anxiety. She focussed on the crowd and began to carefully scan each face, trying to find the one which had caused her such alarm. This was difficult because her hands were shaking so badly.

It must be Wolf, she decided half an hour later when she finally located his face amongst the crowd. What a weird coincidence. For a moment panic took over. 'Nigel, I'm not feeling so well, this cold … you stay here, like a dear, and I'll see you at the hotel.' She thrust her binoculars in her bag and fled.

To Eleanor's amazement she, and everyone else, were locked into the stadium. The police had firmly padlocked every exit. 'For security,' they explained after a translator had been summoned. The translator was a pleasant young man who tactfully offered the toilet, the rest room, the first aid depot – all of which Eleanor refused – so he showed her back to her place with a polite bow. She could leave only when it was over.

Nigel looked up in surprise. 'We're all locked in,' she explained. 'Very strange! Hardly what one expects … but in the East …?' She shrugged.

As Eleanor sat listening to the speeches, she came to terms with the fact that Wolf was real, he had co-existed with her, in another part of the globe, for twenty years. He was not the phantom who haunted her dreams, ruined her days and made her flesh crawl. Somehow, Eleanor's images of Wolf had come to an abrupt full stop, on the day she last saw him. In her mind he had not aged, nor changed in any way since then. But twenty years was a long time, and the Wolf she was surreptitiously studying through her binoculars looked prosperous, well-dressed, self-assured and healthy. Not the crippled, drunk, heart-broken man, she had last seen sobbing in her factory. She felt comforted by this, and less disturbed, for some reason.

She turned to Nigel. 'Guess what?' she said with a false laugh. 'Wolf Muller is over there. Take a look.' She passed the binoculars. Nigel recognised him, she knew from the stiffening of his body and the tense look in his eyes.

'Nonsense,' he said. 'Doesn't look a bit like him.'

'The face immediately under the woman with the red hat,' Eleanor persisted. 'Did you see the red hat?'

Reluctantly Nigel looked again. 'I can't see him,' he said flatly.

After that Nigel mopped his brow several times and Eleanor could feel his dismay in every jerky movement he made. She wondered if Nigel expected to receive the beating he had been promised twenty years ago. Absurd really. Just as silly as she had been. Let him sweat, she thought. Why should I console him?

The cold began to bite as Eleanor stood through two hours of speeches, but at last the flame was delivered to figure skater, Sandra Dubravcic, who ran the flaming brand up a great staircase of brilliantly changing colours. The Olympic torch ignited instantly with a roar and Eleanor listened impatiently to Bojan Krizaj, the Yugoslav's main skiing contender, recite the Olympic oath. Then Mika Spiljak, President of Yugoslavia, declared the Games open, and thousands of doves chased balloons into the sky.

It seemed that fate was inexorably pushing them together that day, for Eleanor's queue took ages, and slowly but surely, Wolf was approaching. She could see his fur hat a head taller than the rest of the crowd. She wondered if he had seen her and was pushing a bit to catch up. When she felt a heavy hand on her shoulder it was not unexpected.

'Wolf,' she said.

'Eleanor!'

'Surprise, surprise.'

'It's been a long time. I can't believe it's you,' he said.

Are we going to proceed from one cliché to the next? Is this how one copes with life's disasters – by uttering phrases of the utmost triteness, for comfort and for familiarity? Eleanor wondered. She turned to Nigel, but there was no help from that quarter, she could actually smell his fear.

'So what brings you here?' Wolf said, taking her arm and steering her firmly towards the exit.

'My daughter Jacqui, is competing – in the British team – she's a downhill skier.'

'Strange coincidence. So is my fiancée.' He laughed.

434

That was not the laugh she remembered. It was without mirth and rather cruel. So he has changed, Eleanor thought. 'Your fiancée?' she echoed foolishly. Then she frowned. Not one of them was over the age of twenty-four.

'Yes,' Wolf said, smiling happily.

Eleanor shrugged. 'Good luck to you,' she said.

'You must both come and have a drink with me,' Wolf went on, smiling more pleasantly now. The three of us – together again. Delightful.'

Delightful? Eleanor looked up suspiciously. Surely he could not have forgotten their last, bitter meeting. To Eleanor it seemed only a short while ago.

'I … I can't. I have a prior engagement,' she said, sounding artificial and silly. She saw him smile mockingly. Strange how his face had hardly changed, but his hair was speckled with grey and his nose seemed larger than she remembered. He looked bonier, but very fit and she gained the impression that he was wealthy, although she was not quite sure why this was.

'I must be going,' she said. 'I'm meeting my daughter.' That was a lie. She had the impression Wolf knew it was a lie from the strange look he gave her.

'Tomorrow then.'

'Well, I really don't know.' She paused in her flight towards the taxis and turned slightly. Gundelfinger had taught her never to run away, but to face the trauma head-on. 'Maybe. Well, all right,' she said.

Wolf gave a funny half-bow. There was no trace of his Austrian accent nowadays, yet she still remembered that foreign gesture. 'I can recommend the Café Constance. First class food. Not international, of course, but very good local menus. See you there at eight.' He turned and shook her hand. 'Or would you like me to pick you up? Nigel, too, of course.'

Why Nigel? she wondered. 'All right with you, Nigel?' She turned and was amazed to see that Nigel had turned deathly white. What a coward the man was. He could only nod, wordlessly.

'Good,' Wolf said. 'Good! It will be just like old times.'

'Heaven forbid it should be like old times,' she told Nigel angrily, as they climbed into a taxi.

CHAPTER 63

3 pm, Thursday, February 9, 1984

By all logical processes, this kind of weather should have turned the Games into a fiasco, Rob thought gloomily as he pushed his way through the jubilant Yugoslav crowds towards the outdoor speed skating rink. It was the second day of a howling blizzard, but typical of the attitude of the proud and joyful citizens were the antics of some of the yellow-jacketed workers at the outdoor ice track, who were playing the fool while battling to keep the ice clear of snow. No one was moping or complaining, and the obvious and almost childlike pleasure the Yugoslavs were exhibiting, was catching. I'm in Disneyland, he thought, smiling in spite of the cold.

The women's 1500 metres speed skating trials had been repeatedly cancelled, but a slight easing of snow got the starting gun off in double quick time before another few tons of the white, messy stuff wrecked the ice. All the same, conditions were still so bad, it was almost impossible to see the race unless you were a competitor, Rob reckoned. By now he had pushed to the front of the rink and he was feeling cold and missing his lunch and wondering why he had come, when he could have joined the rest of the squad in a good, hot meal at the Olympic Village after training.

Then he saw the lovely, leggy Karen Enke striding powerfully over the ice and Rob forgot his hunger. It was easy to pick her out, she was a head taller than the others, and she was smiling, lit up with some inner happiness. Because of her height, she'd been slower off at the start; she only got going after the first hundred metres, she was slower at the bends, too, and she could not get into the really low crouch speed skiers favour, but her talent and her long legs won out and Karen finished an exciting first.

Later, when the smiling, jubilant spectators were filing out, Rob heard English voices behind and turned to see Megan, arm-in-arm with a shorter woman, muffled in furs, whom he recognised from press photographs to be Nikola Petrovna, Megan's Russian skater. They were both excitedly discussing the race.

'Hey there, Megan. How're you doing?' Rob tried to be polite, but found it impossible to tear his eyes away from the exquisite beauty of the slight figure clinging to Megan's arm.

As Megan introduced him, Rob suddenly found himself under the suspicious scrutiny of two grey-clad, stern-faced militia, one of whom was female.

'They're being great really,' Megan apologised ten minutes later, when she and Rob were drinking coffee in the Zartra complex overlooking the Kosevo Stadium. Nikki had left to change for her practice session, accompanied by the policewoman. 'For once, Nikki's not complaining,' Megan added. 'The Russian athletes have been giving her the cold shoulder, and she's upset and a bit scared. I hope it won't affect her performance.' She smiled a little uncertainly. 'I don't understand why they're going to so much trouble, but there's no way we can lose these guards. To tell the truth, we tried.' She looked up at him frowning as she remembered Ian's annoyance. 'They want to make sure she goes back the same way she got here.' Megan fell silent, remembering her many attempts to raise Zoran Banski on the telephone, all of which had failed. Then she turned her attention to Rob. 'Aren't you supposed to be training?' she asked.

'Got back at two-thirty. Thought I'd skip lunch and take a look at this Karen Enke everyone's talking about. Glad I did. She's pretty tremendous. I was lucky to meet you here,' he went on. 'Something has been annoying the hell out of me.'

Megan looked up inquiringly at the tone of his voice. Rob was seldom angered by anything.

'I believe you signed up the British team with Magnum Sports,' he said.

'That's right.'

'Well, this is what I overheard.'

He was talking too fast, the words spilling out, and Megan wondered why he should get uptight about an incident that was rather commonplace – in her world, at least. Then she remembered last year when Rob had been so upset at Jacqui's trauma. Hadn't he come over to London during the year? Yes, that's right, he had checked with Maureen for the whereabouts of Jacqui. Suddenly Megan felt sorry for Rob, knowing that Jacqui spent most of her spare time during the World Cup Circuit with Wolf Muller.

'No kidding?' she said when he finished reciting his story. 'Well,' she hesitated. She wasn't sure how frank she could be. 'All Adele's really trying to do is hang on to her job. The company's been taken over fairly recently, by a US finance group. So far it's been operating under the old management team, but everyone's expecting the axe to fall anytime. No one knows who'll go and who'll stay, so they are all jockeying to score. That's pretty tough, you'll admit. Not that I like Adele Loots. To tell the truth, she can be pretty sneaky at times.'

'Who took them over?' Rob asked.

'Ah! That was the big questionmark. Even Adele didn't know. For some reason, the new owners were trying to keep it confidential, so I asked ISA's legal department in the States to check around. I'd thought of pushing for more sponsorship, but I had to know who I was dealing with. Anyway the outcome was rather startling so I've finally decided to lay off that company for a while.'

'Come on, Megan. Stop stringing it out,' Rob said, smiling to take the rudeness out of his words. 'You've got a hungry, tired man here.'

'Okay,' she smiled sympathetically. 'Magnum Sports were taken over by the First Industrial Finance Company, who are totally owned by Gifford International, who, in turn, are a subsidiary company of Mountain Oil Inc. Chairman, Wolf Muller. And I guess you know of Wolf Muller,' she said with a wry smile, 'since he's been master-minding Jacqui's coaching, although I haven't been able to work out his angle as yet.'

Megan's triumphant smile faded in the face of Rob's misery. He grimaced with disgust, climbed slowly off the bar stool, and fumbled in his pocket.

'Coffee's on ISA,' Megan said quickly.

'Thanks,' Rob mumbled. 'I have a score to settle with that bastard. Now I can beat him up for something, instead of nothing.'

'Oh hell,' Megan murmured as Rob left hurriedly. 'Perhaps I

should have kept quiet. 'Give him one for me, Rob,' she whispered, as she went to watch Nikki's practice.

7 pm, Thursday, February 9th, 1984

The restaurant was blatantly ostentatious, with elaborate crystal chandeliers, tapestries on the walls and heavy gilt candelabra. The ornate decor was contrary to the Slavs' prosaic taste, and Eleanor gained the impression that the Café Constance had been hastily created to make rich Westerners feel at home. She smiled inwardly; the Slavs would do anything to please the West. Even the handsome, tall waiter in his green velvet jacket and pin-striped trousers, who looked like a wrestler, was doing his unsuccessful best to appear obsequious, which was probably the way he imagined waiters behaved in the West. Non-alignment was all very well, but they needed dollars to make it work.

Eleanor sat at the table booked by Wolf, sipping the excellent *Travarica*, a high-octane plum brandy which they supplied as an *aperitif* before every meal. It was an acquired taste, she decided, and she had acquired it. She was feeling pleased that she had been brave enough to come, and confident that this evening's conversation would heal the pain of old wounds and exorcise the ghost which Gundelfinger's meddling had evoked. The room was buzzing with conversation in a dozen different tongues and the conversation was not all about sport, although she heard the names Haemaelainen and Enke mentioned several times, but was mainly about the amazingly low prices of the leather goods and antique jewellery that could be found in the Turkish quarter. 'Really for nothing,' she heard the shrill, clipped accent of a British girl at a neighbouring table.

God, but she was hungry. She had missed lunch to watch Haemaelainen's brilliant win of the women's ten kilometre cross country competition held in blizzard conditions at Veliko Polje, and after that she had driven to Trebević to see the first heats of the men's *luge*, which had frightened her nearly to death. Things could be worse, she had thought at the time. Jacqui might have chosen *luge*.

She glanced at her watch. Both Nigel and Wolf were late and she wondered if she could order a roll, and then decided that it might be more polite not to.

At that moment she felt a hand on her shoulder. 'Am I late?' Wolf pulled back his chair and sat down. She glanced up, flushed and looked away again. It was odd to think that once she had loved and bedded this good-looking man who was both familiar and strange, all at the same time. His eyes had not changed a bit, she thought. They were still the same deep blue serious eyes she remembered so well, but his skin was coarser, not old looking, and he seemed broader. After a couple of veiled glances she decided that he went regularly to a gym and trained with weights. On the whole, she thought, he had weathered better than she, and God knows she had tried everything.

'Where's Nigel?' he asked impatiently.

'He's never on time,' she said slowly. She glanced nervously around, realising that she had nothing at all to say to this man. When Nigel suddenly appeared in the doorway, she raised her hand and signalled gaily with her fingers. Nigel was looking apprehensive, and she wished he could put on a better show.

The waiter arrived promptly and handed round embossed leather menus printed in four languages, and for a while they were silently engrossed in the absurd translations.

Eleanor ordered, *skamplignje*, followed by *lubatac*, a local fish she had never tried and *sarma*, which, translated read: spiced, minced lamb parcelled in vine leaves, and tried to make helpful suggestions for Nigel and his delicate stomach. Eventually the waiter departed leaving Eleanor to wonder why Wolf had asked for a magnum of champagne to be brought to the table later. In the meantime he had ordered a bottle of *Samotok*, a locally-made, mellow white wine.

There was a long and painful silence, and Nigel cleared his throat several times.

'We ought to have a plenty to talk about Eleanor,' Wolf said eventually, looking grave and slightly arrogant. 'We're in the same line of business. I don't know if you heard that I took over Magnum Sports recently.'

Eleanor felt startled and showed it. She took a gulp of wine and then paused to sip more gently. 'This is really excellent,' she said. 'Here's to Magnum Sports.'

'I suppose in a way, you might call us competitors,' Wolf went on. 'Although to tell the truth, most of my interests are in oil nowadays.'

440

'I'm very glad ... ' Eleanor searched for the right words, 'that you have prospered.'

'Of course it wasn't easy to get going after the crippling blow you dealt me.'

Eleanor stared straight at him, but Wolf was innocently eating his *musule*. She would allow him one moan, she decided, and this was it.

The first course arrived and Eleanor was glad to have something to do besides talking. She was hungry, she remembered, and the scampi was excellent. 'This is about the best I've tasted,' she said and broke off as she noticed Nigel scowling at her.

'Well, the main thing is, you survived,' she said crisply, turning to Wolf. 'And I'm glad,' she added generously.

'I would have thought you'd hardly welcome the competition.'

Eleanor snorted with genuine mirth. 'Magnum are not our competitors. I mean, I don't wish to appear disparaging, but their sales are a tenth of Vanguard's in hardware, while in clothing they've hardly begun. Still, they make a good ski,' she added placatingly.

'Just wait,' Wolf went on with an agreeable smile. 'I have big plans for Magnum. I bought the company for a song. Did you know they were in financial difficulties? Labour problems mainly,' He turned and gazed at her, his long blond eyelashes almost shading his eyes and Eleanor remembered how she had loved this secretive look of his, but today there was something menacing about his expression and this made her feel sad.

'I'm shifting manufacture to the Far East, renting out part of the Scottish plant and keeping the rest as an office for sales and accounts.'

She nodded politely and turned her attention to her food. As Wolf proceeded to bore her with his plans for sponsorship and expansion, she was reminded of the old Wolf in Denver, and his grandiose schemes which had so often failed.

The waiter came and left, and Eleanor dug her fork into her fish and prodded it tentatively.

'You weren't listening, Eleanor. What were you thinking about?'

Frowning blue eyes; lips set into a tight line; he was becoming more familiar every minute. 'I was remembering the

441

pickling plant,' she said. 'You were always talking like this, but things didn't often turn out as you had imagined. I was remembering the chutney. The chutney saved us.'

'I've learned a lot since then,' Wolf said with a brief laugh. 'As a matter of fact,' he went on in a bantering tone of voice, 'I'm in the throes of taking over another, much larger sports company. I intend to merge them both. Magnum will soon be one of the world's leaders.'

Eleanor's heart lurched and her stomach knotted with panic. Surely not? Surely he wasn't talking about her company. It couldn't be Wolf. She laid down her fork and glanced wildly at Nigel, but he was staring hard at his plate and would not look into her eyes. Never Wolf, she thought desperately. He would not side with Nigel. He had never liked Nigel. Unless, of course ...

She turned to Wolf and saw that his face was alight with amusement. To Eleanor's horror she felt her eyes burning and then one great tear rolled down her cheek, tickling as it went, and splashed on her fish. There was no point in trying to ignore it, she knew that Wolf had seen. She fumbled in her bag for a tissue and dabbed her eyes.

'I was warned that the enemy would be coming out of the woodwork soon,' she said bitterly. 'You don't look like a woodworm, Wolf.'

'You don't look like a cheat,' Wolf said quietly.

'Don't you like your fish, Madam?' the waiter asked urgently, startling her. 'It's very good. Taste it!' Perhaps he was a student, or a labourer. Half of Yugoslavia seemed to be helping out here.

'I love it,' she said tonelessly. God damn Wolf and Nigel. She'd eat every last bit of it. She set to, with renewed vigour, picking each morsel of flesh from the bones. The waiter was right, it was delicious. 'I'd love some more wine,' she said pointedly to Wolf, and he called for the wine waiter, but a voice inside was saying: Careful Eleanor, you haven't won yet. You'll need all your wits to bluff your way through this.

The wine list arrived and Wolf studied it thoughtfully. 'Now, if I remember, Eleanor, you liked something a little drier than the *Samotok*. Perhaps some red, to go with your *sarma*.' Finally he ordered a local equivalent of *St-Julien Bordeaux* saying, 'I seem to recall that was your favourite.'

'I'm surprised you remember,' she said uneasily.

'Eleanor, I have a remarkably good memory – for some things. You might say – like the proverbial elephant – I never forget.'

Eleanor picked up her glass, sipped gently and laid it down again. Glancing at Nigel, she noticed that his brow was beaded with moisture and he was fidgeting nervously. He would not meet her eyes, but instead stared intently at the reproductions on the wall. Then he took out his handkerchief and mopped his brow.

'I had no idea you were interested in art, Nigel,' Eleanor said scathingly. 'Quite a good reproduction of Barye's *Stags* don't you think. But perhaps the green is overplayed – a problem with reproductions – and of course the lighting doesn't do it justice.'

Nigel mumbled unhappily and to her surprise, she noticed Wolf smiling quietly to himself. He seemed amused. Good! Let's see how much he's enjoying himself by the end of the evening, she promised herself.

'You were telling me about your expansion plans,' she said, seizing the initiative, 'and your takeover bid. Of course, you always were a big talker. I, too, have a good memory, you see. With you, reality was always a little hazy. Tell me, are the oil companies purchased yet, or still in the pipeline?'

'Ha, ha! Very funny.' Wolf was grinning approvingly. 'She hasn't quite lost her touch, Nigel.' For the first time he stared long and hard at Nigel, who looked up flushing horribly.

'Quite, quite,' Nigel said, looking relieved as the fish plates were cleared away.

'I've been seeing a great deal of you and Vanguard in the press lately. Quite honestly, Eleanor, I was amazed you insisted on hanging on as chairman. Youth! That's the order of the day. You should have coaxed in some new blood. You and Nigel – well, you're just a bit *passé*. Wouldn't you say so?'

Nigel looked shocked, 'Come on now, Wolf, we're none of us pushing retirement age. Good for another few decades.' His eyes met Wolf's steel-like gaze and for a moment Nigel seemed genuinely shaken.

Watching them, Eleanor felt puzzled. A strange alliance from which Nigel was unlikely to prosper.

'There's something atavistic about *homo sapiens* obsession

with sport,' Wolf was saying. 'A primitive lust for the hunt – it's in all of us. Did you know that in many African tribes, their chiefs were obliged to commit suicide when their first grey hairs appeared. You see the chief symbolised the vitality of the tribe. The Zulus were one of them. Rather amusing, I thought, but it explains shareholders' unease with ageing management. Particularly ageing female management. That sort of thing makes a takeover bid very much simpler.'

Eleanor gritted her teeth and forced herself to keep quiet.

'Of course, it's a little different for men,' Wolf went on smiling happily. He broke off as the waiter brought their main dishes and a magnum of champagne. Wolf picked up his glass to taste it. 'Superb,' he purred. Turning to Eleanor, he said: 'To tell the truth I ordered champagne for a double celebration. I'm getting engaged shortly, to a lovely young girl. She reminds me of you, Eleanor, in your heyday, although it's hard to see the resemblance nowadays.'

Eleanor flinched. She no longer had to pretend she was upset, because she really was. She could not blame Wolf for harbouring so much hatred. After all, that had been her intention. She had wanted him to feel as cheated and as abandoned as she had felt, all those years ago. But somehow, over years, her hatred had changed to grief and guilt. The business had never compensated her for the loss of Wolf, but at least she had known that he was suffering as much as she was. So much hate, she thought, on both sides, and so unnecessary. How can I bear it, she thought. She wanted to run away, but she could not leave now, there would never be another opportunity to convince Wolf of her invincibility. She was the winner, she had to remind herself, although she felt like the loser.

She shot a sly peep at Nigel and saw that he was smiling to himself, while Wolf was obviously having the time of his life. He lifted his glass for a toast.

'Here's to youth,' Eleanor said quickly, cutting in on him. 'I'm glad you had the sense to pick someone young, at last. Isobel was far too old for you. But of course, she was well enough endowed to satisfy the most primitive fecund longings.'

A glass fell and shattered somewhere. It seemed very far away. She hardly noticed the waiter rushing to mop the champagne from the table and pick up the pieces. Only she and Wolf existed – the rest was superfluous. Wolf's eyes were gazing at her with horror and shocked recognition. 'Did she ever marry you after you lost the company?' she went on sweetly. 'She told me that you were selling out in order to rid yourself of an onerous marriage and business partnership.'

She felt a hand on her shoulder and, looking up, saw Nigel standing there. 'I'll leave you two to your memories,' he said pompously.

'Sit down, Nigel,' Wolf snarled.

Dignity fled and Nigel crumpled into his chair.

'I had no idea you'd met Isobel,' Wolf's voice was husky, his eyes looked bewildered now and the sweat on his forehead glistened in the candlelight.

Ah, Eleanor thought. Now we're evening the score. All the same, she wished she had not told him about Isobel. 'There's no point in dwelling on the past,' she said briskly. 'It was a hundred years ago, and I was young, as you mentioned, and desperately in love with my husband.'

'Very desperately,' Wolf agreed solemnly, 'as later events proved.'

'For goodness sake, you two,' Nigel cut in on them in a fit of temper. 'I was under the impression this was to be a business meeting.'

'Were you?' Eleanor said brightly, trying to look surprised. 'Why would you think Wolf and I would have a business meeting?'

'Nigel, why don't you shut up?' Wolf said rudely.

Nigel blanched and subsided into silence.

'I don't know why Isobel should be relevant after all this time,' Wolf said, regaining his poise. 'We were talking about the takeover bid – for Vanguard.'

'Were we? I knew nothing about it. Rather a lot of bad publicity, I thought. At the time it upset me no end and then it stopped – just like that. You see there was never any danger, Wolf. Between Nigel's and my own share holdings we have the majority,' she bluffed. 'Quite honestly, I could never work out what it was all about?'

'Let me enlighten you, Eleanor. It was about treachery, and underhand business dealings and the morality of revenge.'

This is it, she thought, smiling falsely and bravely.

'Let's drink to the future,' Wolf went on, grinning savagely. 'To your happy retirement, Eleanor. To make the matter even clearer – *you're sacked*!'

'Sacked?' she queried. 'I don't understand.'

'It's quite simple. I hold the controlling interest in Vanguard. I'll make you an offer for your shares. It will be about as good as the offer you made me. Or you can hang on to them, if you prefer. They won't be worth all that much in the future, though. I have plans for Vanguard you wouldn't believe.'

'Maybe I would,' she said sharply. 'But first I'd like to see proof of your ownership.' She wondered why she could not stop shaking. Anyone would think I had lost, she thought bitterly. And would have, if it weren't for my daughter and Ian Mackintosh.

Wolf ignored her. 'Here's to you, Nigel, the new managing director.'

She glanced at Nigel inquiringly.

'Eleanor,' Nigel began, with a big brotherly expression on his face, 'you may be feeling a little hurt, but I can assure you, I made the right decision. Quite frankly you never did appreciate my management ideas, nor my marketing flair. Lately, I'm sorry to tell you, you've lost your verve.'

Wolf cut in on him. 'I had thirty-eight per cent of your stock until recently, but with the acquisition of the NFF Trust's five – very smart of you to snaffle half from under my nose – and Nigel's proxy I control fifty-one per cent of Vanguard's equity.'

Only fifty-one per cent! Eleanor tried not to gasp with pleasure. Less Nigel's eight left Wolf a balance of forty-three. The vital statistics were overwhelmingly in her favour. She knew now that she was absolutely safe. She glowered at Nigel, wondering how long it would be before he sensed deception.

'Hang on a minute, Wolf. That's not quite the whole picture,' Nigel said hurriedly. 'You had my proxy, until you purchased my shares outright, ten days ago. NFF were going to give their proxy to the highest bidder – remember? So why did you say you purchased half of NFF's holding? I don't understand … ' His eyes began to register alarm.

'What the hell are you talking about, Nigel?'

'Wolf, you know perfectly well your London lawyer brought me your bank guaranteed cheque, and I handed him my share certificates,' – his voice tailed off lamely – 'as we arranged on the telephone.'

There was a long silence. Unexpectedly Wolf laughed. 'I've got to hand it to you, Eleanor,' Wolf said. 'You haven't lost your touch.'

'Will someone tell me what on earth is going on?' Nigel said. He grabbed his glass and drained it at a gulp.

'Nigel,' Eleanor said quietly. 'I found out about you and purchased your shares. The script is with my lawyer.'

'How much did the bastard get?' Wolf growled.

'Sixteen million.'

'My way, he'd have got fuck all and so would you.'

'This champagne is too good to waste,' Eleanor said, picking up her glass. 'Here's to revenge. May it always be as sweet as mine was, twenty years ago, Wolf. Pity yours lost out.'

Nigel stood up shakily, looking like a corpse. 'I'll leave you two to scrap about who's paying the bill,' he said. 'I'm leaving.'

'Oh Nigel,' Eleanor called out sweetly.

'I resign, Eleanor,' he said quickly.

Eleanor looked archly at Wolf. 'I'm surprised at your choice of business partner,' she said.

'I knew he'd sell you short for cash and power, just as he sold me short years ago. When I approached him he jumped at the chance of being Chairman. He was a fool to trust me. First him, then you! That was the plan. I aimed to ruin both of you. There's another round coming up,' Wolf told her gloomily, as Nigel staggered out. 'Let's hope you manage to keep your cool.'

He was about to stand up when a hefty push knocked him back into his chair.

Eleanor looked up in amazement as a tall athletic-looking young man gripped Wolf's shoulder hard, and tipped the contents of a full bottle of champagne over his head. 'Thrills and spills,' the young man was saying. 'Here's a taste of your own medicine.'

The room was very quiet, the hum of conversation had ceased as every face turned towards Wolf, watching expectantly. Wolf looked dazed, as if he could not believe what was happening.

Then his hand snapped up grabbing the young man's arm. 'Friend of yours?' he asked, looking deceptively mild.

'I've never seen him before,' Eleanor said, 'but he's a friend of mine.'

Her words were lost in the confusion. The champagne-bottle

was hurled out of Rob's hand, and landed amongst the tables. Then Wolf punched Rob hard twice, in the jaw and the chest.

Rob hardly noticed. He lunged back and moments later the two of them were staggering across the crowded floor, exchanging blow for blow. The young man seemed to be winning.

By the time six burly waiters had managed to separate them, blood was pouring from Wolf's nose, his eye was badly bruised, and he looked groggy and puzzled.

'You're right, Wolf,' Eleanor said, helping him back to the table. 'Youth counts.'

'All right,' Rob said, struggling in the grip of the waiters. 'I'll behave. Let me go.'

'He's my son,' Eleanor said. 'Merely a family quarrel. I'll settle for the damage.' The waiters stepped back uneasily. Rob was pale and still angry, but he sat next to Eleanor, without looking at her, as two uniformed policemen walked into the room.

Wolf took out a handkerchief and held it to his nose. 'What the hell was all that about?' he growled. 'Or perhaps you'd like to reserve your excuses for the court case?'

'That will be a pleasure,' Rob said. 'I'll be able to tell them how Magnum Sports runs its athletic teams. How their PRO told the girls to have accidents to improve television viewership. How's that for press headlines? Let me tell you this,' he went on furiously. 'If Jacqui so much as grazes her knee, I'm gonna punch your head off. Next time there won't be any waiters to hold me back.'

'So you're Rob Scott,' Wolf said, standing up unsteadily. 'A bad loser, if you don't mind me saying so.' He grinned lopsidedly and handed his credit card to the manager. 'Charge for the meal and the damages,' he said. 'Be seeing you, Eleanor.'

'What was he talking about – loser?' Eleanor said, laying one hand on Rob's arm. Then she laughed. 'The conceit of him. Don't worry, you definitely won the fight. He was quite groggy – didn't you notice? If that's what he said to the British team, he deserves all you gave him.'

She chuckled happily and did her best to charm Jacqui's young man. She wondered why he seemed so unhappy as he told her about his home and his factory. Eventually she sent him to call a taxi and show her into it. So this was one of the young men her daughter loved. She wondered who the other man was. He'd have to be pretty terrific to beat Rob Scott, she decided.

CHAPTER 64

Friday, Febuary 10, 1984

It was the third day of the Olympics and the blizzard that had lashed Sarajevo unmercifully since the opening of the Games, showed no sign of abating. Temperatures had plummeted, snow ploughs were working round the clock and visibility was reduced to a few metres.

Megan had hired a car, and driven Nikki to Mount Yahorina. Twice she had skidded into snowdrifts, but Nikki's obliging guards had parked and pushed her car back on the road. They arrived before nine am, anxious to find a good position near the last gate, but conditions were appalling. When they heard that the race was cancelled, Megan felt relieved and drove on through the snowstorm, to Trebević where the bobsleigh and *luge* events were to take place and where she knew she would find Ian.

Nikki's enthusiasm for bobsleigh was nil, so Megan left her at the nearest hotel, together with her guards.

Oblivious to the weather, Ian was excitedly watching the early, two-man bobsleigh trials. It was the first time Megan had been to Trebević and she felt a thrill of fear as she examined the steep concrete structures, lined with snow and ice and tipped at an insanely dangerous angle down the mountainside.

She walked up hundreds of slippery steps that followed the route of the track and eventually found Ian near the starting point. He was in a huddle with some of the American bobsleigh technicians. The cold never seemed to worry him; his sheepskin jacket was hanging open over his sweater, and his fur hat was pushed up on the back of his head as his blue eyes glowed with amusement. He looked tanned and healthy and overflowing with vitality. Ian was cracking jokes with the Americans as he watched the antics of the Russian team, trying to transport

450

their new and top secret bobsleigh from the van to the starting hangar, without allowing close inspection by rival teams. Bobsleighers and technicians alike were crowding around their craft hoping to shield it from curious rivals and the press photographers. Megan could only see flashes of red from the long bullet-shaped contraption as it passed.

'The Soviet's secret weapon,' Ian told her without looking round. He clicked his camera each time a part became visible. When the bobsleigh was hustled out of sight he turned, grinning, and hugged her close to him as he introduced her to the team. The Western teams were behaving like schoolboys, laughing and jeering at the Russians and their 'cigarski' as they called the Soviet's bobsleigh but there was an envious glint in their eyes.

'Is it special?' Megan wanted to know.

'What the Russians are trying to do,' Ian explained, 'is copy Formula One racing cars of the late sixties. Consequently, they have stability problems, just as those earlier racing cars did. Last year in Winterberg, they rolled several times and later, at Cortina, they had to withdraw after a couple of bad smashes. Now there's rumoured to be a mysterious knuckle joint in the suspension which will make their craft stay on the track. We'll see!' He grinned to show that it was all in fun, but Megan could see that the teams took their sport very seriously indeed and the Americans were looking gloomy.

'Once the Russians get their design snags ironed out, they'll probably beat the world,' a reporter told her. 'That's why they've bolted on the fins and front wings. You'll see when they come past – if you're quick enough.'

'Where's Nikki?' Ian asked casually.

'I left her at that restaurant by the river with the unpronounceable name, guzzling Russian food.'

'The Vidikovac?'

'That's it. They have a Russian *smörgasbord* and she's tucking in – groaning with pleasure, last time I saw her.' She gestured towards the snow-covered park where the restaurant stood on a hilly slope overlooking the city of Sarajevo and outlying suburbs.

'With her guards?'

'Of course, with her guards. She can't avoid them.' Megan looked up sharply, and saw Ian frowning and once again she had the impression that Ian was worried about Nikki, although, when she questioned him, he denied this.

'A strange sort of sport,' Megan was thinking as she watched the track. Every few minutes a bobsleigh would hurtle past at over 160 kilometres an hour with the crew leaning from side to side at such exaggerated angles, it seemed that their heads must surely smash against the ice-covered cement banks. Megan, decided that bobsleighing had very little to do with human endeavour and a great deal to do with technical expertise. It did not appeal to her, she was far too frightened for the crews, and she was beginning to wish she had not come when she heard a quiet voice behind her.

'Megan Carroll?'

Megan had hardly noticed the short, squat man edging through the crowd towards her, until he spoke.

'So I find you at last. I must talk to you privately somewhere.'

The familiar accent and broken English brought a vivid recall of her hurried flight from Sarajevo a year ago and her traumatic interview in the airport lounge.

It was Zoran Banski, but he looked older; his face was thinner and the skin dropped in sad folds around his jowls. He's not well, she thought, and remembering that he was Michel's uncle, as well as head of the security police, she smiled warmly.

'Miss Carroll, I have been waiting for your fiancé, Commander Mackintosh, to look the other way.' He spread his hands in a gesture that might be imploring her forgiveness for his deceit, or his dismay at her choice of a fiancé, but either way, it was a friendly gesture, and his brown eyes shone with warmth and humility, reminding Megan of a lost dog.

'Tell him you are going to the toilet, please, and walk slowly down the steps towards the First Aid Depot. I will find you there. The information I wish to give you, concerns the safety of your friend, Nikola Petrovna. She is your friend, quite apart from your client, is that not so?'

'Yes.' Megan breathed in a deep, sharp gasp of air. She gained the distinct impression that the information would not be welcome. She did not know why that was, perhaps it had something to do with the compassionate glint in his eyes, or his apologetic manner.

'Good. Michel said I could trust you.'

'Michel? Is he here? I haven't seen him?'

'No. He telephoned.'

Nikki will be furious, Megan thought as Banski pushed back through the crowd. She had been grumbling about Michel's delayed arrival. There was a roar and a gasp from the crowd as another craft came hurtling down the slope.

Banski was slumped on a bench, smoking a cigarette. He smiled dismally and offered her one.

'No thanks.'

'Neither should I,' he said mournfully, 'But there are times when I lose my will power, when the pressure builds up – like now. I will be glad when the Games are over.' He coughed noisily and wiped his mouth with the back of his hand. 'Well, now, this is not a very pleasant business, Miss Carroll. No one likes to hear bad news about the people that they love.'

Love? Megan wondered. But there was no time for idle conjecture, for Banski was off, speaking quickly and softly with that impression of veiled strength which had so intimidated her a year ago. The same strange hesitation as he searched for words, the sudden rush of speech when he found them.

'Her real name is not Nikola Petrovna,' he was saying, 'but Nikola Petrovna Kuznetsovna. Petrovna was her mother's maiden name, and Nikola dropped her patronym for her skating, perhaps because she found it inconvenient, or intimidating. Does Kuznetsov mean anything to you?'

'It sounds familiar ... She broke off, frowning and tried to remember where she had heard the name before. What was it Ian had said a year ago in the Café Constance? *She'll never be permitted to leave the Soviet bloc because of her father's politics.* 'I sort of knew that Nikki's father was a well-known dissident,' she began cautiously, 'I guess it explains a lot.'

Banski laughed softly. 'Is that what Ian told you? On the contrary, my dear. Nikki's father was one of the most powerful men in Russia. I use the past tense, because Nikki's defection ruined his political career. That is why she was persuaded to defect. Why else should she have been transported to the West by a British motor boat, submarine and helicopter? It was an Admiralty ploy right from the word go.'

'But that's not what they told me,' she reminded herself.

'Did you ever wonder why Nikki was given such magnificent treatment in the West – or why they wanted her?' he went on.

453

A gentle hand was placed placatingly on her sleeve.

'It was because of the publicity,' Megan explained as if to a child. 'Ian told me everything, when we became engaged. He was sent to organise her defection because of the publicity ... it's good for Western morale, and by the same token bad for Russian morale when a top performer defects to the West.' It sounded a bit weak, even to Megan. She couldn't remember whom she was quoting: Ian, or that strange guy at the Foreign Office with the baby face and the shrewd eyes?

'And did you really believe that, Miss Carroll?'

'Is there some reason why I should not?' Megan asked coldly, but a voice inside her was shrieking. You're damned right – I never believed it.

'Sergei Stephan Kuznetsov,' he began wearily. 'The bright, ruthless, ambitious anti-West politician, tipped by experts as the next leader of the Communist Party, was Nikki's father.'

Megan gasped. 'Nikki never mentioned her father ... ' she said after a while. She sat silently contemplating the ramifications of this information. She had a vivid image of Nikki's laughing eyes, and her joy this morning at discovering the Russian food.

'It had to look right. The world's sportsmen and women are politician's natural prey. And why? Because they command the public's attention. The point was, it had to look as if she did it all herself – for ambition – for greed – for freedom, as she was coached to say in the lovely Kent cottage, where they kept her for two weeks before releasing her into your care. Her greed for the good things in life were well-publicised in press reports – ah yes, it was all magnificently handled.'

He broke off abruptly and glanced at his watch. 'I don't want to keep you too long,' he murmured, 'but there are things you must know – she must know ... '

'I remember something,' Megan interrupted him. 'I remember seeing something on television: *The rise and fall of Comrade Sergei Stephan Kuznetsov.* Where is he now – Nikki's father?' she asked.

'He's dead. I don't think Nikki knows. I'm afraid you'll have to tell her this bad news. The matter has not been released to the public yet. Kuznetsov became ill recently and was confined to a sanitorium, where no doubt his eventual death by heart attack was hastened. His supporters blamed him for their failure to gain control. 'You see, Nikola's defection, plus constant publicity about her lifestyle, detracted from her father's credibility and gave his biggest rival the slight edge he needed to oust Kuznetsov from power. Need I tell you that his rival is comparatively pro-West and willing to co-operate on any number of important matters, particularly defence. Kuznetsov was the only man in Russia who believed his daughter's defection was a brilliantly planned and executed coup by the West to bring about his downfall.

'The whole idea emanated from Mackintosh, I'm told. He did his job remarkably well. A man you can feel proud of, my dear. He'll get another medal when this is over.'

The relentless, persuasive voice seemed like a hammer knocking at her head as, blow by blow, she learned of Ian's deceit and of her own contrived connivance in Nikki's manipulation.

Megan glanced around wildly, longing to see Ian, hoping that Banski had nothing new to add. Yet, she had a disturbing premonition that the story was far from finished. Why was Ian guarding Nikki again? *Why was he here?* She could feel fear sprouting from a bud of conjecture in her stomach to a monster plant that surged into her bloodstream, moistened her hands and feet, gnawed at her stomach and trembled in her bowels.

'Nikki has become useful again. If she wins a medal the Soviets are prepared to exchange her for five British jounalists captured last year in rebel territory in Afghanistan and accused of spying.'

'You're lying!' Megan gave a little cry and subsided into silence.

'My nephew, Michel, is a clever boy. I used to think he would be on my staff, but no, he had to go to the West, to be a journalist. He has just returned from Washington where he has excellent contacts.

'Of course, Nikki's return won't help her father, since he is dead, but she will be forced to make some anti-West statements and tell the world she feels happier and freer in Russia. Afterwards, who knows what will happen to her? The Soviets have always been tough on defectors.'

'I don't believe you,' Megan said firmly. 'Ian would never ... never ... ' To her grief, shame was added. She broke off and shuddered.

Banski ignored her. 'It is planned that after the ice skating exhibitions on Sunday morning, Nikki is to be drugged and shipped home, together with the rest of the Russian team. Presumably they have some sort of timing to ensure the safety of the British journalists.'

'No ... No ... ' As Megan's voice rang out loudly, Banski's fingers dug into her arm.

'But, my dear, Miss Carroll, don't be so afraid. It is precisely for this reason that she is being guarded day and night. I, Zoran Banski, have personally guaranteed the safety of every competitor in our city. This type of political hooliganism cannot be allowed to take place on Yugoslav soil.' He stood up and thrust his hands into his pockets. 'I have a private plane standing by to take Nikki to Belgrade and from there she will be escorted onto an aircraft, together with you, Miss Carroll. Once she is back in Paris, Michel will guarantee her safety. He has obtained false papers for Nikki and he intends to hide her for a year, until the British authorities give some guarantee of her safety and her long-promised passport. We are assuming that you will help us there. Michel is hoping that she will marry him, because then no one could believe that she had returned to Russia willingly. So Ian's project would be quietly dropped.'

Megan's mind was in a turmoil. What else could she do? Surely Ian could not be a party to this monstrously inhuman plan?

'Trust me,' Banski said. 'Ian has never been frank with you, my dear. Not once.' He seemed to be reading her thoughts. 'Remember that until Saturday Nikki is perfectly safe. The Russians want that medal almost as badly as Nikki does. Now it's up to you – you must persuade Nikki to give up her dreams; exchange fame for life and liberty. She must return to France before the trials.'

He turned away and then halted. 'You still have eight days,' he said.

Nikki was in the dining room, laughing uproariously while trying to give some of the members of the Canadian ice hockey team Cossack dancing lessons. The hotel had chosen Russian folk music as a suitable background for their *smorgasbord*. It was quite a party, perhaps all the more so because there was no sign of any Russians.

Megan managed to corner Nikki at last. 'We must go,' she said. 'I have to talk to you.'

'Oh,' Nikki pouted and shook her head. 'You have no capacity for having fun, Megan. Don't be a ... what is that word ... ?'

'Spoilsport!' One of the boys quickly obliged and Megan flushed angrily as she took Nikki's arm.

'And now, my dear Megan, what is it that has made you so grumpy?' Nikki said laughingly as they drove out of the car park and took the road to Sarajevo.

Was it true? Megan agonised. Was Banski lying? Or perhaps Michel had been misinformed. Could the man she loved so desperately, really be this unscrupulous? She must tell Nikki everything, but she hardly knew how to begin. 'Nikki, tell me the truth,' Megan blurted out after a long silence. 'Is your name really Nikola Petrovna Kuznetsovna?'

Nikki turned pale. Then she nodded. 'Yes, but I have dropped the last name. This is what they told me to do – they say it is such a ... mouthful ... ' she giggled, 'for Westerners.'

Megan skidded, drove to the side of the road and parked. She noticed that her hands were shaking and she pushed them into her pockets.

'They said ... ? Of course, it's always *they*,' she retorted bitterly. 'Nikki, listen to me. This time you must tell me who *they* are.'

Nikki sat glowering at her – her face a mask of suspicion and secrecy.

'Nikki, help me. You must understand that I'm just as involved as you are.'

Nikki glanced at her in surprise, noting her white face and eyes bright with unshed tears. 'Ian?' she whispered.

'I never knew – not for sure,' she added hastily. 'The people who helped me to defect were all people I did not know. Listen to me Megan, it was like this ... '

She explained about the whispered voices, the note in her locker, the accident which put her in the team at the last minute, the TV team in Sarajevo, all of whom spoke Russian and how they drove her rapidly to the coast where a launch met with a submarine at sea, and afterwards a helicopter which flew her to the house in Kent. Everyone was so kind, everyone spoke Russian, but she never saw one of them again. 'Ian was never there,' she added.

'Not even in Kent?' Megan pressed her.

'Just one very kind lady, who helped me with English, did my hair, taught me some useful things, like how to order in a restaurant, and so on. "A short course in being Western ..." ' She giggled again. 'And then there was you – and Maureen.'

'Did you know why they wanted you to defect?' Megan pressed on mercilessly. There was that look again. That look of monumental obstinacy. Nikki was not going to let go of her guilty secret without a struggle.

'*Da, da*, because I will win ...'

'No, Nikki, because your father had to be discredited, because he was violently anti-West and tipped to head the Communist Party. You were used and so was I. All your publicity – your debut at Earl's Court, your television interviews, even your film – it was for the publicity. That's all. It wasn't to help you, or to help me, but to topple Kuznetsov, your father.'

And for that reason I was used and helped, befriended and bedded and I fell in love. Good grief! I had to go and fall in love.

'Nikki, just for once stop kidding yourself. Deep inside you always knew this. Didn't you?' she persisted as Nikki gazed furiously out of the window.

'Good grief, Nikki, what do I have to say to make you face facts?' she cried out after ten more minutes of fruitless questioning.

She sighed. She was playing this wrong. Maybe the truth would get through to her. She began to relate word for word, what Banski had told her and when she reached the part about Kuznetsov's death, she did not falter. Nikki, you must understand, it was Ian all the time. He arranged your defection, your publicity, everything, he was in charge of the operation and now he's going to exchange you for some British journalists. You are to be sent back to Russia ... to face God knows what ...' She broke off and made a conscious effort not to cry.

'I never suspected Ian,' Nikki began in a small voice, until that day ... you remember ... the guards were removed ... Ian no longer wanted to help with my career ... of course I had heard the news in English. Only a small mention, but enough ... all those things put together. You see, I could no

458

longer pretend to myself.' She sat in silence for a while watching the dusk spread quickly over the distant city until it was lost in misty shrouds.

'It was even more hurtful, because it was Ian,' she went on in a quiet voice. 'I even suspected you, too, dear Megan. Now I can see how wrong I was.

'For a while I wished to be dead. But afterwards I saw things differently. I thought – everyone's been using me for their own purpose – but what about me? What about Nikola Petrovna? What is it that Nikola wants? That terrible week when I lay in hospital, I decided to win. To show them all ... the Russians and the West ... that I am not just a pawn in their war games. I am the world's best. That I deserved this chance to prove it.'

'And your father?'

'I hated my father,' she said flatly.

She would hang on to her hate, Megan thought sadly. It was her only defence, but there must have been a thread, however nebulous, that caused her to attempt suicide when her father's career ended because of the scandal of her defection.

Suddenly Megan understood the reason for Nikki's relentless training, and her newfound discipline and determination.

'Nikki, listen to me,' Megan said urgently, 'you and I are returning to the hotel to pack. We are taking a private jet to Belgrade, and from there we'll catch the evening flight to Paris. Michel will be waiting for you with forged papers. You will be safe with Michel. Now don't argue. Just do as I say.'

'Of course, that is impossible,' Nikki turned towards Megan looking panic-stricken. 'Weren't you listening to me at all?'

Megan sighed. She leaned forward and turned the ignition key, but Nikki laid one hand on her arm.

'There's no hurry, Megan. I'm not going. I intend to take part in the skating trials and I intend to win.'

'Nikki!' Megan cried. 'Climb off your high horse. It's your life we're talking about. They won't be too pleased with you in Russia. You know how they treat defectors.'

Nikki shrugged and looked resigned. 'So ... if that is my fate ...'

Megan leaned back, closed her eyes, took a deep breath and remembered every selling technique she had ever used. She reminded Nikki of her fame and her half-a-million dollars in her trust account, which would be hers when she turned pro.

459

She told her how much more famous she would be after going into hiding. She promised to extract the British citizenship from the Foreign Office, if she had to go to the Prime Minister. Afterwards she could not remember half the things she had said, but knew that they sat there until much later and they were both shivering with cold.

'Next year at the World Championships, you'll show them all,' Megan said confidently as she steered the car back on to the road.

'This time?' Nikki said stubbornly. 'Why is it that you cannot understand me correctly, Megan? Is it because you do not want to understand?'

For once Megan was at a loss for words on the long drive back to their hotel. Well, she still had eight days, she reminded herself, as she tried to quell a feeling of panic.

CHAPTER 65

Saturday, February 11, 1984

Day after day, the Women's Downhill race had been postponed due to gale force winds, but at last the wind had dropped and the various squads were waiting apprehensively on the summit of Mount Yahorina for the fateful decision. They were all uneasy for the piste was a dangerous one, promising a hazardous race.

Jacqui had closed her mind to personal questions. Emotionally she had blanked out. Mother's confession and Wolf's treachery were too much to handle. Only skiing was real, meaningful and pure, the rest of her life was a mess. She had one desire and that was to win. This was it! Her big chance. She had to win. She was willing herself to go faster than she had skied in her life. Win! Win! Win! She whispered the magic word under her breath.

For the past twenty-four hours, technical preparations had been hectic, but finally the weather had fooled them all. Hours ago, there had been an unexpectedly thick fall of snow on the summit, covering the night's brittle icecrust. What had promised to be a fast and aggressive course was buried beneath several inches of the cloying stuff. The back-up boys were furious; racks of skis cannot be carried to the top of the course, and consequently, technicians have to select the right skis beforehand, based on information being sent down by two-way radio. Their findings were now out-dated by a matter of hours – a nightmare for the servicemen responsible for last-minute selection of the skis available on-site.

The European teams' technicians were muttering under their breath about their hours of testing, wind-tunnelling, computers and videos, at the mercy of the elements and their far from perfect skiers. Acts of God must be tolerated; human error made them very angry.

Jacqui had drawn thirteenth position, so she had the advantage of watching the skiers who went down before her for clues about the course and the snow. Her chances were further enhanced by the weather which had largely negated her competitors' superior technology.

She eyed the piste critically. She was in that curious state of absorption which marks the serious skier. She looked dazed, but she was far from dazed; she was at one with the elements; moving into harmony with the coming race. She would know instinctively how to go faster at each part of the course, picking up a hundredth of a second here, a hundredth there, fighting for every split-second gained. There was always a voice saying: you could have done better, but by then it was too late.

As the reports from the first skiers came back, Jacqui's unease deepened. There were patches of ice, intermingled with soft snow, and several gates were almost entirely obscured.

No skier, unless he is extremely foolish, would race downhill in thick fog, that was an elementary rule.

Standing at the finishing gate watching the piste, Wolf had an uneasy feeling in the pit of his stomach. His prospects had turned a complete somersault since the fateful dinner with Eleanor two nights ago and he was feeling wretchedly depressed as he gloomily considered how his plans had failed from the outset. Each time he set a trap, he fell into it himself. Someone up there loves Eleanor, he thought ironically.

He had never been able to harm Jacqui, this vivacious lovely girl, who was now so angry with him. His plans to take control of her shares had fizzled out, for he had found he could deny her nothing and his desire for her to fall in love with him had backfired, for it was he who had fallen in love so deeply. He cared more for her than for his own life, and far more than he had ever loved Eleanor, he suspected.

Knowing that Jacqui detested her mother, he had prepared his ground well, never letting her forget the woman who had ruined his life, betrayed him when he was crippled and stolen his business. Jacqui had learned to despise this other woman, and he had longed for her to learn that it was indeed her own mother who had behaved so despicably towards the man Jacqui loved.

Yet now Jacqui knew the truth, she had turned against him. Why?

From Jacqui's frequent complaints, he had assumed that Eleanor was pitifully lacking in maternal instincts, and that this angered Jacqui. Yet here was Eleanor, not five yards away, white and trembling with agitation as the first skier collided with a gate and was carried off on a stretcher. She was scared half to death for her daughter and it showed.

His hopes for regaining Vanguard had been foiled by Eleanor's usual cunning, but the real reason was giving Jacqui back her shares. Surely Jacqui knew that? For some curious reason he was relieved.

Eleanor was waiting near the last gate in the forefront of a huge crowd which seemed to be half pressmen, and to her annoyance, Wolf was standing quite near to her. She had no wish to see Wolf again, he was a painful reminder of old wounds and silly dreams about what might have been. She could not understand why she had spent most of Thursday night crying, she should have been crowing with elation. To hell with the man! But right now she suspected that his defeat in the takeover bid was hardly uppermost in his mind. He was staring up at the starting hut with a look of agony in his eyes, and she assumed that he must love the young skier he was engaged to very much indeed. The thought was strangely hurtful.

Eleanor herself was sick with fright. Consequently, her rash was playing up and she had developed acute hay fever, and she knew why – she was scared for Jacqui and feeling guilty. She regretted making her daughter the Vanguard champion in their international advertising campaign, for Jacqui would be inspired to take chances, and conditions were abominable. Three girls had already missed the gates, and several had fallen. If only they would stop the race. They should have cancelled long ago.

Number Thirteen: Jacqui shot out of the starting hut and down the mountain, gliding fast and dynamically towards the first bend. Her style was one of constant flowing movements of the body and awesome speed. From each fragment of time she must squeeze the maximum thrust forward and downwards.

At the first gate she launched into a turn by a lateral step on one ski, then continued the turn with skis together, weighting both of them – the mark of a supreme technician – followed by an explosive up-weighting. Her body was now totally erect, in suspension, zooming down, exploiting every facet of her skill as she moved towards a speed of a hundred kilometres an hour, her skis airborne for several metres at a time.

Reality shredded and flowed away as the mist settled thicker, blotting out vision. Around her there was nothing but whiteness; her sensation of movement was diminished because there was no sight of passing anything. The cloud swirled thicker and closer and Jacqui lost sense of her whereabouts in the swirling sea of fog. She thought she knew where she was ... Or did she?

Suddenly the gate loomed before her, where it should not have been. She had to make it. She flexed her knees violently, pressurising the ski on its balance point, felt her body propelled violently downhill as she came into the full curve, and centrifugal force and gravity exerted a punishing propulsion. She made one last, violent effort to push her outside ski forward to obtain more curving.

Then she was flying out of control, through the white hell, not knowing which was the ground and which the sky. She felt a razor-sharp ski slice her knee and her arm, as she fought her fall with all her strength, jaws and fists clenched. Flashes of feeling! Flashes of light! Reality was a series of concussions as sky and snow met to pummel her out of existence. She opened her mouth to scream, but her mouth was filled with snow.

It was Wolf who raced across the piste to reach the fallen girl, long before the stretcher bearers arrived. Eleanor, who was hanging on to the fence to stop herself from falling, could only mutter: 'God, let her be all right. Let her be all right.' Her grief outbid all other sensations or emotions, even the horror of Wolf, tears streaming down his face, bending over the unconscious figure that was her daughter and the girl he loved.

'Oh God! Oh God!' she wailed. The full horror of the situation was lost in her fear for Jacqui. Then she set off after him, in an awkward shuffling run through deep snow in her moon boots, panting as she watched the stretcher bearers wrenching Jacqui from Wolf's unwilling arms and zooming down towards the First Aid Depot in the orange chalet, with Wolf racing after them.

'I knew this would happen,' Eleanor sobbed, as she slumped on a bench in the hut and tried to make some sense out of the kaleidoscope of images around her: white-clothed figures rushing in and out from another room; the doctor and his nurse cutting away the fabric of Jacqui's ski suit; Jacqui, white-faced, eyes closed, a sleeping child, but so white – the blood so red. It had gushed out of her wrist with such force, but now it had stopped from the tourniquet and the doctor was stitching and binding. Eleanor turned to Wolf and saw his grief and his expression of anxious caring – a well-known, well-loved expression. This is my punishment, she thought dully. He has fallen in love with his own daughter. Now my deceit has caught up with me.

'She'll be all right, won't she?' she murmured, fighting for control. 'She'll live?'

How could they be so calm?

'The doctor is doing all he possibly can,' the interpreter, who had just arrived, told her breathlessly. Eleanor searched for reassurance, but found none. The doctor looked anxious, the nurse, coldly efficient and detached, the interpreter was gazing unhappily at Wolf who was crying as he spoke to her in a low voice.

Eventually the interpreter turned to her and translated the doctor's quiet words: 'Shock, concussion, bad bruises and loss of blood. When the mist clears we shall fly her to hospital for skull x-rays.'

Eleanor felt that she was hanging on to the very lip of sanity. She was being punished for her greed. Of course it was her fault Jacqui had fallen. Criminally thoughtless of her to have blurted out her life story to the poor child, just to ease her own conscience and right before the race. Could she not have kept the burden to herself for a few weeks longer? And now? One thing was sure, Wolf must never know, or they would never be free of him. He must be sent away. Perhaps Jacqui would help her?

At that moment, Jacqui stirred and groaned. She opened her mouth hand licked her lips. Wolf bent swiftly to lift her head and touch her lips with a glass of water. She opened her eyes wide and stared as if she didn't believe what she was seeing. 'Wolf, Wolf,' she murmured, 'where are you?'

'Don't worry,' the interpreter said. 'She's hallucinating, but she's coming round.'

'They should have cancelled that race earlier,' Wolf growled. 'She was doing marvellously. She would have won ... fantastic timing ... but they should never have raced in that mist. She didn't know where she was ... never stood a chance.'

'They've cancelled,' the interpreter said as she hung around in the door. 'It will probably be a few days before this fog clears, so the event may be delayed for a few days.'

'Then she'll make it,' Wolf said. 'She'll be better by then.'

'You monster,' Eleanor sobbed, but Wolf was not listening to her. His hands were clasped over Jacqui's, his face looked anguished, his cheeks were wet, Eleanor noticed and his lips were moving over and over.

Good God, he's praying. He cares and he doesn't even understand why, yet he loves her with all his heart. The fog was thicker now and they seemed to be wrapped in a cocoon of whiteness. They were up in the clouds, floating in time and space, transported to a supernatural place where right and wrong were taught in practical lessons: where the morality of truth and the results of treachery were demonstrated in pain and suffering. An elementary lesson in the physical reality of fatherhood was taking place in front of her eyes. She felt she would go mad.

Jacqui groaned and both parents jumped and peered over her.

'Where the hell is Nigel?' Wolf grumbled. 'What sort of a father is he, anyway? He didn't come to watch her race.'

Eleanor gave a long shudder. 'Don't you understand,' she said, feeling defeated. 'Would she be lying here if she were Nigel's daughter?' Her voice rose to the edge of hysteria. 'Goddamn you, Wolf, she'd be out shopping,' she was half choked with her tears, and trying to hold them back. 'She'd be having tea with her friends, or playing tennis, or at a discotheque, or any number of safe, sane occupations young girls love. Oh God!' She covered her face with her hands and stumbled back until she collided with the bench. Then she sat down heavily. 'God knows, I've tried. I forbade her to ski, but your genes, your rotten genes drove her to do all the things you used to do. Can't you recognise your own genes? For God's sake, she's got your hands, your teeth, your foolhardiness, your

466

insane craving to be the best, your recklessness, your obstinacy.' She was yelling, but she did not care. 'That's why you fell in love – for Christ's sake, because she's a replica of yourself. Have you ever loved anyone besides yourself?'

Wolf gave one long ugly sob, and then he took a deep breath and made a visible effort to control himself. 'I'm going to kill you, Eleanor,' he said wiping his cheeks with the back of his hand. 'All those wasted years – and I begged you.'

'You blame me. You dare to blame me?' she began with mounting fury. 'I never wanted you as her father. You build things up, only so you can have the pleasure in knocking them down: businesses, women, marriages ... it's your nature to do this. You would have destroyed her, too. Just as you destroyed me. I had the right to take what was mine – my baby and Vanguard. Isobel had everything else.'

'I never loved Isobel,' Wolf said softly. 'I used her ... to prove that I was still a man ... you were determined not to let me find out – you'd taken over – remember? – like you always do – even sex. When I walked out of that relationship I was a whole man, ready to take up where we left off – before the accident. I told that to Isobel and she cried. I suppose that's why she came to see you – out of spite.'

Eleanor was not listening. She was wrapped in her own morbid self-analysis. 'I was keeping the good news about the baby for your birthday,' she was saying monotonously.

'My little Jacqui,' Wolf's voice was cracking and he broke off and cleared his throat several times. There was a kind of puzzled pleading on his face as he turned back to Eleanor. 'You'll never know how I loved that girl. It was like getting a second chance.'

'Don't kid yourself, you would soon have tired of her.'

They bludgeoned each other, word for word, blow for blow, and when Wolf told Eleanor about the shares, she said:

'You must be the devil himself to use this child to ruin her mother.'

'If I was, you made me one.'

Wolf was beaten. 'Eleanor,' he begged, 'let's make an end of this. Now.'

But the day had not done with Wolf. With a sudden shock he saw that Jacqui was staring at him: had been staring for how long?

467

He saw how white her cheeks were, but her eyes blazed with fury. 'Go away,' she said, in a whisper. 'Just get the hell out of here. I never want to see either of you again.'

He felt his heart hitting his ribs and heard Eleanor's gasp turn to a sob. Then the roar of the helicopter rescued them all from each other.

CHAPTER 66

Sunday, February 12, 1984

Unbelievably the sun was shining and the bare branches of the tree outside the window saved the ward from being totally antiseptic. The bed looked inviting to Megan, who had hardly slept for two nights. She had been watching the Women's Downhill yesterday, when Jacqui cartwheeled past and she had waited outside the First Aid hut in the thick mist for what seemed hours, until she had news of her. Later she had driven to the hospital to see if she could help, and Eleanor had broken down and told her the story and she had promised to try to help her daughter cope with the situation. Now she was watching Jacqui until Eleanor returned from a hasty trip to the hotel to bath and eat.

Megan knew she had a dose of flu coming. Her throat felt rough, her nose was burning and her eyes felt filled with gravel. Jacqui was out of danger, thank God, so Megan could dwell exclusively on the problem uppermost in her mind – Nikki's safety. For Megan, the Winter Games was unrelieved hell.

But she could not help thinking how lovely Jacqui looked with her ringlets spread over the pillow and a faint blush staining her pale cheeks at last. She looked angelic.

At nine o'clock Jacqui opened her eyes and surfaced to the real world. She looked startled. Megan reached forward and gripped her hand. 'Everything's all right,' she said comfortingly. 'You're coming along just fine and there's nothing to worry about.'

'Don't be trite, Megan,' Jacqui answered. 'Can you see any water around?' Megan reached for the glass and tilting the girl's head, gently tipped the water towards her mouth.

'Thanks.' Jacqui leaned back and frowned as she stared at the ceiling, and after a while she turned her eyes questioningly to Megan. 'You heard the news?'

469

Megan nodded, wondering how much it would be wise to reveal. Megan had hoped Eleanor would return before Jacqui woke, but when she spoke again, all she seemed interested in was when the race would be run. 'D'you think I'll make it?' she whispered softly.

'Maybe. I'll try to find out when it's scheduled,' Megan said. 'I really think you should rest now, Jacqui and not worry about the race.'

'God, sometimes you sound just like my frigging Mother,' Jacqui retorted with a sigh. She closed her eyes and smiled.

Clearly she was out of danger. 'Rob was here yesterday,' Megan said. 'He seemed pretty cut up to see Wolf with your mother and he left. Would you like me to contact him?'

'No, what for?' Her mouth shut in that obstinate, tight line Megan knew so well. 'Just find out about the race,' she said. 'I've got to make it.'

Eleanor returned shortly afterwards and Megan left and found a taxi to drive her out to the Igman Mountains where she had arranged to meet Ian.

It was forty-eight hours since Zoran Banski had spoken to her, and she had thought of little else since then. She did not know what to do, whether or not to believe this strangely humble Security Chief. But why should he lie to her? She could not make up her mind about Banski and her thoughts swung, pendulum-like, from one extreme to the other. At one moment she would decide that it was merely a Soviet ploy to persuade Nikki not to compete in the Games, but when she would remember so many strange, unaccountable things Nikki and Ian had said during the past year and she would find herself sweating with fright. In particular one memory was uppermost: at the film set ... what was it Ian had said? *Try to get the girl's skating shots finished before February, you may not get another chance.*

Damning certainly. But was it really Ian's brain child from beginning to the sordid end, as Banski insisted?

As the taxi laboured up the steep mountain road, she became increasingly apprehensive. She had never succeeded in hiding her feelings from Ian, and for the past two days she had been giving a false impression of happy optimism, trying to pretend that nothing was wrong. It was a strain. Now she could blame her gloom on the flu, she decided, so she could be thankful for that, at least.

470

Ian was standing near the finish of the Women's Cross Country trials. His mouth was set in an angry line and his eyes were dark with sadness. It was strange the way Ian's face could show conflicting emotions simultaneously. Today his unruly hair was sticking out from the crown of his head and every few minutes one hand would go up and try to push it down. He looked round at her impatiently. 'The press are turning this into a circus,' he muttered. He bent almost absent-mindedly to kiss her and caught some of the tension in her face. Then he looked at her, really looked at her, and his expression changed to one of compassion. Such a strange look. Did he sense what she was going through? He caught hold of her hand and thrust it into his pocket and held it tightly. Warmth and comfort flooded through her, and for a few minutes she was able to forget her nightmare situation. How could it be true? Banski must be wrong. She longed to blurt out her story, enlist his support and help. They loved each other, surely they could help each other. But she was not sure and her doubts were driving her crazy.

They stayed long enough to watch Marja-Liisa Haemaelainen's thrilling victory, and then Ian wanted to drive on to Mostar for a late lunch.

During the long drive, she rifled through her memories: Ian guarding the osprey in eight hour shifts regardless of the weather; Ian birthing the foal of his favourite mare with gentleness and skill; Ian sitting unmanned and hopeless on the bed the night she had cried at Aviemore. Was this the man who was sending Nikki back to face the anger of the Russian establishment and almost certain destruction? No, she screamed inwardly. No! No! No!

On the other hand, Ian had lied to her, manipulated her, used her and her business, pretending quite shamelessly that he loved her, until at last he had fallen in love – in reality. She had been only too willing to forget the past and plan the future, lulled into a false sense of security by Nikki's well-being and happiness. Nothing had changed, really, she reminded herself miserably. Ian was still the arch manipulator, Nikki was still the pawn, but this time she was to be sacrificed.

She could not stop castigating herself. Why had she forgiven Ian so easily? Ian was still manipulative and he was turning a living, loving, beautiful girl into an object to be used. So what

471

was new? What a fool she had been, but only because she loved him and she had so desperately wanted to believe in him.

But now she was forced to acknowledge that deceit was inherent in his trade – Nikki's happy ending would be the very last consideration for Ian. He was driven by some secret commitment to whom – to what? To Queen and country, to his naval career? What was it that was so sacred to Ian, he would sacrifice his friends, even his home? She should have been warned – after all she had read his family history in the books she had found in the cellars. Wasn't it Dougall Mackintosh who had abandoned his family to destitution, and his estate to the Crown, when he returned to France with the young Prince Charles after the battle of Culloden.

So now she was forced to play the same game – Ian's game – in order to save Nikki. Why should Nikki be more important to her than the man she loved with all her heart? But it wasn't just for Nikki, she thought sadly. It was for herself – for morality – or goodness. She could not live with herself if she abandoned goodness.

Megan glanced at her watch; it was nearly two. Nikki would be coming back from the ice rink after her training time. She planned to visit Jacqui, and spend the rest of the afternoon shopping. Megan had felt uneasy about leaving her, but Ian had been so insistent and after all, she had reasoned, Banski had assured her there was no possibility of danger until after the finals.

She was jolted out of her misery as the car swung off the main highway and on to a farm track. They were driving along a curved gravel road full of bumps and ruts, covered overhead by bare branches of the tall bare spruces, dripping with melting snow.

'For goodness sake, Ian. You'll damage the car,' she gasped.

He frowned, hating to be criticised, particularly over his driving. They skidded and turned and bumped along the country track for another ten minutes beside a wide and strongly flowing river. The River Buna, Ian told her, and swung unexpectedly into a gravel car park.

'This is it,' he said. She could see from Ian's face that he was on the defensive. His eyes gave him away. When he was hurt, he would narrow one eye slightly, as if in a permanent flinch, while the other stared coldly hostile and ever-watchful.

472

If only she were a better actress. Ian already knew that she was holding something back. She would have to be more careful. Outwitting Ian at his own game, would not be easy.

There was a low wall ahead and looking over it Megan saw several stone fish tanks fed with river water from bricked canals. She saw long, speckled shapes, in the dark water and for a moment she glanced pityingly at the trout, so graceful as they jerked forward in short sharp bursts of nervous energy, and paused again, still with fear – trapped!

Inside a shed-like building beyond the tanks was a restaurant for locals: a long low room overlooking the river, with whitewash walls and bare wooden tables and benches. There was a delicious smell of frying trout and Megan forced her regrets aside. She was hungry. The waiter, who was also the chef and the proprietor, brought a jug of Travarica and two glasses. There was no menu because there was only one dish.

She gazed across the table at Ian. He was studying her carefully. She stared back, feeling nervous; fussed around the table with her hands. Usually Ian did not bother to refill her glass, he did not like her to drink, she knew, although he had never said as much, but today he was refilling her glass after every sip, while he kept her amused with stories of his previous visits here.

Good grief, she was thinking, either the man's innocent or he's the most superb actor. But of course he's a good actor, she remembered with a pang of misery. He acted out the freelance writer bit and kept it going for months. Looking across the table at him she felt such an ache. She loved him so. How could she face a life of separation? But how could she live with such a monster? Her mental agony had turned to physical symptoms, a lump like lead in her throat and her chest, numb fingers and mouth, she felt as if she had been caught in a snowstorm and was slowly succumbing to hypothermia.

She gulped too much *Travarica*, but when the food came she could not eat. She tried a few times, then laid her fork down and leaned back sighing with despair.

'Don't you think it's time you told me what's wrong?' Ian said. She looked up startled, but there was nothing besides worried concern in his eyes.

'Why Ian ... nothing. Nothing's wrong. Just the flu,' she said. Then, because she had drunk too much on an empty

473

stomach she added: 'Ian, if you had to choose between your career and morality, which would you choose?'

He frowned, his eyes narrowed. 'I would never have to make that choice. Whatever it was I had to do would be the right thing; although at times the morality of the action might not be apparent. It's a matter of trust. I trust my colleagues and superiors. As I trust you and you, I hope, trust me. Are you getting cold feet about the wedding?' he added as an afterthought.

'No,' she said miserably.

'Today you're going to see something you'll never see again,' Ian said. 'Let's be happy today.'

'Yes, oh yes,' she said shutting her eyes and meaning it. Perhaps today was all she would ever have.

They left and drove upstream, watching the wide river bubbling over boulders and fallen logs, until they parked in the shadow of a gigantic cliff, too steep for shrubs or trees. From here they walked on, along a narrow track to the base of the mountain.

There was a deep cavern, and out of this black cave surged the river at tremendous power and speed, from some deep underground spring, and over it wild eagles soared and turned. 'Why, it's amazing. Like something supernatural,' Megan gasped.

It was a strange, desolate place, and built out of the cliff was a double-storey structure, freshly painted with a roof of slate tiles, but set into the bosom of a cave, so that the house itself was a series of rooms hollowed out of rock and only the front was built by man. It was called *Tekija*: '*The House of Dervishes*', and it was still the ritual centre for Dervishes today, Ian explained. The old Turkish peasant woman who took their money, made them thick black coffee and explained in broken English that she cared for the shrines of two holy men in the room above.

Megan walked around the rooms in awe, examining the brilliant Persian carpets, the intricately wrought iron work, the carved wooden ceilings, the ceiling of the Turkish bath studded with stars, the scrolls and the elaborate mausoleum.

'This has been a holy place for man since neolithic times,' Ian said. He pointed to a sign in a niche beside the entrance. It read: '*Mutu kable ente mutu: die before you are dead*'. Above the door of the guest room, that served the Dervishes for rituals was a prayer which read: *'Oh You, who opens all doors, open the best door for us.'* The sabre-and-mace relief on the wall of the mausoleum symbolised the link between the spiritual and the military.

Perhaps it was the *slivovitz* or the strange situation in which she found herself, but Megan lost her courage. She was unwilling to let go of her love. Just one more day, she told herself. What harm could one more day do. Then she would face her problem head-on, and anyway, it was important that Ian should not suspect that she knew.

So finally, after they had driven home, she went willingly and lovingly to his room in the hotel, and as the door closed they clutched each other and then she struggled out of her clothes, her hands trembling with haste.

There must be nothing ... no ... nothing at all between them, as if it were some strange ritual. They lay body to body, savouring the sensual touch of skin, the trembling of flesh. She felt his loins quivering against her thigh.

Oh, but she must have him, every last part of him must be examined and kissed and cossetted. Was this the last ... the last time ... a voice was asking?

She loved each part of him so desperately. She moved her lips over his stomach which was taut and strong, and up over his broad chest and kissed his strong neck, and his lips – soft and sensuous lips. She smoothed her fingers over his broad brow and ran them feverishly through his hair. 'Oh Ian, Ian, I love you. Remember that, won't you. I love you,' she whispered sadly.

'Don't talk. Just love,' he said, caught up in passion and a strange sense of needing.

She caught his buttocks with her legs and bound him down and into her, and tightened her arms around his neck. Oh, but she would be one, she would ... she would. If she pushed harder, and tighter, perhaps they could be forever moulded into one, never to be parted. She sighed and swayed to his rhythmic thrusts, and when at last he came, something intensely sad broke inside her and she burst into a frenzy of sobbing.

'No, don't,' she cried out in alarm as she felt his inevitable withdrawal. 'Please, don't.'

So Ian stayed, and soothed her and finally she felt him coming to life and they started all over again.

She was insatiable, her instincts cried out for more and more reassurance, for only when she held him captive between her thighs, was he really and truly possessed by her.

The hours passed the moon rose and the sounds in the hotel gradually ceased. Ian fell into heavy sleep while she lay anxiously watching his face in the dim light. She was searching for some sign of evil, which should surely show, but she saw only her beloved Ian, kindly, over-sensitive, loyal and true.

She wanted to cry again. She was faced with a decision that she was unable to make. Ian or Nikki? She remembered the quotation on the wall of the *Tekija*. '*Oh, You who opens all doors ...*' she prayed.

She could not help thinking: it's like the British, linking moral, military and religious codes into one. Ian's tradition of service was as sacred as any religion could be.

She propped herself on one elbow and bending over him, kissed him on the mouth. He stirred sluggishly and murmured something.

Then the startling blue eyes were looking up at her. 'I warned you,' he said. 'I warned you not to get involved and I begged you to give me a year to get out of all this. Go home, Megan. Go home and wait.'

So it was true. Feeling heavy with misery she went into the bathroom to shower and when she left Ian was asleep.

CHAPTER 67

Monday, February 13, 1984

It was a narrow, crooked cobbled street between tall buildings, built close together, some of Austrian descent, graceful and quaintly European, others starkly modern and utilitarian – the new identity – and this unlikely mix housed the Sarajevo hospital complex towards which the taxi was edging, hooting and dashing through the traffic.

It was the fourth time Eleanor had been here since her daughter's accident two days ago, but Jacqui had been sleeping most of the time. She was out of danger, the doctors had told Eleanor and could leave soon. It was just a matter of her depression, they said. The car halted at casualty entrance, and Eleanor jumped out briskly and looked around. There was a sudden hush amongst the patient Slavs queueing to sign the visitors' book and collect their passes. Conversation faltered, eyes turned surreptitiously, glances of envy, and admiration, but mainly longing. She was not cowed, nor patient, defeat had not touched her eyes, and her bearing was firm and aggressive. She might as well have arrived from another world, so striking was the contrast.

Eleanor joined the queue hesitantly, but after a while the women immediately ahead of her politely called to the guard, who ran to fetch a translator, who removed Eleanor from the queue and led her into the hospital.

Jacqui was lying in bed, gazing out of the window. She looked forlorn, her face was still pale and she had been crying, Eleanor could see.

'Jacqui darling,' Eleanor's rich, deep voice was like a breath of warm air from Monaco, and for a moment Jacqui smiled slightly then she turned away and closed her eyes.

'You can leave today, darling. The doctor assured me that

you're out of danger; you're only a little weak. We could catch tomorrow morning's plane, be home by afternoon. What do you say?' She squeezed her daughter's hand.

Jacqui frowned. 'Are they holding the race today?' she asked.

'No. It's been cancelled – again. There's no date set as of one hour ago.'

'Then I'll stay.'

'Whatever for? You can stand all day and see nothing. Winter sports are best viewed on the TV screen. Let's go home, darling,' she coaxed.

Jacqui shook her head obstinately and pulled her hand away.

Eleanor rummaged in her bag and produced some sweets and fruit juice. 'Unbelievable,' she said. 'You can only get the fruit and vegetables in season and right now nothing's in season. They don't import a damn thing – or so it seems. The waiter acted like I was crazy when I asked for tomatoes in my salad. He explained that tomatoes don't grow at this time of year – as if I was some sort of an imbecile.'

'It's all right. I don't feel hungry,' Jacqui said tonelessly. 'You don't have to stay, Mother. I feel very tired.'

'I'm not in a hurry,' Eleanor said. For a while mother and daughter sat in silence. 'Jacqui,' Eleanor said at last, plucking up courage. 'I always wanted to tell you about ... everything,' she began. 'I'm sorry I left it so long. I never could pluck up courage, I thought you would hate me.'

The words came tumbling out, the guilt, the excuses, the explanations, the long and tedious self-analysis, but mainly the guilt.

'Mother,' Jacqui said eventually, peering intently into Eleanor's eyes. 'Don't take all the blame. Yesterday ...' She turned her head round sharply and stared intently at her mother. 'Yesterday I heard everything. Wolf wanted to ruin you – he nearly succeeded – that's the sort of man he is when he doesn't get his own way. He's spoiled and arrogant and ... and I love him in spite of it all. After all he's my father,' she whispered. 'And anyway, who says you have to love a saint. All the same,' there was a glimmer of a smile in her eyes now, 'it can't have been easy being married to Wolf.'

Eleanor took a sharp intake of breath and squared her shoulders. 'Funny ... you block out the things you don't want to remember. I always thought about the good things and I guess I

forgot how fractious he could be when you tried to oppose him.'
She broke off, remembering Gundelfinger and all that she had
told him. She had never run Wolf down; never told him of her
fears of Wolf when she had beaten him at his own game and
grabbed Vanguard. It was that, more than anything else, which
had propelled her move to Monaco.

'You did what you had to do, Mother. It was long ago, before
I was born and it has nothing at all to do with me.'

'No, Jacqui, you were part of it all – the innocent victim. Oh,
but I've always sensed ... well, never mind ...' She sighed. 'If
only you would stop blaming me.'

'I never blamed you,' Jacqui repeated obstinately.

'If I could stop blaming myself,' Eleanor hiccupped, took out
her handkerchief and blew her nose loudly. 'Excuse me, dear. If
we could just be closer.

'Do you know what I was thinking, Jacqui,' she began again
in a voice that was falsely bright and a smile that was more of a
grimace. 'I was thinking that when we get back, we could take
a holiday together. Perhaps we could go to Denver. Did you
know I met your young friend, Rob Scott? I think he's
tremendous, I really do. He told me about the skis he makes in
his factory and I couldn't help thinking how exactly right he
would be to fill the gap Nigel has left. That is if you two are
really serious. Are you serious?'

'Oh Mother ...'

Jacqui pressed her eyes tightly together, blotting out sight,
but nothing could block out Mother's voice, bombarding her
with promises, bribes, compensation, regrets.

Would it make her feel better, Jacqui wondered, if I said: as
mothers go you were a disaster, but I'm getting to understand
you, and if you'd just shut up, I might even get to like you?

But Mother would not shut up, she was still planning Rob's
future when Jacqui fell asleep.

It was dusk and no one had turned on the light. Snow was
falling and Jacqui could see the flakes spinning through the
bare branches of the beech tree outside her hospital window.
Something had woken her, but she did not have the energy to
turn her head around.

Then she realised that someone was holding her hand too

tightly. She wished whoever it was would go away. She could not take any more emotional drama or demands. She felt inadequate to cope with the situation, but the relentless pressure on her hand, was urgently requesting some recognition, some responsive twinge, which she could not give.

Eventually she turned her head and looked into Wolf's eyes. How grave he looked. He was not trying to smile and that was a relief.

'That's my girl,' he said forcefully. 'It takes more than a few cuts and bruises to knock my girl out. That's what I told the doctor. I told him I'm taking you home, tomorrow. We can be on the morning flight, Jacqui. What do you say to that?' His voice was confident, but his eyes beseeched her for mercy, for love, for forgiveness. 'I can't wait to show you my oil wells – our oil wells, everything that's mine is going to be yours, you know that don't you, honey?

'I want you to know that I love you to bits. I always did, maybe I was a bit confused about the way I loved you – after all, it was a confusing situation.' He laughed falsely and increased the pressure on her hand.

'It's all right,' she whispered. 'You don't have to explain.'

'Oh, but I do. All my life I wanted kids, but after Eleanor and I split up, I didn't feel much like marrying – not until I met you that is. Ha-ha! Bit of a joke really, isn't it? You and me meeting up like that, but the point is, I learned to love you.' His voice faltered for a moment and Jacqui heard him take a deep breath. 'Never mind what sort of love – that's not important – love's love! There's no two ways about it. And, honey, now I know you're my daughter, I understand why we always seemed so much alike. Same blood – literally. I'm going to be a good father, Jacqui.'

'Is this you talking, Wolf?' she whispered in amazement. 'It doesn't sound a bit like you.' Jacqui looked up in fright. 'Wolf, please, don't try to act out the good guy. Don't turn into someone else. Please. I know you very well and I love you just the way you are.'

'You do? Somehow it's hard to believe,' he said, his voice twisted with grief. 'Look, I want you to know that the oil wells are still there – still yours. They were always meant for you.'

'Oh Wolf, don't talk about it, please.'

'Father! Call me Father! Dad! Any damn thing. Oh Jacqui. I

480

can't tell you what I felt when I realised that you were my daughter. For a moment I wanted to kill Eleanor, not because she'd kept you from me all those years, but because we had the same blood, because I realised I would never be able to ...'

'Sh! don't talk about things like that,' Jacqui said.

'Oh God, Jacqui, I love you, kid,' he whispered.

Jacqui turned her head away. All she wanted was to be left alone. 'I'm tired,' she said.

'There's something I have to tell you,' Wolf went on relentlessly. 'I want to explain why your mother and I ...'

'You told me everything in Arosa,' she said, trying not to cry.

'But perhaps it wasn't the full story. In a way, it was more like this ...'

Why must I listen to him? It's not fair, Jacqui thought desperately, as his tortured voice went on and on. She was feeling on the edge of panic. Is this the age when people have to set the record straight? she wondered. Was that the reason for Mother's skin eczema? I must try to lead a blameless life, she thought desperately, because it all piles up; nothing is ever forgotten or forgiven. She closed her eyes and tried not to listen.

'By the way honey,' he said much later. 'I bumped into your boyfriend, Rob Scott. We had a few words – nothing serious. To tell you the truth I like him. He's just the sort of young man I'm looking for to head my oil consortium – of course, he'd have to learn the business first – if you and he are serious, that is.'

Not Rob, Jacqui thought. You can't have Rob. He's too nice – much too nice for my family. Then she fell asleep.

Wolf was lying in bed naked between the sheets, saying to himself: 'daughter, daughter'. He thought of the virginal white nightdress, and the way her neck moved so gracefully, when she turned her head on the pillow, her beautiful profile with the sloping, exotic nose, the slightly slavic eyes. God knows where she got them from, and the halo of dark ringlets lying on the pillow. She was even more beautiful now, because she was paler and thinner; the hollows in her cheeks and the smudges under her eyes increased her womanliness. Oh God, she's my daughter, he murmured, but that slender, exotic body kept

481

floating into his mind, as she had been ... Oh, those lithe and supple legs! Daughter! Daughter! Then he thought about Rob and his jealousy and his youthful vigour. Agony!

Abruptly he pushed back the blankets, swung his legs out of bed and fumbled for the light switch. It was two am. He had to have a drink, but instead of dialling the bar he dialled reception. A sleepy voice answered eventually. 'Put me through to Eleanor Douglas,' he said, low-pitched and ashamed.

'Who is it? What's wrong?' Eleanor sounded agitated and for a moment Wolf nearly replaced the receiver.

'Eleanor ... Oh God ... listen ... it's me ... you've got to help me,' he said.

There was only a momentary hesitation. 'I'm in room 503,' she said and her voice was soft and strangely girlish. 'I'll leave the door ajar.'

CHAPTER 68

Tuesday, February 14, 1984

Rob wanted nothing more than to get the race run, and the day over and done with. Then he would take the first flight out of Sarajevo and forget Jacqui. From then on it would be business all the way, and for that he needed a medal – any medal – but he knew that he could not beat Switzerland's Max Julen, who had set the pace in the first run of the Men's Giant Slalom race, with 1:20:54. So he would fight for second or third place, and he thought he stood a good chance. His timing in the first race had been good. He had been fourth, and since the top five went down in reverse order on the second compulsory race, he would be second down.

For a few moments he stood outside the starting hut, gloomily surveying the *piste*. It was a bad one. The hill's vertical three hundred and eighty-three metres commanded a set of unusually tight gates. Not only that, but a sharp opening section was followed by a short flat, giving way to a finishing slope culminating in a *steilhang*, or steep wall of extreme severity. The army had been out since dawn, compressing the course, and they had decided, for reasons which escaped Rob, to hose the surface to reduce rutting. The upshot of all this water was a glittery, grainy surface with skiers struggling to hold their edges, like mountaineers on an ice wall.

Beyond the piste, the grim scene exactly mirrored Rob's mood, steep and barren white slopes against a sky of burnished lead. There were about thirty thousand spectators, Rob reckoned gloomily, and from the sound of things they were all locals, for they were nosily rooting for Jure Franko, Yugoslav's national Downhill champion. He doubted Jacqui was there. Why should she be? Rob had visited the hospital three times, since her accident, and on each occasion he had seen Wolf

Muller holding her hand, and once he had seen Wolf in the hotel restaurant, arguing with Jacqui's mother. From their serious expressions and sharp voices, he assumed it was the marriage settlement which was under discussion. He had read somewhere that the rich married the rich, regardless of any other considerations, such as love or happiness. Well, to hell with them all.

He turned back to study the piste once more. He would do well, because he had to do well, because a medal would mean millions to his business and because he wanted to show Jacqui and her family exactly why he had come to Sarajevo. Anyway, it was his kind of snow.

Afterwards, Rob remembered very little of the top part of the course, he seemed to have skied down in a daze, he was hardly bothered by the turns, but coming into the final straight there was just one critical patch to the finish. Every muscle was screaming with the effort of keeping low and straight, but the last bump caught him out of sync and the impetus shot him into the air. Keep straight ... keep straight ... he was screaming, but he knew this error had forced him onto the back of his skis and lost him precious time. From then on he was struggling for control.

Once through the finish gate, Rob knew he had skied well, but how well? He hardly dared glance at the time clock, but as he wrenched off his helmet he became aware of an excited buzz from the crowd. Perhaps he would make the first eight in spite of his imagined failure. He had to force himself to look up; 2:41:75. He did not know what his position was, but he knew he was fast and amongst the leaders.

He was third and he had won a bronze medal. Julen was first. The applause, however, was not for Julen or Scott, it was for Jure, the tall, good-looking Slav who won the silver, the first medal of any kind the Yugoslavs have ever won in a Winter Olympic.

The American squad caught up with Rob as he was walking towards the bus and dragged him back to the TV cameras. He said a few words and then, as he was lifted shoulder high, he caught sight of Jacqui: a red, knitted cap, brown eyes solemn and sad, a face white as snow. Thank God she was out of hospital. 'Hey, fellows, let me down,' he pleaded, but he was chaired protesting towards the bus.

Now he'd never find her, he thought, cursing under his breath, but to his surprise she was there, tailing along behind, looking forlorn and slightly scared and he wondered why.

'That was swell,' she said. 'I was so scared for you ...' She broke off and looked away and a slight shudder wracked her body.

'Good to see you,' he said catching her hands in his. His fingers felt hers under her gloves, searching for a ring. No ring! Was that a good sign, he wondered? 'Surprised you're still here.' He pulled her beside him, linking her arm in his. 'I thought you'd be back home by now. I heard about the accident. Glad to see you on your feet,' he said. 'Everything okay?' He was damned if he'd tell her how often he had paced the hospital grounds wondering whether or not to go in.

'The Women's Downhill is delayed; if they hold back long enough, I might make the team. I'm hoping ...'

He looked down at the red ski hat bobbing up and down at the height of his shoulder. She had guts, he thought. That was what had attracted him to her in the first place.

'Rob, I just wanted to see you and tell you what's been happening to me. It's pretty dramatic in a way. For me, that is ...' She smiled wistfully and Rob felt his stomach lurch. 'Wolf ... that is, Wolf and I ...'

'Don't talk,' Rob said. So that was that. Tough! He'd never been a coward, so why did he feel like breaking down and crying like a small kid.

'Come with me on the bus, Jacqui,' he said. 'They're pretty swift with doling out the medals every evening at Skenderija. We could take a taxi and look around the place first. Then I'll get the medal and we'll say goodbye. What d'you say?'

What a crazy fool he was, hanging on to the last seconds, as if they were the last moments of his life ticking away, but how could he say goodbye? He'd never been a quitter – never given up on something he wanted this badly. Fight, he told himself. Don't give up without a fight. There are four more days. Anything could happen in four days.

They sat side by side on the bus and Rob reached out and grabbed her hand. She did not pull her hand away. Then he slipped an arm around her shoulders and hugged her against him. This was her place, tucked in close to him where he could keep an eye on her.

'Rob, there's something I have to tell you,' she said. 'I haven't told anyone else, but it's too much for me to handle ...' She stopped, lips trembling, eyes downcast, he could see her lashes quivering, and the blood flushing her cheeks and her palms were suddenly moist in his. 'Oh Christ,' she whispered.

'Not now,' he said, glancing over his shoulder. 'Not here. Later.' He knew what she would tell him. His stomach felt leaden, there was a lump in his throat and his eyes were burning. Why did he love this crazy kid so badly? What was he doing here with her?

He stared blankly out of the window at the route lined with flags of every nation at regular intervals. The snowy brambles made a lace edging to either side of the road, and the mountain slopes were thickly covered with wolf and bear spoor. He felt content with the warmth of Jacqui's body pressed tightly against him and he had the absurd impression that this feeling was going to last forever. He closed his eyes and thought: I must remember this day; this is going to be the best day of my life. There will be nothing else. I must remember every part of it.

After a while some wild ideas flitted through his mind. Could he kidnap her? She was running scared, he could feel that. Would Wolf Muller be able to care for her the way he would? He could feel the tension and the fear throbbing through her. And no wonder. Marrying a billionaire twice her age was enough to scare any girl. What if he beat the shit out of Muller? Could he scare him off? No, from what he had seen of that bastard, nothing would scare him off.

He wondered if he should say something to make her feel better. Something like: it would never have worked, Jacqui, you and I. You're just too damned rich. I couldn't imagine you washing dishes. No! Goddammit, it would have worked and why should he try to make her feel better. Yet she was suffering and he longed to help her.

Murder! The thought thrilled through him and for a few seconds he contemplated the joy of Muller buried six-foot under.

'I guess you're still angry at me throwing a couple of punches at your Wolf Muller. Well, I want you to know I'm not sorry ... not a bit sorry. I wish I'd killed the bastard.'

He felt her involuntary withdrawal and the tension. Why did

486

he have to spoil their last afternoon, Rob wondered? Something in him had to keep on digging at his pain.

'Rob,' she said softly. 'I have to warn you, Wolf is going to be around for a very long time. He's part of my life.'

After that they continued in sulky silence, past the Igman Mountain where the cross-country Nordic events took place and the ski jumps had been constructed. The mountain slopes were thick with beech trees, gaunt and brown against the snow – like a dead forest. Rattling on, over thirty-five kilometres of winding mountain road, past the quarry and alongside the frozen River Kroupac, until the bus deposited them at the Olympic Village.

They found a taxi nearby. 'Take us to see something ... anything,' Rob said in a voice that was husky with pain. 'And get us back to Skenderija in time for the ceremony.'

They drove for a long time in silence. Content with the close proximity of each other's bodies, hands clasped. 'I can't put it off any longer,' Jacqui said eventually. 'I've got to talk to you. You asked me to marry you. You said I had to make up my mind here in Sarajevo, and I've decided to do you a favour and say 'no', because you're a real nice guy ... far too nice ...'

'Don't ... ' he burst out. 'Don't lie, Jacqui. Don't try and dress it up. Here, hang on.'

The taxi had parked at the curbside of a snowy expanse of what was probably lawns under plane trees and sweet chestnuts. 'You go that way,' the driver said, pointing towards the dim shape of Mount Igman, heavily shrouded in mist.

They walked stiffly, each wrapped in their own separate misery, along the three-kilometre pathway through the park and Jacqui began to talk. She had to talk, she explained, had to tell someone, so she told Rob of her fears and expectancies and of her revelations, which of course, she had instinctively known inside herself, but never been able to put into actual thoughts or words. 'So you see he's my father and there's even worse to come.'

As she talked on and on, Rob wondered if the accident had unhinged her mind. Joy had burst in on him, somewhere amongst the shrubs and trees; love had resurged into a great fiery ball; their future looked like a beam from a searchlight pointing straight to heaven; the problems which she was listing so poignantly, were merely shadows which paled to transparency in the beam of love he was projecting towards outer space. What was she babbling on about – oil wells? And Father? And the need to protect him from Father and Mother. And Mother's determination to buy out his plant.

Oh boy! That glorious, wonderful, beautiful word 'Father' which had knocked Muller and his expectations into a bog. For a moment he felt a beam of pity. Father was gurgling in the mire, before he even got into the act, but if he was very good, and well-behaved, and kept his oil wells tidily out of sight, they'd let him view the children from time to time. They'd even call him grandpa.

'Jacqui,' he said cutting in on her. 'Look at that! Look at that spring. I've never seen anything like it.'

Gigantic gushes of water were pouring out of the frozen earth, forming pools and islands, as the jets spurted – gurgling, bubbling frothing and foaming – from some vast, compressed subterranean river, bubbling free and joyful, unconstrained, to roll over snowy slopes into a deep channel, forming the famous Bosnia River. They wandered hand-in-hand amongst the leaping fountains of water.

'So that's how rivers are made,' Jacqui said, gazing breathless and over-awed.

'Will you marry me?' Rob said, slipping his signet ring over her finger. 'Say yes. It's Valentine's Day.'

'After all I've said. Could you bear it?' Jacqui replied, her eyes shining.

They ate *baklava* and ordered some wine to celebrate, and strong black Turkish coffee and watched the river forming and rolling on, never ending, but Jacqui was not her usual pert and arrogant self and Rob wondered what else was wrong. She seemed tense and preoccupied, and every now and then a shudder would shake her body and Rob watched and said nothing. One step at a time, he thought. When we're married and back home, she'll get over whatever it is that's worrying her.

'Let's go,' he said. 'Let's fly back to Denver. I'd rather you saw my place before we're married. I don't want you to get any false impressions. It's not Monaco, but I love it. I've got a feeling you're going to love it, too.'

'I still have to race that race,' she said. 'It's still there. It will be there for the rest of my life if I don't do it.' There was that

488

look again, the terror he had seen before the tensions, the shaking hand and moist palm, as she tried to explain about the awfulness of being trapped in a world of whiteness, of losing awareness of movement and earth and sky, at over a hundred kilometres, when one mistake can trigger the end of your world.

She was all snarled up by the accident and there would be no peace for Jacqui until she faced the terror head-on. 'I don't expect you to understand,' she said miserably. 'After all, they don't and they're my own parents. So why should you?'

Watching her, Rob thought: I can only help you to do what you have to do, by doing what I have to do as well as I possibly can, but he said: 'I'll be right there, Jacqui, and you're going to be all right.'

CHAPTER 69

Wednesday, February 15, 1984

Michel arrived at Sarajevo Airport at ten o'clock in the morning. He had his return ticket for a flight later that day and a one-way ticket for Nikki, made out in the name of his wife, Nikola Juric. He also had her photograph and name stamped into his passport. This had cost him fifty thousand French francs and a delay of three days while he unearthed the best forger in France. He had taken a taxi from the airport to the hotel, and found Megan who had repeated her conversations with Nikki, and explained angrily why she had been unable to persuade her to leave Sarajevo. Right now Nikki was rehearsing, Megan told him.

He found Nikki at Zetra Stadium in the midst of a difficult set piece and watching her he could only gasp with wonder at her sheer artistry and her amazing courage. That was Nikki, he thought smiling ruefully: infuriating, spoiled, disloyal, greedy, and rude, but when she skated, one became totally bewitched. You forgave her everything, because Nikki was someone special. Sometimes it was hard to believe she was really human when she was on the ice.

The moment Nikki caught sight of Michel, she whooped with relief and zoomed to the edge of the rink to throw herself at him across the barrier.

'I thought you would never come. I missed you. Oh, darling, darling Michel, how I missed you. Just imagine if you had not seen my performances,' she babbled on breathlessly. 'Tomorrow is the figure skating; on Friday there's the short programme, and Saturday the long programme – that's the real thing,' she said joyously and spinning around in front of him. She counted off the days on her fingers like a child. But then, Michel reminded himself, she was a child; far too emotionally immature to be faced with such a tragedy, or to make the right decision.

Michel pulled himself up short. He was making excuses for her – *again*. He always did that. In his heart he was feeling deeply hurt, not exactly angry, for anger was a difficult emotion for Michel to sustain. All his life he had worried about this and he had been ashamed of his gentleness. When he sat in front of his typewriter he could be cruel, or cutting, or quite ruthless, but not in real life. Right now he longed with all his heart to feel furiously let down; to cleanse his system of the poison of compassion and understanding with a flood of temper. 'Violence was a cleansing force,' he had read that somewhere and he understood how it was, but it wasn't in him. Oh, if he could only shout her down, beat the hell out of her, force her to give in. But he could only be gentle and try to woo her with the logic of his understanding.

So he tried. 'I've come to take you home,' he said carefully for starters, not wishing to give voice to his insecurity.

He tried again when she came off the rink and marched, eyes smouldering, lips pouting, to the changing room and he, following behind her like a cocker spaniel, pleading all the while. He tried once more when he led her to the café for the coffee and cake she demanded and later, when he had her in his car, he really put his heart into it.

'It's the only way,' he repeated. 'We can be married, or not, as you wish. We could even marry to make you legally French. I could give you a divorce, later, if that was what you really wanted. Anything! Only come with me to France – now. I'll look after you. I'll hide you, and in a year's time, when this is all blown over, you'll start again, just where you left off. You're only seventeen. Good God, you'll be eighteen and famous. Do it, Nikki. Do what I say. It's the only way.'

All this he managed to say, in short bursts between her complaints, refusals, tears and tantrums.

Then she exploded. She was like a vision of stormy seas, crashing breakers and foam lathering. That was Nikki in a fury, he thought wonderingly.

'How can you dare to say you love me. Wicked lies! When you know that I would be destroyed, utterly destroyed.'

'Nikki, just this once, cut out the melodrama,' he said urgently. 'We're talking about your freedom, maybe even your life. Your father's supporters would take their revenge, and your father's enemies would be even worse ...'

Nikki was humming as she studied her fingernails, but Michel ploughed on desperately. 'You know what happens to defectors and you of all people, would be punished. Nikki, for God's sake, listen to me,' he pleaded. 'You've been headline news for a year – all those statements about freedom in the West, freedom to develop your art, your escape from petty tyranny. Have you any idea how many enemies you've made?

'They would force you to make a statement saying you had been kidnapped and then you would conveniently disappear – to Siberia; or an asylum where they give you these terrible drugs ... within a month you're a grinning vegetable.'

He was getting nowhere. She could think only as far as Saturday and her precious gold medal. Michel was beginning to feel increasingly desperate. 'You've got everything going for you here.' He tried another approach. 'You can turn pro, make a fortune, be a film star. Nothing's changed.'

'If I'm not a gold medalist then there's little point in turning pro,' she said with sudden peasant shrewdness.

'Goddamn it, the Olympics isn't the only thing in the world, what about the European championships, the World championships?

'You must choose now,' he said bravely. 'I won't have you staying here a day longer. For the last time now I'm asking you – begging you – to come. What's it going to be – life or a gold medal?'

She giggled. 'I choose the gold medal,' she said. 'You sound just like that funny television programme.' Suddenly she was laughing at him. She could be so absurdly serious about nothing and then joke about life and death. At that moment Michel longed to put his hands around her throat and shake some sense into her. But he would never do that. It was not his way.

'Michel, will you please take me back or I will lose my next practice time – and I don't want to do that,' she whined.

Cursing himself for his compliancy, he turned the car and drove rapidly back to Zetra Stadium. It seemed that there was nothing more to say.

Then, after a long silence, Nikki laid one hand gently on his knee. 'You don't understand me at all,' she said quietly. 'Why

492

can't you see that if I prove to myself that I am the best in the world, then whatever else happens I can at least live with myself. Loving you has nothing to do with it. You understand? Nothing!' Her lips folded into an obstinate curve.

Michel sighed. She was intense on keeping up appearances. That was what it boiled down to – her major preoccupation all the time.

He parked the car, followed her up the stairs to the changing room, and paced the passage while she changed. There was so much he should say, but he felt impotent and inadequate to cope with the situation. In all his life he had never felt such a failure.

'Goodbye, Nikki,' he said in bitter humiliation. 'I won't be staying. I came to fetch you and now I'm going back to Paris.'

She was lost, he thought sadly as he walked away. Why was it that he understood her so well? That damned Russian fatalism was leading her straight to disaster, but even while he was arguing with her, he knew how she felt, and what she meant, and that she would never give in. Nikki would never count the cost in pursuing her target. A typical Russian trait – that was what made them so formidable.

He turned at the top of the stairway, and waved. God damn it, she was lacing her boots again. Not even looking his way. Couldn't she wait another minute, just to wave? He would drive to the airport and take the first available plane. Wipe the dust of Sarajevo off his feet forever.

There will come a day, he thought, as he started his car, when I will no longer forgive myself for my passivity.

CHAPTER 70

Thursday, February 16, 1984

It had stopped snowing two hours ago and although state meteorologists predicted gale force winds and the possibility of further snow, bus loads of women skiers were moving towards Mount Yahorina. At last, after six consecutive cancellations, the Women's Downhill Race was scheduled to take place today.

The convoy moved laboriously up the slippery snowbound mountain pass, with frequent halts to wait for snow ploughs to move out of the way. No one seemed to mind. There was a good deal of laughter and singing as the squads battled to keep their spirits soaring. Jacqui sang, too, in a desperate bid to hang on to the present, live only for this moment, to focus her attention on what was around and about her, in order to avoid the confusion within.

Time and again she failed and her thoughts homed back to the previous evening. Wolf had invited her, together with Mother and Rob, to dinner at the Holiday Inn Hotel. A strange gathering, but it had not taken Jacqui long to realise that the event had been jointly planned by Mother and Wolf who were conspiring to quiz Rob about his prospects, his background and his intelligence. Evidently he passed their critical tests, for Wolf had looked gloomy and Mother had been radiant.

Nevertheless, it had been a torment for Jacqui. Wolf was strangely changed, and it hurt. It was almost as if he were ashamed of loving her. All through dinner he had carried on like an actor at his first dress rehearsal, acting out diverse parental roles as if he could not make up his mind which one fitted. To Jacqui it seemed that he was making a first class fool of himself, while he talked down to her as if she were a cretin child. Finally she had stormed out of the dining room in a temper and ordered a stiff scotch in the bar. Wolf found her there eventually, and that had surprised her, too, for she had expected Rob to come. Wolf had sat opposite her, stared at her gravely and said: 'Goodbye, honey. It's not working.' Then he had leaned over the table, cupped her face in his hands and kissed her long and hungrily, oblivious to the crowded bar.

'Wolf, don't go,' she had begged. 'Please don't go. I need you. All these years I've longed for a father, now you want to leave me ...' and she had burst into noisy tears.

'The way you were acting in the dining room I thought you couldn't wait to see the back of me. As for Rob, he was smirking from ear to ear. I'd like to beat the shit out of him.'

'You spent the night with Mother, didn't you?' she accused him, feeling hurt and jealous.

'Yes I did,' he said gently. 'Jacqui, I'm going to say something that might hurt you. Part of the reason why I love you is because you're the toughest, bravest, most talented girl I've met and a hell of a lot of fun to be with. But let's face it, part of it was from loving your mother. You're just like she was. It was like having another chance – only, of course, I'm not as young as I once was. You know something? It's probably just as well or we'd ... Hell, let's not go into that.'

'It's hard for me as well as you,' Jacqui had whispered, feeling sorry for herself. 'How about we help each other? I think we'll make it. But for God's sake, cut out the Daddy bit. To me you're Wolf, you've always been Wolf, you always will be Wolf.'

Wolf had shaken his head and stared long and sadly at her. 'I'm not much of a father, am I Jacqui? But don't worry, I'll get better with practice.' Then he smiled and something of the old Wolf was back in his eyes. 'As my first fatherly act, Jacqui ...' He had reached forward, taken her glass and drained it at a gulp. 'No hard liquor for you, my girl, until you're twenty-one. And no hard feelings, I hope.'

She wanted to say: That wasn't what you said in Mègeve, when you were trying to make me drunk, but that would have been hitting below the belt. Instead she whispered: 'I'm jealous of Mother. Can you believe that anyone could be jealous of their own mother?'

'Can you believe anyone could be jealous of their own son-in-law?'

'Yes,' they said together and grinned and after that it had

been all right and they had walked back to the dining room arm-in-arm.

It had been funny to watch Mother, who was no longer the Mother Jacqui knew. She had turned into a silly, middle-aged teenager, flushing every other sentence, fluttering her eyelashes at Wolf and leaning over in her disgusting dress, showing everyone her fat breasts. She had lost her rash, she kept saying proudly. Jacqui wished she'd shut up about the goddamned rash.

Mother still loved Wolf — anyone could see that. A real one-man woman. Jacqui's image of her mother had done an abrupt about-face, leaving Jacqui feeling insecure, and strangely vulnerable. It was as if Mother were the child and she the adult.

There was another unscheduled stop. Jolted out of her reverie, Jacqui leaned forward and blew warm breath onto her window and smeared a circle to peer through. Suddenly she was looking into the slanting black eyes of a peasant woman trudging past, herding her flock of goats. She was heavily lined, and poorly dressed in dark blue broadcloth trousers, and a waistcoat over her white calico blouse and embroidered scarf. For a few seconds their eyes were locked and they exchanged a solemn greeting, one woman to another, worlds apart, yet, in a way, indivisible. Then the woman lifted her hand and smiled, showing gaps where her teeth should be. She called out: '*Dobrodosli, dobrodosli*,' — welcome — and her broad peasant's face lit up with pride — pride for the Games, for the competitors who had journeyed to her home from all over the world, and for their achievements.

For some reason Jacqui found that her eyes had filled with tears. I'll be racing for her, just as much as for myself, she thought.

They reached *Rajska Dolina* — Paradise Valley — in the shadow of Mount Yahorina, where the last gates were situated and went on upwards to the crest of the mountain pass where the *Mladost* hostel had been built. Behind it were the starting huts. The girls piled out feeling bruised by the road. They laughed and shouted to raise their spirits before the race began.

Jacqui emerged from the bus like a sleep-walker. She hardly noticed the dark clouds gathering, obscuring the summit, or the

496

trees bowed by the wind, but she saw the waiting crowd far below. Her family would be there. She thought of Mother and her lonely quest to build Vanguard into the greatest sports company in the world, and of Wolf who had found that love was stronger than hate, and Rob who had been unable to deny love, and of the peasant woman with her murmured greeting, and of the Slavs and their slogan: *You are beautiful — we love you.* And she thought: I love you too. Because she wanted to give something back, and because all she had to give was skiing, she murmured: 'Just watch me! Just watch me go!'

She burst out of the starting hut with a hosanna of joy, straight and pure and fleet, and skimmed down the mountain, like a lark released from a cage, like an arrow shot from a marksman's bow, like a cheetah homing on its prey, lusting for life, thrilling to every split-second of it, devouring each moment. Thrusting forward like a prayer of thanks for the gift of life and the supreme thrill of being alive.

That night the family celebrated Jacqui's third place, and her fastest ever timing, her engagement to Rob, and her departure with him for a holiday in Denver.

CHAPTER 71

Friday, February 17, 1984

It is a strange thing about the Winter Olympics, but the Games seemed to start winding down almost before they are started. They were nearly all gone – all the stars: Gunter, who had won a silver medal in the Men's Downhill yesterday, Debbie Armstrong, Bill Johnson, Rob Scott, Wolf Muller and the Douglases – all gone. The streets were emptying, and the Yugoslavs watched wistfully as one plane after the next taxied out of Sarajevo. With only three days to go, even the tourists were starting to leave, for there were many who came for particular events that were now completed.

What will it be like when we are all gone, Megan thought sadly? It would seem like a ghost town with all these empty hotels and unused facilities.

There was certain dogged desperation in the behaviour of the Slavs. They refused tips, gave extraordinary service, welcomed each new task with joy, exuded warmth: 'Come back! Come back. We love you. Not goodbye, only *au revoir*.' Cana told every guest as they were leaving.

Their desperation seemed to echo her own inward fears and gloomy premonitions.

This morning Megan was on the way to Yahorina to watch the Women's Slalom trials. She had an Italian client competing and although she was very young, in fact, only sixteen, Megan had high hopes for her. She would not win, of course, but if she made the first fifteen, Megan would be pleased.

As she hurried out of the lift, Cana waved urgently from reception. 'Megan, dear Megan,' she said when she had rushed across the foyer to catch up with her. 'When are you leaving? Only on Monday morning? Well, that is good because we must meet before you go. We must have a drink together. I want to

498

talk to you. Please Megan. I can meet you at any time. You are my dear friend.' She had looked imploringly at Megan, while she plucked her sleeve.

Such a waste, Megan was thinking as she arranged to meet her at six pm in the bar. Cana had a rare and delicate beauty. Her skin was as pale and unblemished as a young girl's and her large amber eyes were set wide apart under her thick, straight brows. Her forehead was wide and smooth and her honeyblonde hair tumbled back to her shoulders. Beauty, however, was not an asset in Yugoslavia.

As Megan called a taxi and drove off, she wondered where Ian was. Lately the tension of having to pretend that nothing was wrong was almost unbearable. She sighed and glanced out of the taxi window. A blizzard was threatening and towards Mount Yahorina the sky looked black. Perhaps they would cancel, but there was so little time left.

Megan leaned back and closed her eyes and once again ran through her arrangements: tomorrow morning, both Megan's and Nikki's suitcases would be placed in the boot of Banski's car, but Megan would pretend to Ian, that they were planning to leave on Monday morning, as they had originally booked. Megan would watch Nikki's performance from a reserved seat beside the entrance to the wings. She would wait long enough to see the final scoring, but when they called the winning three back, Nikki would not be there. Instead, Megan and she would run to the dressing room, and together with the police guards, they would leave by the fire escape and take Nikki to the waiting police car where she would be driven to the airport in her skating costume. She would change later in the private jet supplied by Zoran Banski.

They would be in Belgrade by 7.30 pm to catch the last Air France flight to Paris, from where they would go by train and hovercraft to Dover. Once there, they would be driven by Maureen to her aunt's cottage in Wales. No one would find her there. No one knew where it was. And Nikki and Maureen would remain there until Megan had extracted some sort of safe conduct and assurances from the Foreign Office. She and Michel planned to pull in the full weight of the British press to help pressurise the authorities.

It would be all right if Nikki reached Wales, but to her mind they were taking an unnecessary risk in waiting so long, before leaving. What chance would Zoran Banski have against the combined cunning of the Russians and the British? *What chance do I stand against Ian?*

It was snowing heavily by the time the race began. Although she had a good position at the finishing gate, she could not see the competitors until they came into the last schuss. It was abominable weather and the television crew and commentators were in despair. Her Italian client did well to come in seventh, Megan thought. She knew she would prove her worth in the Cup Circuit next year.

Later that evening, she met Ćana in the bar. Ćana was longing to find a job for her daughter in the West, she explained. The girl was an unemployed electronics graduate, learning to be a chambermaid, because there were no other employment opportunities. She was a very good skier, Ćana told her proudly, and a linguist. She could type, speak, write and take shorthand in English, but if she ever landed a job she would be one of the lucky ones.

Megan did not know what she could do about it, but she promised to make inquiries when she was back in London.

Ian joined them shortly afterwards. He had spent the day watching the Russian team winning the 75-kilometre cross-country relays and he was disappointed that the Norwegians had not scored.

'Well, we must be going,' he told Ćana. 'I've booked a table at the *Sentada* restaurant for seven.'

'Ian, I don't feel so well,' she began. 'I'm sorry, but I think I'm running a temperature. I have a tough day tomorrow, so if you don't mind, I'll go straight to bed. Have a good evening.' She hurried out, grateful that Ćana was there to stifle further arguments, but Ian caught up with her at the lift.

'Megan,' he said urgently, gripping her arm. 'What's wrong with you? What's wrong with us?'

She looked up guiltily. 'When we are back in London,' she said. 'You and I and Nikki,' she added with heavy emphasis on the last word. 'Then I'm sure it will be just like ...' she searched for the right words, 'like old times,' she said lamely. 'And we'll be married,' she added in a breathless rush.

'Come now, Megan. You don't really believe that I can be controlled by that kind of moral blackmail, do you?'

He smiled. It was a strangely intimate smile, implying secrets shared, and sadness shared. Then he watched her quietly for a long time while she dug her finger frantically at the lift button.

There was the strangest glint in his eyes. Not the face of a loser, she decided. His eyes were glowing with that secret, mocking look she knew so well. His brown hair was brushed back and gleaming in the neon lights. How could you fight someone when you knew and loved each part of him so intimately? God damn him, he was so polished, so sure of himself, so outrageously clever. 'Just remember that I love you,' he said. 'I haven't changed. Whatever happens, Megan. Remember that.'

The lift doors slid open silently as Ian turned away. Megan stepped inside feeling cold with fear.

CHAPTER 72

Saturday, February 18, 1984

Zetra Stadium, with seating capacity for eight and a half thousand spectators, was packed with a noisy, jubilant crowd, many of whom were obviously American. Megan tried to look like just another happy tourist, but she was rigid with tension, as she twitched and fidgeted, crossed and uncrossed her legs, and wanted nothing so much as to grab Nikki and run for it. All this waiting was playing havoc with her nerves, but their plans had progressed smoothly so far. She was sitting in a ringside aisle seat, near the exit to the dressing rooms and toilets and she could see one of Nikki's bodyguards standing there. The other, a woman, was waiting in the dressing room. Megan had not seen Banski, but she had checked that his car was parked in the official car park, close to the fire escape exit, with her luggage and Nikki's in the boot.

There was no earthly reason to be alarmed, but Megan could not banish a sense of dread which had been creeping up on her all day. Ian, for instance, seemed to be backing off – giving her space in an excess of polite concern, which was not Ian at all – it was almost as if he knew. Sometimes she would find his eyes fixed upon her with a curiously thoughtful expression, as if he was trying to make up his mind about something. To add to her unease, Nikki was far from cooperative. Megan was tired of Nikki's over-played martyrdom. She seemed to welcome the prospect of punishment and disgrace in her homeland. 'What is to be, is to be,' she repeated monotonously several times a day. Megan found Nikki's obsessive, oriental acceptance of her fate baffling and downright irritating.

She gestured to one of the polite ushers who were patrolling the stands selling chocolate and local brandy, and bought four bars. Nikki would be ravenous after her performance; she always was. She would be able to nibble in the car.

Megan willed herself to relax and concentrate on the coming performance. She had to admit that Nikki's prospects were good so far. She had excelled in the compulsory figures, which made up thirty per cent of the overall marks, and her short programme of free skating figures had again indicated her superior ability, for she had scored three sixes and six five-point-nines, with an outstanding performance of technical skill. The longer free-skating programme today, would determine the remaining fifty per cent of her marks, but Megan knew that the total of marks given to date only offered guidance towards the final position. Points were not the deciding factor. The result would be determined by what the experts called the majority placing system.

Nikki was very much the favourite tipped to win. Most of this was due to her ability, but it was also partly due to the extraordinary worldwide publicity she had received. Megan knew that there is no other Olympic Sport as intensively predetermined as ice skating. The four years between the Olympics, is spent building up a new generation of world champions. By the time the Games open, a rigid pecking order has been established which creates extraordinary demands on the favourites, but by the same token, the odds are in their favour. This afternoon, Nikki was expected to produce something quite extraordinary and she knew it. At the same time, she was expected to win a gold, a psychological advantage which affected both performers and judges.

It was a pity Eric Lamont was not here, she thought, but he dreaded flying. She knew he would be watching the television screen, and praying for Nikki right now.

Megan glanced across the rink to the nine judges. Six of them were Europeans, three from behind the Iron Curtain. Would this affect Nikki's marks, Megan wondered? They all looked tense and stern. This was a gruelling test for both skaters and judges and the responsibility was mind-boggling.

Nikki's music began: Nielsen's *Flute Concerto*, and Megan heard a few gasps from those in the audience who thought it a strange choice, but Megan agreed with Eric, the music was strangely unfamiliar, weird and way-out, acutely precise and in a way characterised Nikki's unique style of dancing.

There were more gasps in the applause as Nikki skated out onto the rink, for she seemed to be naked, clad in an ultra thin,

503

white leotard with a few flimsy drops of green muslin. She was an enchanted sprite, haunting the wastes of snow and tundra, she had escaped from her prison of ice to dance briefly until she was caught and imprisoned again. After only a few seconds, her ecstacy and her terror were transmitted to the audience. Nikki glided effortlessly into a series of risky and technically demanding moves, which included three triple jumps and a triple toe loop in combination with a double jump that she performed faultlessly in the opening seconds. She cleanly landed four more triples, including one in a combination with two other jumps. She had a knack of making the axels and the salchows and her own inimitable Cossack whirl look simple, while her joy in skating was transmitted to the audience. She was putting on the best performance of her life.

Soon Megan could no longer evaluate Nikki's dance in terms of technical ability. The illusion had taken over as the sprite danced as if her heart would burst, jumping, twirling, racing, spinning; packing a lifetime's joy into a few precious minutes of freedom. Each movement seemed more daring than the one before. Was she really human? Is this really Nikki? Or had she been bewitched? She saw total commitment in Nikki's eyes; she was entranced; captured by her role; pale and gasping, until at last she moved into a scratch pin in which she became a total blur.

It was over – freedom, laughter, movement, and now she had to face her punishment. The sprite crumpled into a tiny ball on the ice, moving her arms protectively over her head, and there was a long, frightened hush. Then Nikki looked up laughing, jumped to her feet and curtseyed to a great roar of approval. The scores were flashing up, six … six … five-point-nine … six …

But Nikki had fled.

Long before the applause ended, Megan was running headlong through the exit to the women's dressing room. There was a man there. Good grief, she thought, what was he doing in the women's dressing room? Concern changed to alarm as she saw he was bending over the policewoman who was lying unconscious on the floor.

'Nikki,' Megan screamed, long and loud, fearing the worse.

There was no answer.

'Nikki!' Her call became an agonised wail as she raced

through the door to the toilets, thrust them all open, but there was no one there.

Megan ran back to the policewoman. A crowd had collected, but no one spoke English and the woman was slowly opening her eyes and looking dazed. Megan ran out of the dressing room, pushed her way through the crowd to the fire escape. The door swung open, but there were no footprints in the snow. Nevertheless, she ran down and round the corner to the waiting car. This was what they had arranged, but Nikki should have been with her. 'Oh God, Oh God, Nikki, where are you?' she sobbed.

Banski's driver was reading the newspaper.

'Where is she? Where is she – for God's sake?' she cried out breathlessly as she approached the car. A second later the driver was speaking into his two-way radio in Serbo-Croatian, but Megan could not understand what he was saying.

'Will somebody help me?' she sobbed. 'Help me?'

Then Zoran Banski arrived. He looked pale with anger and shock. She had never seen him look so upset.

'Go back,' he said. 'Go back and wait – in the restaurant. No one came out. She could not have gone past the exits. All guarded – she's still inside the stadium.' He broke off and spoke urgently and rapidly into his radio. Then he noticed she was still there. 'We search – we find. Please wait in the restaurant, Miss Carroll.' His brown eyes stared compassionately at her, as if to summon the comfort his broken English had failed to convey. 'They'll never get out of Yugoslavia.' He placed one hand on her shoulder, but Megan did not feel comforted. She had failed and Nikki was lost. A feeling of desolation was welling up inside her.

The audience moved out noisily, and the skaters and their coaches moaned at the delays as the police examined identification. Then there were only cleaners and police, and as the hours passed, hope dwindled and died. Eventually Banski acknowledged defeat and insisted that she return to her hotel.

There was nothing left for her to do now except to find Ian.

She found him in the bar. He was leaning forward with his elbows on the table, and he looked deep in thought. An untouched glass of Scotch was pushed to one side. He turned his head slightly as she approached and gazed up at her from under his thick brown brows. He looked half defensive, half aggressive, but his grey eyes were framing a question. At that moment he seemed to Megan like some evil creature peering out from under a stone. Then he smiled. More than anything else, it was the innuendo in his smile that turned grief to rage.

'I'm going to ruin you,' she snarled, in a voice that was rough and grating. 'God damn you!' She leaned forward and slapped his face hard, and watched his eyes change. The guilt and defensiveness fled, replaced by anger. One arm shot out grabbing her elbow and she found herself hurtling through space to sprawl on the chair opposite him.

'Why don't you sit down?' he said smirking.

'You're contemptible,' she almost screamed. 'I won't let you get away with this. I'm going to the press.' Her hands gripped the table. She had to use all her willpower not to strike him again. 'Michel will help me; we'll tell the world about you and your fine naval friends. How you use innocent, defenceless women?' She gave one loud sob and pushed her hand over her mouth. 'Where is she? What have you done with her?'

'Who? Oh Nikki? You took over, didn't you? You should know? She's halfway to Russia by now I should think.'

'Devil! You're unspeakably evil.'

He caught hold of her wrist and gave a hard shake. 'Did it ever occur to you that Banski might be pro-Russian?'

Megan crumpled suddenly, anger gone as she buried her face in her hands.

'Then he wouldn't have told me about you – you and your despicable plans. Oh, I hate and despise you,' she muttered.

'Why wouldn't he?' his mocking voice went on relentlessly. 'It was one way to get Nikki to Russia, without the Russians fulfilling their part of the bargain.'

'You admit it?' She looked up hating him more than ever. 'You dare to be so ... so matter-of-fact about this terrible plan of yours. Did you ever stop to think of how it would be for Nikki – alone, frightened, with no one to turn to. God help her, what is she going to do?' She began to cry quietly, wiping her cheeks with the back of her hand.

'Do-gooders! God protect me from do-gooders. Megan listen to me ...'

'Go to hell. Stop trying to switch the blame on to that poor little man who tried so hard to outwit you. Zoran Banski is my friend and he's Michel's uncle.'

Now, at last she had shaken him. He was staring at her in disbelief.

'Tell me this. Was it really you who thought up the plan to swop Nikki for five British journalists?'

'Yes.'

'Then all the rest is incidental.'

'One life for five. She's a gold medalist. No one will harm her.' Megan considered Ian's statement, but after a moment rejected it.

'No,' she said. 'You're kidding yourself, Ian. Have you really convinced yourself of that? Tell me then, what do you say when you shoot people – that they'll be happier in heaven? And when they're maimed or blinded? That all the latest books are in braille, or that modern wheelchairs are such fun to operate?'

'Shut up,' he said. 'I warned you not to get involved.'

'Ian,' she said, stonily pronouncing her own life sentence to exile. 'I love you, but not enough to forgive you for what you have done.' For a moment she hesitated. Then she decided that there would never be enough love for that. 'You have your code,' she went on, 'discipline, tradition, patriotism, dying for the cause whatever that may be. But I have mine. Mine is very simple. I try not to harm people and I feel responsible for those who cross my path. Not the whole world – I'm not big enough – but just the few I come across. I could not live with someone who was destroying my code, because that would be like destroying me.

'As I see it, all your bravery, your intellect counts for nothing. *You* are nothing.'

She closed her eyes tightly. Tried not to hear his footsteps leaving. When she opened her eyes at last, Ian had gone.

CHAPTER 73

Sunday, February 19, 1984

It was the last day of the Winter Olympics after a night that seemed to have lasted all winter. Megan had not slept, she had spent the night pacing her room and flying with Nikki to God knows where – Siberia, Moscow, Lubianka prison? She had, after all, read her spy stories and she knew about these things: about drugs and beatings and hypnosis, and she had watched Nikki, pale and hauntingly lovely, but with her green eyes blank as a painted wall, walk zombie-like to a tall platform, stare down at a sea of hostile faces and read haltingly from a prepared statement into a microphone: 'Comrades, I have returned to Russia to be truly free, because I am an artist and I must be free.' She had watched the long prison train, with barred windows, racing through snowy tundra to Siberia. All this she had witnessed and she had not even slept yet. The real nightmares would come later.

It was eight am and Megan was too tense to be tired. When the phone rang, she flung herself forward and grabbed the receiver with shaking hands.

'No news, Miss Carroll, I am sorry to wake you.' It was Zoran Banski's voice. 'Will you please come down to reception?'

She found him huddled in an armchair near the information desk, drinking a cup of black coffee Cana had brought him. He looked haggard and close to collapsing.

But they were all magnificent actors – every last one of them, Megan reminded herself. Ian's words were knocking around in her head in disjointed fragments: *'You played along with the wrong side ... the Soviet bloc ... took him at face value ...'*

But his ulcers must be real, Megan thought. Banski's pupils were dilated with pain, his face the colour of dough.

'We have failed,' he was saying bleakly. 'Airports, seaports, major roads, customs' crossing points – are at every frontier. The British or the Russians, or, the two of them together, outwitted my men.' He grimaced and fumbled in his pocket for a bottle of pills, shook a few into his hand and flung them into his mouth. 'I am sorry. So very sorry. This is something which I was sure would never happen.'

Once again her eyes scanned his face with unconcealed suspicion. His own eyes were registering first shock and then compassion. He understands, she thought, feeling sick. His words had voiced the death sentence. Her love was to be executed without mercy – at once – no time for mourning. She said bitterly: 'Ian Mackintosh is as clever as the devil and twice as evil.'

'My dear Miss Carroll, do not give up hope. We shall continue the search until we find where she is. It is not the end. Perhaps – because she is British – we may get her repatriated.'

Should have been, Megan thought sullenly, but where are her passport and her citizenship papers? Ian had thought of everything.

'I have a message from Michel,' Banski went on. 'He flew to Belgrade this morning. He has good contacts there. He will try to find out where his fiancée is – and whether or not she is in Russia. Afterwards he will fly to Paris. He says goodbye.'

'Goodbye,' she repeated and shook her head as if dazed. So many goodbyes. It was all so final.

What if Ian were right? She thought in a last ditch appeal against the death sentence. Well, what if he was? Blackening Banski would not make Ian any purer. She had liked the little man when she had first met him, but that was a long time ago.

'What do you think happened?' she asked.

He sighed, spread his hands palms uppermost and shrugged. 'I think the British found out about your plans and brought their plans forward by a few hours. Don't you?' he said softly. 'I think Miss Kuznetsovna is in Russia now and those five British journalists are on their way home.'

He glanced up and saw the guilt in her eyes. 'You must not blame yourself,' he said too quickly. 'It is I who am to blame. I should have insisted she left earlier.'

He was trying to console her, but she remained unconsoled.

'I could have expelled her, but that would have caused an international incident.' He was floundering now, utterly trite and broken phrases: 'outraged ... on Yugoslav soil ... rest assured ... given time ... buffer zone ...'

'Shut up,' she cried. 'What's the good of words?'

He beckoned to Cana who carried Megan's suitcase out from the back of her desk. 'Goodbye, Miss Carroll. I'm sorry to have failed you. I will keep Miss Kutznetsovna's suitcase, in case we find her. I can return it to you later if you wish. Naturally you will be kept informed. Anything! But of course Commander Ian Mackintosh will let you know – I have no doubt.'

Who the hell was Ian Mackintosh? Did she know him? Someone from way back – a memory of her youth. 'Yes, very well. Whatever you think best.' She spoke quietly, but she felt outraged. That he should dare to suggest that she and that bastard! She drew in a deep breath and said: 'Goodbye, Mr Banski.' She hoped she sounded calm and controlled, for she knew she was toppling on the lip of hysteria.

She stood up in a daze and walked away.

As Zoran Banski watched her go, he looked sad. She should never have been exposed to this exercise in the first place, he thought. She was far too vulnerable.

'Oh God, Nikki. Poor, poor Nikki.' Megan wanted to show some sign of her grief, to cry or to wail. She felt she deserved to suffer, but sorrow, like pain, she discovered, cannot sustain itself for long periods, but prefers to attack in short, sharp shafts, incapacitating its victims, leaving them dazed and shocked between each thrust.

Megan felt numb; a walking corpse, devoid of feeling or of any emotions. The rest of the day passed slowly, it took about a hundred years. She took a taxi to Bjelašnica, to watch the last Alpine event, the Men's Slalom. She saw the Mahre brothers come first and second and her own two clients, one Swiss and the other a Norwegian, zoom home in the first fifteen.

Then, because she had nothing better to do, she taxied back to town and walked the streets of the Turkish quarter. Somehow she had to pass the day, and the next. That would be her life from now on, she decided. As long as she lived she would merely pass time until she was old. She would go back to London and become famous and successful; there would be many more stars; many more profits; she would become the caricature of a successful business woman.

She walked as far as the Zetra Stadium and because she had tickets, she joined the queue at the entrance. Once inside the empty seat beside her – Nikki's seat – was like a finger pointing an accusation. It would be there beside her wherever she went.

The ceremony began with an exhibition of modern dancing on ice to pop music, but Megan was seeing Nikki, as she had first seen her, together with Ian, in this very stadium. Two large and cheery bears, twice the size of men, frolicked around the rink waving to the packed stadium, and at last the finale was ushered in by a crowd of happy children in blue and white striped costumes who danced with the bears and Vucko, the wolf, the Game's mascot.

She heard the speeches, watched hundreds of balloons rising, saw the Olympic flag being lowered to half mast – it would remain here until it was taken to Calgary, Canada for the next Olympics – and when at last the Olympic flame flickered and died, it seemed to Megan that for her, too, everything sacred had died here in Sarajevo.

EPILOGUE

Monday, March 15, 1985

It was over a year since Megan had visited Yugoslavia, but their domestic airline's service had not improved. Take-off at Belgrade had been delayed by fog for three hours, and the flight had been bumpy and uncomfortable; it all seemed a conspiracy to make Megan feel depressed; she'd had too much time to remember Sarajevo and its imprint on her life.

Leaving ISA, even for a week, had not been as easy as it used to be. Her business had become too cumbersome and her staff of fifteen too demanding for her to take a holiday. But without ISA she would never have survived those first few bitter weeks in London, when she returned alone from Sarajevo a year ago. London, without Ian and Nikki, had been like being reborn into a new and hostile world. She had felt like a leaf untimely shed, drifting in the wind, without direction or any reason for existence. For months she had no social life; she lived and worked amongst strangers. She suffered and it showed, but there was no one close enough to her to notice. If Maureen had been there it might not have been so bad, but Maureen was running the Johnny Bart Gym in Monaco.

Eventually, with willpower and courage she had brought herself under control. The new, tough, self-sufficient Megan Carroll was a personality she alone had built and she felt pleased with her creation. Loneliness had been one of the many flaws she had eliminated in her precise and efficient manner. There was more to life than playing helpmate to some arrogant male. Men were fine as a diversion and for relaxation, but like social drinking they should never be allowed to take over.

The plane was buffeted by turbulence as they swept low over the Dinaric chain. Staring down at the misty mountains Megan shuddered slightly and tried not to remember too much. She

513

felt vulnerable. She was going back, and Megan never went back.

It was all because of a letter from Michel. *'I have a client for you and news of mutual friends ...'* he had written and much more. She knew his tantalising letter by heart. What on earth was Michel doing in Sarajevo? She had tried to contact him many times in the past year. After the Winter Games, Michel's magazine had published a really tremendous article about ISA London and her role in its development. She had wanted to thank him, but he had quit his job at the sports magazine. However, Michel's letter had brought about a relapse in her newly acquired control and she'd caught the first plane to Yugoslavia. Oh Michel, how can you do this to me?

The plane landed smoothly in spite of the turbulence, but the moment she stepped off, the harsh emotional climate hit her like a slap in the face. Drab faces, bleak eyes, the total lack of comfort, the utilitarian decor – nothing had changed. There was a queue of migrant Slav workers in their cheap shiny suits, en route to jobs in Düsseldorf; their families looked desperately sad and watching them Megan felt a tide of compassion race through her.

Oh God, why did I come back? She could explode with temper at her own stupidity. She did not want to feel anything – ever again. Feeling absurdly overdressed in her fur coat and hat, Megan pushed her way to the luggage ramp.

Zoran Banski was waiting outside and the sight of him brought a lump to her throat. Crazy really, but he was part of the Sarajevo nightmare. He looked fitter than before, and he was smiling happily. 'I have retired,' he told her. 'I am the family odd job man, and driver. I wanted so much to see you again.' His melting brown eyes gazed shyly at her. Suddenly she was clasped in his arms, being kissed on either cheek.

She clutched him back. He was, after all, a link to the past. Suddenly they were old friends, which was strange, because they never had been friends before.

'Where are you taking me? Where's Michel?' she wanted to know, as she settled into the front seat of Banski's old Lada and tried to shift her bottom to a place of comfort amongst the broken springs.

'Michel is waiting at the Hotel Yahorina. You remember it, yes?'

'So, what's it all about, Mr Banski?' she asked as he started the car.

'You'll see?' Was all he would say. He was taking her to Michel. That was all. But first they must have a tour around the Olympic Village – for old time's sake.

It was then that Megan noticed Banski's Olympic tie and the five circles on his tie-pin.

'It was fantastic, yes?' he said three times. And later: 'There's not a day that passes when I do not remember the Olympics and how beautiful it was. Indescribable! Something you are lucky to experience once in a lifetime. None of us wants to forget.' He gestured towards the faded pastel-painted blocks, paint peeling, balconies filled with washing; the shops and restaurants beneath, empty and shuttered. 'The kids that live here are called the *Olympians* by their school friends.'

There were a few snowflakes whirling in the air and a thin covering of snow lay in ditches and gutters. But this time she could see more of the fields and woods and the beauty of the countryside. There were women huddled in scarves and shawls hoeing the frozen fields, and curious, conical-shaped haystacks and an extraordinary number of half-built homes along the way.

Banski was in a hurry. They rattled and bumped up the steep and winding mountain road towards the famous skiing sites. The roads, hurriedly completed only eighteen months before, were already falling into disrepair with gaping sinkholes, deep ruts and cracks; signposts and flagposts were leaning over at all angles, like drunks remembering better days; the *pistes*, so hopefully prepared, were criss-crossed with tracks of wolves and bears, but not of skis, while ski lifts rocked in the wind and the huge hotels stood empty and shuttered.

Suddenly Megan experienced a vivid recall of the joy, the crowds, the skiers and their army of trainers and back-up men. Every man, woman and child had joined together in one foolhardy onslaught to woo the world. They had been fired with enthusiasm, and a feeling that all this would last forever: one fantastic, larger-than-life happening.

Now the bubble had burst. Suddenly Megan's eyes were filled with tears, for she, too, shared a feeling thread with this poignant city. She remembered the hope the elation, the feeling that from now on nothing would ever be the same again and the Slavs' whispered message to the West: *'You are beautiful, we love you, come back, come back.'*

So much for love, Megan thought grimly.

'What are we? Just gypsies.' A nation of gypsies. No wonder we are so poor,' Banski lamented, pointing at the erosion and the derelict construction.

She'd had enough. Oh Lord, she thought, it was so depressing. She wanted to go home. But at last she saw that they were driving into the car park of Hotel Yahorina and for a moment she was immersed in memories of Jacqui and her last race.

The hotel was deserted, but far away behind the fir trees, she could see some skiers plunging down the mountainside. 'A few locals and one visitor,' Banski explained with a wry smile. So we are keeping one ski lift running.'

Always 'we' never 'they' she thought with a surge of irritation.

'Consequently,' he went on. 'This hotel is still open and I have booked you in. You will have lunch here.'

'You're joining us, of course.'

'No, not this time,' he said, smiling obsequiously. Funny how his gentle manner had seemed so intimidating when he was Chief of Police, she thought. Now he just looked sweet.

'But tomorrow ...' he was saying. 'Tomorrow we are all having lunch together.'

He took her suitcase, signed her in and ushered her into the diningroom. 'Until then,' he said with a bow.

The hotel smelled of dust. The windows were dirty and so were the carpets. It was cold and not enough lights were switched on. Ugh! she murmured and shivered.

Obviously she was expected, because one table was dusted, and set. She heard footsteps at the far end of a long corridor and Michel hurried towards her.

'Michel,' she called and ran to hug him. 'Where've you been? What are you doing here? D'you know how many times I've tried to contact you. Oh Michel! Why didn't you write before? Now tell me all about it ... you have news ... don't keep me in suspense.'

'First things first,' he said. He reached down and kissed her. 'I've just finished my novel,' he said proudly. 'That's why I didn't come to the airport. I wanted to finish off before you

516

arrived. I've a contract from the publishers. It's to be published in November,' he said, his eyes glowing with pride. 'I'll be glad to get back to Europe. I feel like an exile in my own home. Can you believe that?'

I believe you, Megan thought, but she merely smiled and said: 'There's a good many stories waiting for you. Remember Rob Scott? I suppose you know he married Jacqui Douglas. Well, he's learning to run Vanguard's marketing now. His skis are Vanguard's new prestige line. There's a good story there. And Jacqui – remember Jacqui? – she persuaded her father to back her in launching a chain of budget-priced ski schools for youngsters in the most unlikely places. She likes to do her own thing. Did you know Eleanor remarried her ex-husband? Oh Michel, I have so many stories for you.'

Michel had ordered for both of them and now the food was arriving: a varied assortment of Turkish specialities which Michel regarded mournfully. 'I can't tell you how I long for French cuisine,' he said sadly. 'You've got to help me. I want to go back to France and for that I need you.'

'I'll do anything I can, Michel,' she said. And I mean it, she thought. That's what's strange about it.

As Michel began talking, Megan lost her appetite. She missed the point to begin with. Perhaps because she was feeling a little tired. Michel kept mentioning his wife, who wanted to come to the West and who could skate. But really, Megan must come and see how good she is. When he took out his photographs, Megan gasped and sat with her mouth hanging open stupidly. Nikki's eyes smiled up at her, Nikki's hair, Nikki's smile.

'Oh God, Michel. It's Nikki. Tell me how you found her,' she said, leaning back and closing her eyes.

'Nikola Petrovna Juric, my wife,' Michel said happily. 'And she was never lost. I kidnapped her.' Then he smiled nervously. 'Didn't you guess?'

'No,' she burst out. Then she recovered herself. 'I mean how could I have guessed? I thought the Russians had. Oh Michel, I've been so unhappy.' She took a deep breath. 'Couldn't you have told me?' she asked.

'I'm sorry, Megan. We owe you an apology, but we were afraid to trust you, because of your association with Ian. That is, your former association. We only found out about you and Ian splitting up quite recently.'

Megan nodded noncommitally, while Michel floundered on. He decided to change the subject. 'Nikki was in the grip of some masochistic urge to suffer, and this was compelling her to take her punishment. She wasn't going to escape with you – I think you guessed that much.'

'I sort of suspected,' Megan whispered. 'That's why ...'

'We both know Nikki and her damned Russian fatalism,' Michel went on, interrupting her. 'She'd got it fixed in her head that she deserved to be punished because of what she had done to her father. I suppose they told you that he died. I tried to talk some sense into her, but I failed, so I had to use force. Of course, most of the refreshment vendors were old friends. We grabbed her, knocked her out and carried her off in an empty wine barrel.' He broke off as the waiter brought some more wine. 'I took Nikki to an old farmhouse that belongs to my family and kept her prisoner for weeks.'

Michel chuckled. 'To be honest we've had fun.' He broke off thinking that it was really because they both recognised it as an interlude, not a way of life. 'But now my book's finished, I want to return to Paris.' Then he smiled sadly. 'My uncle provided Nikki with papers, so that we could be married and after that she had French nationality, so there's no problem there,' he added morosely. 'Except that she won't go back – she's scared stiff. She feels she's no good – that she can't get back to what she had. She's out of practice, I admit that, and a little plumper, but otherwise ...'

He broke off and smiled. 'You'll see for yourself in the morning. I've arranged a short performance at Zetra. I'd be grateful if you'd handle her career again, Megan. She wants to turn pro.'

Nikki's lucky to have Michel, she thought. 'So that's it?' Megan asked.

'That's it,' Michel said.

'I am very happy for you both,' she said solemnly. 'I can't wait for her to come back to London. It's been lonely,' she admitted.

'And you?' he asked. 'How are you keeping? Are you married?'

'No.'

'Going steady?'

'Nothing like that,' she said crossly. 'I burned my fingers with Ian. I just work nowadays.'

'Nikki said you were a one-man woman.'

518

'Nikki said that? No kidding? Were you talking about me?'

Michel flushed and then grinned. 'Once women get married they turn into regular matchmakers. I don't know why that is, but it always seems to happen. Ian's been here, by the way,' he said, after a short awkward pause. He thinks she's still as good.'

'Ian!' she gasped. 'He's been here. And you actually speak to him. You're quick to forgive. I wouldn't forget so soon.'

'He was merely doing his job.'

'It was his idea in the first place,' Megan said bitterly.

'There's such a thing as regret, remorse, shame. Call it what you will. You see Ian was given the job of rescuing five journalists held by the Russians and Nikki seemed a heaven-sent opportunity: one Russian for five Britons, one of whom was his best friend.'

'You don't have to make excuses for him to me,' she said angrily. 'It's of no interest.'

'He paid the price. He was in hospital for six months with a bullet in his back. 'You see, last year, after the Games, Ian went back to organise a rescue mission, which didn't come off too well. I don't know the details, but two men, including Ian's friend, were killed and Ian was injured. The other three were brought out.'

'I don't want to know about Ian,' Megan said, feeling her carefully built defences crumble about her. 'Michel, please stop it.' Suddenly she felt tired and dispirited.

But Michel would not stop. 'Officially, Ian came to Sarajevo to make a documentary film, but it was really to recuperate and to try to get news of Nikki. Zoran told me he was here and I decided to approach him directly and ask him if it would be safe for Nikki to return to Britain.'

'You're brave,' she said bitterly.

Michel frowned at Megan. He was hoping to see signs of a change of heart, but Megan was staring stonily ahead, her hands resting in her lap, her eyes cold as ice. 'He's a hell of a nice guy, Megan, when you get to know him,' he added.

'Does anyone ever get to know him?'

'There's one sure method – go hunting with a guy and you get to know him pretty quickly. There's two sorts of men, you know. Those you would go hunting with, and those you wouldn't. Our bears can be pretty scary.'

'And you go? He's here?'

519

Megan stared accusingly at Michel and saw his cheeks flush and his eyes turn away evasively. What's he so goddammed guilty about? she wondered. Then she thought: they've cooked this up together – the three of them. *That's why I'm here.* Michel couldn't deceive a child – not like Ian, who was a past master at deception. 'Michel, do they have a toilet here?' she asked in a harsh voice.

She fumbled up the dark staircase to the door. The toilet was thick with dust and there was no towel, but it was as good a place to cry in as any other. So' she cried there for a long time, together with the crumbling plaster, the broken chair, the tap that had no top, and the toilet that would not flush. Eventually she powdered her nose and returned to the table.

'So why are you telling me all this?' she asked harshly. 'There must be a reason.'

'Yes, there is.' There was that shifty smile again.

Suddenly Megan felt two hands on her shoulders and reached up wonderingly. Her fingers recognised those well-loved hands with the black hairs curling round his wrists and the efficient black watch with multiple dials and the ribbing of his ski jacket – those hands that were clasping hers so tightly.

She opened her mouth to speak and closed it again. The emotions warring in her mind were too powerful to be voiced. Anger was uppermost and sadness. Then there was her longing, and fear of losing out again, and the memory of her physical need that had kept her moaning Ian's name night after night for months. What could she say? After all, they were not alone. So she said: 'What a surprise, Ian, after all this time.'

And he, for the want of something better to say, said: 'How pleasant to see you again.'

'I hear you were injured – nothing serious, I hope.'

'I recovered.'

'So I hear.'

Ian sat down, smiling politely, and Megan stole a quick look. His eyes were shining with that strange, intimate kindliness that was so deceptive. Just the sight of him made her catch her breath. How thin he had become, and much paler. He needed a hair cut, she noticed, and his beard was a disgrace, curling halfway down his neck. He saw her frown, and his hand went up to smooth it back. He looked older. It had not been a good year for Ian, she could see that, and she longed to comfort him. Absurd really. She must pull herself together.

'You're looking ...' they said simultaneously, and broke off to glare at each other.

'The skiing's particularly good at this time of the year,' Ian began in his best British manner. 'I've always thought the late snow to be the best of all.'

'That's what the experts say,' she answered brightly.

'You've come to see Nikki skate, I hear,' he went on, signalling to the waiter. 'Are you planning to stay over for a few days?'

There was a long pause.

This is it! This is the moment when I make or unmake my life. Where I live, what I do thirty years from now, all this will depend upon my answer. And what can I say?

She thought about the family history she had unearthed in Ian's cellars, piece by piece, book by book, about the spinning loom and the Highland herd and the endless ships, and the deer which Ian had shot for the table. She remembered the rows of patient faces hanging in the long gallery. Would she be there, too? Was that what she really wanted out of life – a straitjacket of family traditions? Titles and glory, medals in a class case and memories of daring-do to talk about on long, lonely winter evenings? And then she thought: perhaps Aviemore would be as warm as a tropical island with Ian's love beside me. Oh Ian, she thought. Do I really love you that much?

But it seemed that she did for she heard her voice saying: 'Possibly,' as if of its own volition. 'I was thinking that I might,' her voice went on. 'After all, it's a long way to come just for a night. I could get some skiing in myself. I've been working too hard lately.' Oh, traitorous voice!

'There's some pretty good runs around Yahorina,' Ian told her, relaxing visibly. 'If you have time, I might be able to show you around.'

'I guess I could find the time,' she murmured, frowning at her hands as if they offended her.

'Okay, this is where I say goodbye,' Michel said. He jumped up briskly, knocking back his chair.

'Just like that. No kidding? You're leaving me ...' Megan looked up in alarm. She had no defences. She could not be left here alone with Ian. She was about to protest, but broke off

521

when she saw Michel's face. She thought: Good grief, he's going to burst into tears. How awful!

Michel hurried off to find Zoran. He did not look back. He had this terrible weakness: happy endings made him cry. He took out his handkerchief and blew his nose vigorously.

'Don't worry. They'll be all right,' Zoran said, clapping Michel on the shoulder. 'And you'll be all right, too. You and Nikki. But what about our poor Sarajevo?' He gestured towards the pistes ... the mountains ... the forests. She's been forsaken and she's pining. Will the bridegroom ever return? I doubt it. Not soon ... maybe never.'

Michel was not listening to his foolish old uncle. He had the capacity to weep at almost anything emotional. His wife was always laughing at him, but to Anglo-Saxons it would seem disgraceful. He was afraid that Megan had seen and he did not wish to appear so Slavic in front of his two good friends, both of them the epitome of the stiff-upper-lip brigade. He knew they would sit there forever, and talk about the snow and the wild life and the mountains. It would take a few days before they got around to making love. Oh well, they had plenty of time.

He was quite wrong, he discovered from the hotel manager the next day. It only took them half an hour.